"What have you done, Keka?" I said, voice trembling.

All this time I had thought he was apologising for turning some of my Swords against me, not for something I had not yet seen. "What have you done?"

He repeated the mangled apology and got to his feet as a torrent of footsteps entered the room, carried on a tide of strange voices. A Kisian soldier gripped my upper arm, digging in his fingers as I fought to remain kneeling.

"I have not been released and cannot move," I said as another took the other arm. "Let me go! Where is Emperor Gideon?"

"Waiting for you outside, of course," came a voice from the door. "You are needed at once."

"Why?" I demanded, not meeting Leo's gaze as I was hauled up lest he read the fear in my mind.

"For the ceremony." Leo smiled and gestured to the dim sunlight seeping in through the nearest window. "The weather is fine, Levanti and Kisians alike have gathered, and we cannot keep His Majesty waiting, now, can we."

Having been set unceremoniously on my feet by grasping hands, my gaze slid to the back of Keka's turned head. I bit his name from my tongue. A plea would achieve nothing beyond my own embarrassment. If execution was to be my reward, I would die proud and unbreaking. I had retained enough Levanti for that, pride and honour etched upon my bones.

Praise for
THE REBORN EMPIRE SERIES

"With prose that rises above most novels, Devin Madson paints evocative scenes to build an engaging story. Highly entertaining, *We Ride the Storm* is certainly worth your attention and Madson is an exciting new author in fantasy."
—Mark Lawrence, author of *Red Sister*

"Intricate, compelling, and vividly imagined, this is the first in a new quartet that I am hugely excited about. Visceral battles, complex politics, and fascinating worldbuilding bring Devin's words to life."
—Anna Stephens, author of *Godblind*

"An utterly arresting debut, *Storm*'s heart is in its complex, fascinating characters, each trapped in ever-tightening snarls of war, politics, and magic. Madson's sharp, engaging prose hauls you through an engrossing story that will leave you wishing you'd set aside enough time to read this all in one sitting. One of the best new voices in fantasy."
—Sam Hawke, author of *City of Lies*

"A brutal, nonstop ride through an empire built upon violence and lies, a story as gripping as it is unpredictable. Never shying away from the consequences of the past nor its terrible realities, Madson balances characters you want to love with actions you want to hate while mixing in a delightful amount of magic, political intrigue, and lore. This is not a book you'll be able to put down."
—K. A. Doore, author of *The Perfect Assassin*

"Darkly devious and gripping epic fantasy boasting complex characters, brutal battle, and deadly intrigue. *We Ride the Storm* is breathtaking, brilliant, and bloody—it grips you hard and does not let go."   —Cameron Johnston, author of *The Traitor God*

"Fans of George R. R. Martin's Song of Ice and Fire series will appreciate the feudal political maneuvering, shifting alliances, and visceral descriptions of combat and its aftermath in this series starter."   —*Booklist*

"Madson has built a living, breathing world of empire and fury. *We Ride the Storm* grabs you by the throat and doesn't let go."   —Peter McLean, author of *Priest of Bones*

"Madson cleverly uses the characters' distinct perspectives to piece together a crafty political chess game."   —*Publishers Weekly*

"A slow-building tale of court intrigue that picks up lots of steam on its way to a shocking finish."   —*Kirkus*

WE CRY FOR BLOOD

THE REBORN EMPIRE: BOOK THREE

DEVIN MADSON

orbitbooks.net

Copyright © 2021 by Devin Madson
Excerpt from *Legacy of Ash* copyright © 2019 by Matthew Ward
Excerpt from *Son of the Storm* copyright © 2021 by Suyi Davies Okungbowa

Cover design by Lisa Marie Pompilio
Cover illustration by Nico Delort
Cover copyright © 2021 by Hachette Book Group, Inc.
Map by Charis Loke
Author photograph by Leah Ladson

SCI
FIC
MAD

Orbit
Hachette Book Group
1290 Avenue of the Americas
New York, NY 10104
orbitbooks.net

First Edition: August 2021
Simultaneously published in Great Britain by Orbit

Orbit is an imprint of Hachette Book Group.
The Orbit name and logo are trademarks of Little, Brown Book Group Limited.

The publisher is not responsible for websites (or their content) that are not owned by the publisher.

The Hachette Speakers Bureau provides a wide range of authors for speaking events. To find out more, go to www.hachettespeakersbureau.com or call (866) 376-6591.

Library of Congress Cataloging-in-Publication Data
Names: Madson, Devin, author.
Title: We cry for blood / Devin Madson.
Description: First edition. | New York, NY : Orbit, 2021. | Series: The reborn empire ; book 3
Identifiers: LCCN 2020057292 | ISBN 9780316536417 (trade paperback) | ISBN 9780316536424 (ebook)
Subjects: GSAFD: Fantasy fiction.
Classification: LCC PR9619.4.M335 W43 2021 | DDC 823/.92—dc23
LC record available at https://lccn.loc.gov/2020057292

ISBNs: 978-0-316-53641-7 (trade paperback), 978-0-316-53640-0 (ebook)

Printed in the United States of America

LSC-C

Printing 1, 2021

For M, first and forever my baby, for being so patient with me and with life. And for always bringing cheer and joy wherever you go.

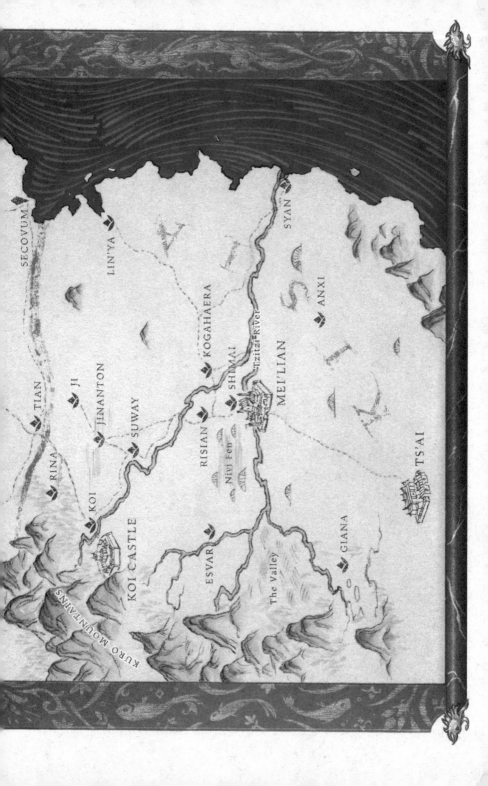

CHARACTER LIST

Levanti

Torin

Rah e'Torin—ousted captain of the Second Swords of Torin
Eska e'Torin—Rah's second-in-command (deceased, Residing)
Kishava e'Torin—tracker (deceased)
Orun e'Torin—horse master (deceased, Residing)
Yitti e'Torin—healer
Jinso—Rah's horse
Lok, Himi, and Istet—Swords of the Torin
Gideon e'Torin—First Sword of the Torin, now emperor of Levanti Kisia
Sett e'Torin—Gideon's second and blood brother (deceased)
Tep e'Torin—healer of the First Swords
Tor, Matsimelar (deceased), and Oshar e'Torin—the saddleboys chosen by Gideon to be translators
Nuru e'Torin—self-taught translator never used by the Chiltaens

Jaroven

Dishiva e'Jaroven—captain of the Third Swords of Jaroven
Keka e'Jaroven—Dishiva's second, can't talk. Chiltaens cut out his tongue.
Captain Atum e'Jaroven—captain of the First Swords of Jaroven
Loklan e'Jaroven—Dishiva's horse master
Shenyah e'Jaroven—the only Jaroven Made in exile

Ptapha, Massama, Dendek, Anouke, Esi, Moshe e'Jaroven—Dishiva's Swords

Other Levanti

Ezma e'Topi—Exiled horse whisperer

Derkka en'Injit—Ezma's apprentice

Jass en'Occha—a Sword of the Occha

Captain Lashak e'Namalaka—First Sword of the Namalaka and Dishiva's friend

Captain Yiss en'Oht—First Sword of the Oht, fiercely loyal to Gideon

Captain Taga en'Occha—First Sword of the Occha and Jass's captain

Captain Menesor e'Qara—captain of the Second Swords of Qara

Jaesha e'Qara—Captain Menesor's second

Captain Dhamara e'Sheth, Captain Bahn e'Bedjuti, Captain Leena en'Injit—other Levanti captains

Senet en'Occha, Jakan e'Qara, Yafeu en'Injit, Baln en'Oht, Tafa en'Oht, and Kehta en'Oht—imperial guards

Diha e'Bedjuti—a healer

Nassus—Levanti god of death

Mona—Levanti goddess of justice

Kisians

Miko Ts'ai—daughter of Empress Hana Ts'ai and Katashi Otako

Emperor Kin Ts'ai—the last emperor of Kisia (deceased)

Empress Hana Ts'ai—deposed empress of Kisia

Prince Tanaka Ts'ai—Miko's twin brother (deceased)

Shishi—Miko's dog

Jie Ts'ai—Emperor Kin's illegitimate son (deceased)

Minister Tashi Oyamada—Jie's maternal grandfather and minister of the right

General Kitado—commander of Miko's Imperial Guard (deceased)

Minister Ryo Manshin—minister of the left, chief commander of the Imperial Army

General Hade Ryoji—former commander of the Imperial Guard

General Tai Moto, General Rushin, General Senn Mihri, General Yass, and General Alon—southern generals of the Imperial Army

Captain Soku—one of General Moto's men

Lord Hiroto Bahain—duke of Syan

Edo Bahain—duke of Syan's eldest son

Captain Nagai—one of the duke's men

Governor Tianto Koali—Governor of Syan

Lord Ichiro Koali—Count of Irin Ya

Lord Nishi (Lord Salt)—a wealthy Kisian lord who believes in the One True God

Chiltaens

Cassandra Marius—*Chiltaen whore and assassin*

The hieromonk, Creos Villius—head of the One True God's church (deceased)

Leo Villius—only child of His Holiness the hieromonk

Captain Aeneas—the hieromonk's head guard

Kaysa (She)—Cassandra's second soul

Swiff—one of Captain Aeneas's men

Others

Torvash—the Witchdoctor

Mistress Saki—Torvash's silent companion

Kocho—Torvash's scribe and servant

Lechati—young man in Torvash's service

THE STORY SO FAR...

Dishiva e'Jaroven is named the head of Gideon's Imperial Guard, but the return of Dom Leo Villius soon becomes her sole focus. People are poisoned and holy books are burned and she's sure he's the enemy no one else can see. After Gideon's marriage to Lady Sichi, a translator is poisoned while stealing her a holy book, and sure it contains something Leo doesn't want them to know, Dishiva seeks to have it translated.

As a prisoner of the Witchdoctor, Cassandra undergoes experiments that pull her soul in and out of her body. She plots escape while learning about her condition until she is accidentally catapulted inside Empress Hana's body. Kaysa—the other soul inhabiting Cassandra's body—runs away, leaving Cassandra behind.

On the run in her own empire, Empress Miko travels with Rah to Syan, seeking the aid of Grace Bahain. They discover Bahain plans to take the empire for himself, killing the Levanti, and with Edo's help, Miko and Rah escape. Together they trudge through the wilds of Kisia, both intent on getting back to Mei'lian. Miko to free Minister Manshin, her only remaining ally, and Rah to save his people. On the way, they are attacked by Jie's soldiers, and Miko lets herself be taken to save Rah's life.

Finding his Swords setting fire to Mei'lian, Rah frees Minister Manshin before challenging Yitti for the captaincy. Sett interrupts to ensure Rah's failure, and is killed for the dishonour while Rah, badly injured, is further exiled from his people.

With Jie's political career hanging on Miko's death, she has to fight for her life and kills him. Now the last remaining member of the imperial family, she woos Jie's southern army to her cause, and for the first time since escaping Mei'lian, she has some hope for the future.

When the Witchdoctor gives them up, Cassandra and Hana find themselves stuck with the hieromonk and on their way to Koi. After killing him, Cassandra puts Hana in the hieromonk's skin to take charge of Chiltae's plans herself. But when they arrive in Koi, they find Leo Villius taking over the Chiltaen army and barely escape alive.

Increasingly not himself, Gideon orders Dishiva to attack a deserter camp, but she finds a horse whisperer there and refuses to kill either her or the Levanti who just want to go home. There she learns that the holy book says Leo will have to die three more times to become a god and build his holy empire.

1. MIKO

I loosed an arrow, heart thrumming in time with the bowstring. It hit the target with a satisfying thud as I took another from the barrel. Around me camp noise swirled on, while like two statues, Minister Manshin and newly promoted Minister Oyamada stood watching. Neither had addressed me since arriving, instead keeping up a stiff flow of conversation.

"And wine?" Manshin said.

"Some," came Oyamada's reply. "We will have to be careful in its distribution, especially heading into winter. Rice too. Millet we have in greater abundance, also beans and dried meats, and we can make use of any river we pass."

Manshin grumbled as I loosed another arrow into the rapidly filling target. A small crowd of soldiers had gathered to watch, quietly murmuring amongst themselves.

"Steel?"

"Of course. And…arrows. Wood for defences. We have plenty of wood and metal in the south, you know."

"Too bad we can't eat them."

"We are not lacking in food," Oyamada said. "Wine will just need to be rationed. Wise if you want your soldiers to stand upright."

Minister Manshin shifted his feet, a sidelong look thrown to the watching men. "And never could you more clearly prove you know little about how armies work, Excellency."

"I have commanded—"

"Troops of guards hired for trade caravans do not count. You focus on maintaining our supply lines, I'll decide how to make use of them."

I loosed another arrow and turned before it hit the target, catching Minister Oyamada opening his mouth to retort. "Your caution is very wise, Minister Oyamada," I said, glancing a look of censure at Manshin. Of the two I trusted him more, had been with him longer and needed his skills, but without Oyamada I would have no soldiers. We had seen Jie's body off that morning, back to his mother to be laid to rest. Under other circumstances he would have been buried in the imperial gardens, but smoke still rose from the burning ruins of Mei'lian.

Both men bowed, Oyamada with something of ironic thanks, Manshin in stiff apology.

I drew another arrow, increasingly aware of the swelling crowd around us.

"Majesty," both ministers said, their first sign of unity. "We ought to call a meeting before the generals begin to worry," Manshin added. "They may take being kept waiting as a sign of disrespect."

"I don't intend to keep anyone waiting." I nocked the arrow, while lying at my feet, Shishi's tail stirred on the churned mud. "But neither do I want to be at a disadvantage at our first meeting. So, I am going to see the rest of the camp. And meet some of my soldiers."

"Are...you sure that's wise, Your Majesty?" Oyamada made all too obvious a twitch in the direction of our audience.

"Yes. If I have to sit in a stuffy tent while men talk down to me, I will first ensure I understand what they are talking about. We will meet tonight. I'm confident you will help them accept this decision, Minister Oyamada."

He received my confiding smile without returning one of his own, but taking it for the order it was, he bowed and departed.

"You need to give him time," Manshin said once he was out of earshot. "You killed his grandson only two days ago."

"And you need to not belittle the skills he brings to our cause."

A humourless smile turned his lips, deepening the dark rings beneath his eyes. "You mean the money he is bringing to our cause."

"His cause now too."

Manshin bowed in acknowledgement and I took another arrow from the barrel. A gust of wind whipped through the narrow mud patch, flapping my surcoat about my feet and ruffling Shishi's fur. I nocked, compensating with barely a thought, and loosed—the whole process second nature, as meeting with generals had been second nature to Emperor Kin.

Despite the wind, the arrow hit more or less where I had intended—more than could be said of my plans.

"You cannot rely on your prowess with a bow to impress the generals, Your Majesty," Manshin said, eyeing the watching soldiers. "At best they will see it as intimidation, at worst as a reminder of your father."

"Of Emperor Kin? I see no issue with that."

"Not who I meant."

"No," I agreed. "But here and now I have only one father and he was Emperor Kin Ts'ai. Only one brother and he was Emperor Jie Ts'ai. My mother was a traitor. My twin a fool. These are the truths I have to live if I want Kisia to survive. But since I also need generals who will listen to me, who know they cannot walk all over me as I am sure they intend to, I will do everything I can to give myself an edge."

He nodded. "They will push to see how much power they have, and will hate you if you give them none and hate you if you give them too much."

"And hate me if I hit this target and hate me if I don't. Hate me if I act like a woman and hate me if I don't." I nocked the arrow. "I know this won't be easy, Minister. But knowing they will hate me no matter what I do is more freeing than you might imagine."

I drew and loosed, taking joy in the thud of arrowhead meeting hemp coil. Minister Manshin watched, his brow furrowed.

"I can do this," I said. "You took my armour in Mei'lian so I might live to fight another day; surely you did that because you believed in me."

The watching soldiers could not have overheard, yet Manshin lowered his voice, almost losing it in the general chatter. "I fear they will not put aside old wounds," he said, "whatever the feelings of the common soldiers. Whatever the needs of Kisia. These are southern men whose homes and families have not been threatened. To them the loss of Koi is something to cheer. Emperor Kin stoked the division in his ongoing war against your mother."

I sighed. "I will not forget, but if I am going to rule Kisia that means all of it, not just north of the river." I lowered my bow, disliking how different it felt in my hands. In leaving Hacho in Syan I felt like I had left behind part of myself.

"Walk with me, Minister," I said. "I wish to see the camp and talk to my soldiers as Emperor Kin did."

"As you wish."

A boy took my bow, but I left the bracer tied around my wrist as a reminder of my skill. Had Kin considered such details? I had never before wondered how much had been true and how much constructed, the real man an enigma.

As I made to leave the training area, chatter rose from the gathered crowd, and with Kin's performance in mind, I said, "Thank you for attending my practice. Tomorrow I will see how many arrows I can split."

This was received with more surprise than excitement, but I needed to start somewhere.

"You ought not play for them, Your Majesty," Manshin said as I fell in beside him, our boots sinking into the mud. "Emperor Kin would never have done so."

"But I am not Emperor Kin."

"As you continue informing me, but as a woman you must demand the respect due to you even more than he had to as a commoner."

"But he wasn't respected because he demanded it. He was respected because he earned it."

Manshin walked on in silence, hands clasped behind his back and his head high, the weak sunlight only serving to deepen the lines about his face. Being imprisoned by the Levanti had taken its toll, leaving a slimmer, harsher man walking with me, a man who might now be questioning the sacrifice he'd made to save my life. My soldiers were not the only ones whose respect I needed to preserve.

The row of tents along which we walked had been set upon grass, but the walkway between them was a muddy trough. Soldiers bowed as we passed and I nodded and smiled to them all, feeling like I was in a parade rather than strolling about an army camp.

"How do I make the focus on them, not on me?" I said as we turned into a wider channel that was equally muddy. A pair of boys scampered past carrying trays of food, eyes widening at the sight of me. "I want to . . . talk to them. Get to know them."

"Then talk to them."

"But what do I say? Court small talk is all about weather and hair and what an unfortunate colour of robe so-and-so has chosen today. How did Kin do it?"

"By asking them about themselves and remembering things so they felt important. There is nothing men like better—especially soldiers—than talking about themselves."

I had never heard him say anything so cynical, and my laugh drew the attention of a young soldier just stepping out of his tent. He flinched at the sight of me. Bowed. Stammered "Your Majesty" and stared at the ground, twisting his tunic in his hands.

"I must be quite the fearful sight to earn such a response," I said, approaching with Manshin in my wake. "What is your name, soldier?"

"Tanaka Ono, Your Majesty."

He said it with such consciousness, such reluctance, that I was grateful for his thoughtfulness even as the name sheared through my skin, my flesh, my bones, to strike deep into my heart. My forced smile trembled. "Tanaka," I said. "One of my favourite names. And where are you from, Tanaka Ono?"

"From Anxi, Your Majesty. At least, I was born there. I grew up in a small town to the west you've . . . probably never heard of."

"Try me."

He seemed to consider if this was some sort of test, but said, "Boruta, Your Majesty."

"Ah, one of the many towns catering to travellers along the fur trails, famed for its warm baths and excellent wine."

The further widening of his eyes was as satisfying as the thud of an arrow hitting its target. "Yes, Your Majesty, that's the one."

"Well, given the beauty of your home, we are doubly fortunate to have you with us."

With that, I nodded to him and continued on with the minister. "That," I said as we walked away, "was easier than I thought."

"For the most part they are men of simple needs, Your Majesty. However, I'm surprised you'd heard of so small a town."

"I haven't. I guessed its attractions based on the general character of the area." An area I had recently walked through in my under-robe with only a Levanti for company.

"I am not sure if that makes your display more or less impressive, Your Majesty. Ah, here are the two generals who weren't present for our...display the other morning," he added, nodding at a pair of men in fine crimson surcoats, talking together near the quarter-master's tent. "The taller of the two is General Senn Mihri, while the other is—"

"General Moto."

One of the two generals Jie had expected would control the empire in his place.

The pair bowed as we approached.

"Generals," Manshin said as we halted before them, he at his ease while I pretended I was oblivious of both men searching my features—no doubt to ascertain how much an Otako I was. "I present Her Imperial Majesty, Empress Miko Ts'ai."

They bowed again, murmuring "Your Majesty," and when General Mihri went to speak his name, I said, "General Senn Mihri, youngest son of the great General Mihri. As famed for his leadership skills as for the quality of the horses bred on his estate west of Anxi. You were promoted after an engagement against the mountain tribes in 1370 and have been stationed there since, defending our western border."

I lifted my chin. "You served my father, the great Emperor Kin Ts'ai, with strength and honour, and I welcome your continued service to the empire."

The hardened soldier's brows lifted, and in a gruff voice he said, "Many thanks, Your Majesty."

I turned my attention to General Moto, who before I could speak, said, "My name is General Moto, Your Majesty. Commander of the forces stationed at Ts'ai since the last border skirmish with Chiltae in 1385."

If he had hoped to leave me nothing to say, he reckoned without the wealth of detail Minister Manshin knew about the generals under his command.

"General Tai Moto," I said, noting he was shrewd. "First of his family to achieve the rank despite the second sons of the Count of Tatan having served since the family took the title in 1236." I owed too many hours of memorising family names and honours for that one. "When you were a captain in Mei'lian's standing battalion, you defended my father against a pair of assassins who attacked while he was inspecting plans for rebuilding the city's defences."

And as I had to General Mihri, I lifted my chin and said, "You served my father, the great Emperor Kin Ts'ai, with strength and honour, and I welcome your continued service to the empire."

No surprise this time, but with the appreciative nod of a move well played, he smiled and said, "Many thanks, Your Majesty."

We left them and walked on, sure they were watching us as we departed. Once we were well out of earshot, Manshin said, "Well done, Your Majesty."

"Oddly, that was easier than talking to the soldier."

We walked on, stopping here and there to exchange a few words with captains and common soldiers alike, even with one of the boys who sped about the camp carrying messages and supplies and food. When I greeted him, he stared open-mouthed for many long seconds before stammering, "Your Majesty. What...what can I do for you, Your Majesty?" with a deep bow.

"Tell me about you."

"About...me, Your Majesty?" The poor child looked horrified.

"Why don't you start with your name."

"A-Ani, Your Majesty."

"And where are you from, Ani?"

"I don't know, Your Majesty, but...but I was living on the streets of Mei'lian when the recruiter found me."

Had someone asked me whether poor people lived on the streets of Kisia's cities I would have said yes, their existence impossible to avoid, but with a jolt of shame I realised not only that I'd never spoken to one before, but that I'd never asked myself why they were there at all.

Another thing I would have to change.

We spoke a little longer, but he got no more comfortable, so I let him escape back to his task.

"I'm unsure what that conversation achieved," Manshin said, having stood like a stern statue beside me the whole time. "You don't need the favour of those who don't fight for you."

"But without these boys, would the camp run as smoothly as it does?"

"No, but that is for the generals and the quartermaster to control."

The argument didn't seem worthwhile so I let it drop, though Ani's simple admission that he didn't know where he was from lingered long on my mind.

We had almost done a full lap of the camp when Minister Manshin nodded at two men sitting before a cooking fire like common soldiers despite their generals' regalia. "I think I told you about General Yass and General Alon, our two barbarian generals."

"You did," I said. "But if they fight for Kisia and live in Kisia, how is it we still call them barbarians?"

"The term is not used in disrespect, Your Majesty, merely to indicate they are not Kisian."

"What makes one Kisian, I wonder," I said, more to myself than because I wished an answer.

"Being born here is a good start."

I had no time to retort before the two generals rose from their meals, and in a hurried under voice, Manshin added, "I've been informed both refused to give allegiance to Emperor Jie. You must tread carefully with them."

"Is treading carefully the best way to earn their respect?"

"No, but with them, demanding it is the surest way not to get it."

There was no time for more as we came within earshot and the two men bowed, which seemed like a good start. At first sight there was nothing about either to mark them as *not Kisian*, as Manshin put it, except that General Yass had shorter hair than was fashionable even amongst soldiers, and General Alon wore a full beard. And when they opened their mouths, their southern Kisian accent was heavy.

"Your Majesty," General Yass said, and where another general might have filled the brief silence with an observation or question, both men merely stood waiting to be informed what I wanted. There was something both uncomfortable and wonderful about men who did not fill silence for the sake of it, talking to no purpose.

"Ah, you like your speaking direct, I see," I said. "Rather than court chatter."

"We have neither of us been to court, Your Majesty," General Alon said, and it was odd not to clearly see the movement of his lips and the lines about his face. In its way, his beard was a mask. "We are but simple soldiers."

"Then allow me to get to the point," I said. "As I'm sure you understand, new emperors, and empresses, usually request an immediate oath of allegiance from their generals as a way of feeling...less vulnerable. I understand my brother requested this, but I will not as it goes against your ways to give loyalty that has not been earned. The very honour that makes this so gives me confidence you won't betray me, and I trust that if you have a problem with my decisions you will afford me the same degree of plain speaking as I have afforded you."

My heart hammered throughout this speech as I hunted their expressions for some sign they understood, that they appreciated my decision, but their faces were implacable. And when I finished they merely bowed, more acknowledgement than anything, and I wanted to be sick.

Until General Yass said, "Your plain speaking is appreciated, Your Majesty. We may give no oaths to those who have not earned them, but we fight for Kisia, so while you fight for Kisia you will find us at your side, sworn allegiance or no."

"And we don't stab people in the back," General Alon said, with a gruff laugh. "We stab them in the front."

My relief was potent and I couldn't but grin, an expression that would have horrified my mother. "You served my father, the great Emperor Kin Ts'ai, with strength and honour," I said as I had to the others. "And I welcome your continued service to the empire."

"Your Majesty," they said.

We walked on, leaving the generals to their meal, and once we were out of earshot, I awaited a compliment on how well that had gone. But Minister Manshin maintained a noncommittal silence, not even pointing out other leaders or areas of the camp as we went.

"No congratulations on my handling this time, Minister?"

"I feel there is a line between being too distant and too...forward, Your Majesty."

"There was something more forward about my interaction with them than any others? I am afraid I don't see it," I said, stung by the injustice.

I looked up, but he didn't meet my gaze as he said, "They conduct themselves differently, but you are their empress. This is Kisia, not the mountains. It is weak for you to conform, and in your position, indelicate to speak so to barbarian men."

His tone chastened, yet his words filled me with a frustration I could give no voice to, could not even explain, let alone argue over.

"Only the barbarian ones?" I said, keeping my question deceptively cool.

"Let us say *especially* the barbarian ones."

"Are they more dangerous to my virtue?"

He looked down at me, a scowl cutting his brow. "This is hardly a useful conversation."

"No, you're right, it's not." I stopped walking. "I'm feeling fatigued and will rest in my tent until it's time for the meeting."

Minister Manshin bowed. "Your Majesty."

I walked back to the central tents alone, caught in my own abstraction. Everything was noise and movement, but it seemed to calm the thoughts swirling through my head, thoughts I could barely catch let alone dwell on, such did anger speed them from my grasp.

A soldier stood guard outside my tent, bearing the expression of one with something important to say. I let go a reluctant sigh. "What is it?"

"Your Majesty. You have a visitor."

"A visitor? Who?"

"That would be me."

I spun, breath catching at the sound of so recognisable a voice. At his ease a few paces away stood General Ryoji. Ryoji who had trained us. Ryoji who had been my mother's most loyal guard. Ryoji into whom I had stuck a blade the night I had protected Emperor Kin against Mother's coup. For all the good it had done.

He didn't look any worse for it, but he had aged since I'd last seen him. Or perhaps it was merely that I'd never seen him out of uniform.

Despite the way we had parted, despite everything, it took all my self-control not to run to him, not to touch him to be sure he was real. Not to demand news of my mother and how he came to be here. The answers would hurt too much, and too many people were watching. I was fast learning there were always people watching in an army camp, much like at court.

"General Ryoji," I said with great self-control. "It has been quite some time since I last saw you."

"Indeed, Your Majesty." He bowed, and I could not but think of how long he had bowed to my mother and called her Majesty. "You are remarkably difficult to find."

"I was unaware you were alive, let alone looking for me." I turned to the soldier standing guard. "Have someone bring food and wine to my tent. General," I added, gesturing an invitation to enter. "Do join me."

He bowed again. "I would be honoured, Your Majesty."

The interior of my tent owned few comforts of rank amid the practicalities of life in a military camp. Especially a military camp where I was trying to prove myself useful and necessary, not merely a figurehead sitting on a nonexistent throne.

No finery, but there was a table, and I gestured for Ryoji to sit. He hesitated, something of a wry smile twisting his lips. "What a reverse this is."

"Isn't it," I agreed. "I must admit I prefer the power balance this way around."

"So did your mother."

He seemed to regret the words the moment they were out of his mouth, his smile fading into wariness.

A hundred questions banked behind my teeth as I sat down, intent on maintaining my imperial bearing whatever our history. He had known me from a child, but I would give him no reason to look at me and still see that child.

"Well," I said. "I think you owe me quite the tale, General, but first, where is she?"

He bowed his head. "I don't know."

I had not been prepared for grief and ought to be glad I'd been spared it, yet this ongoing limbo was somehow worse. "You had better explain yourself."

I hoped I looked as grim as I sounded, hoped he had not forgotten the blade I'd stuck in his flesh. I wanted to trust him, but I was well past trusting people merely because I hoped I could.

Letting out a sigh, General Ryoji ran his hand along the tabletop as though smoothing wrinkles from the wood. "I tried," he said, the words a whisper. "I tried, Miko, I really did, but they came so fast. One moment the city and the castle were secure, then they were inside slaughtering everyone. I'd headed for the gates at the first sign something was amiss and by the time I realised how bad it was I couldn't get back to..."

He stared at his own hand sliding over the table. "We were overrun. There was nothing I could do. I ought to have fought and died, but...it seems my loyalty to your mother is stronger even than my sense of duty and honour."

I refrained from pointing out his support of her coup had been evidence enough of that.

"I took a Chiltaen uniform from a fallen soldier and got out into the city. I began planning how to get back in to save her, but by morning they had already left."

"They?"

"I understand the hieromonk took her south with him. I followed their trail, but it went cold at Suway. What little was left of the northern towns were in no state to remember anyone passing through, or perhaps they weren't following the roads, I don't know." His hand stilled and he looked up. "I went every direction I thought they might have gone and found nothing. I don't even know..." His gaze flicked away again. "She was suffering a bout of illness the night they took Koi."

I thought of my mother banked up by pillows with Master Kenji kneeling at her side, thin trickles of blood draining from pinpricks in her arm. She had always been so well I had thought it a ruse to gain pity.

"She was really sick?"

General Ryoji nodded. "The Imperial Disease."

Of course I had heard of it, had seen it listed often enough in our family history to ask what it was. No one seemed to know, only that it had plagued the Otako family for a long time. Fatigue. Weakness. Slowing of breath and vitality. Nothing seemed to help.

"How long?"

"Had she had it? A few years, getting slowly worse. Each bout more debilitating than the last and getting closer together. With care Master Kenji thought she had a year left, maybe two. Without his care..."

He left the words hanging, the rest of the thought not needing to be spoken aloud for how completely it filled my mind. Without care she could already be dead.

"By the time I gave up trying to find her," the general went on, not wanting to dwell on the fear that must have been in his mind as much as it was in mine, "Mei'lian had fallen to the Chiltaens and my search for you turned up as little as my search for your mother. Until now."

"Well," I said when I could swallow the lump forming in my throat. "For what it's worth, it's good to see you again, General."

"And kind of you to call me so when I am now a mere commoner."

He would have to earn my trust, but he was as useful as his presence was comforting. I allowed myself a smile. "Not a kindness, merely an acknowledgement of your continued position."

He looked up so sharply he banged his elbow on the edge of the table, shock and pain mingling in his face. "You want me to...?"

I hadn't realised how much anger I had been carrying toward him until its knots loosened in my gut. "Yes," I said. "Despite what happened at Koi, I wish you to command my Imperial Guard. Unless you wish to keep searching for my mother."

He breathed a bitter laugh. "I fear continuing to throw myself at the impossible would be to allow grief to consume me."

I wasn't sure what to say. He had never spoken about his relationship with my mother, the secret everyone at court knew but only whispered.

"Don't worry, I don't mean to get sentimental on you," he added. "There was always a level of mutual ambition in what we had, but you don't spend that much time with someone without developing more love than you ever planned to allow them." He let go the elbow he'd been rubbing and met my gaze. "If you will have me back I will do all I can to serve you, Your Majesty. Your mother made a promise her child would sit on the throne and we cannot let her down now, can we?"

I ran my gaze along the table of generals, each quieting as they took their places, gazes flitting Minister Manshin's way as they waited. General Moto in particular I watched, wary.

Once they had all stilled, I cleared my throat and began. "Welcome to our first council meeting," I said. "I believe I have met you all, so we can get straight to the most important business."

In the pause before I went on, a few murmurs sounded as they quietly questioned this woman who would sit at the head of their table and dare to lead them when Minister Manshin was far more qualified and sat right there.

"The Levanti are consolidating their hold on the northern half of our empire," I went on, determined to be taken seriously. "There is a chance Chiltae may regroup and attack them, but it seems more likely after losing much of their army they will hold their borders and stay out of this. It would be an easy enough battle to get these barbarians"—I winced at the word, but there could be no space for nuance, no accepting they were no such thing when I needed to rally an army against them—"out of our lands were they not allied to a number of northern lords. Some may have joined out of a pragmatic wish to not be trampled, but others appear to have eschewed loyalty to the empire for power and personal gain. Chief amongst these being Grace Bahain."

No muttering followed. They had all heard, but for a moment I was sitting across from Edo at Kiyoshio Castle as he wrote this treason for me to see. The realisation of having no allies left, of being wholly alone, had hollowed me with a fear I had not yet shaken.

"We cannot strike at them head-on with such support," I said. "But we may be able to if we can peel Bahain away from his new emperor."

"Attacking Kogahaera would be suicidal," General Rushin said.

"Not Kogahaera. Not yet." I shook my head. "Syan."

A moment of utter stillness held them in its grip, before they looked to Manshin to see if he'd heard my mad utterance. When he gave no sign of surprise or derision, the complaints began.

"I'm sure you must realise Syan is one of the most fortified cities in Kisia, Your Majesty," General Moto said.

"The castle is behind at least three layers of walls."

"It has never been conquered!"

"Yes, even though pirates have raided the city for decades, the castle has never fallen."

I weathered their exclamations, much like Kiyoshio weathered the furious sea, and waited for them to die away. Eventually they did, perhaps because they had uttered every complaint there was, or because one by one they noticed I was sitting, untroubled, waiting patiently for them to finish.

"We are going to take Kiyoshio," I said when they fell silent.

"May we ask how, Your Majesty?" General Mihri said. "You have a plan, perhaps."

"Yes. I do."

Now they were all listening.

2. DISHIVA

*D*on't go back," Jass had said, yet here I was. *"There is nothing you can do."* I could only hope to live long enough for him to say he'd told me so.

I knelt on the floor, breathing slowly in and out. My knees ached and my stomach was on fire, but I could barely keep my eyes open.

"Captain Lashak and her Namalaka will have to stay behind," Gideon said over the crackling fire. I yearned for its warmth, but dared not edge closer. "They have only just returned and someone must remain. More refugees from Mei'lian arrive every day. The city is getting full."

"Yes, it is a testament to your people's faith in you, Your Majesty," Leo Villius replied. Only days ago his mouth had slackened in death. Days? More like a lifetime of kneeling in shame. "But with all deference to Captain Lashak, do you think she and her Swords can be useful here? They can raise tents, but they are not skilled builders and cannot speak Kisian." Here the assiduous speech paused, and not for the first or even the hundredth time I imagined ripping out that golden tongue. "I can assure you, Your Majesty, my people do not mind doing the work. In fact, at such times I feel God's servants are more useful than soldiers."

Say no. Say no. He's either going to kill the people or turn them against you.

"There is wisdom in what you say," Gideon said. "And if Captain Lashak goes that will be two Swordherds as well as half my guard."

You shouldn't send any of your guards!

"I would be more confident in the success of three contingents of Swords," Leo said, my existence continuing to be ignored. "But if there are no others nearby..."

"Captain Taga's last message had her and Menesor e'Qara near Suway."

Stop telling him where they are!

"I have not heard from Atum e'Jaroven—" A pause proved my presence had not been forgotten. "I could recall the Injit, but despite the destruction of Mei'lian, I cannot be comfortable with the rumours that Empress Miko has been hailed ruler in the south."

"It is troubling," Leo agreed, and I could almost have believed he meant it.

For a time there was nothing but the slosh and clink of wine bowls and the slow chewing of two men hardly paying attention to their meals while the room filled with the scent of sweet and spicy meat and ginger soup. My stomach rumbled.

At length a maid scratched at the door and came in, the old reeds crackling beneath her careful steps. Cups and plates clinked as she gathered them, and over their symphony Leo spoke again. "It would be well, I think, for you to be seen out amongst the refugees this morning, Your Majesty."

The words were a suggestion but did not sound like one.

"Yes," Gideon said, his thoughts sounding distant. This was the man who had come so far for his people, to better our place in the world and give us power over our own future. Yet here I was kneeling in shame while Leo Villius sat in a place of power.

If you can hear me, Leo, I am going to kill you again. And again if I have to, however many times it takes before your god gives up on you.

Leather creaked as Gideon rose from the table, letting go a long breath. "I will meet with the refugees who arrived overnight."

"As you wish, Your Majesty."

Fabric rustled. Footsteps crossed the floor only for one set to halt before me. I did not look up. Was not allowed to look up. But all too well could I imagine his mocking smile. Not so long ago I had punched that face until it broke, until it could not smile anymore. Little good it had done.

"Tired of kneeling yet, Dishiva?" spoke that hateful voice, all tender sweetness.

I did not answer.

"When I first returned I wanted to watch you die," he went on. "Until Gideon condemned you to kneel. Never had I thought to find a Levanti custom I liked more than your head chopping, but here it is—kneeling in shame. How long, I wonder, will you survive so? How long until fatigue and thirst and hunger drive you mad and destroy you as you let them destroy me? How long until you throw away your precious honour and stand up to defend your *life*?"

Still I did not answer, but my blood boiled with hatred for this man who would not die. I could leap up and strangle him, but would achieve only ruin.

"I hope I am here to see you break. To sink yourself in the eyes of your heathen gods like poor Rah. There could be no greater justice."

Only the mantras I had learned for my Making kept me kneeling as he loomed over me. "Well done, Dishiva. I'll ask someone to watch you while His Majesty is not here. Wouldn't want you able to move."

He walked away, pausing to speak to whoever was on duty outside. They ought to be my Swords, but Moshe had planted a seed of doubt even about Keka, and I didn't know who I could trust anymore.

As Leo's footsteps faded away along the passage, someone entered. I tensed aching muscles and refused to look up, not even when boots stopped before me, the red bands around their ankles very familiar.

Keka. Ever silent now, though I could still remember the sound of his laugh barking into the wind as we rode out on hunts. It felt like a lifetime ago.

"How long?" I said, quiet enough not to be heard from the door. "How long have you hated me? Since I chose to follow Gideon? Since I could not stop the Chiltaens cutting out your tongue? Since we were exiled? Or from the moment I was named captain instead of you?"

The question hung in the musty air.

"You could have challenged me. You can't have been afraid you wouldn't win."

Still no reply, not even a grunt, and I could not look up—would not.

"I'm sorry I failed you, my friend." I could not keep the catch from my voice, for whatever he might have incited, whatever had happened in that clearing near the deserter camp, I had loved him like a brother.

Keka moved and I tensed already tense muscles as he bent one knee after the other, settling on the matting before me just out of reach. And there he stayed kneeling with me, palms up in a silent gesture of apology. Words that had come so easily before failed me, and I blinked back tears.

Neither of us made a sound for what felt like hours to my long-suffering knees but could only have been one at most. The guards did not change, and from outside came no sound but the ever-present hubbub of activity in the yard, none of it as loud or present as every inhale and exhale of Keka's breath. I could have wished to remain so forever, but time doesn't work like that. The longer away you wish something the faster it comes, and all too soon footsteps thundered along the hallway, all quick, purposeful strides heralding trouble.

"Go," I said, and looked up, the urge so great I could not fight it. "Don't be found like this."

I had seen those dark eyes laugh, had seen them scowl and smile and wince and widen in fear, but never had I seen tears pouring from them, never had I seen his shoulders shake or his mouth open slack in silent distress. As the footsteps drew closer, he held out both hands, palms up, and uttered the first attempt at speech he had made since the Chiltaens had taken his tongue. The words were not clearly enunciated, and yet their meaning was as clear as that of his gesture.

"Sorry? What have you done, Keka?" I said, voice trembling. All this time I had thought he was apologising for turning some of my Swords against me, not for something I had not yet seen. "What have you done?"

He repeated the mangled apology and got to his feet as a torrent of footsteps entered the room, carried on a tide of strange voices. A Kisian soldier gripped my upper arm, digging in his fingers as I fought to remain kneeling.

"I have not been released and cannot move," I said as another took the other arm. "Let me go! Where is Emperor Gideon?"

"Waiting for you outside, of course," came a voice from the door. "You are needed at once."

"Why?" I demanded, not meeting Leo's gaze as I was hauled up lest he read the fear in my mind.

"For the ceremony." Leo smiled and gestured to the dim sunlight seeping in through the nearest window. "The weather is fine, Levanti and Kisians alike have gathered, and we cannot keep His Majesty waiting, now, can we."

Having been set unceremoniously on my feet by grasping hands, my gaze slid to the back of Keka's turned head. I bit his name from my tongue. A plea would achieve nothing beyond my own embarrassment. If execution was to be my reward, I would die proud and unbreaking. I had retained enough Levanti for that, pride and honour etched upon my bones.

Leo's smile stretched, though to call it a smile was unfair to sickening sneers. "Ah, there we go, the great Levanti martyrdom. It truly is impressive that you've made a culture out of suffering." He laughed at his own wit, and when I made no reply, spoke in Kisian and gestured to the soldiers. The grips upon my arms loosened. One spoke a question, and with his travesty of a smile not leaving his face, Leo nodded. The soldiers let go and stepped back.

"Better," he said in Levanti. "Now we walk. You will walk on your own, won't you, Dishiva?"

For the barest second our eyes met and I tore my gaze away with a jolt of panic. *Don't think about her. Don't think about her. Don't think about her.*

"Yes," I said, rolling my shoulders and straightening my back. "I will not be dragged like an animal."

Like an honour guard, a few soldiers went before me while others remained, their confused looks flicking Leo's way. He waited for me to move with enough patience to shame a drying riverbed.

There was nothing to do but follow the guards with what pride I could gather, my stomach empty and my heart heavy. Massama stood guard outside, and in the moment I passed she sucked in a breath to speak, her hand twitching, only to leave me walking alone.

I had lost track of time while kneeling. Night had come and been chased away by morning. Now, thick cloud obscured most of the sunlight.

"There is, I'm afraid, no time for you to bathe," Leo said, walking alongside me down the narrow passage ribbed with thick beams. "But fresh clothes are waiting."

I wanted to ask who needed fresh clothes to die, but would give him no such satisfaction. Not for the first time I hoped I was right and he needed eye contact to read my thoughts.

Don't think about her. Don't think about her. Don't think about her.

"You will have to change quickly, however. We have kept His Majesty waiting."

I bit my lip, the pain making it easier to keep my tongue behind my teeth. He smiled anyway, radiant smugness louder than words.

The guards marched ahead along the passage and down the stairs, turning into a small room off the main hall, across from the open doors where an impatient hubbub of voices wafted in on damp air. "It looks like your fresh clothes are still on their way, so you get a moment to wash after all. Fortunate, really, given how... pungent you smell."

The little room was empty of all but a pair of candles and a basin of steaming water. There had been no time to wash since I had returned to Kogahaera, and the blood and mud and filth of all that had happened since Jass and I had carried Leo broken and bound through the caves was still stuck to me, each a memory I wished I could wash away. Yet I hesitated.

Beside the open door, Leo went on smiling. At my back the Kisian soldiers stood shoulder to shoulder. There was no escape.

"You don't have to wash, of course," Leo said. "But you will have to change clothes. I assume you would rather take care of that yourself than have many helping hands."

I gritted my teeth. "If you, or any of them, touch me, I will take as many of you with me as I can."

"So dramatic," he crooned. "You almost make me want to try it just for the sport. Unlike you, however, I am capable of delaying satisfaction for much greater gratification later. So do, please, wash and change before we are summoned by His Majesty."

I distrusted his *we*. I distrusted everything about him, but it was stupid to stand there and risk his mood turning.

With my head high, I stepped inside, firmly closing the door behind me. As fast as I could, I stripped off my filthy, blood-crusted armour and my stained underclothes, all of it stinking of sweat and mud and horse. Underneath it my body was surprisingly clean, but I was glad to whisk a damp cloth over my skin to wake myself up.

The door opened as I wiped my feet, and I spun ready to punch the intruder only to draw up short at a maid's squeal. She dropped a pile of clothes and dashed back out, leaving nothing but a small gust of wind making the candle flames dance.

As clean as I could hope to get without exposing myself more, I picked up the clothes. A fresh under-tunic and some tight Chiltaen leg coverings, plain armour, and...A white sash and mask fell softly to the floor and lay turning gold in the candlelight. I stared, sure I could feel Leo's smile radiating through the closed door. He was out there waiting for me to object, to refuse, to give him the satisfaction of forcing them upon me. All to humiliate me before death like a cat playing with a mouse.

In silence I dressed, disliking the strange fabric and the unfamiliar cut of clothes made for someone smaller and thinner than I. At least it would soon be over. A deep part of my mind rebelled, shouting this could not be the end, I would not die like this, not here, not now, not ever on the whim of an evil so insidious it refused to die. I tried to calm the rage with mantras as I dressed, time stretching thin between the flickering candles.

The tap came as gentle as the beat of bird wings, but his voice was hard with malicious humour. "Time's up, Dishiva."

The door swung in, sending dim daylight pouring into what had become my little sanctuary. It fell upon the mask and the sash on the floor, and Leo showed his teeth. "Ah, of course, you don't know how to wear them properly; foolish of me to forget you were not born one of us. No matter, we will soon fix that."

I had expected a very different reply, and looked up. I met his gaze only for a moment, a moment that jolted me back against the wall. The candle fell, hissing into darkness and leaving Leo lit from behind, godlike.

"There is no reason to be afraid," he crooned, stepping forward. "What the One True God wants to see in your thoughts he will, whether you let me in or not. Once you muse on that truth you will realise how comforting it is, how content you can be when you let go, when you stop fighting and flow upon the tide of God's purpose."

His words crept under my skin like my mantras.

"And God has a purpose for you, Dishiva, as he has a purpose for all," he went on, taking another step. "A purpose that will be remembered long after we are gone, the effects of our lives left to ripple on as Veld's once did, building all that makes this world great and good."

He picked up the sash and mask. I was trapped, but the warmth of his voice was comforting like a protective mother. "Here, let me do this for you," he said, sash held out.

Deep down where my rage lived, I screamed and fought and would have bitten his hand rather than let him lower it over my head, but with my eyes caught to his and the sound of his voice filling my ears, I could not move. The sash settled over one shoulder, and like a hypnotised child I threaded one arm through so it could fall diagonally shoulder to hip.

"I'll hold on to this until after," he said, lifting the white mask. "Come with me."

And I did. Moving through a dream, I let him set my hand upon his arm and lead me out past the guards, though the touch of his hand and his proximity made bile rise in my throat.

Outside, murmurs filled the yard. A raised stage stood shoulder high, surrounded by a sea of Levanti and Kisians, soldiers and refugees, looking up to the commanding figure of Gideon in his layers of imperial crimson silk. His gaze pinned me as we stepped out into the light, and every voice faded into silence.

What are you doing? I demanded of myself. *Run!*

But the deep fear and anger was nothing to the peace. It hung about me like a drug, infusing every thought with its insidious belief this was meant to be.

Heads turned, and though I ought to fight, to kick and bite and scream, I walked on at Leo's side bathing in the disgust of every Levanti sneer. I caught sight of Lashak, her stare a horrified thing mingled with confusion, and I wished she could feel the peace and be comforted by it as I was.

A low hum rose from the whispers, becoming something like a wordless chant as the crowd parted. It seemed to come from all around us, but as we drew closer to the stage, a group of pilgrims appeared, along with Lord Nishi and his ever-growing number of servants, joining their voices to the song.

Don't do it! Don't go! This is madness! I shouted, but I might as well have been two separate people for all the heed I paid. We had reached the stage, leaving all chance of escape dwindling to nothing.

The stairs creaked beneath the guards' heavy treads as they mounted the platform. There was nothing permanent about the construction, the stairs shaking beneath my feet even as my legs trembled to hold my weight. Leo tightened his grip on my arm.

"My people!" Gideon called, stepping to the edge of the stage, his outstretched arms spreading cloth like webbing—a crimson bat ready to take flight. "These are difficult times, beset by evils. As a prisoner I fought to save you from Chiltaen tyranny, and now as your emperor I can do no less than fight on for peace and tolerance."

Having reached the top of the stairs, I gazed out over the sea of watchers, and a sea it was, for there were more people at Kogahaera now than ever before, more Kisians displaced from their homes and more Chiltaens come to join Leo's faith. When Gideon spoke again in their language instead of ours, a murmur of amazement spread.

"The Kisia I dream of is one where we can all—Kisian, Chiltaen, and Levanti alike—live side by side not regardless of our differences, but celebrating and accepting our differences," he went on, none of it sounding like the beginning of an execution.

"Smile, Dishiva," Leo whispered as Gideon repeated his words in Kisian, gesturing to the silent figure of his empress standing behind him in equally glorious regalia. "You are about to be very famous indeed. Whatever history may forget about these events it will not be me and it will not be you."

"We are new to these shores," Gideon went on in Levanti. "And we can only truly make a home here if we accept some of your ways as our own. I took on the title of emperor. I took a Kisian wife. And now we must give something back."

With my hand caught to Leo's like it had been buckled, I searched the crowd for faces I knew and begged silently for help with all I had. But there was no help.

"Step forward, Dishiva e'Jaroven," Gideon said. "Captain of the Third Swords of Jaroven and of my Imperial Guard, defender of all I have built."

The peace on which I had floated dropped away and I stood naked of all assurance, staring out at the crowd but not really seeing them. Whatever Leo had done, however he had clouded my mind, he had cruelly stripped away. Now, seconds from an unknown fate, I had the barest moment in which to make a choice. Fight, risking death and exile and harm to Gideon, or let myself become something unthinkable in the hope of lessening the damage.

It was both the hardest choice and no real choice at all.

I stepped forward.

"To forge stronger ties between our people, we are here to celebrate Captain Dishiva e'Jaroven's decision to take oath as Defender of the One True God, to become a bridge between Levanti and those of the faith."

Gideon repeated the words in his second language, but even as the strange sounds washed over me, all I could hear was their echo in my head. A defender of the One True God. The One True God.

He turned his gaze upon me. No smile, no cruel sneer, nothing but hard, implacable determination to succeed, and I could not even hate him for it. He had come too far, risked too much, dreamed too high.

Beside me Leo said, "Kneel, Dishiva."

Fight or submit. The choice had already been made and I knelt, as much a martyr as if it had been my execution.

"I call upon the blessings of the One True God," Leo said, and though he must have shifted into Chiltaen at some point to hold the crowd, time seemed to have lost all meaning. There was just me and him and the hard wood beneath my knees. "That he may protect this warrior who gives herself body and soul into his service, as she fights to protect him and his humble servants upon this mortal plane."

The silence of so many held breaths sucked at my attention, but I kept my eyes upon Leo's feet and dared not move.

"Do you, Dishiva e'Jaroven, swear upon life and honour to uphold and defend the faith of the One True God?"

The words stuck in my throat with a disgust I could not swallow, a disgust that had nothing to do with the gentle people whose faith I was taking on and everything to do with the man standing over me.

Let him think he has broken me. Let him think he has won.

"I swear upon my life and honour to uphold and defend the faith of the One True God," I said, my dishonour ringing through the yard to be chased upon a tide of Levanti murmuring.

Nearby, Oshar translated, calling in Kisian to the watching people.

"Do you, Dishiva e'Jaroven, forsake your position as commander of the Imperial Guard and captain of the Third Swords to give your honour to the protection of God?"

I swallowed a mouthful of self-pity with my bile. "I do."

The translation rattled on, the only sound to break the silence in the yard.

"As the highest-ranking priest present, it is my great honour to accept your pledge on behalf of my absent father, the hieromonk of Chiltae, and on behalf of the One True God himself, in whose service I am sure you will make all Levanti proud."

The collective hum rose again, Oshar translating over the top. Within the hum a single voice chanted, its meaning shearing through my skin and into my heart. Levanti had such chants for summoning the attention of the gods, and though this one soon rose into a song it was no less beautiful than our own for being different.

I flinched at the touch of fabric against my face. Pale, soft fabric, suffocating like a cloud.

The mask.

I clamped my lips as Leo wrapped its ties around my shaved head. Light bit through the narrow eye sockets that thinned the world to a narrow band, and there was no way to breathe but through the weave. No way to be seen as anything but a faceless servant of the One True God.

I was Levanti no more.

"Rise, Dishiva, Defender of the Faith," Leo said as the song faded away. "And take your honoured place."

I stood, faceless before the masses.

Applause rose from the crowd and Leo leant close. "Now in God's name you can bless the Swords marching south to root out those deserters and their beloved whisperer."

I turned, shock pounding through my veins.

"You are not good at lying," he said. "And before you ask how I intend to force your hand, remember what levers I have at my disposal. If you refuse to comply with my plans, I will kill every one of your Swords and their horses. I will butcher even your dear Itaghai, and I will make you eat him. Don't think I can't."

I thought of the dreadful peace under the effect of which I might have done anything.

He straightened, adding his own applause to the tumult in a rhythm that seemed to mirror the panicked racing of my heart. "All praise Dishiva, Defender of the One True God!"

3. CASSANDRA

The cart jolted to a halt, and while Captain Aeneas leapt onto the road, I stabbed the driver through his ribs.

Was that really necessary? Empress Hana asked, though it was less a question than a need, for her own conscience, to register displeasure.

"Would you rather he blabbed everywhere about the two Chiltaens and their heavy box? I don't know about you, but I'd rather not be found by—"

You seem to be forgetting you're no longer in your body, Miss Marius. I am not Chiltaen.

I gave the empty road the look I would have given her. "I had not forgotten," I said, patting her blonde curls with my bloodstained hand. "I look more Chiltaen in your skin than I ever did in mine."

Her knees clicked as I forced us to rise, and setting a boot to the carter's back, I kicked him off the box. The body landed on the road with a fleshy thud. Captain Aeneas had walked a few paces away and knelt on the damp grass to murmur his evening prayers. I rolled my eyes. Evening gloom was setting in and the air smelled like rain, but at least the horizon was empty of pursuit. Wherever Leo was, it was not here.

Yet.

While Captain Aeneas prayed to the dying sun, my gaze slid

to the long, coffin-like box in the back of the cart. It hadn't moved since the carter had helped the captain lift it in this morning, and yet... Even looking at it made the hairs on my arms stand on end. It was just a box, but the thing inside was alive and listening and, worst of all, seemed to be waking up.

I climbed down, wincing and hissing at the pains in every joint. I wanted to sleep, but there wasn't even the semblance of a shelter, and the box needed to be moved, a fire built, and the ox and cart tended.

He can do it.

"Not without help."

He'll have help. Put me in the carter.

I stared at the carter's body, and to hide my annoyance that the idea had not occurred to me, said, "An empress doing manual labour?"

In the silence, a chill wind rushed past my ears.

I was not born an empress and I will not die one. Just put me in the corpse.

It was only a few steps to the body I'd kicked onto the road, but it was more steps than the empress's aching body wanted to take. I envied the freedom she was about to have as I bent to touch the man's lifeless cheek. The loss of her loosened the tension across my shoulders, but did nothing to lessen the fatigue hanging about my neck.

Like a waking cat, Empress Hana stretched the body's limbs in the last of the light. Her first attempt at speech came out as a gurgle, but she coughed as she hunched off toward the trees and soon had it working. By the time Captain Aeneas rose from his prayers, she had returned with an armload of wood scavenged from the damp forest floor. Before I could point out how useless damp wood would be, he was already shaking his head.

"We don't need a fire," he said, the gathering shadows making art of his scarred features. "We stop only long enough to rest the ox." He glanced toward the box as he spoke, its stillness eerie. The sharp wind tore at my skin with its icy hands. "And to feed him."

Hana dropped the wood. It landed on the dead man's feet, but she seemed not to notice. "I want an answer first. You think we can use him to stop Leo Villius, yet you're a believer in the faith. Why do you want him stopped?"

The captain did not meet her gaze. She pinned him with the unnerving stare of a dead man and waited.

"His father is dead," I said. "So surely he will be the next hieromonk of Chiltae."

His scowl deepened. "Even were that true, the hieromonk of the One True God ought to work only for his faith and his people, not for…power and glory," the captain said. "The holy empire is a thing of the past from which we ought to learn, not something to emulate whatever the…connections and…similarities." He trailed off. "I am not good at expressing myself about such things."

He went to tend the ox, and I suppressed the urge to follow. "At least I think we can trust him," Hana said in the carter's croak.

"*We*? After all that shit back in Koi, I'm not even sure I can trust *you*."

Leaving her to glare after me, I walked her aching limbs toward the closest tree and sat. The ground was cold and wet, but I could not find the energy to care and leaned back, watching the stiff-limbed corpse help Captain Aeneas free the ox from the shafts and lead it to water.

I closed drooping eyes, only to see a city street bustling with people—Chiltaen people in Chiltaen clothes, walking a Chiltaen street beneath a Chiltaen sky. Quick breaths came and went from my lungs, tasting of thirst and stale bread. Across the road a tall building rose from a nest of bare trees, its single spire reaching higher into the sky than any building in Genava.

I muttered a prayer and it was my voice that emerged as unsteady steps took me out into the crowded square. A shoulder shunted me sideways, sending pain through my injured leg, but Kaysa kept balance and walked on toward the church doors.

With a shout I awoke, jolted back to where Captain Aeneas and the dead carter were lifting Septum's box from the cart. I hauled myself up and only remembered my body's aches when pains pierced my knees and ankles. Hissing swear words, I hobbled across the muddy field as fast as I could, which was not at all fast once the first rush of panic wore off.

They had set the box down by the time I arrived, out of breath and sweating despite the cool night air. "Kaysa is in Eravum. At the church. If we hurry we could get there before she moves on."

The captain and the empress shared a look. "I thought you might ask to go after her again," the empress said. "But it's too dangerous. Leo Villius is looking for us, and he and everyone else knows what I look like. This"—she pointed at the box—"might be the only way we can nullify him."

"Why do you care? You were ready to die not so long ago."

Empress Hana narrowed her eyes. "And you wouldn't let me go. You told me I had a duty to my empire. To my daughter. And you were right."

"You do. I don't. It's not my empire and she is not my daughter."

"No, but that's my body you're walking around in, Miss Marius."

The silence could not have been deeper had the wind itself held its breath. I glared at the empress, but every argument sounded petulant, and beneath Captain Aeneas's gaze I could say none of them.

"I don't want to be stuck with you any more than you want to be stuck with me, Miss Marius, but there are more important things than either of us. And getting this...man back to Torvash is one of them."

I wanted to say Captain Aeneas could do it on his own. I wanted to say there was no evidence the seventh Leo would be of any use and the hieromonk had been no paragon, yet all those words went as unspoken as the rest.

It was the captain who broke the silence. "We cannot stay much longer," he said, having taken to the *we* much more confidently than I had. "We must feed him and restock and get back on the road. I'll fetch the running lantern." He walked away toward the front of the cart, leaving the empress and me standing awkwardly together.

"I'm sorry we can't go after her yet, Cassandra, I know—"

"I don't need your pity."

She scowled. "Solidarity is not the same as pity."

"It is when it's empty words."

"Empty words? When I have given you more autonomy over my body than—" She snapped the dead man's jaw shut. "If you try to run, I'll shove you so deep into my mind you won't even remember who you are."

She ended on a hiss as the captain returned, a lantern swinging in his hand. Its light glared into my eyes as he set it atop Septum's box. "I have some bread and meat left in my pack." He paused. The light was too bright to see his expression. "Normally I wouldn't be worried, but given what happened back in the hut..." He trailed off, but even without his words I relived the moment when the unmoving body had turned its head, had looked at us, *really* looked at us.

"I think between the two of us, Cassandra and I can keep an eye on him while you feed him," the empress said. "Give Cassandra your dagger; she is by far more skilled than I."

I hated her vote of confidence as much as I hated the look of shocked question the captain threw her way. "Are you sure? Is that—?"

"Yes, do it."

And as though she in her stiffening skin of dead flesh was his empress rather than an enemy, Captain Aeneas took the dagger from his belt and held it out. Almost I did not take it, but though I glared at the empress, I closed my—*her* fingers around the hilt made warm against his body. "Try not to hurt him if you don't have to, but…"

"If he's trying to strangle you, stick him in the arm?"

A smile flickered. "Something like that."

He pulled a wrapped package out of his bag. My stomach rumbled, but the food was not for me. Captain Aeneas picked up the lantern. "If you would lift the lid for me, Your Majesty."

"Indeed. Ready, Cassandra?"

"Yes, *Your Majesty.*"

She ignored my sarcasm. "Good. On the count of three. One, two, three."

With the strength of the carter's limbs it took little more than a grunt of effort to lift the lid, leaving lantern light to fall upon the man in the box. He was pale and thin with knotted hair and the wisps of a beard growing long upon his chin, but it was Leo from the tip of his straight nose to the bright eyes. Everything but the expression. Septum showed by not so much as a twitch that he saw us, not even flinching when the captain swung the lantern into his face.

"Food," the captain said, and ripped off a piece of salted beef. Septum did nothing as it was held toward his lips, but when Captain Aeneas said, "Open," the man in the box opened his mouth. The captain dangled the beef just inside and said, "Eat." Leo Septum closed his mouth, taking the meat and chewing. A second piece of meat was proffered once the first had been swallowed, and was eaten without further sign of life. Captain Aeneas had said he had been so all his life, like an empty shell, and watching him eat only at the captain's command, I could imagine his mother's horror at being presented with a silent baby that grew into a silent, empty child.

I shivered, wishing I could blame the cool gusts of wind dancing around the open field.

"Eat," the captain repeated, this time with a small chunk of bread. A glance up at the empress in her carter-skin proved I was not the only one wishing themselves elsewhere. I adjusted my grip on the dagger.

Septum chewed. Septum blinked. On command Septum took another bite while the empress and I stood watching, stiff and tense despite the pain and fatigue in every joint.

"Eat."

More pieces of meat and bread disappeared and my stomach gurgled. By the time the captain had finished, the cool night seemed to have frozen me in place. My grip on the dagger hurt to loosen, and I could not relax. With a nod from the captain, Empress Hana lowered the lid. A thud of finality and I could no longer see Septum, but his face seemed to be burned onto my mind, and I could not look away.

"We should eat and get moving," the captain said, holding out the wax-paper parcel.

"And when do we rest?"

He shrugged. "You can sleep in the back of the cart if you wish. Your Majesty, how long are you able to remain in that...form?"

"Puppeteering the dead, you mean?" she said. "I think a full day and night would start pushing the limits. It got pretty uncomfortable in the—the last one. By the end."

I stared at the box lid rather than the captain. The last body she had worn to its limits had been the hieromonk, something Captain Aeneas was better off not knowing.

I thrust the captain's dagger into my grubby sash and opened the wax paper to reveal leftover meat and bread. Both were dry and stale, but food was food, and I shoved a chunk of meat in my mouth.

"That's my dagger, Miss Marius."

"I know," I said, mouth full. "But you've got a sword and I don't, so I'll keep it."

He narrowed his eyes.

"Just for now," I added. "Until I can find a better one. What do you think I'm going to do, kill you?"

"The thought had crossed my mind."

"Oh, don't worry, Captain," the empress said. "Miss Marius likes you rather too much for that. Although she will no doubt stab me for saying so."

It would have been very satisfying indeed to plunge the knife into her dead body and watch the blood pour out, but to do so would only prove her assertion and she knew it. The dead body smirked. "Thank you for that childish utterance, Your Majesty," I said instead, aiming for awful dignity, and in her body it might just work. "But if we could focus on the task at hand, that would be good. I have my own body to be getting back to."

I pulled the captain's dagger from my sash and thrust its hilt into his slack hand. "Now you need have no concern over your safety; I shall just have to pray for mine."

Refusing the empress's assistance, I struggled onto the box seat, swearing all the way. "Your stupid body and its sore everything. Even your eyelids hurt—how is that possible?"

It was impossible to tell how late it was by the time Captain Aeneas had hitched the ox back to the cart. We were ready to go and the empress had settled on the hay beside Septum, yet still the captain fussed around at the ox's head.

I rolled my eyes. "I thought you wanted to get moving."

"We will in a moment."

"You needn't worry I am about to embarrass us both by

confessing a love for you I am far from feeling, whatever *Her Majesty* says. You're not a shit of a man, that's true, but it's far from the same thing. Now get the fuck up here so we can leave before Leo catches up with us."

Captain Aeneas tightened the ox's harness quite unnecessarily and cleared his throat. "My thanks," he said. "I strive to live by God's maxims."

"Oh yes, must be easy with all the killing and taking orders from madmen," I muttered to myself, and behind me the empress snorted.

Captain Aeneas, not having heard, jumped onto the box and took up the reins. But before he set the animal walking, he turned and fixed me with a serious look. "You aren't the terrible person you think you are either, Miss Marius," he said, temporarily taking from me all power of speech.

I dozed through the night to wake in the morning and wish myself dead. My mouth was dry and sticky and my head hurt, and I opened my eyes only to close them again. The sun was too bright, and I was leaning on Captain Aeneas's shoulder.

Shit. I tried to sit up, and everything spun.

"Whoa, no, no," the captain said. "Lie back down. I assure you it is not uncomfortable, and you have been very unwell."

I set my head back on his shoulder, hating him for his easy strength in that moment as much as I hated the need for him to provide it.

"Majesty," I managed to croak. "You can take your body back now."

"Unfortunately I'm going to have to join you soon." The carter's voice crackled. "This shell hasn't much left in it, but I will wait as long as I can. I think the strain of having both of us in there makes the illness worse."

"Worse? Then you can piss off," I said, accidentally drooling on the captain's shoulder and not finding any energy to care.

"Why thank you, Miss Marius. Do continue with what you were saying before you were interrupted, Captain."

Captain Aeneas cleared his throat. "Well, I don't know how to tell them apart except for Unus and Septum, so for ease let's just say Cassandra killed Sextus and the Levanti emperor killed Quin. The last I heard, one of them had replaced Quin at the Levanti court—Quator, let's say. We just left one in Koi—Tres. Unus has not left Chiltae, as far as I know. That leaves Duos still at large and unaccounted for, which is worrying. But—" He took a deep breath. "They seem to be attempting to re-enact the six deaths of Veld from the Presage. First killed by his leader. The hieromonk paid Cassandra to do it, but it is essentially the same thing. Then cut down in a throne room. Dying in a cave with a defender shouldn't be too difficult, but—"

"Are you telling me they are . . . sacrificing their lives to replicate a story in your holy book?" the empress croaked.

"They're one soul in seven bodies; I don't think they would see the loss of some of those bodies the same as we would see the death of brothers."

"But why do it?"

"I'm not sure, but being seen as a reborn servant of God would grant enough influence to ensure his elevation to hieromonk, and if he can follow Veld's footsteps all the way he could rebuild a holy empire."

Silence fell as we each considered these words, at least as far as our minds would allow, which for me was about three seconds. "But it's a book of stories; the One True God is just a threat to keep people in line."

Captain Aeneas's hands tightened on the reins, and I deemed it time to sit up straight, or at least as straight as I could.

"Miss Marius," he said stiffly, keeping his eyes on the road. "You may choose to believe or not as it suits you, but if we are to be stuck travelling together, I would request you not to mock my faith. All that's important here is that Leo Villius most certainly believes it and is acting on it, lacking as he is in your expertise on the subject."

I rolled my eyes, but it only made my head hurt all the more. Pulling my knees up close, I huddled into a ball on the hard bench beside him and thought of Kaysa. Chasing her was what I ought to be doing, not sitting around being lectured by a man so stubborn he could look at Leo and still have faith. What real god would allow his priesthood to become so villainous?

"I think...this...body...is almost...done..." Empress Hana said some hours later, having remained in it as long as she could. "Give me...your...hand."

I looked at the trees and dreamed of running, but this body held me prisoner and there was no escape. Slowly I unfolded my arm, reaching over the cart wall toward her. The empress did not take it. She stared at me with the carter's eyes, and I failed to suppress a shudder. Skin so pale and sickly, yet there was a dark patch like a bruise on her cheek where blood had pooled as she lay down. Its deep purple hue made the bloodless lips and crusted eyes look all the more terrible.

"What?" I said.

"You hesitated."

"Moving your arm hurts."

Those lifeless eyes narrowed. "You'll forgive me if I don't trust you, Miss Marius. We will go after your body as soon as this task is done, you have my word."

"And you'll forgive me if I don't think your word is worth much right now. This body of yours could die before ever we reach Torvash and then—"

Captain Aeneas hissed. "You never know when he might be listening."

My gaze fell to the long wooden box beside the empress, who despite her dead skin had leaned as far away from it as possible. It had an aura about it.

"Does he hear all the time?" I asked. "How does it work?"

"How the fuck do I know?" the captain said. "I'm just a soldier who takes orders from madmen, remember?"

"Yes," I said as I held out my hand again to the empress. "You are."

She took it. For a moment I was clutching dead flesh before I drew the largest, deepest breath I could take, expanding not only my lungs but my heart and my stomach and my hands and my feet, swelling everything to twice the size. And like a deep breath it felt so good to breathe in, to suck deep of life, but the moment I could not let it go and was forced to hold it in was agony.

I groaned, but it was the empress who swore. "This...is getting worse."

"Yes, it is," I agreed, letting go the empty corpse's hand. "We could go get another."

I'm not going to keep killing people so I can walk around in their bodies.

"You wouldn't be killing them."

Then whose hand is this? She lifted our right hand up before our face, its skin crinkled like we had been sitting too long in the bath. *And before you say we killed the carter, that was different. We needed the cart and couldn't leave behind a witness.*

"Suit yourself. Doesn't matter to me if we end up dead."

Captain Aeneas half turned, watching us from the corners of his eyes.

With the empress back inside the body we had been forced to share, the world was louder and brighter, warmer and harsher and tighter as though the air itself had closed in. The jolting of the cart was more painful, the stink of the ox more unbearable, and despite the fast-approaching winter there was enough warmth in the sun's light to make my eyes droop, followed by my head. And in the darkness swarming upon us, Kaysa walked and talked and lived the life that ought to have been mine.

She groaned, rubbing her eyes so hard little shoots of pain and colour marred the darkness. "I know you're there, Cassandra," she said. "You're like a... prickling in my head. If you're trying to use our apparently impossible-to-sever connection to find me, it won't work. I'll just keep moving. I'd rather run forever than live imprisoned in your head again."

I wanted to reply, but my sleeping consciousness owned no lips.

"Nothing?" she said. "How nice to have you silent for a change. Now why don't you go away and leave me alone?"

She folded her arms, but even had I wanted to leave I didn't know how. It wasn't like our situation came with instructions.

A heavy sigh. "Fine. Stick around. Watch me go to prayers, you might learn something." With a grunt of annoyance, she pulled open the door and stepped into the hallway. Blades of light sheared through the narrow windows on one side, and she walked through them past door after door, owning the quiet grace of one who didn't want to disturb God's nap.

"Is Empress Hana still stuck with you?" she murmured to herself after a pair of priests had passed with nods. "If so, I feel sorry for her."

Kaysa walked to the end of the passage, carrying me with her in her mind if not her body. "Makes it easier for me if you are, because that sick body of hers can't be long for this world. What happens when it dies, I wonder. Do you die? Or would you just live on, hanging around in the dead flesh?"

I didn't want to think about it, but her thoughts drifted back to the days she had spent inhabiting Jonus's body after death, after his limbs had stiffened and his blood cooled and the Kisians had carried him to Koi as a trophy.

"I'll leave you to think about that, shall I?"

She turned at the corner and stopped.

"Hello, Cassandra." Leo stood in the middle of the passage, faintly smiling. "Or would you prefer I call you Kaysa?"

Kaysa did not move, did not answer.

"Surely you remember me," he said, taking a step forward. "My name is Dom Leo Villius, and you stabbed me in the heart and cut off my head."

"No...I...I..." she stammered. "I didn't—I..."

"Ah, of course, not you, not you," he agreed, all smiles and calm, soothing words. "Not you, but it was those hands, was it not? Was those eyes into which I looked and begged."

She ought to stand her ground, to assess her options while showing no fear, but with every step he took closer she retreated. "What do you want?" she said, and my lips trembled on the words. "Cassandra isn't here. It is just me now, and I have come to seek forgiveness of God and live a life of repentance."

"Do you trust God, Kaysa?"

A nod, yet she shivered.

"Do you believe everything happens the way God intends for a reason?"

Another nod, another step back.

"Then why are you afraid of me? I'm a true child of the faith, sent back again and again to fulfil his purpose, and yet you retreat like I'm diseased."

A priest stepped into the passage only to halt. "I heard—Oh, Your Holiness, I did not know you were here. May I be of assistance?"

"You may escort this woman to my carriage, and if she gives you trouble you have my permission to use force." He might have been praying over a dying man for all the solemnity the words carried, yet there was no mistaking his meaning. The priest froze in a pose of indecision, one hand hovering in the air between us.

"Holiness? Forgive me, but if the lady does not wish—"

"She is hardly a lady."

"Your Holiness, I really—"

Leo turned to the man. "Bring. Her."

The priest's voice became a dead monotone and he gripped my arm. "Yes, Your Holiness."

I slammed my foot into his instep and pulled free as he yelped. Someone shouted after me as I dashed back along the passage, but the words vanished beneath the pounding of my feet and the ragged drag of my breath.

Another door opened and a priest looked out, brow creased, but no sooner did I part my lips to beg his protection than he intoned, "Yes, Your Holiness," and lunged. His fingers caught my cloak, but I wrenched free and ran on.

"Yes, Your Holi—" I slammed into a man at the corner, throwing him back against the wall with a crack of skull on stone.

"As Your Holiness commands." Two priests strode toward me, their eyes glassy, and terror stole all thought, leaving me a sack of instincts. I ducked and rolled between them, the stone sending shoots of pain spreading through my skull. Cassandra had always made it look so easy, damn her.

I sped for an arch leading into the garden as another man stepped into the passage, wearing the mask of a high priest. "What is happening here?" He peered through the fabric slits, eyes darting and alive, but he would soon turn against me like all the others, so I elbowed him in the gut and ran on.

Dashing through the garden, I hunted another arch, a door, a vine I could climb, anything that would let me escape, but I was surrounded by sheer stone walls.

Dom Villius, at an easy pace, stepped into the garden, surrounded by followers as lifeless as puppets though they walked and talked like men.

"Ah, you cannot escape, my dear," he said. He looked too big for the space, his voice overloud. "As there is no way out it really is easier, for all of us, if you just come with me. You wouldn't like any harm to come to that body now it's finally all yours, would you?"

I backed against the wall, the stone cold. "Why do you want me?"

"Why? Because you are far more useful than you think. And because we can't have Cassandra going and doing anything foolish now, can we?"

He stopped and held out his hand. The priests ranged behind him, standing perfectly still in the way people didn't.

"What's wrong with them?"

"Nothing is wrong with them; they are just obeying. Would you like to learn too?"

Come with me.

I stepped forward before I could stop myself.

That's it. Come closer. Take my hand.

I reached out.

Yes.

"No!" Leo screamed, pulling away. Behind him the priests shifted awkwardly like men waking from sleep.

"No, stay back," Leo said, thrusting out a hand as one drew close. "Keep away, I—"

Crouched upon the grass, his chest heaved and he pressed one hand to the side of his head, the other shaking as he kept it stretched out to guard against them approaching. They looked at one another, looked at me, and did not move.

Leo lifted his head, his eyes dark, haunted pools as they met mine. "Please, Kaysa. I need your help."

I jolted awake, my heart pounding so fast I was sure for a terrible moment it would fail.

"Miss Marius?" Captain Aeneas. "Is everything all right? You shouted in your sleep."

"It's Kaysa. He found her. We have to go back. We have to save her."

"Who has her? Leo?"

"Yes. Unus. I'm sure. You said he was different and this one was different. They're at Eravum. We have to go back."

He looked at the box, but it was the empress who spoke. "No. We keep going. There's nothing we can do to help her now."

What? You saw him. You saw—

"Yes, I did, better than you, apparently. How can we fight a man who can control people? No, we go to Esvar. We see what we can find out. It's the only way."

Fuck that.

I made to move, but the empress stuck out one of our arms. "Please tie me to the cart, Captain."

"But Your Maj—"

"Just do it. Now."

4. RAH

A camp full of people stared at me. No, not a camp, a settlement. These Levanti had built huts and palisade walls, and I stared as I was carried along, people bustling out of our way. It wasn't that Levanti didn't know how to build. We built temples and groves, and when we wintered, we often made storage huts, but this looked so...*permanent*.

"Out of the way, out of the way," Yitti grumbled as he and Himi set me down beside one of the fires. "Make space, damn it, surely you've seen an injured man before."

The curious onlookers didn't disperse, merely stepped back and stood watching and whispering.

"Why are they all staring at me?"

Yitti tilted his head. "Because you're Rah e'Torin. Or because your face is a mess. You choose."

Since Yitti had won our challenge, it ought not to have been his job to pick me up off the forest floor and carry me to safety, but he had, and I had not yet found the voice to thank him. My ability to speak seemed to dry up completely when a man in all-too-familiar clothes stepped forward. I had worn just such a band of knotted fabrics around my waist and carried just such a bag, half healing satchel, half horse box, with a special pocket in the side for writing implements and the book every whisperer carried to note the seasons and the grove produce, the movement of herds through their areas and the interchange of blood from one herd to another. I had left mine behind the day I had run from Whisperer Jinnit. The notes of an apprentice whisperer exiled far from home would be an interesting read. It took the unanimous vote of the whisperer conclave to exile one of their own.

As the man approached, a faint frown marred his otherwise handsome face. His head was shaved, and given how closely he appeared to adhere to tradition, the mark of an apprentice whisperer was sure to be upon the back of his head. I could still recall the light touch of Whisperer Jinnit's brush as he painted mine on every morning, taking his time about it and humming, though I had been restless. No doubt he had been trying to teach me patience.

"Ah, a new arrival," the man said. "I am Derkka en'Injit, apprentice to Whisperer Ezma e'Topi."

"Whisperer." My mouth was dry. "A whisperer here?"

"Yes, she'll be along in a moment. Nothing interrupts her daily check of the horses, so for now you'll have to put up with me."

Yitti had already dropped his own satchel and was pulling out a wooden bowl and thread and bundles of herbs. "There's no need for you to do that, Captain Yitti," Apprentice Derkka said. "I am well able to take care of him."

"I'm sure you are, but I inflicted the wounds, so I'll tend them before I go."

The apprentice's brows rose, and getting no explanation from Yitti, he looked at me. "I challenged and lost. My name is Rah e'Torin."

Despite the onlookers and the mutterings, he looked genuinely surprised. "Well, the famous Rah e'Torin, what a pleasure to finally meet you. That explains all the interest." He jerked his head in the direction of the crowd. "You're rather famous around here."

The apprentice set his satchel down on my other side and began to unpack.

"Rah!" Tor stood over me, his mouth open like he had seen a ghost. My first thought was joy to see him safe, but a smile hurt my bruised face and I recalled the circumstances under which we had parted. His shock became a sneer. "Well," he said. "Injured and in need of saving again. What stupid thing did you do this time?"

It was highly disrespectful, but I wasn't a captain anymore. Wasn't anything. Still, Yitti looked over his shoulder. "Mind how you speak there, boy," he said.

Tor huffed a laugh, but said no more.

"It's probably best if you lie down while I—while *we* see to these wounds," Yitti said, beginning to examine each one. "I did quite a good job."

"Yes, best to lie down now rather than risk hurting yourself if you pass out," Derkka said. "Here, Tor, why don't you sit and keep him entertained while we get this done."

Tor looked like he would rather have done almost anything else, but the suggestion of an apprentice whisperer is no suggestion at all. He plonked down on the dirt beside my head with a mutinous scowl. "As you wish, Apprentice." He saluted. "As long as it's understood I take no pleasure in it."

"Oh, go stick your head in a water barrel," Yitti said.

Tor settled stiffly and opened his book. It took me a moment to recall Tor had been taught Chiltaen, but despite my curiosity, I didn't dare ask about it. Then I couldn't. Yitti had prised open my leg wound to see how bad it was, making the world spin. Darkness crawled in on a hundred reaching fingers, stealing me away.

———————◆———————

"'And he will'... or maybe it's 'he *has* a blade made... forged... by gods'... no... 'by the one god...'"

Scratching sounded near my ear. My legs were aflame. Yitti and Derkka seemed to be arguing about something, but it was Tor's voice I latched on to. "A temple? A camp? A house? Fuck this stupid language."

I tried to ask for water, but a dry death rattle emerged from my lips. The boy didn't hear and I tried again, opening my eyes upon light so bright I closed them with a wince. I was still outside, the crackle of the nearby fire unchanged. Perhaps I'd been out only a few minutes.

"Oh, you're awake, are you?" Tor said. "We seem to be making a habit of this. Not the empress stitching you up this time, so you may as well pass out again."

I glared at him, but the face haloed in bright sunshine looked not the slightest bit contrite. "You did better when she was stitching, but I guess you wanted to impress her, huh?"

"Did I really do so wrong by you?"

Tor looked away. "You should have fought for your people, not for her."

I let out a heavy breath, trying to ignore the tugging and burning and itching that infused my legs. "Because all Levanti are worth fighting and dying for? Even when they choose poor paths? Or because all Kisians are evil and have no right to fight for their lands now we are here?"

He stared down at the book, eyes glazed. For a moment I wondered if he would apologise. Would see my point. But Yitti shooed him aside to examine my face. The feeling it was swollen and wrong and crusted in blood kept the memory of Sett before me, smashing me into the road with furious fists.

"You're going to have a few scars here," Yitti said, touching split skin beneath my eye. I winced. "And maybe here." He touched my jawline. "But otherwise once the swelling goes down you should look your ruggedly handsome self again."

Despite our challenge, despite our disagreement, he was trying to make me laugh. But my thoughts had caught on Sett. He had wanted me to lose, wanted Yitti to kill me. And I had killed him for it.

Yitti's smile faded. "You didn't do the wrong thing."

"That's a careful way of saying I didn't do the right thing either."

"Sometimes there isn't a right thing. Now close your eyes so I can clean your cuts without burning them."

Having both Derkka and Yitti working on my wounds was an exhausting barrage of pains, and while I didn't pass out again, I kept my eyes closed long after it ceased being necessary. I focussed on breathing deep, steady breaths, but restlessness infected me. Gideon was in danger. The Levanti with him were in danger, and here was I lying around, useless and injured.

"Is it really necessary to redo that?" Derkka's voice came through the gathering mire of fears.

"Yes, it needed more."

Yitti's words owned no disrespect, but I could imagine the apprentice's scowl. Whisperers were the most highly trained healers, to whom all others deferred.

"I am well able to attend to his injuries properly."

"Yes, Apprentice, but so am I. I think it ought to be tighter."

The tension between them stretched over me, and two pairs of hands went on applying salves and stitches and bandages like two crows fighting over a corpse.

They might have continued until I had no flesh untended, had Istet not approached. "Captain," she said, and I opened my eyes. She glanced down, but of course she wasn't addressing me. "Captain," she repeated. "We ought not linger here."

"You can leave the rest to me, Captain," Derkka said. "You cannot be afraid he is going to die now."

"I wasn't worried about that." Curt words, edged in the anger I'd seen back in Mei'lian. Smoke had risen around us as we fought for the Second Swords, his reason the right one, mine far more selfish.

"Yitti, will your path take you near Kogahaera?" I said.

"No, rather as far away from it as we can go."

He was shoving things back into his satchel, and I gripped his arm. "Please, Yitti," I said. "He's in danger. They all are. Please. I can't get there like this."

Yitti stood, pulling from my hold. "I have to go."

I struggled up onto my elbows, but could rise no farther. "Yitti—"

"No, don't get up, you fool; you're being held together by bandages."

"You'll help?"

He grunted a noncommittal sound and, slinging his satchel over his shoulder, strode away.

"Yitti!"

I tried to rise, but Derkka pushed me back as the world spun. By the time it stopped, Yitti was gone.

"No, the one with the *t* is 'bird,'" Tor mumbled beside me, following it with Chiltaen words. Empress Miko's inflection had been different, but she had muttered to herself a lot too.

"*Iidoa,*" I said, the first Kisian word that came to mind. "*Iidoa lo kaan.*"

The empress had greeted everyone with some variant of those words, as had Leo. Tor looked over the top of his book. "*Esh lidoosa ma sa mara.*"

He rolled his eyes at my blank stare. "After all this, you speak to me in Kisian? You wished me good fortune, so I told you to get fucked. To fuck a sea urchin, more precisely."

He lifted the book only to immediately lower it again. "Did she teach you that? Or did you just pick it up while following her like she was a mare in heat?"

She had been so warm beneath me that night in the cart, her breath dancing across my cheek, her lips a temptation away.

I made no answer, but Tor laughed. "Missed your chance, did you? Of course you did; if there's one thing you're good at, it's messing things up. The phrase you want is *Ao gasho te remeste mot, kaa lo kiish ao falachu sho loa-da.*"

"Why? What does that mean?"

"It means 'I can't stop thinking about you, please take pity on me and take me to your bed,' though I might have used rather coarser words. I am but a humble barbarian after all."

A laugh made my throat hurt and sounded like grinding river rocks, but it spread a reluctant grin across Tor's face. "Damn it, Rah, just let me hate you."

"I'm not stopping you."

Derkka cleared his throat. "You should let him rest now, Tor. I'm all done."

———◆———

Horse Whisperer Ezma e'Topi stared across the fire. After her apprentice had finished his ministrations, I had dozed for a while, left alone in the centre of the camp while Levanti went about their tasks. When the sky darkened toward evening, Tor covered a pair of saddles in a pile of old horse blankets to prop me up, the young man surprisingly loath to leave my side.

Ezma was a tall woman, her jawbone headpiece making her even taller. I had once asked Whisperer Jinnit if it was heavy, and he had said it weighed the same as the job's responsibility, but less than its honour, and I had not bothered to ask again. He had always stooped beneath its weight, but Ezma showed no sign of bending. She stood straight and proud and strong, a true leader in a time when the fractured Swordherds needed leadership more than ever.

"Rah e'Torin," she said, a touch to her long hair the only sign of ill-ease she showed. "A pleasure to meet a man I have heard so much about."

It ought to have been a gratifying speech, but it made a sick feeling squirm inside me. I had done all I could to avoid horse whisperers since returning to my herd, everything about them reminding me of the time I had spent training, of the days I'd wandered the plains alone and the shame that had grown daily heavier since.

I swallowed all of it down in an attempt to look confident. "Whisperer," I said, lifting tired arms to salute. "Forgive me not getting up."

"You're badly wounded?"

Derkka had surely explained my injuries already. "Not so much badly as in far too many places."

"Inflicted in a challenge, I understand."

Food was cooking and Levanti gathered around the other fires, but as she spoke I became aware all activity had quietened, even those barely within earshot stilling to listen.

"Yes." I thought of Sett, of his head rolling onto the road, and immediately tried not to think of him again. Nor of how Gideon would react to the news his blood brother was dead. At my order.

Ezma took a few steps closer and sat down, not quite across the fire like in a challenge, but close enough that my heartbeat sped to an anxious pace. No smile, no welcome, just a hard, determined look I did not like. Surely I had not been there long enough to earn her dislike.

"I have heard much about you, Rah e'Torin," she said, her tone friendly enough. "There are even some members of your former Swordherd here. And Tor, of course."

She nodded at the young man still sitting at my side, and he saluted.

"All of them," she went on, "have quite differing opinions about you, and I find myself unsure whether you are a threat to my people or not."

"Your people?"

Ezma waved a hand. "A figure of speech. *These* people."

Horse whisperers were our guiding hands, the last bastions of law and health, able to be consulted about everything from where to winter to the choice of breeding stock, but the one thing they weren't and could never be were leaders. They were solitary, owning no herd allegiance, only responsibilities.

They weren't meant to live within a herd, and watching the way others reacted to her arrival—casting down their gazes and gathering around her—I could see why. Levanti society was pragmatic, no one given power that could not be easily taken away. Being good at your job was requisite to keeping it, yet here was an exiled horse whisperer being treated the way Kisians treated their empress. The way Chiltaens had treated Leo. Like a walking god.

She accepted a plate of food without thanks. Comfortable in the knowledge of her entitlement.

My ill-ease deepened.

"Tell me, Rah e'Torin," she said, setting the plate on her knees. "What do you want? Do you want to return to Kogahaera when you are well and serve Emperor Gideon? Do you want to go home? Or do you want to inspire your own uprising of Levanti to take over new lands?"

"I want to save my people."

"That's the same answer Gideon would give. The same answer I would give. What does saving your people look like to you?"

I could tell her about Gideon. About the Kisian plans to use us as the Chiltaens had, but doubt itched at the back of my mind. I met her questioning gaze and tried to tell myself my distrust of her was built on my dislike of Whisperer Jinnit, but imagining him sitting with the conclave and judging Ezma unworthy of her position steadied me.

"I once believed ideology could save us," I said, choosing my words carefully. "That all we had to do was hold to our ways and our honour, and that would be enough. It had always worked before. But did it work because it was the best way to survive? Or because we had never truly been tested?"

She did not interrupt when I paused, just waited expectantly.

"I would no longer make any decision based on ideology," I said. "When a different decision could save lives. So you ask me what saving my people looks like to me? It looks like as many of them as possible getting out of this mess alive, whatever it takes."

In the silence, I became aware of how many people had gathered to listen, and as I was unable to see their faces beyond the firelight, it was even more like a challenge, each of us speaking our arguments so the gathered Levanti could vote upon a leader. But she was a horse whisperer and I was no one.

"That is not very enlightening, Rah e'Torin," Ezma said after a time. "You are, in fact, an unpredictable horse. A troublemaker. Our ways and tenets and ideologies are important because they bring people together for a common cause, and unite—"

"So does the desire to survive."

She lifted her brows, the pair of them vanishing into the shadow thrown by her headpiece. "I do not appreciate being interrupted, Rah e'Torin. You are not a captain here. You have no standing at all. I ask these questions because you have a history of going against your herd masters' orders, and I wish to understand why."

"With all due respect to your former position, you have no standing here either, exiled horse whisperer Ezma e'Topi."

I ought not to have said it, but her words filled me with silent rage made worse by weakness. I could not get up and walk, let alone fight, but I would be damned if I would let this woman, condemned by every whisperer on the plains, question my loyalty.

"Just so, Rah e'Torin. Just so." Ezma smiled, and without giving me even the smallest bit of satisfaction, she took food from her plate and ate, paying me no further heed. Levanti remained gathered around her, hanging on every word she wasn't saying. Beside me, Tor went reluctantly back to his book.

From beyond the firelight, a Levanti approached with a plate of food. "Honour to you," she said, setting it down beside me and holding a prolonged salute. She walked away before I could reply, but she was replaced a moment later by another. A second plate of food, a longer salute. "Honour to you," he said, and was gone.

Tor stared at his book with the determination of one refusing to comment. Ezma watched yet another approach, her features stern.

She had said some of my former Swordherd were present, yet I wasn't prepared for the sight of Amun carrying a plate toward me. Amun, who had refused to fight for the Chiltaens. Amun, who had been left behind and thought dead.

"Honour to you, Captain," he said, saluting as he set the plate down. Before I could think what to say, he walked away.

Across the fire, I met Ezma's gaze, a flash of something so like hate in her expression that it startled me. I had done nothing. Said nothing. Yet this horse whisperer, who ought not to care for such things, was angry at the respect being shown me.

"What are you reading?" I demanded of Tor, anything to remove myself from the uncomfortable scene that was brewing.

"It's the Chiltaen holy book." He held up the cover. "Dishiva gave it to me to translate, and it's fucking hard because I don't know all the words, and some of it seems to be literal and some of it is just made-up nonsense."

"Dishiva gave it to you? Why?"

"She didn't exactly say, but Dom Villius killed Matsi because he didn't want any Levanti to read it, so it must be important."

I hunted his face for a lie. "Dom Villius killed Matsi? You mean Matsimelar?"

"Redcap poison painted on the book's cover." He looked up.

"Oh, I forgot you liked Leo. I guess your record as a bad judge of character continues."

"It wasn't him I liked," I said, though it was a lie. "He was going to set us free. Going to let us go home." I glanced at the still form of Whisperer Ezma just beyond the dancing flames. It was almost dark now, her features lit more by the fire than the day's light. The distant hum of chatter around us ought to have been relaxing, a reminder of home, but Tor's words had left me cold. Even the breeze swirling past had more bite.

"This sentence makes no sense," Tor said with a frustrated growl. "What is *chasine*? It's not 'enemy,' it's not 'friend,' it's not 'soldier.' They taught us all those words. Normally I can get at least a sense of meaning from the rest of the sentence, but this could be anything. Someone or something stabs him in the back."

"Empress," Whisperer Ezma said.

"What?" Tor realised who he was talking to. "Pardon, I mean, what did you say, Whisperer?"

"The word you are wondering about." Half her face seemed to be engulfed in flames for how brightly it lit her. "It's 'empress.' Veld is stabbed in the back by an empress. Although it's not the best translation."

"You know what's in this book?" Tor sounded shocked.

"I've been here a while, young Tor, so yes, I know what's in that book. And what it's really meant to say." She got up as she spoke and strode toward one of the nearby huts. She returned carrying another book. At first I thought it must be her whisperer's notebook, but as she drew close, the firelight danced upon a dark blue cover. Levanti notebooks were always undyed, made to be functional and sturdy in the ever-changing conditions of the plains.

Without a word, she held out the book to Tor, and having looked a question up into her face, he took it and flipped through the pages.

"But this..." Tor began and stopped, staring at the words. Still standing over him, Ezma watched with a gaze all too like a hungry animal, her eyes alight. "This is the same book. Or almost the same. But it's in Tempachi."

He looked up and she nodded. "It is. I got that from a travelling merchant some years ago. The Chiltaens like everyone to believe they're the centre of the world, that the faith of the One True God originated here, their priesthood the ones through whom God communicates, but in truth they are some of the most recent converts. This book is older than the one you have and truer to the original."

"And we can read it." A note of excitement entered Tor's voice as he hunted the right page. "Ah! Here." He muttered, running his finger along a line of text. "'And the woman both god and leader did thrust a blade into his back'! I see, 'god and leader,' like a Kisian emperor or empress." He looked up. "I have to tell Dishiva. If I leave now, I could catch up with Captain Yitti. Yes, that's the best, I'll—"

"No."

Ezma's calm words were made of steel.

"No, Whisperer?"

"No," she repeated. "It is not our place to interfere with such things."

"But if I don't warn her—"

"This is one of the points upon which both the religion of the One True God and the tenets of whisperers agree. It is not our place to interfere with the fates. We must watch and record and guide when asked for guidance, but never interfere. Never change the course of history."

"Even when it means people may die?"

"Even when it means people may die, yes, young Tor. You have a lot to learn, and I am glad to have you under my eye while you do."

She held out her hand. Tor hesitated, but gave back the Tempachi copy. "You are a good soul, Tor. Perhaps we will make a whisperer of you yet. Now, I think Rah is in need of proper rest. Why don't you help him to one of the huts so he may sleep away from all our bustle and noise."

Tor stood, saluted. "Yes, honoured Whisperer, I will, but Dishiva begged me to let her know if—"

"No." Her smile vanished. "Dishiva e'Jaroven must be left to follow her path without our interference. There are many things you do not understand, but I am your whisperer and I advise you not to make any attempt to communicate the contents of this book to anyone in connection with Dishiva." She set her hands behind her back, moving her book out of sight. "One of the others can help Rah to shelter. If you're already struggling with difficult thoughts, it's best to keep you away from corrupting influences."

"Corrupting—"

"Derkka!" She spoke sharply, many Levanti turning to stare. Her apprentice approached with quick long strides. "Rah e'Torin needs to rest," she said as he saluted his willingness to serve. "Help him to one of the huts. Tor is going to help me with my evening rounds."

"Yes, Whisperer."

Ezma made to leave, but looked down at me, caught to the ground by my injuries. "You have no place here, Rah e'Torin," she said, her low tone chilling bones I had thought could get no colder. "No position or honour. For the sake of my people, I will make sure it stays that way."

5. MIKO

Two days without rain in the storm season was unusual, three a rarity. Four seemed like a gift from the gods, and while I sat in the dark with my bow across my knees, I thanked them in silent prayer. All around me, soldiers shuffled and sniffed and cleared their throats, waiting for the night to grow old.

"It's almost time, Your Majesty," General Rushin whispered, his outline all I could see in the low light. "Are you sure you wish to remain?"

"I am, General."

"As you wish. I feel I would not be doing my duty if I didn't at least mention the dangerous nature of the mission and how unnecessary—"

"So I have been informed many times. Thank you, General."

The man bowed and moved away toward the stairs, leaving me to smother my fears with a reminder that it was another Emperor Kin these men wanted, not an aloof Otako. If anyone with the loyalty of the army could take and hold the throne, then it was the loyalty of the soldiers I needed, not just their generals.

Jie's words echoed in my mind, words that haunted me in every quiet moment. *"No child can lead Kisia in battle. No child can rule in a time of war. But tell me, sister, how many times have you been told you cannot rule because you were born a girl?"*

All to prove a woman could do it too.

I squeezed the bow's upper limb, the wood squeaking in my sweaty grip. I turned, catching General Ryoji in the corner of my eye, looking his old self in his imperial uniform. His return had not gone as well with the southern generals as I had wished, and had his position given him any real military power they would have rejected him outright, however much I favoured him.

The drunken merriment two floors up was growing wild. What had started as talk and laughter punctuated by footsteps had transformed into shouts and song, screeches and shrieks of mirth, and thuds as men fell over their own feet. I'd only had that much to drink once, when Ambassador Goro retired to take the position of Lord Chancellor. Tanaka and Edo and I had been sent away after the official dinner, but Tanaka had hidden a bottle in the knot of his sash. I could not recall much else, only that the laughter had been followed by a whole day of being sick and a week of lectures from our tutors.

I made my way across the cellar to the foot of the stairs where General Rushin stood with one of his commanders, a man whose name I could not recall but whose thick eyebrows were impossible to forget. "Are you ready, General?" I said, able to look him straight in the eye without having to incline my head. I suspected anyone who measured us would find me taller by an inch.

"Yes, Your Majesty," he said. "I judge it to be about time."

A chink of light shone beneath the door at the top of the stairs. "I will go up first."

"As you wish, Your Majesty," he said, nodding stiffly to General Ryoji as he joined us. The general nodded back, and tapping my quiver, I passed General Rushin and started up the stairs. No one called after me, and with my heart thudding hard I gripped my bow and climbed on, leaving the sounds of adjusting armour and clinking weapons behind. A pair of soldiers stood watch in the upper cellar, shafts of light falling through the floor to stripe crates and bar-rels and sacks and an old table hacked up for firewood. The revelry overhead easily drowned the noise of soldiers preparing to kill below.

"Majesty," the soldiers whispered, and nodded to General Ryoji behind me.

"May the gods speed my arrows and good fortune keep you both," I said to the soldiers, and made for the second stairs, stom-ach churning and Ryoji in tow. I had not let myself think about what could go wrong, but now that I stood at the base of the stairs, panic flared and my feet stuck to the floor. Overhead someone stomped the beat of a lewd song.

I could change my mind. I could send Ryoji up first. I could decide the plan worked best without me and maybe it would, but I had received oaths from men who had not wanted to give them, and if I did not find a way to make them want to follow me, I would soon have no army and no allies. Again. I had to lead.

So there, in that close space filled with the smell of wine and sick and sawdust, of reeds and mud and smoke, I let go a long breath and thought of what Rah would do. What needed to be done, always, whatever the cost. Perhaps if he was still alive somewhere, he might one day approve of this night's work.

I set my foot on the bottom step. Then the next. And the next. Halfway up, I drew an arrow and nocked it, keeping my bow low at my side and my breath even. Another step. A crash sounded overhead. A laugh. Someone shouted for more wine while another bellowed out the first line of "Itikata's Triumph."

The next step creaked beneath my foot, but the noise above drowned all. Another step and I could reach the door, its latch a worn, rusting thing barely keeping the door closed, let alone locked. The landlord was an old sailor, his job to keep His Grace of Syan's sailors happy whenever their ships docked at the Tzitzi Knot. He probably had no fear of common thieves.

Reaching around me, Ryoji thumbed the latch and the door opened a few inches, sending light spilling up his sleeve. I nudged the door the rest of the way, bracing for a shout, but the celebrations went on. The stairs emerged behind the bar, no more than half a dozen paces from the bottom of the next stairs leading up to the overnight rooms. They were not brightly lit and no one was expecting an attack, two facts upon which we had based the whole operation. Yet as I made to step out, footsteps sounded atop the upper stairs and a sailor bearing the Bahain sigil appeared, his arm around a young woman in a thin, brightly coloured robe tied with the black sash of a night worker. He had been laughing, but his smile died at sight of us. I drew and loosed without thought, and before my arrow had made half the distance, Ryoji was already moving. Like a wolf he sprinted low, covering the distance between stairways in a bound. My arrow hit the sailor's throat, blood spurting, and no sooner had the woman drawn breath to scream than Ryoji's blade punched into her throat. He caught her as she fell forward, lowering her down to die beside the fallen sailor.

It had taken mere seconds. Around us celebrations went on, but there was no retreating now. Holding my bow in line with my body, I took the four paces across the floor from the top of one flight of stairs to the bottom of the next, and not a single person kneeling around the tables drinking and dicing paid me any heed. I was but a shadow in the corner of their hazy awareness.

"She did not need to die," I hissed as I crouched next to the general. "Can we try not to kill—"

"Yes, she did."

He spoke so harshly I was taken aback. My hand froze in the act of drawing another arrow.

"You had not prepared a second arrow and her scream would have alerted everyone to our position." A grim smile flickered across his face. "As the commander of your Imperial Guard I cannot hesitate when it comes to your safety."

He was right and I hated it, as much as I hated the strange feeling that he was two different men. There was the Ryoji I'd grown up with, more teacher than soldier, a mild man of the imperial court and my mother's lover—never a cold-blooded killer. The night of Mother's coup he had shown another side, and here it was again. It ought to have been comforting that he would kill to protect me, but the feeling I didn't really know him gnawed at my confidence.

Thrusting the doubts away, I drew an arrow and nocked, briefly considered my choice of target, and loosed through the railings. My aim was good, but my choice was poor. I ought to have started with someone on their own, have sowed confusion before panic, but instead I chose the biggest, brashest looking man in the room, standing atop a central table singing the "Triumph" at the top of his lungs. The arrow dug deep into his throat, cutting the song off mid-note. He gasped, pawing at the shaft, and every single member of his carousing audience turned, dozens of bleary eyes finding me in the shadows.

"Shit." I nocked and loosed another into the closest sailor. It pierced his neck but not his throat, and as shouts rose, Ryoji slipped behind me to guard the bottom of the stairs, short blade in hand. "Shit, shit!" I nocked and drew and loosed as fast as I could, my arrows sailing into a mass of angry drunks rather than panicking ones. Weapons were pulled from belts and bags and no one was running for the door. Every single one was coming for me.

I could not look, could only focus on my bow and listen to the grunts and gasps and meaty thuds that told me Ryoji was alive and fighting. Two minutes, I had told General Rushin. Two minutes to sow discord and panic as a lone archer in the shadows. It had not seemed long enough, but now every second was a second too long.

With Ryoji guarding the stairs, some sailors rushed straight at the railings and tried to climb, and had they not been the worse for drink they might have succeeded. But they were too slow, and I had spent too many dull mornings practicing while a servant counted how long it took me to empty the arrow barrel.

A guttural cry drew my gaze. Ryoji had his blade through a tall man's eye and had drawn a dagger to stick in another's gut. He did not wait even a breath, just pulled them both out, kicking the one with the opened guts in the knee.

Steps thudded along the upper passage. Two men appeared, but drew out of sight as my first arrow hit the wooden beam. I nocked another as they charged, sending it through the front one's eye as he clattered toward me, all spitting rage. The force threw him back and his companion tripped, tumbling to meet an arrow nocked and loosed at very short range.

At the bottom of the stairs, Ryoji was no longer alone. Soldiers—my soldiers—were streaming through the cellar door, filling the room with a full symphony of blood and pain and death as bodies fell. I half drew another arrow before letting the string slacken. I couldn't risk hitting my own men.

Beside me, Ryoji let go a held breath, and in silence we stood watching the bloody end of Bahain's sailors. One minute celebrating, then you're dead on the floor, bleeding out in a pile of vomit and spilled wine.

A portrait of Emperor Kin hung on the far wall, watching. As the farthest port upriver any warship or trade galleon could go without smashing its hull to pieces, the Tzitzi Knot had long been a watering hole for the Imperial Fleet. He had built it, and would only have hated me all the more for tearing it down.

First lesson in battle is not to dither at the opening. Move a piece before your enemy moves it for you.

"Check all the upstairs rooms as well as the ones on this level," I said, pulling myself back to the present as the last of the sailors hit the floor. "Any who got out will have run straight into General Moto, but some might be hiding. Check, double check, and prepare to burn the place."

However much I called them enemies, the walk to the door was a trek over dead and dying Kisians, and I tried not to look at their faces or think about the families they might be leaving behind.

After the cloying stink of blood and bile, the chill night air was a welcome relief, though I shivered in my sweat-drenched tunic. Despite the lack of rain, the ground was soft, every breath tasting of mud and rich loam. Insects buzzed. Distant voices murmured. And nearby, water sloshed and the clonk of wood on wood echoed as the ships bumped against their docks. It was all too peaceful.

With the moon but a sliver in the sky, I didn't see General Moto striding to meet us until he loomed out of the darkness. "Your Majesty," he said. "My men are standing by." He had been positioned in the lea of a storehouse across the road, and by the way he and his soldiers were hovering impatiently there couldn't have been many escapees.

"Good." I kept my voice low, hoping he would take the hint. The dock was far enough away, but anyone could be hiding in the darkness. "Do you have the uniforms?"

"They should be here momentarily, Your Majesty."

"Good."

I moved on a little distance and stood watching the shadowy activity while I waited, trying to appear as calm as Ryoji did, though my hands were shaking and the longer we stood there the less sure I was my knees would keep holding me up.

"Are you all right, Your Majesty?" he asked in a low voice.

"Fine. Why?"

"You're breathing very fast. If you want my advice, you should walk it off. There's a good reason most generals never stop moving once a battle begins."

I thought I wouldn't be able to walk a step, but once I started moving back toward the inn, I began to feel better. Ryoji kept pace, half a step behind. I'd often seen him walk just so with my mother. With Emperor Kin. Even with Tanaka.

"If you would deign to take another piece of advice, Your Majesty," he said as we approached the busy inn, bustling now with soldiers searching every room and preparing to set it ablaze.

"That depends what it is, General. The most I can assure you is that I will always listen."

"Don't take part in the attack on the boats."

"You don't think I can do it?"

"Did I say that?"

"You insinuated it."

He looked steadily at me in a way that reminded me of the time when I was five years old and had loosed a blunt arrow at his leg, or when I had tripped over while sparring and almost sliced his ear off, or when I stuck my knife into his arm when he tried to stop me escaping Koi with Emperor Kin. And still he had come back.

"One thing you need to learn," he said, stepping back into that mentor role we both knew so well, "is that a leader doesn't do everything themselves. You won't win your soldiers by always being there. Always being at the front, especially when the task is one you're not well suited to."

"I can—"

"The time it would take to fit a sailor's uniform to your figure well enough to pass for one would endanger the rest of the plan. You have done your grand, valiant fight; now let others do theirs. You don't have to do everything to be a leader, you just have to be there cheering others on."

Between the buzz of the inn fight wearing off and General Ryoji's dampening words, I felt like I was shrinking. I hated that he was right, but knew I ought to be grateful I had someone who would speak to me as Miko Ts'ai. Perhaps tomorrow I would be able to thank him. For now I could only nod and stride back across the main street of the small, manufactured village.

While we watched, flames began to curl from the upper windows of the alehouse. At the other end of the short street, torches danced around the moored ships like fireflies. And yet despite the distant sounds of fighting and the muted roar of fire, where we stood the little village was still and quiet. Barely a breeze gusted about us, ruffling my sweat-dampened hair.

"Does it ever get any easier?" I said, watching the battle on the docks like it was a miniature play. "Standing back here and watching. Waiting. Hoping for the right outcome."

"No, Your Majesty."

"I didn't think so."

We watched, listening to the fighting, until it calmed into the splash of heavy objects hitting the water. As we strode toward the docks, the objects being thrown overboard resolved into bodies. They hit the man-made bay and disappeared in a splash. A swarm of torches climbed all over the ships—as many as twenty in all, stretching away into the darkness—while on the dockside under the light of a single torch, Minister Manshin held court with the two generals who had come with us on this mission.

I strode toward them, keeping my bow in my hand and drawing myself up, glad for once of my over-great height. Manshin bowed as I approached, causing the other two to turn and bow with varying degrees of depth and alacrity.

"They had no idea we were coming, Your Majesty," Moto said. "My men were easily able to get through the dock gates wearing Bahain's uniforms, and once the sentries were dealt with, we could just walk in."

"The plan has indeed been an unmitigated success, Your Majesty," General Rushin added, a glance and a nod to Minister

Manshin boiling my blood. This was my army, my plan, not his. "We have had minimal casualties, and once Moto's men finish clearing the ships we will have enough at our command—"

"How many soldiers can be transported on each ship?"

The men looked at one another, and my grip on my bow tightened. "Two hundred on the larger ships," Moto said. "Maybe seventy on the smaller sloops."

"Keep three sloops and burn the rest."

"Burn them?" Moto looked to Rushin and then to Minister Manshin. "Burn them? Why would we burn ships? We *need* ships, Your Majesty."

"We need enough ships to carry a small army without being seen as a threat," I said. "Despite our care to ensure there were no survivors, there is still a chance Grace Bahain will hear of this. If we can pass it off as the opportunistic work of angry southern loyalists rather than a concerted plan, we have a better chance of seeing out the rest without opposition. If they don't know this was us, they won't know we're coming."

Manshin's eyes fixed on me and his lips turned into a grim, understanding smile. Moto was not so quick. "But, Your Majesty, why should we burn them?"

"Because it is not something we would do," Manshin said. "Which is exactly why we should do it."

"Fill the smaller ships with enough men to make the attack on Syan and burn the rest as a decoy," General Rushin said, mulling over the words. "Yes, as much as I hate the idea of losing so many valuable ships, it is not like the Bahains haven't got plenty more where these came from."

He nodded at Manshin, and I forced their attention back to me, saying sharply, "Good, it's agreed. Load three sloops, burn the rest. I will command one, General Moto another, and General Rushin the third."

Lips parted to protest, but before either general could speak, Minister Manshin said, "You have a different mission in mind for me? This was not part of the original plan."

"No, but it occurs to me a second decoy with what's left of our soldiers could put them off further. If you head back to Shimai and cross the river before marching east to Syan, you can serve the dual purpose of making our plan less obvious and picking up any soldiers north of the Tzitzi who are loyal to our cause." There had been rumours of resistance pockets, but until now we'd had no chance of getting to them.

Moto rocked back on the heels of his boots. "Oyamada already has the bulk of the army heading for Kogahaera. If we send much of ours away too, what do we do if three sloops of soldiers are not enough to see out your plan?"

My plan, now that it was being questioned.

"We don't have enough soldiers to take Syan front on," I said. "So if an attack by stealth fails, it won't matter where the army is."

Silence met my words, but slowly Moto nodded and I released my tight hold on my bow. They had listened. Perhaps only thanks to Minister Manshin's initial agreement, but they had listened and agreed and all three made gestures of assent.

"All right," Moto said at last, something like excitement gleaming in his eyes as he looked over his shoulder at the moored ships. "I'll give the orders and we'll get moving. Best for the three ships to sail away as the fires draw attention. We'll load the boats full of soldiers and provisions, and when we're ready to go we'll light the rest."

He bowed and stalked away toward the ships.

"I will gather my men," General Rushin said, and with a bow and a murmured "Your Majesty" strode off toward the alehouse. Shouts rose on the wind as orders spread, cheerful in tone, so well had the mission succeeded.

Manshin lifted his brows. "Are you sure you do not wish my company upon the rest of the mission?"

"Yes, because I need someone I can trust to lead part of the army without fearing they will run off with it and fight for their own cause instead of mine."

"Then I will gather men and move out at once. Best not to risk being seen here." With a bow he departed, leaving me standing a moment alone in the aftermath of our success. A success that had come at the cost of many Kisian lives. With the first flush of battle having past, the breeze was icy upon my lingering sweat and I felt flat and weary while my army broke up around me. Groups hurried here and there in the firelit night, shouts ever on the air. But there was organisation amid the seeming chaos, and I was impressed at the speed with which these generals could work under such conditions.

Minister Manshin and his portion of the army were soon gone, leaving General Rushin and General Moto gathering supplies from the surrounding buildings and arguing over which ships to keep and which to burn.

"The three-master would make a good, quick leading ship," General Rushin was saying when I joined them.

"Says you with your excellent knowledge of ships and sailing." General Moto's cynical tone was more than I had energy to deal with, and I let them nip at each other while I thought dreamily of finding something soft to curl up on as soon as we were aboard.

"I know quite as much—"

A crash rent the air. Flames roared. Something enormous smashed into the side of the dark storehouse, sending fire and embers flying from the crest of an orange wave. Another hit the alehouse, fire meeting fire in a blinding burst. As though spat from a dragon's mouth, another fireball whistled through the air, growing larger as it dropped toward us.

"Run!" It might have been me who shouted, or Moto, or both of us as cries rose all around. He grabbed my arm, or Ryoji did, the confusion nothing to a moment later when the fireball landed at the end of the short street. There were no sounds but the smash and crack of wood and the roar of flame, no smell but burning flesh and hair and smoke, nothing to see but darkness and fire and death. Screams erupted as shards of burning wood flew like knives from the wreckage. Heat seared my back and cut trails in my skin, and every breath I sucked stung.

"Get on the boats!" Moto yelled, my ears ringing around the sound of his voice.

"What? They might catch fire!"

"Lesser of two evils right now, go!"

I could not feel my legs, yet when I ran they were there beneath me, seeming to belong to someone else. Another burst like the crash of thunder shook the ground. Heat bloomed against my neck and I ran into a panicked crowd of soldiers speeding all directions, the shouted orders barely audible beneath the storm of footsteps and cries. At the nearest ship, Eyebrows was frantically waving soldiers aboard, so many cramming on to escape the raining fire that they pushed and shoved with nothing like their usual discipline.

"Too full," Ryoji shouted as I headed for it. "This way."

I followed him away from the chaos and the lights and into the darkness, soldiers falling in with us as we passed. General Rushin was there with some of his men, and nearby, General Moto was shouting, "Pull back! Onto the ships! Move move move!"

Ryoji jogged on, passing crammed gangplank after crammed gangplank as another crash slammed into the stones. The ground shook and screams mixed with the roar of fire as a great flaming ball of sticks and straw and pitch hit the dock and rolled, shedding embers, into the closest ship. It took out the gangplank, knocking soldiers into the water and coming to a smashing halt against the side of the hull.

"We need to get on board a ship!" I shouted to Ryoji's back. "Before another one of those—"

He pointed into the darkness at the end of the dock and broke into a sprint. Footsteps thundered behind me—a tail of soldiers following their empress's lead, even if it was in retreat.

Ahead, a small sloop came into sight at the end of the wharf. A few torches bobbed upon its deck, and half a dozen soldiers were hurrying up the gangplank.

Ryoji waited as I caught up, out of breath. The gangplank was narrow but had a railing on one side, and gripping it with a trembling hand, I made my way up onto the deck. It hurt to let go, and I looked down at the blistering sores on my palm even as shouts swirled around me.

"To the oars!"

"Raise the anchor!"

"What?" I turned. "We can't go until everyone is aboard."

"If we wait, no one will get out of here alive."

I turned to protest and found not Ryoji but General Moto behind me, bent over from exertion. "Who is attacking us?"

"Some of Bahain's men must have made it to the watchtower," Moto said. "It's usually unmanned, but it houses a trio of catapults with enough range to hit ships and crossing armies."

Another ball of flame hit the ground, so close to the riverbank that the initial impact sent sprays of embers hissing into the water. A chunk flew off, taking out the mast of the nearest ship and scattering chips of fire across the deck.

"Then they know who attacked them, and as soon as they've run out of things to lob at us, they'll go straight to Bahain."

General Moto had no answer, nothing but a grim set of his teeth as together we stood in the centre of a storm of action. Beneath our feet the deck rocked with the gentle swell and vibrated with running steps, while shouts rang in my ears even louder than my fearful thoughts.

All along the wharf ships were pushing out toward the turbulent waters of the Tzitzi River, yet it would all be for nothing if those men got to Grace Bahain. By ship we could make it to Syan before him no matter how fast he marched from Kogahaera, but a swift rider carrying a message could warn those at Kiyoshio Castle that we were coming.

There was nothing I could do. There was no getting to them. No going back.

"Cast off!" General Moto called, all other words stolen by the crash of another flaming ball hitting the deck of a ship almost at the river. Fire rained over the sides, but not before setting the whole ship alight. Dark shapes leapt into the water, and soon the sails were like great burning flags.

"Row, row!"

I stood silent as the ship burned. I stood silent as the shadowy remnants of my army disappeared amid the nest of flaming buildings. And I stood silent as General Moto ordered our ship on rather than back, to safety rather than to save, and I felt sick.

Here was one lesson Emperor Kin had left out of his mock tuition. An emperor could have no heart.

 # 6. DISHIVA

Everywhere I went, stares and whispers followed. I had been set free after the ceremony, but it hadn't taken long to realise it was no freedom at all. With a few words and a change of attire, I was Dishiva e'Jaroven no longer.

I could talk to anyone, but they would not meet my gaze through the mask. I could go anywhere I wished, but the Levanti would eye me warily until I left. Even my own Swords. Keka's Swords now, whatever my heart cried about captaincy having to be challenged for. It was little comfort that I would have lost such a challenge anyway.

By early afternoon the yard was busy with Swordherds preparing to ride south against the deserters. Yiss en'Oht was in charge, and I leaned against the stable wall and watched her bustle about giving orders. Many eyes turned my way, but no one approached, not even Lashak, until Yiss broke away from her Swords and strolled toward me.

"Defender," she said, making a little bow rather than a salute. "I require one of your three traitor Swords as a guide. Who do you think would be best able to fulfil the task?"

"Traitors?"

"What else ought we call Swords who deliberately go against their emperor's orders?"

"Since we've never had an emperor before, I think—"

"I don't have time for this," she snapped. "I need a guide. Through the swamp."

"Are you planning to walk everyone in along a single narrow track?" I enjoyed the sound of my own sneer even through the hated mask.

"No."

I lifted my brows, but it was a moment before I realised she couldn't see them. "Then what?"

"I don't mean to tell you, Dishiva of the One True God. You are no longer one of us, so I cannot trust you with anything it's not necessary for you to know."

It stung, but I wouldn't let her see it. "As you wish," I said. "Loklan likely recalls the way best as he was up front when we went through, but Shenyah was to be apprenticed to our tracker due to the sharpness of her night vision, and Esi has the better memory."

Yiss narrowed her eyes but said nothing, and not for the first time, I wondered if we were on the same side. She had always been fiercely supportive of Gideon, but she had no love for Leo and his religion. Surely even she could see just how much influence the priest had gained. A desperate urge to grip her tunic and hiss in her ear that I had been forced to do this against my will flared and had to be fiercely swallowed down, Leo's threats all too fresh in my mind.

She strode away to where my three Swords stood in an awkward little knot awaiting their fate. A hand to Loklan's shoulder chose him to lead them through the swamp, and my heart, which already seemed to be a shattered mess of its former self, broke anew at the look he flicked my way. Not the disgust everyone else seemed to feel, not even anger or mistrust or fear, but hope. Damn him, but he still believed in me, still thought me his captain, and that faith, that loyalty, was more painful than all the scorn because I could not show him I valued it.

I stared back as emotionlessly as I could until he turned away, his fleeting look of disappointment impossible to miss.

Powerless to do anything but watch, I soon escaped back to my room. There, I paced my frustration. Whatever those Swords had been made to believe, I had seen the deserter camp. They were not traitors, were not planning to attack us or destroy all Gideon had built. They just wanted to go home. I knew I ought not to doubt the intentions of those under Yiss's command, ought not to even doubt Yiss, but too well could I remember the sense of peace Leo had given me, and how much I had wanted to cling to it even as he stripped it away. I had thought myself weak for having succumbed, but if Gideon could fall under his spell, what hope was there for any of us?

Hot panicky breaths made my face sweat beneath the mask, and glad to be alone, I untied the strings.

"Dishiva?" Lashak stood on the threshold, wary. "Or should I call you Defender of the One True God?"

"No!" I said, goaded to speak before I could stop myself. "I mean, yes, you should. It is my position and I am proud to—"

But she closed the door, half a dozen steps bringing her close enough to grab my loosened mask. The fabric fell from my face, leaving me meeting her stare without its protection. And with the feeling of one made naked and vulnerable, I knew the depths of my own fear.

"Oh, thank the gods," Lashak hissed, and letting the mask drop she gripped my face in both hands and planted a kiss upon my lips. "I had begun to fear I really had lost you." She kissed me again, a little laugh coming out as she drew back. "What the fuck are you doing playing that little shit's game, Di?"

"He will kill all my Swords and our horses if I don't. I have to pretend, to protect Gideon and you and everyone. I have to do this. I have to *be* this."

Lashak stepped back, looking me up and down as though

hoping to see the lie writ somewhere upon me, and finding none, she pressed a shaking hand to her mouth. "Fuck, you mean it."

"Yes."

"And the deserters?"

"Have to be destroyed or we all die. Us or them."

"Surely he doesn't mean—"

"He does, Lash, he does." I gripped her shoulders. "Don't you underestimate him for a moment. He can read minds. He can control your thoughts. He is like the sickness taking over back home except he's a person."

"Then we ought to kill him."

"I did."

Again, she leaned back, assessing me head to foot, and before she could speak, I went on in a hissed whisper. "I killed him, Lash, I did. Just before you were sent to Mei'lian to oversee the burning. And when I came back…"

"His god really is bringing him back to life?"

"Yes. No. I don't know. I don't know how he does it, only that he does and there's no stopping him. And now that you know, you're in danger." I pressed my hands to my face. "We all are. Oh shit, Lash, he'll know I told you and he'll kill everyone. Even our horses. We're so fucked, oh I wish you hadn't come." My breaths came fast, too fast for comfort, and the room began to spin. "We're all dead now. What are we going to do?"

Pain radiated through my chest and I couldn't feel my legs, every breath fast and shallow.

"Calm down, Dishiva, hush, it's all right, we won't let him. Breathe now, come on, try to relax."

I dropped onto the reed matting, my vision sparking and my attention skittering at every sound outside the door, sure he was coming, sure any moment we would be dead, the sense of doom so heavy it pressed me into the floor.

"No no no, breathe with me, Dishiva, breathe," Lashak said, kneeling before me now. "You are stronger than this, you can do it. Take a breath and hold it."

I tried to do as she bade me, but the air rushed out of my lungs as if loath to stay. I couldn't blame it. I was a death sentence to all who came near me now.

"Breathe in," she said, rubbing circles on my back like we did for injured horses. "Hold it just one second and let it out, then try to do two the next time."

"He's coming for us, Lashak, he's going to kill you and kill me and kill all of us and—"

She struck my cheek and I flinched, holding a breath from the shock. It was enough to ease the tension in my chest.

"We are the Swords that hunt," Lashak began to chant, stopping at the end of the line to take a breath and slowly letting it go with the next words. "So your hands may be clean." Another breath. "We are the Swords that kill." Breath. "So your soul may be light." She nodded encouragement as I breathed with her this time. "We are the Swords that die. That you might live." Nodding again she started over, and little by little, focusing on the words and my breath, my body let some of the tension go and my panic eased enough for me to sit and face her across the dim, unlit room. Out in the yard, the rest of the Levanti went on about their tasks unaware.

"Now, let's get one thing straight, Dishiva," Lashak said before I could speak. "No more apologies. No more blaming yourself for putting me in danger. You aren't doing that, he is, got it? Besides, I'd rather be in danger and here for you than leave you to bear this alone."

Her words made tears prick the corners of my eyes. I blinked them determinedly away, hating the way crying always made saliva thicken in my mouth like date paste.

"You are my friend and that's more important than my life, all right?" she went on. "Now, we are pretty clever, you and I, so what are we going to do about this? And no, 'nothing' is not an option."

"You have to go to the deserters and warn them," I said, and already having said too much I dared more. "They have a horse whisperer."

Lashak stared at me. "A horse whisperer?"

"Yes. Exiled here, before our time, I think, but still a whisperer and the closest we have to the sort of help we need. We can't let her die."

"I can send someone—"

"No. You have to go."

She tilted her head, her way of asking silent questions.

"You can't risk telling anyone else about this." My words were so low I wasn't sure she could hear them. "Leo has people everywhere. You ask someone else to go, you risk them being one of his. It has to be you. You're already in danger, and whatever you say, I don't want to be responsible for your death. That's not something a friend should have to bear."

She blew out a breath and nodded, her mouth a grim line. And without her having to say so, I knew what she was thinking, that to abandon her Swords was the height of dishonour for a captain. But there was a horse whisperer, and there was no overstating the danger she would be in if she stayed.

I didn't tell her she would have to stay with the deserters. I didn't have to.

"I'm sorry, Dishiva."

"No," I said. "I'm sorry."

"We'll get rid of him, won't we? We'll kill him? Properly."

"We will."

A single, sharp nod, and she turned to look at the door. "I had better go before anyone gets suspicious."

"Right."

I didn't want her to leave, didn't want to be alone, but to stay risked too much. "If you can get Shenyah or Esi away from watching eyes, one of them can guide you in, but I don't know how you'll do it without being seen and—"

I could feel the panic building again. Lashak gripped my arms. "Really? You're choosing this moment to doubt my skills? Shame on you, Dishiva e'Jaroven."

That made me smile, a pained, twisted thing, but all I could do was nod and trust her. With a parting kiss she left me to my solitary fears, to my pacing and my panic, sure any moment Leo's reprisals would come.

Hours passed. Yiss and her army filed out through the gates, leaving the yard quieter than it had been in a long time, and I began to hope I had gotten away with telling Lashak after all.

Until I peered out my door in the evening and saw, pinned to the wall opposite, a Mask of God. Its eye slits watching me.

A warning. I doubted there would be another.

I paced through the night, expending my nervous energy. I had been untethered from my own life, left to float in the same space I had occupied but without purpose. My Swords gathered in the kitchen for their evening meal, but I was no longer their captain. Levanti sat around fires out in the yard, but I was no longer welcome. And whatever the needs of my body, I could no longer find a partner to satisfy them with. I was alone. But it was all the worse for being alone while surrounded by my people.

There seemed no way out. Leo had found out about Lashak, and next time there would be consequences. But what was I to do? Sit in my room and accept myself beaten?

Giving up felt wrong, and I paced all the faster, wishing there was a simple answer and knowing there wasn't. Anything I did risked the lives of others. Risked our horses and our future, but every time I didn't speak let Leo get one step closer to possessing us completely.

"*No more apologies,*" Lashak had said. "*No more blaming yourself for putting me in danger. You aren't doing that, he is, got it?*"

How much easier to have been riding toward battle. Every Sword rode knowing they might never come back, but at least they had chosen to ride. Here the choice was all mine. Doing nothing would lead to our enslavement. Yet the weight of all their lives, their futures, would fall upon my shoulders. My scales. And like the deaths of Swords in battle, I had to make peace with that.

But first I had to test how far Leo would let me stretch my freedom.

The following morning, adorned in the regalia I was not allowed outside without, I strode to Empress Sichi's door and tapped on the wooden frame. Voices inside stopped abruptly, and when the door slid it was with a degree of wariness. Nuru peered out. She flinched and stepped back, jaw dropped.

"Hello to you too, Nuru," I said, loud enough to compensate for the mask. "I'm here to see Empress Sichi."

At least my tone must have been unchanged, for her surprise soon became a scowl. "Empress Sichi already has a visitor, Capt—Def—Dishiva."

A spike of fear it was Leo flared and died as I peered around her. A dark-haired young Kisian sat with her, keeping his gaze to his tea bowl. From inside, Sichi spoke and Nuru answered with my name, and with a heavy sigh, she drew herself up.

"Where is the Motepheset Shrine?"

"What?"

Nuru rolled her eyes. "I want to be sure it's you. Where is the Motepheset Shrine?"

"A day's ride east of the Hamat Grove. If you climb onto the roof you can see the ocean."

"And where does the whisperer conclave meet?"

I stared at her a long moment. "I don't know. Only whisperers know that."

Nuru spoke over her shoulder, and Empress Sichi's answer was somewhat resigned. Nuru stood aside to let me in.

I had wanted to take the damn mask off so many times since Leo had first tied it around my head, yet somehow Sichi's calm scrutiny as I entered was almost what broke me. I tightened my hands to fists and bowed. "Your Majesty."

"Captain."

In anyone else I would have excused the error as a lack of Levanti vocabulary, but I was coming to realise Sichi was a smart woman who never did anything without good reason.

The man with her turned, and I was surprised by the sight of Grace Bahain's son. I had never spoken to him, only knew him by sight—a gently spoken young man with a soft smile. This he favoured me with, though his gaze skittered about my face, trying to find some feature of the mask to settle on.

"Dishiva," Nuru said, having closed the door and joined us. "I don't think you've met Lord Edo Bahain. He is Grace Bahain's son and heir, and Sichi's cousin." Nuru spoke to Lord Edo in much the same tone, and I heard my name as he must have heard his.

"Do remove your mask and join us, Captain Dishiva," Nuru said for Sichi, gesturing at an empty cushion beside the table.

It was a test. I could see it in the steady way she watched me. If I complied, they knew I was still myself. If I didn't then I was Leo's puppet. Well, I had wanted to see how far I could push my freedom. I was not outside. I could not be expected to drink tea with it on. And Leo never wore his in Sichi's presence. Time to see if I was to be held to his own standards.

I slid the mask down around my throat as he often did, my heart thumping hard. *"I will kill every one of your Swords and their horses. I will butcher even your dear Itaghai, and I will make you eat him."*

Sichi's smile was grim, but she nodded as I knelt to join them, my knees weak. She poured me a bowl of tea and slid it across the table, speaking all the time.

"I am glad to see you have some mind of your own," Nuru translated. "But tell me, why agree to that ceremony?"

"You speak like I had a choice," I said sourly, but at least she hadn't assumed me lost as so many of my own people had. "I'm afraid I'm endangering you by being here."

"As I am endangering you by letting you stay. He is watching me. Ever since he came back."

Nuru finished translating this as Sichi refilled Lord Edo's bowl, a brief exchange between them going untranslated.

"He knows what we did," I said.

"He does," she agreed through Nuru's lips. "But he doesn't dare harm me or seek to use me. We think it's because his hold on everything here is still too tenuous to risk Grace Bahain's wrath." She gestured at Lord Edo. "Edo tells me my uncle is very unhappy with Dom Villius's current position."

I turned to Lord Edo. "He doesn't trust Leo? Can we use that to be rid of him?"

The young man looked to Nuru, the speed of the conversation frustratingly slow. "He has tried talking to His Majesty," came his eventual answer. "Tried pressuring. Tried just shutting the man out, but Emperor Gideon is tenacious in holding on to him."

I thought of the peace that had come over me, of how easily he had been able to make me do whatever he liked, but no sooner had I thought to tell them than I couldn't. It made no sense. Easier to believe I had been dehydrated and starving. But how else to explain the change in Gideon?

"Have you noticed that Gid—Emperor Gideon has been...different recently?" It was a risky question, but it was risky even being present, and the opportunity for allies could not be passed over.

Sichi and Nuru shared a look. "We were going to ask you the same question," Nuru said. "Sichi has not seen him since the ceremony and does not know him as you do."

"He was your captain."

This she conceded with a shrug. "I was only a saddlegirl, and the Gideon I knew back home isn't the same man you got to know here."

"Was he ever one to take advice? Or orders?"

Nuru considered this a moment before shaking her head.

"Then I have no doubt Leo is doing something to him," I said.

Both Sichi and Lord Edo had watched our exchange, and Nuru quickly summarised it for them in a few lines of Kisian that made both look all the more grim. When she finished, I gave voice to the question I could not answer. "What does Dom Villius *want*?"

At Nuru's translation, Lord Edo shrugged. "Power," Sichi said. "Control."

"But doesn't he already have that?"

This time Lord Edo spoke.

"Lord Edo says the political situation in Chiltae has always been very complicated," Nuru said, rather than translating his ongoing speech word for word. "He says they don't have a central ruler like Kisians, and access to...being a ruler? I think they must have many, decided by money. Yes, nine high rulers, the nine wealthiest men in any given cycle."

"Why must it always be men?"

Nuru shrugged and went on as Lord Edo continued in his soft voice. "The...second tier?...are the next nine wealthiest men, and while the top three haven't changed for a long time the rest move around a lot, and they fight to be in the Nine. Trade wealth is everything."

"What about the church?"

Again Lord Edo gave his little shrug. "That's even more complicated," Nuru continued, staring at his lips. "The church is relatively new but has gained such popularity with the common people that some members of the Nine defer to the hieromonk rather than risk... I think he's saying the common people attacking them, but we don't have a good translation for that. An uprising is perhaps the closest, the whole reason we have a challenge system."

"So he wants real power and he's taking it through Gideon." I sighed. "And he's died some of the same ways as Veld in their holy book, which will make people think he is also a god. He can read our minds. And if we kill him, he comes back. Excellent."

In the silence, Sichi refilled everyone's tea bowls. "Do we have any other allies?" she asked, having blown the steam from the top of her tea three times. "Or is it just us?"

It was my turn to shrug. "If they knew all this and believed it, the Levanti would be against Leo. Especially if he's getting into Gideon's head. There's..." I spun my bowl slowly on the table. To speak of Levanti affairs to outsiders felt strange and wrong. "There's something like it going on back home," I said, unable to meet their gazes as Nuru translated. "Gideon calls it a sickness. It's why we're here. Both why we were exiled in the first place and why he's trying to build us a new home. Our herd masters seem to have been infected with... something that turns their minds far from what's best for their people. If they knew it was happening here too..."

I couldn't finish. I wasn't even sure what most of them would do. My own feeling was one of suffocating dread and helplessness, not anger. And if I wasn't alone in that, perhaps knowledge would not spur the Levanti to do something, but to fracture and break.

"My answer is complicated too," Lord Edo said, only to pause and glance at Sichi, seeming to ask permission. She gave it with a nod, and with his gentle grimace, he went on in an apologetic tone. Though who he was apologising to, I wasn't sure. "My father is no true ally," he said through Nuru's lips. "He has no interest in playing second to a Levanti leader. Sichi already knows this," Nuru added on her own before going on. "He took advantage of the opportunity to be rid of the Ts'ai and wound Kisia so he could take the throne and put it back together again himself. He intends to marry Empress Miko and get rid of you all—at least he did. Between me having helped Miko escape him and Leo getting in the way, his plan is a mess."

I could only stare from him to Sichi to Nuru for a full minute after she finished the translation. He had spoken so calmly I could scarcely believe he had just admitted his father's treachery.

"Nuru," I said. "Do correct me if I'm wrong, but are they saying that Sichi's uncle is planning to get her off the throne he worked to put her on in the first place?"

"Yes. It's complicated, but yes. Emperor Gideon and Sichi are meant to solidify the empire by doing all the fighting and dying, then he swoops in and saves Kisia from them and us."

"But she's his blood."

"Yes."

I closed my eyes a moment, unable to imagine how twisty Grace Bahain's mind must be to have come up with such a plan, let alone execute it.

"As for the rest of the Kisians here," Edo went on after a pause, "most of them are here because they have alliances with my father, through family or trade or debt, and would likely do whatever he told them to. They would happily get rid of Dom Villius, but that would give them more power. We may not like it, but Dom Villius's power here has been severely curtailed by Father's, and Father's by Dom Villius. Which of them is ultimately worse for you all I'm really not sure."

I had not thought I could feel more helpless, but these words sank me beneath a very dark cloud. I had a small group of allies, but our enemies were more numerous and powerful, stretching well beyond Leo. In fact, Levanti allies seemed to be nonexistent, and my heart ached for everything we had hoped to build. The road to that dream was longer and more treacherous than ever before, and the end goal far less desired. Why stay here if the sickness could come with us? Why stay if we were so unwanted that even our allies would seek our destruction?

A sharp rap fell upon the door, and I turned to Nuru before she could rise. "Why are there no guards outside?"

"Because His Majesty, in his infinite wisdom, has decided it looks as though she doesn't trust his people or her own if they're there."

"But he still has guards."

"Naturally." Nuru rose as a second, more insistent knock sounded. No sooner had she slid open the door than Grace Bahain pushed past and strode in, his eyes flying about the room and landing, scowling, upon his heir.

He spoke, a tirade thinly veiled in stiff formality, first at Lord Edo and then at Sichi, and desperate to know what he was saying, I glared at Nuru until she shifted beside me. "He opened with a complaint that he has been looking all over for his son and didn't think to find him gossiping with women, which neatly allowed him to switch to demanding of Sichi where her Kisian women are and berating her for preferring Levanti to her own people. She said the Levanti are her people too, which is why I love her."

With someone translating his words for a stranger, Grace Bahain drew himself up and stopped speaking to them as though they were disobedient children.

"But I did not come to quarrel with you," Nuru translated in a low voice when he went on, far more moderately. "Rumour has it, Miko Ts'ai has taken command of the southern army Kin's bastard was leading. The sources are confused whether he is still alive or not, but either way she's unlikely to wait until after winter to move. She has your father with her."

I watched him speak, hunting any part of his son's calm, thoughtful manner and finding none. Grace Bahain was a man of fine features who nevertheless could not be called either handsome or beautiful, no matter how decorated his robe. He failed too at the Kisian penchant for moderating tone and expression, even his attempts belied by flashes of anger or contempt flitting across his features.

Sichi's sharp response made him scowl.

"She said if he hoped her to have insight into her father's plans, he ought to consider that Miko would be the one in charge." Nuru lowered her voice to the barest whisper as Bahain snapped back at the empress. "He reminded her she wouldn't be where she is without him and"—Nuru grinned—"she replied that he wouldn't have his position without her either, and now that she's an empress the only person who outranks her is her husband. She said, 'Apply to him if you want me given orders.'"

I could see why Nuru liked her so much. Even Lord Edo struggled to hide a smile. It didn't last. His father soon bore his heir off, and no sooner had the door closed behind the two Bahains than Sichi was up, pacing out the anger she had been hiding, hissing to Nuru all the while. I didn't need a translation to understand.

Needing air, I drew my mask back up and left them. It was drizzling out in the yard, lightly enough to be pleasant, but I couldn't avoid the effect my arrival had on the other Levanti. Some let their gazes slide over me like I wasn't there. Some pointed and whispered. Until Anouke fell into step beside me. As one of my Swords it ought not to have been a statement, but Leo had changed everything.

"Captain," she said in something of a mutinous tone. "What's going on? What's with all this all of a sudden?"

She gestured at my attire, her contempt almost too much for my resolve. I could tell her I had been forced into it, that it was all part of Leo's plan, but truth spoken only to soothe my pride was dangerous. So though it hurt like every word was a blade in my throat, I said, "It is as you see. I am the bridge between peoples. The Levanti Defender of the One True God."

"But aren't we meant to be joining the Kisians, not the Chiltaens? Why not swear to some Kisian god instead of joining Dom Villius?"

Pride at her shrewdness mixed with annoyance as we walked on past the main stables. Levanti hanging around the open doors watched us like they might watch a Hoya match, waiting to see the outcome. Itaghai was in there. I could just walk in and take him from his stall, could saddle up and ride and ride until I was so far away all this faded into a distant nightmare. The urge was great, but instead I kept walking and said, "I am sure we will build many bridges with the Kisians too."

Her reply was cut short as panicked shouts burst from the stables. Everyone in the yard sped toward the doors, hearts pounding with the fear for our horses we all held close.

Shouted questions rose around me as we crammed into the dim stable, all fresh straw and lamp oil and the blissful scent of animals. And the heavy thuds and cracks of hooves kicking floor and wall amid scuffs of straw.

"What's going on?"

"Whose horse?"

"Call a horse master!"

I had barely registered that the commotion was happening outside Itaghai's stall before the sounds stopped, leaving only the voices and the thump of my heart. Struggling to breathe, I ripped my mask off and pushed through the crowd, feeling like I was no longer in my body for how stiffly my limbs moved, mere numb lumps of flesh attached to a core of fear.

I saw the head first, protruding from its stall. Still. Lifeless. Large eyes glassy and staring, a string of foam dangling from its nose. For a heart-stopping moment, I was sure it must be Itaghai, until I saw the streak of dark hair. Motep, Katepha e'Jaroven's horse, in the stall next to mine. Katepha was there, head to his horse's back as it lay lifeless in the mess of straw and foam spittle.

Itaghai's stall remained closed, a Levanti I didn't know reaching over the door to calm him with a gentle hand, while on the other side another horse lay dead, an Injit sobbing at her loss.

I ought to have stayed. To have taken over comforting Itaghai. To have been there for my people. But the realisation this was no accident hit me like a stone, and panic gasping its ragged breath up my throat, I pushed back through the murmuring crowd of onlookers, desperate for air. For space. For accusing eyes not to fall on me.

Two horses had died, and whatever Lashak had said, it was my fault.

7. CASSANDRA

The Witchdoctor's house sat atop a hill overlooking the town like a scraggly blackbird watching its nest. I had hated everything about my time there and had hoped never to go back, but here we were because fate hated me.

The time since we'd left had not improved it. The gardens were still overgrown, the carriageway pocked with potholes, and the roof was missing tiles, but Captain Aeneas didn't slow our pace. Empress Hana sat in her new flesh suit looking as grim as only a dead body can. Which, it turns out, is very grim.

"Every time I leave this place, I think I'll never come back, and yet I keep returning," she said, her voice constricted in the aging corpse. It had been too hard on her body for us both to remain in it long. "Like I lost something here and can't escape until I find it again."

I was curious about the place and her memories of it, but I had learned since falling into Empress Hana's body what true fatigue was. It clouded everything, slowed everything, and in this state, I could well imagine not having the energy to give a damn about a tree growing through the floor.

"I don't see anyone," she added as the cart jolted and swayed up the carriageway, its violent shifting sure to break a wheel. Even the prospect of being thrown out onto the road could not rouse me to care.

"The Witchdoctor doesn't like visitors," Captain Aeneas said. "He isn't likely to send out a welcome party. More likely to hide and pretend he isn't home."

I imagined the perfect god-man sitting crouched in a cupboard like a child, and managed a breathy snigger.

"Oh, you're awake, Miss Marius," the empress said, looking around, her dead eyes slow to move. "I had thought you were asleep."

"No one can sleep with the cart rocking like this," I said.

Having jolted and bumped all the way, the cart finally pulled up at the main gates. Beyond sat the courtyard carved with Errant boards where the hieromonk had stood when he came for us. The feeling my life was going in circles could not be suppressed.

"Still no sign of anyone," the empress said. "This does not bode well."

She leapt onto the pitted drive and strode through the gates with the fearlessness of someone who was already dead. Halfway she looked back, shrugging jerkily. "They might be inside, but at least no one else seems to be here."

Small mercies.

Captain Aeneas hauled himself off the driver's box with a grunt of effort. "Here, I'll help you down," he said, coming to the back of the cart. "Whether or not there's anyone home we ought to stay a night and rest. We might find some papers too. He seemed the note-taking type."

"I don't need help," I said, hauling myself into a more upright position.

"Oh yes? Able to just…jump down and dash off, I'm sure. But let me guess, you just don't feel like it?"

"No need to be a sarcastic arse."

"No need to be a pain in my sarcastic arse." He held out his hand. "Come on, I'm too tired for this."

He looked tired, the dark rings under his eyes having aged him ten years in the space of days. Sleep had been impossible and we had rarely stopped moving, always afraid Leo was hard on our heels. And if the Witchdoctor wasn't home...I couldn't think what we would do next. Or where we would go.

I took his hand, allowing him to pull me to my feet. Shaky feet. I had to lean on his arm while the world spun, darkness crawling in at the edges of my vision. He waited patiently, his expression all concern. "Just light-headed," I said. "I'm fine."

"Yes, absolutely fine. I'm not at all worried you're about to drop dead on me, oh no, not at all."

"That's not comforting."

"Wasn't meant to be. I think we're beyond trying to comfort each other, Miss Marius. Here, hold the side of the cart while I jump down, then I'll lift you. With your permission, of course."

He said the last with such thick condescension I wished I had the strength to hit him and not fall over. As it was, I gripped the cart and let him lift me down, feeling as light as a broken bird.

"Are you able to walk? Or do you need my arm?"

"I can walk," I said, though I managed more of a shuffle.

The empress had disappeared inside, but the total lack of sound was not promising. Despite the Witchdoctor's small staff, the house had never felt this dead before.

By the time I had shuffled halfway across the courtyard, loosening stiff joints and muscles as I went, I was sure we were alone. The last hope died when the empress emerged and shook her head. "No sign of them. And it looks like they haven't been here for at least a few days. There are corpses in the workroom, but they look... oozy."

"Delightful."

"You can't tell me you're squeamish about dead things, Miss Marius."

I met her gaze, coming as it did through the slightly bulging eyes of a dead traveller, his skin pale and waxen. "There's dead and there's dead."

"What wisdom. I shall have to remember that one."

"My, aren't we snarky today."

She tilted her head. "Might that have something to do with not getting any rest and being on the run from a religious zealot we don't understand?"

"Nah, I think it's because we're all cunts."

The empress's eyes narrowed, but she turned away rather than rise to my bait. "I'll search the kitchens for food. You should rest."

"Telling me what to do now?"

"While you're wearing my body, you're damn right I'll tell you what to do," she threw over her shoulder. "This one isn't going to last much longer, and you need to rest or mine won't be able to support us both."

It was true, but I was getting sick of always feeling weak and broken, of not being able to do the things I needed to, a walk from the cart to the front door the extent of what my energy would allow.

"I know having to take care of yourself is a new concept to you, Miss Marius, and it's frustrating when you're used to being able to do so much more. It took me a long time to make a sort of peace with it. Now come. I'll help you to a sleeping mat. Food. Rest. Then maybe we can find out what the Witchdoctor knew about this bastard."

———————◆———————

Kaysa was in my dreams again. Or rather I was her in my dreams, my bound hands numb in my lap. A carriage jolted beneath me, but over the rattle and clatter a voice droned. Leo sat opposite, the holy book open on his lap. Sitting at his ease, without his mask, with his hair tousled and his foot upon the seat, he owned a stormy beauty at odds with the lifeless version of his face I was used to seeing on Septum.

"A man does kneel at the dawn and the dusk and thank his God for the night and the day, the sun and the moon and the stars," he said, the words washing over me like a warm blanket. "Though he kneels with others he is alone, one man in the eyes of God as the man beside him is one man and the man beside him is one man, all through the gathering."

Leo glanced up. Our eyes met. His, deep pools into which I could fall—green, I noticed for the first time, flecked with a golden brown. Did all their eyes look the same? The thought was sleepy and sluggish, and I could not look away. He had begged for my help. No one had ever needed my help before. No one ever needed *me*.

"We are many," he went on. "A congregation of ones, together even when we are apart. Whenever he kneels and gives his thoughts and his heart and his body to God he is not alone; though he kneels upon the cold ground and the morning fog covers all from his sight, he is not alone. Never will he be alone again."

He closed the book, but the feeling of warmth and peace that had crept over me remained long after he stopped. I don't know how long we sat there together, only that when at last the warmth began to fade, when the lassitude ebbed, I felt abandoned. Until like a body breaking the surface of a dark sea and gasping for breath, I was free.

I jerked awake. Late afternoon sunlight crept in through a high shuttered window.

"Ah, good," came the empress's rumble. "I've brought food. You need to eat, and don't tell me how exhausting it is and how you don't feel like it because I know, Miss Marius, I know exactly how this illness works and how it seeks day by day to kill me. But no medicine Master Kenji or the Witchdoctor ever gave me did more good than food, so shut up and eat even if you have to nap again straight after."

I didn't have the energy to argue. She had managed to cook some rice and soup, some salted fish and a green vegetable I could only call limp. And tea. "I don't like tea."

"You don't, perhaps, but my body is used to a steady diet of tea multiple times a day, and think how awful you felt when you couldn't have...what was it called? Stick?"

"Stiff."

"That. Drink and don't complain."

"I am not a child." She helped me to sit, her hand cold and stiff and unpleasant to touch. "Is it weird telling yourself what to do?"

She tilted her stiff neck. "A little, yes, but as I have spent a good portion of my life telling myself off and beating myself down, it is not so very strange. Although..." Again with the stiff attempt at a wry smile—one side of the dead man's face seemed to have stopped moving. "I am a good deal kinder to you in my skin than I ever was to myself."

I knew that feeling, but could not say so, could not open the raw wound that had always lived at my core. A wound around which I had built Cassandra Marius, to protect the little girl who had been spat on and shouted at for being different, who had always known she was wrong, broken, unnatural, wicked. Every punishment had been earned. And when there had no longer been anyone around to punish me, I had punished myself.

Under the empress's watchful gaze, I fed her body, and then I slept. This time Kaysa was alone but for distant chatter and laughter. A horse snorted. Nearby a fire crackled and someone sniggered at a crass joke. The artificial darkness around me smelled musty. A tent, perhaps. Mud. Leather. My hands were still bound, but I was not thinking of escape. He would just find me again. And he had asked for my help. Asked *me* for help.

"It's an army camp, Cassandra," Kaysa said in a low voice. "I don't know where."

I tried to ask what he was doing. Why he needed help, but while I could hear her and see her and feel her, she seemed too far away to hear me. She closed her eyes, and as she too drifted off, we were together no more.

Moonlight crept across the floor when I woke. A lantern had been left, and a spare robe garnered from somewhere. Taking up the lantern, I shuffled into the passage.

The room in which the great tree grew enthroned looked no different to the first time I had seen it. Water still pooled on the stones, and its roots curled around railings and pillars, turning the space into something like a forest cavern. Its boughs spread out like beams, while its leaves fluttered against pinpricks of night sky. Again I couldn't swallow the feeling I was going around in circles achieving nothing. I had been here before. Done this before. Ought to have been capable of so much more.

As I crossed the damp, blossom-covered floor, the blessed sound of voices came along the passage. Captain Aeneas and the empress were in the workroom, sitting at one of the benches with a pair of lanterns and a pile of books.

"Found anything?" I said, shuffling in.

"There aren't as many notes here as I had hoped." Captain Aeneas didn't look up from the book he was flicking through. "But we might find something."

"Not many notes? That's quite the stack."

"Most are books by other people," the empress said. "About all sorts of subjects. One of them is about the anatomy of legs."

"Legs?"

"Yes. The author seemed particularly fascinated by frogs, but it is hardly useful in this case."

I leaned on the bench beside her. "Oh, I don't know. Perhaps I could put you into a frog."

Empress Hana looked up, her dead face ridiculous with its mouth half open in an odd shape. "Can you do that?"

"Put you in a frog? I don't know, I've never tried. Shall we find one and see?"

"No, let's not. I have no desire to get stuck in a frog for the rest of my life."

She went back to the book. Pages rustled amid the gentle flare of lantern flame, until she went to grab another book and her jerky movements knocked a pile onto the floor. "Are you all right?" I said. "You don't want to get stuck in that thing either."

"Nor do I want to be weak when there's still so much to do," she snapped.

I didn't have as strong a connection to her as to Kaysa, but I could remember the pain of Jonus's body tightening and decaying, the feeling of being trapped. Of suffocating. Would she have stayed there forever? I had tried not to think about it at the time, too afraid of the answer. What happened to Deathwalkers when they died? Did we just . . . fade away like everyone else, or were there Deathwalkers trapped in corpses all over the world, slowly going mad?

I shuddered, but rather than answer the question in the Empress's hard gaze I grabbed a book off the stack and opened it. Its spine cracked.

"*A Comparative Anatomical Guide to the Animals of the Sands,*" I read aloud. "Where are the Sands?"

The captain shrugged. I flicked a few pages, almost every one of them covered in additional information or corrections in a variety of inks.

"What is . . . whatever Leo is, called?" I said, causing them both to look up. "I'm a Deathwalker," I said, realising it was the first time

I'd owned the description aloud. "Kocho said he was a Thought Thief, and you said the people who used to own this house were Empaths, but what is Leo? What is the opposite of a Deathwalker?"

Captain Aeneas screwed up his face, all lines and scars and fatigue in the lantern light. "I don't recall anyone ever saying it. We weren't allowed to speak of it."

"That's unfortunate," the empress said in her dead voice. "Because Miss Marius makes a good point. Knowing its name would make it easier to find references to him. Do you recall any of the other names? There's a sheaf of papers here about Saki, but that's all I've seen about any of these...conditions."

Conditions. She made it sound like an illness, but it wasn't something one could catch or be cured of; it was how I had been born, how *we* had been born, and to speak of it like a disease made me squirm. What I could do was monstrous. To live the way Kaysa and I had was terrible. And yet...

"Is one of them a Ghost Hand?" Captain Aeneas said, leaning close to the lantern to read a line scrawled in the margin.

"That sounds familiar," I said. "I think Kocho mentioned them as an...overincarnation? But he said we weren't like that. He said they have birthmarks on their wrists. Leo and I are just... abnormal."

Captain Aeneas snorted. "You can say that again."

"You watch it. Just because I am trapped in this weak body doesn't mean I can't still jam a knife between your ribs when you're not looking."

"And how far would you get if you did?" It wasn't even a challenge, just an exhausted piece of truth that left us all quietly turning pages.

"What if there's nothing here?" I said once I had flipped through two more books. "What if we're just wasting time? We could be farther away from Koi by now, we could be—"

"Where exactly?" Captain Aeneas lifted his brows. "Where do you think we can go that's safe? We're in Kisia, which may be marginally safer than Chiltae because fewer people give a shit about Dom Villius, but it is also woefully thin of allies. If you want to be safe, leave me here with Septum and run."

That a few seconds of silence passed proved how tempting it was, but Leo might still follow us, we'd lose our only potential weapon, and he had Kaysa.

I shook my head. "It's too late now. Tempting as it is."

"You just want your body back," the empress said. "This sudden selflessness has nothing to do with stopping Leo or helping anyone."

"Like you're any better. You only want to help because you feel guilty for ignoring your daughter. Had you paid more attention to what was going on perhaps none of this would have happened."

Silence stretched between the lanterns, strained like a tightening string. It snapped when Captain Aeneas closed his book and stood. "I'm going to check on Septum. Don't kill each other while I'm gone."

As his heavy footfalls faded into the depths of the house, I picked up another book, expecting the empress to do the same. Instead she cleared the dead traveller's throat. "In sharing my body you are privy to certain thoughts and feelings I would not have chosen to share with you," she said. "They are also incomplete thoughts and memories and feelings not always containing correct context, if what I see of your mind is anything to go by. That being the case, I would prefer if you did not use ill-gained and incorrect knowledge about the inner workings of my mind to bludgeon me with shame to make yourself feel better."

I parted my lips—her lips, I reminded myself—but she lifted a hand. "No, I don't want you to lie and say that was not the purpose. Nor that you were only trying to help. If you can't see that you're trying to beat me down and assert dominance in this...relationship...I will have to take full control from here on."

Her scathing attack on my character hurt more than the fear she tried to cow me with. I thought of the kind priests who had taught me how monstrous I was, how ignorant I was to the evils I had brought on myself. I had hated my home, but mere weeks at the hospice had been enough to make me wish I could go back. And oh how they had held it over me. *Learn to be better and you can go home, Cassandra. Let us teach you. Let us guide you to God.*

"I'm sorry," I said. "I shouldn't have said it."

"No, you shouldn't," she agreed, but went on staring at me, her protuberant eyes growing glassy.

"Stop staring at me like that, it's creepy."

She looked away. "I was merely marvelling at the sight of Miss Cassandra Marius apologising."

"Well don't get used to it," I said. "It doesn't happen often."

"No, but that means I can trust that when it does, you mean it."

I couldn't think of an answer, couldn't make sense of the weird squirming feeling my guts were writhing, and rather than focus on it I took up another book. *Gender All Around Us* by Essa Yirin.

A quick flip through uncovered no mentions of any soul abnormalities, and I set it aside. "What are we really looking for?"

"Some understanding of what Dom Villius is and how his seventh body can be used against him."

"But against him how? To kill him? To get inside his mind? To control him? We don't even know what he is trying to do, really, do we? Beyond the whole recreate the deaths of Veld nonsense."

"He attacked us at Koi."

"Yes, but why? And why kill Commander Aulus? The Nine have been aligned with the church of the One True God for decades; it's hardly like they would refuse him anything he wanted. And if war with the Levanti is what he wants, why?"

"They did kill a large amount of the Chiltaen army."

I shrugged. "So? He isn't a general, he's a priest. And besides, retribution is not one of the lessons taught by his god. God is merciful and forgiving, not vengeful. I might hate the church, but their actual teachings aren't terrible."

As though summoned by mention of his religion, Captain Aeneas stepped back in, looking more exhausted than when he had left. "He's fine," he said, before I could ask. "But I think we should all rest. In the morning we can gather what supplies we can find and keep moving."

The empress rose stiffly from her seat. "I think we should also leave a message for Torvash."

"Leave a message saying what, Your Majesty?"

"That we were here. We could ask him to leave any information with someone for us if he sees the note. I haven't given any thought as to who, and of course he might not return, but the chance of answers is surely worth the risk of leaving evidence we were here."

Captain Aeneas nodded slowly. "Yes, but I too am not sure who we can trust. And if the note falls into Leo's hands it could put the person we've chosen in danger."

"That's true." She scowled, the expression all the more frightening on a face losing its muscle tone. "Something to think on."

"Indeed."

Empress Hana reached her dead hand out to me. "It's time, Miss Marius."

"Can't you wait until we reach our sleeping mat?"

She gave me a long appraising look, but nodded, and leaving the last of the books unchecked, we left the workroom, heading back toward the main stairs.

"I've heard many stories about this tree," Captain Aeneas said as it appeared at the end of the passage. "A tree larger than any in all

Chiltae, which cannot be cut down. Its trunk and branches break even the sharpest axes."

"Really?" I said. "I've never heard of it. It sounds like nonsense, a proud man's excuse for why he let a tree grow in the centre of his house."

"Lord Darius Laroth would have been the first to disparage his forebears," the empress said, shuffling her corpse along. "But he told me that story when I asked about the tree. He said people once came from all over the empire to try to remove it, but no one succeeded."

"Why isn't it more famous?"

"Probably because that was a long time ago, so it stopped being an attraction and just became a thing that was."

I looked at the trunk. Like every other tree, its bark was rough in some places, smooth in others, all ridges and divots and knots. The branches swayed like supple limbs, nothing about them stiff and unyielding.

Captain Aeneas saw us safely to our room and bade us goodnight. Again the empress held out her hand, and I could give no excuse to put the reunion off except that I feared how much it was going to hurt.

A single touch began the great inhalation, my entire body breathing in and swelling, capturing not air but the essence of another person, so large a thing that for a moment I was sure my skin would split like overripe fruit. It didn't, but everything felt tight and strange and wrong.

The dead body dropped to the floor, all stiff and pale, with waxen skin and staring eyes.

"We ought to have done that out in the passage," I said. "I don't really want to sleep in the same room as it now it's..."

Empty? You're right. Gosh, I was looking bad, wasn't I?

Though every part of me ached, I bent to grab the man's boots and used the last of my strength dragging him into the hallway before lying down to sleep.

———————✦———————

We found the workroom empty the following morning, and with nothing better to do while waiting for the captain to wake, I settled at the bench and pulled another book toward me.

"*Essays on the History and Evolutionary Anatomy of Northern Dragons.*"

What a life Torvash has led.

"Kocho said he's lived a really long time. He isn't human and doesn't age like we do."

Yes, he told me too. I find I envy Saki just a little, you know, being right here at the cusp of knowledge.

"I don't know, he's a grumpy shit too."

But never at her.

She was right. They had made quite the odd pair.

I pulled another book off the stack.

"*Mystics and Memaras.*"

I flicked a few pages, but most of it seemed to be about the religious practices of a group of people I'd never heard of. I set it aside and took up another, finding increasing amounts of nothing useful.

"You're up early."

I hadn't heard Captain Aeneas's approach, but I had grown so used to his voice I barely flinched. He brought in a tray of steaming food and set it on the bench. "Breakfast," he said. "And when I went out to the stables to check on the ox, I found this."

He held out a dirty book, its pages all bent and smeared with I didn't want to know what. "It looks like a notebook. Perhaps they left in a hurry and dropped it. Or it could be nothing. It's written in Kisian and I don't know Kisian."

He sounded embarrassed. It was not an uncommon language to

learn in Chiltae, but most Chiltaens stuck with knowing the differences in our spoken languages and left it at that.

"Here." Empress Hana stretched out our hand for the book. "Let me see."

Our stomach rumbled at the smell of the food, but ignoring even the steaming pot of tea, she flipped through the book, trying to touch as little of each page as possible.

"It's recently dated," she said. "Looks like it might be some notes they took about you, Cassandra. Oh, look." She pointed at a neatly transcribed line detailing Saki's first attempts to move my soul in and out of my body.

"What does it say?" the captain asked.

"It says, 'While Saki has been unable to permanently re-anchor the soul, there is the strong possibility that, in the same way Deathwalker Three is able to move her second soul into the dead, Saki may be able to move a second soul more permanently into a vessel made empty by other means. While I have many theories on how a body may be emptied of its soul without damaging the physical construct of the body itself, the easiest way to test this would be to use the empty vessel that is the sixth body of Memara 21.'"

She looked up at the captain. "Sixth? Does he mean Septum?"

"It sounds like it, though you're right. Septum ought to be the seventh."

We could put a soul inside Septum? I said.

"I think that's what he's saying, yes, but I can't say I'm any more keen on being inside that... thing than I was being inside a frog."

Captain Aeneas tapped the table. "He is not bad, Your Majesty, just... empty."

"Exactly," I said, taking back control to speak. "That's why I heard the death song coming from your hut back near Koi. It wasn't because anyone was dead, it was because there was an empty vessel. The soul must only stretch to six divisions and after that..."

"A hollow shell." The captain's voice was equally hollow.

"Yes, but a living hollow shell," I said. "One that won't disintegrate on us. You could use Septum to walk around until we're able to get Kaysa back."

Silence hung while the empress considered this. I could feel her trying to figure out whether her distaste for the idea was because it was a bad idea, or because the body belonged to Leo Villius.

"I am…not entirely sure that would be wise, Your Majesty," Captain Aeneas said. "You remember I said they are connected? They know what each other knows and feel what each other feels, and if you were inside that mind it could be…"

He seemed unable to find a good word and let the sentence fade away. "Could be…?" I prompted. "Overwhelming? Destructive? Because if you don't have a good reason why it's a bad plan, I can give you one why it might be a good plan. If they are so interconnected, even one minute inside that body could tell us everything he's planning and where he is. You might even be able to feed him false information about our whereabouts."

"You might be able to," the captain said. "But there is just as much chance the body could shape the soul." He huffed out a breath. "Usually you take over dead bodies. Bodies that aren't connected to a soul, aren't alive. There is no danger to you in getting in there and…making it walk around." He paused, but soon went on rather than examine his own blasé attitude to walking corpses. "Septum is not only alive but connected to a living soul, so you'd be sharing a body connected to Leo in the way you and Miss Marius are currently connected and—" He bit his lip and wouldn't look at us. "And I hope you will excuse me for saying so, Your Majesty, but the sharing of a body with Miss Marius has… changed you. Changed both of you. You are…day by day…little by little…becoming the same person."

Our joint horror ran the same path to denial. It couldn't be true.

I still felt like me. She still sounded like herself. It hadn't happened with Kaysa, had it? I'd always been me, and she had always been her irritating self, just a voice there to berate me. The only existence I had allowed her.

"I do apologise most sincerely for the observation, Your Majesty," the captain said, bowing. "But I really did not feel comfortable letting you consider this option without knowing. There is a chance you could get…stuck. You could cease being yourself. Unus is…"

He didn't need to finish that thought. We had seen him. We had seen him enthral a whole church full of priests like puppets in a play.

"I take your point, Captain," the empress said stiffly. "Thank you for the warning."

"Your Majesty."

Saying no more, we ate and flipped through the notebook. Most of it was observations on the experiments Saki had carried out on me. It was all very interesting, but added nothing to what we already knew or suspected. Yet the word *Memara* kept nagging at me.

"Memara 21," I murmured, setting the muddy book aside and hunting back through the stack I'd already checked. "Memara 21. Ah! *Mystics and Memaras*, I thought I'd seen that word before. Perhaps after all the religious bits there'll be something about what Leo is."

"We'll have to take it with us," Captain Aeneas said, licking the last of his meal off his fingers. "It's time to get moving. But first we should take the rest of this food to Septum. Will you come and…?"

"Make sure he doesn't leap out to eat your face off?" the empress said, tucking the book into her sash.

"Yes, Miss Marius, exactly."

She took his proffered dagger rather than correct him.

Septum's box had been left on the back of the cart. Leaving the stable doors open for light, the captain climbed up with enviable ease. I had to be helped up, Captain Aeneas taking my hand with a little bow of apology. Never to me, I realised, always to her, as though he was not only apologising for having to touch her hand but for the very fact I was with her at all.

"When you're ready," he said, stepping closer to the box.

I tightened my grip on the dagger. "All right, go."

Captain Aeneas lifted the lid. There again the pale, unmoving form of Leo Septum, staring at nothing despite the lid opening like a door to the entire world. He showed no interest in the new sights or sounds. Even the smell of the food had no effect.

"Eat," the captain ordered, dangling some salted meat above his lips.

The empty shell ate, chewing long and slow like he had all the time in the world before finally swallowing.

"Eat."

And on it went until the plate was empty. Setting it down at his feet, Captain Aeneas adjusted his grip on the coffin lid and prepared to lower it.

"Ah, Captain, always so caring and considerate," the body said, fixing its gaze on his face. The voice rasped and the words slurred like his lips were out of practice.

"Leo," Captain Aeneas said, the words strangled.

"Yes, Captain, it's me. I'm outside the house and would like my brother back now."

8. RAH

I wanted to stay awake, but when you push your body too far it demands what it needs. The moment Derkka laid me down in one of the huts my whole body gave up on wakefulness.

Fears followed me into the darkness. People walked the paths of my memories, all as clear as if they had been sitting before me. There, Whisperer Jinnit commanded me to repeat the harvest calendar for our grove again and again while he sat listening for the inevitable mistake. Every mistake had to be followed with a prayer to the gods, but the prayer came out in a tumble of hoarse gasps, and there was old Herd Master Sassanji sitting before me, sharpening Snakegrass on his knees.

My trembling fingers found skin and I tried to hold on, to beg, to plead, to explain. "I'm sorry, Herd Master, I did not mean to cause such trouble. Please don't exile me."

The old man laughed and he laughed and he laughed at this little boy kneeling before him in trouble for having almost hit three Swords with a speeding barrel wagon. With Mother dead it was Gideon who sat supporting me, his hand holding mine and an indulgent smile on his face.

"Please. I don't want to be sent away."

Then the heavy weight of Horse Whisperer Jinnit's hand was on my shoulder. I ought to have been proud, and I was in a way, but it was the pride of a martyr, built on the stubbornness of an indoctrinated child.

Gideon had not tried to talk me out of it. We were to leave at first light. The gods only knew when I would see my herd again, or Gideon. We must have had the same thoughts, yet no such words were spoken. We were Levanti. We had to do what was required of us.

"Here, take this." He had given me a tunic, not a new tunic but one with little rips along the neckline and a bigger tear up one side fixed by inexpert hands. It was the tunic I'd always pinched from him whenever I felt sad, whenever I missed my mother or the world seemed bleak and pointless in the way the world sometimes does. He'd gotten annoyed at me and I'd been unable to explain, unable to give voice to the uplifting sensation in my chest when I wore it, when I breathed its scent and felt its soft fibres against my skin, so I had said something childish, that it was mine now, or that I wore it better, or that he had stolen it from me in the first place, and in our scuffle it had ripped right up the side and he'd fumed and called me an irritating child. I'd fixed it so poorly, taking care over every wonky stitch. To have it in my hand again, smelling like him, feeling like him, stole my voice.

He hadn't come to see me off the next morning, though I had turned to look a hundred times as the herd grew ever smaller in the distance.

I woke in a sweat of panic, disoriented in the smothering darkness. The tunic was in my saddlebag and it suddenly seemed important to be sure it was still there, but as I patted shaking hands around the hut, it all came back to me. My saddlebags were with Jinso in Syan, and I was unwell from lack of food and rest and too many injuries in a camp run by a horse whisperer I wasn't sure I could trust, while Gideon was in danger and I couldn't get to him. And in the darkest hours of the night, I could not but wonder if he could be saved at all. Or if he even wanted to be.

I dozed through the night and the following day, not fully waking until golden evening light filtered into the hut and the smell of cooking once again filled the air. A whole day? Two? I ached all over, every wound and sore muscle creating a symphony of pain, and yet I berated myself for such weakness when everything hung in the balance, when at this very moment things could be happening I might have prevented.

Someone had left food and water beside my sleeping mat. I managed to prop myself up enough to eat, yet despite my hunger my stomach seemed to have shrunk, and I soon felt sick.

Outside, the quiet chatter over the cooking fires sounded cheerful and welcoming, and I lifted a leg in an attempt to rise. A sudden spike of pain made my head spin.

I tried again, but every part of me was achy and sluggish, and I fell back onto the blanket with a gusty exhale. Footsteps hurried past the door, but no one looked in.

On my next attempt to rise, I managed to roll before the pain sent my head spinning toward darkness and I had to stop and steady myself, breathing slowly. When the sick feeling retreated, I pulled myself up, but as I bent my good leg beneath me my head spun again. Having waited for the dizziness to pass, I eventually managed a step outside. Though to call it a step was optimistic, a shuffling limp a better description of my poor progress.

I couldn't tell how late it was, but it didn't look like the evening meal was in progress yet. Tor sat by one of the fires with the Chiltaen holy book open on his lap as though he hadn't moved. An adapted Hoya game was taking place in an open area nearby, attracting a simple audience, while others sat around chatting and taking care of small tasks. The whole effect was so like being back with a herd that my heart ached.

Heads turned as I approached the closest fire, conversations trailing off. A few people began to rise to help me, but I lifted a hand in refusal and lurched on alone. I made it, but every part of me seared and ached and shouted that I was a fool to have moved.

"How are you feeling?" Tor said once I was down and catching my breath. "You look shit."

"Thank you. I feel shit. But I would rather feel shit out here where I can see what's going on."

There was no sign of Whisperer Ezma, nor her apprentice, though I made doubly sure before I said, "Why was she exiled?"

"I don't know. I haven't heard."

"Historically, I can think of only two others who have been exiled," I said in a low voice. "And neither was exiled with their apprentice leaving a grove untended. That he's here is almost worse than that she is. Worse still, to have been here longer than we have, yet I don't recall a whisperer being exiled within my lifetime. Do you?"

"No, but my lifetime has been considerably shorter than yours so far."

"A bit shorter, not *considerably*."

"Considerably," Tor repeated without pity.

Before I could ask what he thought of the whisperer owning a copy of the holy book, a pair of young men approached, saluting and seeking permission to sit by us. I gave it, and no sooner had they sat down than another arrived. Followed by Amun. He sat by me as one of the other newcomers—Diha, her name was—asked if I'd had my wounds tended that day. "I am—I *was* the healer of the First Swords of Bedjuti. We don't really have positions here, but I would be honoured to tend you. Of course, if you wish to wait for Whisperer—"

"I would rather not trouble her," I said, too fast for politeness but too sore to care. "If you could, I would be very grateful."

"Of course, Captain. I'll get my bag."

She was up and off before I could correct her, leaving a short, awkward silence to fall between me and Amun. As his former captain I ought to have said something, but everything sounded trite in my head.

When Diha returned with her bag, she started by looking at the cuts and bruises on my face. Lifting the bandages, she whistled. "This is some impressive work. What happened?"

"Someone punched me."

She laughed. "A lot, by the look of it."

The feeling of Amun's gaze on me intensified, and the urge to confess what I had done to Sett burned up my throat, but if the story hadn't gotten around, perhaps I could be free of it just a little longer. "Yes, it was a lot."

Diha cleared her throat. "I'm not used to having such a large audience while I work."

I looked up. Not only had the circle seated around me grown, but at least a dozen more had gathered, standing around us, and forgetting the past awkwardness between Amun and me, I turned to him and said, "Why is everyone standing around?"

"Because you're the great Rah e'Torin."

"Last time I checked I was an outcast; that's not very great."

His smile was a sad thing pressed between thin lips. "Ah, but there is no love here for what Gideon is doing and you stood up to him, at least so I hear. You challenged him?"

"And lost. I challenged Yitti and lost too."

Amun shrugged. "No one else has dared. Levanti are used to having leaders they can respect, and when one falls they replace them with another. You make a fine replacement."

"I thought Ezma was doing that job," I said, keeping my tone light.

"There is great comfort in having a horse whisperer around, but what we need is a herd master who can unite us. So far we've had no consensus on a herd master, so Whisperer Ezma fills the role as best she can."

"Ah." No wonder she didn't like me.

"All right," Diha said, patting something pungent onto the cut beneath my eye. "Arms next. Sleeves up or tunic off. Probably best to just take it off so I can check there's no new internal bleeding we should worry about."

All too many people were standing around, but with Diha's help I struggled my tunic off. I hadn't gotten a good look at any of my wounds while Yitti and Derkka were tending them, but I looked now at the spread of bruises mottling my chest and could only be grateful I hadn't broken a rib.

Diha checked them all with a judicious prod, found every sore spot on my abdomen and, with a satisfied grunt, moved on to my arms. The exhaustion of being worked over began to take its toll, and I leaned against the pile of saddles and blankets Tor had built the previous day and let the chatter wash over me. Having been separated from other Levanti so long, it was a pleasant sound, none of it tense or important, just the everyday talk of herd members gathered around the fire after finishing their tasks. I could have dozed off lulled by their voices had Diha not been poking all my sorest spots.

By the time Whisperer Ezma approached, there were so many people gathered around me that she had to thread her way through, turning her shoulder and sliding between chatting Swords.

"Ah," she said, looking down at me. "I see you are feeling a little better, Rah e'Torin. I ought to have guessed when I saw so many had abandoned their tasks who I would find. Tor, Amun, I require your assistance. The rest of you ought not crowd Rah e'Torin so much. He needs rest."

She wove her way back out of the crowd, both Amun and Tor rising, a little reluctantly, to follow her. They shared a look, but only Amun glanced at me, something of a smile there before he was gone.

Diha kept working. Some of the crowd dissipated, but probably not as many as Ezma had hoped.

"Do you know why Whisperer Ezma was exiled?" I said to the healer.

"No," she said. "I don't think she's talked about it. And it's not the sort of thing one can ask a horse whisperer."

"I would. If she's going to lead us we need to know."

Her curious look was hard to decipher, and she went on working through my injuries. Ezma kept both Amun and Tor busy all the while as though punishing them for talking to me, and my dislike of her grew.

Despite Diha's handiwork, Derkka insisted on checking me over before the evening meal in the privacy of my hut. No doubt he had something he wished to say, so I let him help me back to my mat, but he said nothing, just began the task of checking over my wounds in silence.

"Why were you exiled?" I said, once it was clear he had nothing to say.

"That," Apprentice Derkka said, putting more pressure on my leg wound than was needed, "is quite a disrespectful question."

"I don't see that. As it takes a full conclave of horse whisperers to exile one, the reason you were exiled seems important. Central, even, to whether we ought to trust you."

He poked harder.

"And you need not tell me you were exiled because Whisperer Ezma was exiled," I went on. "Because on no prior occasion was an apprentice deemed untrustworthy to continue their whisperer's work."

At least this time I had the satisfaction of seeing him flinch. He jabbed one of my bruises. Deliberately trying to hurt me? Or merely angry at my questions?

"Diha has already done a thorough job of this," I said. "Why were you so intent on checking me over again?"

"Because it's my job," he snapped. "As it is Whisperer Ezma's job to guide the Levanti, and your job to lie there and shut up because you aren't even a captain anymore. You're an exile from exiles and have no voice here."

I had not arrived with any intention of staying, let alone leading, but the man's aggression goaded me to say, "There are no herds here, so I have whatever voice my people choose to grant me. You, on the other hand, are holding on to your voice through deceit."

Derkka sat back on his heels. "Deceit?"

"What else can it be called when you refuse to explain your exile? That you wish to keep it a secret surely means no one would want anything to do with you if they found out."

He gripped my thigh, fingertips digging hard into the broken flesh. I couldn't swallow my gasp, but gritted my teeth rather than satisfy him with a pained cry. "Shut. Up," he snarled into my face. "Or I will make you. There are all too many ways I could kill you here and now and make it look natural, your wounds having been too great. A bleed in your gut we didn't find. Such a pity."

I could not speak, so intense was the pain shooting through my leg and up my back. He let go, but it didn't ease and all I could do was breathe.

"Good. Now, you seem to be developing a fever, so I've brought you a tonic for that."

"Fever?" I managed. Apart from the sharp pains I felt fine.

"Yes, it's come on rapidly and needs to be tended before it takes you from us."

He slid his arm under my shoulders and lifted me from the mat, pressing the mouth of a flask to my lips. Bitter liquid poured down my throat before I could think better of swallowing it, fear kicking in only in time to spray the last mouthful over him.

Derkka laughed. "Nice try, but that's not going to make any difference to you or me." He dropped me back onto the mat so hard my teeth snapped together. "Good night, Rah."

I tried to roll. To get up. To speak. But already my tongue felt furry and my body weightless, as though I could float up into the sky like the woolly seed of the silk tree. This time my dreams owned no Gideon, no Master Sassanji or Whisperer Jinnit, just the swirling dust of a dry plain as thousands of Levanti hooves thundered toward a destination I couldn't see.

I arose from my dreams a few times, mostly to silence, but sometimes to voices—many unknown to me, often chanting prayers. Sometimes I thought I heard Tor. Or Amun. Or Ezma. Sometimes it was Derkka there to pour more of the bitter liquid down my throat.

"Only one healer is needed here, Diha," he said once, his voice piercing the haze around my head. "I know his health is important to many, but you can safely leave him to me."

Even when I woke enough to know myself, I felt too ill to move or call out, too weak. I hadn't enough strength to fight him, nor enough voice to cry out for Tor, and sank again and again into the strange darkness of my own head.

Until someone shouted. I couldn't make out the words, but another cry followed and I lay caught halfway between sleeping and dreaming while other people's fear washed over me. It seemed to drop into a lull, or maybe I did, until another shout shattered the peace. Running steps spread a widening sphere of panic. Hooves gathered. Sacks were dragged. Tents were rolled and tied. The noise pecked at me incessantly.

I rolled, trying to get up. The room swam as it had the last time I'd tried to rise from my mat, but this time it was like someone had stuffed my head with wool.

While the panic mounted outside I struggled upright and sat as best I could with my leg wounds screaming. I made it onto my knees as footsteps approached. "Rah? Rah! You're awake!"

A face swam in and out of focus before solidifying into Tor. "Are you all right?"

"I'm fine." My voice was the dry croak of a dying animal. "Or I would be without Derkka."

A frown fluttered over his face at the apprentice's name. "Derkka?"

"What's going on out there?"

"Gideon's Swords are on their way. Dishiva must have betrayed us."

"Not Dishiva. She wouldn't," I said—a mantra of hope more than anything else. Could I have been so mistaken in everyone?

"Captain Lashak is talking to Whisperer Ezma right now, but Shenyah e'Jaroven was with her and said Dishiva took the position of Defender of the One True God, and...I..." His grip tightened on the holy book in his hand. "There is mention of a defender in here, and it...doesn't end well. But she was against him. He killed Matsi. If she's been forced into this I have to warn her what the book says."

As he spoke, Tor bustled around the small space gathering things into a sack—food, water skin, gloves, even the holy book, which he wrapped in the dirty remnants of a tunic. "She must have been," he said more to himself. "It's the only thing that makes sense."

"She could have succumbed to the sickness, like Gideon seems to have."

Tor stared at me, his mouth hanging open. "I...don't even want to contemplate that."

"We have to."

He drew a breath and let it out in a gust of air. "But if I doubt her...who do I tell about this? While you've been sick I've been thinking, Rah, what if...what if he's only being resurrected by his god while he dies the right ways? If he messes one up maybe he's dead forever."

My instinct was to stand up for Leo, to explain as I had to my Swords that he was a priest, not a soldier, that he was only interested in peace, not death, but the words dried like so much sand in my mouth. What a naive fool I had been, tricked by a mild, soft-spoken manner and a gentle smile. Part of me didn't want to believe it was true, wanted to say there were two sides of every story, but Matsimelar was dead and Dishiva could be in as much trouble as Gideon.

"You need to go," I said. "You need to warn Dishiva if you can." He parted his lips to speak, but I hurried on as a terrible idea occurred to me. "You need the other book. The one Whisperer Ezma has. If you're quick you can use the panic to get into her hut and steal it and—"

"Steal from a whisperer? Are you mad?"

"No. You know I'm not. How many days have I been out?"

"Two." Tor looked away. "We didn't think you'd make it."

I gripped his wrist. "There was nothing wrong with me. Derkka forced something down my throat, and I haven't been properly awake until now. He seems to have forgotten me this time."

"He's scouting out the attack, but...you're not serious. Why would he—?"

Hurried footsteps emerged from the noise outside, and I tightened my grip on his arm. "Get the book. Take—"

The hut darkened as Ezma passed the threshold. She halted a few steps in, not with the look of one brought up short, but of one cynically unsurprised. Guilt coloured Tor's face. "Well," she said. "This looks like a pleasant discussion I have interrupted." Her gaze dropped to the book in Tor's hand. "You had best hurry out of here, Tor e'Torin. The traitors could be here as soon as night falls, and you don't want to still be here when they come."

"I came to help Rah. He's better."

"How herd-minded of you, Tor. But you needn't worry, I am here now and I will ensure everyone gets out safely. You must leave with the others."

"But—"

"Now, Tor. We cannot have dithering while an army of traitors rides to destroy us. Go as I have told you."

His gaze flicked my way. He licked his lips. And with a sharp little nod, he saluted. "Yes, Whisperer."

Tor strode toward the door, his eyes on his feet and his hands clenched upon the holy book. A brief flash of darkness and he was gone, leaving the evening light to spill in with the ongoing noise. Outside, panicked footsteps and shouts had risen to a furore, but I faced the horse whisperer with what calm I could. "You had Derkka drug me. Why?"

She closed the space between us and, taking a knife from her belt, held it out to me. I stared at the hilt, knowing what it meant.

I didn't take it. "I'm invoking *kutum*," she said, holding the blade steady.

I stared at her rather than the blade. "That can only be invoked by a herd master with the support of two-thirds of their matriarchs and patriarchs."

"But there are no herd masters here. Only me."

"I know, but there should be. Horse whisperers are never leaders; it's not our way."

"It is my way. And you are in the way."

"I guess that answers my question."

Still I did not take the blade, but rather than force it into my hand she dropped it onto the ground at my feet without breaking eye contact. "Call this my thanks, Rah e'Torin, for showing just how easily Levanti can be led and changed. You can kill yourself or die fighting, whichever suits you best, as long as you die."

Ezma stepped back, no hatred in her face as she saluted in farewell, just a genuine look of kindness and thanks that chilled my skin. "Goodbye, Rah."

She was gone before I could call her back, and chill fear settled like iron in my bones. *Kutum*. We only ever invoked it in dire situations, when the fate of the whole herd relied on speed or a frugal spread of food and water. In no other circumstances could a Levanti think of leaving behind the wounded and the sick and the old. The Torin had never needed it in my lifetime, but there had been a terrible famine within the memory of our elders, during which at least a hundred old and infirm Torin had been Farewelled by a horse whisperer, a death ritual performed to end life honourably. The thought of it always made me shudder. Whisperer Jinnit had spoken of it as a sacred rite, but I had silently vowed never to perform it.

The panic had stilled outside, just a few last desperate dashes around the camp ensuring everyone had what they needed. Except me.

My legs wobbled beneath me as I climbed my hands one after the other up the door frame, but once I was standing, I wanted nothing more than to sit and never move again. But I was a dead man if I did. Ezma would see to that, even if Gideon's Swords did not.

Holding the door frame, I hobbled a step out onto the soft, muddy ground. A few Levanti lingered, some injured and slow, others still packing supplies, while a steady stream of deserters on foot and on horseback departed through a gap in their palisade wall. At the base of the hill, the gates remained closed.

"Everyone out!" someone was shouting. "Make south for the river. Stay quiet and keep together!"

A great black horse trotted into view. Ezma sat easily in its saddle, her jawbone headpiece reaching for the grey sky. It barely seemed to wobble atop her head as though it grew from her skull. Derkka followed on an equally grand animal, riding with the same assurance and pride, his circlet of knuckles shiny with wear. A pair of emperors in their own empire.

Ezma's gaze slid toward me. I shrank back into the shadows, but her horse slowed enough to make her apprentice look around. His stare fixed on me and a question seemed to hang unanswered, until with a little shake of her head, she urged her horse on. Her apprentice followed and both disappeared through the gap in the wall, leaving a mournful silence in their wake.

I let go a breath and almost my shaking legs collapsed beneath me. But for the door frame I might have fallen, yet I could not take it with me and I could not stay. Jammed into my belt, Ezma's knife hung heavy, an ever-present reminder of everything she had said.

Taking a deep breath, I let go the door and hobbled out into the damp evening, my feet squelching in the mud. Each step was more of a fall, hastily curtailed by another step, and they shuddered their force through me. I could not stop. The momentum pulled me on and I had to keep going until my searing limbs gave up. I fell. Mud splattered into my face and I breathed it in, the stink of it filling me with loathing. For Sett. For Ezma. For Derkka. For this place and its endless rain and most of all for myself and my useless body. I pounded the mud with my fists.

Another Levanti on horseback and two on foot hurried past. None looked my way, but why should they? During *kutum*, injured Levanti were dead Levanti, and what was I but a stubborn man who refused to die? *Not yet. Not yet,* I chanted to myself, looking at the blade of Ezma's knife bumping against my thigh. She thought me a danger to her plans, but whatever it took, I was going to survive this. Perhaps. I'd made it only half a dozen paces from the door.

A man in worn leathers hurried toward the gap in the fence. "Amun?" My voice cracked on his name. "Amun!"

He looked back. Hesitated. Our eyes met, and while I knew what I wished to see in his expression, the distance made such detail impossible. Yet I hoped he might turn, might help me, until with a little shake of the head he turned away.

"I'm sorry!" I called after him, words I hadn't been able to say earlier. He flinched as they struck his back as hard as an arrow, but he did not stop and the trees soon swallowed him.

I let out a shuddering breath and, with shaking arms, lifted myself onto my knees. Damp mud chilled my skin as it seeped through the wool. It felt foul, but I began to crawl, walking both arms forward and dragging my knees to catch up, the effort of moving even short distances enough to make angry tears well in my eyes. And the bump of the blade grew more and more pronounced, like a voice becoming ever stronger. *I'm here. I'm here. I'm here.*

But I did not want to die. I would rather jam the tip in Ezma's neck than my own.

I reached the gap in the wall as the sun slipped into the trees. My knees stung from cuts and scrapes, and because things could always get worse, it began to rain. Just a light, teasing drizzle, but I had spent enough time in this wretched place to know it was merely the prelude to a downpour. At least in the rain I would be harder to see, making my slow escape through the marsh like a dying animal.

I felt like one, fatigue setting in before I had made it farther than a few lengths into the trees, followed by the first gnawings of starvation.

I'm here. I'm here. I'm here, said the knife, hitting my thigh. *You could end this now.*

Chill wind rushed through the trees, bringing a squall of rain to pepper my back, all sounds of life disappearing beneath its whistle and the ferocious snap of leaves overhead.

Night crept through the sodden forest, throwing long shadows, and as they began to blur into darkness, I could only continue straight and hope. For what? To find the Levanti who had deserted me? To find Kisians? To somehow find food and water and a place to survive the inevitable winter? I wasn't supposed to be eking out an existence, I was supposed to be fighting, supposed to be saving my people. Saving Gideon. As he had once saved me.

"I will not die," I hissed to the drizzle, and gripping the nearest tree for support, I pulled myself upright. Mud smeared the front of my tunic and my pant legs, weighing me down. "I will not die."

In the last of the light there was no sign of life. All I could do was keep following the hoof marks and hope.

Shifting my hand from tree to tree, I limped a little way on until my legs cramped and I fell, hissing, back into the mud. "Fucking stupid place," I spat through gritted teeth as I tried to loosen the spasming muscles. "Fucking—" I gasped and hissed and tried to breathe, to focus, but the cramping was like animals gnawing on my flesh.

Eventually it loosened and I lay, chest heaving, on the ground, too afraid to move lest it happen again but knowing I must. Any search from the camp would spread this far and farther, and I needed to keep moving. But I didn't. I lay staring at the cloud-covered night, mouth open to catch the cool rain, and thought of the blade Ezma had given me. Rain spattered into my eyes. Animals made small noises in the undergrowth. And still I did not move. It would be so much easier to die, but every time I thought of drawing the blade, I hit a nugget of iron in my soul, a truth harder than any fear.

I did not want to die. Especially not for her.

With a grunt of effort, I rolled over, elbows sinking into the mire, and kept going.

A shout sounded in the distance. It could have been a distressed animal, but my heart raced and it came again. The deep voices of men calling to one another through the trees. Hoofbeats vibrated through the ground, and I sped my pace away from them.

Gideon's Swords had come.

Hands, knees. Hands, knees. Hands, knees. The fabric of my

breeches had torn and warm blood seeped out, but I crawled on, too afraid of what would happen if they caught me.

Now with every bump of the blade against my leg, I changed my mantra.

I will not die. I will not die. I will not die.

The shouts drew closer. Footsteps thudded through the trees. A call—Kisian. A reply in the same tongue returned before Levanti words stained the night. "More tracks," someone said. "And here."

"Some here too. Looks like they were dragging something. Hey, those idiots are just walking all over them. Stop walking on the tracks!"

A flash of light made grey shadows of everything, leaving my eyes to readjust and my hands to hunt the muddy hoofprints. They were becoming sludgy pools. If I went downhill much farther I might find myself swimming in bog water, but there was no going back with so many lanterns flashing between the trees.

"More tracks! They definitely went this way, or at least some of them did."

I stilled while they drew nearer, but they turned and seemed to be moving away so I crawled on.

Another shout had me freeze, holding my breath and lying low. Mud smeared the side of my face as I listened. Kisian. Two voices. Three. Footsteps, and the creak of a lantern handle. Did they even understand why they were hunting their emperor's people? Or maybe after all we'd done, they no longer needed a reason to want us dead.

Low talk approached. I dared not move, but there hadn't been time to shift into the trees, and any swing of a lantern could find me. The footsteps drew closer. I could not keep holding my breath and let it go slowly, chest aching from the effort and the cold that cut into me like knives. More low words. The clink of buckles. The footsteps stopped. Turned. Light gleamed off the mud.

I closed my eyes, breath ragged. Boots sank into the mire beside my head. Something jabbed me in the back, and I could not keep the gasp of shock from my lips. A shout, Kisian words sent hollering through the trees. I winced as a hand gripped my shoulder and rolled me over.

The tip of a thin blade hovered before my eyes, the Kisian face above it lit by an upheld lantern. More footsteps approached. And before I could do more than think about using the knife in my belt, more faces appeared. The first Levanti sneered. "Well, if it isn't Rah e'Torin," he said, and catching my name, the Kisians repeated it like an echo—*e'Torin, e'Torin, e'Torin*, until it faded into the night. "The emperor will be very pleased to see you after what you did. You're going to be torn apart. Although it looks like someone started the job for us." The unknown Levanti gestured at my wounds, while the Kisians milled around like a flock of viciously armed owls, their eyes gleaming in the lantern light.

"Arron!" someone called as they approached. "Is it really him?"

Another head popped into view. For a moment she stared down at me, then laughed. Her face was vaguely familiar, but I knew neither of them, nor the third Levanti who came to stand over me. "Well, won't His Majesty be happy with us."

The one called Arron agreed. "A reward, perhaps, for finally bringing in the enemy."

"The enemy?" I croaked. "The Chiltaens are our enemies. The city states are our enemies. What does it say about your emperor that his greatest enemy is someone trying to hold on to our traditions?"

"You killed Sett."

"For cheating during a challenge!" I tried to rise, hot with anger, but the blade swung before my face and I fell back. "He threw aside all honour."

Arron spat, the wet glob hitting my cheek. "He did what he needed to be rid of you. That is real service. Real honour."

The spit ran down the side of my face as I stared up at features twisted into a hatred so strong it stank. "Is that what you learned at your herd master's feet? Is that what your matriarchs bade you uphold? Other Levanti have never been our enemies. We—"

A boot jammed hard into my side and I coughed up pain, vision sparkling.

"Your time for talking is done," he said. "As will be your time for living. Get him up on my horse and we'll head for camp. Let the others hunt for the rest."

They gripped my arms and hauled me up. I could have gotten to my feet, but there was petty joy in making them lift a dead weight.

Nearby, a Kisian shout rose over the trees. The Levanti ignored it, but the Kisians pointed the direction I had come. Rapid words, broken off as the same shout came again, like an impatient order, sending them all off at high speed.

"Hey, come back!" Arron called after the retreating lanterns. "Where the fuck you think you're going?"

One turned, beckoning the Levanti to hurry. Arron looked at the other two. The woman shrugged as best she could with her hands gripping my upper arms and her muscles straining.

"Idiots," Arron muttered, hooking the lantern he'd been carrying to the side of a distinctly non-Levanti saddle. "The sooner they learn basic orders the—"

An angry roar erupted from the trees and barrelled into him. Together they collided with the horse, sending the lantern swinging as the animal backed and snorted. Someone screamed. The other two Levanti let me go as the scream became a gurgle, and I looked up in time to see blood splatter the horse's knees. It reared, legs kicking. The others scurried out of range as it landed with a crunch of flesh and bone. The lantern smashed, leaving a bright flare choking my sight. Hoofbeats thudded off into the distance, while above me the two Levanti let go shuddering breaths. "Arron?"

Only the distant thud of hooves sounded in reply.

"Who's there?"

"Show yourself, cowa—" The words ended in a gurgle and thud. Fabric flurried nearby, before hurried steps sped off into the darkness.

But I was not alone. "Who's there?" I said, sure I could make out a vague outline in the dark.

"It's me, Captain."

A pair of hands took me beneath the shoulders, helping me up. "Amun?" I said. "By the gods, Amun, am I glad to see you."

"As I'm glad to see you still alive. No, you and I have a lot to say to each other I think, but this is not a good place. Let's do the talking thing later, yeah?"

"Yes," I said. "Less talk, more running, or...limping. Please help me get the fuck out of here."

9. DISHIVA

I couldn't sleep, could only lie and stare at the pattern of light and shadow on the ceiling and see the glassy eyes of dead horses. In the panic after I had made it back to my room, I had told myself I would not do anything else to incur Leo's wrath, the pain of seeing others mourn their animals too heavy to bear. But slowly anger had returned. That's what he wanted me to do. He wanted me to give up. He wanted me not to fight. I had to find a way to get rid of him, whatever the cost.

It was both easier and much *much* harder knowing I was gambling the lives of others and their horses, the only way to continue to stop thinking of them as Levanti, stop thinking of them as family, stop thinking about them as people at all. But how long could I spend lives like coin and not become a monster?

The room darkened and the door slid open a crack, sending my heart into my throat. "Dishiva?" hissed a voice. "Are you in there?"

I knew that voice. It sounded worried and unsure, but the very sound of my name on those lips lessened the weight pressing me into the floor.

"Jass."

He stepped inside, a shuttered lantern giving vague shape to the room as he closed the door behind him. It lit the shadowy form of his face too, his thick brows drawn low. And there just inside the door he stood with his muscular arms crossed over his chest as though attempting to keep out the cold.

"I saw Swordherds leave," he said at last. "Heading south. What did you tell them?"

"I didn't tell anyone anything!" I sat up, stung by the accusation in his tone.

Jass dropped to a knee, setting the lantern down. And there beside my mat lay my mask and sash. He picked up the mask, the weak light seeming to further contort his disgusted features. "What is this? Are you one of them now? Are you Leo's puppet too?" He dropped it and sat back, running a hand over his scalp. "I trusted you, Dishiva. I told you where they were because I believed you meant them no harm. That your loyalty to Gideon would stop short of slaughtering your own people."

"How dare you. How dare you walk in here and berate me with no idea what I have been through. Of what happened. You have no idea what it's like. What he's capable of."

Jass held his ground, breathing hard in anger as he said, "I told you not to come back here. I told you—"

"And I told you I could not abandon my Swords!"

He stared at me as I stared at him, his eyes shadowed pools in the low light, his breath a gust of emotion that brushed my cheek. The world seemed to shrink, closing in until it was nothing but him and me in the darkness, the roar of our anger having left something hot in its wake. With every deep drawing of my breath tension mounted, until with a small quirk of his boyish smile, Jass said, "Damn you, Dishiva." And kissed me. A fierce kiss tasting of anger and frustration and need and the desire to feel alive in each other's arms whatever tomorrow might bring.

But as he gripped my wrists and pushed me back onto the mat, his weight on me in the shadows, I was back on that cold ground in Chiltae. Chained. Beaten. Exhausted. The commander yanking down my breeches while all around me Levanti howled their rage.

I cried out, recoiling. Tearing my hands loose, I shoved him away and wriggled free, scurrying for the corner where I curled my knees up, every breath ragged and quick.

"What happened?" he said, just a voice disembodied by eyes squeezed shut. "Dishiva? Are you all right?"

But in the darkness behind my eyes was the memory I could never escape, no matter how often Lashak and I had talked of it, had tried to stop it from having any hold over us. The weight of them. The force. The helplessness of being chained to the earth. The shame. While my people had sung for me, I had cried for myself.

Those same bitter tears spilled now as I tried to control my rapid breathing, tried to calm myself with reminders I was safe, lie that it was.

I flinched at Jass's gentle touch. "Dishiva?"

He didn't press me, just maintained the gentle pressure on my arm, a reminder he was there when I was ready. I wished I could tell him I appreciated it, but panic suspended my voice and for a time all I could do was remember to breathe.

"May I hold you?" he said when I had steadied myself.

I shook my head, hating the idea that I needed a man's comfort to soothe a man's wrongs, but when he said, "You don't have to do everything on your own," I reminded myself that he was also a Levanti, not just a man. "Needing help is not weak."

Levanti rarely did anything alone, yet somehow the idea that I alone was responsible for carrying this weight had rooted deeply, and it was with an effort that I nodded and allowed him to wrap his arms around me. There against his body—a seemingly immovable force in that moment—I let flow the tears I had been holding until there were none left to cry, until the world was quiet but for the steady thump of his heart.

"The Chiltaens hurt you, didn't they?"

It was hardly a question at all. The words vibrated deep in his chest, full of understanding, needing no answer. Yet I nodded. He deserved more, but it was all I had.

"I heard it happened to others," he said. "And you've always been so intent on being in control that I wondered. I'm sorry."

"For guessing, or because it happened?"

"Both. And for reminding you of it just now. And ... for coming in here shouting at you. I feel ..."

Still melted against his chest, I said, "Helpless and frustrated. I know the feeling."

For a time he said nothing, the pair of us sitting there caught to each other in the darkness, just breathing and existing, until at last I spoke the words he needed to hear. "I didn't tell them anything. Leo heard the directions you gave me when we carried him out to the cave. And he was here, Jass. We left his body in the cave, and by the time I got back he was sitting with Gideon like he had been here for hours. How can that be?"

Jass shook his head, the stubble of his chin scratching against the stubble of my regrowing hair. "I don't know. I didn't leave straight away either. I'd forgotten my knife and went back. It took me ages to find the cave, but I eventually did and he was still there. Faintly smiling and starting to stink."

"How does he do it? How does his god know where he is?"

"I don't know," he said, his breath warm against the side of my head. "I'm sorry I doubted you."

"No, you're right to doubt everyone who has been near him." I pulled out of his embrace enough to look him in the eye. "He changes people. Controls people. He ... put this blanket of peace over me to make me compliant at his ceremony and it was like I was dreaming, half of me sane and screaming at the other half, but I could not stop myself being led, being controlled, and it was ..."

I couldn't find words for the fear, not just for myself but for everyone caught in his influence. How many had he worked that sorcery on? How many was he still controlling? "I keep wondering if this was how our herd masters felt, if somewhere deep inside they were still utterly themselves and hating every word coming out of their mouths. Then we abandoned them."

"They exiled us."

"But did they exile us? Or did someone else exile us with their voices?"

"That," he said after staring at me for a time, "is a horrible thought." Jass looked at the mask and sash still lying on the floor. "So he made you a...priest?"

"I don't know what it is really. A prestigious position within the church, but he gave it to me just to be cruel. Because I didn't kill the deserters. Or more likely didn't kill Whisperer Ezma. I think... I think he wants to get rid of anyone who could be a threat to his power, and Levanti who don't answer to Gideon are dangerous. Whisperer Ezma doubly so. I...I told Lashak about her. I hope she was able to warn them in time."

He had no answers, and again we sat in silence with our thoughts, my imaginings too dark to share though his were surely as grim. "It's dangerous for you here," I said after a while. "I'm not your captain anymore so I can't order you to go, but you should."

"You'll always be my captain, whatever title Leo saddles you with. You should come with me."

I shook my head. "Oh, how I wish...you know I would if I could. But if I don't fight him, who will?"

He straightened, taking my face in his hands. "I know," he said, a wry smile on his lips. "You wouldn't be my Dishiva if you walked away when you could help people. Your Swords and your people and...what is right, what you see as duty, are more important to you than your life. But by all the many gods that look down on our folly, I worry." He tightened his hold on my cheeks and looked into my eyes, his own made all the darker by the shadows. "Promise me you will take care. Promise me you will consider that...sometimes there is nothing even you can do to mitigate the damage. Sometimes you have to accept the world is just a shitty place and some people are monsters and we are powerless to change that. Promise me."

Promises were just words, words that could make him feel better about my choice, but I could not utter them when they would be hard to keep. I was already walking a dangerous line with Leo. "I...cannot stand by and let him, let anyone, harm us without challenge, Jass."

He sighed, dropping his hands. "I ought to have known you would say that." He passed a hand over his eyes. "I wish I could help. Wish I could be here for you rather than—" He turned, seeming to struggle with some feeling he could not express. "He knows, doesn't he? I was there when he died; he knows me. My reappearance would immediately put us both in danger and achieve nothing."

"You help by staying out of sight. If you take some supplies you could hold out in the caves, get out anyone who wants to leave."

Jass nodded. "That will be enough for now. Just don't get yourself in trouble or I'll have to come running to the rescue, danger or not."

I touched his cheek. "How lucky I am to have such a guardian."

"What sort of man would I be if I left you—left anyone, to face this on their own?"

"A smart one."

"Yes, as you would be smart if you just let it all go and came away with me now. Somewhere. Anywhere. But...neither of us are going to do that, are we?"

"No. No, we're not."

"What fools we are." His words had grown thick with emotion, and he pressed his lips closed upon a grief he dared not voice, a fear that surely filled him as it filled me. That things were only going to get worse from here. That perhaps this was the last time we would see each other.

———————◆———————

The following morning, I awaited my punishment for talking to Jass. I watched Leo walk here and there, nodding to me as he went, but nothing happened. Had my transgression not been enough to incur his wrath? No. If I knew anything for sure it was that Leo wouldn't pass up a chance to hurt me, which only left one option. He didn't know. The great Leo Villius was capable of reading my mind, but he was not omniscient. Could not be everywhere at once. Was still fallibly human.

It gave me more hope than I'd carried for a long time.

Despite my new-found knowledge, I dared not go see Sichi again without good cause, leaving me caught alone with my thoughts. I needed a plan. Leo wanted power. Wanted control. Gideon was the wedge splitting Kisia. Splitting Chiltae. The seed of chaos Grace Bahain himself had planted to take the throne. Talking to Gideon seemed the only option, and yet having seen him at the ceremony it was no option at all.

I went to see Itaghai, knowing he at least would treat me no differently. I took off my mask as I approached his stall and received his snort of greeting, a playful nudge of his nose all too like a cheeky 'Who are you, stranger?' that tears pricked my eyes. "Yes, I know I haven't been to see you much. Things have been a bit… strange. You can't tell me the horse masters aren't taking good care of you though."

There were other Levanti around and I told myself they had no reason to stare at me, but it did nothing to alleviate the feeling they were watching to see if I was still Levanti beneath the mask.

"What do you think of these horse houses?" I said, my cheek against him. "Do you think you'll be so unused to the rain falling upon you that you'll want one forever? I'm not sure how we'd move around the plains dragging a stable."

They were silly words, but the thought of being back on the plains, of travelling again, of being everything we had been, struck me with a mixture of homesickness and ill-ease I was unprepared for. I had not thought myself so changed. Had we all changed? The breakdown of our Swordherds, the lack of trust. We weren't the same people who had been exiled anymore.

I stood breathing in the comfort of Itaghai's scent for a long time, might have remained all day had not a commotion grown outside—the sort of troubled voices that boded ill. It was no longer my job to ensure Gideon's safety, but I could not let go the belief he was our only way through this, so I drew up my mask and stepped out into the yard.

Grace Bahain's soldiers had their own camp, but an inordinate number of highly ranked Kisians stood in the courtyard. Lord Edo's presence at the head of the group eased my fears, though I could not ask him what was happening, could only wait and watch.

As I crossed the yard, Keka emerged from the main doors closely followed by Oshar, the youngest of the Chiltaen-trained translators. Keka looked grand sweeping down the steps in his surcoat but flinched at sight of me. I stared through my mask's narrow slits, the effect sure to be unnerving.

"Lord Edo," Oshar said as they halted before the Kisians.

"Oshar. Captain," Lord Edo returned, before launching into their reason for coming. Keka stood stiff while he waited, and I took the opportunity of edging a little closer. Glances shied my way, but who was going to tell me to leave?

"Grave news has come from the Tzitzi Knot," Oshar translated. "I must see my father at once. He was meeting with the emperor. If you would inform him I'm here, I need not tramp my muddy boots through the manor."

His boots were muddy, but I wondered if he had another reason for keeping the conversation outside, perhaps to avoid Leo's presence. Whatever the reason, Oshar carried the message inside, leaving Keka to stand watching the Kisians with an air of mistrust Lord Edo ignored.

While we waited, I caught sight of Nuru edging her way through the crowd. Some Levanti had gotten bored and were wandering back to their tasks, but a few seemed determined to stay, and Nuru ranged herself among these as unobtrusively as she could. No doubt Empress Sichi was watching from her window.

When Grace Bahain emerged he waved the crowd away with an imperious hand. The Kisian onlookers obeyed, but most of the Levanti folded their arms and stood their ground. The man chose to ignore them and demanded an answer of his son with awful dignity.

No longer needing to translate, Oshar ought to have whispered to Keka as Matsimelar had always done to me, but with a glance Nuru's way, he translated loud enough to be heard by the closest Levanti. "Riders have just arrived from the Tzitzi Knot, Father," he said. "Our ships were attacked and many of our sailors killed. Most of the ships sank. The men could not be entirely sure, but they believe it was Empress Miko with the southern army."

I needed no translation of the curse words that hissed through Grace Bahain's lips. The man had been so calm and sure and in control the day he arrived, but he had failed to get his hands on Empress Miko. Was losing control of Gideon. The Chiltaens had not retreated from the north. And now his ships had been attacked while he was here trying to keep hold of what power he had claimed.

"Did she take any of the ships?" Oshar said when Grace Bahain spoke, the translation of his question causing the duke to glare at him.

"Two. The rest sank."

This seemed to satisfy, but it was a troubled Grace Bahain who walked out through the compound gates with his son and his soldiers in tow, taking their conversation where no Levanti translator could hear them.

That Empress Miko had struck against us, or at least against Grace Bahain, was worrying. Anything that diminished his power ought to be celebrated, except that without him, Leo would hold complete sway in Kogahaera.

I needed to see Gideon, alone, but to do so would require careful planning. Careful planning soon overset by the day's second unexpected arrival.

We had grown used to Chiltaen pilgrims walking through the gates, but the sight of four Chiltaen soldiers striding in sent every hand to a sword hilt. They did not reach for theirs, as confident of their welcome as the man leading them—a man whose only uniform seemed to be the satchel slung over one shoulder.

"Who in all the hells are they?" someone near me grumbled.

"Who let them in?"

"Have they got a death wish?"

Despite the muttering, no blades were drawn, so little interest did the newcomers show in our existence. Yet I could not drag my gaze from them. Though they owned different faces, these were the very men who had hurt us, and it was all I could do not to leap at them and tear their throats out with my hands. Were others struggling as much as I was? What would it take to make us snap?

Once again, Keka strode down the steps, Oshar close behind, and it was petty of me to wonder whether he was regretting taking my job, but I wondered it anyway.

Oshar demanded their purpose. The young man wasn't threatening, but they had only to look at the number of armed and angry Levanti to know their answer would make the difference between getting out of here alive and not.

The man with the satchel stepped forward to speak.

"He says he brings a message for Emperor Gideon," Oshar said.

"Then tell them to give us the message and get the fuck out of here," Captain Dhamara e'Sheth said, joining the group gathering threateningly close.

Oshar translated, but the Chiltaens didn't seem put out by the reply, calmly holding their ground.

"The message has to be given only to Emperor Gideon. He requests an audience."

"Bes, run and let His Majesty know," Captain Dhamara said. "And Oshar, you tell them that if he wants to see Gideon, his soldiers have to wait outside. I'm sure they'll understand our dislike of the people who enslaved us."

The four soldiers shifted their weight at this demand, but with perfect calm the messenger replied, "As you must understand our wariness of the people who slaughtered our army."

There were mutters. Someone laughed. Eyes turned to Captain Dhamara, and I felt all the more invisible. "Tell him we can ensure his safety only if the soldiers remain outside. It's not negotiable."

This led to discussion between the messenger and his soldiers, but by the time Bes returned to say Gideon would see them, they'd accepted our terms. I wished to send them all away, or even better to run them through and let their blood spill onto the stones, but I was just capable of admitting it was worth finding out what they wanted first.

How brave the messenger had looked striding in with his countrymen, and how small and fearful walking to the throne room flanked by Levanti. I followed, cramming with many others into the long gallery. Not so long ago, I would have stood at Gideon's side, but Keka was there now. And in the place so often possessed by Grace Bahain stood Dom Villius.

Gideon sat upon his throne, his place upon the low dais seeming to tower him above everyone. To the messenger's credit he didn't cower, but he did slow his pace as he walked in and faced the grand picture Gideon made—a warrior upon a throne, bedecked in crimson.

"I come bearing a message from His Eminence, Secretary Aurus, eleventh oligarch of The Nine," the messenger said. "He has travelled into Kisia as a peace envoy and wishes to meet with you, Your Majesty, in person, to discuss terms that would be of benefit to both yourselves and Chiltae. A temporary camp has been erected outside the town of Kima, and he would be honoured if Your Majesty would join him there at the end of the week."

A murmuring tide followed and I glanced at Leo, wondering if these Chiltaens were his allies or his enemies. Ought they be our allies or our enemies?

Gideon sat upon his throne and stared at the man, seeming to consider the request, then without answering, he rose. "I will meet with my council before I answer."

No longer a captain or the head of his Imperial Guard, I could not attend. Only Captain Dhamara e'Sheth and Captain Bahn e'Bedjuti were present, and while Gideon strode away, both lingered to hear the opinions of vocal Swords. Anger formed the backbone of them all, though the desired action manifested as anywhere between "kill them all now" and "take everything they offer and then kill them."

"I don't think the Kisians like this any more than most of the Levanti."

Nuru had edged to my side and stood looking at the loose knot of Kisian lords gathered in one corner. Lord Edo was with them, but there was no sign of Grace Bahain, and without him they looked lost.

"Shouldn't they want peace with the Chiltaens?" I said. "At least while they deal with their renegade empress?"

"Logically, but Sichi says however it might look, Kisians are as ruled by their hurts and their anger as everyone else. It sounds like they've been at war with the Chiltaens off and on for a very long time."

"Can you attend the meeting?"

Nuru shook her head. "Lord Edo might be able to. Grace Bahain seems rather too busy about his own problems to rush back for this."

"Are we worried about Empress Miko?"

"We are . . . undecided if she is a problem or not. Sichi was meant to marry her brother, you know, Prince Tanaka, though he was in love with Edo."

"Is that why she didn't marry him?"

"No. He was executed by his father, not that Emperor Kin was really his father, and she threw her lot in with Gideon." In spite of my mask, she must have been able to see something of my horrified expression because she shrugged. "It's all a mess. If Sichi wasn't the one caught up in it, I would enjoy the ridiculousness of the drama, but she is, so instead I worry."

"Because Kisians are as ruled by their hurts and their anger as everyone else," I said.

"Exactly." She turned her direct stare on me. "We need this treaty, Dishiva. We cannot let our desire for revenge overrule our need for basic self-preservation. No one wants a long-term treaty, least of all the Chiltaens, but removing this danger would allow us to focus on the ones closer at hand."

I'd always looked at Nuru and seen a young saddlegirl, unmade and untested, thrust into an important position because she could speak the right words. Now as she calmly laid the political land-scape before me, I saw someone else and felt ashamed. This young woman was shrewd and determined, not conforming to the Kisian ways so much as choosing her own path, refusing to walk the one set before her by the very leaders who had failed her. Failed us.

"I know you don't have the influence you used to have, but any-thing you can do to persuade Gideon to accept this treaty would be of service to all of us," Nuru went on, unaware I was seeing her anew. "Let us know what you can. I have to go."

Leaving me no time to reply or even gather my thoughts, she walked away, her Kisian robe swishing about her feet. I envied her sense of place, something I'd never thought to feel of an unmade Sword.

I found a small room off the passage where I could await the end of the meeting. It was a calm little room owning a single lacquered table carved in flowers. Two narrow windows looked upon the manor's private garden. *Private* was a good description. I'd never seen anyone use it, not even to walk its neat paths or sit in its little garden house.

When at last voices emerged from the meeting room, I watched a handful of Kisian lords pass first, Lord Edo amongst them, before Captain Dhamara approached, her expression giving no hint of the meeting's outcome. With no sign of Gideon or Leo, I stepped out.

"Captain," I said, falling into step beside her.

"Defender."

I flinched. It wasn't a good beginning.

"Whatever title forced on me, I am still Dishiva, if you would call me so."

She met my stare through the slits in my mask for a long time, before nodding. "As you wish, Dishiva. What do you want?"

"To know what happened in the meeting."

She stopped abruptly and spun on me, sending my heart jolting hard against my breastbone. "And what do you think gives you the right to that information?"

"I am still Levanti. Nothing has changed except that I am forced to wear this...this *thing*. Leo is dangerous, and if you cannot see that then you have your head in the sand."

Dhamara gave a grunt and started walking again. "I can see it. I dislike his presence. I think many do, but it's dangerous to say so without risking..."

I pulled my mask down. "Without risking what?"

She looked along the passage, and although it was empty for now, she steered me toward the narrow servants' stairs. "It is too much like it was back home. There may be no exile here, but wrong words get you sent away. That's what happened to the others. They questioned decisions. Or questioned Dom Villius. And now they aren't here to keep questioning. Gods only know what has happened to Captain Yitti. He didn't even come back."

"That bad?"

"That bad. We stayed here to build a new home, but the troubles followed us. Or should I say, the missionaries followed us. You may not believe me, but I just watched Gideon change his mind about this treaty having done nothing but look at Dom Villius. The man didn't even speak. One moment he was listening to the Kisians—they think he should meet with them, removing the chance of war on one front especially now that Grace Bahain is marching much of his army away to—"

"Away?"

"Yes, to his home, I think. Something about Empress Miko, but it didn't make all that much sense to me. He's leaving some soldiers and his son, not wanting to lose his voice here, I suppose, but either way it cuts our numbers significantly. Which is all the more reason, the Kisians say, to come to an agreement with the Chiltaens so we only need to focus on the Kisians to the south."

It was exactly what Nuru had said. The choice we had to accept for now.

"I don't want to befriend them," Dhamara went on. "I want to kill them. But Gideon was right when he said there's a right time for vengeance and it isn't now. We aren't strong enough to fight on two fronts."

"Everyone agreed?"

"You would think so," she said, and I felt the warm glow of belonging as she once more looked around at the dim stairway before leaning in to confide, "except for Dom Villius. I don't know what he said or did or what he holds over Gideon. I don't know how any of it works, but Gideon had only to look at him and he stopped mid-speech. He said it would be unwise to give the Chiltaens what they want, or some such thing. Said he would send the messenger away with a warning. That we weren't weak. That we wouldn't make deals with people who had murdered Levanti. And that was it. He wouldn't listen to any argument to the contrary and brought the meeting to a close."

I stared at her, her features a collection of worried shadows in the gloom. "Leo doesn't want him to meet with the Chiltaens. That's all the more reason to go."

"You don't have to tell me."

For a minute we stood there at the top of the steps as two Levanti captains, equal and confiding, before the moment gave way to remembrance of all the ways we had changed, and all we had to lose from trusting each other. A frown descended upon Dhamara's face.

"I should go," she said. "Don't make me regret telling you any of that."

She didn't wait for a reply, just spun on her heel and strode out into the passage, leaving me to breathe the musty air alone. I waited, but before I could follow, footsteps passed. "Ah, Captain Dhamara, walk with me," Leo said. "I too am heading out into the yard."

I couldn't catch her reply, but it must have been an assent for I heard nothing more, nothing but my own rapid breathing and thundering heart rate. Had he been waiting for us? Had he known we were talking? Expressing mistrust. Dislike. Fear. At least there were lots of people in the yard. What could he do? Convince Gideon to send her and her Swords away seemed the most likely, further cutting the number of Levanti around Gideon.

Gideon.

Leo was out. I could go now, talk to Gideon, persuade him to change his mind. Gods, it was a risk, but I had to do something. Allowing myself no time to even think, I stepped out of the stairway and hurried in the direction of Gideon's rooms, praying he would be in and I wouldn't have to go in search of him.

Massama and Sipet were on duty outside his rooms and shared a look as I approached, such wariness from my former Swords causing me a deep stab of sorrow.

"I need to see Gideon," I said. "Now. Is he in?"

"He is, but he doesn't want to be disturbed."

"If I walk in are you going to stop me?"

The two Swords looked at one another, but it was Sipet who shook her head. "No, Captain."

Captain. It was the belief I needed. The faith that I was still one of them. "Thank you."

Leaving them to close the door in my wake, I stepped inside. Gideon sat alone at his table, no meal or papers, nothing but a bowl of wine. Head in his hands, he didn't look up, just stayed like a hulking bear in the shadowy corner.

"Gideon?" I said, dispensing with his Kisian title.

He looked up, his gaze hazy as though in the short time since the meeting he'd drunk enough wine to knock out a horse. Yet his eyes focussed on me after a few moments and he blinked. "Dishiva?"

He had stood so strong and sure before the messenger. Had shamed me and proclaimed me Defender of the One True God without so much as a catch in his voice. However often I had disagreed with him, Gideon had always been a stony force against which the world battered its troubles in vain. The leader who would always stand strong for us.

This was a different man.

Shaken, I stepped closer like one approaching a wounded animal. "Yes, Herd Master," I said, checking my mask was around my throat rather than over my face. "It's me. Are you...all right?"

"Fine." He cleared his throat. Blinked. Seemed to be pulling himself together, and I hated how much I wished I could believe him, wished I could let him carry this weight alone.

I knelt in front of him. "You're not fine. It's Leo, isn't it? You don't have to lie to me. You feel like you're shouting at yourself, but you can't make yourself hear it through a furry blanket of peace."

The eyes Gideon lifted to mine were wide and darting. "How do you know?"

"I've felt it. He did it to me. He's doing it to you, infecting you with the sickness that has been poisoning the minds of our herd masters back home. Gideon, you have to get rid of him. You have to send him away."

"I've tried." His voice cracked upon the whisper, his sunken eyes wide. "I've tried. When we're alone he just laughs at me. If others are around the words don't come out. Or I contradict them straight away like I can't make up my mind. Maybe I don't want him to leave because if I did surely I would say so?"

I gripped his trembling hands. This frightened Gideon was not the man I needed, whatever satisfaction there was in knowing I had been right. "No," I said. "He's just inside your head. Controlling you. He wants you to doubt. To send us away. To ruin everything. He needs to go. He's a danger not only to you but to all of us, to everything you've been trying to build."

"I wanted to give us a home. A place in history. A place where we could have some control over our futures." He looked up. "You have to kill him."

"I tried," I said. "He came back."

Gideon let out a deep breath that fluttered on the edge of panic and I couldn't blame him, but by the gods we were running out of time. "Gideon, listen," I said. "You have to agree to meet the Chiltaen envoy, now before he comes back."

"He won't let me."

I had to stop myself from shaking him, from demanding to know whether he was a Levanti, a Sword, a herd master, an emperor, only the recollection of what it had been like under Leo's spell granting me the compassion to keep my frustration between my teeth. "All right," I said. "Then make me your ambassador. Give me the power to accept on your behalf. To organise the journey to Kima. He cannot be in two places at once."

Gideon, tall, grand, strong Gideon who could mesmerise a room with just his words, looked at me with wide eyes and hopelessness, and I knew not whether I most wanted to hit him or mourn the change Leo had wrought. The leader he had stolen from us.

"Please." I tightened my grip on his hands. "If you haven't the strength left to fight, let me fight for you."

He looked away. "What if I give orders against you? What if you get hurt? I'm scared of him, Dishiva. Scared of myself."

"I've made the choice. I know the risks."

"But no one else gets to choose."

The quiet words spoke deep into my soul, touching all the

doubts I carried. Safest not to fight. To let Leo have his way, let him control Gideon to his own ends and hope for the best, but as I had dug in my heels and refused to let him beat me, I refused to let him beat Gideon either.

"Think of it as a battle," I said. "When you lead your Swords into battle you know there may be casualties. The battle is against Leo. And it's your people you're fighting for."

He stared at me, saying nothing, his brow creased. He must have known, as I did, that it was not only his people he would be risking, not only me, but himself. If he did something Leo did not want him to do, how much would the God's child tighten his grip on Gideon's mind and soul and voice? Would there be anything of Gideon left when he was done?

After a long silence, Gideon drew himself up, a man pulling himself together with a deep indrawn breath. "Massama. Sipet," he called, his voice more like the Gideon I remembered.

The door slid and the two Swords stepped in. "Your Majesty?"

"Bear witness for us," he said, rising to his feet like a figure unrolling from child to man before my eyes. "I am naming Dishiva e'Jaroven as my ambassador to Chiltae. A permanent appointment. Announce it. Also run at once to the Chiltaen messenger and tell him we will meet the peace envoy."

Both Swords stared at him, open-mouthed, and might have stayed so had he not hurried them out with a request to know what they were waiting for.

"Yes, Your Majesty. At once, Your Majesty."

They were gone on the words, and Gideon gripped my arm. "You had better go too," he said. "Fast. Put as many orders in place as you can for the journey before he finds you."

"Yes, but... will you be all right?"

"No," he said. "But that's something both of us have to accept. Go. Fight for us all."

I stared at him, hating that it had come to this, hating that there was no other way. This was not the future we had dreamed of. "I'm sorry," I whispered.

"So am I."

I left, not daring to look back lest the sight of him stole my resolve. I had to get as much done as I could before Leo discovered what had happened, so I ran, keeping to the narrow passages and the servants' stairs.

"His Majesty travels to Kima," I called as I walked through the barracks, sharing Gideon's plans with as many Levanti as possible to force Leo's hand. "All his imperial guards will travel with him, leaving first thing in the morning. Be sure you're ready." I would find Keka later, but for now I sped along, through the barracks and up the stairs to the yard, repeating the words over and over and leaving a curious commotion in my wake.

The yard was already full of noise. Massama was climbing down from the low stage Leo had used for the defender ceremony, and all eyes turned my way. Grateful I'd left my mask off, I strode out. There was no time for second guessing, no time to doubt or even to care what they all thought of me. This was our chance to rip away some of Leo's power.

"As ambassador of His Majesty Gideon e'Torin, I have orders to ensure everything is ready for His Majesty's departure tomorrow morning," I said. "We travel to Kima to meet with the Chiltaen envoy."

Captain Dhamara hurried over amid the chatter, and I was glad to see her unharmed. "He goes?" she said, seeming to need more assurance.

"He goes," I said. "You and Captain Bahn will stay to ensure nothing goes wrong in our absence. We take Keka and his guards, as well as Empress Sichi and Nuru. Oshar stays with you."

"That works well. I don't know what you said to him, but thank you." She walked away on the words, speaking to the Swords gathering around her.

"So wise of His Majesty to have named you his ambassador." Leo stood in the doorway, eyes glinting through his mask. "I ought to have thought of it myself. My, my, quite the busy little bee you are, Dishiva, Defender of the One True God." He pointed at my throat. "Careful. Your mask has slipped."

Without another word he walked past me, anger in his every step. And although a part of me cheered to have so enraged him, to have achieved something, I couldn't but dread the outcome.

We found Captain Dhamara's body the following morning, hanging from the rafters in the stable as though she had taken her own life. Maybe she had, but it was my fault. I knew in the same way the deaths of the horses had been my fault, my every transgression eliciting a greater consequence until at last, he would come for me.

I sat nearby while her second took her head, every slice of the blade seeming to dig into my own flesh. I tried to tell myself that meeting with the Chiltaen envoy was more important than a single life, but as I watched her soul be released to the gods I couldn't believe it.

10. CASSANDRA

We could see them through cracks in the gate—a gathering of soldiers on the drive and before them, Leo. Leo who I had travelled with. Had laughed with. Had killed. I had to remind myself he wasn't really the same Leo at all.

"Shit." Captain Aeneas ran his hand through his hair. "Shit."

Gripping his sleeve, I dragged him away from the gate. "We need a plan."

"What plan? We're stuck here," the captain said. "We'll have to fight or give him up. That's at least a dozen soldiers, maybe more, but if we bottleneck them somewhere and—"

"No." An idea was forming in my mind, slowly coming into focus.

"No? There's no other way, Miss Marius."

"Yes, there is. Listen." I glanced around to be sure no one could hear us. We were in the middle of the courtyard, surrounded by mossy Errant boards carved into stone, a smattering of puddles, and nothing else. Even beyond the gates the soldiers had yet to make a sound. "Can you carry Septum? Without the box, I mean."

Captain Aeneas frowned. "Yes, I suppose so, as long as he stays calm."

"We'll have to hope so, because this is the plan. You take him out of the box and carry him the fuck out of here. There are so many back ways in and out of this place they can't be guarding them all. While you escape, we'll hitch the ox up to the cart and drive the box out to Leo. If we waste enough time trying to make some sort of deal, which is exactly what Empress Hana would do—"

Excuse you.

"—it could be ages before he realises Septum is gone."

"But what about you?"

"I need my body and Leo has it."

The captain's eyes narrowed. "Your Majesty?"

I let the empress take control of her own skin. Her words might damn my plan, but he would refuse without her assurance. "As we have agreed that attempting to get inside Septum is too dangerous," she said, "it seems this really is the best thing we can do to help you, Captain. In this state we are little more than a dead weight ourselves. I don't know where you mean to go or what you mean to do, but do what you feel you must and get Septum out of here. We'll play decoy."

He drew a deep breath and let it go in a gust, squinting up at the sun as though seeking strength from his god. When he lowered his eyes again, he nodded. "If that is your wish."

"It is the only way. But we have to move fast."

Leaving no time for him to change his mind, we hurried back toward the stables. He had backed the cart into the main building, but the ox was in the little yard chewing feed that looked none too fresh. "You get him, we'll hitch this boy up to the cart," the empress said, nodding to the captain and striding on toward the animal like our knees weren't aching and our arms weren't heavy sacks of grain.

"I should—"

"No, thank you, Captain, I know how to hitch an animal to a cart."

He nodded and ducked in through the stable door.

He thinks I'm talking.

"Yes, probably, but do you know how to deal with animals, Miss Marius?"

No. I'm a city girl and you're an empress; we're both fucked.

"Not at all. I've told you I wasn't born an empress. I grew up on a farm in the Valley, in secret so no one would know I was still alive and come after me."

So Emperor Kin wouldn't know you were alive and come after you, you mean. That worked out well.

She didn't answer, but little flashes of memory filtered into my mind. Standing before the hated Emperor Kin upon his throne. A beautiful man with violet eyes like Saki's, except where she often looked blank, this man mocked. They were there together for a moment, the man with the violet eyes and the emperor, before they faded into the damp stable yard where the ox munched away without a care in the world.

Who was that?

She busied herself getting the ox moving toward the gate. She could have pretended not to know what I meant or ignored me completely, but once we had the animal out of the yard, she said, "Lord Darius Laroth. The last owner of this house. It's been a long time, but being here...There are a lot of memories."

And a lot of regrets. I felt them, each like a little blade in my heart, except I could not understand the pain. They were not my memories. Not my regrets.

"So many."

The words were whispered as though even she did not want to hear her own truth, and blowing out a heavy gust of breath, she hustled the ox into the stable.

At least regrets were something I was fast coming to understand.

Captain Aeneas emerged as we reached the door. He had Septum slung over his shoulder, a sack tied over his head. A good idea, but I couldn't tell him so. He had been the hand of the hieromonk, but somehow we had developed enough mutual respect that parting like this felt wrong. Fortunate perhaps that there was no time for long goodbyes. No time to linger at all.

"Good luck," the empress said, and I was glad of her steady voice as she handed him the book about Memaras we'd found. "Take this. It might help."

"Thank you." He tucked it into his belt as I had done. "And good luck to you as well, Your Majesty. Miss Marius. May we meet again soon under better circumstances."

A nod. A bow. And he strode away toward the house.

We returned to the task of hitching the ox to the cart. Our arms trembled with the effort of lifting things, and our fingers felt fat and slow and stiff at every knot, but I had to admit the empress seemed to know what she was doing. She must have really lived on a farm.

"You think I would lie about it to look interesting, Miss Marius? Make up a story that gave my enemies fodder to throw against me? 'What more can you expect from a common farming woman?' 'There are probably more bastards all over the Valley. She had to learn her promiscuous ways somewhere.'"

People are awful.

"Yes, Miss Marius," she agreed, tugging tight the last knot. "They are. Which is why we have to find the ones we love. The good ones. And fight for them with every last breath in our bodies."

She was speaking of her daughter. I had no such person. It had been just me for so long, and when I had lived at the hospice, I had only ever wanted people dead. Monsters, all of them, though it had been me they gave that name. Yet by the light of her determination, I could see what it might feel like to have something to fight for. To have some*one* to fight for. It looked frightening. A determination built on a foundation of fear she had to carry around, a fear she had to breathe every moment of every day. She could fail. Her daughter could die. And she would have to live with that.

Empress Hana pulled our body up into the cart and took the reins. Glad to think of something, anything else, I said, *You know how to drive a cart too?*

"Of course. Don't you?"

City girl, I repeated. *I can ride a horse and I know how to flag down a sedan chair.*

"You are more high-class than I am, Miss Marius. You ought to be the empress."

She set the ox walking, jolting the cart out through the big stable doors and into the courtyard. We glanced back to be sure we still had the box, its presence unsettling despite being empty. There was no going back. This had been my idea, but it was starting to feel like the stupidest idea I'd ever had. Would Leo really be tricked by us stalling for time?

"Probably not," Empress Hana said. "But we have to try to give the captain what time we can however it turns out."

At the gates we stopped and jumped down to open them, knees aching. A quick peek showed they were still out there, waiting calmly, though it had taken us some time to get the ox hitched up and the cart moving.

The lock on the gate looked new, as did the hinges, so well-oiled the ancient doors made not the smallest squeal of protest as the empress pulled first one open, then the other, one eye on the unmoving soldiers. None had drawn weapons. They just stood like statues, only their clothing shifting with the breeze.

The empress climbed us back up into the cart and took the reins, our hands shaking. Leo was standing close enough we could have shouted a greeting. Instead we let the ox carry us on toward an inevitable sense of doom.

The back wheels jolted over the divot at the gates and onto the drive. Out on the gravel, with his white robe eddying around his legs, Leo Villius raised his hand. A gesture of welcome. He was smiling. Just like my Leo had smiled at me.

My Leo. What a pathetic thought. He had never been the friend I had started to think him.

Behind him two dozen soldiers drew their bows.

Are they going to...?

They nocked arrows. Leo still smiled. Still had his hand in the air, the other behind him. "We request a—"

The soldiers lifted their weapons.

"Shit!"

I dropped the reins and rolled off the box seat as two dozen arrows thudded into the cart like the furious hammering of a woodpecker. I hit the ground hard, all breath knocked out of me, and for a stunned moment could only lie face to the damp dirt and struggle to draw breath. More arrows clacked as they left their quivers to be loosed into the air, falling like rain.

Finally able to move, we scrambled under the cart as they fell, hitting the wood overhead and sticking in the dirt. The ox bellowed. Its hooves stomped as it backed, the wheels scraping past us. And with a low of pain, it bolted. We threw our hands over our head as the cart tore away, wheels grinding upon either side. As soon as sunlight struck us, we scrambled up and ran. They could have loosed arrows into our back but they didn't, whether by choice or because they were too busy dealing with a frightened ox bearing down on them as it bolted down the drive.

I closed the first gate and ran for the second, all the time expecting soldiers to push through. The second slammed hard, making my fingers tingle as I fumbled with the lock. It clicked closed and I dropped to my knees, breath coming fast and ragged through our gaping mouth.

And outside, nothing. No movement. No arrows. Not even the lingering sound of the cart in the distance.

I pulled us up with the help of the gate, legs shaking, and peered through a crack in the old wood. For all the activity outside we might never have gone out there. They stood in the same formation, Leo at the front. He tilted his head as though to better meet our gaze, and I pulled back.

Did he read our mind? the empress asked. *You said you wondered about that at Koi, but... we weren't even close this time.*

"I don't know. I don't know how it works. I don't understand him at all, but we need to find another way out."

I could not calm our breathing and staggered away across the courtyard, chest heaving. We had woken feeling well rested, but now our legs were dead weights against which we fought to keep moving, and fatigue was like heavy armour, a cloak of steel weighing us down at every step.

By the time we reached the manor door there were still no sounds beyond the gates.

"What are they waiting for?" I said, turning back.

For us to surrender, perhaps.

"We could have been about to. We had the box with us and everything."

Then perhaps we are merely a mouse for him to enjoy teasing before he eats us.

"Lovely. You know I didn't get into this business so I could be chased around Kisia by a madman," I said as I stepped through the door. "Or get stuck in a god-man's house. Or walk around in the body of an empress."

It was dim and chilly inside despite the sun bearing down on the courtyard. The last time we had fought for our survival in this house it had been dark, but at least we hadn't been alone. Knowing it was just us was far more frightening.

You know how we went upstairs last time, the empress said. *To climb out through the window in your room.*

"Yes, but I don't think we could manage that again without the extra body."

And we'd probably just break a leg. No, I was thinking about how we saw Saki and Kocho and Lechati up there, heading the other way along the passage. Do you think... maybe there is a secret way out of here? They did mention a door more than once, and not like it was an ordinary door. But... a Door.

They had. And they had been up there though the second floor of the manor couldn't own a way out.

"It's worth looking. I don't have a better idea."

Having taken a moment to steady ourselves upon the wall, we pressed on into the house. At first I couldn't get my bearings, could only follow the passage, its shadowy boards a trail from which I could not venture, but the smell of the tree soon drew us toward the stairs.

So why did you get into this killing people business?

"What?"

You said you didn't do it to get stuck here, but I imagine the list of reasons you didn't do it for would be rather long.

"I—" Why had I? It had been an expedient use of my talents and interests, a way to earn money, but a younger, naive Cassandra had dreamed of better things. Of being able to change the world with the slip of a blade. Of making a difference. Before all such thoughts had slowly been ground down beneath the wheels of the everyday reality that was life in Chiltae. "I... I don't really know."

You should know by now you can't hide your thoughts from me.

Ahead, a growing echo of footsteps saved me from answering. Just one set of steps, but they were drawing closer.

Leo?

I shook my head slowly and dared not speak, dared do nothing but hope as a figure appeared, silhouetted against the bright light of the tree hall. A figure carrying something large over its shoulder.

"Captain," I said, not caring that the relief was palpable in my voice. "What are you doing? Why are you still here?"

"Majesty? Well, it looks like neither of us was successful. There's no way out that isn't guarded. I've been all around this damned pile and out into the gardens, and there's nothing."

I pressed a finger to my lips and nodded at Septum's legs, caught to the captain's chest by one strong arm. "You ought perhaps not say that so loud."

"I don't think it matters now."

"Well... we have... an idea, maybe, I don't know, but..." I grimaced at Septum and the captain nodded, seeming to understand.

"After you, then," he said, nodding, his usual bow impossible with the heavy weight of a man slung over his shoulder.

A man who cleared his throat. And spoke. "Are you hiding yet?" Septum said, the words muffled by the sack over his head. "Shall I come find you?"

Distant thumping rose upon the end of the words. The battering of many weapons upon wooden gates.

"Fuck, he's coming."

"Yes," Septum said in that same dead voice. "I am coming, Cassandra. Aren't you hiding yet?"

Captain Aeneas turned on the spot, swinging Septum with him. I jumped back rather than get hit in the face with the young man's swaddled head, but I almost overbalanced and was only saved by the existence of the wall.

"Are they... upstairs already? Shit." Thumps sounded overhead as the captain lumbered off along the passage away from the tree. We followed, only to all but run into his back when he turned. "They're on that side too," he hissed, the crashing of timbers growing loud ahead. "Let's try out the back."

But halfway to the garden door, the cracking of wood echoed through the house and we spun back, hunting impossible sanctuary as thudding footsteps joined the smash of broken wood and shouting.

"Quick, in here," the captain said, dashing toward the workroom. "The door looks stronger than the others."

I hadn't noticed but he was right. Whether it had always been so or the Witchdoctor had changed it, the door to his main workroom was not the traditional thin wood-and-paper affair of most Kisian houses, but a sturdy swinging door made of thick, dark wood.

Something smashed nearby. More shouts and running steps thundered toward us, and using desperation to pull together enough energy, I hurried after the captain. He closed the door behind us, locking it. Not that it would keep them out for long.

"It should keep them busy for a while," Captain Aeneas said, "but we should barricade it and ... and decide what to do next."

"What we should do next?" I said, leaning a moment against a workbench while the room spun. "What choice is there at this point?"

But the captain wasn't listening. Still with Septum slung over his shoulder, he carried a chair to the door and set its back beneath the handle. A workbench followed, its legs squealing on the floor. Whatever his reason for not putting the young man down, Septum spoke no more and made no attempt to move, though I could only guess where his eyes were looking beneath the sacking hood. Or rather try not to think about it at all.

I straightened up, caught by a horrible idea. Could this one read our minds too? And if he could, was the Leo out there hearing everything I was thinking?

Time to stop thinking then, the empress said. *What a great idea.*

"It's his eyes," I muttered. "So dead and yet..."

The sack-covered head turned toward me as I spoke.

"Fuck this." I grabbed the nearest chair and half carried, half pushed it across the floor to join the rest of the furniture.

Is there anything we can use as a weapon? On ourselves, if need be.

I looked around, the empress's words only adding to my thumping fear. Getting caught might mean getting to see Kaysa, but it also might not. Having something we could conceal, could be sure of just in case, would make whatever came easier to bear.

"Some of these potions must surely be poisonous."

One wall was covered in shelves, holding books and jars and bottles and little labelled samples of god only knew what. One looked like a dried heart.

If not, broken glass in the right place can do a lot of damage.

"To him or us?"

Either. Both.

I dragged myself to the shelves. Most of the bottles had labels, but that didn't help me understand their contents or purpose.

Just grab something.

A pair of longish glass rods stood in a jar, and preferring something I could at least pretend to hold like a dagger, I grabbed them both.

The thundering footsteps echoed all around us now, rising like a storm. It sounded like a hundred soldiers or more, all converging on us at once.

Something collided with the door, shaking the mountainous barricade. Captain Aeneas was scribbling something on a piece of paper against one of the walls—there being no bench left that wasn't a part of the barricade—and paid no heed.

"What are you doing?"

He threw a significant look over his free shoulder and jerked his head at Septum before returning to his task. The empress had suggested we leave a note for the Witchdoctor, but there hadn't been time to consider who to forward information to. Who would even understand it? Or care? To most Chiltaens, Leo Villius was a god-like figure, and no communication from a Witchdoctor would convince them otherwise.

Another thump against the door shook the whole room.

Dropping the quill, Captain Aeneas folded the paper three times and shoved it into one of the books on the shelf, a corner sticking out, before putting the book back upside down, in the wrong place, and poking out.

"The man is a perfectionist," he said. "That'll drive him mad until he fixes it."

Subtle enough to keep it safe from Leo, but obvious enough for the Witchdoctor. "Smart."

"How surprised you sound, Miss Marius."

I was oddly pleased he knew I was the one who'd spoken.

Another fierce impact shook the door. They were getting faster and harder, rattling the hinges. A stool atop the barricade tumbled off, snapping a leg as it hit the floor. A side table followed, spilling papers and quills and ink from a drawer.

Gripping the glass rods, I stood before the door, a soldier awaiting the end. Except I wasn't a soldier. I was an assassin. A survivor.

I looked at Septum.

Cassandra.

"What? They'll have him once they kill us. Better they don't."

Leaving her no time to object, I snapped one of the rods and lunged at Septum, only to be brought up short like a rope had hitched around my wrist. My hand yanked back, rod dropping to the floor with a clatter.

What just—?

"I have a better idea," the empress said, speaking as much to me as to the captain, who was looking at us like we'd gone mad. She nodded at Septum. "I think it's time to find out what happens when you put me in there."

"I'm not sure that's wise." The captain backed away. A piece of the door splintered off, flying past him like a loosed arrow.

"I'm not sure standing here and waiting for them to come to us is wise either."

Captain Aeneas hefted his sword. "Small doorway," he said.

"That won't be enough. There are dozens of them. You'll have to be very lucky. Are you...very lucky, Captain?"

He met the empress's gaze and it was the empress he stared at, receiving the full force of her imperiousness. Or rather the full force she could manage while we felt faint enough that standing was an effort almost beyond us.

The man sighed. "If you...if you think it worth trying, Your Majesty, I will not stop you. I can only...caution against what seems like the very worst idea you've ever had."

"Oh no, nothing can be that bad."

Captain Aeneas stood in the centre of the room, facing the barricade with his sword slack in his grip, and grimaced at our shuffling approach.

Are you sure about this? I said, wondering if she wasn't giving back control of her body because she thought I'd stop her. *What if you get stuck and can't come back?*

"Is that better or worse than dying here without trying?"

I don't think Leo wants us dead.

"My body doesn't care what Leo Villius wants. It will die soon either way."

I grimaced. And we did grimace. Switching control was getting faster and easier, and I thought about what Captain Aeneas had said about us getting more alike. He was struggling to keep track of who he was talking to, and I was seeing more of her thoughts and her memories. If her body lasted, would we eventually become one mind? One person? Why hadn't it ever been like that with Kaysa?

I'm ready, Miss Marius.

The hooded figure was before me, seemingly lifeless but for the slow rise and fall of his chest against Captain Aeneas's back. "We don't have to do this."

A heavy series of thumps sent more pieces of wood flying. A crack appeared near the hinges. *Yes, we do. Don't dither, Cassandra. And don't get sentimental on me now.*

I reached out and pressed two fingers to the only bit of skin visible at the man's neck, between the sacking hood and his tunic. I had expected it to be different, or perhaps not to work at all, but exactly as if he had been a corpse, she slid out like a descending chill.

The thumping stopped. For a moment I didn't move, didn't speak, just stood frozen with my arm half raised, the silence stretching. Captain Aeneas turned to look at me, careful not to upset the now far more important burden over his shoulder. "What happened?"

"I don't know," I said. "Empress?"

No reply. No movement.

"Perhaps... that's what he was afraid we would do all along," the captain said.

But something wasn't right. "Hana?"

I pulled the sack off Septum's head. The young man didn't move, didn't flinch, but his eyes were staring from his head as though he had seen a terrible sight, as though someone was burning his toes but he wasn't allowed to move or scream or pull away. "Hana? Are you—?"

His mouth stretched open at an angle, producing a shape like a malformed oval melted in the middle. And he screamed. It wasn't a human sound, rather something monstrous, grating and shrill and wrong like a whole flock of birds in pain, and I pressed my hands over my ears in a vain attempt to stop it ripping through my skull.

Banging added to the din as the soldiers out in the hall began hammering furiously on the door, more cracks spreading across its surface. Another stool fell. Followed by a small cabinet with glass doors that shattered. A hinge squeaked and strained. And still Septum went on screaming and screaming, barely seeming to draw breath.

"Get her out! Get her out!" It took a few moments to realise Captain Aeneas was shouting at me, the rhythm of his low voice lost in the din. Upon his shoulder, Septum writhed like a weak kitten and he needed both arms to hold him, weathering the young man's rage as he beat his fists upon the captain's back. "Get her out!"

I gripped a flailing hand.

Nothing happened.

"Hurry up! Get her out before they're through!"

The cold fingers slipped through my grip and I snatched for them again. Never had it taken effort to withdraw either Kaysa or Hana, but trying to pull the empress free now felt like trying to wrench a nail from a board, all continuous strain and a tight, squeaking pressure. I had to control the urge to yank physically back and concentrate on it with my mind, with my intent, with my soul.

A board broke off the door, dropping onto the workbench still pressed up against it. "What's the problem? Hurry up, Cassandra!"

I couldn't explain, could only grip the sweaty hand in both of mine and hope it wouldn't slip free, forcing me to start again. She was almost with me. Almost.

My chest swelled. My mind swelled. Everything grew tight and sore and wrong like a doll with too much stuffing, and as the screaming stopped coming from Septum's lips it went on inside my mind and I dropped, spraying bile on the floor.

"Do you have her?"

I stared at the shifting floorboards. Captain Aeneas seemed to have six legs.

"Do you have her?"

I tried to speak, to nod, something that might answer his question, but whether or not he saw he must have understood for he did not ask again.

"Can you stand?" he said instead. I wanted to laugh, but it was more bile that dribbled from my lips. Empress Hana had stopped screaming, but her thoughts were a mess of noise and I could not find space to think as they flickered through my head. God. Pain. Emptiness. Our stomachs hollowed with a hunger we couldn't sate.

Wood splintered. Faces shifted in the dim passage beyond, an army of ghosts more than men.

"Can you stand?" The captain gripped our arm, dragging us to our feet. Trembling. Aching. More bile just sitting there in my throat. I began to sink down, but he grabbed my arm again. "Just one more minute."

The top hinge squealed loose, and gingerly Captain Aeneas loosened his grip on my arm. "Just one minute," he repeated, a man trying to convince himself as well as me. I forced myself to remain standing though my knees ached and my legs trembled, though the room spun and my stomach churned and the empress's thoughts swirled on, snatching at horrors. "Just one more minute."

It was like a trance, standing there immersed in pain and watching the door break apart, the furniture splintering and shattering and tumbling off the hastily made barricade. As a bit of the main workbench smashed, I thought dreamily that the Witchdoctor was not going to be happy, and only the pain in my gut stopped me laughing.

"This is unacceptable," I muttered as Captain Aeneas positioned himself between me and the door. "How can one be expected to work in such a mess. I must insist—"

The door burst open. The workbench squealed back across the floor. Soldiers jostled in the jagged opening, and only then did I realise Captain Aeneas had sheathed his sword.

While the first soldiers pushed through the remnant furniture, the captain took Septum off his shoulder. And with an inhuman grunt of effort, threw him right at them. They flinched, one trying to catch him while another tried to duck, a third making no move at all, and all of them getting a hundred and thirty pounds of lifeless young man to the face.

In the same moment, Captain Aeneas turned, ramming his shoulder into my gut and lifting me off the floor. Four long, jolting strides and he leapt. Glass and wood shattered around us, but there was air and sunlight and the whip of reaching branches as the captain sped on, my chin against the sweaty fabric clinging to his back. The world spun. The vibration of his running steps made everything hurt, made me yearn for death, and yet I was flying.

11. MIKO

Rain sheeted diagonally across the deck, turning everything beyond the railing to a dull grey. The wind howled and the ship rocked, and as I sat huddled in a dead sailor's storm cloak, I thought of another time I had been battered by this coast. That time Shishi had curled up at my side and Rah...Rah had kept lunging to vomit over the edge of the little boat. Now I had an army. Part of an army. What was left of part of an army.

The thud of a rowboat returning trembled through the deck, and I stared, detached and numb, as a handful of soldiers threw down ropes and shouted and did other nautical things.

After a few minutes of watching men shout at each other through the storm, water running in rivers down their cloaks, General Moto approached and I knew my moments of peace were over. "Majesty," he said as he strode in beneath the awning, spraying rain from his clothing with every movement. "No sign of Grace Bahain. Nor does it appear they have strengthened their defences. Your army is known to be marching on Kogahaera."

At least that meant Minister Oyamada had not run into trouble. I let out a long breath. "You are a very good bearer of news, General," I said. "You do not hold one in suspense, you just...blurt."

He put back his hood. It seemed to have done little to protect his face, droplets of rain sparkling in his eyebrows and on the emerging bristle of his unshaven cheeks. "I don't believe in giving someone time to brace themselves. They inevitably imagine quite the wrong thing. You can thank many years of living with my wife for that; I have only to take a breath for her to assume the worst possible words are about to come out of my mouth."

It was difficult imagining him as anything but a bluff soldier, and the knowledge he had a wife, probably children too, made my stomach tighten. If we failed tonight, they would lose their father.

The general made a gruff little harrumph as he sat down on one of the crates and seemed to chew on air as he thought, perhaps annoyed with himself for having been so open, or worried I would not take the rest of what he had to say so well.

"We can't wait for more definite news," he said at last, with the same rushed directness. Behind him a fierce squall made the returned scout clasp the railing. A pail scraped across the pitching deck. "We have to strike now or—"

"I agree."

Moto pushed out his thick lips, his eyes narrowing a moment as he made mental readjustments for the rest of the conversation. In a detached way it was amusing to unbalance him so. "We have only two ships, however, and the men are shaken and undersupplied."

"All the more reason not to delay."

"There is only one problem, Your Majesty," he said, his gaze skittering away over my shoulder. "We don't have enough soldiers to take Syan, even from the port. Not even if we assume Kiyoshio Castle only has a minimal garrison at present. It would take double the number we have. Probably more." When I said nothing, he waved his hands, the gesture vaguely apologetic. "I'm sorry, Your Majesty, but unless you have another clever plan..."

"I am so glad you asked," I said. "I may not be very experienced with troop movements and field battles, but I did not grow up in the shadow of Emperor Kin for nothing. We are not going to attack the port. We don't even have enough men to take the city, let alone breach the walls of Kiyoshio. So we are going to take Kiyoshio first."

I enjoyed his long moment of open-mouthed confusion too much to explain further until he snapped his jaw shut and demanded to know how.

"Using the castle's own harbour."

"It's little more than a cave, too small to bring either of our ships in."

"Yes, I know. We'll row out."

His lips did their thinking wiggle again. "That harbour is the most protected in the empire. They'll sink any approaching boat the moment it's within range."

"Not if they think we're part of their fleet."

"Even their fleet puts in at the main port. The harbour at Kiyoshio is only for members of the family and their closest allies. Even if they have received no warning from Bahain, they won't believe we are close enough allies to dock under the castle."

I pulled at the singed threads of my crimson sash, the fire damage seeming to have come from the mouth of the Ts'ai dragon itself. "Do you know the basic naval code?"

"Yes, it's mostly the same as the military code, but for a few variations. I don't know the variant for docking at Kiyoshio, however, so unless you do, we—"

He narrowed his eyes as I smiled. "Ready the lanterns, General. We have a castle to take."

We had played in the empty palace halls. We had played in the gardens. And every summer we had sailed a little boat out into the centre of the pond. It hadn't been much more than a pond, perhaps too deep for us at the time but not for a grown adult, its width side to side little more than a few lengths of our oars, but to us it had been as big and dangerous as the sea. Full of fabled monsters and pirates, of fish so big they could not be reeled in and sea people who spoke in streams of bubbles, it had been our favourite place to sneak away between lessons. Now as I listened to the general's orders and the rhythm of footsteps crossing the deck, it was Edo and Tanaka I could hear.

"*Lower the boats!*" *Tanaka shouted, standing proud at one end of the ship, a hand outstretched in the direction of oncoming pirates, the other hooked into his sash.* "*Archers at the ready!*"

"*Yes, Captain!*" *Edo cried, the boat wobbling as he sat.*

"*Ready, Captain!*"

Tanaka had lowered his arm and rolled his eyes at me. "*You need to speak in a deeper voice, Koko. Imperial Archers don't squeak.*"

"*I didn't squeak!*"

"*You did. You said 'Ready, Captain,'*" *he repeated, lifting his voice mockingly high.* "*Soldiers don't talk like that.*"

"*They might if they were women. And besides, I didn't talk like that and you know it; you're just cross because I hit more targets than you this morning.*"

He had opened his mouth to retort, but turned as Edo began stomping, his sandal meeting the bottom of the boat with a hard clack. Once. Twice. A third time. A succession of short, staccato snaps followed by another long then short then long, and while Tanaka watched, he repeated the pattern.

"*What's that for?*"

Edo had flushed, his foot halting before the last hard snap. "*It's a call for help,*" *he said.*

"*What is? Stomping your foot?*"

"*No, the pattern. When ships are in trouble, they flash the pattern and wait for help. At least Father's ships do. It might be different for different fleets.*"

"Oh!" *Tanaka's face had lit up.* "You mean it's like a secret code?"

"Well, I guess."

Tanaka had completely forgotten our argument, completely forgotten the game, and sat on the rowing bench opposite Edo with a hungry look on his face. "What else can you say other than 'help'?"

"Your Majesty?"

Pulled from the past, I looked up, heartache lingering. One of Moto's soldiers hovered at the edge of the awning, seemingly unsure if he was allowed to step beneath out of the incessant rain. It had followed us into the night, but despite how much I wanted to be warm and dry and not feel like my skin had grown as swollen and saggy as my clothes, it was a blessing to our plans.

"Yes?"

The man bowed. "General Moto sent me to tell you he's ready, Your Majesty."

"Thank you," I said, forcing a smile through my heartache. "Tell him I shall be with him in a moment."

He flicked his gaze toward me and away, murmuring thanks and bowing again before backing out into the pelting rain. I let go a sigh and went back to smearing blood and ash onto my face and arms so I would look like I'd been in a fight.

When I joined General Moto, he stood at the railing staring at the lights of Syan growing closer as the wind pushed us toward the city. "I would deem my duty undone if I did not once more, most strongly, counsel against this plan, Your Majesty," he said without pulling his gaze from the wild sea. "If the storm does not drown you, the Bahains certainly will."

"Thank you for your warning, General Moto," I said. "But once again I shall choose to ignore it. Do you know how many times I could have given up? I could have been a docile daughter and married Dom Leo Villius, though it would have made no difference. I could have let my mother kill Emperor Kin, though that too would have made little difference. I could have run away after the siege of Mei'lian, but I came back. I could have let Grace Bahain take the empire, but I refused. There is always an easier way, but easy isn't the same as right. There is a chance this will go horribly wrong, but the prize is worth the risk, wouldn't you say?"

The general met my gaze, sea spray and rain whirling through the golden halo of lantern light behind him. "You have more wisdom than I expected from a young woman your age, Your Majesty. And in truth I agree. The prize is worth the risk, which is the reason I am only counselling you to reconsider, not ordering my men to turn this ship around."

"Against my orders?"

"You do what you think is right and so do I. That's why Emperor Kin disliked me so much and kept me stationed as far from the capital as he could. For all his low birth and soldier's blood, he didn't like being disobeyed or hearing anything more than 'Yes, Your Majesty.'"

"Then we are going ahead with this, General Moto?"

A small smile quirked his lips. "Yes, Your Majesty."

"The boats are ready?"

"Yes, and my best rowers are wearing the few uniforms we had left bearing the Bahain sigil, but there aren't enough for the soldiers in the second boat. They'll arrive a little behind you in the hope they aren't noticed."

Not ideal, but we would have to make do and hope the combination of rain, surprise, and small numbers would work in our favour. "All right. If everything is ready, put the red glass in and we'll get this over with."

"Lower the red and give me the plate," he said to the soldier beside him.

"Yes, General."

Even over the crashing waves and the clunk of oars in the waiting boat, the grating of metal on metal made me shiver as the red glass frame dropped in front of the lantern. Where golden light had spilled onto the waves there was now a stream of blood. And into Moto's hand landed a broad metal plate. "Damn, but this thing is heavy," he muttered. "Why do sailors always have to make everything so thick and sturdy?"

A few laughs sounded in the small crowd gathered behind us.

"All right, Your Majesty. What is it you would like to say?"

———————— + ————————

Rain pattered heavily onto the surface of the ocean, an angry barrage that stole all other sounds from the night. Waves crashed against the sides of the boat, rocking us sickeningly, and with my hands tied I could not swallow the fear I would be thrown overboard into the dark, storm-swept sea.

With both General Ryoji and General Moto too recognisable, I sat in the company of soldiers they trusted but I did not know. I had a part to play, so I had let them help me into the rocking boat and tie me up and sat with them now as they rowed toward the great, towering black crag that was Kiyoshio Castle.

No one spoke. Even had there been anything to say, the roar of the wind and the rain made it impossible. All I could do was watch the castle draw ever closer, occasionally glancing back to be sure the other boats still followed and our ship had not foundered. There was nothing to see but a hulking outline and a collection of ships' lamps, while the boats following were a swarm of low-hovering fireflies caught in our wake.

I stared at the night and tried not to think. Not to worry that the code had changed. That I had misremembered it. That we were all about to drown.

Do not worry about things you cannot change. That had been the wisdom of our tutor, Master Ukiata. Had it been one of Emperor

Kin's lessons he would no doubt have added, *but change things you would rather not worry about.*

We drew close enough to see inside the cave mouth, all light and hazy shapes through the downpour. I couldn't tell if a few guards awaited us, or many. How many were stationed here without Grace Bahain? Was Edo still at home?

No, I told myself, asking questions I could not answer was a pointless exercise in mounting anxiety. All I could do now was hope the answer was no.

The looming castle blocked most of the sky from view, the rain lessening as we rowed into its protective lee.

"We're almost there, Your Majesty," said the soldier sitting beside me. Captain Soku, maybe. There were so many of them to remember.

"Yes, I can see that, Captain. I assume we are all ready."

"Yes, Your Majesty."

The soldiers were getting restless as we approached the harbour, its opening all too like the open maw of a beast. Lights flickered inside, and as we drew beneath the overhanging rock, the rain finally petered out. I had left half my armour behind to look more like a prisoner, but even without it the weight of my saturated clothing was uncomfortable. For the others in their full armour it must have been almost unbearable.

None of them complained. None of them moved. There were a few men standing on the dock watching us approach, and we were on show now, acting the roles we had to play for this to work. Mine was to scowl and sit proud, shooting looks of disdain, which suited me just fine.

Captain Soku glanced my way, but I just straightened my back and squared my shoulders and glared around. Boats roped to their mooring posts bobbed up and down on the swell, while a party of guards stood on the dock, unsurprised at the sight of me. They looked like a welcome party, though whether they had believed our message or not I couldn't tell. Until one smirked.

"How lovely to see you back again, Your Highness," the man said. He looked familiar, but I couldn't recall what part he had played in my escape from the castle a few weeks before. "It seems you didn't get as far away as you would have liked."

"That's *Your Majesty*," I snapped.

"Grace Bahain has given his oath to Emperor Gideon. Our empress is Empress Sichi e'Torin, may she live forever. You are nothing." The sound of Sichi's name sent a worried chill through me. I couldn't but think of that morning in the bathhouse when she had begged me for information and wonder what had been in her mind. Had she abandoned us for a surer prospect? Even if that prospect was a conqueror from over the sea? I had only to think I couldn't believe it of her to remember how much I hadn't thought myself capable of. There is no limit when you're truly desperate. Jie's death had been proof of that.

No, don't think about him. Don't think about how he had kicked and struggled and gasped against the pillow as I pressed it against his face.

The boat bumped up against the stone quay, and one of my soldiers threw out the mooring rope with the skill of one who had done it before. No doubt General Moto's doing. After Jie's fear the man would be the next emperor, I had determined to be careful, but I couldn't help respecting him. Even liking him.

With the rope caught and tied, my soldiers began to disembark. Only half a dozen guards had been waiting and were soon outnumbered, but they could have been fooling us as we were fooling them. The passage beyond the closed door could be full of armed men.

When it was our turn to climb out, Captain Soku gripped my elbow. Playing my role, I yanked my arm free, almost sending him overboard. "Don't touch me," I said. "I can stand on my own."

"Then get moving," he said, a pronounced sneer in his voice. "We don't have all night."

Exactly like a woman walking to her execution, I strode to the front of the rocking boat and made to step out, but with my arms tied I could not balance myself and would have fallen had the captain not been behind me. The gentle way he steadied me gave the lie to his earlier act, and I stepped out with renewed confidence. Behind me the last of our soldiers followed. Fourteen in all, as many as we could take without risking the appearance of something more sinister. Even so the greeting party eyed us warily. "A lot of guards for one woman."

"Not just one woman," the captain said, having stepped out behind me. "For a princess with a reputation for escaping. We thought it wise to be on the safe side rather than let her get away again. His Grace would not have liked that news, I think."

The speaker lifted his chin in reluctant agreement, but eyed us with no less suspicion. I had told General Moto to mention injured soldiers as well as a prisoner—*long short long long long*—in the hope they would not take amiss the appearance of other boats on their way, but it had been a risk. We needed to get moving, needed to get through the door—repaired now, I noticed, after Edo's soldiers had smashed it in an attempt to stop me escaping—before the others drew close enough to be seen without the right sigil.

Their attention had begun to shy toward the incoming boats, so I stepped in front of them. "Well? What is it you intend to do with me now you have me? Am I to be executed? Or is His Grace wishful of selling me to the highest bidder?"

I dared not suggest I knew what Grace Bahain really wanted, but by the renewal of the man's sneer he knew a tactical marriage for power was in my future. "Oh no, he has something much better in store for you, Your Highness. Take her upstairs. Keep her tied up. We don't want to risk her escaping."

"Or what? Grace Bahain will have your head?"

A flicker of fear, there and gone to be replaced with a snarl. "Get her out of here."

His gaze shied back to our second boat gliding in beneath the overhanging rock. The Bahain sigil gleamed on the rowboat's prow, and the figures inside sat still and quiet, no reason for him to doubt, yet my heart raced and I wished my hands were not so tightly bound. It had been for my safety as much as for the ruse, General Moto had said when I suggested a pretence. The Bahains wanted me alive, and if all went wrong and I got trapped, they wouldn't harm someone who wasn't fighting.

It hadn't filled me with confidence.

One of Grace Bahain's real soldiers unlocked the harbour door and leaned against it, my heart exulting as it squealed open.

Four of his men went before us, and Captain Soku let four of our own go before shoving me in their wake. The rest came after, while the splosh of oars and the thunk of a wooden hull meeting stone echoed behind us. Someone spoke. It sounded like a question, but over the footsteps of the soldiers in the tight passage I couldn't make out words. The splashing grew quieter, and I risked a glance back at the open door.

A shout echoed, followed by another. And in its wake, chaos broke out behind us. My fear that the last two boats weren't close enough to avoid a barrage of arrows from the upper battlement was soon overwhelmed by shouts of "Traitors!" ringing along the passage. One burning torch behind, one ahead, and in the dim space between them, my soldiers turned on Bahain's. Captain Soku thrust me out of the brutal scuffle, and I fell against another soldier as someone cried out. Grunts and the wet, meaty sound of cut flesh filled the close space, stinking of blood.

I spun to the man I had fallen against. "Quick, cut my ropes."

No sooner did the ropes fall than Captain Soku gripped my shoulder. "Stay with me, Your Majesty. The rest of you, go ahead.

We have to secure the castle while we still have some element of surprise. Go go go!"

Soldiers hurried away and I made to follow, reaching for the short blade concealed beneath my robe. "With all respect, Your Majesty," the captain said, still holding my arm, "you must wait."

"I am quite capable of—"

"I'm sure you are, but they are in Bahain uniforms and can get a lot more done without being suspected. If you go with them, they are more likely to die."

I hated how right he was and that I ought to have thought of it myself.

Back in the cave, the last of Grace Bahain's guards were dead, and our third boat had arrived, spilling more soldiers onto the stone pier. Wherever the secret lookout was stationed, he had surely run for help by now.

The second load of soldiers hurried toward us and pressed past in a thin snake of seawater-clogged hair and leather. Once they had passed, I made to pull out of the captain's grip, but he did not let me go. "You said I could not join soldiers wearing the right sigil, but those men have no sigil at all. If you wish to stop me you will have to come up with a better excuse."

"A better excuse than that my general ordered me to keep you out of the fighting?"

His expression was hard to read in the dim passageway, but I thought I caught a wry smile. "Yes," I said. "A better one than that. But you can tell General Moto I am flattered by his solicitude."

I turned away as he laughed, and hurried after my soldiers.

Noise echoed along the passage, bouncing from the stones in a way that made it impossible to know where it came from. Grunts of effort and running steps came from everywhere and nowhere all at once, and I hurried on, trying to recall the way Edo had brought us the night we had escaped this place.

I met only corpses before I found the winding stairs leading to the highest parts of the castle. My men had been given orders regarding what defences to take out and how to signal to the main ship so more soldiers could come safely ashore. They did not need me but I hurried on, desperate to be there, to be part of it, to *prove a woman could do it too*. Jie's words went on haunting me.

The upper passages of Kiyoshio Castle were dark, no lanterns lit in the Cavern or any of the upper chambers. But there was noise and flickers of torchlight, and I hurried on toward the yelps of surprise as my men cut their way through Grace Bahain's guards.

They weren't to harm Edo if they found him, but in the darkness, would they be able to tell? "Edo!" I called in the direction of the Cavern. "Edo?" I thought I had seen someone move, but no one answered.

I strode along the shadowy passage, looking into every open doorway. "Edo?"

I stuck my head into the narrow room where I had taken a bath. "Edo?"

Someone whimpered, hands clasped over their mouth. I stepped inside. They pushed back against the wall, feet slipping on the floor in an effort to gain purchase. A pale skirt flapped and I held out both palms to show I carried no weapon. "I won't hurt you," I said. "Do you work here?"

I tried not to think of the serving girl who had attacked me, who had come so close to throwing me over the edge of the balcony onto the rocks below. I hadn't even heard her body land over the rush of the chill sea wind.

Another whimper was the only reply. Probably not a killer. I took a step closer. "I promise I won't harm you or allow my men to do so. Just tell me, are either of your masters at home?"

She paused her attempt to push through the stone wall.

"Grace Bahain. Or Lord Edo. Are they here?"

For a long, anxious moment the girl just stared at me, before very slowly she shook her head. Relief slumped my shoulders. I wasn't sure what I was more grateful for, that there would be fewer soldiers without Grace Bahain, or that I didn't need to fear my men would end Edo's life. I had already lost one brother. I didn't think I could survive the loss of the only person I had left who felt like family.

What little light had been filtering in from the passage vanished. A soldier stood in the doorway, but I couldn't tell by his dim silhouette whether he was theirs or mine.

"Well, well," the man said, the voice familiar. "If it isn't Empress Miko all alone. Making my job all the easier."

I drew my short blade and backed a step, eyes on the newcomer though it was too dark to see more than his outline. He hefted his own short sword. "Going to fight me, Your Majesty?"

"If you make me, I won't just fight you, I will kill you."

He laughed, a sound all the more terrible for the genuine amusement it held. "Just because you were trained to fight doesn't mean you can beat a man."

"Then why are you looking warily at my blade instead of attacking me?"

"Because I'm not an idiot."

"Yes, you are, because while you're standing here wasting time, my soldiers are taking your castle."

No flicker of concern, just another gentle laugh. It made my skin pimple. I wanted to ask what was so funny, ask what he wanted, but dared not sound worried. And then I couldn't because his laugh broke and he lunged, jabbing his blade toward my unguarded shoulder. My dodge was a desperate thing and I staggered back, hitting the wall within a few steps, so small was the room.

The soldier followed, still blocking escape through the open door. But the maid scrambled to her feet and ran in a flurry of pale linen. The soldier's gaze flicked her way and I thrust my dagger at his gut, only to have it almost knocked from my hand as he slammed his forearm into my wrist. I ducked out of instinct and felt something brush my hair, but rather than risk standing into his strike, I charged at his legs, knocking him into the wall. A grunt of air burst from him, but he wasn't winded, and thrust me back with a slash of his blade. It grazed my arm like a stinging trail of fire and I fell back, breathing hard.

Here a lesser man might have boasted or goaded me, wasting time on self-aggrandisement, but my assailant merely licked his lips and stepped cautiously closer. Beyond the blocked door, I could hear shouts and running steps, but calling for help might bring the wrong people.

Another step. A spin of his blade. I tried to think of all the lunges and guards and parries and dirty tricks General Ryoji had taught me, but everything slipped from my mind like it was full of holes, leaving me staring at the man with my jaw slack. Perhaps noting my stupor, he feigned a lunge one way and thrust the other; I only reacted to the first movement and couldn't stop the short blade slicing a cut into my side. He stepped back without so much as a grin, but instead of sticking me with it again he stiffened with a rattling gasp and staggered. I leapt back, blood weeping through my shallow wound as the man fell, first onto his knees and then his hands, an arrow protruding from his back.

A new figure stood in the doorway, one whose silhouette I would have recognised anywhere. "General Ryoji." Once again, I kept myself from running to him like a child in need of reassurance.

"Sorry I took so long, Your Majesty," he said, stepping in and making short work of slicing the dying man's throat. Blood ran onto the stones. "You ought not to have been on your own."

Almost I snapped that this wasn't the time for scolding, but someone else appeared in the doorway with a lantern, and I was glad I had kept my mouth shut. "Ah, there you are, Your Majesty,"

General Moto said. "It looks like the garrison here is severely depleted and we've had an easier win than—"

He broke off, perhaps realising I wasn't listening. I was staring at the dead soldier on the floor. His voice had sounded familiar, but I hadn't been able to place who he was. Now, as General Ryoji rolled him over, I recognised Captain Soku.

"But—"

General Ryoji cleared his throat, the look he shot me full of warning as he let the dead man roll back onto his face. "Sorry, General Moto," he said. "You were saying?"

If the general had noticed anything amiss, he didn't show it. "I was merely informing Her Majesty that we have taken the castle without significant losses. How long we can hold it with so small a force if Bahain comes to oust us is, of course, a different matter. But for now, we can count this as a victory."

The words washed over me, losing all meaning. General Moto formed something between a smile and a grimace. "It has been a long and difficult few days, Your Majesty. Perhaps you should rest." He looked at Ryoji. "Find somewhere for Her Majesty to rest and ensure she is well guarded, just in case we have missed someone or one of the servants is particularly loyal."

Not a fear I needed planted in my head, but General Ryoji nodded.

"I'll take it from here, Your Majesty," General Moto said, and I could only nod and was still nodding when his voice faded away along the passage.

All the while, General Ryoji watched me. "This man tried to kill you?" he said.

I nodded, not sure I was capable of words.

"He's one of ours, isn't he? He was with you on the boat."

I nodded again and managed to add, "He sat with me on the way in and seemed to be...to be in command."

He had even let me go off alone. Had he tried to talk me out of it knowing I would refuse? Had it made him feel clever?

"You think he's one of General Moto's men?" I said, when General Ryoji didn't answer. "Is that why you stopped me speaking?"

"I don't know. But it's my job to ensure your safety and I'm a suspicious bastard, so don't say a word. The last thing we need is for whoever he works for, assuming he was taking orders from anyone at all, to know we know. Let them think we are none the wiser."

It was a clever plan, but I was sick of clever plans. Sick of having to doubt the loyalty of everyone, sick of wondering if a knife waited in every shadow. I had grown up worrying about death every day, and it was not a state I wanted to return to.

"I'm going for a walk."

He straightened up to join me.

"No," I said. "I just want... a moment to myself. No one will try anything now."

He gave me a look.

"I know you'll have your men watch me from a distance anyway, or pretend to be servants, so just do that to make yourself feel better and let me have a moment to myself."

General Ryoji bowed. "Yes, Your Majesty."

Leaving him in the doorway of the small bathing chamber, I walked back along the upper passage toward the now lit Cavern at the end, ignoring the sounds of life all around me. This ought to have been a moment to celebrate, and by the sounds echoing through the great castle, somewhere someone was, but our success sat like a lump of cold coal in my gut. Out beyond the balcony the sea raged and the storm blew, just as it had while Edo and I had eaten together the last time I had seen him.

I blew out a held breath and gazed around. The Cavern looked the same as it had that night, its walls of dark stone cold and severe despite the light and warmth of the braziers and the crackle of reeds underfoot. So many times had I imagined this place. So many dreams where I had become the duchess of Syan after Edo or his father had regained approval at court. It had all seemed so simple then, because even if Emperor Kin never allowed it, Tanaka would when he took the throne. After all, what could please him more than having his best friend and his twin sister marry and hold the fortress at Syan?

I thrust out a hand as though I could push away the memory of my naivety, but no matter how tightly I screwed my eyes shut it was still there. Even without the war, it would never have happened. It had never been me Edo loved.

"Miko Ts'ai, Lady of Kiyoshio," I said, mocking myself. "Just not the way you thought."

It was late, but no one seemed inclined to rest. There was too much to do. The castle had to be searched, the flags changed, messengers sent, the rest of the soldiers to ferry in off the ships and the city to be made sure of before any loyal watchmen thought to resist. Trembling servants brought food, my reassuring smile having little effect. I bathed. I ate. I sat and stared out at the night. I walked around the castle in a numb state and checked in with General Moto enough times that he began to counsel me, with the directness I had previously applauded, to get some sleep.

"Are you planning to seek your mat as well, General?"

"I will get an hour or two once I'm confident we are secure here until reinforcements arrive."

"Have you sent messengers to Manshin and Oyamada?"

A sharp nod was his first, impatient answer, but I was not satisfied and lifted my brows. "And?"

"And I am concerned that our inability to wait for a reply from Minister Oyamada before striking may mean Grace Bahain leaves Kogahaera before Oyamada gets near it. Minister Manshin may be on his way, but the chances he's picked up enough soldiers to hold against a siege are slim."

"This castle is well fortified, and we've sent messages."

"It is and we have."

"But you're still worried."

He chewed on his lip and huffed out a breath. "Not worried, Your Majesty, just concerned enough to make sleeping in the darkest hours more difficult. But I've never been very good at sleeping after a battle. We'll know more in the morning."

The possibility we had walked into a trap of our own making made my heart race and the walls close in around me. "Your Majesty?" Moto's voice seemed to come from a long way away, the vision of him blurring. We had almost died getting the ships, almost failed before we had begun tonight, and all of it might yet be for nothing. Or worse than nothing. Death came to everyone, but if Grace Bahain retook his castle our fates would be far worse.

"Majesty?"

Someone laughed, and it took me a few moments to realise it was me.

"Perhaps a rest, Your Majesty," Moto said. There was a hard edge in his voice, but I couldn't stop gasping breaths. They didn't come out as laughs anymore but with a ragged edge of panic.

"Pull yourself together," General Moto snapped as the sound of hurrying footsteps approached along the passage. "The most important part of being a leader is looking confident no matter how you feel, is continuing to walk and talk and carry on no matter who or how many you lose or how close to death you come. If you want to lead soldiers, you have to remember that."

"*There are no gods. Only men,*" Emperor Kin had said. "*But if you can give people hope then you can become something close to divine.*"

But as I looked at General Moto, I thought of the captain who had tried to kill me and couldn't but recall one of Kin's other lessons. *Lesson number four. Sometimes those who seek to help you are the worst enemies of all.*

12. RAH

We didn't speak as the night wore on, Amun navigating the fenland as quickly as he dared in the eternal drizzle. There was little moonlight to see by, but after an hour spent looking over his shoulder, tensing at every narrow miss with a tree or low branch, I began to relax. Not once did he panic, his swift skill at changing direction impressive even for a Made Sword.

Confident in his ability, I let fatigue overtake worry and set my cheek to his back, holding tight. But I could not rest. Blood was oozing from a wound somewhere, mud was heavy all over me, and painful spasms of cramp kept surprising me with their ferocity.

And I couldn't stop thinking about Ezma. She had wanted me dead, and I was grimly determined to go on disappointing her.

"Whisperer Ezma is going to be angry with you for coming back," I said when Amun slowed to navigate a tight clump of trees.

"She'll be far angrier with you for not being dead." He turned his head so I could hear him better. "Isn't exile the punishment for disobeying *kutum*?"

"It is. I can be an exiled exiled exile, lovely. We're going to need new words for this."

His shoulders shook with silent laughter. "Enemy of the people?"

"Yes, very good. Ezma will like it."

Laughter faded from his lips, and I remembered the way we had parted as I hadn't before and wondered if it was in his mind. "I'm sorry," I said, still leaning my cheek to his back. "For leaving you behind back in Chiltae."

"You didn't. I chose to stay. In hindsight it wasn't the smartest decision I've ever made, but I couldn't think of anything but losing Hamatet. If it hadn't been for the Sheth seeing the bastards coming and dragging me with them over the walls, that would have been it. Thought I'd found a good place with Whisperer Ezma, but... *kutum*...Fuck."

His eloquence perfectly summed up my feelings, and with my head still resting against his back, I chuckled, too relieved and exhausted to be angry anymore.

"I don't know what we should do though," he said, reminding me of the yawning sense of hopelessness lying at the end of every possible path. "Following them sounds unwise. Fuck going to Kogahaera, but could we make it home? Just the two of us with one horse?"

I was too tired to find the words to explain why I couldn't leave yet, why despite everything Kogahaera was exactly where I needed to go, so I said, "First we get through the night alive. Surely they would rather chase the bulk of the deserters, but..."

"But you are Rah e'Torin and some of them really hate you."

I thought of Sett spitting his anger. Of Yitti's disdainful look. Of Istet's sneer. I had never set out to make myself an enemy of my own people.

When Amun spoke again, I might have missed it had my cheek not been pressed to his shoulder. "For what it's worth, I don't hate you," he said, the words vibrating through his back. "You were a good captain and a good friend, and I'd like to have that back."

The simple words left me speechless, but thankfully he didn't seem to need a reply, speeding our pace to a trot through the mire.

It was hard to tell how much time passed between sluggish thoughts, every doze both a second and an eternity. Amun must have been exhausted, but he did not stop to rest, just kept on, his frequent glances behind us waking me more often than our sudden turns or his occasional gasp as a tree appeared from the night.

Dawn found us eventually, early grey light the first hints of its arrival. Slowly the world appeared from the darkness, first as shadows then shapes, and before I was ready to face the new day, it had come. Yet still Amun did not stop. The horse needed rest. We needed rest. But he kept on alternating between a walk and a canter wherever the fen allowed.

"Do you think they're following us?"

"I keep hearing night calls," he said. Even in profile he looked tired and worried. "I could just be imagining things, but...why wouldn't they follow?"

We used the calls of plains creatures in night ambushes, each having a different meaning, varied by pitch, but there were enough animals in the fen it could mean nothing. Yet when a *tila tila* sounded in the distance, both Amun and I stiffened. Did they have those birds here? Back home, at least to members of the Torin herd, it would have meant enemies sighted, and Amun sped again to a canter, chill morning air cutting at our cheeks.

Another call sounded closer. Amun changed direction sharply and my grip slipped. I had to throw myself forward to grab hold of him again, my heart racing. The trees to either side of us remained empty. Behind too. "Nothing," I said, my lips by his ear to keep the words as quiet as I could. He gave the slightest of nods, discernible only because I had my chin on his shoulder.

The horse thundered on, though I could feel it beginning to tire. We ought to stop. But even as I began to hope the two calls had just been a coincidence, a third sounded close by. A flash of brown and crimson flickered through the trees. There and gone. I hadn't seen many coloured birds in Kisia and didn't try to convince myself it had been one. Especially not when it came again, keeping pace.

"They're here."

"I know."

Amun pressed his knees in hard, and the horse lunged forward at a speed we could not maintain, not with the dense cover and two riders on its back. Our pursuers had the advantage of only riding one warrior to a horse, and would catch us eventually no matter what we did.

"Shit," Amun hissed, no doubt having the same thoughts. Our horse was flagging, and neither of us was well-armed or in a good state to fight multiple opponents. "Shit shit shit."

He made another sudden turn through a dense thicket. It left the flash of crimson behind, but it wouldn't be for long, and Amun urged the horse to a mad dash, the animal speeding as fast as it dared through the trees and over fallen trunks, around pools and through dense foliage damp with morning dew. There was nothing quiet about our progress, but if the Levanti giving chase were travelling as fast, they would have little to hear but the wind in their ears and the thud of their own hooves. Sound is useless on horseback, as every young Levanti learned in their earliest tracking lessons.

"Hold tight."

The warning came a moment before Amun yanked the reins, sending our mount off at a sharp tangent, hooves skidding in mud. He ducked as a laden branch brushed its leaves over our heads, leaving us to emerge on the other side with water droplets glistening in the short bristles of his hair. Shouts echoed through the fenland around us, but when I looked back it was to see nothing but the bluster of trees in the wind, the gathering dawn turning everything bright.

"Anything?"

"Can't see any, but I can hear them."

He flicked his gaze up at the sky, turned sharply again, and plunged on. I wanted to ask where he was going, if he knew where we were, but all I could do was trust he had a plan.

Another flicker of movement upon our left. Not crimson this time, and I wished I could convince myself it was anything but a fellow Sword hunting us down. No sooner did I part my lips to warn Amun than he said, "I know," and turned again.

I swallowed the urge to demand what he planned to do about it. Easier to handle the pressure when you're the one in control, I reminded myself, but it didn't make me feel any better.

When next he glanced at the sky and made a sudden turn, I was sure he knew where we were. Something about the way he looked about, scanning the trees, looking up at the sun and down at the tracks in the mud. Mud... it was all mud now, mud and pools of water, and had I not known we were travelling east I would have assumed we were heading deeper into the fen, not out of it.

A flicker of sparkling blue showed through the trees. Not someone following, but a river. The river we had followed with General Kitado and Empress Miko, all the way to Otobaru Shrine and on to Syan.

Our horse splashed through a particularly deep pool of water, wetting our legs. We weren't in the fen anymore at all. We were in wetlands bordering the river, farther from the camp than I had thought.

"You have a plan?" I hissed in Amun's ear. "We can't outrun them."

"I know," he said. "I have half a plan."

Half a plan would have to do.

A shout cut over the rapid thud of the horse's hooves as we crossed a brief stretch of solid ground only to splash into another pool of water, narrowly missing a tangle of twisting branches more bird's nest than tree. A shadow flickered behind us, and Amun must have heard me gasp for he urged the horse on faster, turning away from the river. Here every breath was full of mud and salt water and a stagnant kind of rot that tickled the nose, a smell that reminded me of another time I had been injured and on the run from my own people.

Amun wound through a series of dense copses before bearing sharply away from the riverside pools onto a narrow track. It twinged the same memories as the smells. This was the way to Otobaru. Perhaps if we could make it to the shrine we could... what? Fight? Hide? Neither would be an option if there were enough of them. But continuing on was increasingly not an option either.

The track was freshly churned, the hoofprints wet and gleaming in the morning light. They wound on ahead toward a sharp corner. The road to the shrine was close.

"Yes," Amun said, exultant. Although if the tracks belonged to Ezma and the others, we would merely be exchanging one death for another. "Is anyone close enough to see us?"

I turned and, holding tight, hunted the surrounding trees. Dawn light filtered through at a sharp angle, making odd shadows of the morning, but there were no flitting shapes of horses or flickers of colour.

"No. But I'm sure they're not far behind."

He grunted, and at the sharp right turn in the track, he yanked the horse left and plunged us into the trees, their thin branches whipping our arms and legs and probably his face. He slowed as suddenly, reining in to a complete stop. And there in the middle of the dense foliage we stood still, breathing hard and sweating despite the morning chill.

I parted my lips to ask what he was doing, but he twisted in the saddle, shaking his head in warning. We listened. Leaves rustled all around us, and now we had stopped, insects buzzed into our faces, but for a while there was nothing but our ragged breathing. Then hoofbeats. Slowly rising above the other sounds, the growing thunder of them muted only by the mud over which they travelled.

No shouts, no cries, just a concert of hooves hammering the track growing closer and closer.

Amun tensed, seeming to hold his breath as if, even at this distance, they might still hear him. Through the thick stands of trees and fluttering branches, swift shapes passed. I started counting them only to stop as they melded into a continuous line. Two dozen, maybe more, following the track. Slowly the hoofbeats began to fade, and Amun relaxed. "Well, that's good for now," he said, "but how far will they go before they wonder if they've missed us and send some doubling back?"

"At the speed they were catching up? A few minutes."

He nodded, grim. "We need another plan."

"We need rest. Somewhere safe."

"What place is safe?" Amun ran a shaking hand over his face. His other hand still held the reins and was equally unsteady. It wasn't the trembling of fear, I thought, watching it, rather the shakes of a man who has exerted himself too much on too little sustenance and rest. Our horse was sweating too and could not be pushed much farther.

"Well we can't stay here, but ... I don't think it's safe to catch up with the others."

"Whatever gave you that idea?" Amun laughed wildly, before snapping his mouth shut. "We aren't safe anywhere. I don't know where we ought to go. Or even ... or even what we ought to do." He ran his hand over his face, and it was a man much older than his years who looked back at me. "Fuck this, Rah, this is horseshit. How do you just stubbornly deal with this? Every time I try to do the right thing, shit goes wrong and ..."

He trailed off, looking away.

"Because doing the right thing in difficult times is almost always the hardest of all the choices you can make. You think rising high in the eyes of the gods is easy?"

"I don't care about gods. I don't…I don't even believe they're there. I tried to just leave you behind, you know. I tried. I tried to tell myself Whisperer Ezma had a good reason for calling *kutum*, but I couldn't deal with the little voice of doubt in my mind. Because the voice of doubt was proof I could do something, and if I didn't I would think about it every day for the rest of my life. And that would be worse than being exiled by a whisperer, because who do we really have anymore except ourselves? Except the few we can cling to. Can trust."

"I don't know," I said, the truth a pain in my chest. "I don't know. This whole thing is a mess, but we will figure it out, Amun, I'm sure of it. Things will get better. We will find a path. Whether here or back home, we will find the right path. For now we just need to get out of here and find shelter."

Amun didn't immediately answer, but neither did he set the horse walking again. Instead he sat pushing his lip between his teeth with a shaking finger. He gnawed at the skin, not seeming to realise he was doing it.

"We have to go back," he said at last. "Go home. This isn't our home. These aren't our people. If we can find out what is wrong on the plains and fight the city states, we could put things back the way they were and be true Levanti again."

When Tor had brought up fighting for the plains I had refused because to do so would require uniting the Levanti, breaking down everything we were to create a new whole. But if we couldn't fight for the plains and we couldn't fight for this new empire, what was there left to fight for? Was it time to just let the Levanti way of life die away to nothing but a memory? Should we? Could I?

"We need to survive the day first," I said, refusing to make a decision yet.

Amun set the exhausted horse walking, the animal reluctant to move. "Where to, then?"

I was tired. I was done with running, with being chased by my own people, with trying to find safe shelter. But I didn't want to die. We needed rest.

"We could head toward Otobaru," I said.

"The shrine?"

"You know it?"

"I've hunted out this way a few times. There are some abandoned huts along the riverside. I sheltered in one when a fierce squall blew up while I was gathering crabs. We could go there and hope they think we wouldn't be mad enough to stay so close."

"Or that they decide chasing Ezma is more important."

Amun grimaced, because we both knew if they caught her a lot of Levanti would die, and we were neither of us so detached from our heritage to accept that without pain.

We saw the hoofprints first. Then the footprints. So many they churned the mud to a cratered mire.

"They had Kisians with them," Amun said. "But they can't have walked this far overnight."

He had been letting the horse walk at an easy pace, the morning peaceful with the rush of the swollen river roaring by. Every bush and tree seemed to be full of bugs and birds making the insistent sounds of life, but there was no sign of people.

A hut emerged from the morning haze, but where there ought to have been relief at finding shelter, my stomach only tightened. Amun had tensed too, but whatever our private thoughts we said nothing, the eeriness of the day demanding silence. Even the birds had stopped singing.

"I think—"

An arrow plunged into the mud in front of us. The horse backed. Someone shouted from the trees in Kisian. Having found one dark figure in the branches I soon found many. One in almost every tree. How long had they been watching us, just waiting?

More appeared ahead of us, a group emerging from the trees with arrows nocked to their bows. That they hadn't drawn made it the friendliest, most trusting greeting I'd received in a while.

The men in the trees blended in, but the ones ahead wore Kisian military uniforms exactly like those we had fought as we travelled south with the Chiltaens, conquering their lands.

Their leader, a step ahead of the rest, set his hands on his hips and spoke, slowly, the tone of a man speaking to someone old and hard of hearing.

Amun made a disgusted noise in his throat. "Why do they always think we're idiots?"

"Don't you ever think they're idiots?"

"Ha! Sometimes. What do you think they want?"

They hadn't yet lifted their bows, but that wasn't reassuring. "A reason to kill us, I think," I said. I gripped the edge of the saddle and began the painful process of dismounting, always a difficult task when injured but doubly so when there's someone before you taking up all the wiggle room. I kneed Amun in the back by accident, but he remained proudly upright in the saddle while I climbed down, hoping my knees wouldn't buckle.

My knees buckled. I would have fallen into the mud had Amun's leg not been there, saving me from an ignoble fall that would have robbed my planned speech of its authority.

With a hand on Amun's knee to steady my shaking legs, I stepped forward a pace. "My name is Rah e'Torin," I said, hoping my name and tone would mean something even if the words did not. "We are not your enemies. We aren't loyal to the Levanti in Kogahaera. Nor to the others who came this way." The words were making no difference. Arrows remained nocked and fatigue was fast sapping how much I cared. It was time to risk all or nothing.

"Both Minister Manshin and Empress Miko know me, if you answer to either."

Those names caused more muttering, and I watched their weapons rather than their faces. One by one, the bows lowered like weights pulling down their arms.

The man I had deemed their leader repeated Minister Manshin's name, pointing into the trees.

"He's here?" I said. Could we be so lucky? But what was he doing here? Was Empress Miko with him? Or had he been too late to save her? I hated how much hope and fear seared through my heart. I had tried not to hope I would see her again, tried not to think about the evening in the bathhouse or the night lying beside her in the busy inn.

"Who is he?" Amun said as the soldiers pointed again, seeming to invite us—demand us even—to follow them.

"He's…sort of like a second to the empress, I guess. Gideon locked him up in Mei'lian and I let him out, so he owes me a debt."

"A give us shelter and supplies kind of debt or a stab you through the ribs while smiling at you kind of debt?"

I looked up at him. "I…wish you hadn't put that thought in my head. The former, I hope. I helped the empress at a difficult time too, so I would like to think they aren't about to order us filled with arrows."

"You've been busy."

It was just a statement, yet I caught disparagement in the tone and hoped it was my imagination. My own doubts. "Busy making friends and enemies in all the wrong places," I said. "Here, help me up. If nothing else the minister ought to be able to keep us from being torn apart by other Levanti."

"As long as we aren't about to get torn apart by Kisians instead. In this state you'd probably fall over if you tried to fight, and I'd be little better."

The Kisians watched us expectantly, still holding their bows. The ones in the trees perched like hawks ready to dive.

"I really don't think we have a choice," I said.

"No, that seems to happen all too much around here." With a grunt of effort, Amun helped me back up into the saddle, and with a nod to the Kisians, we followed their lead off into the trees.

———————◆———————

I had expected to find a handful of Kisians with the minister, but there were more than I had thought possible gathered in such a tangled, out of the way place, a ragtag collection of men in different uniforms. Even more surprising was the presence of Tor. He stood talking to Minister Manshin away from the clusters of tense soldiers awaiting orders, the others with them having the look of commanders. A map sat on the ground at their feet, and their intense discussion only ceased at our approach.

"Rah. Amun," Tor said, glancing up with neither interest nor surprise. "Did you get separated from the others?"

"No. Ezma called a *kutum* and left me to die." It had been too long a night for anything but blunt honesty.

"What?" His shock drew the attention of some of the Kisians. Minister Manshin's gaze flitted between us despite the disinterest of his expression. "Amun?"

Having halted our horse, the Sword before me folded his arms. "You think he's lying?"

"No, I—no." Tor grimaced at me. "Shit."

"Yeah, shit," Amun said, and it had been so long since anyone had stood up for me that it felt like an entirely new experience. "Where were you?"

"Here, obviously. I was trying to get to Kogahaera, but—"

Beside Tor, Minister Manshin pointed at us, demanding answers. The man I had last seen leaving the prison cells beneath the palace did not smile. He didn't look like he knew how, but he hadn't scowled at us or ordered his men to run us through, which was a good start. And he remembered me. "Rah e'Torin," he said after getting an answer from Tor.

"Minister Manshin," I returned as Amun made to dismount. I wanted to get out of the saddle, was as sick of riding as the horse must be of carrying us, but I did not want to appear weak before the man I had to bargain with, so I stayed where I was, looking down at him. "We do not mean you or your soldiers any harm," I began, though the first question I longed to ask was whether he had helped Empress Miko and if she was all right.

The minister looked healthier than when I had last seen him but hardly more rested, the skin beneath his eyes dark. Those eyes looked me up and down now, lingering on my injured leg. Tor translated, "You're injured."

"I am. By my own people, not yours."

His expression didn't change. "What are you doing here?" the minister said, Tor managing something of the man's tone. "You are alone?"

"But for Amun. We are trying not to die. What are you doing here?"

He stared at me without blinking. "There are some of your people at the shrine," Tor translated. "A lot of them. We were passing nearby and stopped to see if they were a danger or not."

"Whisperer Ezma?" I said to Tor, who nodded.

"I was in the middle of explaining they would do no Kisian harm if left alone when you arrived." He looked to Manshin as the man spoke and added, "The minister wants to know if you are part of the group at the shrine."

"If he means the deserters, tell him no. Their leader and I disagree on something rather fundamental."

"Enlighten me," the minister said. "What is this fundamental point?"

"My continued existence."

His brows rose, and at any other time I might have been glad to have elicited a reaction, but my whole body was heavy with fatigue and pain and a dull ache had started in my ear like someone jamming a stick in there.

"He wants to know what you want," Tor said. "He's quite busy."

"What I want? We aren't here by choice. His men insisted. We want safety. And rest."

"And food," Amun added. "I could eat a whole deer."

"If I ask him to let you go, will you be heading to Kogahaera?"

"Kogahaera?" Amun said. "Why would we go there? From one snakes' nest to another."

Tor glanced my way, and I wondered how much of my intentions he had guessed. Had he overheard me begging Yitti to ride that way to help Gideon? Or was he just hopeful I would carry a message to Dishiva?

Both of them stared at me, the Kisians getting restless behind Tor as Minister Manshin's expression soured. "I don't have a plan yet," I said, a conversation about Gideon the last thing I wanted to have standing right there. "Right now I just want to not—"

"Minister!" A Kisian sped down the nearby slope, kicking up leaves and almost losing his footing in his haste. "Minister!" He halted, breathing heavily and pointing up the slope. He went on, and all Amun and I could do was watch for the nonexistent reactions of the gathered Kisians and wait for Tor to tell us what was going on. I hated relying on him, both for my sake and his, and tried to bury my impatience.

"This is ridiculous," Amun muttered. "We should have taken our chances against the arrows."

Tor glared at him while the Kisians went on talking. "It sounds like Gideon's Levanti have caught up with Ezma's. The man says there are more Levanti coming, that the road is thick with them. He says it looks like the ones in the shrine are preparing for a fight, and he doesn't understand why."

"Shit," Amun said. The word was getting a lot of use today and it wasn't even noon.

Ezma had called a *kutum* against me, but the Levanti following her only wanted peace, wanted to go home, and the thought of them dying here on these shores at the hands of other Levanti made my stomach churn. This wasn't how it was meant to go. Surely wasn't what Gideon wanted. He had wanted to build a new home for his people, not bury them all.

Minister Manshin had been watching us impatiently, and broke in with "Why would Levanti fight and kill other Levanti?"

"Because we aren't and never have been a unified people," I said, leaving Tor a moment to translate. "We are separate herds not used to taking orders from someone who isn't a member of our herd, and this is not how we live. I am happy to give you a history lesson another time, but if we don't move now there will be a lot of dead Levanti on the other side of that hill and still enough left to make you wish you hadn't stopped here."

I looked from Tor to Amun. "I have an idea."

"Oh, here we go." Tor rolled his eyes. "Who are we saving now?"

"As many as we can."

"We can fight any who are left," Minister Manshin said, and glared at Amun when he laughed.

"But you don't want to have to," I said, more statement than question. "Perhaps you're hoping they'll make an end of each other, but it won't happen. Gideon has more Swords than the deserters. They are more prepared to kill. We need to splinter them."

The minister looked unconvinced.

"You think they don't know you're here," I said. "You think you can just lie low and wait for this to pass? It's too late. They are Levanti. We hunt and we track. They might not know how many of you there are, but you can be sure they know you're here, and once they deal with Ezma and her deserters they will deal with you.

So you can fight them, run, or lend me a few of your archers and let me talk to my people."

Before Tor finished translating, Minister Manshin had turned to his men, their discussion a low rumble the saddleboy made no attempt to translate. Standing beside our horse, Amun shifted his weight—a man wishing he was anywhere but here. Perhaps wishing now he hadn't come back for me at all.

"What are you going to do?" he said, leaning close. "They've all just tried to kill you. You think they'll listen now?"

"Guilt is a funny thing. And only Ezma tried to kill me. You can't have been the only one who thought the *kutum* was wrong."

"No, but she didn't announce it widely, just informed anyone who suggested helping you. The story will get around fast though. If you stand up to her it'll be divisive."

Tor wasn't looking at us, but I was sure he was listening, caught between the two conversations as he was caught between two worlds.

I shook my head. "We are too divided already. Until I know what her intentions are, it would be wrong for me to step in and try to destroy the respect due a whisperer."

"She wanted you to die."

I thought of Sett, never far from my mind. "She's not the only one to want that."

A grimace was all Amun managed before Minister Manshin turned from his discussion, a sharp nod accompanying his decree.

"I will lend you my archers," he said. "But if this does not work, Rah e'Torin, should they all turn on us, I will give you to them, debt or no, rather than risk the lives of my soldiers."

By the time Tor finished his translation, Manshin was already striding around giving out orders, and I could make no objection. It was a wise call given the circumstances, but a buzz of nerves jangled up and down my arms.

"Rah?"

I turned and the dull tension in my ear became a sharp stab of pain. I hissed, and had to ask Tor to repeat his question. "He wants to know how you plan to get up the slope."

How bad must I look for Minister Manshin to doubt my ability to walk? Was it just the muddy bandages on my legs? Or did my face still look as much a mess as it felt? Sett had beaten his fists into my cheek and my nose and my jaw, rage stealing his ability to aim for the same place enough to do greater damage.

Doubt seeped its lead fingers into my heart. If I could not walk, could not even stand, what Levanti would look at me and see someone worth listening to? But the Levanti at the deserter camp had brought me offerings of food, saluting their respect as I lay by the fire. Perhaps it would be all right. After all it was Ezma they really had to listen to.

I assessed the hill, dotted with its broken statues. We had gone around it with the empress, joining the road because the slope down into the shrine was too steep. Now it was crawling with more well-concealed Kisians, some in trees, others lying flat, watching the direction of the shrine.

"It's too steep for the horse," Tor said, his tone possessing a note of resignation.

"I'm going to need help." I hated to say it, but there was some relief in the admission, in not having to keep pretending.

"Lucky us."

Amun shot him a reproachful look, but the saddleboy ignored it. He watched the Kisians bustle around us, Minister Manshin striding about giving orders like we were the eye of a storm.

"I hope you know what you're doing," Tor said, not turning to look up at me. "Gideon's Swords no doubt have orders to capture or kill you."

"I noticed. Hopefully we have retained enough of ourselves that this will work."

"How so?"

"Assuming it works, you'll soon see."

"And if it doesn't?"

"I won't have embarrassed myself by explaining it to you only to be wrong."

He looked up, a quizzical smile twitching his lips. "Priorities."

"Always. Here, help me down."

"But surely it's too embarrassing to need help getting down from the saddle."

"Ah, but you see, I am a warrior injured by the feuds of my people, and that, I think, could work very well."

Amun laughed, but there was nothing amusing about the pains that assailed my body as they helped me down, my every limb having stiffened into place during the night. To make them move again was like tearing open old wounds.

It took the combined assistance of both Tor and Amun to help me walk, although to call it walking was generous. Each with an arm across my back and a hand beneath my shoulders, they took most of my weight, all but carrying me up the ever-steepening slope. There were a number of good vantage points along the top, the minister had said, spots where we could be as high as the shrine roof and see what was happening below. I would have to shout, he said, but, seeming to understand some of my intent, added that the sight of me up there with Kisian archers along the ridge would be impressive.

Tor and Amun spoke in strained whispers as we made our way up the hill, swatting branches out of the way and staring at the ground in the hope of avoiding hidden rocks and divots. Kisians climbed all around us, as silently as so many men couldn't, their movement a continuous rustle like an endless gust of wind. My ear continued to sting its sharp pain, and though I was taking little of my own weight, the mere using of my legs had me gritting my teeth. Which hurt the bruises along my jaw.

This had better work was all I could think, because if it didn't, I was done. I couldn't fight. I couldn't run. I could not even think about what I would do or say to protect my life if Minister Manshin sacrificed me to protect his soldiers. I was just a haze of pain and exhaustion being half carried, half dragged through the undergrowth toward a moment that would decide too much.

Otobaru Shrine sat in a hollow. High ground on one side protected it from the west while the river protected it to the south. Only one road connected it to the rest of the empire, an overgrown thoroughfare as abandoned as the shrine itself.

The peak of the ridge was a narrow strip, crumbling away beneath our feet, but Minister Manshin had been right—it was the perfect vantage point from which to witness what was happening below, and an even better place to be seen from. Not so high I would be just an ant against the sun, but high enough everyone could see me.

The shrine stood below, the main building standing at the edge of a courtyard full of smaller outbuildings. We had built a fire in that courtyard and shared food with some Kisian travellers, but now the courtyard was full of Levanti—horses had been gathered in groups and fires built. They had planned to spend the night, confident Gideon's Swords had not followed. Until they had. They filled the road, as many of them as there were deserters.

It was a terrible place for a battle, yet Ezma had no choice but to rally the deserters to protect themselves. Had there been more time, archers could have climbed the slope and the shrine, could already have been picking off riders, but the enemy was coming too fast.

Enemy. It never ought to have been this way.

Minister Manshin halted beside us, a little out of breath but nothing compared to the huffing of the two men who had helped me get there. "Anytime you're ready, Rah," Tor said. "We can't keep holding you up forever."

I had thought to stand on my own once we got to the top, maybe a hand on Amun's shoulder all I would need to keep me steady, but my shaking legs made a mockery of all such plans.

Down below, Levanti were beginning to point up at us. More and more looked up, and Minister Manshin hissed words I didn't need translated. If I was going to speak, I had to do it now.

I swallowed hard, spikes seeming to have formed in my throat at so many watching eyes. I could not recall ever feeling so nervous, not even the night I had challenged Gideon for leadership. I had been carried by anger then, now I was empty.

"Levanti!" I called before I lost the moment. "For those who do not know me, I am Rah e'Torin, once captain of the Second Swords of Torin."

Down in the courtyard and out along the road faces turned up, weapons stilled, but there was a restlessness, a muttering, a few pointing up at the great number of Kisians ranged around me along the ridge.

"I am no one," I went on, glad the Kisians couldn't understand what I was saying. "No leader. Nothing in the eyes of the gods. And yet my soul will be lighter than yours, for I have not so forgotten our ways." More muttering. I shouted over it. "When we have such divisions, we do not resort to violence. That is not our way. Levanti life is the only thing more precious than food and water. Each of us takes many barrels of water and baskets of food and years of training to create, but only one stray thought to destroy. Put down your weapons and perform a Fracturing, or the gods themselves will see you are no longer Levanti but merely murderers."

I hoped it would work, hoped the threat of Kisian archers would speak for itself, but most of all I hoped we were not so lost.

Most of them were faceless figures from this distance, but I stared at Ezma, her jawbone headpiece standing above the heads of the others. *Come on*, I urged. *Be a horse whisperer.*

At the head of Gideon's Swords, their leader walked their horse forward. It was Yiss en'Oht who shouted back, her voice carrying well, a damning snap of words upon the air. "I have given orders and they will be obeyed, because that, Rah e'Torin, is truly the central tenet around which our society is built."

"On the plains, yes, but not here," I called back. "Obeying orders without question can only exist when one has confidence in the morality and wisdom of the Levanti giving the orders. We obey orders because our challenge system ensures the best person for the job is the one doing it. Only your own Swords can have that confidence in you, but since the orders come from Gideon, only his Swords can have confidence in them. Everyone else standing with you has no reason to obey and ought, by our tenets, make up their own minds. But really, it's not even Gideon giving the orders, is it? Who are you really obeying? Is it Dom Villius who wants you to slaughter your own people? Or is it Grace Bahain?"

So many swords had been drawn and arrows had been nocked, a poor choice of words all it would take to turn a tense scene into a bloody one. I had said all I could. It was up to them now.

I stared at Ezma, willing her to move, to do the right thing, while beside me Amun hissed a string of swear words like they were prayers. Until at last she stepped forward and laid one of her swords upon the ground before Yiss. The captain looked at it. Behind her, restless horses with restless riders made an undulating sea upon the road.

I was too far away to catch Ezma's words, but it didn't matter. As long as the Swords behind Yiss could hear, could see a horse whisperer standing before them. In this moment it didn't matter why she had been exiled or even that she wanted me dead. I just needed them to listen to her. Needed them to choose their own paths.

A blade clanged onto the road. Another followed. A horse near the front of Yiss's army walked forward, passing her to join Ezma.

Yiss shouted, a shrill rage drowned beneath the movement of more Levanti crossing the narrow space between armies. I had wondered if a proper Fracturing would work, whether people would cross both ways believing themselves safe whatever their choice, but there was too much fear for that. Why join a shrinking army even if you believed in their ideology? You were just going to lose.

Manshin rumbled something beside us.

"He wants to know who is still a threat," Tor said. "What should I tell him?"

"Tell him none of them."

"But Yiss might—"

"She might, but she has to be allowed to walk away. Those are the laws of a Fracturing. He won't understand, so tell him none are."

Tor relayed my words while below on the road Gideon's Swords were breaking up from behind now too, some of the Levanti turning at the back to ride away. Where they were going and who they believed in I couldn't know, capable only of relief there had been no bloodshed. At least not today.

"And what will those Levanti do?" Tor translated for the minister.

"Ezma's? That will depend."

"On?"

I turned my gaze on Tor, Manshin watching from behind him, his jaw clenched and tense. "On what the minister intends."

13. DISHIVA

The rain held off as we rode north, a small cavalcade. Sichi accompanied us, carried in her silk box while Gideon rode ahead, Leo at his side. Keka and my—*his* Swords rode behind Gideon and Sichi, and no longer having a place within even this patchwork herd, I kept Nuru company beside Sichi's box.

"You're going to have to explain it like I'm a child," I said, interrupting Nuru's explanation of the Chiltaen political system. "As soon as you start using words like...*secretary* and *oligarchy*...I'm lost."

The young woman sighed. "All right," she said, staring at the road stretching endlessly before us. "Imagine the whole of Chiltae is one herd. They have a central leadership. Do you understand that?"

"Yes, of course I understand that."

"Good. Now, they don't have one herd master or emperor, they have nine. They all have equal power, and decisions are made by majority."

"Like at conclaves."

"Exactly. I'll just call them leaders for now since the names confuse you. Nine leaders. They aren't chosen by the people though, as we do; they are decided by wealth. The nine families with the most money have a representative leader."

I stared at empty space beside her head while I considered this. "You see, that's what I thought you said before, but it made no sense. How would giving leadership to rich people make sure everyone else is all right?"

"I asked that. Sichi says it doesn't, but then neither does giving all the power to an emperor ensure common folk are looked after."

"Better to not have such a distinction between rich and poor."

"I said that too. I got a funny look."

"Empress Sichi doesn't agree?"

"Not really. I think they're all so entrenched in their ways they think that it's normal for there to be rich people and poor people, lords and servants, and so struggle to consider a more equitable way to live."

I looked at the silk box and tried for a moment to imagine Sichi living a herd life. It was a strange image. I couldn't but wonder what skills she had been taught, or if her childhood had been devoid of all such lessons beyond stitchery.

"Anyway," Nuru went on. "Nine rich men, and yes, they are all men. And the next nine most wealthy men account for the...second tier of leadership. Like our matriarchs and patriarchs, I guess, except it's also based on money, not wisdom."

"Can they challenge?"

"In a sense. Because it's always the nine richest; if you lose your fortune you lose your place, and it's given to the next person. Or if you get lots of money you can take someone else's place."

"Is money all they think about?"

"I think they're big traders. Lots of ships. Access to both the Eye Sea and the...other sea along the Ribbon. I think they make people pay money to use the Ribbon too, because the other way through the Jaws is really dangerous." She must have caught my confused look, for she sighed and added, "I don't really understand it all myself," giving lie to the confidence with which she'd explained it. "But that's what I got from Si. I asked a lot of questions and she was very patient, but I'm still trying to make sense of it."

Not for the first time, the incompatibility of our cultures seemed insurmountable.

Ahead, Gideon rode, tall and confident, toward our destination. I hadn't been able to talk to him alone since he'd named me ambassador, barely been able to catch his eye, Leo ever-present. Had I outsmarted him? Or was he letting us meet the envoy for his own reasons? With his faint smile and his mind reading, he was a fabled monster used to scare children, leaving me unsure if my fear of him was proportionate to his abilities or not.

Dom Villius looked around and seemed for a moment to stare at me, though with his mask on it was impossible to be sure.

"Do we know who Gideon is meeting?" I said, unable to sit with my thoughts of Leo for long before a deep sense of despair began to rear. "This envoy?"

"Excuse the words you don't understand, but his name is Secretary Aurus. As in, *secretary* is his title and Aurus is his name. He's one of the lesser nine."

"So he's rich, but not the nine-richest-level rich."

"Yes."

"Is that a good thing or a bad thing?"

Nuru shrugged. "Sichi doesn't know enough about the olig— the leaders to be sure. She thinks as an initial meeting it's good, but the Nine and the lesser nine are divided. Some of them follow Leo's church, some don't think the hieromonk should have any say in the movements of the army. Since Leo didn't want us to come, this Secretary Aurus may be one of the latter."

"An ally?"

She gave me a look. "He's Chiltaen. *Ally* is probably the wrong word."

Nuru was saved a snap of temper that had everything to do with me and nothing to do with her words by the noisy return of a pair of scouts.

"Your Majesty," one said, a little out of breath as he came within earshot, his horse sweating. "We found a small, hastily abandoned camp not far off the road ahead. Levanti."

"Are you sure?" Gideon said.

"Yes, Your Majesty. Laid out like one of our camps and with *shem* still cooking in the pot."

No Swordherds were meant to be in this area. Nor were the deserters.

"How many?"

By this time the scouts had drawn up before Gideon, the whole cavalcade halting and glad of the rest. It had been a long day on the road, travelling with so many like travelling with a herd, except that not everyone put in equal work.

"By the hoofprints, maybe only half a dozen. We tried following them but lost the trail, so I'd say they don't want to be found."

The only unaccounted for Swordherd were the Second Swords of Torin, but I had only to think that than to wish I hadn't.

A short conversation between Gideon and Leo took place in Chiltaen, while the thud of hooves from behind heralded Lord Edo passing the increasingly anxious cavalcade upon the grass, a question on his lips the moment he joined his emperor.

"Can you hear what they're saying?" I asked Nuru.

She shook her head. Empress Sichi's box had been lowered to the road, and the lady was peering through the side curtain. Nuru spoke to her and it was Sichi's turn to shake her head, but the mention of Lord Edo's name held the expectation he would explain later. And barely had we started moving again than he fell back to ride beside Sichi. He kept his voice low, but not so low Nuru couldn't catch what he said.

Gripping Itaghai's reins to enforce my own patience, I awaited a lull in their talk before demanding a translation.

She hadn't been wary of our surroundings when explaining the Chiltaen leadership, but this time Nuru looked all around to be sure she wouldn't be overheard and still lowered her voice. "There is talk of Rah. Both he and the rest of the Second Swords disappeared after he challenged Captain Yitti in Mei'lian and when—"

"Wait, what? When was this?"

"When they were burning the city. Captain Lashak brought back the news. It must have been while you were kneeling."

She said it as though I'd just been out for a walk, no weight in her tone for the shame kneeling was to us.

"Rah was there," she went on. "He challenged Yitti for the captaincy of the Second Swords of Torin and lost, but Sett shone light in his eyes—"

"What?" I interrupted again. "Sett e'Torin shone light in Rah's eyes during a challenge?"

"Yes. That's what I just said."

"But that's so dishonourable! Who would do that?"

"Sett, apparently. Rah had him killed for it."

"Killed?"

Nuru gave me another of her looks that made me feel like a child. "It was well within Rah's right as the wronged challenger."

"Of course it was, I'm just shocked."

"Shocked that Sett would do such a thing or shocked that Rah would?"

"Either. Both. Gods, what a mess."

"Indeed, now if you've finished interrupting, I'll continue. After that they all disappeared. The Second Swords didn't return with Lashak, and no one knows what happened to Rah. Perhaps they joined the deserters or are on their way home."

She paused there a moment to catch something in Lord Edo and

Sichi's conversation and, seeming to deem it unimportant, blew out a heavy breath.

"And Gideon thinks this camp..." I began and couldn't finish.

"It's not big enough for a whole Swordherd, or even half one, which they must have been reduced to by now. But if Rah was his stubborn self and chose to stay, perhaps with a few loyal others..."

She too seemed not to want to finish that thought, leaving the consequences of finding Rah here playing out in both of our heads. Rah was a stubborn, honourable man, one who could turn an already dangerous situation into something far worse, and yet I couldn't but wish for him. For someone I could trust, whose shoulders could bear some of the weight of responsibility I carried alone.

A small camp had been set up outside the town of Kima, and I recognised it as a Chiltaen forward camp, the sight chilling my blood. Their tendency to build camps ahead of themselves had always appeared overconfident and risky, but I realised to them it was no risk. What did rich leaders care if slaves and lowly ranked soldiers were killed? More important that everything was already in place for said rich leaders when they arrived.

We were greeted by a man called Captain Leveret who, despite the number of Chiltaens he appeared to have under his command, did not look at all happy that we had arrived first. His ill-ease was more than shared by us. Free as we were, being back inside a Chiltaen camp, being around Chiltaen soldiers and the smells of Chiltaen food, dug up all too many memories most of us would have liked to forget.

Despite every fibre of my being wanting to escape, I tried to focus on Leo, to watch him with his own people. Most Chiltaens knelt before him and kissed his feet, gathering around him and treating him like the god he wanted to be, but while the companions he had brought with him still treated him so, these new Chiltaens paid him no heed. Not his supporters then. A small amount of my tension loosened.

While we awaited the envoy, we were shown to tents. There were pens for our horses and firepits already burning, and I found some peace in being surrounded by Levanti voices despite the Chiltaen trappings.

Until a shout made me drop the bowl of soup I'd been cradling. Those sitting around the fire with me all looked up, a few losing their bread into their bowls, Nuru the only one too focussed on the task of gathering Sichi's meal to immediately attend. A group of Levanti hustled past, shunting shadowy figures toward Gideon's tent. A crowd of onlookers tailed them, and abandoning my meal, I leapt up to follow.

"Gifts for His Majesty," a rough voice said as the two leading men halted outside Gideon's tent, saluting to Anouke and Eppa on guard. "We found them."

Employing my shoulder, I reached the front of the group as Gideon emerged, Leo at his side. And down onto the dirt at his feet were thrown four Levanti. Bruised and bloodied and filthy, their hands tied behind their backs. Their hair was just too long to make out their brandings, but too well did I know their faces.

"Yitti," Gideon said, standing over them.

Yitti—Captain Yitti now, I reminded myself, the man no longer Rah's healer but Rah's replacement—Himi, Istet, and Lok e'Torin, four of Rah's former Swords, and I hated how relieved I was that Rah was not among them.

"Gideon," Captain Yitti said, no respect in his tone.

"You didn't return to Kogahaera."

"No. We didn't."

Gideon folded his arms, becoming a broad, immovable wall of crimson silk. "Of all the Swords I thought would desert, I never thought it would be you. Any of you," he added, turning his glare along the line of beaten Swords. Istet spat blood at his feet, but Gideon didn't move, didn't acknowledge the disrespect with anything but a dismissive glance. "A shame my own herd are so short-sighted."

He looked at the men who had brought them in, who stood like hunters over their kills. "Just the four of them?"

"Three others. Ptahphet is bringing them."

"Rah?" The question burst from Gideon, a breathless, desperate demand that drew Leo's attention. His frown was there and gone in a flash, but while he could regain control of Gideon, he could not retract the question.

Yitti's bloodied lip curled. "Dead, if your *army* has done their job," he said. "You probably don't care anymore, but I hope you live long enough to regret him even if you haven't enough soul left to regret the rest of us."

"Lock them up," Gideon said, his moment of honest emotion gone. "We will take them back to Kogahaera with us. Their deaths must be seen. Must be witnessed. A warning to others who would take our future into their own hands by throwing the rest of us under the cart."

They were hauled to their feet, arms so tightly bound that but for the thickness of the gathered crowd they might have overbalanced and been unable to save themselves. The closest Swords jeered and spat at them, hissing condemnations at these Levanti traitors, but beyond the central core of hate and anger, discontent muttered its way through the crowd. I had been a captain too long to miss the signs, to ignore the prickling of my skin as small groups broke away whispering.

Gideon surely noticed, but with Leo at his side and in his mind, smothering everything he was, he did nothing. Together they walked away, leaving the Second Swords of Torin to be dragged off by those Levanti who had found a hateful sort of joy in the cruelty absolute loyalty allowed them. The leader who had brought us all together, upon whom we had heaped our hopes, had become the wedge that would drive us all apart if I didn't stop Leo soon.

———————————✦———————————

By evening it was clear the envoy was not expected until the following day, but when Swords and soldiers alike made for their tents and the camp quietened, I could not rest. Could not be still. I strode the edge of the camp under the watchful eyes of the Chiltaen guards on duty, up and back, up and back, a caged animal with a burning purpose but no agency, trapped by everything except bars.

I needed to get rid of Leo. I needed to save the Second Swords from execution. I needed to make sure we left this place with a treaty. But all the success I'd felt having Gideon name me ambassador had crumbled. Momentum had gotten us here but could carry us no farther, not while Leo had his claws so deep in Gideon he had become a puppet.

I pressed my palms to my eyes, hard enough that bright colours darted in the darkness. Gods, I wanted to close my eyes and open them upon a new day, this nightmare nothing but a memory. I had thought being enslaved was the worst that could happen, but at least we had all been united then, had all wanted freedom. Now it was each other we fought.

The Second Swords of Torin had been penned near the horses, and once the camp was quiet and the lamps in Gideon's tent had been extinguished, I went to see Itaghai. He was happy to see me, but wasn't fooled, treating my distraction with nudges for attention.

"Just hush a moment, will you?" I said, patting his neck. "There are some Swords locked up over there and I need to see if I can..."

I trailed off. What could I do? I'd been given the power to organise this meeting, but I could no more order the captured Swords released than I could fight those guarding them. Both the most and the least I could do was check that they were all right for now, a plan so pathetic I almost retreated rather than carry it out.

Leaving Itaghai to sulk, I made my way across the grass to where Yitti and his Swords had been dragged. My steps faltered as I neared, not because their guards glared at me, not because *they* glared at me. The sight of the chains holding them to the ground reminded me all too viscerally of those nights imprisoned within Chiltaen camps. Only momentum kept me moving through the horror.

"Defender," one of the guards said, his tone one of wary respect. Not one of my Swords, I noted, not even one of Gideon's usual guards, and I thought of the Swords who had first stepped into such positions when Gideon had taken the throne, their loyalty an excuse to revel in chaos, and the opportunity to take power our society didn't usually allow.

Not knowing his name, I saluted. "I have a few questions for the prisoners," I said, not waiting for them to step aside but pushing through with all the assurance I possessed, hoping the sneering words would make them see me as an ally in their hate.

Neither stopped me, but where no amount of insistence from them could have, the hateful glares of the captured Swords halted my steps like I'd walked into a wall.

"Captain Yitti," I said, trying to swallow the feeling I was going to be sick.

Chained to the ground, the man looked up at me unblinking and said nothing. I had so much I wanted to say, so much to ask, but the guard's stare was like a blade between my shoulders, stealing my voice.

I crouched as close to Yitti as I dared. He had the look of a man who would tear my throat out with his teeth, and I couldn't blame him.

"Why didn't you come back from Mei'lian?"

Behind the captain, Istet barked a sharp laugh. "See? I told you it was Dishiva behind that mask. It's the way she walks."

Chains clinked as Himi elbowed her twin. "Well, excuse me for not ogling arses as much as you do. I found it impossible to believe that someone so abused by the Chiltaens would become one of them."

I had been chained to the ground just as they were now, and I couldn't look at the stakes hammered into the dirt between them. "I am not one of them," I said, vibrant hurt overtaking my calm. "I am a prisoner here as much as you are; my chains are just made of fabric and guilt."

Himi's eyes narrowed, but she didn't speak, owing me nothing.

"Are you... all right?" I said, aware as I asked how foolish it sounded.

"Oh, very excellent, Captain, yes," Lok e'Torin grumbled.

"Hush," said a woman beside him whose name I didn't know.

"Well, what are we supposed to say to that? I thought being prisoners of the Chiltaens was the worst that could happen to us, but prisoners of Levanti? Some of them from our herd?"

Captain Yitti adjusted the way he was sitting on the dirt. "If you've nothing of use to say, Dishiva, do fuck off. I have no information for you no matter what sort of martyr you claim to be."

The woman beside Lok spat at me and I fell back, as shocked by her anger as my own. That my suffering was invisible didn't make it any less painful. How I wanted to shake them, but it wouldn't help them to acknowledge I was hurting too.

Behind me one of the guards hissed to the other, something of ill-ease in their tone. Half a dozen Swords had gathered before them, bright-eyed and belligerent. "This is wrong," one of them said. "We shouldn't have attacked the deserters, and we shouldn't kill Levanti just because they want to go home. Let them go."

"That's not your decision," a guard said, standing his ground. "Take it up with His Majesty."

Around us, Chiltaen soldiers who had been minding their own business drew closer, watching warily, their hands all too close to their weapons. One spark was all we needed to tear ourselves to pieces before the envoy even arrived.

"His Majesty." The man spat. "It isn't our way to have a majesty."

"It isn't our way to fight each other when we can talk either," I said, eyeing the Chiltaens closing in. "Fight for what is right only after all possibility of talk has failed. I'm sure Emperor Gideon will be happy to hear your thoughts."

Whether it would have worked without the Chiltaen onlookers didn't matter; it only had to work because of them, because the tension was growing taut and I feared how much hate and anger we all carried. I needed to walk away, to calm the situation, but I could not leave without turning back to Yitti one last time. "I will not let you die," I whispered, pulling down my mask enough that they could see my face. "I will do everything I can. I promise."

"We aren't afraid of dying," Yitti said. "Only afraid to die like this. For nothing."

For nothing.

I carried the echo of those words with me away from the pen and back toward the tents, muttering remaining in my wake. So much of what we had fought for, had died for, had strived for now seemed to have been for nothing. We had to stop letting it be true.

Secretary Aurus arrived the following afternoon, his travelling group far smaller than I had expected. Unlike us with our whole cavalcade of Swords and servants, he travelled with half a dozen guards, a collection of men who looked like scribes, and a short train of pack mules led by slaves. He was welcomed by Captain

Leveret as we had been, though while only Chiltaen eyes had watched our arrival, our whole party was added to the number watching his. Despite the interested stares of Chiltaens, Levanti, and Kisians alike, the man appeared unconcerned.

He was tall for a Chiltaen, his short hair more brown than sandy, and his attire was one of the most glorious I'd ever seen. At a glance it was made from dozens of layers of different-length fabrics with folds and embroidered hems gathered around him, but on closer inspection it was only two garments atop his breeches, one white, one gold, both draping asymmetrically around a thick belt inlaid with slices of glittering gemstones.

And this a man not wealthy enough to be one of the nine leaders of Chiltae.

"Secretary," the captain said. The rest of his words were in Chiltaen and lost on me, but the respect he showed the newcomer bordered on obsequiousness. He and his companions were shown to tents on the opposite side of the camp, the divide narrow but present.

"It sounds like the meeting will be in about an hour." I jumped at the sound of Nuru's voice beside me, the mask I was forced to wear having stolen my periphery vision. "Sichi isn't allowed to attend. As usual. She requests you come to see her afterward to let her know the details."

"Are you and Lord Edo not to attend?" I said, still watching the envoy's people being shown to their tents on the other side of the camp.

"I will be too busy translating to watch expressions. And yes, Lord Edo is, but he can only report what happens from a Kisian point of view. As Gideon is not Kisian, she would appreciate your thoughts as well."

"I'm not sure Gideon is Levanti either at the moment," I muttered.

I felt rather than saw her turn to look at me. "What do you mean?"

"Are we being watched?"

"Not by anyone of note."

I dared not look around. "Leo hasn't left his side since he named me ambassador for this meeting. I think... whatever it is that Leo does, he's got Gideon on a short rein now. He doesn't want us here. I don't think this secretary is a friend of his."

"All the more reason to make him a friend of ours then."

She walked away, her abrupt manner leaving me feeling the full weight of the responsibilities I carried alone.

A large tent had been erected in the centre of the camp, and as the hour of the meeting approached, slaves and servants began to bustle in and out in preparation. Gideon had not left his tent since we'd arrived. He would attend with Leo in tow, and unable to exclude him, the meeting would surely go exactly how Leo wished, ending with no treaty. It felt foolish to hope for a better outcome, yet we could not come this far and leave with nothing.

If only my plan had been more than a few reckless ideas.

All too soon it was time to go. A buzz of tension and excitement had fallen over the camp, even the Chiltaen soldiers who maintained it halting about their work to watch as we gathered. From our side, Gideon in his imperial regalia, Leo in his mask, Lord Edo and Lord Nishi in their Kisian robes, Keka, Nuru, and myself, all entering the tent to find Secretary Aurus and a single scribe already seated at the table. Food and wine had been set out, less a meal than a display of finely painted dishes with little morsels set in the centre. One of them looked like a dish of flowers carved from fruit.

"His Imperial Majesty Emperor Gideon e'Torin, first of his name, Lord Protector of Levanti Kisia," Nuru said as Gideon entered, before repeating the words in Chiltaen. She did the same in introducing me as both defender and ambassador, before introducing the others in simple terms.

Secretary Aurus and his scribe had risen to their feet at Gideon's regal entrance and bowed now, uttering a respectful greeting. A sweep of his gloriously clad arm and a slight smile invited us to join him even before Nuru translated, and I took a place at the table kneeling beside Gideon. He didn't so much as glance at me. Leo knelt on his other side with Lord Nishi, while Lord Edo took the final place beside me, leaving Keka and Nuru to stand.

While wine was poured, both Gideon and Secretary Aurus seemed content to sit and wait in silence, a general shuffling of fabric and clearing of throats the only sounds in the candlelit, silken space. Outside, the camp presumably went on about its tasks in the bright afternoon light, but it all seemed a world away.

When at last the servant stood back, Secretary Aurus treated us to another smile. It looked genuine, if my experience of Chiltaens was anything to go by, and a little of my wary dislike faded.

"I am honoured that you have agreed to meet with me," Nuru translated for him. "Especially on such short notice and given the prior...history between our two peoples."

I heard the quiet pause in his words though Nuru spoke them more harshly. It was not an admission of wrongdoing or an apology, but that he wasn't refuting his own involvement or pretending it hadn't happened was better than nothing.

"I am not sure how much you know of the history between Chiltae and Kisia," Nuru went on translating. "But it is a long and bloody thing, each war being followed by periods of short-lived peace sealed with a new treaty and, often, a political marriage. We freely admit we came out of this conflict as the losers and as such are making the first gesture toward peace."

It sounded like a fair speech to me, but the little grunt of air that left Lord Edo's nose made me wonder whether it was unusual, even in such circumstances, for them to admit defeat.

Gideon made no reply, but for a long time sat staring at the man across from him, tension mounting. Despite Gideon's size and stature and the sure knowledge he was a capable warrior, Secretary Aurus managed to meet his gaze with an impressive degree of calm, waiting while, beside me, Lord Edo fidgeted with his wine bowl.

"And what," Gideon said when eventually he spoke, "do you intend to offer us in return for this peace?"

"We offer the same peace," the secretary said. "A peace that goes both ways. Chiltae is a rich nation, one you would benefit from trading with, one who will not long be weakened by the losses you inflicted upon us. I assure you it is as much in your interests as in ours, especially with winter coming." He gave a little shrug. "Don't worry, I am sure we will fight again one day. There is no such thing as lasting peace in this cursed land of ours."

"Peace," Gideon said after a time, and I wondered whether it was as obvious to others as it was to me that it wasn't him speaking. He had always drawn us together as much through inspiring words as actions, and now here he sat barely managing single sentences as though they were being dragged from him. "That is all?"

For the first time since we'd entered, Secretary Aurus turned to Dom Villius at the emperor's left hand, answering as though he had been the one to speak. The smallest of gestures, but I held my breath. Perhaps this man understood. "The Nine have authorised me to negotiate terms in good faith," he said. "Trade routes. Goods. Merchant galleys. A bride. There are many options, each from wealthy houses that will bring much fortune to your coffers besides making you an admirable empress."

"I already have an empress."

The secretary's brows rose before Nuru translated, and again I stared at him, increasingly sure he understood a lot more than he wanted us to see.

Lord Edo spoke and I caught Sichi's name. Whether for us or for the show of maintaining Gideon didn't speak Chiltaen, Nuru translated this too. "His Imperial Majesty allied himself to my family by wedding my cousin, Lady Sichi Manshin."

"Ah a pity," the secretary said, though he didn't sound disappointed. Or surprised. "We shall keep our rich brides and may argue over the rest."

"No."

Gideon snapped the word, dropping the smile from Secretary Aurus's face. "No?"

"No. There will be no treaty. There will be no promise of peace. Not unless what you have on offer is the entirety of your lands and your people. We already have an alliance with Dom Leo Villius, and given the political situation in Chiltae that is of far greater value." Gideon settled his hands on the table. "Curiosity made me accept your proposal to meet, a curiosity that has now been sated unless you have something more meaningful to offer or say."

Secretary Aurus gave back stare for stare, resting his hands on the table in the same confident manner. "Nothing more meaningful to offer, but a question if I might, Your Majesty," he said through Nuru's lips. "On one side of you sits the son of our late hieromonk, while on the other sits a Levanti he seems to have elevated to the position of Defender of the One True God. Are you yourself a believer, or is this an…odd coincidence among your advisors?"

"I am a Levanti."

"Ah, a requirement forced upon you then. How very insidious the faith is."

Gideon rose from his place at the table, causing a small smile to turn the secretary's lips. "This meeting is over."

And that was it. While I had hoped for better, it was no surprise, the whole thing having taken on the appearance of a play. But I was not done yet.

Rising to his feet, Secretary Aurus bowed to Gideon, thanked

Nuru for her translation, and stood watching the imperial party stride out one after another until I was the only one left. I stared at him through the slits in my mask while his scribe shuffled papers, the stare a question I could not ask even had I known the right words. All but alone, the envoy met my gaze, and over the peace negotiations that hadn't even begun, we shared a long, silent stare. And then he nodded. Not a nod of acknowledgement, but of agreement. I nodded back and departed, glad I hadn't been wrong.

———————————+———————————

With the meeting over, the camp was restless. Nothing had changed. We had wasted our time and everyone was keen to get moving, to leave this all too familiar Chiltaen camp behind. It was too late to depart that day, but our half of the camp was soon busy with preparations to leave at first light.

I found Nuru talking to a servant outside Empress Sichi's tent, seeming to be arguing over the tray of food that had been brought to her.

"Nuru."

"I am rather occupied, Captain."

"I need Sichi's help. It's important."

She thrust the tray into the guard's hands with a growl and turned on me. "What is it, Dishiva?"

The servant stood stunned, watching us, but thankfully so few Kisians understood our language that I sped on. "I need to meet with Secretary Aurus. Alone. I'll be watched, will be seen if I go to his tent, but—"

"If Sichi invites both of you to her tent, it will be less noteworthy and may not get back to Leo or Gideon. I'll see to it."

"Seems like you're seeing to a lot of things." I glanced at the servant. "Is everything all right?"

"No, not really, but... here isn't really the place to talk about it."

Nuru always looked so confident and sure and angry at the world that the sight of her biting her lip in a worry she could not contain reminded me just how young she was. Too young to have so many responsibilities thrust upon her. "Then walk with me," I said. "No, don't argue. Sichi will be just fine for five minutes and you will feel better for it. Come."

Gripping her arm, I bore her away from the fine tents, away from the curious gazes and the proximity of Leo, out toward the horse pens where the scent of hay and horsehair held a trace of home.

"All right, spill," I said throwing her a brush as we reached Itaghai's side. "What's wrong?"

Nuru caught the brush and glared at it like it had offended her, but she took it firmly in her grip and started on Itaghai's side without answering.

"Come on, it's not like you have another confidant besides Empress Sichi."

"That you're the only person I can confide in does not make you someone I *want* to confide in."

"Is it Sichi?" Nothing. "Is it Leo?" Still nothing. "Gideon?"

She huffed an annoyed breath. "It's all of them. Do you remember that seven days after the marriage ceremony, Gideon was supposed to untie her sash and...and bed her to complete the rite?"

"Supposed to?" I'd been kneeling when the sevenday had been up, but the next time I'd seen Sichi she had no longer been wearing the white sash.

Nuru gave me a long look over Itaghai's back. "I don't know what you've heard about Gideon, but...well the whole time I was a saddlegirl with the First Swords of Torin, I never once heard of him lying with anyone. Sex just...didn't seem to interest him, and that doesn't seem to have changed. Whether he's incapable, not interested in anyone, or just not interested in Sichi..."

"He hasn't tried? For the sake of the rite?"

"No."

"Did you ask him about it?"

"No, I didn't want Leo hearing about it. So I asked Tep, since he's been the healer of the First Swords for years. He laughed at me." Nuru glared at Itaghai's back, her hand working fast with the brush. "He said I ought to have been with the First Swords long enough to realise Gideon has only ever been *Rahsexual* and told me to untie her sash and bed her myself. So I did."

I'd not heard it put that way before, but the moment she said it I knew it for truth. I'd not been with Gideon as long as any of his Swords, but long enough to know there was only one person he truly cared for.

"That's good advice," I said. "So what's the problem?"

"Leo. He knows. In the way he knows everything. And the Kisians are so... *Kisian* that it could ruin not only their marriage, but her as well, and have her thrown out of her family. He says he will if she doesn't promise to marry him should anything happen to Gideon, but not only is he awful and she hates him, but she is afraid that making any such promise would be as good as stabbing Gideon in the back. Someone like Leo doesn't ask for something like that without having a plan in place to make it happen."

Her tide of admissions ended of a weak huff of frustration all too like a sob.

"Well," I said, words momentarily abandoning me. "That's some shit. Why does he want to marry her? I mean, I can see why you like her, but Leo isn't exactly the sort to be... in love. There must be some reason why *her*."

"We think so too, but gods only know what it could be. Or why I told you. It's not like you can do anything about it."

"Not right now, but you feel better having let it out, I'm sure, and we're more likely to find an answer together."

"I want the answer to be 'No, fuck off,' but she's considering letting him bed her as a sort of unspoken promise no matter how awful it would be, and whenever I get frustrated and say Levanti would never let such a thing happen she snaps at me. I am told this is quite normal in Kisia and if I don't like what she is forced to do I should leave."

For a time we stood brushing Itaghai together, nothing more either of us could say that would be of use. I wished I had advice, or could fix this as I wished to fix everything else, but I had no answers for anything, only ever more problems.

"I should get back to her," Nuru said after a while. "I don't want her to worry."

I let her go and stayed brushing Itaghai for longer than he needed, the mindless task providing no answers or ideas, only more questions. The evening meal was in progress by the time I made my way back through the camp, yet few Levanti had gathered around the fires. A group stood forming a circle between two of the larger tents, their sombre expressions sending my heart racing.

I ought to have known what I would find in its centre, ought to have known I was due another warning, that Leo would not long go without punishing me and every Levanti who got in his way.

At the centre of the circle knelt a Bedjuti, bloody blade in hand as he took the heads of the Swords laid out before him. The very Swords who had stood before the captured Torin and called for their release. Who I'd sent to see Gideon.

Though I'd not seen Leo around the fires, though he was probably still in Gideon's tent, I felt the prickle of his gaze upon my skin. He wanted me to stop. Wanted me to look at the tears of my people and listen to their mourning songs and stop. But as I stood there letting their pain wash over me, it was anger it fuelled. Anger and determination to beat him no matter what it took.

With summer long behind us, the nights were getting cold, my skin pimpling in the chill wind. Nuru came to fetch me, and by the time we reached Sichi's tent, my hands had turned to ice. The light spilling through the opening was inviting despite what I feared to find out inside.

Although Sichi's guards nodded as we went in, the empress was not there. Only Secretary Aurus, rising to greet us. "Ah, Defender e'Jaroven," he said. "I hoped to be able to speak to you."

I halted a step inside. "You speak Levanti."

He acquiesced with a little bow. "Not perfectly, such that I am glad for your translator." He gestured at Nuru. "But yes. I learned with Legate Andrus and a few others. Many of my..." The secretary looked to Nuru and said a word in Chiltaen.

"There isn't a Levanti word for that," she said. "Probably best translated simply as 'fellow leaders.'"

"Ah. Then many of my fellow leaders thought, when Gideon first arrived, that the Levanti presence here would be short-lived and insignificant. A few of us were more...forward-looking."

"You could have spoken Levanti at the meeting."

"And Gideon could have spoken Chiltaen. Yet instead we maintain our formalities."

At that, Secretary Aurus graciously invited us to sit as though it had been his own tent. In Kisia it was customary to sit at a table and be served tea, but Sichi's tent had been furnished with a trio of long bed-like chairs. He reclined upon one, but Nuru and I just sat.

"How long has Leo Villius been with you?" he said, taking up a glass of wine from a side table.

"In total or just since he last died?" I said, as much to see his reaction as to clarify what he wanted to know.

"Ah." He swirled the wine, looking at it rather than me. "You are aware then, of his...oddities."

"Hard not to be when you've seen him die twice."

"Who killed him?"

I glanced at Nuru, wondering if I ought to be so open with this man. He was no friend of Leo's, but he was still a Chiltaen. She gave an infinitesimal shrug, and deciding the information could do no harm, I said, "Gideon the first time. In Mei'lian. I did the second time." I kept the information about the cave and the holy book to myself, only willing to trust this man so far.

"Ah." He seemed to like that sound. "I have not seen him die myself, but I understand one of the assassins I hired achieved his death, before she disappeared. Every assassin I've sent after him didn't come back."

"You need better assassins."

"These were some of the very best money could buy, I assure you. Would either of you like some wine?" Secretary Aurus lifted his glass. "I find all conversations about Dom Villius require wine."

"You know he can read your mind."

He took a large gulp of wine, followed by another. "I know. Fortunately, our late hieromonk, Leo's father, was able to discover from a man who studies people like Leo that he requires a..." He waved a hand, trying to find the right Levanti word. "...an amount of closeness," he settled on. "In order to look inside our heads. My guards are well versed in this and will ensure he isn't close enough to hear what we are talking about."

"We cannot always keep him at a distance."

"No, but he also cannot penetrate deeper than your surface thoughts. He uses certain phrases and questions to bring the information he requires to the forefront of your mind so appears to have more skill than he actually has."

I leaned forward, elbows resting on my knees. "Why are you telling me this?"

"Because right now, Defender, you and I both have the same enemy, and it's not each other."

"You could have left us to deal with him. Surely you would rather he break us than strengthen us."

A smile twitched the secretary's lips. "I enjoy the Levanti direct-ness. You're right. I wouldn't care if him being a danger to you did not also make him a danger to us. Excuse my own directness when I say the Levanti empire is weak. The Kisian Empire is weak. And now thanks to you, we are weak. There has never been a better time for Leo to thrive."

"Can I take from those words that you have no intention of attacking us despite our emperor's refusal to sign a treaty with Chiltae?"

"The Nine are never unanimous about anything and often take actions that aren't...agreed, even with a treaty. So as you can make no promises for your people, neither can I, but at this point enough of us feel it is Leo against whom we must fight." He took a sip of his wine, followed by a larger mouthful. "You know he has com-mand over a coalition of the Chiltaen army? Their commanders are intensely loyal to the church and followed his father, but we understand he has them now. They were last seen outside Koi. We had a commander in place who was not so keen on continued war, but...we have reason to believe he is no longer in command."

His words chilled my blood. "Leo has an army?"

"It is not so much his as is led by a group of men more faithful to their god than to Chiltae. And it's currently in Kisia somewhere. I wish I could tell you where."

I wished I could believe he was being entirely honest, but between a natural scepticism and a visceral dislike of uniformed Chiltaen men, I couldn't. It was all I could do to remind myself that the actions of one Chiltaen ought not condemn them all.

I eyed him across the carpeted space between us. "You didn't expect us to agree to a treaty, did you?"

The secretary smiled, spreading his hands in a wry sort of

acknowledgement. "If Dom Villius had let us make such an agreement, I would have wondered how he intended to turn it to his advantage. In truth, I'm surprised Emperor Gideon came to meet me at all. Or...was allowed to come meet me, perhaps I should say."

"You know what he does."

"I know enough."

I twisted my fingers together and couldn't meet his gaze. "We are only here because I and...others made great sacrifices to ensure we came. To not let Leo Villius destroy everything we have worked hard to build."

The man's pitying smile made me wish I had kept my mouth shut, made me wish I had not tried so hard to trust him, to think well of him, but he didn't mock me.

"You are a credit to your herd, Defender Dishiva," he said, the words sounding honest enough. "And I wish I could give you the assurance you came for, but all I can do is warn you of the dangers—"

"Which we already knew."

"Which, for the most part, you already knew," he admitted, not put out by my interruption. "And assure you that Chiltae wants him gone as much as you do and we will do all in our power to ensure it happens. Sadly, so little is in our power while he remains at a Levanti court deep within Kisia. Thus, I hand the problem over to you."

"For which I cannot thank you."

Secretary Aurus sat up. "I don't expect your thanks. I can give you nothing but information. In that capacity, I intend to remain here at this camp some weeks should you require anything that could assist in the...speedy removal of our mutual problem."

"Don't attack us," I said, standing to depart. "That is the only way you can help."

He got to his feet as well, setting his wine glass down on a side table. "I can give my word on that for now, at least for all parts of our army we command. Most of which you destroyed."

"I hope you don't expect an apology after everything you did to us."

I hadn't meant to bring it up, but the anger always lived just beneath my skin, an ever-present heat I could not shake and didn't want to. The rage gave me purpose, helped me feel alive and connected to my people.

"I do not," he said, his sharpest tone so far. Satisfying to know we had left them their own anger to carry. "I do not feel there is anything left to say, so I will bid you goodnight, Defender, before anyone gets suspicious of our meeting."

Stiffly courteous, we each thanked the other. A bow. A salute. And Nuru and I were back out in the chill night air. She bade me goodnight and I walked slowly in the direction of my tent. Although I had given Gideon's a wide berth on the way over, it was late enough that Leo might well be asleep, so I risked the more direct route back. Keka was alone on duty outside, faint light dusting his feet.

I strode over, always more aware of the fabric over my face whenever I caught Levanti grimacing. Keka grimaced now, unable to meet my gaze.

"I'm going in to see Gideon," I said, not a request or a question but a statement of fact. He could refuse, but I thought of the man who had knelt with me while I knelt, his palms open in silent apology, and it was that man who stepped aside for me now.

Inside, a single lantern burned on the table, throwing its light over Gideon sprawled upon the faded carpet. Foam spilled from his slack mouth, and in a heartbeat I was back in Kogahaera watching Matsimelar and Jass struggle to breathe. To live.

"Gideon!" I dropped beside him, heart in my throat. "Gideon!"

His eyes flickered and his back rose and fell so little beneath my hand I wouldn't have felt it had I not been seeking a sign of life. Relief flared, only for every part of me to tense as Keka entered in a flurry of canvas. He stood a moment on the threshold, staring at Gideon, and the fear that he had done this faded at his blatant shock.

"He's still breathing," I said, getting a hand under his shoulder and levering him onto one side. "I'll steady him here. Get your fingers down his throat. Now!"

Keka didn't need telling twice. It was not a technique we learned as part of our training, but it needed little finesse, and as I had jammed desperate fingers down Jass's throat, he thrust his into Gideon's slack mouth, keeping his head tilted. Thankfully he did, for Gideon retched, spilling partly digested food and wine, bile, and foam out onto the carpet, narrowly missing our knees.

We held him steady until he had finished purging and his shoulders began to shake, his every indrawn breath a rattle that sent vibrations through his chest. And while he breathed, Keka and I breathed with him. I had been too shocked upon entering to consider the implications of finding Gideon in such a state, to even consider how long he might have been lying here slowly dying. That he'd been given a low dose of redcap was clear, as clear as the warning that next time he would not be so fortunate. That I was fast running out of warnings.

In silence, Keka and I cleaned Gideon up and got him to his sleeping mat, a rag doll of a man where our strong, proud leader had once been. I tried to tell myself it wasn't my fault, that it was Leo's doing, but losing Gideon wasn't just gambling with one life, but with our whole future.

We left Gideon to sleep, stepping back through the canvas and into a cool, calm night that made a mockery of my hot skin and panicking thoughts. "No one can know," I hissed, gripping Keka's sleeve as he went back to his post. "That's what Leo wants. To spread fear. To destabilise us and destroy our faith in our leaders." I tightened my hold. "We can't let him destroy us, Keka. We can't. This isn't for me. It's for all of us. For the whole future of the Levanti people."

14. CASSANDRA

I sat with my back to the side of the cart, rocking with it as it rolled along the rough track. Soldiers marched alongside, their footsteps barely audible above the storm of many. Drizzle fell on their helmets and dusted their shoulders, and it had dampened my clothes and my hair but had not dampened the unsettling warmth I felt watching Leo riding with them.

No one had ever needed me before. Not in the way of one needing care and protection like a child. But Leo did. He had broken again this morning, the occasions he escaped their hold coming closer together, though he struggled to hold them off longer than a few minutes at a time. Minutes he sometimes used to talk. To explain. Or to sob like the broken creature he was. Before he was gone again. Back behind the faintly smiling mask.

He wore it now though no fabric covered his face. The faint, confident smile, knowing everything. Seeing everything. I longed to peel it away to let free the smothered man underneath so I could fix him. Could help.

Cassandra would have jeered at the very thought, never inclined to help anyone, to love or care or protect. I'd sometimes wondered if we were opposite forces somehow, her whole purpose to destroy, mine to protect and nurture. How different things might have been if I'd been stronger. If I'd understood what we were sooner.

Leo's gaze was on me, and I turned away, fearing what they might read in my mind. Safer to look ahead at the soldiers. They stretched far ahead of me, a long dark trail across the landscape, broken up by carts and siege weapons, horses and banners and commanders in green and blue cloaks. I hadn't asked where they were going. It didn't matter.

I had a purpose now.

———————◆———————

The jolting carried on into wakefulness as though I dragged the dream with me. I wondered muzzily if I was still asleep and tried to blink to check, finding my eyes crusted and sore. Only the sun-warmed wall against which I leant provided any comfort.

Hoofbeats grew louder, clacking on stone, only to soften again into the muted thuds of a horse upon grass, and I tried to open my aching eyes. Wind whipped into them, and the sun was too bright. I closed them again with a sharp gasp.

"You awake?"

The voice rumbled through my back. Captain Aeneas was behind me, and I realised he was the warmth against which I leaned.

"Yes," I said, or tried to say. It came out a dried rasp like one of the empress's failing corpse-skins. "Where are we?"

"I'm not sure yet. We're heading east."

East. I tried to recall where we had been that we were travelling east, and it took a few long minutes for the memories to return like a sluggish stream in high summer. The house. Leo. Septum screaming. I'd almost lost Empress Hana inside his skin.

"How are you feeling?"

A groan was all the answer I could give. The empress's body was slowly waking, each part registering voluble complaints as it roused. There appeared to be stinging cuts upon one of our arms and another on our forehead, but most of the pain was deep inside our bones. It was the leaden weight of fatigue, like this damned disease was slowly eating us from the inside. Her beautiful, proud outer shell would be the last thing to go.

"Here." Captain Aeneas pressed a water skin to my stomach and I managed to take it, realising he'd had his arms around me. Jolting. Reins. The captain behind me. We were riding. Foolish it had taken me so long to realise.

I tried to pull the stopper out of the water skin, but it was stuck too tightly.

"Here," he said again, and lifted it to his mouth, yanking the stopper loose with his teeth before handing it back. "Drink your fill. I don't need any and we'll soon find more, I'm sure."

The deep rumble of his voice seemed to surround me, comforting like a warm blanket I sorely needed. Despite the sunlight the air felt chilly, although the captain stank of sweat.

I lifted the water skin to my parched lips, but it took all the energy I possessed to keep it there, letting the water dribble into my mouth. It was hot and tasted unpleasant, like over-steeped tea. I was too thirsty to care and drank greedily, even the empress making no complaint when some spilled down my chin and neck and onto my clothes. She hadn't spoken, but I could feel her there, hunkered down in the back of my mind like a wounded animal.

Are you all right? I said.

I had the feeling she nodded, as much as one can nod without a head to move. The images that had come back with her from Septum had been mangled and strange, loud things, his inner voice perpetually shouting, thoughts rendered in thick, scrawled strokes in his head. Not single lines, but every line of thought coloured over again and again in a mad rush to be heard.

Was it just loud?

She laughed, but it owned no humour. *You have no idea what that word means.*

I had thought that inside Kocho's head too. Able to hear all the thoughts in the room as though everyone had been speaking. No wonder he'd spent his whole life trying not to hear them.

That's exactly what it was like, but... worse. Oh, so much worse. I can't even...

Her memories of it were there if I wanted to see them, too raw and fresh a wound for her to hide away, but... I shied from their brightness, their heat. Even my curiosity would take me no closer.

Wise woman.

I rested the half-empty water skin in my lap and let my head fall back against Captain Aeneas's shoulder. Bright sunshine seared through my eyelids and I kept them closed, content for now to trust in where he was taking us. East. The Witchdoctor's house had been as far west in Kisia as I had ever been, making east everywhere else in the empire.

I think I could have controlled the body eventually, Empress Hana said after a time jolting on with the gait of the horse. *It was starting to feel more... natural. He fought back, but the shred of him in there is so weak.*

Why did you scream?

I didn't.

She had been winning. It must have frightened Leo. Frightened him enough to elicit the flickers of rage I could see as she turned the memories over in her mind. In our mind. It was beginning to feel more like one room owning two occupants than two rooms, and it ought to have frightened me more.

Don't worry, Miss Marius, it's a far greater loss for me than you, I feel. You are at least going up in the world.

I didn't deign a reply.

———————◆———————

"The man must kneel at the setting of the sun as he kneels at its rising, setting his knees and his feet and his hands upon the ground, along with his head and his heart."

Leo held the book easily, its cracked spine upon one hand. We had stopped for the day, and outside the tent the soldiers were busy with soldiery things, but here, out of the wind and the drizzle, he sat on a pile of cushions and leaned toward the lantern.

"And with head and heart connected through the ground and the air and the flesh, through the breath of God in—"

It had felt like I was sinking into a hot bath, but at the sudden cessation a chill shivered from head to toe, and I woke from my pleasant stupor. With a gasp, Leo pressed his hand to his head, leaving the book to fall open upon the ground.

Outside, the sounds of the camp continued unabated while he breathed full, deep, shuddering breaths and let the air go in a burst, only to suck more in. It wasn't the even rhythm of a man in pain, yet he kept his hand pressed to his head and hissed.

"Leo?"

"Read," he said through gritted teeth.

"What?"

"Read! Please." It was a desperate gasp, and he kicked the book toward me. He caught the corner, spinning it around, but it was all he had. Hands gripping his hair, he lay across the cushions and did not move again, the rise and fall of his chest all that proved life.

Seconds dragged by. Outside, the world went on.

"Please," he said, little more than a whisper.

I reached for the book, half expecting him to lunge and snatch it from my hands the moment I touched it, but he let me pull it toward me.

It was a nice copy, its leather cover indented with gold leaf, but its corners were scuffed and some of the gold had flaked away, its spine rubbed smooth with the touch of many hands. I opened it to the devotional lessons he had been reading, still expecting him to lash out at any moment.

"The man must kneel at the setting of the sun as he kneels at its rising," I read, hesitant though the words were well known to me. "Setting his knees and his feet and his hands upon the ground, along with his head and his heart."

I read on, and he lay and listened and his breathing eased.

"And with head and heart connected through the ground and the air and the flesh, through the breath of God..."

Grass tickled my face, and this time I felt more awake as I rose out of the dark sea of sleep. The droning voice remained. More distant. Not mine anymore, but the tone was the same and I rolled my head. Captain Aeneas knelt nearby, chanting his prayers. The sun was setting, lighting the sky in pink and orange.

"Do Kisians pray at specific times of the day?" I asked, to think of anything but the dream that wasn't a dream, not because the answer interested me.

If you don't care about the answer, we could talk about something else.

"Like how you came to marry Emperor Kin, despite the whole hidden upbringing on a farm thing?"

We pray whenever it is... seemly or convenient to pray.

"That's a terrible answer."

It's honest. We have long assured our people their emperor is their god, which meant diminishing the importance of all the other gods to be beneath the emperor. People uphold old traditions out of habit now, but rarely have the faith that once went with it.

"But that means you worship a man. Men are not worth worshipping, you know."

I know. Oh, trust me, I know.

"What about Katashi Otako? What was he like?"

Silence filled the joint space we shared in her head, but I could see flickers of a handsome man, his smile lopsided and a single dimple peeping mischievously beside it. Him sitting. Him riding. Him holding an enormous bow and hitting a target with three arrows, each one splitting the one before it. Oh, how he had laughed. How he had looked at me. How he had loved me.

My heart ached with a love I had never known. Never felt.

I made him a promise, that our son would sit on the throne when he was gone. And I failed. Tanaka was so like him. Whenever I was with him, I could almost believe my beloved Katashi walked again.

"You still have your daughter."

If she is alive. Yes. I ought not to have neglected her, but…grief is…a powerful force, Miss Marius, more powerful than love, I think. More maddening and destructive, and it does not go away. Not ever. Not really. There is always a memory preparing to ambush you when you least expect it, and just when you think the pain has lessened it is back as harsh and bright as ever. And when you're married to the man who destroyed the man you love, when you're married to a man who would do anything to see your son fail, it is impossible to move on. To let go. To change. I have made many mistakes, but they did not come from a place of malice, I hope you can see that. I hope at least you can see, you who has access to all of this in my head, can see I never meant things to go like this, never meant to weaken the empire or see it fail. I never meant to harm my daughter in uplifting my son.

Her words were desperate, seeking atonement, and I felt a raw, hot sense of pride that this woman, of all women, gave a shit what I thought of her.

Captain Aeneas went on with his droning prayer amid the gathering twilight, and I nodded, our hair catching on the grass. "I know," I murmured. "There is still time, you know."

Time? That's one thing we're fast running out of. Don't give me false hopes. Even if we found your body tomorrow, I don't think mine has long left.

"Has it ever felt this bad?"

Never.

Captain Aeneas bent his head to the grass and held the position for a few moments, before rising slowly to his feet. He threw a hand out to grip a nearby branch, steadying himself.

"The horse needed a rest," he said, indicating the animal munching on grass nearby. "I stole it," he added, answering a question I hadn't asked. "I have begged forgiveness, but there really wasn't another way we were getting out of there."

"How did we?"

"The element of surprise, I think. Having held on to Septum so long, I think they were shocked I'd let him go. Or maybe they only wanted him and don't give a damn about us. Either way..." He shrugged. "There has been no sign of them yet. And we have no Septum to give our position away, so I'm mildly hopeful."

"You shouldn't have done it."

He didn't insult both our intelligence by asking what I meant. "It was the only way."

"I am not important."

"It isn't about what is most important but about what is right."

I laughed, but it hurt. "Admit you had no choice and I'll at least admire your honesty."

His severe expression wavered on a weak smile, but he said nothing.

"Where are we going?"

Captain Aeneas rubbed the back of his head, looking away into the distance to where a dirt track vanished into the trees. "I thought about it while I was trying to find a way out with Septum. Where could I go? To whom? I no longer know which members of the church I can trust. Which Chiltaens I can trust. Dom Villius is sure to have followers even in Kisia, while I have no allies, am nothing but a soldier. Then I thought, who has the strongest interest in Leo not fulfilling his purpose? And who is strong enough, powerful enough, to make a difference?"

"We're going to Mei'lian." It was the empress who spoke, a jagged edge to her voice I doubted the captain would catch.

"Yes, whoever is emperor, or empress, of Kisia is the only person we can beg aid from now. And with you, Your Majesty, well…"

"Depending on who is sitting on the throne at this moment, my presence could be quite detrimental."

The captain grimaced. "Surely not after they hear what we have to say."

"Perhaps. But this is…quite a danger to bring to anyone, even an emperor."

Despite her worry, a bubble of excitement was building in my stomach. Mei'lian meant information. We could find out what had happened to Miko. Perhaps see her again. Help her. Keep our promise to Katashi. A child of our blood safely on the throne.

"It is an emperor's lot to deal with troubles." Captain Aeneas brushed the dirt from his knees. "Someone has to, if they want Kisia to survive."

"Why don't you support Leo? You're faithful to the church; don't you want what he is trying to achieve? Or is it…just because he's…" I left those words hanging rather than attempt to describe all Leo was. I had never thought myself monstrous despite my strange affinity for the dead, but him…It wasn't what he *was* that made him monstrous, but what he had chosen to do with it. All I had done with my ability was attempt to survive.

Captain Aeneas squatted beside me, his scarred face lined with fatigue. "You know how I said I believed he was trying to…remake Veld's empire?"

"Yes."

"Well, I have another reason for thinking it's important we reach whoever is sitting on the throne right now. Do you know any scripture, Your Majesty?"

"Very little," she replied through our lips.

"Then I will explain."

"I see you don't bother asking how much scripture *I* know, Captain," I said.

He had the grace to look sheepish, but he shrugged. "If I have to explain to Her Majesty anyway, it didn't seem important. Like I said before, I believe Leo is attempting to recreate the six deaths of Veld. He has already been struck down by the head of his family, and in a throne room while standing up for his people. I mentioned the cave, but while I don't know if he has done that yet—"

"He has."

The words came out of my mouth, but were not mine.

"Did you…?"

The captain left the question unfinished, his meaning clear. Empress Hana looked away. "I saw…memories. There was a lot of pain. It seems to have been one of the Levanti who did it. I think he was surprised, truthfully. I think he was expecting to have to orchestrate that one himself, and was thankful he had not already done so when it happened. It has him wondering whether…wondering whether he isn't orchestrating at all, but whether he really is Veld reborn, destined to live that cycle over again."

Captain Aeneas gave a little shiver despite the warmth of the day and the sheen of sweat on his brow. "That answers many questions, and only makes me more determined to reach Mei'lian as soon as possible. Because the next death, the one after the cave, is most commonly translated from the old language as being stabbed in the back by an empress."

Silence fell over our little patch of wilderness. Stabbed in the back by an empress. Literal or figurative? It didn't really matter in the end. "You think if we can get to Mei'lian and tell the empress *not* to do it…"

"He has a way of…manipulating people to do things they don't want to, but if he isn't allowed near her he can't make it happen."

"So if he is relying on hitting each of these deaths, we need to get to Mei'lian, or wherever the court is currently situated. We need to find my daughter and make sure she cannot be manipulated into anything that could lead to this outcome."

Captain Aeneas smiled. "So, do you think you can go on a bit farther tonight?"

"Yes. Let's get to Mei'lian as soon as we can."

We rode until there was no light left to see by. A fishing village on a tributary of the Tzitzi River offered a small inn, and we took it gratefully. Hot food. A sleeping mat. And the glorious anonymity of being no one in a chattering crowd. With a scarf around the empress's golden hair and shabby and tattered robes, I felt completely invisible.

I sank onto the floor before the table and leaned on it gratefully, chatter washing over me as completely as the scent of fish and wine and sour mushroom stew. It had been nearly twenty years since I'd left the Valley, since I'd last smelled that particular combination of scents, and the warmth of nostalgia filled me, tinged with grief for times passed.

Except you never lived in the Valley. We really need to get you back in your body soon.

It took me a confused moment to realise what she meant and to shake loose the belief I had lived her life. Panic sheared through me. I was losing myself. Was this how Kaysa had felt? But she had always been so determinedly herself, and in a way, we *had* shared every experience of our lives.

"Are you feeling more like me, or is it just…?"

No, I think it's just you. Perhaps souls meld to their host bodies.

"That makes sense." I didn't want to think about it, but it was hard not to wonder what it would be like when I no longer remembered who I was, who I had been. Would we even know there had been two souls here? Or would the empress forget me? Left with nothing but a tendency to swear more often.

I'm not sure I like the sound of that.

"Ha, well, I'm not sure I like the sound of being you forever. You're not exactly fun."

And you are?

"I'm lots of fun."

I doubt all the people you've killed would agree.

"No, but..."

But there was no one else. I had not seen my family since they sent me away. Had not had a friend since the Blessed Guards who'd taken pity on me at the hospice and taught me how to hurt people. Hadn't had anyone at all except for Mama Hera, and calling her either family or friend was laughable.

Empress Hana didn't laugh. *Friends are hard to make and harder to keep. It takes a degree of trust neither of us possesses.*

I was getting too tired to sit straight and lay my head upon my arm. Captain Aeneas hadn't yet returned with our food.

"I think perhaps you are my friend," I said, closing our tired eyes. "I've tried so hard to hate you because hating is easier."

Hating is so much easier, she agreed. *And you are easy to hate, Miss Marius, but...yes. I think I would be lying if I did not admit I feel the same. I would not have trusted you by choice, but we got stuck together, and you aren't half as bad as you think you are.*

I had no idea what to say, had no experience in...being myself in such a situation, but the Cassandra Marius I had put on every day like a protective skin seemed to have been left behind somewhere along the way.

"Thank you?"

She laughed. *You are terrible at this. Thankfully it looks like the good captain has procured wine because we both need it.*

Captain Aeneas was winding his way across the floor between other tables, the small tray in his hands bearing two bowls of broth and a flagon of wine. No meal made in a palace kitchen could have looked more appetising.

"Sorry for the wait," he said, setting the tray down. "I got to talking to the man who runs this place. Very full of news he was when I said we'd come from the Valley and wanted the local gossip."

He settled himself opposite, kneeling easily on the sticky wooden floor. He poured out a bowl of wine and offered it to us, before pouring another for himself. We took the bowl, desperate to burn away the taste of those strange words of friendship.

Having taken a gulp of his own, the captain continued. "He says the Levanti hold the north still, and not too much information is coming from that way. But he says *Empress Miko Ts'ai* was at Achoi, just south of the capital, not so long since."

"Achoi? But why there?" the empress asked, masking an excited shiver at the sound of her daughter's name. She was alive. She was the empress. There was still time.

"To take back Mei'lian, I think. The story gets a little involved, and none of the locals could agree on the details of who did what, but it seems that boy who was calling himself Emperor Kin's son is dead, and the city—"

He stopped abruptly, the smile that had dawned at the good news fading away.

"The city?" Hana prompted with something like her old iciness.

"It's gone. Burned to the ground."

"Gone? The whole thing? The whole city? What of the palace and the houses and the market squares and—"

"I only have gossip to go on, Majesty," he said, lowering his voice. "But it was one of the few points these men were in agreement about. The whole city. Every last house. Gone."

The empress reeled, and though I was sure Captain Aeneas went on speaking, we heard nothing, saw nothing but a parade of places and people and events, everything from the gardens in the palace to the silk market, to the shrine at Imperial Square. Gone. How could it all be gone? How could it all have burned? Even the palace? The Crimson Throne? The imperial graveyard. I had farewelled Katashi there.

"I'm sorry," she said eventually, putting a hand to our thumping temple. "I...What were you saying, I...did not hear."

She was still listening to the memory of chattering crowds and music coming from the teahouse across from a particularly fine maker of northern sweetbreads. A crier had stood on the nearby corner, coins clinking into his purse as people stopped to tip him for his work.

"I said I was sorry for the bad news," the captain said. "It is extremely unfortunate, and I know—"

"Unfortunate? That would be accidentally tipping out a basket of eggs. This is a city, Captain, a—"

She stopped as tears pricked our eyes and choked our throat. There were no words strong enough to give voice to the depth of this new grief.

"Where is the empress? Where is my daughter?"

"They weren't sure." He grimaced. "Only that she was at Achoi with her army. I feel sure if we head that way, we may be able to find out."

I nodded, conflicting emotions both oceans deep making my heart ache. The whole city gone. But Miko was safe. Not just safe but...thriving, it seemed, getting on with the business of ruling despite how little Kisia now looked like the Kisia she had known, the Kisia I ought to have left her.

More grief sat inside that raw wound, but I would not examine it, could not. Too many emotions already filled me, each weighing more than I could carry. Enough she was well, for now. Enough there was hope I would see her again.

We ate our soup in silence and drank our wine in deeper silence still, Captain Aeneas seeming to be flagging at last. He had so often appeared an unstoppable force, a man who did not know when to give up, did not even acknowledge the need to lie down and rest. I had watched it ravage his face, bit by bit, but now, perhaps feeling safe for the first time since I had found him sheltering in that little shed with Septum, his eyes were drooping.

"Thank you, Captain," the empress said when the meal was eaten and the evening had worn on around us. "Thank you for... not leaving us behind."

His brows rose, but he covered his surprise with a little bow over the table. "You're welcome, Majesty. Septum was important, I'm sure of it, but together you and I can make sure Dom Villius doesn't achieve his ends regardless. Will you sleep now? I find myself quite done in."

"What a lovely understatement. I may have to request the support of your arm up the stairs. One last service before you retire to your well-earned rest."

"Of course."

———————————————✦———————————————

We rose before the sun and were gone from the town by the time it was waking, fishermen heading to the river in the half-light as we rode out along the narrow road. East. East to Miko. East to the future.

I look forward to hearing how you explain my presence to your daughter, I said as Captain Aeneas sped the horse to a canter. He had pushed it hard the previous day, and likely we would not get as much out of it today, but an early burst of speed would brighten the mood.

No doubt you will think of the crassest thing possible to say, she replied. *Just to punish me.*

We were once more sitting before Captain Aeneas on the horse, his arms reaching around us to the reins, forming a protective cocoon. Against our back his warmth radiated, and the steady thump of his heart and the gust of his breath in our hair was comforting. All the tiny signs he was alive and present.

Crassest thing? Did you know, if you kill a man when he's hard it stays that way for a while, I said.

That is certainly . . . enlightening.

It can leak too.

I think you have made your point now.

If you were brought up on a farm, surely you haven't always been this stuck-up.

Well, fuck you very much indeed, Miss Marius. If only Mama Orde could hear you say so; she was my foster mother, you know, and a very proper woman. The tutors Lord Laroth hired for me all bemoaned my lack of grace and sensibility. I was a vulgar girl who spent too much time climbing trees and kissing the field boys.

A boy with a face made amorphous by time leaned to kiss me as though afraid of getting too close with his body. Almost immediately he was gone, replaced by Katashi Otako. Strong, handsome, gentle Katashi. The weight of his body. The lines he traced across our skin with his tongue. I had pleasured many a man in my time, but even a glimpse of what she'd had with him made me yearn in ways I hadn't known I could. I remembered pressing myself up against him, remembered asking him to touch me, to kiss me, to take me. It took the sharp pierce of grief to remind me I'd never met him, that it hadn't been me at all.

Perhaps you'll agree stuck-up *is hardly the right word.*

Were you really fucking everyone at court?

And I thought you had already reached the heights of crassness with your previous utterances. What a question.

Call me curious, I said. And we're running out of time, I thought to myself, or maybe to her, I couldn't tell anymore. Could only tell the lassitude consuming us had nothing to do with the gentle sway of the horse, or the sun that had barely started to rise on a chilly morning.

No, she said. *I was not. I considered it numerous times, as a way to build alliances, but...I had made that choice once and slowly broken that man's heart. I didn't want to risk doing so again.*

Before I could ask who she meant, Captain Aeneas turned the horse off the road. A stand of drooping willows stood in the damp ground this side of the track, and he wound our mount through the hanging fronds toward a small clearing.

"Where are we going?"

"Just here. The sun's almost up and I must pray."

It had been years since I had given up anything but the occasional pretence at prayer. I had gone through the motions for any clients who had expected it of me, but of my own volition I hadn't knelt to make faith with the rising and setting sun since leaving the hospice. Even so, I felt a strange tug to join the captain as he slid from the saddle.

As soon as his feet met the ground, he turned to help us down. He showed no sign he expected us to join him, instead helping us to the base of a tree where the strength in our legs gave out and we slumped back, the trunk not as warm as the captain's chest but as strong and reliable.

Eyes closed, we listened to his footsteps move away through the grass, willow fronds swishing. His murmuring voice soon added to the music of the morning.

"He's a...surprisingly good man," I said.

He is. Something I find I am coming to appreciate more and more in my old age. Or perhaps it's just the gratitude speaking. In this state we couldn't make it to Achoi without him.

"Old age," I scoffed. "I'm older than you."

Then your existence in my head surely increases the average age of my thoughts, yes?

"I'm not sure brains work like that. But I can tell you like him."

We like him. We like his goodness. What a shock that is after all the people I have thrown my heart at over the years.

"And all the people I haven't."

Flickers of sunlight began to light the inside of my eyelids. Birds were dancing through the willow thicket, singing their morning song along with the captain's prayers, and in the distance the rush of the Tzitzi was comforting.

Grass rustled. A light tread approached. I opened my eyes to greet the captain's return even as I caught the sound of his voice still droning on.

Leo crouched before me, his smile that of an old friend. "Good morning," he said, his tone pleasant. "How lovely it is to see you, Your Majesty."

Captain Aeneas still knelt some way off, his head bowed. A soldier stood mere paces away from him, his presence halting the cry of warning in my throat. If I spoke, he would be dead before he could rise from his prayer and draw his sword. Perhaps it was only me Leo wanted.

"You are very selfless," Leo said, keeping his voice low. "A shock really when I know you have Miss Marius in there with you."

His words stung as I had not thought they would.

"You think your sacrifice can spare him?" he went on. "He knows quite as much as you do, information I cannot allow the world to know. I am sure you understand."

"What do you want?"

"To control the information," he said. "To control my image. Image is everything in the business of belief." Behind him more dark shapes moved beyond the willow fronds. Captain Aeneas murmured on, and I tried to recall how long the standard morning prayer went.

"Usually for about seven minutes and twenty-five seconds unless one speaks it very slow or very fast," Leo said. "But I know the captain for a very pious man who often adds an extra prayer on the end and occasionally a personal word or two. So, we probably have about three more minutes before he stands up."

"Are you going to kill us?"

"Oh no, not yet."

He wanted us alive. I reached for my knife. His closest soldier was far enough away and—

The point of a dagger touched my throat. "Oh no, no, no," he said, smile vanishing. "Don't try anything like that. You aren't *that* useful. Why don't you give me the knife so we don't have to risk a scene?"

Captain Aeneas had stopped his murmur. In a moment he would dip his head to the ground and rise, and our time would be up. Would he even get the chance to fight? Would it matter? Perhaps it would be better if he didn't, better if we both just gave ourselves up and hoped to fight another day. We were outnumbered.

But we had been going to see Miko.

Heedless of our safety, the empress lifted her foot into the groin of the man crouched before us, and when his blade dropped from our throat, she kicked him again. And despite his pretence at godhood, he was man enough to gasp and wince and whiten and fall down on one knee in a moment of blinding pain.

We ripped free our dagger. He had turned as he crumpled, displaying the expanse of his back. I lifted the dagger in my weak arm and—

No! No, we cannot. Stabbed in the back by an empress, remember?
Whatever the technicality, everyone still calls you an empress.

I fumbled, the handle slipping through my grip even as Leo roared and spun back, all pain and anger and determination not to die, not to fail. It turned him from the mild-mannered man of God into a hissing, spitting animal, and he gripped my wrists so hard I was sure the weak bones would snap.

"Oh, you think you know so much," he said, forcing a laugh through his lingering pain. "You think you can stop me?" Eyes wild, he twisted my arms and I cried out, too weak to fight him, to do anything more than wriggle and kick, and I hated how little power I had. How little strength.

Captain Aeneas must have heard us for he was up now, two shocked steps having brought him close before he reached for his sword. An arm snaked around him from behind, and in a flick of silver a blade slid across his throat. Blood blossomed from nothing, spilling down his neck and onto the collar of his plain tunic. He stared at me as his blood ran out, his eyes wide and his lips slightly parted. The arm let him go and he stumbled forward. His blade fell heavy upon the ground and his knees followed, seeming to shake the world beneath me. But even as my lips parted to speak, to beg, to apologise, to say something, anything, the light faded from his eyes and he fell forward, his head almost within reach, his hair sticking up like pale blades of grass in an otherwise green glade.

The river went on rushing by. The birds went on singing. The willow fronds danced. And before me Leo was smiling again. "Well, that's one problem solved," he said, letting me go and sitting back.

"You said you wouldn't kill us." My voice was a quiet, broken thing. I could not stop staring at the back of Captain Aeneas's head. Only moments before we had been musing on how lucky we had been, how much better the world was with a good man in it trying to do the right thing.

"Oh, that I wouldn't kill either of you two." No apology, nothing but a broadening of his smile. "He wasn't very useful."

"You mean his faith was too strong to be corrupted?" I spat.

His smile broadened like a wolf's. "Ah, I missed your bite, Cassandra. I look forward to hearing much more of it."

He stood, and I wished I could kick his knees out from beneath him, but my legs were too weak. I wished I could strangle him, but my hands were stiff and trembling. I wished I could ram my fist into his gut and steal his blade, slicing his throat and jamming the tip into his eye, but every joint was a searing pain and I could not move.

"Poor, pathetic Cassandra." Leo looked to the closest soldier. "Bind her up and bring her. Leave the captain for the birds."

15. MIKO

Syan ought to have been easy to hold once we took the castle, but we had not accounted for the city's governor. Messages had gone out to every authority informing them I was in possession of Kiyoshio and had taken the place of their lord, and even General Moto had expected little fight. The arrival of the first message left him staring.

"Governor Koali has written back, Your Majesty," he said, not lifting his gaze from the paper in his hand. "He seems...disinclined to accept your position here."

He had been briefing me on the overnight situation when the messenger arrived. "He says while he acknowledges you to be in possession of the castle, he cannot acknowledge you as his lord and so requests that you remove yourself from his city."

General Moto's hand dropped, and he stared at me as though expecting me to tell him it was a hoax, so ludicrously did his jaw hang open.

"His city?" he said when I made no answer, my heart beating too fast to speak. "*His* city. You would think Grace Bahain didn't exist. Or that he's never heard of the right of conquest."

The general noticed the messenger was still present and flapped the missive at him. "Why are you still here? Did he request an immediate reply?"

"No, my lord. I... I was also asked by the captain at the gate to inform you and... and Her Majesty that there are people outside." He trailed off into a mumble under General Moto's stare.

"People? What sort of people?"

"Angry people. I... I understand they are city folk who have gathered at the gate to shout and... and throw things, my lord."

I had been picking at breakfast when General Moto arrived, and now I pushed the tray away, sure I was about to be sick. Taking Kiyoshio ought to have been a smart play, striking at Grace Bahain's home to draw him out only to crush him between two halves of my army, but with our timing out and the loss of so many at the Knot, we were vulnerable, trapped animals at the edge of the world. And without the city on my side, we couldn't keep Bahain out.

"Thank you, you may go," General Moto said, and the man bowed three times before hurrying away at the same speed he had arrived.

In his absence, the general read the message again as though it might contain different words.

"More trouble," I said, prompting disclosure though I felt ill. "What are your thoughts?"

"My thoughts are full of more bad language than my wife would ever countenance me uttering aloud, Your Majesty, but they paraphrase as this being a big problem. We don't have enough soldiers to take the city by force. But if we don't have the city, we can't defend ourselves. The first defence of Kiyoshio Castle is the Syan city gates."

"Gates they could open for Grace Bahain if they wished?"

"Indeed. Perhaps if Minister Manshin gets here in time we could take the city with the combined force and—"

"No."

General Moto clasped his hands behind his back and straightened. "No, Your Majesty?"

"No, whatever their allegiance these are still my people, and I will not have my soldiers kill innocent civilians to take over a city."

"We're at war."

"But I am not at war with my people. I am at war with Grace Bahain and all the other Kisians who have sworn oaths to a false Levanti emperor. I am at war with the Chiltaens who marched across our border and conquered the north of my empire. I am at war with everything that threatens Kisian lives, but never with Kisia. An emperor serves his people. The day the people serve the emperor is the day the empire falls."

They were Emperor Kin's words, one of the lessons I had held close as I tried to navigate the turbulent waters of this war, and while General Moto gave no sign of recognising them, at least he bowed his acquiescence. "Then we had better write a very convincing reply to get Governor Koali on our side."

"Ought I meet with him?"

"I don't think that's wise, Your Majesty. It would be both dangerous and demeaning for you to go to him, and in bringing him here we would be exposing how few soldiers we actually have. We will write back."

It took a long time to compose a suitable reply, stating the rights of conquest and the authority I had as empress of Kisia, invoking Emperor Kin's name where possible and closing out with a recommendation that he make peace with the change as Syan had prospered under his governorship and it would be a pity to have to replace him.

For the rest of the day I entertained myself imagining his grovelling capitulation, but when a reply eventually came General Moto looked even more grim. "It says, 'Kiyoshio Accords paragraph six, line two.' And was delivered with this scroll." He held it out. "I took the liberty of reading the part in question, and well, I think we can blame years of pirate raids for this."

I found the line.

Where the Master of Kiyoshio Castle does not hold the title of duke as bestowed upon them by an envowed Emperor of Kisia, that Master has no authority over the city or any of its inhabitants and will be treated as an invader.

"We aren't going to get him," I said, dropping the scroll on the windowsill. The distant lights of people holding torches outside the gates went on bobbing around like a swarm of fireflies. "Beyond keeping the city gate open, can he harm us here?"

"Not directly. He has his own personal guards along with those who protect the city, but it's not enough to go up against our defences. The danger is not immediate, but if you don't get Governor Koali on your side soon, a protracted siege will be the best possible outcome."

"Fascinating how it changes from being our problem to being my problem as soon as there's trouble."

He drew himself up and tucked his hands behind his back as he always did when defensive or annoyed. "A mere figure of speech, Your Majesty. This is naturally everyone's problem."

Despite his assurance, I lay awake long into the night, thoughts bouncing from Governor Koali to the absent Minister Manshin to the crowd outside the gates and inevitably back to the staring dead face of Captain Soku. I couldn't rid myself of the fear General Moto wanted me gone, and only the knowledge that General Ryoji himself stood outside my door allowed me eventually to sleep.

Like a morbid rooster, General Moto once again heralded the morning by reading the messages that had arrived in the night and discussing plans for the day. I stared at my uneaten food and listened, a heavy sense of hopelessness weighing upon me.

"There has been no further communication from Governor

Koali," he said, seeming to be running through a mental list with his customary way of blurting information. "It may be best to consider another missive. Or perhaps it is time to risk sending for him to meet in person, if we—"

A soldier hurried in. "There you are, General! Your Majesty!"

"What is it, man?" Moto asked, annoyed.

"It's...he's..." The soldier gasped a breath. "At the gate...just arrived..."

My heart stopped on the words, sure now it had all been for nothing. Bahain was at the gates. Governor Koali would let him in and we would all be dead by tomorrow.

"Who is at the gates?"

The soldier let out a long breath. "Minister Manshin. And some Levanti."

"What?" I said. "Captured Levanti?"

"I...don't think so, Your Majesty. Some of them look injured, but for the most part they look...friendly. No, not friendly, but not a threat. They seem to be here by choice, with the minister."

"How many?"

"A hundred and forty or fifty? Maybe more, it's hard to tell, Your Majesty, I'm sorry."

I leapt up, straightening my sash and surcoat. "Where's Manshin?"

"I don't know, Your Majesty," he said, following me out into the passage. "They had only just given the order to open the gates when I came running, so he may still be in the courtyard or..."

"Did you make sure they put down their weapons before allowing them inside?" General Moto demanded, keeping pace more easily than the younger man despite the thickness of his figure.

"Yes, General. The one that can translate relayed the request. They didn't seem pleased, but when the one with the big bone crown and the injured man put theirs down, no one argued."

"Bone crown?" I said. "Did the translator give his name?"

"Tor, I believe, Your Majesty."

My breath caught in my throat and I hurried on, as fast as I could without breaking into a run—something my mother would never have done. People wait for empresses, she would have said; be an empress. With the general following, I sped down the stairs, only slowing to a proper walk as I descended into the entry hall. None of the torches were lit, but the room was full of light and people, and I tried to remember to breathe as I hunted the gathering for—

I pulled in a breath and held it, my heart thumping. Rah. There. Alive, clearly injured and changed in the short time since we had parted, but alive. Since the fire at Mei'lian I had feared the worst, and my legs trembled with relief as I let go that secret dread. It had been a long few days, and I just wanted to sit down and spill tears, to let the fear and the gratitude, the sorrow and the excitement drain out. But I was an empress. I could no sooner do that than I could run down there and throw my arms around him despite the promptings of my joy.

I swallowed a manic little laugh as they all looked up, one after the other. Rah had been speaking to Tor and was one of the last, but the smile that lit his bruised features had the same effect on me as a dozen bowls of wine. I'd have had to bite my own lips off to keep a smile from spreading them, however briefly.

"You stand now before Her Imperial Majesty," General Moto intoned from behind me. "Empress Miko Ts'ai, first of her name, Lord—" He faltered just a moment. There had never been an empress who ruled in her own right before. "—*Lord* Protector of the Kisian Empire."

I had not wished to be announced so grandly, yet the proclamation steadied me as nothing else could, returning my thoughts back to the ceremony of the imperial court. I might have railed against the stiff etiquette in which my mother had schooled me, might have slipped away to spend every moment filling targets with arrows, but the imperial ways still lived in my blood, its habits hard to shake.

Drawing myself up, I sailed down the stairs as my mother might once have done, halting on the third step from the bottom, which she would have insisted on, and stood a proud statue before the Levanti, gaze deliberately skipping over Rah as I swept the gathered warriors.

I turned toward Tor, the only one I knew for sure would understand me. His jaw set and he met my gaze with defiance. No doubt he was thinking of the last time he had been in this castle. "Tor e'Torin," I said. "Introduce your companions to me."

The young man stepped forward, pushing loose strands of wet hair off his face. "Yes... Your Majesty." There was a note of gritted teeth in his reply, but he turned to the tall woman in the centre of the group, a crown of bones atop her head. She had the presence and appearance of a queen, yet what little I knew of the Levanti had led me to believe they had no such thing. "This is Horse Whisperer Ezma e'Topi." He gestured to the man beside her. "And Derkka en'Injit, her apprentice. Rah e'Torin you already know, and—"

"And which of them speaks for you?"

Tor opened his mouth and closed it again, looking from the tall woman to Rah and back at me, every eye on him, every ear waiting.

Shit, I thought as no answer came. *They aren't united.* That was a problem. Had they all been united behind Rah I would have felt more sure of them, but nothing was ever easy.

General Moto cleared his throat, and seeming to realise he had gone too long without answering, Tor said, "The Levanti do not follow a single ruler as you do. Some of us wish to fight, and some of us wish to go home. For the purposes of discussion, however, you should perhaps address yourself to Whisperer Ezma."

General Moto touched my elbow and I turned my head enough to catch his low whisper. "Offer them sanctuary here for now. We need time to discuss what to do with them."

What to do with them. I bristled at the implication they were things to be used, but his words were wise all the same. We didn't know their intentions.

I needed to talk to Rah.

"My soldiers will help you find stables for your horses. And sleeping quarters," I said. "While we are safe here, you are safe with us."

Tor passed the message on, and relief rippled through the gathered Levanti. They began to move about, heading for the doors, low talk spreading. Rah's gaze was on me, but I couldn't risk looking at him again and was grateful for the appearance of Minister Manshin stalking across the hall.

"Your Majesty," he said with a bow. "Congratulations on your conquest."

"If we can hold it. Any news of Bahain?"

"He is a day behind us. Maybe two."

"And Oyamada?"

Minister Manshin shook his head. "I sent messengers, but I doubt they will reach him in time. With the supplies and the foot soldiers, he would be travelling much slower than either of us. He may only have reached Shimai by now."

General Moto cleared his throat. "Well then, if you don't have a whole extra battalion or two out there, Minister, we may be in trouble."

"We may be in trouble."

"Maybe," I said, watching the Levanti milling around the doors. "Tell me, Minister. How many soldiers is each Levanti worth in the saddle, do you think? You may have brought with you quite the army after all, so long as we can get them to fight for us."

The Levanti refused proper rooms in the upper castle, instead making their own dormitory spaces in the outbuildings around the stable yard. I didn't like it, but it created separation between them and the Kisian soldiers filling the guardhouses and barracks, and that was for the best.

I found Rah sitting in the stable yard, basking in what was left of the day's meagre sunshine while a Kisian physician checked a wound on his leg. Tor was with him, providing the necessary translation.

As I crossed the yard, eyes swivelled to stare, and I regretted the impulse of coming in search of Rah amongst his own people. At the growing hush, he looked up. Our eyes met. And though I felt an almost overwhelming urge to look away from so direct a gaze, he showed no sign of discomfort, just watched me approach with a guarded look made fierce by the bruises fading on his face. Beside him, Tor seemed to find the mud-streaked stone safer to look at.

Heart thumping like a war drum, I stopped beside the physician. My guards' boots scuffed as they halted behind me. Rah's steady gaze hadn't shifted.

The physician looked up. "If you don't mind, you're in my li— Oh, Your Majesty. I'm sorry, I did not realise it was you, I—"

"Even an empress is capable of blocking the light." I stepped to the left, making Rah turn his head to keep me in his line of sight. "Is that better?"

"Y-yes, thank you, Your Majesty. I will soon be done. These are unpleasant wounds, but they have been surprisingly well cared for."

Tor grunted, and I met his scowl with an apologetic little grimace, which only made him look away again, seeming to hate the very sight of my face.

"Rah," I said, finally facing the reason I had come. "It's good to see you again."

He lifted his fists and pressed them together in the Levanti sign of respect. "Empress Miko."

Tor had not translated. Many times I had imagined being reunited, wondering how Rah would look and what he would say, forgetting that however well we had come to understand each other in gestures and simple words, for any conversation more nuanced we needed Tor. It was daunting, especially with so many people watching. I could not mime anything, or butcher Levanti words in an attempt to remember things he had taught me. I had to be dignified and proud, and I began to wish I had not come at all.

I turned to Tor. "Tor e'Torin," I said. "I would greatly appreciate if you could translate for us."

"Fine."

I could have stared him down for so disrespectful a reply, but I knew as well as he did just how much I needed him. "Thank you. Let him know I am happy to see him again and ask how his wounds fare."

I ignored the roll of his eyes and watched Rah's features as Tor passed my words along in Levanti.

"He says it is also good to see you, Your Majesty," Tor said. "He feared for you when you parted. His wounds will soon heal."

Relief warmed me. Whether at the knowledge he had cared what happened to me, or that his wounds would not long keep him from being able to fight, I wasn't sure. It was a mercenary thought, but I was running out of options.

"I am glad to hear that," I said, hating such stiff formality. I had sat naked in a bathhouse with this man, had shared meagre meals and a single sleeping mat, but here we were, empress and warrior, and all too many eyes were watching. I cleared my throat, hoping to loosen some of my awkwardness. "I understand you were of some help to my minister on the way here. Might I enquire where you were going when you ran into him?"

I wished the question unasked as soon as I spoke it. It didn't sound like something a curious friend would ask but rather a suspicious interrogation. Tor made that little frown of his.

"As he helped us," was Rah's reply through Tor's lips. "We weren't going anywhere. We were... undecided as to our next steps when we came across your soldiers and our people near the shrine. But I am sure Minister Manshin has already told you what happened."

He had, but I hadn't been able to make much sense of it. That Rah hadn't been travelling with either group of Levanti was clear, but why not? And why had he offered his help? And why had two angry factions of Levanti listened to him? Manshin had shrugged when I asked, all too willing to put it down to the unknowable Levanti culture.

The physician shuffled back and stood. "All good for now, but it will need new bandages tonight. And tomorrow it should be left to air if possible." He spoke to Tor as though he were Rah's keeper.

"Thank you," Tor said, showing the physician more respect than he showed me. Stiff, reluctant respect, but respect all the same.

"Anytime; I take my profession very seriously." He bowed to me. "Your Majesty. With your permission, I will move on."

"Indeed, thank you."

Another bow and he was gone, leaving me standing awkwardly to Rah's side like I had attempted to creep up on him and been caught in the act. I looked around at our audience. Most were Levanti, and not many were close enough to hear what was being said, but the interest with which they surveyed me was troubling. Could nothing ever just be simple?

"Your people," I said, gesturing around at the gathered Levanti. "What is it they want here?"

"The answer would change depending on who you asked," Tor said, answering the question himself. "As I said before, the Levanti have never been a united people. We follow our herds."

"But now your herds are divided? You are both Torin, but how many of these men and women are Torin too?"

"About three, Your Majesty."

Rah tilted his head, the look of a man trying to understand.

"The largest number of any one herd here are the Bedjuti," Tor went on. "But they only make up maybe a quarter of our total numbers, the rest a combination of Swords from all different herds."

Somewhat emboldened by the fact no one watching could understand our conversation, I said, "And how many of them follow Rah?"

"Right now? None. He hasn't put himself forward."

"And if he did?"

"If he chooses to fight for you?" Tor folded his arms. "There are some here who are angry and want to attack Gideon. There are some who want to liberate the Levanti they see as being forced to fight for him. There are some who are just following Ezma because she's a horse whisperer and they don't know what else to do. Some just want to go home. If Rah makes a stand he might get half of them. Maybe more. Maybe less. I don't know. He is well respected, but Ezma is a horse whisperer."

"You don't know?"

"Levanti don't pick sides until forced to do so."

"A fine luxury."

He gave me a look brimming with disdain. "Hardly. It's necessary for survival. People who pick sides too early tend to make poor choices. They also make factions and divisions, and those factions and divisions make internal wars, internal wars that no herd can sustain. We don't have the resources for ideology."

Although he had said nothing insulting about my people, his ongoing disdain made the information more like an attack, and I bristled. "Is that a jab at the way my people deal with conflicts, Tor e'Torin?"

"No, but if you must make this about you then by all means take it as criticism. From what I've learned about both Chiltae and Kisia, internal divisions are the reason for almost all your problems."

I wished I could slap him, but gods damn the man he was right. Whatever his reasons for disliking me so much, he had not attacked me with baseless insults, and somehow that was worse.

"I thank you for your honesty," I said, forcing a smile I was far from feeling.

"Better you understand what you're asking of him before you ask it."

Rah looked from me to Tor and back, frowning, and I realised I was glad he couldn't understand what we had been saying. Whatever my need for soldiers, I was happy to see him for himself. I had told myself I wasn't going to see him again, and hadn't realised how much I had been hoping it was untrue.

Despite all the things I needed to say as an empress, right now I needed to be Miko more. Nodding to Tor, I said, "Thank you, you may leave us. Rah." I gestured away across the yard. "Are you able to walk with me?"

Rah nodded and got carefully to his feet.

I was a tall woman, a tall Kisian, but I had forgotten just how completely the Levanti towered over us. Tor only had an inch or two on me, but Rah was half a head taller, and he wasn't the tallest. I looked up to his face as he joined me, only to look away in confusion, my cheeks growing hot. It was the serious, intent look he always had, seeming to both consider me and look right into my soul at the same time.

With my two guards trailing at a discreet distance, I set off across the courtyard at a slow enough pace I hoped Rah would not struggle. He made no complaint, and I was reminded how indefatigable he had been on our seemingly endless walk across southern Kisia in the rain. It had been daunting and uncomfortable, tiring and depressing, and I had feared all the way that I would never find allies again, that I had lost, but with him there, every day had been a little brighter. A little easier.

Having no idea what I wanted to say or what he would understand, I said nothing. Until the silence became uncomfortable and I glanced up, catching a smile. "Hello," I said in Levanti, just as he had taught me around one of many meagre campfires.

The first smile had been encouraging, but the next lit the day. His eyes crinkled at the edges and he breathed a half laugh, his whole being more alive in that moment than I had ever seen him. "Hello," he returned, his Kisian accent far better than my Levanti. "How are you?"

Had I taught him that? I didn't think so, yet he'd picked it up all the same. "Good. Well. You?" I said.

He shrugged and gestured at his various wounds, but despite them he smiled and said, "Good," as I had done, following it up with another shrug and some Levanti I didn't understand.

I tried to think through all the words he had taught me, but short of listing unconnected terms like *fire* and *rain*, I had nothing. So I spoke in Kisian and hoped he would understand the sentiment, if not my actual words.

"Thank you for rescuing Minister Manshin," I said. "He came just when I needed him most and...helped." Oh, to be able to tell him all about Jie. Would he think me monstrous for having killed a child? Surely he would. It had been him or me, yet whatever my excuses, Jie had been a child and I was not. A moment then to be thankful he couldn't understand me.

I stopped walking and turned to him, and knowing myself free from anyone who would overhear us, free even from being understood by the man before me, I found I could speak more honestly than I had for a long time. Perhaps ever.

"I've missed you, you know," I said, looking up into his face, his smile fading into its usual serious concentration. "Missed the sight of you always there, missed the sound of your voice and the comfort of... not being alone when I ought to have felt more alone than ever. I say... I say Minister Manshin helped me when I needed it most, but I would not have even been there, perhaps not even been alive, if not for you. You saved me." He tilted his head, and I reddened and looked away, fearing his judgement on my feelings. "Shishi and I owe you a great debt."

"Shishi?" His face brightened as he latched on to a familiar word and looked around the courtyard.

"Oh, she's not with me, I couldn't bring her on the ship, you see..." Despite that truth, danger felt like a foolish reason to have left her behind after everything we had been through together. "She is with Minister Oyamada. But if all goes well..." I couldn't finish that thought. Too great were the chances it would not go well at all.

Turning away, Rah beckoned me to follow, and I caught up as my guards parted to let him through. Hurrying after him was hardly the action of an empress, but his aura of excitement had overcome my need for dignity.

The mixture of discomfort and excitement warred within me all the way to one of the smaller stables. No Levanti bustled here, and it took me a moment to realise it was because this stable was full of Kisian horses. There would be a man somewhere whose job it was to look after them, probably a few stable boys, but for the most part Kisians were happy to let their servants look after their animals. Without Bahain, no one was paying them much heed.

Except there was one Levanti horse, and at sight of him I hurried toward his stall. "Jinso!"

I rushed in, genuinely pleased to see him. On that first journey to Syan, his great size and strength had helped me feel less like a weak, frightened girl stubbornly running from inevitability.

Jinso lowered his head and nuzzled me as I drew close, giving me such joy to have been remembered that I turned to Rah. My heart surely stopped at the intent look on his face. It made my breath come in shortened gasps, and the hand on Jinso's neck felt fuzzily like it didn't belong to me anymore.

We were alone but for Jinso, together in this confined space as we had been in the bathhouse, and as he had stared at me then he stared at me now, and I realised he was never going to move. Whether it was his sense of honour or respect or something deeper and more cultural, he was never going to kiss me if I did not kiss him.

The realisation was both paralysing and thrilling. The power was mine, but if I was not brave enough to use it, nothing would ever happen.

The moment of indecision, of heavy-footed fear, seemed to stretch painfully long, but Rah just stood and watched me. Heat filled my body. I licked my lips, and letting my hand fall from Jinso's neck, I took a step closer. Too small a step, but Rah did not run, did not retreat, did nothing but watch me with far more calm than I could ever imagine feeling.

One more step. Just one more. It was like dragging my feet through mud. Time seemed to have stopped, but there were his lips and his face and the warmth of his body and—

I took the final step, close enough that our clothes brushed against each other, close enough that he had to look down at me as I had to look up, that our fingers could have entwined if I shifted my hands. Instead I lifted them and set them upon his chest— gods, were they really shaking so badly? I hoped he wouldn't notice, would just feel the weight of them as I felt his firm muscles, and in a daze, I stretched onto my toes.

At the touch of his soft, warm lips I couldn't think, couldn't move, every part of me ceasing to function. There was just him and me and nothing else. And he had not pulled away. Not flinched.

His hands pressed into the small of my back, sending a thrill not only of touch but of triumph shivering through me. I leant into him, wanting to be as close as I could get and give permission the only way I could.

"Majesty?"

I stepped back, wiping my mouth with my hand, face burning. I couldn't look at Rah, only rage at the destruction of our moment and seethe with shame, sure Minister Manshin knew well what he had interrupted, and if not, that he would see the kiss upon my lips like it had been painted there in brightest red.

He stood in the doorway, blocking the light, silent a moment upon the threshold before he stepped in. Outside, my guards' shadows shifted their weight.

"Your Majesty," Manshin said, turning his shoulder on Rah and addressing me alone. "Governor Koali is here."

"What?" I had expected anything but that and was stunned out of my embarrassment enough to add, "Where? What does he want?"

"I couldn't say, Your Majesty. He's been shown into the Cavern to await you." He glanced at Rah and back to me. "You should come at once."

I hated I could not meet the hard look in my minister's eyes, like I was a child he had chanced upon in mischief. "Of course," I said with as much stiff pride as I could muster, and nodding to Rah like he was no one, like I could not still taste him on my lips, I followed Minister Manshin out into the harsh daylight of a real world where I was an empress and Rah a warrior from a far-off land.

Minister Manshin said nothing as we crossed the courtyard, my guards falling in behind us. I couldn't decide if I was more glad he sought no explanation or bothered by the judgement in his silence. All the way up the long castle stairs without a word, only to break the silence as we entered the main hall.

"You need to be more careful," he said then. "It does your image no good to be seen...fraternising with a barbarian. You are Kisia's empress, not a common whore."

Had he said just the first part I could have agreed. I had been too open, too caught up in seeing Rah again to consider what it would look like going alone into the stables with him, but the second part brought my hackles up. "I have done nothing to make anyone think I have sold myself."

"I am merely representing to you that your behaviour was far from virtuous or circumspect. You cannot risk rumours of a Levanti lover if you wish to stand against a Levanti emperor."

My cheeks heated, and I was glad he had at least waited until we were inside to speak.

"I must most strongly counsel you to keep away from Rah e'Torin," he added. "Even the barest whisper could destroy everything you are trying to achieve, and all of us in the process."

Keep away from him. I had only just found him again. Only just had the joy of seeing him alive, of having the courage to kiss him and feel the strong grip of his arm around me. To give it all up now, to not even allow myself the experience of wanting someone who wanted me, wherever it might lead, made me want to throw all care to the wind and tell Manshin I would do whatever I liked whenever I liked. But I was not so mad. Not yet, though history was full of people who had done foolish things for love or desire.

"Thank you for the warning," I said instead, and as frustrated as I was, I knew I ought to be grateful. Another man might have just let me fall into a mess of my own making and taken power out from beneath me rather than warn of the impending cliff.

We had reached the top of the main stairs, and he paused there to bow. "I am ever here to serve, Your Majesty. Now you must be careful how you handle Governor Koali," he added as he walked on. "He is not only popular but clever and good at his job."

"And loyal to the Bahains."

"And loyal to the Bahains."

We walked a few steps in silence, though nothing about Kiyoshio was ever silent. If it wasn't the waves or the wind it was the echo of footsteps, of guards walking behind me everywhere I went, of servants scurrying or the distant moans of the injured. All of them mixed together now, stirred by the wind.

"Shall I remain with you, Your Majesty?"

"In case I say something foolish?"

"Rather to bolster your appearance of importance," he said. "I am not no one, I believe. It will do well for your consequence to have me at your side."

I shook my head. "Were I a man it would. As a woman it just makes it look like you are my keeper and I your mouthpiece. I will see him alone. Is there anything else you know about him that could be of use?"

We had almost reached the Cavern, its open arch allowing a distant view through the great room and out to the balcony and the grey sky beyond. "I'm afraid not. Without access to the archives..." He trailed off, and for a few steps I could not but think of all that knowledge going up in flames. How recklessly the false Levanti emperor had destroyed so much. "With the Bahains out of favour at court, few of their allies—"

I lifted a hand. We were too close to the Cavern to risk being overheard. "Thank you, Minister. I will take it from here."

Having no imperial regalia, I had donned clean armour and a long crimson surcoat, and as much imperial bearing as I could carry.

I straightened my back and rolled my shoulders as I approached the open doorway, where a waiting servant bowed deeply. "Her Imperial Majesty Empress Miko Ts'ai, first of her name, Lord Protector of the Kisian Empire."

I swept past him on the last words, entering the room with the hope I looked more assured than I felt and wishing, not for the first time, I had paid more heed to my mother's lessons.

Two men rose from the table where a myriad of dishes had been decoratively laid. One man was tall and slim, long of fingers and face with eyelids that seemed too heavy to open all the way, while the other was stocky in the way of a farmer or a soldier, though he wore his double silk robe with the confidence of one bred to money. For a horrible moment I had no idea which one was Governor Koali. They both wore the same degree of finery, they both bowed to the same depth with the same whisper of my title, they stood side by side like equals, and yet only one could be the governor of Syan.

"Your Majesty," the stocky one said as he rose from his bow. "It is quite an honour to meet you at last. We have heard so very much about you these last few weeks. It is most gratifying that rumours of your death were...premature."

The words were spoken with sincerity, but it could have been a threat. There was no time to do more than wonder as he went inexorably on, carrying us forward like a river determined to reach the sea. "I am Tianto Koali, the governor of Syan, and this, if you will allow me to introduce you, Your Majesty, is my brother, Lord Ichiro Koali of Irin Ya, an estate gifted to him for special services to your father, our late emperor."

Lord Koali bowed. "Your Majesty."

They had brought no guards, no scribes, no servants, and despite the fear they ought to have felt upon the arrival of a new ruler, both settled themselves upon their cushions with every sign of comfort. Here were two men sure they could not be touched.

I closed my fingers into fists upon my knees as I knelt, keeping my anger in my hands so it would not spread to my face. "Lord Koali," I said, lifting my chin. "Governor. I have also heard much about you, and I admit I have been curious to see for myself what sort of man manages to serve both the emperor and an out-of-favour duke without earning the ire of either."

"With great tact and skill, Your Majesty. It is not difficult when you hold both men in respect."

A maid poured tea while my hands clenched all the tighter. I could not decide whether the emphasis on *men* or *respect* most enraged me, but after one minute in the governor's company I disliked him and needed him gone. Governor Koali turned his gaze to eye the maid as she worked, but his brother stared across the table at me, his heavy-lidded eyes meeting mine for a moment before slowly lowering down my body in a display of disrespect.

My fingernails dug into my palms, but I did not let my gaze shy away, forcing all embarrassment into anger as I waited for the maid to depart. With no door to close, her footsteps faded away along the passage. The stocky governor turned his gaze to me as his brother had. "Now what were we saying, Your Majesty?"

A disconcerting tactic I had seen Emperor Kin use too many times to be shaken, but his stare was enough to make me want to squirm away.

"Ah yes," he said, seeming to remember. "We wanted to be sure you had heard the news. Grace Bahain is marching this way, and since that means you will not long be with us, we wished to see for ourselves this woman who calls herself an empress."

It was not news, but the carefree, callous way he spoke filled me with renewed dread. I had not grown up fearing constant assassination attempts for nothing, however, and managed to say with quiet calm, "Need I remind you, that although you have taken no oaths, I am still your empress and you must show me the appropriate respect."

"Oaths?" Governor Koali laughed. "This is all very amusing, but we have no intention of doing more than humouring you out of curiosity. Your mother was quite the beauty and ah...well known for spreading her favours. A wise course of action to take yourself if you wish to court the assistance and support of the powerful."

They were untouchable and they knew it. They wanted to be sure I knew it too. Wanted to be sure I knew I was in their power, that they could turn the city of Syan against me the moment

Bahain arrived outside the gate with his army if I did not play their game. If I did not let them demean and embarrass me into my proper place as nothing but an upstart woman. No wonder my mother had chosen to rule from behind the screen rather than in front of it.

"You intend to bow and give your oath to a Levanti emperor?" I said, trying to keep my voice even despite the anger boiling through my body.

"Grace Bahain is our lord," Lord Koali said. "We go where he leads. But surely you are not so averse to Levanti. We saw quite a number of them in the grounds on our way here."

I wondered then if they knew about Grace Bahain's plan to get rid of the Levanti and take the throne for himself. Would they have been so disrespectful if they knew he intended to marry me to further that end? Probably.

The tea was barely cool and I was already out of moves. I did not want to argue or plead, or even bribe them, I just wanted them gone. But like with Rah, I was not allowed to be an individual. I had to be an empress.

"What," I said, drawing on my mother's imperial demeanour, "do you want?"

Governor Koali's brows went up. "In return for our loyalty? Nothing would make me throw my lot in with the losing side."

"We will bow to you," his brother added, tapping the slice of pear in his hand absently on the plate. "If and when Grace Bahain does so and not before. After all, he may be marching here with his army to bow to you for having been brave enough to take his castle when his back was turned."

I could have found more sincerity in a common street swindler. I could have them arrested. Could have them executed. But it would only turn the whole city against me and make it all the easier for Bahain to win.

Governor Koali's smile broadened. "Thinking of killing us like you killed Grace Bachita Ts'ai? Oh yes, we heard all about that. Go ahead if you think there are no others who would take our places. Others who would fight to ensure Grace Bahain's castle does not long remain in . . . enemy hands."

The emphasis on *enemy* ought to have angered me, but it gave me pause. Were they trying to rile me? Trying to make me lose my temper and lash out, giving them the moral high ground over an unstable woman? Perhaps they were even more dangerous than we had thought.

"We are done here," I said, taking refuge in pride to keep my voice steady. "May you have no cause to regret today's decision."

Their smiles were foul. "Oh, I don't think we will. Thank you for your hospitality, Highness. I do hope we will have cause to see each other again soon."

There was nothing I could say, nothing I could do but sit like a statue and wait for them to leave while my thoughts swirled and my skin prickled hot. How dare they? How *dare* they? As though somehow having breasts made me worthy of dismissal and derision.

When General Moto walked in some time later, it was to find me scowling at the table, all the tea and food having long since gone cold and the guards become restless. He waved them out and they departed with grateful bows and low murmurs of "General."

"Well?" he said when they were gone. "How did it go, Your Majesty?"

"Poorly. Governor Koali and his brother refused to bow to me unless Grace Bahain does so, and that was after telling me they only came to see me out of curiosity because the duke is marching here with every intent of absolutely not doing that and they would soon lose their opportunity of staring at my breasts."

Moto's eyes widened, and I had to laugh. "I seem to have been spending rather too much time with soldiers of late. Mother would be horrified. Except she's probably dead."

The anger and frustration I had been holding in burned up my throat and emerged on a sob, half rage, half misery, but there was no time to feel anything when hasty steps were approaching along the passage. Minister Manshin swept in looking grim. "Not a success, I understand. I will gather something of a council so we can discuss further plans."

"Do," I said. "But not yet. First I think it's time to find out if we can count on the Levanti to fight for us."

"You think it's wise to trust them?" It was a simple question, but owned all too much unspoken censure.

"You did at Otobaru," I said.

"I had little choice."

"We have even less now."

He conceded this with a grim nod.

"Have the refreshments replaced, then inform the Levanti horse whisperer I wish to see her."

"Just the horse whisperer?" This time Minister Manshin did glance at General Moto, and I hoped he hadn't told anyone what he'd witnessed in the stable.

"Yes, Minister. Just the horse whisperer. She is the closest thing they have to a leader right now."

———————◆———————

She kept me waiting, and when she finally appeared, she remained standing in the doorway, eyebrows lifted.

"Whisperer," I said. "Come and have tea with me."

Two maids knelt at the table, replacing the cold pot of tea and preparing to serve. I gestured for the whisperer to kneel, but she merely tilted her head.

"Do you understand my language?"

She tilted her head farther, a little smile creeping onto her lips.

Tightening my grip on my sleeves, I looked to one of the maids. "Fetch Tor e'Torin, the Levanti who speaks our language."

"Yes, Your Majesty."

"As fast as you can. Quickly!"

"Yes, Your Majesty."

She bowed and hurried out amid a storm of clinking crockery, leaving the horse whisperer smiling in the doorway. Annoyance boiled inside me and I squeezed my hands to fists, forcing a smile as I gestured to the opposite cushion. The invitation was obvious, and the horse whisperer approached and knelt with a degree of composed strength that would have made my mother weep. Having settled and straightened her crown, she set her hands upon her knees and fixed me with a curious stare.

I maintained my smile though it felt like a rictus. She must have known we would need Tor yet had come without him. It was a bad sign. This tall, capable leader of a woman had no interest in talking to me, and I needed her.

While steam curled from the teapot between us, we smiled in silence. Until, slowly rising from the endless beating of the waves outside, came the rushed snap of sandals. The maid hurried in, all red cheeks and stray hairs. "Tor e'Torin, Your Majesty," she said, the words a breathless gust as she bowed. Tor followed, slowing from his fast walk to a hesitant approach, his eyes darting from me to his horse whisperer and back.

"You sent for me, Your Majesty?"

"I did," I said, gesturing to the end of the table. The second maid had been hovering and hurried forward with a third tea bowl and plate, her cheeks flushed with mortification as she poured for him, her hand trembling. My only consolation was that the Levanti had no idea how smoothly it ought to have transpired.

Once tea sat steaming before a wide-eyed Tor, the maids both retreated. I took up my bowl and breathed in the fragrant steam, letting it relax the tension in my shoulders before I once more faced the horse whisperer over the prettily set table. She had touched nothing. Had not moved.

"I'm not sure what the correct form of address for your horse whisperer is," I said to Tor. "But please begin by thanking her for attending on me to discuss what is to happen."

Tor nodded and translated into the throaty language they managed to make both compelling and poetic. She listened without shifting her gaze from my face, and I breathed another lungful of steam and tried to appear unconcerned.

Once he had finished, she spoke at last. I watched her face. To someone less used to life at court she might have looked impassive, but she had not been trained by a lifetime under watchful eyes. Her nose crinkled in the briefest flash of disdain, before her eyes widened a fraction and her nostrils flared. All tiny signs, but to me they meant a lot. Especially when Tor translated, "This conflict is not of our making."

"Not of your making?" I tensed, tea bowl lifted. "You come to our lands and kill my people, you burn our cities and you tell me this is not of your making?"

Tor may not have repeated my words with the same vehemence, but just as I had not failed to see her disdain, she cannot have failed to see my anger. I had never been as good as Mama at wearing the mask.

"We did not make war on you, the Chiltaens did," he said when at length she answered, and while he spoke, a hard smile set on her lips. "Did we attack your city? No. I have been here ten years and have I, or any Levanti to have come and gone in that time, given you trouble? No."

"Gideon—"

The horse whisperer leaned forward. "Gideon is not one of us," she said in a snarl of Kisian. "He is herdless and unseen by God, as befits a traitor."

"Not one of—?"

"Are you to be held responsible for every Kisian who does wrong? No. Are you expected to atone for their wrongs? No. Gideon was born one of us and has since chosen his own path. It ought not be required that all Levanti suffer for his mistakes."

I set my tea bowl down, taking care with it so I might calm my annoyance. A deep breath made little difference. "I appreciate neither being interrupted nor lied to, Whisperer. My soldiers protected you at great risk. I have taken you into my castle at great risk. I ask to meet with you privately to avoid pressure being put upon you to bow before an empress you do not follow, and yet all I get is contempt and a deliberately provocative charade that has extended embarrassment even to one of your own." I gestured at Tor, who had been staring at his whisperer with his mouth open since she spoke her first words in Kisian. "Unless you intend to disown him too."

She did not flinch, but her smile became something more pugnacious. "You deserve no respect—"

"Men tell me that every day, because I am a woman. That you say so because I was not born of the same people as you is infinitely more sad."

I could almost believe the wind and the waves fell silent, so completely did the room chill. No one moved. In their braziers, coals crackled and hissed.

Eventually the whisperer drew a breath. "What do you want?"

"I respect you and I respect your people, and I will be honest with you now in the hope you will be honest with me in turn. We are in danger here. The men who hold the city this castle stands in are not our friends. The man whose castle this was is marching an army this way. He is loyal to your Gideon e'Torin, so if I understand the relationships correctly, he may be as unkind to you and your people as he will be to me and mine. So I ask if you will fight with me. Against Gideon. Or if not against him at least to protect this castle and your people currently taking refuge here when Gideon's army comes to reclaim it."

Another long silence while Ezma stared down into the dark tea in her bowl, no longer steaming. "You have already spoken to Rah."

"Yes, but not about this. I travelled with him and was glad to see him well."

Still staring into her untouched tea, the whisperer set a hand upon the table and tapped a rhythm with her fingertips. Four beats. *Short short short long. Short short short long. Short short short long.* In the naval code of the Bahains it meant danger beneath the water.

She looked up. "Do you know what a horse whisperer is?"

"Not really."

Short short short long. Short short short long. Short short short long.

"The Levanti do not have kings and queens, or emperors and empresses, nor even lords as you do, as all the city states surrounding our plains do. We value leadership that is earned. Our herd masters and matriarchs are always old and wise and strong and chosen, not born. Same with our Swords. They may challenge one another, and spats of honour are common, but one does not get to be Made as a Sword of the Levanti without earning it."

For the first time since she had started speaking my language, Tor moved. It was but a shift of his weight as though one of his legs had gone to sleep, but it drew a fleeting glance all too like pity from the whisperer before she went on.

"And when a Levanti is wise beyond their years, when they show an innate ability to understand the needs of our horses, when they prove themselves the best of all our people, they are sometimes chosen to be trained as horse whisperers. No longer to travel with a herd but to live alone, serving as healer and guide and judge to all Levanti who come to them regardless of herd. We are part of all herds and of none, and our word is law through which the will of the gods is done. If I tell them to fight they will fight, but if I tell them to lay down their swords they will lay down their swords no matter what Rah e'Torin may say about it."

I stared at her, at her proudly lifted chin and her tightly pressed lips, and saw something of myself in her aging face. Someone intent on being respected for what and who they were, no matter what they came up against. Or how far they were from home.

"And do you intend to tell them to fight? Or not to?"

"That depends. Were I to help you, would you honour the debt when it came due?"

"As far as I am able, yes."

She looked at Tor, who appeared intent on staring at his undrunk tea rather than meet her gaze. Was there more to his discomfort than her pretence at not knowing our language? I wished I could ask, but even if he didn't trust her, I had to. We needed the Levanti.

"I cannot fight this battle," she said. "But if Rah e'Torin chooses to lead my people against this thrall of Gideon who comes for us, I will not stand in the way, however little anyone should risk putting their faith in such a man."

She flicked another look at Tor, but smiled at me. "And no doubt there will soon come a moment when I need something in return."

"Indeed. I am sure it will be a fair trade."

"Naturally." The horse whisperer rose on the word. "If there is nothing else, I will leave you now. There is always much to be done with the horses after prolonged travelling, and I do not like to leave the task solely to my apprentice, as much as I value his work."

"Of course. Thank you for your time, Whisperer."

With a nod to me and another glance at Tor, she turned proudly upon her heel and strode toward the archway, the bones in her crown clicking.

Once she was out of sight, I let out a long breath. Tor didn't move, was staring at his knees like a scolded child.

"You didn't know she could speak Kisian?"

Without looking up, he shook his head.

"If she has been here ten years, I suppose it is hardly surprising."

When he made no answer, I heaved another sigh and slid a plate of skewered fruit across the table to him. "Have something to eat. And I think we could both do with a stronger drink after that."

He didn't answer, and my heart sank. "I know you and I did not get along well the last time we were thrown together," I said. "I was wary and angry, I think justifiably after the fall of my city, but even so I did not treat you with a proper degree of respect, and I'm sorry. I owe Rah more than I can ever repay for staying with me and for saving Minister Manshin, and whatever ill your horse whisperer thinks of him, I will be proud to fight alongside him."

"She is just angry people look to Rah for leadership."

"She dislikes him so much?"

A crease appeared between his dark brows. "As a person she doesn't know him. As competition, she's tried to get rid of him once already." At last he looked up. "All she said about horse whisperers ought to be true, but she is leading these people like a herd master and has been allowed to do so because they have no other strong leader. Until Rah arrived and—"

He broke off, perhaps realising how much he was telling me.

I nudged the fruit platter closer. "So if he did challenge her, do you still think he would only get half of them?"

"Probably. She's still a horse whisperer, but he would have to divide us to do it, and no Levanti does that lightly."

"Even when she is not doing right by her position?"

"It takes a full conclave of other horse whisperers to exile one. At first I assumed she had been caught up in the same…difficult times we were, but to have been here ten years…" Tor closed his eyes and lifted his face to the cavernous ceiling, covered in its stone spikes like an upside-down mountain range. For a moment he seemed to be praying, but tears leaked from the corners of his eyes and he looked altogether younger and more vulnerable than the sneering young man I had first met at the cursed woodcutter's hut.

He blinked fast to stem his tears, and I took up the teapot to refill my bowl rather than embarrass him with my stare. "If Rah challenged her on her exile, she would throw it back at him," he said, a throaty note to his voice he sought to clear with a cough. "He is an exiled exile. Though such things have little meaning now we are so divided. Why heed who is exiled on Gideon's orders if we do not follow Gideon? We have no...no...history, no... example..."

"Precedent?" I said.

"Is that the right word?" He turned a ferocious gaze on me. "Precedent then. Yes. It has never happened before. No Levanti has travelled this far south. No Levanti has been forced to break with their herd. No Levanti has claimed themselves an emperor. No Levanti has...has knelt in a castle having tea with an empress, being spoken to like an equal." He looked away again, his shaking hand lowering his bowl with a clatter. "I don't know who we are anymore. Who I am."

It seemed for a moment he might say more, but instead he picked up a slice of plum and chewed it like it had offended him, all brooding scowl. Not unlike the look my brother might have worn. And for the first time I wondered how old he was. The lack of hair made all the other Levanti appear older, but Tor, like Ezma, had hair so long it looked like it had rarely been cut. Although unlike Ezma, Tor wore his tied back and tangled and seemed to hate it. I had asked before and received no answer, but perhaps now...

"Please forgive my ignorance," I said, dropping the mantle of the empress completely. "But I am unaware of your customs and would like to know at what age you will cut off your hair as the others do? Or is that not something to do with—"

"Sixteen cycles," he said, and perhaps feeling he had interrupted rudely, added, "Your Majesty. That's when we are Made as Swords."

"Made?"

"Branded before the gods, giving our lives in service."

"And you?" I knew I was pushing it. He had sneered at me for such questions before, but sitting alone with the tea cooling in its bowls and the waves crashing against the cliff was different to that rainswept road where General Kitado lay dying. "When will you be branded?"

He didn't answer. If I wanted him to speak, I would have to speak first. Tanaka had been the same, stubborn and proud.

I slid my hands down my thighs, smoothing fabric. "Did you know I was never meant to be the empress?" I said. "Kisia has never had a woman sit on the throne before. It ought to have gone to my brother. I loved him, so that was all right, up until it wasn't." Tor looked up, that deep crease between his brows again. "Until I realised I had just been telling myself it was all right, that I didn't really want it, that he deserved it more, when deep down I knew none of it was true. I was not less worthy. I was not less qualified. It was all right to want it, to yearn for it, to feel...incomplete without it." When he didn't speak, I shrugged. "We all have our—"

"Two years ago." He barked the words, forcing them out. "I should have been Made two years ago. I have lived almost nineteen cycles and still I am not Made. Gideon..." He took a breath and let it go in a rush. "Gideon gave me to the Chiltaens instead so I could learn to speak their language. Knowing how to speak it has kept me alive because I'm valuable, but I would give that up in a heartbeat to be a real member of my herd. Or I would have. Once."

"But you are!"

"No, I'm not," he said, rising so quickly he knocked the table, sending the dishes clinking. "I...I thank you for the tea and the... the kindness, Your Majesty, but I really must get back to my people."

There was nothing I could say. For whatever the gods said about belonging coming from inside one's own heart, I had the same need, the same drive, the same yearning to be acknowledged. To sit on the throne and be properly crowned as empress of a united Kisian Empire in my own right. What wouldn't I give to have it so? What hadn't I already?

——————◆——————

We knelt around the small table, Minister Manshin, General Ryoji, General Moto, and me, the size of our forces clear in the size of our meeting. Had we not been attacked taking the ships, I would have had twice the number, but we had been and now I didn't—the past not a place worth walking.

"At least we need not fear an attack from the sea," Moto said. "Any ships that didn't escape with us surely burned."

Solemn nods agreed. Manshin had chosen a small, out of the way chamber for our meeting, and while there was tea and food there were no servants to pour or clear away. There were not even guards, only a pair of braziers fighting back the castle's pervasive chill. Manshin, it seemed, was taking no risks.

"It is a small consolation," he said, "when we are so precariously positioned."

"I could wish for more soldiers," Moto agreed. "But this castle is more fortress than palace. Almost as impenetrable as Koi."

"And look what happened there."

"Well yes, Excellency, but that was thanks to a traitor. We do not—"

"Don't we?" Manshin looked around the table. "This castle has been held by the Bahains for sixteen years, and they have not been hated masters. Whatever his loyalties, Bahain is a fine warrior and tactician, and he, like his predecessor Lord Toi, defended this city from roaming pirates with his own sweat and blood. We have been here a day and you think there is no one here willing to open the castle gates to him as Governor Koali will open the gates to the city?"

I thought of all the servants who bowed to me in the passages, who made up my sleeping mat and filled the braziers, who brought me food and tea and warm washing water. Somewhere amongst so many there had to be one whose loyalty to the Bahains outweighed all sense of self-preservation. There was always one.

It had started raining again as the evening wore on, and now as the drops pattered upon the jutting stone windowsill, the same thoughts seemed to pass through each of my companions' minds.

"Is there any way we can avoid a siege?" I said. "The harbour is full of ships."

"Ships with captains loyal to the Bahains and Governor Koali, Your Majesty," Manshin said. "At best they will do nothing. At worst they will block all attempts to resupply the castle."

"You mean at worst we have walked into a trap," I said, panic thumping like a drum in my ears. "Governor Koali will make sure the city does not fight for me. The servants may betray me. And we cannot even be sure of our supply line. It sounds like a siege is unwise. The horse whisperer says the Levanti may fight for us. Would meeting Bahain in the field be the best course of action?"

Manshin and Moto looked at one another, while General Ryoji stared at the table. "Even with the number of Levanti here, assuming they all fight, we are still well outnumbered by all reports," he said. "We can hold a siege; it would just be difficult and may last some time."

"Time in which Gideon e'Torin tightens his hold on my empire and the Chiltaens can regroup."

"Yes, Your Majesty, and with winter on its way we will soon be stuck for the season."

"During the best time to push the Levanti emperor, whose warriors have never had to deal with snow."

Outside, the rain went on pouring. Seconds passed, coals clinking in their braziers.

"We could retreat, Your Majesty," General Moto said, his gaze flitting to Manshin. "We could leave a token force so it appears we are manning the castle and slip away during the night."

Retreat. I had known the suggestion was coming yet it was still a punch, and I sat winded. This ought to have been a great success, taking Bahain's castle from beneath his feet, drawing him away so the rest of my army could follow and crush him against his own gates. It had seemed so clever. So sneaky. And now retreat was all they could counsel. They were right; I just couldn't bring myself to say so, to believe it had all been for nothing.

A loud knock shook the door. Ryoji reached for his blade, but Minister Manshin waved him down and rose. The knock came again as he crossed the floor on wary steps to rest his hand upon the pocked metal latch. "Who is it? I gave orders we were not to be disturbed."

No answer came. More bad news perhaps. Or an assassin. Wouldn't that be a way to go out, stabbed at my council meeting before the battle even started.

Manshin leaned closer to the door.

"I am Rah e'Torin," came the muffled voice from outside, followed by the distinct sound of a whisper. "I have a...plan for... the council."

Manshin looked my way, his face deceptively neutral. "Majesty?"

"Let him in. At this point I think we can all agree we need any help we can get."

"Are you sure we can trust him, Your Majesty?" Moto's words were quick and urgent. "His countrymen are allies of the false emperor and—"

"And so are some of ours, General. This war ceased to be

straightforward quite some time ago, and Rah e'Torin put himself at great risk to protect me at a time when no one else, not even my own countrymen"—I nodded at Moto himself—"would. I trust him as much as I trust any of you." I lifted my chin and dared not look at Minister Manshin. "Let him in."

Silenced, Moto made no more complaint, but the look on his face was far from welcoming when the minister pulled open the door and there on the threshold stood Rah. He had shaved his stubble and head since that morning, and wore a fresh set of clothes, but discoloured bruises still traced lines of pain across his face.

All eyes fixed upon him as he walked in, Tor in his wake. He glanced at each of the men in turn, but it was at me he stared and said in his awkward, halting Kisian, "Your Majesty, you must ambush."

A beat of disbelief, then Minister Manshin and General Moto exclaimed in unison, "Ambush? Bahain's army is as good as upon us. We have no time."

"No time. And such a risk as cannot be thought of."

"Not enough soldiers."

"If we had twice the number."

"Or more time."

I let them go on exchanging their complaints back and forth while Rah watched them, Tor hissing translations in his ear. When at last the two older men had talked themselves out, all eyes turned to me. Except for Tor, who seemed intent upon the chisel marks in the ceiling. "Perhaps," I said, "we should hear the rest of the plan before we so loudly condemn it. Do join us, Captain e'Torin."

Rah glanced in confusion at Tor, but after a brief exchange Rah sat upon a spare cushion while Tor remained standing behind him.

"An ambush," I said to the Levanti I had kissed who was now sitting at my council table. Even Mother would have laughed at how twisted these knots were getting. "How? Where? Grace Bahain has many men."

Tor relayed my question, his gaze determinedly fixed upon the window. Rah nodded and spoke slow enough for Tor to translate as he went. "Ambush in the night. Tomorrow night. You say he will be here the day after tomorrow. He marches fast. But no commander takes unrested soldiers into battle unless they must. They will camp. They will be tired. They will not make fortifications or expect attack when they know, as you do"—Rah gestured here to the two men who had spent the last few minutes listing everything wrong with such a plan—"that to attack would be foolish when you have big, strong walls you can hide behind."

My advisors bristled at the word *hide*, but they let the Levanti keep talking. Tor spoke my language, but it was at Rah I stared, watching the energy and passion in his every expression.

"On the plains we have a form of night attack we use against raiders from the city states, called *ekkafo*; it means—" Rah waved a hand as he sought words to explain it and eventually looked to Tor for help. The young man who had stopped translating to wait shrugged and said, "It means something like 'night song,' but it involves a lot more stabbing and blood than singing, so don't get the wrong idea. We've..." He paused, swallowed. "*Swords* have been able to decimate large bands of Korune and Tempachi with relatively small numbers. It would not be possible to teach you the song or the precision of navigation required in so short a time, but as long as your soldiers are willing to follow a Levanti leader, Rah believes he can adapt the strategy effectively to use small groups rather than a hundred-odd individuals."

At this, both Levanti turned their gazes around the table to await a response. They acknowledged the men, but ultimately settled their attention on me as the decision maker, and I had fought so hard all my life to have my opinion even noticed, let alone respected, that their calm acknowledgement of my authority made my heart thud all the more fiercely.

"How many soldiers would you need?" I said, forestalling my advisors' questions.

"As many as you have. But they must be able to take orders from us without question or delay."

"Are we seriously considering this option?" General Moto said with a little laugh. "Seriously considering risking the lives of our soldiers on...singing?"

"It is not just singing," Tor snapped. "It is a...precision man... manu...strategy that would have you shitting your pants and running if we used it against you. It's been cloudy. There's little moonlight. They won't be able to see a thing without lighting torches, and that'll only make them a bigger target. It'll work even better if you have a lot of men who are good with bows and can pick off any sources of light."

I could lead the archers. Rah could lead a manoeuvre no Kisian army would ever expect. Together we could do this. Could salvage success from disaster. A sense of hope flared within me, all the more intoxicating for being him and me, like we were a foretold force that together could change the course of history.

Minister Manshin cleared his throat. "We need to know more about how this works, Your Majesty, else I cannot advise it. We need Grace Bahain to bow to you or be bartered back to the false emperor, *alive*, and we cannot simply"—he glanced at the scowling Tor—"trust they have a plan that will work."

"I don't intend to," I said though I bubbled with excitement. "They will explain the plan in great detail, and we will execute it. No, General Moto, I will not take the safer route when retreat would give my people little reason to follow me. I have had too many losses. Too many retreats. It's time to make our enemies fear us."

16. DISHIVA

I t was no unified herd we led back to Kogahaera, each day upon the road more divided than the last. I swung hourly between pride that so many Swords looked upon the chained Torin and saw it for the horror it was, and wanting to shake them all until they could see their enemy wasn't Gideon, but Leo. Leo and the Swords who were taking the opportunity to revel in cruelty. They gathered around Yitti and Lok and the twins, harrying them to walk faster and hissing at them for traitors. It was an ignominy no Levanti ought to bear, but the Torin stood proud and walked in silence.

Keeping to the back of the cavalcade, I watched the movement of Swords, gathering to mutter and whisper, an endless dance of hooves upon the road. At our head, Gideon rode, paying no heed to any of it, and I couldn't but wonder what was going through his mind. The part of his mind that was still him.

I watched and I worried and I waited until the shadow of Koga-haera City came into view, our walled compound sitting like a duckling beneath its wing. With our destination in sight, I urged Itaghai to a trot and, moving onto the grass, passed the staring, muttering mixture of troubled Levanti and wary Kisians.

Gideon didn't so much as turn his head as I reined in beside him.

"Defender Dishiva," Leo said, greeting me with an inclination of his head as though he had been the emperor. In every way that mattered he was.

"Your Majesty," I said, ignoring Leo like the annoying fly I wished he was. "What do you intend to do about the unrest caused by your plan to execute the Torin?"

A flicker of expression crossing Gideon's face rewarded my bluntness, yet it was in an emotionless voice he said, "Anyone to whom the execution of traitors is a problem is themselves a traitor."

"Ah, so this is going to be a very large execution then. It is going to take you quite a while to take the heads of at least half your supporters."

"Burying them will be easier."

I knew they were Leo's words, but could not stop disgust flaring through me at such calm dismissal of our beliefs coming from Gideon's lips. "Of course," I bit back. "I'm sure Rah would agree with so reasonable an efficiency."

The moment the words were out of my mouth I wished I could call them back. Even as Gideon's eyes closed in pain, Leo smiled the most self-satisfied smile I'd ever seen lips produce, physical distance all that kept me punching it off his face. Not a moment went by when I did not wish Gideon strong enough to fight back, but in all too real a way, he was our shield, forcing Leo to focus on him so completely that he could not turn his ability upon the rest of us. And I had hurt him for it.

To push my point further would be to fight with Leo through Gideon and achieve nothing, so I let Itaghai fall back.

Returning to Kogahaera brought mixed emotions. The heavy sense of dread I had expected, but the relief of homecoming I had not. When had I started thinking of it as home? As a safe place I understood, at least when compared to the Kisia outside our walls. After the conversation with Secretary Aurus, I even had some small degree of hope for the future. Hope that whatever threats Leo made, whatever he was forcing Gideon to do, he was fallible. He had weaknesses. And we had allies.

The gates swung open upon a familiar yard. A yard that might have been a comforting sight but for Yiss en'Oht standing in the centre, a leader welcoming us home. Had any other captain stood thus, my sense of hope would have swelled, but Yiss had refused to question Gideon's orders, had led an army against peaceful deserters, and I could not but eye her return with misgiving.

"Your Majesty," she said, saluting as Gideon rode in through the gates. "Your return is well timed. I was on the verge of sending a messenger after you."

"You have news of the deserters?"

"Yes, but that can wait." Yiss's feet shifted, something uncomfortable in her stance. I braced myself for bad news. "Traders from Risian report a Chiltaen army is camped a few days west of here, making a nuisance of themselves among the refugees from Mei'lian who went north. The news is all over Kogahaera, and many of the refugees who came here are already leaving. Some of our... Kisian allies are also... conspicuously absent as of last night." She looked to Edo as she spoke. He would need it all translated, but when it was he would surely feel the same slow sinking sensation I had felt with every new pronouncement. She hadn't even reached the outcome of her attack on the deserters yet.

"A Chiltaen army?" Nuru said as she accompanied Sichi's travelling box into the yard. "West? Not the ones we just came from near Kima?"

Yiss turned a sneer on her. "Not the same ones, saddlegirl. I am not a fool."

"They may not be the same, but we have equally no cause to be concerned by them," Gideon said, reining in. "They are allies of Dom Villius and are not our enemies."

I thought of Secretary Aurus's warnings. Leo's army. An army he could use against us if we didn't do what he wanted, if Gideon rebelled. If I kept getting in his way.

Gideon dismounted before his most loyal Sword captain, the yard slowly filling around him as the tail of his cavalcade made their way through the gates. "And your mission, Captain?"

"I request to discuss it in private, Your Majesty."

"No." Gideon seemed to enjoy the damning syllable, standing before her with a slight smile while one of the serving boys led his horse away. "Here. Either you have successes to be celebrated by your herd, or failures to bear to them."

Yiss drew herself up, and I couldn't but feel sorry for her, whatever her mission had been. "The deserters got away, Your Majesty," she said, meeting his gaze so intently she need not see the gathering crowd, need not see them turn grimaces to each other. "They were warned we were coming."

"By who?" Leo this time, but she kept her gaze on Gideon as she answered.

"By Lashak e'Namalaka."

I hoped it was only my imagination that made it feel as though many eyes turned my way.

"There is more," Yiss went on, seemingly inured to her fate now and determined to have it all out despite the talk growing around her. "They have an exiled horse whisperer."

The words dropped like broken water barrels onto the stones, a gasp spreading through the Levanti. They hadn't known. Of course they hadn't known. And now each of them had to contend with the confusion such a discovery wrought within them as I had done. An exiled horse whisperer.

"She called a Fracturing," Yiss said. "We lost many and had no choice but to walk away once we were outnumbered. Rah had Kisians with him as well, and fighting them seemed...unwise."

"Rah?" Once again, Gideon snapped out his name as a question before Leo could quell it, a desperate flicker of fear twitching his features.

For the first time since beginning her report, Yiss looked around at the crowd of Levanti onlookers, her gaze a question. Was he really sure he wanted her to speak in front of so many? However unwise it was, Gideon's desperation to know what had become of Rah would keep him from fighting Leo's seeming desire for nothing but chaos and disunity.

She cleared her throat. "Yes, Your Majesty. It would appear he continues to be a thorn in your side. I don't know in what way he is allied with the Kisians who threatened us, but the Fracturing was instigated on his words."

While she spoke, the last of the cavalcade had been riding through the gates, leaving the arrival of the chained Torin Swords ill timed. Or perfectly timed, perhaps, if divided Levanti was Leo's current goal. Yitti led them in, head proudly raised, and all the muttering and whispering that had followed us back from the Chiltaen camp erupted again, leaving Gideon and Yiss the centre of a hissing sandstorm.

"Keep them under guard," Gideon said as Levanti stepped aside for the prisoners to be brought through.

"That's it?" Yitti called after Gideon, his voice hoarse. "That's all we get? No discussion? No appeal? You call us traitors, but you are the very greatest traitor of all, and the gods will ensure you suffer."

Gideon had stepped toward the manor doors, but he looked back over his shoulder in a way so aloof and uncaring I felt cold to my bones and had to remind myself this wasn't our Gideon anymore. This was just Leo's Gideon-shaped puppet now.

"Prepare for their execution at sunset."

I found Jass in the caves, packing supplies into half a dozen satchels. At the sound of my steps he looked up, hand skimming to his sword hilt. "Dishiva." His hand dropped as he stood, the pair of us closing the space between us with hurried steps. "You're back."

Our arms slid around one another, and there with our chins upon each other's shoulders we clung tight to this fleeting comfort, this one thing that hadn't been taken from us. Need held us there long after we ought to have parted, like starving animals eating their fill.

When at last I stepped back, unable to keep the smile off my face despite all the news I carried with me, I gestured at the satchels. "Jass en'Occha's rescue service is going well then?"

His sombre expression split into a grin. "I should start demanding payment in jerky. I've helped about a dozen through so far, too terrified to walk out through the gates lest they be hunted down like the deserters and—"

"They survived. The deserters. There was a Fracturing. And Rah was there. And Kisians."

"Hold up, slow down, Di." Jass gripped my arms, his firm hold steadying me. "Start at the start."

I told him about Yiss's news, about the Chiltaen army and the envoy and the Torin Swords condemned to execution that night, and as it all spilled out of me I had the doubtful felicity of watching his expression run a full gamut of emotions from surprise to horror, relief to fear. At least I no longer felt alone.

"I think I'm about to get a lot more people through here," he said when I finished. "What a mess. I'm sorry, I know you really believed in him. In this."

"The worst is that I still do. There's a way through this, a narrow, difficult path like that—" I pointed to the crack between the first and the second cave, barely wide enough to squeeze through. "It's so close I can feel it. If I can just get rid of Leo for good, then Gideon could do this."

His smile was a pitying thing. "I wish that was still true." He let me go and turned around, staring out into the dim cave. "Gideon has to go."

The words echoed around us unchallenged, and only once they had faded did Jass turn back to face me. "You know it's true. It's been true for a while. Even if you could get rid of Leo. Even if Gideon was still the same man. Even if you could convince everyone it was all Leo's fault. Gideon's reputation is too damaged. People might still believe in his ideals, in his plans, but not in him."

I closed my eyes, but couldn't block out the truth of his words, a truth I had known and yet refused to accept or acknowledge. In continuing to shield us from Leo, Gideon had sacrificed everything.

"We can't kill Leo without him coming back," Jass said, softly now. "But we can kill Gideon."

Such a suggestion ought not to have been able to come from Levanti lips, but so much had we changed, had we been shaped by the need to survive and by the Kisians around us, that I was not even surprised. It was the easiest way. The neatest fix, and yet I shook my head. "No. He deserves better than that. He brought us this far. Sacrificed so much. There has to be another way."

Jass pressed a sad smile between his lips. "I'm sure there is, but how is the fighting against Leo Villius thing going?"

I'd had such hope, yet the answer was *terribly*. Horses and Swords had been sacrificed to his increasing warnings, but all I had achieved was a vague peace with a Chiltaen who wasn't even a threat, and further division. I had risked the lives of others, yet when it came to sacrificing Gideon's to the greater good of my people, I recoiled. I had believed in him, in his vision, with every shred of my being.

"If Gideon died, Leo would just turn his focus on whoever next opposed him," I said, staring into the shadows as I worked my way through an idea coalescing in my mind. "If I'm right and he can't focus his...manipulation on more than one person at once, then—" I snapped my gaze to Jass's worried face. "I should have done this days ago."

"You're going to challenge him."

"I'm going to challenge him."

Jass blew out a long breath and ran his hand over his face. "It's not the worst idea you've ever had—"

"Thank you."

"—but it's close. All you would really be doing is exchanging Gideon for yourself. Why not let this dream die? Why not go home?"

"Because I'm not ready to give up on us. On this, and neither should you."

It wasn't a good answer. I knew it wasn't, but I couldn't put into words the complex depths of my feelings. About our herd masters on the plains. About fighting for the right to exist. We deserved a future no less than any other people—*that* a fight to which I would give my life.

My hands trembled, and I closed them to fists. "You don't have to stand with me," I said. "You can leave if that's what you want, but you can't talk me out of doing what is right. If we can split Leo's attention, if I can—"

"I get it," Jass interrupted. "I don't like it, but I get it. It's very... you."

"I can't tell if you mean that as a compliment or an insult."

"Neither can I." His laugh was strained. "Either way I'm not going anywhere. Having almost died, and helped you carry a very broken body out of your room, I feel like it would be pathetic to walk away at this point. If you're trying to push me into leaving, you might have to be more aggressive. I'm a stubborn bastard and I like you. So don't die. Or become Leo's puppet."

Reciprocal words hung on my tongue, but I could not speak them, too close would they be to a promise I couldn't make.

"I'll try," I said instead. "I should go. The sooner I do this thing the sooner I can order the Torin released and try to pull us all through this in one piece."

Jass's smile had a wry edge, my lack of response not having gone unnoticed. He saluted. "May the gods watch over you, Captain."

Captain. It was a retreat to a former formality, one I had to accept because there was no time to do anything else. Somehow I had become the Levanti empire's last hope.

No guards stood outside Gideon's rooms. It was a bad sign. I knocked, just in case, and receiving no answer, slid the door to peer in. Empty room, empty table. The room hardly looked lived in at all—a very Kisian space in which Gideon temporarily existed.

Standing in the doorway, I ran through all the places I might find him with evening drawing close. It no longer mattered that Leo would be with him too, the beauty of the challenge that regardless of what Leo might want, Gideon could not refuse it without forfeiting his position outright.

Running steps broke upon my thoughts, and I turned as Nuru came pelting along the passage, skidding to a halt out of breath before me. "The execution," she said, bending double and gasping. "They've brought it forward. It's... it's happening now. Outside."

"What? But it's not—"

"I think Leo must have thought you would try to stop it. Come! Now!"

He already knew my plan.

No more time to think, only to run. Along the passage and down the stairs, blindly sprinting in Nuru's wake out into the bright daylight. I blinked, seeing nothing but brightness and flickering shapes, shapes that slowly coalesced into figures—Kisian and Levanti alike—gathered in a mass before the low stage. Noise hit me like a sandstorm, nipping and tearing at my skin. Groups of Levanti were shouting at Gideon, at Keka standing at his side and the Second Swords of Torin upon the stage, even at each other—this moment the knife edge upon which our future stood.

Beside Gideon, Leo smiled.

"No," I growled, pushing out into the crowd. "You can't take this from us. I won't let you."

Confused Kisians watched on, jostled about amid the raging crowd. Lines of them stood between groups of Levanti, Lord Edo in the centre of it all, keeping his soldiers calm in what could easily have turned into a brawl, if not a massacre.

We reached the stage as a pair of axe-wielding Kisians managed to make their way through, only to find Sichi blocking the stairs. With her arms thrown wide she scowled like a protective hawk, the fluttering of her robe like ruffled feathers. She was shouting, not only at the Kisian executioners but at Gideon, at the crowd, at all who would listen, and though I could not understand her words, they rang with vehemence.

"Gideon, remember that day you named me ambassador," I said, not caring who heard me. "You told me you were afraid this would happen. Afraid of what he would make you do. This is exactly that moment and you need to fight it! Please!"

He was listening. Staring. Intent. Almost I could see the battle rage behind his eyes. Could see his struggle. Against the voice. The peace. The weight of everything that was Leo inside his head. And even before he spoke, I knew he would order their release. That he would win this fight. That he could. He was Gideon e'Torin. Our emperor. Our herd master. Our chosen one.

Until he turned. And met Leo's gaze.

"Kill them."

"No!" I screamed. "Stop! I challenge you, Gideon e'Torin, for the right to lead this herd."

The words were out, leaving my whole body thrumming with the knowledge of what I had done. What I had said. All around me Levanti stilled in a moment of silence.

I dared not look at Leo. Dared not look at Yitti and Himi and Istet and Lok, knowing too well their lives now sat upon my shoulders. Upon my voice and my soul. Upon my ability to speak to my people and earn their respect.

"Do you accept the challenge?" someone close to the stage demanded of Gideon.

He had to. Had to accept the challenge or forego his position. No matter what Leo could make him do or say, those were our laws, and whatever had changed in the way we lived, those laws were so ingrained in all of us that no Levanti could follow a herd master who did not abide by them.

"Yes," Gideon said, so completely without thought that I wondered if Leo could have altered his reply had he tried, or if there was some deep, incorruptible part of us even he couldn't reach. "I accept the challenge."

Noise rose as the Levanti spread, shouting for a fire to be built, while the Kisians all looked at one another in confusion. The axe-wielding soldiers sweated as they looked from Gideon to Edo and back, unsure what they ought to be doing, while the crowd around them dispersed.

"Except."

Such a small word. He didn't shout it, yet it froze all who heard it, even the Kisians, their hands reaching for their weapons.

"Except," Gideon repeated, Leo ever a statue at his side. "That Dishiva e'Jaroven, by the very laws she claims to challenge me by, is not allowed to make such a challenge. She is no captain. No matriarch. No member of a hand. She is, as Defender of the One True God, not even Levanti anymore in the eyes of our gods, and as such she cannot challenge me. Kill them."

The words seemed to reverberate, quietly spoken yet the loudest sound I had ever heard, vibrating their meaning down through my limbs and into the very ground on which we stood. Behind the Second Swords, Gideon's most loyal supporters stepped forward. I made it two steps toward the platform before one plunged a blade into Yitti's side. Yitti threw his head back, his shock and pain mirrored on the others' faces as Levanti, people who ought to have been their friends, their allies, stuck blades into their backs and sides and throats. Hands bound, Yitti fell to his knees, wide eyes staring as blood spilled from a slash across his neck. For a moment he seemed to stare at me, but his gaze slid out of focus and he toppled. The thud of his body hitting the wooden platform echoed upon silence—the sound of Levanti Kisia's ruin.

17. RAH

The castle's great entrance hall was full of soldiers, each one sitting cross-legged or kneeling on the stones, even their leaders. I had never seen a stranger training session. A few hundred Kisians crammed into the space repeating Levanti words and phrases loud enough to echo to the high stone ceiling. They had not taken to the idea with any enthusiasm, but what had started as a mumble had eventually become a disciplined shout.

"Wait!" they cried in unison when Minister Manshin, standing a few stairs from the bottom, shouted the equivalent in Kisian. Tor stood beside him, but he hadn't needed to correct the minister for the last ten minutes. Perhaps there was a chance we could do this after all.

"Close attack!"

Amun leaned close and whispered, "You think they'll remember once we're out there in the dark?"

"I hope so."

He grunted. "At least if we don't pull it off, we'll be too dead to look stupid."

I tried not to think about it. Going through Grace Bahain was the only way we were getting to Kogahaera. Since the run-in with Yiss en'Oht's Swords, riding to Kogahaera to free the Levanti still in thrall to Gideon had become a goal for many, and one I could encourage. They didn't need to know I had a different reason for wanting to get there.

"Down!" the soldiers shouted. It seemed to have become something of a competition who could shout it first and loudest, and however strange it was listening to Kisian men chant Levanti commands, at least they were taking it seriously.

"Full chaos!"

They seemed to like that one best. Tor hadn't told them it was a distraction of last resort and not something they were likely to enjoy.

"Do you think the elders who created *ekkafo* ever thought we'd teach it to outsiders?" Amun said.

"We aren't teaching it to them. We're just using them as extra sword arms because we're short-handed."

"They'll want to learn it once they see it in action."

He was probably right, and though I was proud of our ways, the thought of teaching the sounds to anyone not of the plains made me twitchy. I couldn't say why, but it felt wrong. It was one thing to make use of it under our command, but to gift it to others? I hoped Empress Miko wouldn't ask.

I thought of her standing before me in the stables, her hands on my chest as she stretched up to grant the kiss I had wanted all too much yet known I ought not take, because no matter what Gideon was attempting or what we had achieved in this hall, there was no place where Levanti and Kisia met. We were two people from vastly different worlds with different views, two people who couldn't even understand each other properly. Yet I could tell myself that a hundred times, could believe it with my entire being, and one look at her little scowl of determination had me wishing it untrue. It had taken all my self-control to hold back, to let her make the choice, only for Manshin to walk in. She had been right in front of me, offering comfort and affection and warmth and wanting all I had in return, until she had stepped away and taken that warmth with her.

"Silent!" The word rang to the high ceiling, and trying to think of anything but their empress's lips, I looked out over the miniature sea of Kisian soldiers and wondered which ones would be heeding my commands tonight. I could only hope they were as good at fighting as they were at memorising. And that my body wouldn't let me down. The wound in my leg still ached.

Seeking somewhere to sit, I turned toward the great staircase. Ezma was there in its shadow, and before I could look away, she beckoned. I'd managed to avoid her since saving the deserters at Otobaru Shrine, unable to trust myself to be respectful knowing she'd had me drugged to keep me out of the way before taking the opportunity to leave me for dead. She seemed to have forgotten those details, bestowing a smile on me as I joined her.

"Whisperer," I said. She deserved no respect, but I would not demean myself by calling her anything else.

"Captain Rah," she returned, perhaps for the same reason. "Do you really think this travesty is going to work?"

I clamped my teeth together, loosening the bite when a sharp pain ripped through my ear. It was gone as soon as it had begun. "What travesty? A horse whisperer hiding in the shadows?"

I was beginning to really hate her mocking look. "Or a Levanti captain making eyes at a foreign empress. Whatever will our Swords say when they discover they are really fighting for your cock?"

"They are fighting to protect themselves and their people. Show me how my cock makes that untrue."

Ezma folded her arms, looking me up and down.

"What do you want, Ezma?" I said. Behind me, the chanting of Levanti words went on. "Why are you here? Why try to get rid of me?"

"I'm keeping the oath I made when I became a horse whisperer," she said, ignoring the second question. "That's all I have ever sought to do."

"You swore to lead when whisperers should never do so? And to leave Levanti who threaten your control behind to die? That's not the oath I was taught."

Ezma tilted her head. "You were taught?"

I looked away, annoyed with myself for having said so much, but her mere existence seemed to make my blood hot.

"Who taught you the oath of a horse whisperer?"

There was no going back now. "Whisperer Jinnit," I said, meeting her gaze squarely. "When I was his apprentice."

Ezma took a step back, annoyance passing unchecked across her face. "You?" she said. "You were an apprentice? When? How?"

"I was chosen at nine years old, the same as all apprentices. Because I had all the ideal traits."

"But you failed him."

"No. I was a good apprentice. He said I would make a famed horse whisperer one day. It just…wasn't what *I* wanted." I had only ever admitted that to Gideon. The shame of having run away, of having let down my herd, had trapped me in silence. It was a weapon she could use against me, but doing so would mean having to admit to others I had the makings of a whisperer. The sight of her expression changing from a sneer to a snarl as she realised this gave me a fierce, angry joy.

"A false whisperer," she said. "To add to your other crimes."

"I am not a false anything. But you are. Why were you exiled?"

Her eyes narrowed. "That is no one's concern."

"You don't think so? What crime can have been so bad you were sent away, not just for a cycle, but for ten?"

"What makes you think I didn't just choose to stay, as Gideon did?"

"Abandoning your duties. I don't think that's any better."

I stepped closer, all too aware of the tight skin over my healing wounds hampering my movement. "These Levanti have followed you because they want someone to believe in; they don't ask questions because they fear the answers would return them to a state of hopelessness. You think it's because they trust you, because they love you, because they need you." I shook my head. "You're wrong."

She lifted her chin. "Threatening to challenge me?"

"Only if you force my hand," I said, Amun's warning that it would be all too divisive still fresh in my mind. She ought to know as well as I did how greatly it would weaken us.

Behind me the gathered soldiers shouted, "Down!"

I disliked the smile gathering at the corners of her lips. "There's a lot more going on here than you have any idea of, Rah e'Torin. Consider that a warning. I won't let you get in my way, nor your empress."

I left her in the shadows, telling myself it was all bluster, yet her warning gnawed at me as I walked away. As I reached the base of the stairs, the Kisian soldiers rose from their places, stretching and talking and making their way toward the meagre sunlight offered through the open door. The sunshine called to me too, reminding me that Jinso was in the stables and it had been too long since we had ridden out together, but with an army on the way there was nowhere safe to go.

Two men had joined Tor and Minister Manshin on the stairs. One was called Moto, I had learned, and led most of the soldiers. The other was General Ryoji, commander of the empress's personal guards, and despite his penetrating stare, she seemed to trust him the most.

He was speaking to Minister Manshin, Tor watching but not translating, leaving me caught between confidence it was of no importance and an intense desire to be reassured. I managed to settle on the former until Empress Miko's voice made my gaze snap to the top of the stairs. She descended, her pale robe reminding me of the one she had worn while trekking through the mountains. It had no longer been white by the time we'd reached the inn, but the unexpected collision of memory with the current moment set my skin on fire.

The empress glanced at me only to look away as fast. Clasping her hands before her, she spoke to her generals while beside me, Tor still said nothing. It wasn't until I nudged him that he said, "They're talking about the ambush plans. The minister is pleased with how the soldiers did today and hopes with a brief revision before setting out they will be able to do their job well enough. Like there can really be such a thing as well enough in an *ekkafo*."

"We'll make it work," I said, quietly enough not to interrupt the flow of their conversation. But Empress Miko turned at the sound of my voice as I had at hers. She looked away again, leaving me all the more attuned to her presence than I had been before. To the proud way she stood and spoke to these experienced men, to the sleek way the robe fitted her body, drawn in at the waist by a crimson sash like a slash of blood, to the way she kept her head turned toward me enough that her profile all but glowed against the dark walls beyond.

The conversation went on, and I clenched my fists and released them again, irritation building. I had come up with this plan, yet here I was standing awkwardly on the outside of the conversation. I knew, logically, they could not always leave time for translation, that it was a lot of work to heap on Tor's shoulders, but that didn't help the tension growing in my body like a stretching bowstring.

"They don't agree on how to divide the soldiers or where the empress and her archers ought to be," Tor said eventually. "But they do all seem to agree there's nothing more to be done right now and everyone should eat and rest."

They all watched Tor finish his translation, and having so many eyes on me did nothing to ease my annoyance. I stared back at each Kisian general, only the empress's apologetic smile keeping me from snapping something I would be glad they could not understand.

"Rest is good," I said. "But why are they all staring at me?"

Tor shrugged. "To see if the great Levanti leader has any words of wisdom? They're talking like they're so kind in deigning to listen and consider your plan, and in letting you and the rest of the Swords fight for them. You should probably thank them if you want them to like you."

I shot him a look. "No. Tell them my people will need good food and rest, as well as adequate supplies to ensure their weapons are in the best condition. Tell them we will gather at sunset to go over the plan."

A smile flickered across Tor's face as he translated this. I watched them bristle, petty joy warming my heart. Miko twitched her own amused smile, and I fought not to grin back.

At an order from the empress, we were dismissed. General Moto and Minister Manshin stepped away together, while with a lingering look my way, the empress and the head of her guard made their way back up the stairs, leaving Tor and me at the bottom, the room around us far emptier than it had been ten minutes before.

I watched the empress until even the sweeping hem of her robe was out of sight.

"Remember the phrase I taught you," Tor said. "Say after me: *Ao gasho te remeste mot, kaa lo kiish ao falachu sho loa-da.*"

"I am not so lacking in either honour or pride. You, however, lack respect."

"Respect for who? I assure you I respect the empress enough to wonder what she sees in you when you can't even talk to her. The great Captain Rah e'Torin, exotic piece of manflesh."

"Respect for me," I said coldly.

"Why, because you're leading the collective Swords tonight? So what? You're not my captain, because I'm not a Sword of the Levanti. I'm just a useful mouthpiece." He walked away.

"We can fix that, Tor," I said. "We can fix that right now if I can find the right tools."

The unmade Sword stopped, glancing back over his shoulder. "You could, but it's too late. How can I give my life, my soul, in service to something I don't believe in anymore?"

What was there to say? His words hurt to the core, but my pain was nothing to his. When had he realised how he felt? That the person he had been born and the person he had been forced to grow into no longer matched? Was there any bottom to that well of grief?

"I'm sorry."

"You didn't do it."

"I'm still sorry it happened. And that if there was something I could have done, I didn't."

After a moment's indecision, he walked away and I let him go, as much because I couldn't think of anything to say as because he needed time and space to be alone. And I needed to rest.

Shivering from a combination of cold and lingering exhaustion, I set my foot on the first step and began to climb to the castle's heights. Most of the Levanti had refused rooms inside, preferring to sleep in tents or beneath the stars as herds were used to, but I had been by myself too long, without my herd too long, and had grown used to being alone. To silence. To the inside of buildings rather than braving the rain and the cold air. Perhaps I was slowly losing everything that made me Levanti and would soon feel like Tor. I told myself there was much more to feeling Levanti than sleeping on the ground. If only I could believe it.

I hadn't long been asleep when a gentle knock woke me. A figure slipped furtively in and I had my knife out before the door closed, my heart thumping hard despite there being nothing threatening about the cloaked figure carrying a tray. It didn't slow its heavy thud when Empress Miko set back her hood. If anything, it sped.

She paused her approach, eyeing the blade. I lowered it and, drawing the required blood from my upper arm, slid the knife back into its sheath. It stung a little, as it always did when the first blood seeped out. The empress didn't move.

"Tradition," I said, though she wouldn't understand. "*Ildoa.*"

"Hello," she said. "You, well?"

I nodded, hoping I looked better than I felt. My brief sleep had been undisturbed and might have been restful had Gideon and Ezma not haunted my dreams and left me unsteady.

Approaching on bare feet, Empress Miko held out the tray to show why she had come. It held a trio of dishes—one fruit, one a sort of flavoured nut, the other fish. And tea. I hadn't enjoyed tea the few times it had been offered to me, but cold seemed to have settled like fog in my very flesh, and I could do with something warm to drive it away.

She set the tray on the floor beside my sleeping mat and, dragging over a discarded cushion, settled herself on the other side. It made me think of the inn where we had eaten until we could eat no more, sharing each other's words. We had talked until suddenly the room had been full of tension and lacking in air. This time her very arrival seemed to have stolen it all away.

Watching me warily, the empress pointed at each of the foods and named them, only *fish* a word I had heard before. And tea. She poured some and I took up the tea bowl as I had seen her do many times, held cupped in my hands to warm them. She smiled, nodding, and picked up her own. My heart drummed a loud tattoo that ought to have sent quakes across the cup's surface.

Empress Miko blew the steam from her tea, once, twice, three times, always three times, even for hot food. I wondered if it was a Kisian tradition or merely her own habit.

Still nursing the tea, she spoke in a slow, considering way, while I watched for meaning. She seemed to have come for my company rather than because something was wrong, but I couldn't shake the fear her sudden appearance had sparked.

She sipped from her bowl and shot a furtive look at me over the rim like I was a wild creature who might bolt at any moment. Yet I was the one who hadn't moved, who sat watching while she fidgeted and shifted and sent her gaze dancing from me to the tray and the mat and the walls. The only place she didn't look was at the door.

More words. And gods I wished I could understand them and for a brief moment was envious of Tor having been force-fed their language, no matter what it had cost him. They started slow, her words dragging their considered meaning across my mind and leaving no trail of understanding, but they grew faster, more manic, her hands beginning to shake. She gestured at her lips and at me and flung her hand in the general direction of the courtyard, and finally I possessed a glimmer of understanding. Was she apologising for a kiss it had been hard to stop thinking about?

She set down her tea, leaving her hands to flutter nervously in her lap, her words descending into a mumble.

I reached for her hand, as much to draw her attention as to offer reassurance. She flinched and looked up, hope and fear in her eyes. "Miko," I said, liking the sound of her name on my tongue without its title. "You don't have to apologise."

She drew closer, that tiny movement the question she could not ask. A warning of what she wanted. A request for assurance it was what I wanted. The excruciating slowness of having to communicate consent without words was a whole new experience.

A little closer still. Her eyes had fixed on my lips, every lash on her lowered eyelids a fine trail of dark ink. She had felt so warm against me in the stable, but the chill gulf between us now was more tantalising. My skin tingled its anticipation as little by little we leant in until our lips brushed and our quickened breath shared the same air.

I slid a hand into her hair. It was soft and tangled about my fingers, the sensation odd after many years of lying with Swords whose scalps prickled beneath my touch.

Bowls clinked as she pushed the tray aside and pressed against me with enough strength that it was difficult to hold my ground as our kiss grew fiercer, deeper. I had to press back against her as her hands ran over my chest and my back and my arms—everywhere her eyes had hunted that night in the bathhouse. That had been my naked flesh, my exhausted, broken soul, yet this was far more intimate, the trailing of her fingers gentle as she laughed something against my lips.

She pushed me back onto the sleeping mat, laughing again as I grunted out a lungful of air. A laugh that faded into something far more serious when she felt me hard against her. I wondered then if she had ever lain with a man, or anyone, and while she wrestled with her own thoughts behind a glassy smile, I realised what we wanted couldn't happen. How could I ask her where she was in her cycle? How could I be sure it was safe? Impossible enough to consider adding an unaccounted-for child to a herd; how much more so to consider adding one to this situation?

Whatever her thoughts, she did not draw back. Like a fighter choosing to charge in despite their fears, she kissed me again, all ferocity and determination, and began untying her sash.

Her robe was open before I could stop her, nothing but bare skin beneath and oh how much I wanted to touch it, to touch her, to run my hands over her curves and revel in her strength, to share this human joy with her when we both needed it so much. Instead

I clenched my fists in a moment of frustration strong enough I wished I could scream, and drew back.

Her expression made me hate my lack of words all the more, so suddenly unsure she was, a question there I could not answer. I wanted to reassure her that I wanted this as much as she did, that it was nothing she had done, but the longer I went without speaking, without being able to explain, the more uneasy her expression grew until she drew her robe closed with shaking hands.

The room had felt so warm, but now the damp chill returned as she stood and backed away, her hair falling in a tangle over one shoulder. Words came to my lips, gabbled explanations she would never understand, but every attempt made no difference.

Before I even finished, she turned and hurried to the door, and I bit back an urge to throw caution to the winds, to call her back and take her in my arms. The door slid open and she was gone without looking back, leaving me lying dishevelled on my sleeping mat, aching with a need I could not sate and a frustration I could do nothing about. It had taken Tor years to learn their language to the level he had, even with a knack for such things.

I lowered my head onto the pillow and let out a slow breath, sleep very far away. In another life, Gideon would have laughed. Laughed until he couldn't breathe, like he had the night I'd failed to realise Khanum had propositioned me and I had unwittingly turned him down after weeks of determined flirting.

Somehow, thinking of Gideon only twisted the knot of tension all the tighter. I ought to have been there when he needed me as he had always been there for me, but I hadn't been able to see past the ideals I had dug my feet into, refusing to move. Now it might already be too late.

This ambush had to work.

———————◆———————

The sun was setting when I left my room. It had taken longer than usual to prepare, every piece of clothing and armour seeming to press upon one or other healing wound like reminders of past failures. I had taken my time, checking and rechecking the position of my blades, pointlessly wishing over and over I still had the one I'd dropped back in Tian what felt like a lifetime ago. How different everything had seemed then. How sure I had felt.

The castle hummed with activity. I passed a dozen Kisian soldiers in the passage, all silent, anxious, unsure, but it was the first Levanti I met that made my stomach do a nervous flip. Tor stood at the top of the stairs, hovering as he so often did, knowing he would be called on to translate sooner or later and as resigned to it as he was angry.

"Rah," he said.

"Tor," I returned. "Sleep well?"

He shrugged, not looking at me but down at the busy hall full of as many Levanti as bustling Kisians. "Like a baby."

"You woke every hour screaming? I can relate."

"It went that well, did it?"

"Nothing happened. Where's Ezma?"

Another shrug, something pettish in the gesture. "I haven't seen her. She isn't going."

"I know."

"But she's sending Derkka to watch you."

"I know."

He looked at me for the first time since I'd joined him. "And what will you do if this fails and she uses it against you?"

"That I don't know. But it won't fail because it's win or die at the hands of Grace Bahain, and I am not dying here."

Tor made no reply, and together we stood watching the activity down in the hall. The Levanti were gathered in small groups, while the sea of Kisian soldiers flowed around them. From this distance at least it looked like respectful cooperation.

I heard Miko before I saw her, and I must have flinched, for Tor looked around, one brow raised as her orders echoed through the hall. She had changed into her armour, but wore no crimson as a mark of her status, only the dark greys and browns of someone intending to move around in the dark and not get caught. The only thing that differentiated her from her soldiers was the great bow upon her back.

Nerves jangled around in my gut. Ambush nerves, I told myself, understandable when there was nothing routine about this and I knew none of the Kisians under my command, but my gaze skittered to the empress every few steps, dreading the moment she would see me. Would she glare at me? Ignore me? I deserved both and worse.

We were almost at the bottom of the stairs before she looked up, and meeting my gaze, held it with her chin jutted. "Captain Rah," she said, such chilly words that Minister Manshin's brows shot up. I could only hope my face gave nothing away.

"We are in the process of dividing our soldiers into the twenty-seven small groups you requested," he said, Tor translating with a little sigh. "Each group has been allocated a commander for you to communicate with, who will also take control and attempt to keep to the plan should anything happen to the lead Levanti. They all understand how this is supposed to work, so I feel we will give a good account of ourselves."

The empress stared at nothing while he spoke. All around her preparations were ongoing, a whole group of Kisian archers making final checks of their bows and arrows.

"If you could be sure your people are ready to go within the hour," Manshin added. "We ought to arrive by midnight. Any later and we'll be rushing our plans."

"We'll be ready," I said. "I will make my rounds now."

It felt like being a captain again, walking from group to group, seeing they had everything they needed. Those riding were out checking their horses, while the rest had to be sorted into groups. Two for each of the twenty-seven groups of Kisians, two smaller groups on horseback, and some archers were all we had, but with luck and a lot of cooperation from the Kisians, it was all we would need.

"Captain," Lashak e'Namalaka said when I stopped by her group. She had Shenyah e'Jaroven with her, along with her allotted Kisians.

"Captain," I replied, saluting her as she had saluted me. "Are you prepared?"

"We are, but having abandoned my Swords, I am no longer a captain."

"Neither am I, but that does not mean you don't deserve the honour of the title. I know you did not abandon them lightly."

She grunted a short laugh. "I was never really sure about you, but I can see why Dishiva likes you."

"Likes me so much she stood by while I was removed from my position and thrown in a cell?" I said, shocked by how strongly the anger prickled inside me. "No, don't answer that. I understand my choices were hard to follow and not always right, but this is hardly the time to discuss it."

Lashak tilted her head, examining me. "Neither were hers. Or Gideon's. Or anyone's. We do the best we can with what we have, but given all that's happened, it's never likely to be brilliant, is it? Is there any such thing as the right choice in any situation anymore?"

"Maybe. Sometimes. Like what we are doing tonight. Protecting ourselves."

"But are the Kisians marching this way even interested in us? Are we protecting ourselves or protecting these Kisians against other Kisians?"

"If you don't wish to fight—"

"Oh, I'll fight. I've seen enough of Grace Bahain that I'll enjoy sticking my blade into him."

"They want him alive."

She puffed an annoyed gust of breath. "Do they understand how hard that is in a night ambush?"

"I did explain. They still want him alive."

"Yes, but we don't. See? Shit just isn't as straightforward here as it was back on the plains. Or even as it was when we were all prisoners. The more fractured we get, the more complicated this war or...whatever it is gets, the less there can ever be a straightforward decision. And you know what? It's fucking awful."

I laughed because it was either that or cry. "It is," I said. "Thank you for sharing your wisdom."

"Wisdom? My frustrations more like. Either way, you can be sure of my support in anything that helps our people, especially if it helps Dishiva get the fuck out of there. We are heading to Koga-haera after this, aren't we?"

"I haven't heard Whisperer Ezma's thoughts on it, but that is certainly the empress's plan. And mine."

"And she'll keep to it whatever the outcome tonight?"

"She wants to oust Gideon so she can focus on the remaining Chiltaen and Kisian threat."

Lashak waved a dismissive hand. "It's all complicated nonsense, their politics, don't try to explain it to me. I stood in Gideon's throne room and listened to all those lords argue and look daggers at each other, always crowding around him in the hope he'd favour them above the others. Or they did until Leo became the only person he took advice from."

I had been about to move on, but her words stayed my feet. "How is he? Gideon."

She tilted her head again, eyes narrowing. "Different. Stubborn. I don't know. Sometimes he seems the same, and sometimes I look at him and don't see a Levanti anymore. It hasn't even been that long, but fuck it feels like forever since we crowned him, so full of hope for something greater."

I had so many questions. I wanted to know if he was healthy, if he ever spoke of me, if he knew about Sett, but there was no time, and what could I have done with the answers? To know he was alive was all I could handle right now.

With the hour almost up, many groups had begun moving toward the gates, but I found Minister Manshin and the empress still inside, Tor hovering.

"Tell them we're ready to go," I said.

Tor relayed the information, and with a sharp nod, the empress strode away, shouting orders as though I no longer existed.

"Remember we need Bahain alive," Manshin said, but didn't stay to await an answer, following his empress.

Around us, the tense buzz became a storm of footsteps and talk as everyone still inside made for the doors. I went to follow, but Tor grabbed my arm. "I...I heard you trained to be a horse whisperer," he said.

"Heard that, did you?" It surprised me Ezma had told anyone, let alone that it had gotten back to Tor.

"What was it like?"

I had expected him to ask why I had failed the training, but my answer would have been the same. I thought of the grove with its stands of trees, of the echoing stones of the old shrine, of the cold floor and the silence and the loneliness. The heartbreaking, desperate loneliness. Having not only to learn and work and pray and learn some more, every single day without pause, but to do it for...no one. There was some theoretical time in the future when I would be a horse whisperer, when Levanti from all different herds would need my advice, but there was no herd to sweat for, no herd to strive for. Just Whisperer Jinnit and his sour expressions.

"It was...lonely," I said, wishing there was a stronger word for the depth of isolation I had felt. A horse whisperer, always to stand apart, never to be part of a herd, never to love or be loved, never to have loyalties to anything but the honour of the task, never to fight for anything or to strive for betterment, merely to be the enduring, ongoing statue of Levanti values. "Really lonely."

Tor nodded, digesting this. I had the feeling more questions were coming and was glad there wasn't time. "Take care of you, huh?" I said as I prepared to join my group of soldiers.

He gave me one of his looks, part scowl, part long, judging stare. "Yeah, don't worry. I'll take care of your empress. Don't fuck this up, huh?"

I was getting used to his habit of biting back and shrugged. "You can always make a run for it through that drain if I do."

He snorted a laugh, unable to crush his grin. "Fuck you," he said, affection in his tone no matter how reluctant it sounded. "Go away."

He turned away to join the empress, double blades hanging at his hip, and though he had not been Made he looked every bit the warrior he wanted to be. There was no time to tell him so, no time to do anything but hurry out into the yard where Levanti and Kisians gathered in a buzz of low-voiced anticipation. Minister Manshin strode about checking the groups were together and prepared, setting his hands on shoulders and giving nods of encouragement as he passed. My group were waiting beside the gates. Their leader—Captain Kofi—nodded in greeting. Amun saluted. "Captain."

"Ready?" I said as the gates swung ponderously open.

Amun nodded.

"You're in command if I'm injured or...you know, die."

"As long as you promise not to get injured or die, that's fine."

I laughed, touched by the sincerity beneath the humour. Amun might not want to lose me, not want to take over, but at least I knew he could. The Torin herd learned *ekkafo* as children, its sounds and its motions and its tale taught through dance.

As we strode through the castle gates, a cohesive group despite our differences, I thought of the first time I had learned it. I had been too young to join Gideon and the other children in their lesson, so Mama had taken me a little way out of camp and sat with me in the grass, its tips scratchy in the late summer dry.

"The secret to learning *ekkafo* is its story," she had said. "Everyone plays a part, but only one part; you can't be more than one part, just as you can't be more than one person. It starts with the oku owl. She leaves her nest in the east to fly to the west. Do you remember which way is east and which is west?"

I had looked up at the setting sun and pointed. Mama had smiled, warming me inside.

"And while the oku flies, she sings like this." She had made its call, loud and clear like I had heard the other children do. "You try it."

It had taken a few tries and a few frustrated stomps of my feet, but I had finally achieved something that sounded right at least to me. And I had run west.

"The flight of the oku owl scares the mouse." Mama had made a high-pitched trill that wasn't quite a mouse but was more distinctive. And I had wanted to be good enough to join the others, so I had practised that sound too. "The mouse runs for cover at the southern point of the circle. Do you know where that is?"

She had smiled again when I'd known the answer. "The mouse passing by excites the sand cat," she had gone on, and there was another sound and another direction, moving southeast to west this time, and I had told myself I would remember it. Three animals were easy. Except there weren't three. There were twenty-seven. That number had seemed impossibly huge.

"Don't worry, Rah," she had said. "You don't have to remember them yet. I'll help you."

We had darted through the grass together, each of the animal sounds becoming a song on my mother's lips. We must have looked ridiculous, trying to be all the animals at once, but I had felt like I was doing it, like I was part of the herd, like I belonged, and I had been happy.

She was gone now, but the *ekkafo* had long been rooted in my mind, able to be sung and danced without the need to think, yet despite Amun's company the night felt chill and empty in the wake of such a memory.

It took longer than expected to reach the field where Grace Bahain's army had camped. It was slow going in the dark, and we arrived with no time to go over the plan. We had our tasks— the empress took her archers and we split into twenty-seven small groups, each taking the role of one animal in the coming dance.

We had based our calculations on a map the Kisians had provided, but one look at the camp and I knew it all wrong. They hadn't built fortifications, but the field was larger than we'd accounted for and not as round, which would throw out the timing.

"Shit," I said as Amun joined me atop the hill. Below the camp was a constellation of lights in the irregularly shaped bowl between the hills. "We need—"

"I'm on it." Amun crouched and started making something like the right shape out of sticks. He worked with only the barest moonlight, lips moving as he muttered through the problem—a task I'd only ever seen Kishava do as easily.

Other Levanti gathered, keeping back from the crown of the hill. It was dark, but any hint of our presence would only make this harder.

"Something wrong?" Lashak whispered.

"The field is not the same shape as on the map."

"Shit," she echoed.

"It looks like about a ten-second progressive delay to the south,"

Amun said. "But it's irregular enough that such rough planning will only be accurate for the first few passes. If we're lucky."

I'd never had to captain an *ekkafo* on my own, nor with so many Levanti from different herds, and despite the confidence I'd clung to, the enormity of the task swelled over me like a dark tide. We were not enough Levanti leading not enough Kisians, who we couldn't even communicate with. It was going to be a mess. A mess we had to win.

"We could alter positions," Lashak said, glancing back down the hill as the Kisians arrived, a grim army appearing from the night. "It might be easier."

"That would put the cricket and the toad in a lot of danger," Amun said. "Are we *that* sure they don't know we're here?"

The moment's hesitation before anyone answered was answer enough. Lashak nodded. "All right, ten-second progressive delay to the south it is. I'll make sure everyone knows, but we'd better keep moving or dawn will be upon us before we're even in place."

Leaving Amun's oval of sticks upon the grass, we made our way back down the hill, Lashak catching a few words with each of the twenty-seven leaders as we went. By the time we rejoined the Kisians, I had schooled my features into as close an approximation of aloof assurance as I could muster. If they didn't trust us, this would be even more of a mess than it already was.

There was nothing to say. To them the plan was unchanged, so with a nod to the shadowy figure of Tor standing at the empress's side, we began to move out. Leaving one group behind in more or less the place we'd arrived, Lashak took thirteen groups west while the rest followed us east.

The ground was hilly and uneven, dense clumps of damp undergrowth making progress slower than we'd have liked, while thick stands of trees obscured our vision. At the first point in our no-longer-a-circle, we left Emmata en'Injit and her group behind before moving on. The scorpions were next, followed by the asps and the mice, and group by group we left Levanti and Kisians behind until it was just me and Amun with our soldiers in the depths of a silent night.

"Well, may Nassus be with us, I guess," Amun said, looking out toward the enemy camp. My legs ached from so long and arduous a walk, yet somehow the worst was yet to come.

The Kisians fidgeted, eyes flicking warily about the darkness. They didn't appear as out of breath as we were, perhaps more used to the uneven terrain, but that hadn't stopped dark patches of sweat appearing on their sleeves and around their necks. They had opted for lighter garb, and though they would move faster they might soon regret the lack of heavy armour.

Drawing a deep breath, Amun made a cuckoo owl's call as loud as he could, the sound filling me with heartache. No answering call came, so we crouched in the darkness, watching the camp.

"We wait," I said to Captain Kofi, now a terrible time to hope he remembered the words we had taught them.

Ambushes are nerve-racking things, but knowing failure was not an option and every part of this was my responsibility... It was as much as I could do to keep from pacing while I ran through all that could go wrong. Until at last the call of a brown owl echoed its forlorn notes across the field. Lashak was in place. It was time to go.

We weren't the first to run, but ambushes relied on speed. Usually we had horses and could trample over anything in our paths. This time we just had to be fast. Quick kills. Maximum chaos.

I tapped Captain Kofi on the shoulder. "Ready?"

"Yes," he said, and I was grateful for those nights around the fire with Miko for teaching me simple Kisian.

He passed the whispered order on, causing a shuffling of feet and a shifting of armour. Knives were drawn. They had their swords with them, but I had laughed at the idea they could use swords as their main weapon if they wanted to move fast and kill faster.

A third owl sound—the oku owl—echoed across the night, and there was no more time to worry or prepare. Beside me, Amun started counting beneath his breath. Ten seconds passed before the first shout. Even with a good view of the field it was impossible to see their progress, only to hear the footsteps and the clash of metal, the cries and the thuds as Amun went on counting.

The mouse call came on time as the second group entered, followed by the third, more and more cries and thundering steps painting a picture of what was happening.

"Ready?" Amun said, and cried the call of the cuckoo owl to the night sky. "Three, two, one. Go!"

Brushing through the undergrowth, we sped out onto the field, legs pumping, every step vibrating its force through my knees. Captain Kofi and his soldiers followed, sprinting southwest with us as fast as we could.

At the edge of the camp, confused soldiers were lighting torches and scrambling into their armour, and like the rushing of the East-bore, we ploughed through them. There were no faces in the con-fusion, only bodies into which we thrust our blades and ran on, spirits of death in the darkness. Amun ran with me, keeping pace. Shouts erupted around us. Torchlight flared. I darted away from it as an arrow dug into a man's back. I had a split second to wonder if the empress had loosed that one before I plunged on, slashing and stabbing my way across the camp. Past tents and horses, dying campfires and running men. And out into the cool air upon the other side, my hands slick with blood.

Amun slowed and stood puffing beside me. Heavy steps heralded the arrival of some of our Kisians. Captain Kofi murmured, check-ing if we had lost anyone, while Amun counted. Behind us, the noise had grown. Shouts and panic rang loud enough to obscure the *ekkafo* calls, but it ought not matter now we had begun.

While Amun counted, we caught our breath in the darkness, noise filling the shallow valley around us. Ten seconds out, I checked Captain Kofi and his men were ready, and took a last opportunity to wipe the blood and sweat off my hands before Amun reached zero.

With a shout, he charged and I followed, our boots scraping on stone and the chill wind whipping into our faces. Plunging back in like loosed arrows, we hit the soldiers on the outer edge before they saw us, slamming bodily into them. Hip and shoulder to knock them off balance so they couldn't fight back, before a blade to the back of the neck or the throat or the side—wherever was easiest to reach. In. Out. Don't stop to check if they're dead, just run on and hit the next and the next.

This time, some had been able to struggle into their armour and most had weapons, but with us pelting through them in the darkness, they were fractured and couldn't rally. One nearby lit a torch, calling out to gather others. Amun dodged away from him, cutting into my path, but though I almost tripped on his feet, I couldn't blame him. Light meant arrows, and sure enough, the meaty thwack of a point ramming into the Kisian's chest soon sent others running.

We took out as many stampeding soldiers as we could and ran on.

By the time we burst through the other side, my whole body ached with fatigue and renewed pains. Yitti had told me I needed to rest and heal, and once again here I was ignoring his good advice.

Amun started counting as he sucked breathless gasps, crouched in the darkness at my feet. Captain Kofi was a few seconds behind us, his men a trail behind him, counted as they arrived. The man held up two fingers, but it was too dark to see his expression. Two losses? Two extra soldiers? My mind wasn't working fast enough to understand.

Every second we waited replenished my breath but drained my adrenaline, and by the time Amun counted down again, I was stiff and sore. But this was the only way, so I forced myself to move, once more leading my group into the chaos of the Kisian camp.

There were lit torches everywhere now. Someone had stoked the camp fires, and soldiers were clumping together for the small amount of protection numbers offered. Our timing must have been out or some groups had lost track, the camp smattered with our people. Some Levanti, most Kisians in their dark clothing hacking at the enemies they had once called friends.

Letting instinct guide me, I ran our third sprint across the camp, the rush of our charge sending soldiers leaping out of the way. Those caught in our path added their blood to my soaked blade. Mindlessly, I would have continued on for as many sprints as we needed, but Amun's cry shocked me out of my stupor. He stumbled out of sight beside me, and I turned before even thinking that wasn't how an *ekkafo* worked.

He was on his feet again, but two soldiers barred his path, closing in.

"On! On!" I shouted to Captain Kofi, gesturing in the direction we had been running. "Take them and keep going!"

A soldier lunged at me as I shouted, but the captain darted in, plunging his knife into the flesh beneath the man's upraised arm. He screamed as he pulled it out, staggering back, and Kofi stood frozen, a moment of overwhelming horror at fighting fellow Kisians crossing his face before he turned and ran on.

Amun had backed up, drawing one of his swords. Grace Bahain's soldiers edged closer, ready to strike. I stuck my knife into one's back and yanked it free in time to face the other, but as he turned, Amun sliced his gut open. Two bodies slumped dying on the ground between us, leaving us to stare at one another amid the chaos.

"You're not meant to come back for someone in an *ekkafo*," Amun said, breathing heavily.

"And you're not meant to when a *kutum* is ordered either," I said. "Some of our rules are shit."

Amun clapped me on the shoulder with a laugh. "Damn right they are. Now where the fuck were we going?"

All was chaos around us, their Kisians and our Kisians a mess of varied-coloured armour now, nothing organised about the attack. Or their defence. A few soldiers went on grouping together, but many were already dead or wounded, or had fled out into the night rather than stand in the dark and be slashed at from all sides. A dozen had formed up before a commander, his voice raised upon roared orders.

"There he is!" Lashak appeared, her face splattered with blood and her group of Kisians following like stunned sheep. "Grace Bahain." She pointed at the commander. "To me!"

Few would hear her over the furore of battle, but a dozen soldiers couldn't long keep him safe.

"To me! To me!" Lashak shouted again as nearby Levanti gathered. "We take him alive! Alive! To me!"

A sense of triumph bloomed inside me, easing my pains. Here he was, all but alone, his army dispersed and in chaos. We were going to get him. Going to win this.

"To me! Take Grace Bahain alive!"

Levanti and dark-clad Kisians charged at the line of soldiers before the duke, cutting them down and drawing them away. Amun ran in, no doubt expecting me to follow, but I hung back, edging around the gathered mass, eyes on this unknown enemy. He stood bravely now but was sure to run the moment all was lost. Sure to escape rather than let himself be captured, and when he pelted off into the darkness, I would be there.

"You should just let him die."

Derkka stood alone some paces away, bow in hand. No one ought to stop and talk in the middle of a battle, but though fighting raged around us he had eyes only for me.

"Empress Miko wants him alive," I said. "So we take him alive."

"That's a poor reason unless you're a Kisian work dog now."

I bristled at the insinuation, but said nothing. Grace Bahain still stood his ground. Soldiers were falling all around him, the whole like a hazy dream.

"Levanti do not take prisoners," Derkka said, his voice closer now. "Levanti do not trade in lives. He dies or he goes free, those are the only options we have."

"Like you've never done anything dishonourable," I hissed over my shoulder as Grace Bahain shouted to his surviving knot of soldiers, Levanti closing in all around them. "You can just drug him like you drugged me, that'll be acceptable to the gods, right?"

"You're a danger to our people. I ought to have killed you when I had the chance." A bowstring creaked behind me, drawing taut with threat. "Or when it would be deemed an unfortunate battle casualty."

Derkka's feet shuffled behind me. "You wouldn't," I said, my back tingling. Did he believe so strongly in Ezma that he would loose an arrow into my back? There was no less honourable way to attack a fellow Levanti. So long as I didn't turn, the gods would cast him into the shadows if he loosed.

"You don't think so? What is the future worth?"

He loosed. The arrow ripped by my ear, close enough I could feel the brush of air, of its fletching, and the promise of its pain—a pain not destined for me. Slowed by dawning realisation, I watched as the arrow tore between the remaining soldiers, burying itself in Grace Bahain's throat.

"No!" someone cried, other voices rising to join its frustration, but I couldn't move. Couldn't speak. Could only turn to stare at the apprentice whisperer. He met my gaze in a moment of silent challenge, before shouldering the bow and walking away.

Grace Bahain crumpled to his knees, Levanti gathering around him, trying to save the life of an enemy while our kin lay injured all around us. But it was too late.

Grace Bahain was dead.

18. MIKO

We returned to dawn light gilding the ragged edges of Kiyoshio Castle. My soldiers were quietly triumphant, while the Levanti were just quiet. I didn't know enough to understand if that meant anything, and walking at my side, Tor offered no explanation.

We had lost Grace Bahain. I was too tired to wrangle with all the ramifications of such a failure, to consider all the ways things could go wrong from here, could only walk with the weight of it seeming to press me into the ground.

It was hard to remind myself in all other ways the ambush had been a success. No army would march to our gates today.

I had sent two riders ahead to inform Minister Manshin and General Moto how we had fared, so was unsurprised to find the pair of them waiting for us in the courtyard. A courtyard alive with bustling servants dashing about packing carts and rigging out horses.

"Minister. General," I said as they bowed before me. "What's going on?"

"We cannot hold Syan without Grace Bahain," General Moto said. "There is no saying what Governor Koali will do when he hears his lord has died in battle, so it's imperative we leave for Kogahaera at once."

Both men stood tall and sure, seeking no approval. No permission. "Our soldiers have been out all night," I said. "Are you proposing we march without letting them rest?"

"There is no time, Majesty." Manshin's tone held no apology. "Without Grace Bahain we cannot bargain support from the Koalis. We aren't safe here. Not even for an hour. At best we could get caught in the castle, unable to leave. At worst they may incite the people against us."

I didn't like the look they shared before Manshin, hands clasped behind his back, added, "They are not loyal to you. They are loyal to Grace Bahain. You have killed Grace Bahain, which will not give them reason to be more loyal now."

You. I noted the distancing once again.

"A token force is all that's required to hold the castle against Governor Koali, given its fortifications," Manshin finished. "But if you want to march for Kogahaera this season, we go now."

Our success on the battlefield overnight would count for little if we ended up trapped inside our own castle while others fought for the empire. I would have preferred to move at my own speed, not to look like I was fleeing, but it was escape now or end up at war with the city of Syan.

I let out a tired sigh. "All right, we march for Kogahaera. Oyamada must be almost there with the rest of the army by now."

Both men bowed as though the order had been mine from the beginning, and I was grateful for that at least. "I will speak to the Levanti translator and discover their intentions," General Moto said, bowing a second time. "If you will excuse me, Majesty."

Almost I said I would join him, but the set of Minister Manshin's jaw gave me pause. There the face of a man who had something else he wanted to say. I lifted my brows. "There is something more?"

He flicked a glance at General Ryoji beside me. "I would speak alone, Your Majesty."

A burst of panic stayed my tongue, but I managed to nod dismissal to Ryoji. We were hardly alone in a courtyard full of busy people hurrying about their tasks, but the absence of either general seemed to satisfy Manshin. He drew himself up. As if that were needed given his height. "You cannot march west with the Levanti."

It wasn't a question or a recommendation, but a statement of fact, and it took me a moment to be sure I had heard him correctly. "Cannot?" I said, bristling at so stringent a command.

"They are not our allies. They are our enemies."

"Do correct me if I'm wrong, Minister, but without them we would be preparing for a protracted siege right now. If fighting for us when we had not enough soldiers to fight for ourselves does not make them allies, I'm not sure what would."

Around us the Levanti were as busy as any of our returning soldiers, the whole courtyard packed with men I had every reason to be proud of.

"A fight which led to the death of Grace Bahain when we most needed him alive. Killed by a Levanti archer, I understand. It would be of great help to their Emperor Gideon if we were trapped here unable to fight, and that is why you cannot call them allies. You cannot trust them."

"Is that advice more prudence or prejudice?"

Manshin stiffened. "Prudence, Your Majesty. Anyone willing to bow to a Levanti, to take orders from a Levanti, to see their leader marching with Levanti, has already chosen to side with Emperor Gideon. Those who have not want no Levanti here."

"While I take your point, it sounds as much like prejudice as it does prudence, Minister."

He took a small step closer, forcing my neck up at a sharper angle. "I will allow that Rah e'Torin appears to be an honourable man by the standards of such things, but you cannot judge his people by the actions of one man. One man who, if he better understood his place, would not be seen so close to you."

"And you ought not judge them all by the actions of Gideon e'Torin."

"My way is safer."

He was right, but the Levanti were powerful allies, and I trusted Rah more than I trusted most of my generals. To ignore that and brand them as nothing but enemies, nothing but barbarians who had taken our lands, was to ignore the real hurt the Chiltaens had done them, even if that hurt had been inflicted in the process of hurting us. Simplifying it to good and bad was wrong on every level, even if it was how you got people to fight for you. Clear, unassailable lines. Us good. Them bad. Did it matter that it bore no resemblance to the truth?

"I do not pretend to understand the complexities of their culture," Manshin went on more quietly. "But if they want to go home, let them go. That is what I believed they wanted when I let them join me at Otobaru. Ships so they might leave our shores."

"And if they don't want to go? If they want to stay? Or fight their own at Kogahaera?"

He met my direct gaze without any sign of discomfort. "Lock them up. Or kill them."

"No."

Manshin lifted his brows.

"No," I repeated. "I will not be that sort of ruler."

He did not reply, but I was sure he thought *The sort of ruler who keeps her empire?* to himself, and a sick feeling rose up my throat. I made to walk past him, only for him to step in my path as though I had been a common servant. "If your reluctance is due to your personal interest in Rah e'Torin," he whispered, every word harsh, "I must, once again it seems, advise you most strongly against associating yourself with a man whose very presence in your army will forever taint you in the eyes of your own people."

Anger shook me. Embarrassment, too. I knew my face to be growing hot, but there was nothing I could do but meet his stare or capitulate. "You want to know how I feel about him?" I hissed back. "Yes, I do want Rah e'Torin to stay. I trust him. But this is not about him or anyone else. I want to rule an empire built on tolerance, not division. I want to unite Kisia, and if I walk the same path to the throne as Emperor Kin, nothing will change."

"You cannot have ideals until you're strong enough to wear their consequences. What do commoners care for tolerance toward outsiders when they are afraid? When all they see is their leader putting others before them?"

Around us, my triumphant soldiers had joined the preparations, a sense of excitement building that we were moving toward Kogahaera at last. To them we were but empress and minister discussing details, while the very stones beneath my feet seemed to be cracking. I had built everything upon my faith in Minister Manshin, upon our shared purpose. When had our hopes and intentions diverged so completely?

"As always, I thank you for your advice, Minister," I said, determined to be stately and confident whatever I might feel inside. "I will consider your words, but will make no hasty decisions. The Levanti are, after all, the only reason we are not at this moment very dead."

I strode away before I said anything I would regret, and it was a dozen hasty steps before I realised I had no destination in mind. I kept walking because to stop would look foolish, but I felt heavy, disconnected from the people around me, even those who spoke my language and shared my culture. Did they all feel as Minister Manshin did? That the Levanti presence undercut my rule no matter how hard they fought alongside us? Even so, could we as easily attack Kogahaera without them? No matter how you considered it, the answer was no, and I would be a fool to throw away such a comfortable advantage.

"Complaisance is the road to defeat." I couldn't recall who Mama had been quoting every time she'd said that, but it gnawed at me

now as I made for the stairs. Laying siege to Kogahaera with a large army was a strong plan, but what if there was a way to leverage it into a clever plan? Something more I could use against this man who was not only an enemy, but an emperor.

An idea began to form and at last I had a destination.

Maids were in my room packing my clothes, though it wasn't really my room and they weren't my clothes. Wanting to be alone, I took a writing table and carried it toward the Cavern.

"Allow me, Your Majesty," one of them said, following me into the passage.

"No, I can manage, but run and fetch Tor. The Levanti translator. With the long hair." The girl looked like I had asked her to jump off the balcony, but she bowed and hurried away.

The Cavern was empty and cold, two lit braziers doing little to combat the morning chill making its way beneath the balcony overhang. Preferring to keep near the warmth, I set up to work beside one, listening with half an ear for footsteps heralding Tor's approach. Yet having set my brush to the ink, I sat with it hovering above the paper. How did one address a false emperor? A man who was not even Kisian? Who had done nothing to earn the title he chose except to take it by force like Kin had done before him?

I smiled. *Usurper.*

Choosing my words carefully, I began to write. It was not easy to find all the right words, yet I had finished before Tor arrived at the speed of one who would rather be anywhere else. From the doorway he lifted his brows in both greeting and question.

"Tor," I said, realising I had sent for him without considering I was asking a favour. He was not mine to command. "I... I would greatly appreciate it if you could assist me. I have written a letter to your Emperor Gideon—"

"He is not mine."

I adjusted my thoughts. Talking to Tor often felt like one was walking blindfolded across a room with holes in the floor. "My apologies. I have written to the usurper Emperor Gideon, but I would rather it be read by him than to him by someone else—"

"You want me to translate it."

Surely, interrupting was a discourtesy in Levanti society as well, so I let go the hope that after our last conversation his opinion of me, or at least his manner, might have softened. "Yes, please," I said as though I had not been an empress. "If you could rewrite it in Levanti for me, I would be most grateful."

He hovered on the threshold, undecided, and stared at me as though I had said something strange. I had no one else to ask and no way to pressure him even had I been inclined to, so all I could do was smile and hope. Tor parted his lips and I was sure he was about to refuse, but he snapped his jaw closed, nodded, and strode to the desk, all long limbs and sullen scowl.

In silence he took up my letter and read it through. I held my breath as he traced the lines with the tip of his finger. It didn't matter what he thought of it. What he thought of me. Yet it was all I could do not to ask if it was acceptable. Once at the end he didn't ask any questions, just sighed, flipped a length of hair out of his face, and took up the brush.

I paced while he worked, trying to keep my steps slow and my tread soft. Trying not to think about what Minister Manshin had said. About Levanti support. About Rah. Rah, who had invited my embrace, who I had been so sure had wanted me like I had wanted him, until he hadn't.

"What does *ichasha* mean?" I said, turning to Tor. "In Levanti?"

He had been flicking his gaze between my letter and his, slowly translating, but his hands stilled and his brows sank low. "It means 'blood.' Why?"

Blood? I must have misheard because that made no sense, but I could hardly ask him what words sounded like *ichasha* could have been uttered in such a situation.

Anyone else would have taken my silence as the end of the conversation, but not Tor. "Did Rah say that?" he asked, something like a long-suffering sigh escaping with the words.

"Yes." My cheeks heated at the mere possibility we were about to have this conversation. "At least I thought it was, but it doesn't make sense so it was probably something else. Forget I asked."

I busied myself straightening my sleeve, watching out of the corner of my eye for him to go back to the letter, but he didn't move. A long minute dragged by, full of the comfortable sounds of clinking coals, distant activity, and the ever-present barrage of the sea, yet over it all the sound of Tor putting down the brush was the loudest of all. Fabric rustled as he turned to look at me.

"Yes?" I said. "What is it?"

"He wouldn't have sex with you?"

He asked the question with such appalling ease, and my cheeks flamed. I looked away, beginning to stammer out a reproof for speaking so, only for him to talk over the top of me. "Excuse my assumption if I am in error, but we have a few different words for 'blood' in Levanti. *Ichasha* is specific to the menstrual blood a woman loses each cycle of the Goddess Moon."

To ask the question was one thing, but to go on talking about it as one would speak of the weather made me thrust out my hand and squeeze shut my eyes, as though obscuring him from my sight would block his words.

He stopped talking, but the silence was no improvement, and my cheeks stubbornly refused to cool. When I risked glancing at him again, he was still looking at me. The brush lay untouched on the paper. "I'm...sorry?" he said, seeming to be venturing an idea he was unsure about. "Is this...is this something you don't...talk about?"

"No! No, we don't just openly discuss...blood and sex, like we're—"

I turned away. Almost I had called his people *savages*, and I hated how easily the word had come to my lips, but though I had stopped myself, of course he knew what I had so nearly said.

"It is rather more barbaric to suppress discussion of natural and important things, don't you think?" he asked quietly.

I couldn't answer, wished I had never asked, that he would finish the letter and go away, but Tor seemed intent on punishing me.

"Food and water are precious resources on the plains," he said, getting to his feet. "So we cannot just allow a herd to grow without limit. Each season there can only be so many children added to the number of mouths we must feed. Sometimes it's a good number. Sometimes it's a very small number. Either way it is the responsibility of all members of the herd to keep to that number and not stretch our resources, so we are careful. As a bare minimum, Levanti men do not have sex with a woman without asking where she is in her cycle, and Levanti women keep track of their cycle. Do you...do you just have babies whenever?"

There was not an ounce of shame or discomfort in his expression, and I couldn't but hate him for it, and for the slight sneer in his question.

"Do men here at least drink epaya?"

"I...What is that?" I said.

"It's crushed epa seeds, you know, the fruit? Maybe you call it something else here, but it decreases a man's potency."

I screwed up my nose, grateful for any opportunity to shift the subject however slightly. "That sounds foul. What does it taste like?"

"I don't know. I've never tasted it."

There was something guarded in his reply, in the way he fiddled with the hem of his tunic, that made him look young and awkward. This a man I had seen kill one of his own people, who could ride more skilfully than any Kisian I had ever seen and could talk about a woman's blood like it was nothing, embarrassed at last.

"How many cycles old are you, Tor?" I said. As the words left my mouth, I realised how personal the question sounded, especially with his name on the end like I was pulling him close. "I mean, if... if that's all right for me to ask. In your culture."

"I told you already. When you asked if I would be Made."

Somehow the embarrassment of having forgotten, of making a fool of myself, was worse than the conversation about my blood, and I pressed my hands over my face. "You did. I'm sorry."

"Nineteen next season," he said, taking pity on me.

Convention dictated I reply in kind, but silence stretched where my answer should have been. In many ways my age was as much a barrier as my womanhood, but I wanted to tell him. To trust him. Not just wanted to, but already did in the same way I trusted Rah. These men who had no reason to want me ousted from my position, who had no reason to look down on me for what I was, were far more honourable than my advisors, with their predetermined and immutable ideas of what I was capable of.

"I'm... about a year behind you."

His eyes widened a moment, but he coughed to hide his surprise.

"Everyone knows I'm young, of course," I said hurriedly. "If they calculate. But Mama always said most of keeping power is appearing to deserve it, so... please keep that between us."

He nodded with such a fixed mask I couldn't tell if I'd angered him.

"The words you want are *ki ichasha sorii.*"

"*Ki ichasha sorii?*"

"It means you're at a safe point in your cycle, having just finished bleeding or being about to."

I looked away, having forgotten for a moment what had brought us here. It felt like a terrible time to admit I had never paid as much attention as I ought, aside from cursing bleeding days when they arrived for their added annoyance.

"As long as you *are* at a safe point in your cycle," he added, perhaps sensing something of my reluctance. "We take these things seriously. Everyone should."

Two steps took him back to the table and the letter I had all but forgotten. "Here." He held it out. "It is done but for your name."

"Oh, thank you."

He bowed, at the same time pressing his fists together in a Levanti salute. "Your Majesty."

And without asking if I needed anything more, he was gone, leaving me with a slew of complicated thoughts I had very little time to consider. That my mother had taught me so little about the way my body worked beyond how to protect garments against blood seemed suddenly a grievous oversight. And to be worrying about it when I was about to march out with my army, more foolish still. It was not the time, but I couldn't help wishing I had someone I could ask. A female friend who would understand.

There had only ever been Sichi. I had not spoken of our plans that day in the bathhouse, and now she was married to a Levanti emperor instead of my brother. And I had just killed her uncle in an ambush and taken his castle. Not a good time to have such conversations even had it been possible.

I thought of her as I signed my name on a letter to her husband, glad at least that if he was anything like Rah and Tor, Gideon e'Torin would respect her.

———◆———

All was ready when I returned to the courtyard, my soldiers prepared to depart, though carts were still being loaded with what goods we could salvage. The Levanti were mounted but had kept themselves apart. That I registered relief they were still present worried me. What had I thought Manshin capable of in my absence?

As I descended the stairs, my gaze slid to Rah, mounted upon Jinso. At this distance there was no sign of the night's fatigue on his face as he laughed at something said to him, sending my heart fluttering. I berated myself for looking at all. I had an army to lead. A minister to placate. People to rule. The handsome smile of a foreign warrior and Tor's words ought not to be taking up so much space in my mind. But they were. Filling my heart and making me weak and foolish.

I began to tell myself Emperor Kin would never have suffered such thoughts, only to halt abruptly upon the second last step. But of course he had. Why else spend a lifetime trying to destroy my mother for the crime of loving another man? She had thrown it all right back, but no matter what he did he was always righteous and pragmatic, while she was the empire's mad bitch. The injustice of it stole my breath, and for a moment I stood alone though I was surrounded by people, my hands clenching to fists for a rage that didn't belong only to me, but to many.

Even I had treated her like she was mad for crossing a line she'd been goaded to all her life.

Around me final preparations spun on, I the still centre of a whirlwind. Near the gate, Minister Manshin was giving orders. Beside him, General Moto was in conversation with a commander whose name I did not know, but the pair looked at ease in their positions at the head of my army. These were all men who knew their places because their places had been carved for them by dozens, hundreds of men before them. My ancestors had carved a place for Tanaka, but not for me.

I had to unstick my feet from the step and force myself forward, holding on to the bundle of new thoughts to examine later. And for the first time I felt the full weight of my womanhood as I carried every one of the women my family had ignored out into the court-yard with me.

A horse had been saddled for me, and General Ryoji waited beside it, his own roan mare tossing her head in impatience to get moving. "Your Majesty," he said, totally unaware that as I mounted, I saw him with fresh eyes. This man who had been loyal to my mother, had helped her cultivate personal support, whatever it had cost him. The court might have said she was using him, con-trolling a weak man with a love he couldn't let go, but I had seen too much to believe it.

"General," I said, settling into my saddle, the horse lively beneath me. "You told me back at Achoi you never meant to love my mother as much as you did, but if it was not love that started it all, what was it?"

He looked around and back at me, brows raised. "This hardly seems the best time or place to have this conversation, Your Majesty."

"I'm not sure if there will ever be a good time to have it."

Again he looked around, but no one was close enough to overhear. "I...we shared the same ideals. And the same anger. I think...the anger was the most important part. A sharing of hurts with someone when you can't let anyone else see them is a precious thing. First anger, then hurts, then honesty, and you would do any-thing for this person."

"Anything?"

"Anything except the one thing you know they will regret ask-ing you to do when they calm down."

She had stood on the steps and ordered her guards to cut through me if it meant getting to Emperor Kin. Just as she had looked through me again and again, focussing her energy and her plans and her love on Tanaka. But little by little, I was beginning to understand why.

"Thank you, General," I said. "For that choice as well as your answer."

"I...am glad to be of service, Your Majesty."

"Now what's this?" General Moto said to no one in particular. "Looks like trouble."

The inner gates sat open, and a guard was running toward us across the band of grass separating Kiyoshio's double walls.

"It does look like trouble," Ryoji said as we pushed our horses through the mass of gathered soldiers. Many stopped talking to watch, and by the time I reached Minister Manshin by the gates, all eyes were upon the guard's approach. Manshin barely had time to say "Your Majesty" before the man stood doubled over before us, heaving breaths. For a few moments he couldn't speak, and I wanted to shake the words out of him.

"Majesty," he said, having regained the power to gasp if not talk. "There are—townspeople—at the—city gates. Some here too. Shouting. They want you—to answer a charge of—treason, Your Majesty."

"Are the Koali brothers with them, by any chance?" Manshin said.

"I—believe so, Minister."

Minister Manshin looked my way, his expression as close to an *I told you so* as he would allow himself.

"Of what treason am I accused?"

The still-puffing man bowed. "Of killing the rightful—duke of Syan, Majesty. As chosen by—Emperor Kin."

I could have railed that I was their empress and it was me they ought to listen to, that I was the last Otako, that the empire was mine by right, but the divine right of Otakos had died with Emperor Kin, and Kisia would be better for it, for having a ruler with something more than their name to give. The thought that imperial bloodlines were outdated and unnecessary had been brewing in my mind since Jie had said anyone could be an emperor now, but we were at war. Pulling the empire back together required more than a single, glorious win on the battlefield such as any general could achieve. It needed a thousand tiny stitches, like the mending of a torn robe. Each stitch a relationship, a conversation, a moment of compassion and attention, a determination to improve the lives of my people to build a more cohesive, united whole. Mother had long ago taught me how to show people the face they wanted to see, how to talk to people the way they wished to be spoken to, and it was that ability that would be needed here, not the brute strength of a general.

"We will ride out and meet them."

"Are you sure that's wise, Majesty?" Manshin said.

"Talking seems wiser than hiding. You have a better idea?"

"Not to hand."

We shared a wry grimace, and it was reassuring to find myself once again in accord with him, however temporary it might prove. "If we march out at full strength, hopefully no one will be mad enough to try to stop us, whatever Governor Koali says."

Manshin nodded. "Very good, Your Majesty. Shall we?"

I tucked the letter Tor had written safely into my sash while Manshin moved away shouting orders. We were marching out. Tor must have been nearby because shouts soon rose in Levanti too, and the space filled with the jostle and bustle of hooves and foot-steps anxious to be moving.

Rather than look back and risk catching sight of Rah again, I walked my horse toward the open gate. The stretch of grass between walls was empty, but beyond the gates I could imagine people filling the street. Shouting, the guard had said. I knew that sort of shouting.

"We're as ready to go as we'll ever be," Manshin said, returning to my side.

"Then let's go."

General Ryoji fell in on one side, Minister Manshin on the other as we made our way toward the outer gates. Down the muddy grass slope, snatches of distant sounds cutting through the morning. A short, high shout that could have been part of a chant. A low, rhythmic thumping. I forced myself to keep my head up and my gaze forward, to not grip the reins too tight though I feared what awaited us more than I had feared facing the Chiltaen army at Risian.

A sliver of daylight appeared between the gates as we drew close, and with a frightening inevitability they began to yawn open like jaws preparing to swallow us.

Noise rushed through. People clogged the street, shouting, a mass of blue and green and brown robes and tunics, some wearing storm cloaks, others with their heads bare. A persimmon flew toward us, followed by another. Some yellowing cabbages came next. General Ryoji caught one, leaving another to smash upon the wall above us and rain wilted leaves.

General Ryoji ordered a pair of his guards to lead the way and the people parted to let them through, though barely. They went on crowding close, shouting and jeering and spitting their hate at us. I kept my head up and breathed. Just breathed. There was nothing else I could do, nothing I could think beyond breathing and letting the horse carry me on toward the city gates.

The crowd followed us all the way. Fruit and clots of mud flew around us, splattering my armour, but I was a daughter of the Dragon Empress. I had been born to wear the proud mask she had always donned. I retreated behind it, thinking of how often she had worn pride because the only other option had been to break, and I missed her then as I hadn't before. What a moment to feel close to her for the first time in my life.

"The crowd is thickening," General Ryoji said. "Keep close."

We were getting near the city gates, but our pace had slowed to a crawl. There were city guards amongst the crowd now, not shouting and throwing their fists into the air like the people but standing still like the threat they were.

"Careful, Majesty."

The gates were open as they had been when we'd returned in the predawn light, but with the wall of people crushed into the road between us and freedom, they may as well have been locked. And sitting upon horses in front of them were the Koali brothers. They sat in the centre of their own army and looked so damned pleased with themselves. Smug enough that their faces ought to have peeled away in sheer disgust at being involved.

"Stand aside for your empress," Minister Manshin shouted over the furore as the guards ahead of us were jostled, their horses backing.

"We will not stand aside until your empress answers for her crimes."

The crowd quietened to hungry little whispers that gnawed at my skin and picked at my attention.

"The empress is the law."

"Your empress wears no authority. She has not been crowned. Has taken no oath. And in the absence of an emperor upon the throne, our only allegiance is to our lord, Grace Bahain, and his noble family. The very lord your false empress slayed in the night, a crime against the authority of our last true emperor, Kin Ts'ai."

"A lord who has allied himself to the very barbarians who tore through our lands?"

"And your empress has not?" He pointed past us. "Who rides with you? Whose blades struck our lord down?"

The crowd shouted their agreement, pressing in against my guards. Something flew past my eyes to smash upon Ryoji's upraised arm.

"Empress Miko Ts'ai is the chosen heir of Emperor Kin Ts'ai," Minister Manshin shouted. "It is treason to refute that. Stand aside."

"We stand aside when your false empress stands down."

My horse backed as a shout rose from the crowd. "Traitor! Traitor! Traitor!" None of the people were armed, but they pushed and shoved at my guards, edging us back. "Traitor! Traitor!" Like a pack of hungry wolves, they kept closing in. Nipping. Growling. More fruit bounced off my shoulder. Something hit the back of my head, sending pain tearing up into my skull.

I tightened my grip on my reins, knowing I shouldn't but unable to stop. How could I make them understand that I was trying to fight for them? That they would have a Levanti emperor if they did not let me go?

"My people!" I cried, lifting a hand in hope of being seen and heard above the noise. "My people! I beseech you to listen. I go to fight for you. For Kisia. Against a false, foreign emperor who would take our lands from us."

Whether they even heard me I couldn't tell, for still they pressed in, shouting, their faces contorted with anger and a hunger that frightened me.

"Usurper Miko Otako," Governor Koali shouted over the growing noise. "You are under arrest for the highest treason."

"Usurper?" The word had bite. So often had northerners used it against Emperor Kin that to hear it again now from the mouths of my people was like the cracking of the earth, yawning our divisions ever wider. How could I unite Kisia when there was such deep, irrational hatred? What stitches could ever be enough to heal a tear that others were determined to keep ripping asunder? These men who took such joy in the destruction of Kisia's dreams to further only themselves. Grace Bachita had been the same.

As though I stood once more in that throne room, Hacho was

in my hand before I thought to draw her, an arrow to her string. I had soared on rage back in Mei'lian, but it was determined righteousness that carried me now. Serving Kisia meant many different things.

"No!" Manshin cried, but the arrow flew. Another was nocked and drawn before the first hit, diving into Governor Koali's throat. The force threw him back, and he fell from sight beneath the undulating crowd. His brother followed, an arrow in the side of his neck as he turned.

Triumph swelled. Shouts rose. General Ryoji's mount was jostled toward me as the crowd pressed in, no rhythmic chanting now but an eruption of noise with no single voice. Something hit my back. Another persimmon burst on my horse's neck, spilling rotten fruit through her mane.

And the moment of soaring joy at having purged Kisia of another danger crashed into the stones. Of course these people could not see what I saw, only the murder of their lords, and they pushed in, shouting and screaming and baying for our blood. The city guards no longer stood still, but drew their weapons, and with the road blocked, there was no way out and no way back.

One of my guards was hauled out of his saddle amid the shouting. The other drew his sword. And in the moment his blade arced down into the crowd, I knew it had been my hands that tore this wound in my empire, a wound I might never be able to fix.

"No!" I cried as the first citizen was cut down, but as with my earlier words it had no effect. No effect but to draw Minister Manshin's attention amid the chaos.

"Majesty," he snapped from beside me. "We must push through or stand here to be torn apart. There is no other way now."

He was right, but I hated him for forcing me to agree. For making me bear the burden of all the blood to come even if I deserved it.

"Cut a path for the empress!" he shouted, and though I could not have heard the drawing of my soldiers' swords over the noise, I felt it in my soul. The smooth withdrawal of blades from their sheaths like the drawing of a breath, the last moment of calm before the storm.

Before the screaming.

And the blood.

And the death.

19. CASSANDRA

I was sick of being tied up and dragged places, sick of sitting across from men I hated in carriages I couldn't escape. The bumpy, jolting carriage ride seemed to have become my life now, and I could only be glad Leo, whichever Leo this was, showed no interest in conversing. I might not have been able to sleep had I been in my own body, but in Empress Hana's it was staying awake that was hard.

I wasn't sure how many days we were on the road. It was a blur, a nightmare of bumpy roads and bright light flashing through trees and the ever-present memory of Captain Aeneas's dead, staring eyes.

We had been going to see Miko again.

Despite Leo's disinterest in conversation, he sent for a doctor every night, weaving different stories about who I was as they looked me over and gave him advice. One bled me. Another gave us a tonic of cloves that burned our tongue. Another suggested sustaining food and wine and rest, and he seemed the wisest of all, but still Leo pressed on rather than stop a proper night at an inn. And bit by bit I sank into exhaustion. I stopped even wanting to have the strength to kill him, and began just wanting to die.

I had begun to wonder if the journey would ever end, or if I had already died and this was my punishment, an eternal afterlife spent jolting along uneven roads with Leo. But one day we did stop. Not just to change horses or eat, but the sort of stop where there's a grand house and you get half guided, half carried inside, servants bustling. It looked familiar in a way I could not place and did not care to worry about, thinking only that maybe now I could lie down. Could sleep. Could cease waking.

I was led to a small room, the sort kept for a lesser guest or their servants. Enough space for a sleeping mat and a small table and little else, the only window high and narrow up beneath the eave. But there was a mat against the wall and a bowl of washing water, and I couldn't find it in myself to care for anything else.

I lay down. I slept. I dreamed, a bright, hot dream, all searing colours and sounds and smells like Kaysa was shouting. But she wasn't, she was sitting, not drinking though she cupped a tea bowl, listening to a conversation happening behind her.

"She's here. In the room next to the other assassin."

I had joined Kaysa for snatches here and there as I dozed the journey away, but not since the night in the army camp had she acknowledged my presence. I wondered where that army was now, whether I was about to find myself in another siege.

"She seems to be extremely unwell. Would you like me to send for a physician?"

"Yes." Leo, impossible to know which. "I want her alive and well. Fetch someone to her. And make sure she gets served good food."

"As you say, Your Holiness."

Kaysa tapped the rim of the tea bowl, watching ripples shift across its surface. None of the doors appeared to be locked, and no one seemed to be watching her. Was she remaining by choice now? Unlike us she had the ability to fight. The ability to run. And had chosen not to.

Why would I? she said, acknowledging my presence. *When I finally have the chance to help someone. To make a difference.*

To help Leo? He's a monster, I said.

That's rich, coming from you, Cassandra. You don't understand him, but I do.

You're a convert? Leo isn't being brought back by God, Kaysa. He hasn't been given a purpose. He's dying every time. He is just one of seven brothers.

I know.

What could I say to that? I had been ready to fight over it, to convince her, owning an energy here I lacked in my body. Sleep seemed to diminish its demands.

It's not because you're asleep, she said. *You haven't figured it out yet? Haven't you noticed that Empress Hana never joins you here? It's always just you and me. She has the strongest connection to her body; when it sleeps, she sleeps, but you aren't connected to it so your consciousness comes to me.*

That makes no sense.

Yes, it does. You're just a passenger there.

Are you admitting that's my body you've run off with?

I felt my brow crinkle into a frown. She didn't answer.

Why does he need your help?

Because he's not what you think him, she said. *There's a lot the Witchdoctor didn't tell you, which you might have discovered if you'd bothered to read the book you stole from him.*

The book? Do you——?

I jerked awake as the door slid open. "Oh, I'm sorry, my lady, I did not think you would already be asleep."

A maid stood holding a tray, and I blinked a dozen times to bring her face into focus. It didn't help. She shuffled in. "I'll leave the tray for when you're ready, my lady."

She set the tray on the floor and backed out, closing the door softly behind her. No click of a lock. No silhouette of a guard or shifting steps, but in this state, freedom was impossible.

Rich smells wafted from the tray, making my stomach turn. From the next room, a voice sounded through the thin wall.

"A man does kneel at the dawn and the dusk and thank his God for the night and the day, the sun and the moon and the stars."

Leo, the musical roll of his voice as he read a relaxing sound.

"Though he kneels with others he is alone, one man in the eyes of God as the man beside him is one man and the man beside him is one man, all through the gathering."

A second, deeper male voice murmured agreement. "*Next to the other assassin*," the servant had said, and my curiosity was piqued. Other assassin. I'd only ever been a lone wolf.

"We are many. A congregation of ones, together even when we are apart."

I forced myself to eat as much as I could stomach while I listened to the rising passion in Leo's voice, culminating in a ringing silence.

"We will continue our lessons tomorrow," Leo said, his voice moving away. "Until then, you are beloved of God."

A door slid open and slid closed, and footsteps faded away along the passage.

Lessons. Too well could I remember my own lessons at the hospice, seeking to shape me into a useful pawn. I cleared my throat. "It's all bullshit, you know," I said, leaning back against the wall. "Lots of people in the world don't worship the Chiltaen god, and the sun and the moon still go on the same. Besides, if you were beloved of God you wouldn't be stuck here, huh?"

No one answered. Perhaps I had misjudged.

"My name is Cassandra," I tried again, deciding it was safest to leave the empress out of this. "Cassandra Marius."

More silence. I wondered if my neighbour had heard me, and had parted my lips to speak louder when he said, "I am Yakono. Just Yakono."

A Kisian name, but the accent was more Chiltaen and yet

somehow not quite. "Nice to meet you, Just Yakono. You must be favoured for Dom Villius to read to you himself."

A little laugh sounded near. He must have moved closer, was perhaps right behind me, our backs pressed against each other but for the interference of the thin wooden wall.

"I hope I am not so fortunate," I added. "Becoming a priest of the One True God involves a lot of confessions, and no one has time to listen to all my sins."

"You would be surprised how much time I have, Cassandra."

My name rolled off his tongue in a way that sounded more like the traders from the west, and I said, "Where are you from? You don't sound Kisian."

"Neither do you," was his light reply.

"Because I'm not. I'm Chiltaen, I'm just stuck here."

He didn't answer for a while, and I wondered if the question had offended him. "You don't have to tell me, we can talk about something else."

"Why do you want to talk?"

Because you're an assassin too, and I'm curious probably wasn't the wisest reply, so I said, "Is there anything else to do?"

"No, but ... I don't know you."

"I don't know you either. You're Just Yakono and you're not from around here and you're not a devotee of the One True God, or Dom Villius wouldn't be trying to make a convert through preaching the devotional lessons."

Fabric scuffed against the wall as he shifted his weight. "And you are Cassandra Marius from Chiltae, and you are also not a devotee of the One True God or you wouldn't speak so."

"My dislike of the church is baked in deep."

"I thought myself impervious, but ..."

I thought of the way Leo's reading had lulled Kaysa's mind, drawing her in. Waking after such dreams had been like breaking the surface of a dark lake and sucking deep breaths of air. "You find the lessons entrancing," I said, turning my cheek to the wall and finishing his sentence for him. "Intoxicating even. Difficult to shake."

"Yes."

"Well, I would shake you if I could. I'll just have to shout at you through the wall instead."

"If you shout, they'll hear us," came his deep rumble. "If they hear us, they'll move us. I don't...I don't want to be alone."

They were such vulnerable words, and I swallowed a constriction in my throat. "You aren't."

A footfall approached along the passage, and fearing someone had heard us, I levered myself out of my sitting position and lay on the sleeping mat, heart hammering fast.

Someone tapped on my door, and I croaked permission to enter. "I have been sent to bring you to the physician, my lady." The maid from earlier bowed. "Can you walk or do you need help?"

I wanted to tell her the physician could fuck off. I wanted to tell her I'd rather die than do anything to benefit Leo. I wanted to refuse all offers of help because it hurt my pride to admit I needed it, but I swallowed it all.

"I will need help," I said, forcing out the hateful words. The maid entered, clucking about my messy blankets and the food I'd picked at, before offering her hands to help me up. They were rough, but strong and warm compared to my cold claws.

"That's the way," she said as though encouraging a child. "I am sure Master Ao will soon have you better. He's the best physician for miles around."

I could not walk without leaning heavily upon her arm, but she was a sturdy young woman and didn't shrink away, let alone buckle. Leaving the door open, she helped me into a long passage. I'd not been awake enough when we'd arrived to pay attention to our surroundings, but I looked around now, noting the decoration carved along the upper walls and the well-polished floor. A nobleman's country estate?

As we slowly staggered past Yakono's door, I stared at the paper panes and wondered why he was here. Had he been sent to kill Leo as I once had and failed? But if so, why risk keeping him alive? I stared longer than I ought at the door, hoping for a sight of his silhouette through the paper.

"*I don't want to be alone,*" he had said.

We ought not to trust him so quickly, Empress Hana said. *We are in a bad position here, and we don't know who he is.*

I never said I was trusting him.

She spoke no more as we reached the end of the passage and turned into a larger hall. Double doors led out into what would be the public rooms, while another, shorter passage led on into a large sitting room. A breath caught in my throat. There I was, kneeling at a central table with an open book before me. Kaysa, I reminded myself, the sight of me from outside my own skin a strange one.

"Ah, Cassandra. Empress Hana." Leo strode forward to stand beside... Leo. Two of them. They looked exactly the same, down to the colour and sit of their robes and the way they wore their masks loose around their throats. And just when I thought it couldn't get any worse, I saw Septum. Not in his box, but lying upon a divan below a broad window like he was resting.

Three Leos.

"How shocked you look," one said. "Surely this should not be a surprise by now. The dear captain was... not very good at keeping secrets, after all. How disappointed my father would have been in his poor service."

"Poor service?" I repeated, anger vibrating in the words. "Whatever my thoughts about your father, at least he put his faith in the right people."

"Fine words from the woman who slit his throat."

Kaysa had not looked up from her book, but nor had she turned a page since I entered. She had the stilled look of one who is carefully listening while pretending not to. Poorly.

The maid remained in the doorway, no shock at the sight of three of the same man in the one room, only a glassy stare that wasn't entirely present. A dead look, but her pulse throbbed in her neck. The spot from which Captain Aeneas had bled out. As had the hieromonk before him.

"Come and sit," Leo said, indicating the divan opposite Septum's. "The physician will be here soon. I have somewhere else I need to be, but I will leave you in the care of..." He turned to look at the other Leo now standing by the window. "Myself."

He grinned at his own joke while the maid helped me to the divan and, without a word, strode back out. Leo followed, drawing up his mask as he went. I lay down, hoping the other Leo would leave me alone if I pretended to be asleep.

"Really, Cassandra, I am hurt," the Leo at the window said, not turning from the gardens blearily visible through wavy glass doors. "One would think you haven't missed me. That you didn't regret having killed me. That you never liked me at all."

I had liked the Leo I had travelled to Kisia with. The one I had killed. He had seemed to come back to life, but it had been a lie. He had died as surely as anyone I'd ever stuck a blade into. Which brother had he been? A less important one?

"His name was Sextus, and I'm sorry, but you did me a favour when you killed him."

He turned from the window as Kaysa leapt up from the table, the way she wore my body so different to how I had imagined myself. "You're back," she said. "I wasn't sure."

"I couldn't let him know," Leo said, glancing at the door. "He wouldn't have left."

They shared an understanding look, and feeling like I had just walked into a mad world, I stared at them both. "Did he just apologise to me?" I said, trying to prop myself up on an elbow and failing. "What the fuck is going on?"

"I told you there was a lot you didn't know," Kaysa said. "This is Unus, Cass. He's not what you think he is."

He looked the same as the others, owning the same boyish good looks, the same sharp nose and fair hair, the same quirk of a smile, though there was something mesmerising about this one's eyes. "Captain Aeneas told me about him. Unus, the firstborn, the most powerful. Blah blah blah."

"That's both very right and very wrong," Leo Unus said, coming no closer. "We are... rather more like you than it appears. Just... a bit different."

"Like us but different?" I repeated. "Well, that clears that up."

Leo looked away, reddening with embarrassment or annoyance, I hardly cared. Yet in the same way Kaysa wore my skin differently, so too did this Leo wear his differently. All awkward stance and arms folded tightly across his chest.

What did the captain say he was? Hana asked. *A single soul in multiple bodies?*

Yes. And the others have all acted the same. Except for Septum.

"I told you she wouldn't help me, Kaysa," he said. "Let it go. I can do this myself."

Kaysa turned back, but as she went to him, he staggered, pressing a hand to his head, the other held out to halt her. And she did stop, freezing in place with a pitiful little groan. He retreated from her, shaking his head until he hit the closed doors of the balcony with a harsh rattle. It seemed to shake through him, and like an uncurling snake he straightened, dropping his hands and rolling his shoulders.

"Well, that was fun," he said, his tone bright and brittle and hard. "Shall we try this again? How nice it is to see you here, Cassandra."

He strode forward and Kaysa fell back, all but scurrying out of the way of a man she had stood close to only a moment before. Leo glared at her, full of disdain, and came toward me. He lowered himself onto the edge of the divan, his weight depressing the cushion and making me slide toward him. It took far too many strained muscles to stop us touching, a fact he seemed to understand and appreciate with another of his smiles. "Wasted energy, Cassandra," he said, slowly lowering his hand to my cheek. "Wasted energy. When there is nothing you can do in this state to stop me doing anything I like."

I expected his touch to be like static, yet it was just the warm, soft touch of fingers that had never seen a day's hard work in their life. Everything about him was smooth and unweathered and gently mocking.

"What do you want?"

"I am too kind a man to answer you. Isn't that nice?" Someone cleared their throat at the doorway. "Ah, Master Ao. I'm so glad you could come. My friend is ill and in great need of your care."

"Holiness," the man said stiffly, making it clear he had little respect even for so highly ranked a priest. "I shall do all in my power to help."

"Good. I have been informed you are the very best physician in these parts."

"The Manshins certainly thought so."

Shit, Cass, I've just figured out where we are. This is the country estate of Minister Manshin, commander of the imperial army. Does that mean he—? The empress broke off, unable to finish her own thought. But she didn't need to; they were loud enough. If Minister Manshin had formed an alliance with Leo, what would that mean for Miko? Hana had been comforted that Manshin was her daughter's minister of the left, but that comfort was fast turning to a deep, intense fear. And there was nothing I could do.

The physician asked a hundred questions, prodded and poked and listened to the sound of my breathing and my heart. Torvash's examination had been far more comprehensive, had involved temperatures and looking inside my mouth and my ears and checking the consistency of my saliva, and I doubted any human physician would ever come close to figuring this out if the immortal Witchdoctor could not. But I let myself be checked over and swallowed a foul mixture while the man explained to Leo that I had an imbalance of the spirits and would do well for more rest and warm broth and exercise in the coolest part of the day.

Eventually we were taken back to our room to rest, but though our body was exhausted our mind was not, too busy flitting from anxiety to dread and back.

What could Leo possibly have offered Manshin to get his support? Hana said, voicing her biggest worry.

Is it possible Leo is here without permission? I said.

It is, but there's no sign of a fight. And I'd rather consider the worst than hope for the best when it could have such disastrous consequences.

Do you worry he would harm your daughter?

She didn't answer, which was answer enough. After a time, she said, *It's no comfort that Leo wants us alive either.*

No, I agreed. *But did you notice how different he was at first? That's not the Leo we know.*

I did, but I don't know what to make of it. And I don't trust him not to be playing a deep game to get Kaysa on his side.

But why? What can he possibly need her for?

If it comes to that, she said. *What can he possibly need us for? Is it something to do with Manshin? Or am I to be ransomed back to my daughter?*

Whatever it is, it's bad.

Her agreement was a warm, silent thing. *He wants us alive for something*, she said. *We can't just lie here and let him get what he wants, so what are our options? Escape is not one of them. Neither is killing him, though if we had, perhaps Captain Aeneas would still be alive. Or we would all be dead.*

It would be impossible anyway, I said. *Between his mind reading and our weak state, the chances of getting a blade in our hand, let alone anywhere near him, are slim.*

She sighed. *All right. We can't escape and we can't kill him, but we can't do nothing. I begin to get the feeling we aren't getting out of here for a long time. Unless he plans to ransom us, I don't think I'll be seeing my daughter again after all.*

Will we get better? Now we can rest consistently and aren't travelling.

She didn't answer.

You said it came in bouts and you would be well between them.

Still she didn't answer, but our minds were close enough that she didn't have to. Determination was all that kept this body going now.

There had been a time I'd hoped to make a difference in the world, to change Chiltae for the better with my blade as I couldn't with my voice, but here I was trapped and fading, the circular helplessness of my existence coming to a slow and pathetic end. It wasn't what I'd wanted. Wasn't how I'd hoped to die. It had all gone wrong the day I'd accepted Secretary Aurus's contract for Leo's life.

I turned my head, cheek to the wall. "Yakono?"

"Cassandra?" came the rumble of my name.

"You're an assassin," I said, more statement than question.

There was a moment of hesitation before he answered, but no shame nor a single drop of embarrassment or pride when he said, "I am."

"Were you contracted to kill Dom Villius?"

The same brief hesitation, perhaps weighing up his options. "That isn't something I would usually discuss, but I get the feeling you have a good reason for asking. I was contracted to kill him but, as you see, was far from successful."

"Was it Secretary Aurus?"

"How do you know?"

"Because he contracted me too."

I could well imagine the silence was shock, and when Yakono next spoke his voice was tight and high with tension. "When?"

"I don't know what the date is anymore, but before the rains. Before Prince Tanaka was executed. I was to kill Leo in time to give the Nine a reason for war."

"Ah, you were before me. I...had the feeling I wasn't the first. I was warned it was not an easy job, but then we've often had difficult jobs in the past, especially political ones, so I didn't think much of it."

"So they didn't tell you he was all weird and capable of shit that makes no sense like you'd fallen into a story."

"No."

I shook my head against the wall. "Idiots."

I could have let silence fall there, could have laid down to rest, but I wasn't ready to stop talking, having found someone so like me. "I was also contracted by the hieromonk," I said, for something to add to the conversation. "For his son. Just to make things more fun."

"That doesn't surprise me. His Holiness seems to have grown increasingly troubled by his son's popularity. And the number of people expecting him, even pressuring him, to name Leo Villius Defender of the One True God so the succession would be secure. Not that the Nine wanted that. He's not...controllable enough for them."

"How do you know so much about Chiltaen politics when you're not Chiltaen?"

"I investigate thoroughly before every job because you never know what small detail could overset your plans."

His answer made me feel vastly underskilled for my profession, just a blade flailing around in the dark.

"I...haven't ever really talked to another assassin outside my own family," Yakono said after a time. "Usually it worries people, though I don't kill for my own enjoyment."

"Do you enjoy it?" I thought of the thrill I'd had the first time I'd killed for money, the legitimacy of the job wiping away all sense of guilt and leaving only satisfaction. There was joy and power in being no one, a no one who could strike from the shadows and change the world.

"Yes?" he said, the admission wary. "I am trained to do the job and enjoy performing it well. People tell me that sounds cold, but I don't like to pretend for the sake of others' sensibilities."

Laughing hurt every part of my chest and my back and my stomach, but oh how I laughed. How many times had Kaysa told me I was heartless and cold, that we could have chosen to do anything else with our life yet this had been my choice, to fuck and kill people because I was good at both and took joy in being good at both.

"Did I say something amusing?"

Yakono sounded hurt, and I had the impulse to throw my arms around this earnest killer whose face I had never seen because I could hear myself in his voice. I had done all I could to bury my doubt and my shame and the part of me that gave a shit what people thought of me, but it was still there, still bubbling its pockets of self-hatred to the surface like a cruel, jeering swamp.

"No," I said, rolling to face the wall. "No, you didn't say anything amusing at all. I laughed because..." Shame roiled up from that ever-present pit and I shoved it down, determined not to let it show. "Because I am both a whore and an assassin, and I too take joy in a job well done."

Did his jaw drop? Did he smile? Did he wrinkle his nose at the idea of someone selling their body as he didn't at being paid to take life? For all too many heartbeats I waited, worrying, before he said, "I can understand that. Sex doesn't overly interest me, but I am aware I'm rather on my own in that regard."

"A man disinterested in sex? Unique, I would have called that," I said, relief escaping in another laugh.

When he didn't answer, I wondered what he was thinking. Had I upset him? I had a hundred questions about where he had been trained and by whom and why he didn't sound Chiltaen, but perhaps I wouldn't like all the answers, or perhaps he wouldn't like my questions, and I was far too tired to deal with such knotty problems. But sleepy though I was, I wanted him to keep talking. The murmur of his deep voice through the wall was as comforting as the warmth of Captain Aeneas at my back had been. I had never trusted anyone in my old life, ought not to trust anyone now, but the choice to do so was oddly freeing.

"Do you use a blade, Yakono?" I said, pressing my shoulder to the wall and resting my forehead against the wood. "I've generally found it to be the quickest and easiest way. I was never taught fancy things like poisons myself."

"A blade to the inner thigh if I can. With enough practice it can be made almost painless. Poisons are such slow and painful ways to kill. Choking and destroying the digestion and exploding blood vessels. I was taught to dose with a few, but they are not my preferred way."

I had never thought about it before. I'd never taken pleasure in the prolonged suffering of my clients, but in the end, dead was dead, however it was done. That here was a man who *practised* ways to lessen the pain was extraordinary.

"But what did you practise on? People you were paid to kill?"

"Oh no, my master had very realistic dolls made of an assortment of materials, and he would put them in different positions and challenge me to find the right spot with my blade. Sometimes he would time me, or make me do it in the dark. I thought it was a fun game as a child."

"As a child? How long have you been training?"

"All my life. Well, as long as I can remember anyway. I don't recall much from before my master took me in. Once I was older, he sometimes used dead bodies so I could cut real skin. That's how I learned about anatomy."

He spoke of it as anyone might about their childhood, a sense of nostalgia in his words as he recalled better times.

"And you?" he said, shifting against the wall. "How did you learn?"

"I'm... not sure I did. Some Blessed Guards at the hospice I lived at taught me how to fight as a child, but I just figured the rest out for myself, really. I had seen enough dead bodies"—bodies that had called to me, called and called until I had gone to see what they wanted, what they needed, their wounds glaring a history at me from dim alleyways—"to figure out the most... vulnerable places. I just tried it after that. People die if you stick a blade in them in enough places."

My laugh ended on a grimace. How awful that would sound to someone who gave their art such thought and care? Terrible enough that I hadn't been trained, had just... made it up as I went along. Perhaps I wasn't an assassin, only a killer.

"I did that once." His voice sounded a little closer, like he had turned his cheek to the wood. "The first kill I ever did. We'd been contracted for a merchant. He wasn't anyone particularly important, and neither was the man who paid us. A personal vendetta, over a woman, I believe, but we don't ask questions." He paused, and I thought I heard him lick dry lips. "So, my master said it was a good first test for me, to do the job for real and see how it went. I was...

sixteen? Old enough to be capable but not old enough to be wise. I thought I was very *very* good and imagined all the way to the man's house how my master would be staggered by my skill and speed." Yakono laughed, not a bitter sound but one full of humour. "It didn't turn out like I imagined. He wasn't in the place I expected. And my fine plan of quickly nicking his thigh or neck and being gone in a puff of wind was thwarted. He saw me. I panicked. All I could think was that I didn't want him shouting for guards because I had no contract for their lives, and I was so busy focussing on his mouth that I stabbed him in the cheek instead of the throat. By the time I finished I'd put at least eight holes in him."

"I almost sawed through half my first kill's neck," I said. "And I once killed the wrong woman by accident."

"I accidentally caught one of mine while they were using the chamber pot."

I laughed and so did he, a reluctant gurgle of sound as though he knew he ought not laugh at such things, but unable to help himself.

"That I've never done," I said. "I'll make a point of trying it sometime, shall I?"

"Oh no, don't, it's horribly messy and embarrassing. The man was so shocked by someone appearing while he was shitting that he was more concerned with protecting his nether regions than his life."

I could well imagine such a scene and lay laughing gently against the wall, tears tracking down my cheeks. "I wouldn't know what to do."

"Well, I killed him," Yakono said, like there could be no question of proper etiquette in such a case. "But it has always been my habit to lay bodies out respectfully if I have the time, and all the time in the world did not increase my desire to . . . clean the man—"

I could barely see for tears, my laughter a great, racking thing as impossible to control as a bout of coughing.

"—nor dress him again. I wasn't even sure all the right bits of clothing were there. He seemed to have recently gotten out of bed, which was where he was meant to be, and how much I wish I had been five minutes faster in reaching his house—"

I sucked a ragged breath, sure I had never laughed so much.

"—so in the end I was a complete coward and bolted out the window, leaving his servants quite the shock. I had barely climbed down the outer wall before I heard them all screaming."

I gasped another breath, wiping tears.

"Are you all right?" he asked, all worry and solicitude again.

"Fine," I managed between eruptions of laughter. "Just...never heard...anything...quite so funny...in all my life."

He chuckled against the other side of the wall. "I'm so glad my misfortunes could entertain you, Cassandra. It is...nice to meet someone who is not immediately afraid of me. Or who doesn't want to bring some god or other into my life so I will see the error of my ways. My master always said it would be so, and not to trouble myself over the values other people claim yet do not follow. Life and death is a business that would go on without us, he said. Our service allows it to be undertaken with respect and dignity. Well, most of the time. Chamber pot man excluded of course."

After a moment of silence, he added, "My master also used to say I would have to accept less than perfection because such a thing is not possible to attain. I'm still working on that one."

In the silence he left, I slowly calmed my gasps of laughter and I wondered if he had stopped talking to allow me to do so, perhaps able to hear my little fits of coughing through the wall as I could hear the scratch and rustle of his clothing.

We ought to sleep, the empress said, and almost I was surprised to hear her, so little had she been present while Yakono and I talked. *I didn't want to interrupt; you were enjoying yourself. But we need rest if we're to have any chance of making a difference.*

My eyes did ache and I could barely feel the lower half of my body, but I did not want to sleep and leave Yakono alone.

We are no good to him dead, just as we're no good to Miko dead. Sleep now.

She was right and I hated it. Hated the weakness, the disease, that I'd gotten trapped in this body at all.

"I have to sleep now," I said through the wall. "Will you... be all right?"

Had I ever asked anyone that before? The words felt the wrong shape, the weight of them constricting my chest in a way I wasn't sure I liked.

"I will," he said. "But take care of yourself, Cassandra. I would like you to be all right as well."

I could think of no reply and let the empress take over, curling her body up the way it found most comfortable to sleep, and soon drifted off.

———————◆———————

Voices murmured nearby and I glanced up—no, Kaysa glanced up, catching sight of Leo's face in profile. The physician was shaking his head. "No, I have not seen this before, not like this," Master Ao said. "It is a little like fever, and something like exhaustion of the spirit, but neither is accompanied by such inflammation of the joints."

"I thought you were the best physician in this district."

"I am, and I am giving you all the information I have, on the honour of my profession. I have made up some more of the tonic, and you must encourage her to rest. Rest is the most important thing in healing."

"Indeed." Leo's brows sank low. "You may go."

Master Ao drew himself up, and I looked away as he departed. A door opened and closed, and I went on staring at the page. Candlelight flickered across its neat lettering.

"You are reading very intently," Leo said as he approached, very much the Leo I was used to. The Leo who had taken his own head from me and killed Captain Aeneas. "Trying to find a way to fight me?"

He leaned close, the heat and weight and sheer presence of him something I wanted to thrust away. *It's not him*, Kaysa told herself. *Not him.*

"No," she said aloud. "I'm just reading the Presage."

"But of course." His breath was warm by my ear, and I shivered. "Ah yes, a curious paragraph."

My heart hammered, making me light-headed with an intense fear I couldn't wholly understand.

"*The empress with two voices*," he went on. "You are perhaps considering that the old translation states it as the *leader with two words* and wondering how you can convince me to marry the wrong woman and ruin the prophecy."

For a moment I was sure I would be sick. "No, I...I was just reading, I—"

"Of course you were. Perhaps wondering how you could get Unus back. I'm afraid that's not happening. He's got to go, and once Cassandra is feeling better, she will see to it for us. Then I can marry Empress Sichi without him getting in the way."

I looked up into his self-satisfied smile. "But she won't get better."

"Not get better?" He gripped my shoulders, his eyes boring into mine unblinking. "What do you mean she won't get better?"

I knew he could read the answer in my mind, but still I stumbled out angry words. This man had hurt Unus the way Cassandra had hurt me all my life.

"It's the Imperial Disease," I said. "They aren't going to get better. The Witchdoctor says there's no cure, so Cass isn't going to kill Unus for you. And she damn well won't live long enough to help you get rid of Empress Hana's daughter, so you can marry the other—"

His fingers squeezed my throat. "But they aren't dead yet."

Unus, fight back! Kaysa thought.

Leo's fury was like the pressure of a gathering thunderstorm. "You're pathetic. Get out of my sight." He threw us from him, sending Kaysa sprawling onto the floor.

Wake up! Wake up! I screamed in my mind. *Oh shit oh shit, Hana, wake the fuck up right now. Wake up. Wake—*"Up!"

We jerked awake upon our mat in a tangle of sweat-laden sheets. The room was dark, a mere suggestion in the faint moonlight.

What is it? the empress said.

"I know why he wants us," I said, our voice crackled and our eyes bleary. "I saw it. In the dream. With Kaysa. I saw it."

Calm down. What is it?

"He wants us to fulfil the whole stabbed in the back by an empress thing, but more than that. It's Miko. And someone called Empress Sichi. There's a thing in the book, the holy book. He thinks it means he has to marry her, and you're going to help him."

He wants to marry Sichi?

"Yes."

No. No. He can't. Surely Minister Manshin wouldn't . . . She trailed off, disbelieving her own words.

"Marry her and get rid of Miko. Whatever he means by that."

I don't care what he means by that. I won't let him. We need to do something. Now.

"But what?"

I don't know. We closed our eyes upon a room that spun and drew the covers up around our trembling shoulders. *I don't know.*

20. DISHIVA

The cellars beneath Kogahaera were dark and damp and I hated them, but it was the only place we could be sure of not being overheard. The network of caverns and tunnels led from one, but this one was used as a bathhouse. A wooden tub sat in its centre, and a pair of braziers failed to warm the air. A small troop of servants carrying heavy buckets and jugs had been needed to fill the tub with hot water.

"Are we ready?" Empress Sichi asked. She sat in the bath, the better to ensure we weren't disturbed. Nuru sat perched on a stool beside her, translating.

"Can we be any more ready?" The chill of the stones was seeping through my clothing. "The longer we wait the more likely it is Leo will figure out what we're up to."

And Leo would get what he wanted from Sichi.

Since the execution, we'd fallen into a tense stalemate, as many Levanti intent on protecting Gideon as there were Levanti who wished to tear him apart. It might have turned out poorly without the presence of Lord Edo and his Kisian allies, and the Chiltaens marching toward our gates. Kisians too, now, coming from the east with a host of Levanti. There were whispers that Rah was with them. That they had defeated Grace Bahain in battle. That

Whisperer Ezma led them. Their arrival would shatter our peace as surely as the arrival of the Chiltaens, forcing us all to choose who and what we really wanted to fight for.

Herds no longer felt important.

"We can't wait," I said, pushing off the wall. "It's shit and I wish there was another way, but we have to do it. If those two armies get here while Leo is still in control of Gideon, it's gates wide open, and that's bad for all of us."

For a moment we just existed there in silence together, but the moment couldn't last. We had a plan and we had to see it through to whatever end. It risked everything, but so did doing nothing, and there was an odd sort of comfort in that.

Sichi shifted in her bath water, the slosh echoing around the small stone space. "We had better move, or there won't be time to dress before Leo arrives," Nuru translated when she spoke.

Empress Sichi stood, water streaming off her naked skin. A towel sat ready, and Nuru held it up as she stepped out of the tub, the two of them walking through the routine like they'd done this a hundred times before. A murmur. A wry smile. A lingering touch of thanks. I thought of Jass hiding in the caves, and could only hope I would see him again. Would get the chance to discover the depths of what had started to grow between us.

"All right," Sichi said through Nuru's lips. "It's time. I'll keep him as long as I can, but I suggest you move fast. Just in case he sees through me."

Almost I asked if she was sure, and seeming to understand, she flashed a fleeting smile. "Don't worry, Dishiva. I can take care of myself."

"And I can take care of her," Nuru added when she had finished translating. "You get to Gideon and don't worry about us."

There was nothing else left to do. Nothing else to say. Another moment stretched in which it was just the three of us, safe, but it could not last. With one of her flat, wry smiles, Sichi nodded to me and headed for the door.

"Good luck, Captain," Nuru said, turning back as she followed Sichi through it.

"And to you."

The door closed on my words, and I was alone with the empty bath and the shadows and the damp. "Damn it," I hissed, and began to pace. The cellar was small enough that a handful of steps got me from one side to the other and back, doing nothing to alleviate my nervous energy. It was the simplest of plans, but when the man at the centre of it could read your mind, nothing was simple anymore.

I paced until I lost track of time, might have paced forever had not the creak of the door surprised me. A blade was in my hand before I had fully turned, its point levelled. The newcomer flinched, but weak lantern light fell upon Lord Edo Bahain, made sickly green by the cellar walls. His jaw was clenched and his face lined with lack of sleep.

He gave a sharp nod. It was time to go.

I nicked the tip of my thumb and thrust my dagger back into its sheath. My swords hung from my belt too, and though I wouldn't need them if all went well, they were a comforting weight all the same.

Lord Edo held the door open for me to pass into the shadowy passage, and leaving him behind, I started up the stairs two at a time, the sounds of the busy manor growing louder around me. Up and up through the tangle of stairs and passages until I stood in the long upper hall, Gideon's door at the end. I had deliberately gone the long way so I wouldn't have to pass Sichi's door, and not daring to even look at it, I spun toward the two guards outside Gideon's room. Dendek and Anouke eyed me with worried clefts between their brows, Dendek shifting his weight from foot to foot. "Captain," he said.

"I am here to see Gideon."

They shared another glance. It had been a risk trusting anyone else with part of the plan, but Keka owed me. Nothing would ever fix the seam of trust he had ripped, but as Dendek nodded, a little stitch was remade. The door slid open.

Gideon was alone. He showed no sign of life at my entrance, not turning from the window out which he stared at gardens half turned to mud. "Herd Master?"

He flinched.

"Gideon?"

"You're going to betray me, aren't you, Dishiva?"

"No," I said, with a degree of confidence I could only achieve because it wasn't him I was talking to. "I am here to serve you." Oh, how I hoped this would work. That there was still a way to get through to him despite all the damage Leo had done.

He turned a little, enough for me to see his face in profile. He looked the same, all the shapes and lines of his face coming together to create the same man, but even from the side the strain was evident.

"Herd Master," I said when he made no reply. "It is time. Your task is waiting."

"Task?" His brows nested close.

"Yes, Herd Master. You cannot have forgotten. Come. I will walk with you."

He hesitated, confusion giving me a younger, troubled Gideon for a moment. A moment in which I wondered if he had ever looked like that. Hard to believe we had been a part of each other's lives for so short a time, no matter how long it felt.

"Yes," he said at last. "Let us walk. I . . . feel I could do with the fresh air."

Despite his confusion, he looked every bit the ruthless emperor he had become as he crossed the floor, crimson surcoat swirling. I couldn't tell if he wore it perfectly or if it wore him, but I had to thrust away all the memories it brought with it.

Anouke and Dendek watched us leave but said nothing. Did not even move to bow or salute or nod, like they'd been turned to stone. The second of the things I had asked of Keka. Now as long as he had done the third, we could do this.

I had memorised the quickest path to the private garden from Gideon's rooms, but as I took the first turn into a narrow servant's passage, I feared I would forget it all. Walking from one place to another with our herd master would once have been something I didn't need to think about, but now my heart felt like it was made of shattered shards of hot steel.

I didn't forget the way, each passage leading to the next with the echo of Gideon's footsteps trailing behind me. I didn't dare turn in case looking at him broke whatever spell had him following, complaisant like a lamb. We were getting farther and farther from Leo, but it wasn't bringing Gideon back. Was there any of him left to bring back? If I turned to look, how empty would his gaze be?

We met no one in the maze of narrow passages and no one in the gallery that opened onto the garden. It was a tucked-away thing around which much of the manor contorted itself, but no one used it. The servants had a different yard for hanging clothes, and the cooks used a different patch for their herbs and chickens and woodpiles. Even the horses had their own space, leaving this an empty, useless patch of prettiness.

Gideon walked at my side as I made my way toward the little house. Not a house with walls and doors, but with open sides and a roof and vines growing up the outside. It had benches within covered in old cushions, its use as a place to sit. I'd had no time to sit when I spent the last hours of darkness here building the shrine. I had cried the whole time, the instinctive use of such meaning-ful muscle memory taking me back to the plains, to a time when such things had mattered more than politics and the appearance of power. Sichi had given me ink to paint the stones and I'd had to use short sticks for the reaching hand, but I had murmured all the prayers and sung all the songs, and the effort had left me too hollow for pain to touch me.

My handiwork sat in the filtered light of morning at one end of the garden house. Yitti's body lay before it, waiting, and I let out a breath. Keka had done all I had asked of him.

Gideon halted in the doorway, a flash of confusion there and gone. He leaned back as though he might bolt, so I drew my knife and held the hilt out to him. "Your job as First Sword of the Torin," I said. "No one else ought to have the honour."

If Yitti's spirit was present and watching, I hoped he would forgive me. He deserved better than being Farewelled by the man who had ordered his death.

His expression blank, Gideon took the knife and strode forward. Knelt. Crimson silk spread across the wooden floor like spilling blood, but it was a Sword of the Torin who gripped Yitti beneath the shoulders and pulled his stiffened body onto his knees.

In the same way my hands had worked without thinking to build the shrine, so his hands made the first incision. His gaze was fixed on Yitti but in a way that saw nothing at all.

Blood poured onto the wooden boards, missing Gideon's spread knees. It smelt metallic and slightly sweet and turned my stomach. It was always better to Farewell a body when it was still warm, but we'd needed time to prepare.

I watched him work, the ease with which he achieved even the trickiest cuts dragging reluctant admiration from me. But it seemed to be doing nothing. He was just working, slicing skin and cords of muscle and shifting his position to avoid the blood like a man who had done this a thousand times. The frightened Gideon I'd spoken to before travelling to Kima wasn't there.

"I can't help but think that if Rah had joined us when we took Mei'lian, it could have been him lying here," I said, watching for a reaction. Did he hesitate? It was hard to be sure what was a flinch and what was a natural movement of the blade. "I couldn't have forgiven you for that, I think. I'm not even sure I can forgive you for this, whoever it really was who gave the order."

The slightest of pauses as he shifted the position of his blade. But he went on working, eyes glazed. I had no bigger provocation I could use than Rah, but mention of him had done nothing.

Gideon had been angry that night. We had taken Mei'lian. We had overthrown our captors and positioned ourselves to build a new home within the power structures of the empire, but he had not celebrated. Rah had called for him from the cells. He had shouted Gideon's name over and over, and the more he had shouted the more Gideon had paced, hurt and fury in his every step like the wild licking of flames in a storm.

Rah had sung too. His lament had reminded me of my own sufferings, hardening my lingering doubts into assurance, but Gideon had refused to return to the celebration. Refused to eat and drink and instead had sunk onto the stone floor at the top of the stairs and dropped his head in his hands, remaining there alone in his grief. He had eventually returned with his chin set, determined, and not looked back.

Stepping out of Gideon's reach, I began to sing the lament Rah had chosen. I had not his voice, but I pitched it as low as I could and hoped it would do. Gideon had just started on Yitti's spine, a difficult, messy job at the best of times. Harder still if your hands are shaking. His had been so still, so sure, but as I sang on, they began to tremble, fumbling the knife as he went to jam it between vertebrae. The tip of the blade slid into flesh, making a mess of his fine work.

I sang on and Gideon's shoulders began to shake, the whole of him trembling now as he worked the last tricky bits. His fingers slipped and blood sprayed up onto his face, but though he shook and rocked back and forth, hunched as he worked, he remained silent. Until Yitti's head came free. His body slipped from Gideon's knees, but he kept hold of the head and the knife as he sucked a rattling breath wet with suppressed grief, and despite everything, pity struck its discordant note into my heart.

With a strangled cry, Gideon curled in upon himself, upon Yitti's head, blade dropping to the floor as his cry became a guttural roar tearing up his throat until there was no air left to sustain it and he had to draw another wet, rattling breath choked with sobs.

Letting the song fade, I risked a step closer and crouched in front of him. "Gideon?"

He let out another cry, his fingers digging into Yitti's sagging cheeks.

"Gideon. Can you hear me?" I edged closer, reaching out. "It's Dishiva, Gideon. I..."

His fingertips broke the soft skin on one of Yitti's cheeks, and I reached out instinctively to take the head. "Gideon."

For a moment he held on, before letting go and falling back, shaking. "What my people need. What my people need," he chanted. "They just don't see the whole picture. They just don't understand. But you do. You have to lead. You have to do what they need you to do. You have to be strong." The words were barely more than hisses upon each indrawn breath. I set Yitti's head gently on the shrine and crouched beside Gideon. "Is that what he said? Leo?"

At the name he flinched back, hands and feet working fast to push him across the floor, his head shaking furiously. "No no no," he repeated, hands over his head, whole body shaking as he curled ever tighter in on himself. "No, please. No!"

"He isn't here, but..." I wanted to apologise for having left him to bear the brunt of Leo's manipulation, for having walked away the day he named me ambassador, but despite all I knew I couldn't find the strength to forgive him for what had happened since. I reached out, but the moment my fingers brushed his sleeve he lashed out with the bloodied blade. I fell back, ready to disarm him, but the blade clattered onto the wooden floor and his bloodstained hands curled back over his head.

"Gideon…" I closed my lips on further words. What could I say? I had feared to find him empty, but even that fate might have been preferable to finding his mind so utterly broken.

"Dishiva, watch out!"

A rush of footsteps thundered toward us, and there in the aperture stood Leo. Furious, triumphant Leo, his hands balled to fists and his chest swelling. "Well," he said. "How very like you, Dishiva. Always finding a way to mess everything up."

Sichi and Nuru appeared behind him, hovering unsure just out of reach. Lord Edo too, his chest heaving like he had been running. None of them moved as Leo took a step in.

"It was cute of you to think you could keep secrets from me." He shot a pitying look at Gideon, trying to push himself back through the wall, the sound of Leo's voice torture. "But really, Dishiva, you have done me a favour. He was getting to be a liability as fewer and fewer people trusted him, but you, you will make a very nice puppet."

I glared at him. "I will never—" The words choked off as a piercing cacophony of screams ripped through my head, discordant and wrong. I could see the sounds, corporeal like twisting vines, and I swatted at them only to press my hands back over my ears. It didn't help. The screams went on and on, stealing all sense. Beneath their teeth I could no longer feel myself. I was disembodied, floating, yet I could see everything. There Leo, smiling. Always smiling. There the distant, blurred faces of Sichi and Nuru, of Lord Edo, none of them moving. None of them helping.

That's right, the voices stopped screaming to say. *You are alone. You have always been alone. But don't worry, I'm here now. I'm here to help you.*

I stumbled away, or tried to with a body that owned no limbs and no bones and no mind. The voice followed. *You are the saviour of your people, Dishiva. You are the one who knows what is good and right, and the only one with the courage to see it done.*

I tried to speak, but nothing came out. I owned no mouth as I owned no body, yet somehow I was still standing, still staring at Leo.

I know it's hard to be the one chosen to lead your people, Dishiva, to save your people from themselves, but I will be here for you. I will help you. Just say yes so I know we understand one another.

"Yes." I had not thought the word, yet I heard it emerge from my tongue, shaped by my lips, a single syllable I could not retake.

No! I shouted the word to myself, but no sooner had I thought it than it confused me. Why would I refuse what I knew to be right? It had been my life's purpose to serve and protect my people. I was a Sword of the Jaroven and would not back away now, no matter how hard it got.

Good, yes, you are wise, Dishiva. You are the leader your people need right now. What they need more than anything is to be free of their false leader. See how he gibbers and raves upon the ground, guilty of so many transgressions against the soul. Kill him.

I owned no hand, yet the weight of a knife hung from it like it was all I was. A mind and a blade. My purpose clear. Gideon was rocking back and forth in little jerks of terror, his arms over his head bent fully now between his knees, the back of his neck exposed. It would be easy and clean and it would be right. He was the wrong leader for my people. Had led them only into trouble and dishonour. He deserved death.

But it was not my place to give it to him. He had not been tried.

I was no horse whisperer, and with such tenets burned into me, every shred of my being screamed its own revolt.

"No."

This time the word was mine. Leo stopped smiling. The screaming renewed and I pressed my hands over my ears and screamed too, unable to hear my voice, only feel the expulsion of air from my lungs.

You must do it, Dishiva. The hardest things to do are the most important. That this is hard only shows how import—

The screaming twisted into a pained shriek. An oomph of breath leaving a body sounded loud nearby, and fresh blood oozed its reek into the air.

As suddenly, the voices and the haze were gone and I knelt on the wooden boards, hunched over, breathing fast. A heavy thud shook the floor and I looked up, eyes wet. Leo. He lay face down only a step away, his neck at an odd angle and his eyes wide and glassy. Blood covered his back, pouring through dozens of wounds to stain his pale robe. Sichi stood over him, a dripping blade in her hands. She breathed as fast as I did, but her hand was as steady as her gaze, heavy and assessing.

"Are you all right?" Nuru asked, wary.

"I..." Hoarse as it sounded, it was my voice, and I had thought the word myself.

"What happened?"

Nuru hovered with the others, even Sichi not drawing closer despite the protection of the knife in her hand. Between us, Leo Villius went on spilling blood onto the floor.

She spoke first, finally lowering the blade. "Did he...do to you what he has been doing to Gideon?" Nuru asked, the translation more hesitant than the empress's question had been.

"I don't know. I...I don't know." I clenched my hands to fists, hating how much I was trembling. "There were voices in my head, screaming and talking to me and encouraging me to do what was right for my people. They wanted me to kill Gideon and…" Would I have done it? Would they have worn down my hesitancy to the core of anger within? Because beneath it all I couldn't doubt I owned enough rage for anything.

None of them had an answer. They just stared. Gideon hadn't moved. We were like a stunned tableau of fear and blood upon this beautiful background.

"We have to move." It was Lord Edo who broke the moment. Nuru translated, but I was already nodding, sure what he had said.

"Yes, we have to move before we're found like this. Keka can't keep people away long without rousing suspicion. Especially if they heard…"

We'd had a plan for everything up to this, but the plan hadn't included dealing with a dead Leo Villius. I stared at the body. Was he still in there? Or was he even now being reincarnated by his god into another body, the same but whole? I looked away with a shudder.

"We have to hide him," I said. "We can't let his followers find the body."

"But how will we explain where he is?"

"We say he's dead. He killed Gideon, Gideon's guards killed him. The body vanished. Everyone knows he does the coming back from the dead thing, so enough people will believe that if we hide him well enough."

Sichi looked at Gideon as Nuru translated my words. This the man she had married, the Levanti she had staked her future on, and thanks to Leo all her plans lay in ruins. "But Gideon isn't dead," she said, the words cold.

"No. But no one needs to know that," Nuru said. "No one will follow him now. Half the Levanti want him dead anyway. We can hide him in the caves until we figure out what to do with him."

She repeated the words in Kisian and received nods from Sichi and Lord Edo.

"All right, you two get him to the caves," I said, forcing my mind to keep running on, to solve this problem so I wouldn't have to think about how completely Leo had filled my head. "Go via the route we used getting in and out, and hopefully no one will see you. And fetch Tep to him. No one else. I don't trust anyone, but healers are sworn to secrecy."

Nuru nodded. Translated. Discussed a few details with the others I was not privy to, and finally stepped toward Gideon. She took one of his hands and put her arm across his back, speaking softly when he tried to pull away. Lord Edo joined her on the other side, and feeling useless and sick, all I could do was watch them coax him to his feet and know I could not have managed such gentle kindness. But however it looked, however it sounded, when Nuru glanced my way there was a flash of disgust in her eyes, hard and angry. Gideon had been her captain once, and no matter how much Leo had used him, all the orders had come from his lips, some long before Leo had returned.

Guiding the steps of our shrunken, huddled leader, Nuru and Lord Edo hurried away as fast as they could get him to walk, their arms twinned across his broad back. Down the stairs and out of the garden house, out of sight, leaving Empress Sichi and me to Leo's body. I could not look at his face without shuddering, his existence a horror I could put no words to.

Sichi pointed out into the garden, at the pond in the centre. It was a pretty thing, with flowers growing in and around it and an edging of rocks, almost like a sculpture.

"Deep enough?" I said, indicating height with my hands.

She shrugged and nodded, which would have to do.

I didn't want to touch Leo, but I was the larger and stronger of the two of us. So, steeling myself with a long exhale, I bent to pick up the still-warm body, hefting it over my shoulder stinking of blood and incense. He was heavier than I had expected with everything about him so ethereal and unreal, and the first few steps were a struggle until I found the right balance for his weight.

Sichi hurried ahead, still dressed in the layers of courtly robes she had donned to entertain him, her hair pinned up in curls and her face painted. She knelt at the side of the pond and looked in, grabbing a stick to test the depth.

She nodded as I approached, but rather than helping me set him down, she hurried off toward the house. Fearing she had heard someone coming, I dropped Leo's body with a sickening smack of flesh on stone, and quickly rolled him into the water. The pond had a shallow edge for water plants, and at first I achieved nothing beyond getting him wet, but I kept pushing until I was up to my shoulders in the water and he started sinking slowly toward the bottom. He was hardly invisible, but one would have to be really looking, the covering of plants and the swift movement of fish enough to distract a casual glance.

In a flurry of silks, Sichi was back, an enormous rock cradled in her arms. It was leaving clods of dirt on her robe and she'd somehow gashed a finger on its rough surface, but with a grim smile she knelt to drop it in. It hit the water with a *splosh* and sank fast, falling on top of the submerged Leo Villius like a baby held to his belly.

"Not up," she said, attempting an explanation. "Water. Up."

She was worried he would float. Dead fish sometimes did. It was a good precaution and one I wouldn't have thought of.

She got up, brushing the dirt from her robe as best she could and starting for the manor. I didn't follow. There was something else I needed to do first.

When she realised I wasn't behind her, she turned, brows raised, but all I could do was point at the shrine and say, "I'll be there in a few minutes," and hope she understood. Whether she truly did or not, she nodded and hurried away.

I could have left Yitti for later, but if I had learned one thing since arriving on these cursed shores, it was that no one could guarantee *later* would even exist. He deserved respect. And thanks. Our plan had worked. I didn't have space to consider at what cost.

Yitti's head sat discarded upon the floor, and I retrieved it while trying not to see it, that just another hurt to add to a pile of hurts that seemed to have no end.

"I'm sorry," I said. "But thank you."

They weren't enough, but no other words would have been. So I sang the lament and called the gods to witness and salvage his soul, Farewelling him back to the world.

I found Empress Sichi, Nuru, and Lord Edo speaking in low whispers just inside the opening to the first cave. All three grimaced as I closed the secret panel behind me. Deeper into the dimly lit space, Tep knelt before Gideon, propped against the wall, a small lantern beside him all the light we had to see by.

"What now?" Nuru said. "Lord Edo isn't sure he can hold the Kisians through such an upheaval. He thinks this might cause some to defect to Empress Miko's cause, or turn on the Levanti here."

"I don't care who they fight for, but the Chiltaens will be here first and they aren't just coming for us. You tell them that. Gideon was their enemy, the Chiltaens are their enemy, but we aren't."

"Perhaps if we give Gideon to the Chiltaens they'll—"

"Still attack," I snapped, causing Nuru to scowl. "I know you're angry. I'm angry, but handing him over to be torn apart isn't going to stop them attacking us and you know it. Right now we have to stop everyone panicking. Lord Edo can talk to the Kisians. Tell

Sichi she needs to address the Levanti, with you. I can't do it. They don't trust me enough anymore, but many have come to trust her. She has to make them believe she fights for them, that she will stand up for them, that they may have lost him but they haven't lost you or each other. You know...inspirational stuff."

Nuru translated, and though I half expected Sichi to laugh, she gave a sharp nod and turned to leave. A word from Edo stopped her short, and all three of them looked at me. "He wants to know what is to be done if someone asks to see the bodies."

"Refuse. Blame Leo. Lock his followers up to stop them looking for the body. Whatever you need to do. We have to keep peace in here if we are to have any hope of facing the army out there."

Solemn nods met the translation of this, Sichi the only one to reply. "If I write a letter to Empress Miko, will your friend"—she pointed farther into the caves—"be able to carry it to her for me? She may yet prove an ally."

It was my turn to nod, and with glances at each other, the three of them departed, leaving me to the relief of a long, slow exhale. I turned to thank Tep for coming and caught a breath. He still knelt before Gideon, but the small cup in his hand was only ever used for one thing.

I strode over. "What are you doing?"

Tep dropped his hand with a start, the redcap dose sloshing. Despite his shock, his face owned no shame. "Putting him out of his misery, Dishiva." He stared right at me in the disturbing way he had, every line in his face cut deep and set hard. "It will be better for us all."

Gideon sat against the wall, his hands on his head and his head between his knees, gasping for air. Not like someone who couldn't breathe, thank the gods, but like all the air in the room could not satisfy his panic. "Better for him how?" I said, despite how awful he looked. "He would be dead."

"Yes, but dying here and now like this would be better than what many will do to him when they find out he's still alive after what he did."

"He will have to carry that shame."

Tep lifted his brows. "A cruel curse, but it does as much damage to the rest of us as to him. I would rather not risk him returning to his senses and doing us all the more harm."

"I think Leo...broke him."

"Then why not let him die?"

Why not? It would be easier on everyone, including Gideon, and in this state, he might not even fight, might take it gladly. Yet every part of me resisted. It was not my judgement to make. Not his judgement to make. Only a whisperer could Farewell living Levanti.

He must have read something of my thoughts in my face for he sat back, lowering the cup still farther. "Think very seriously about this before you tell me no, Dishiva," he said. "I won't look after him. If you leave me with him, I will do the merciful thing. And he cannot look after himself in this state. Are you going to care for him? Could you?"

I looked as he bade me, but my gaze could not even linger upon Gideon's hunched shoulders without seeing the crimson surcoat that had become such a symbol of his brutality. It ran like blood across his shoulders and down onto the floor, just as Yitti's blood had poured out onto the stones in the garden.

"No," I said. "But I am willing to leave the choice in another's hands." I pointed toward the end of the small cave. "If you walk that way, you'll find the path narrows before opening again into another cave, followed by a smaller one. After that you squeeze through a narrow gap into a big cavern. You'll find Jass en'Occha there, though you might want to call out that you're a friend so he doesn't kill you as you walk in."

Tep set the cup down, but the liquid remained inside, glinting its promise of death. "You want to ask an Occha to take care of our mess?"

"No." I reached out a bloodstained boot and knocked the cup over, spilling its deadly contents onto the bare rock. "I want an Occha to carry a message for me."

21. RAH

Riding west to Kogahaera with the empress was so reminiscent of our march south with the Chiltaens that I was glad they wanted us to keep to ourselves. Each day riding now ended with companionable Levanti talk and songs and stories around the camp fire, uninterrupted by caring what the Kisians thought of us. A few always gathered to watch the Hoya game we squeezed into the evening, but at least they kept their comments to themselves.

Despite the freedom allowed us, there was tension in this combined herd of ours. Ezma rode ahead like the leader she wasn't meant to be, while Derkka brought up the rear like a patriarch. Most of the Kisians were on foot, which kept the pace slow, and without enough horses for all the Levanti there were arguments over who most deserved a mount. Tor hadn't even asked for one, choosing instead to sit in the back of one of the carts so he could continue translating the Chiltaen holy book in peace. Until his services were requested by the empress and he had to jog to the front of the army to translate instructions and plans.

"You'd think he'd grumble more," Amun said, watching Tor stride past us in the wake of the soldier sent to fetch him. He had the book tucked under his arm and a determinedly blank expression on his face. "I'm not sure I would like being summoned."

"Who says he likes it?" I said, glancing across. "At least someone is valuing him. He should have been Made ages ago."

Tor disappeared behind the bulk of the empress's soldiers. "By age, yes," he agreed. "But I've been wondering about that. The First Swords have been here for three cycles, and in that time he and the others trained to speak Chiltaen, not to do any of the things they ought to have been training to do."

"You don't think they're ready? Capable?"

"Maybe not. Whatever that even means now."

"Whatever that means," I agreed. "Here, being able to speak Kisian seems far more important than any of the skills needed back home."

Ahead of us, Captain Lashak rode alongside Ezma, the two conversing with many nods and smiles and little laughs of understanding. The horse whisperer was often accompanied by different Swords, a rotating collection of Levanti seeking her wisdom or approval. Or she theirs.

"What do you think she wants?"

I had been asking myself that question since first meeting her, but it was reassuring to hear it on another's lips. Proof I wasn't being paranoid about her.

"I wish I knew," I said. "Wish I knew why she was exiled. Why isn't anyone else worried what could cause every other whisperer to deem her unworthy?"

Amun shrugged. "They probably don't want to think about it. I know I didn't. I cried when I first saw her. A whisperer here, someone to help us find ourselves again. By the time I wondered why she was here, I already believed in her. I think people are worried though. Especially since the *kutum*. No whisperer should look at a captain and see a rival."

"Unless they don't think of themselves as just a horse whisperer anymore."

We rode on a little way, caught in our own thoughts of what that meant.

"She has an old translated copy of the Chiltaen holy book," I said as tonelessly as I could to get Amun's honest reaction.

I wasn't disappointed. His head snapped around. "She what?" I flicked a meaningful glance at the two women riding ahead, and he lowered his voice. "A holy book? You mean like the one Tor has?"

"Yes, but older. Like... an original. She seems to treasure it."

Amun screwed up his nose and froze there a moment before his face smoothed into wide-eyed awe. "Wait," he said. "Do you think she believes in the whole One True God thing? If she abandoned our gods and our ways, the whisperers would have had to exile her."

"And Derkka," I agreed. "I'd feel sorry for him if he wasn't a shit."

Amun snorted. "Poetic."

"He doesn't deserve the effort it would take to be more eloquent."

"That... is one of the wisest things you've ever said."

It was my turn to screw up my nose. "What a low standard I've set."

He grinned, but the light-hearted mood soon faded back into the worry we seemed to carry everywhere with us now. "But even so, what does she want?" Amun said abruptly. "Why does she want to lead us into battle now when she wouldn't stir from the castle against Grace Bahain? Why is she so often talking to the empress? Is she trying to get something? Do you think if we ask Tor, he'll ask Empress Miko about it?"

I stared ahead at the empress's banner—all I had seen of her for the last few days, barring the occasional glimpse. She was always busy, moving about the camp talking to her soldiers, Minister Manshin and General Ryoji ever at her side. She had no dragon armour to wear now, but she was up there riding as if she did, pride and determination fuelling her every move despite what had happened back in Syan.

"No," I said, trying not to think about the night she had come to my room, about the relationship I could have had with her even now had I thrown away my tenets. "I don't think he would, and it's unfair to ask when it could put him in danger."

"Danger? You think she would take the question badly?"

"I think her minister is displeased with our presence."

"Didn't you save his life?"

"As far as he knows. I think Sett would have let him go, but… we'll never know for sure."

Amun said nothing. He had heard about Sett; everyone had. No deserter would think the worse of me for it, but it wasn't their anger I feared. Each day we got closer to Kogahaera, we got closer to Gideon. I had thought of little beyond helping my people for weeks, about helping him, but that Sett's corpse now lay between us troubled me more than I wanted to admit. Perhaps it wouldn't matter. Perhaps he would not listen to me anymore. Would order me killed on sight. Perhaps it was already too late.

———————————◆———————————

Kogahaera sat on a tributary east of a river whose name I didn't know and didn't care to find out. The city remained a dark smudge on the horizon when we came upon a Kisian camp, the sight of flags and tents sending a jangle of fear through my bones.

"We're about to stop for the night," Tor said, walking back to join us.

"Whose camp is that?"

"The rest of her army. The big part. Led by… Oya… Oyamada? We're still to keep our distance, but there will be a meeting tonight and you're to attend. Don't worry," he added. "I've already been *requested* to translate for you. I'll come find you when they're ready."

"Why are we having to keep our distance?"

"I don't know, Rah, and I don't ask. Learn to speak to them yourself if you want to have nuanced political discussions."

He walked away on the words, his long stride catching up with Ezma after a dozen or so paces. Again the feeling I was reliving the time spent following the Chiltaen conquest could not be quietened. Perhaps Amun felt the same, for he fixed his gaze on the camp and spoke no more.

There weren't as many Levanti as there were Kisians, but we were used to travelling, used to being social on the move, and the chatter and laughter around me didn't begin to fade until the wooden stakes of a palisade wall loomed. I shuddered. Whatever differences we might find inside, that the Kisians and Chiltaens built their army camps in similar ways made my stomach twist.

A chant rose inside as the empress's banner passed through the gate. I felt Amun's gaze on me, but had to keep my focus on Jinso, my steady hand all that kept him from fretting under the weight of my worry. We had ridden into many such camps and never been greeted with respect. What was to say these Kisians would not betray us the way Grace Bahain had planned to betray Gideon?

In Ezma's wake, we rode into the camp, beneath the wooden arch and into a world of mud and tents and staring eyes. The empress and her soldiers were greeted with cheers, but these quietened to whispers at sight of us. I had to remind myself we were the enemy in their eyes. Chiltaen mercenaries, they had thought us, barbarians, not the prisoners we had been.

Beside me, Amun let out a puff of held breath. "I...don't like this."

"Neither do I, but we have to do what we came for. And I trust the empress far more than Legate Andrus."

"But do you trust her generals?"

The answer was no, but I didn't say so.

As the only one able to understand, Tor gave the orders and

instructions as they came to us, directing us to empty tents in a way that only served to set him further apart. To stave off the air of the familiar, I focussed on the tasks I could control. On rubbing down Jinso and making sure he had feed, on sharpening my knife and speaking my prayers to the gods, on checking every Sword was provided for.

At least the food was different to what we'd grown used to with the Chiltaens, and for a time we could settle around our separate fires and pretend we were back on the plains.

Until Tor tapped my shoulder. "Meeting time."

I hadn't forgotten, but I had put off thinking about it, about having to sit there pretending anyone gave a damn what I thought while others decided my people's fate. Gideon's fate.

I set my unfinished meal beside Amun, no longer hungry. "Yours, if you want extra. I have to go find out what the plan is now."

I hadn't spoken to him about my fears for Gideon, only my worries for our people, but something in the way he looked at me, some note of pity, hollowed me to the core. "Good luck," he said, and I could once more see him kneeling beside the shrine in Chiltae, offering Hamatet's soul back to the gods.

I always assumed you would be doing this for me one day. Gideon had smiled, but he'd meant it.

"Rah? They're waiting for you." Tor had taken a few steps away, impatience in every line of his body.

"Yes, I'm coming."

The meeting tent was well into the Kisian portion of the camp, a few minutes' walk we made in silence. All I could think to say was sorry that I needed him to translate for me, but with nothing I could do to fix the problem I kept my mouth shut. It wasn't his job to allay my guilt as well.

The Kisians were even more keen on grand tents than the

Chiltaens had been, the great silken thing Tor led me to like an enormous lantern. Light from inside shone through patterned patches of thinner material, leaving golden dragons and curls of flame to glow upon the dark shell.

Four guards stood outside, none of them familiar. General Ryoji might have nodded, but these men just stared as we approached. I thought to stop and gain permission to enter, but Tor kept walking, a man far surer of his welcome here than of his place in our herd.

I entered the tent a step behind him, momentarily blinded on the threshold. The space was full of light and glints on gold and wine, and all too many stares. Calculating. Assessing. Suspicious.

Empress Miko sat at the head of the table in a glorious crimson and gold surcoat, and though I had planned not to look at her, I stared longer than I ought, the sight of her kneeling there with her great bow upon her back breathtaking.

Nine men knelt with her, Minister Manshin, General Moto, and General Ryoji the only ones I knew. My name was spoken. Theirs followed. Oyamada. Yass. Mihri. I would forget them all in a few minutes. I stopped even listening when I caught sight of Ezma. She was sitting at the opposite end of the table to the empress, still and sure as a rock. She met my gaze with a slight smile. "Rah."

"Ezma." I forced myself to salute though it felt dishonourable to even pretend I respected her.

Talk buzzed around the table, but understanding none of it, I focussed on the empress's voice as Tor steered me toward empty cushions near Ezma. Once we knelt, a maid filled our wine bowls and topped up others. Beside the empress, Minister Manshin addressed the table, and I sat listening to his tone and waiting for Tor to enlighten me.

"He says taking Kogahaera will be more complicated than initially thought," he whispered at last. "There is...oh. A Chiltaen army is camped on the opposite side of the city. Minister Oyamada has been keeping an eye on them, prepared to fight should they attack but making no move without Her Majesty."

"Chiltaens? I thought—"

"That you killed them all?" I flinched at *you*. "It seems not. The minister sounds surprised. They are now discussing what the Chiltaens could be planning, as an attack on a fortified Kisian city this far into the empire is no small thing."

He fell silent, listening as the conversation moved around the table, picked up by each of the men between sips of wine while the empress watched. They addressed her as they spoke, some deferentially, others with minimal respect, all with the confidence of men who existed to be listened to. They spoke too fast for me to pick out any words, but the sound of Leo's name sent a chill rolling down my spine. I reached for my wine bowl.

"Some are suggesting the Chiltaens may want the release of Dom Villius. Though having marched an army all the way here, it seems unlikely they will just leave again even if Gideon gives him up."

It made no sense that Gideon had kept Leo with him having killed him once already, but having done so, the priest was probably the only thing he had to bargain. I didn't say so, sure the men around me had already said it or the empress had already thought it.

"They are agreeing that unless the Chiltaens are there to bolster Gideon's forces—"

I snorted. "Unlikely."

"Their view too," Tor said. "Which means it's wiser to keep out of the way and let the Chiltaens attack the city first before sweeping in to clean up the mess."

"What? All the Levanti inside the city could die if they do that."

"They could die if the Kisians attack too."

"No, because many more of them would surrender to a Kisian

army, especially with us here. How many will surrender to a Chilt-aen army?"

"None."

The intensity of our interchange had drawn attention along the table. The empress lifted her brows, but what could I say? They were right from their own point of view. Why risk greater casualties to fight both the Chiltaens and the city at the same time when they could just sit back and wait to see what happened?

"Do you want to—?"

"No," I said. "I will not bare my pain to people who won't listen."

"Then we ought to fight with people who will," Ezma said, and before I could answer she rose, towering above the table, her headpiece brushing the sagging silk roof. When she spoke it was in Kisian, and I stared, shocked by her ease with the language.

"She is saying that, as many of the Swordherds are outside the city, it would be a good opportunity to gather the closest to our cause. There's a good chance they chose to leave and therefore may be desirous of—"

"Attacking Gideon in retribution," I said.

Tor gave a half shrug. "Something like that, yes."

Ezma finished, leaving the conversation to leap around the table, from General Moto to the empress to others I didn't know and back to General Moto. "Some of them like the idea," Tor said. "The Chiltaen army is sizeable, and we don't know what they intend. More soldiers can never be a bad thing."

"But some of them fear we'll turn on them?"

"Yes, they are mentioning what happened to the Chiltaens at Mei'lian quite often."

"We were their prisoners. They treated us like dirt."

Ezma broke in on what one of the generals was saying, and by the way Tor nodded in her direction this seemed to be the point she was making. Despite interrupting, everyone at the table listened to her, looked up to her standing above them, and let her finish with more respect than I had ever seen them show another Levanti. Clearly the crown and the regal bearing spoke to them.

"She is explaining the position of a horse whisperer and assuring them of her word."

I snorted. The nearest general glanced my way, but no one else seemed to notice.

When Ezma finished, she remained standing, and it was a moment before the discussion was taken up again, bouncing up and back along the table with little sign they cared I was present.

"Let me know if you want to say anything," Tor said. "I grumble about the need to do this, but I'll be your voice."

I thanked him with a murmur, but in truth I wasn't sure what I wanted to say. Gathering up loose herds was a good idea in theory, we were always stronger together, but if they put Ezma in charge of such an undertaking she could gather more supporters for... whatever she was trying to achieve. I didn't trust her, nor her intentions toward Gideon and his Levanti. In my nebulous plans for what I would do when we reached this point, I had always imagined getting to speak to him, to appeal to him peacefully. That I could be overruled by a Levanti majority wanting him and the others dead made me feel sick.

Minister Manshin spoke next, and I didn't need Tor's translation to know he was against the idea. He shot unpleasant looks my way. Whatever rapport I had thought we'd developed seemed to have run out.

"He says the people won't trust us, and they shouldn't either. He's talking about the burning of Mei'lian and his imprisonment. I don't think you're getting any more support from him."

I grunted agreement as the empress spoke, sliding her wine bowl forward on the table. She looked to Minister Manshin, who drew his back toward himself and turned to the man on his left.

"What are they doing?"

"Voting. Yes or no depending on whether they think Ezma should be allowed to round up more Levanti."

As though they had the right to control our decisions.

More wine bowls moved, around the table in roughly equal numbers, ending with one more no than yes. Until Ezma pushed her wine bowl forward, evening the number. One of the generals exclaimed, appealing to the empress, and a flurry of heated conversation followed.

"They don't think Ezma should get a vote, but apparently there is precedent," Tor whispered. "She and you have been invited to this council as allies and so are officially allowed a say in the decision-making process. I get the feeling from the way they're being deferential that the empress could overrule the vote, but I'm really not sure how this works."

After some grumbling, the men finally seemed to accept they couldn't stop Ezma voting, and all eyes turned to me. It was a draw, equal votes either way, and I stared down at my wine bowl rather than risk looking at Miko. She wanted more soldiers. Wanted to be sure of this battle. Of her empire. We owed her that after what Gideon had done to it, but Ezma was not who they thought her, wasn't even who the Levanti thought her, and the idea of giving her more followers chilled my blood.

I reached out and, still looking only at the table, drew my wine bowl toward me. Murmuring broke out above my head, and when I did look up it was to see Empress Miko's disappointment. And Ezma's flash of anger, quickly hidden with a harsh smile.

———————◆———————

Ezma was waiting for me in the shadows halfway back to our camp. "You think you're clever, stopping me from helping our people?" she said as I passed.

I gripped the front of her collar, twisting the fabric in a shaking hand. "What are you doing here?"

"Doing?" she said, her initial shock sharpening to a derisive smile. "Helping my people. Fulfilling my purpose. What are you doing?"

Purpose. Leo had always talked a lot about purpose.

"You were exiled because the missionaries got into your head like they got to our herd masters, weren't you?"

"The Entrancers?" She barked a harsh laugh. "Oh no, they only do that to people who refuse to listen."

My stomach dropped through the bottom of my feet. "Entrancers?"

She gripped my hand and twisted, sending a shoot of pain through my wrist. My hold loosened, she pulled free and straightened her collar. "Yes, Rah," she said. "Entrancers. That's what they're called when they can get inside your head. Gosh, how very adorably pathetic you look when you stare like that. You have no idea about anything you think you understand, little man."

"Get inside people's heads?" I took a threatening step closer, anger bubbling through me. "The sickness. Our herd masters are being controlled and you *knew*? You knew and said nothing?"

She held her ground and shrugged. "Even if I wanted to tell someone, I was here, wasn't I?"

"But you didn't want to tell anyone?"

"Why would I? They're helping us be better."

The knife was in my hand before I thought to draw it, its edge pressed to the skin of her throat. "How many people have died for your idea of *better*?"

She glared back as though the blade wasn't there and hissed through her teeth. "None would have to if they just listened. The missionaries came to me like they came to everyone, but I was wise. I listened and I learned and opened my eyes to a world beyond the plains, to the truth just out of reach. I stopped fighting against God's purpose and became one with it."

I pressed the blade harder into her flesh, my own prickling with the heat of an anger I'd never known. "You carry the name and honour of a horse whisperer, and yet you spit on everything it stands for."

She leaned in, daring me to keep my arm steady and slice deep. A thin line of blood appeared on the blade. "Horse whisperers guide the spirit of our people. I would be spitting on that if I let the Levanti keep believing in nothing."

"In nothing?" For years I had berated myself for having failed, for having shamed my people by abandoning my training, and now here she stood proud of how she had twisted all we believed in. I wanted to hurt her, but even now the dishonour of threatening a horse whisperer warred with the anger within me. "And I thought I had failed the training. At least I knew enough to know I had failed."

Ezma glared her challenge. "The way the Levanti are going cannot last. The world is moving on and we are staying the same. If we don't accept change *all* Levanti will die, our ways lost with us. Gideon chose to do something, even if it was the wrong thing. If you choose to do nothing there will be more blood on your hands than on either of ours."

She stepped back, leaving my blade hovering in mid-air. A trickle of blood trailed down her neck. "Don't worry, Rah, by the time you get back to the plains, if you ever do, you'll be obsolete anyway. The new Veld is going to shape an empire for us."

"You mean Leo. You're one of his followers?"

Her laugh made me feel like a child. "Leo Villius is nothing but a cheat. A pretender. Veld is Levanti. The empire will be built on Levanti land. All this"—she spread her arms and gestured around—"is just the war and politics of people who don't matter."

"Don't matter?" Pain sheared up my arm for how tightly I gripped the knife. "Don't matter? You are talking about thousands of innocent people."

"Then stay here and fight for them. I have Levanti souls to save."

It was my turn to laugh, the sound a bitter thing full of hate. "You think you're Veld?"

"Oh no, not me. But I will be there when they save our people from the Entrancers, taking up their holy empire under God."

"The Entrancers who created this problem in the first place!"

She grinned. "A neat plan, don't you think?"

"Why are you telling me this?"

"Because it's funny. All this information you can't do anything with because it's too late. Look at that pain crossing your face. You want to hurt me so much, but you can't do that either. Not here. You can't do anything at all, Rah e'Torin, because no one is going to believe a damn word you say about me. It's your word against mine, and I'm a horse whisperer. You're just a—how many times exiled?—former Sword captain."

Ezma straightened her clothing, wiped the trickle of blood from her neck, and clasped her hands behind her back. With her head proudly raised, the jawbone headpiece of her calling was imposing, and I couldn't separate the respect I held for her position, for those who gave themselves to such a life, from the disgust I felt for her.

"You just want power, and you'll do anything to get it," I said. "You weren't satisfied with helping people only when they came to you. You only listened to the missionaries because the beliefs they offered you allowed you to give in to your impulse to control."

A snarl creased her face. "Don't assume you know anything about me."

"I don't, but I know what it felt like being all alone, isolated from your herd, belonging nowhere. And to know it would always be like that. People revere you in silence. They come for your help and leave and you are alone again. No power. No supporters. No friends or family or lovers. It's just service and nothing else."

This time when her face twisted she couldn't smooth it, so deep were the creases of hurt. "You have no idea."

"I do. I hated it. That's why I left. You should have too."

"Fuck you and your righteous compassion, Rah. I don't want it. I found my path and I hope you never find yours."

She strode out into the moonlight, leaving me still gripping a knife in the shadows, my every heaved breath containing more emotion than I had space in my body to hold. But disgust and hate and horror all too soon gave way to a gaping hopelessness, because she was right. There was nothing I could do. No one would believe me. I wasn't even sure I believed it. Entrancers? It sounded mystical, but so did a man who could come back to life when he died, gifted new flesh by a god. How could a man like that be a fraud?

"Rah?"

I spun, still clutching the knife. Amun stood behind me, keeping a wary distance. I thrust the blade back into its scabbard and gripped him by the shoulders. "You were right," I said. "She is a believer in the One True God. She thinks there's going to be a holy empire and she is going to help it happen. But...why make a deal with the empress to lead the Levanti into battle?"

For a long moment, Amun just stared, his gaze jumping from one of my eyes to the other like he was trying to read. To catch up. "Perhaps she thinks being in charge will help her protect Leo Villius?"

"No." I let him go and ran a hand over the short hair on my scalp. "She doesn't think he's Veld. She thinks it's a Levanti who is going to remake the holy empire."

"A Levanti? Her?"

I shook my head and started to pace, short distances with furious steps. "Someone else. But she talked about Entrancers, who are the ones getting in the herd masters' heads, Amun; she told me because there was nothing I could do to change it, and she's right."

I stopped abruptly and turned to him. "I probably sound like I'm raving even to you. Who would believe such a thing, especially levelled at a horse whisperer?"

"You do sound like you're raving. But for what little it's worth, I believe you."

His words dropped some of the weight from my shoulders and I drew him to me, squeezing him hard. "Thank you."

"Thank yourself for teaching me to be a stubborn ass," he mumbled into my shoulder.

I let him go with a laugh, my soul momentarily lighter. "You had a good teacher there, that's for sure."

The lightness was short-lived. Amun was only one Sword, and even if I could get others to believe me, what could I do? We needed to get into Kogahaera to save who we could, and dividing the Levanti more would not achieve that. I didn't trust Ezma, but we needed to get inside the city.

"I have to go see the empress."

Amun set his hands on his hips and eyed me suspiciously. "What for?"

"To change my vote. I'll explain later. Do you know where Tor is?"

I started walking away before he could answer. "Probably with the empress already or not far," he called after me. "But wait—" He jogged to catch up. "There's something else. I came to find you because a small group of Bedjuti arrived while you were gone. Only ten of them, don't get excited. They've been scouting in the north and came across a large group of Kisian soldiers seemingly without a leader. Do we . . . do we tell the empress? Do you trust her enough to give her more soldiers?"

I had stopped to listen, but with so much on my mind I could hardly focus on what he was saying. I shook my head, more in confusion than disagreement. "I don't know. I think so? I'll tell Tor. I had better go."

"All right," he said as I walked away. "But you had better explain later! I don't want to be still wondering what the fuck we're doing by the end of the night, all right?"

I waved a hand at him and hurried on, fighting back doubts. I had voted against gathering the other Swordherds because I didn't trust Ezma, because I feared how few would side with me, but there wasn't time for doubt anymore. We needed more Levanti and we needed them now. Needed to get into the city. Needed to go home. Even if I could persuade half the Levanti I was telling the truth, it would be worth the risk.

Soldiers stared at me as I strode along looking for the empress's tent. Many had flags and flapping crimson openings, but only one had General Ryoji standing outside, lantern light lapping at his feet.

"General," I said, catching his attention. "I need to talk to the empress." I mimed talking and pointed at the tent as I said her name, hating how foolish I must look.

But he didn't laugh. He asked a question before thinking better of speaking Kisian at me and held up a hand for me to wait. Having stuck his head inside, Tor emerged.

"Rah?" the young man said. "What is it?"

Almost I demanded to know what he was doing with Empress Miko, but I swallowed the words just in time and said, "I need to talk to the empress. I've changed my vote."

He stared at me a long moment. "Are you sure?"

"Yes. I can't hide behind someone else's army because I'm afraid of my own people."

A slow nod was all I got for my honesty before he ushered me in.

"If you surrender the city," the empress muttered, pacing slowly back and forth across a carpeted floor. "If you surrender the city. If you surrender the city." She stopped and looked up. "Rah."

"You speak Levanti?"

She looked to Tor, who shook his head. "I'm teaching her a speech she can make. To appeal to the Levanti at Kogahaera."

Of course. Stupid not to have thought of that.

Before I could recall why I had come, Shishi bounded across the matting toward me in a flurry of white and tan fur. "Shishi!" I knelt to scruff her ears, letting her lick my face and taking a moment to press my forehead to hers. As joyous as it was to be so fondly remembered, I had come with a serious purpose and soon forced myself to stand. Despite her dog's welcome, the empress lifted her brows in haughty challenge, and I couldn't but think of the last time we had stood so close together. She had kissed me, our mutual desire ending us in a tangle on the floor until I'd tried to explain why we could go no further. She must have thought of it too, for the tension in the lantern-lit tent grew tight and hot. By the opening, Tor said, "Shall I go and—"

"No," I said. "I need you to translate. First, tell her there are some newly arrived Levanti who found a group of Kisian soldiers sheltering in the north. I don't know any details, but if she wants to find them, talk to Amun. Then tell her I'm changing my vote. I agree to the Levanti leaving to gather more allies."

Tor's eyes had narrowed at the mention of more Kisian soldiers and stayed narrowed as he said, "With Ezma as their leader?"

"Yes. With Ezma as our leader and me as her second."

My words were relayed to the empress, who snapped out a question.

"She wants to know what changed your mind."

"Time to think. No Kisians should have to fight Levanti battles. We will do this ourselves."

Empress Miko nodded, her face carefully neutral. I wished I knew what she was hiding behind it, but it would have to wait until this was done. We had both come too far to focus on anything else now.

"I will inform my generals," she said. "You may leave whenever suits you." She didn't add that we had better not betray her or her people, but the sentiment was there all the same.

"Thank you."

It was poor gratitude. She was trusting us, trusting me, with the safety of her empire, and I was only half sure I could keep Ezma from turning the Levanti back upon Kisia. I couldn't say that, of course, couldn't say anything but thank you and goodbye and bow as I left her tent, sure that to stay any longer would see all the truths come pouring like confessions from my lips.

Rather than risk another run-in with Ezma, I sent someone else to her with the message. I hadn't been sure what to expect, whether she would seek me out herself with suspicious demands to know what I meant by it, or whether she would change her mind too and refuse, but all she did was send back a message with a condescendingly worded thank you that made me hate even the face of the Sword who had carried it. We were to leave at dawn.

Knowing I wouldn't be able to sleep, I went to the horse pen. Jinso was still awake, nosing about in the grass, keeping to himself. "Hello there," I said, patting his neck. "We leave in the morning."

I wanted to tell him I didn't know what would happen. Didn't know where we would end up when we walked out of here. That I wanted to leave as much as I wanted to stay, but I couldn't risk admitting aloud how close the empress and I kept coming to having something, only for it to come to nothing. Perhaps it was too late now anyway.

"Rah! There you are!"

I turned, hand falling from Jinso's neck. Amun hurried into the pen, someone following in his wake, their breathing laboured like they'd run a long way.

"What is it?"

Amun halted, taking a deep breath to steady his heart rate while his companion bent double, gasping. "It's Gideon."

"Gideon?" My stomach dropped. Everything seemed suddenly very far away. "What about him?"

"I'll let Jass explain. He just arrived from Kogahaera. Dishiva sent him."

"Dishiva? What's going on?"

Fear thundered through my veins, and I had to keep from shaking Jass to make him speak faster. Sweat ran down his face and his chest heaved, but I would be sick if I had to keep waiting.

"Is he dead? Is—"

Jass shook his head. "No—not dead. But he's—in a really bad way."

One fear lightened, only to be replaced with more. "In a bad way? You mean injured? Sick? Tell me, please."

The man let out a long breath and nodded. "Sick. In the head. I don't know. It's something to do with Leo, but I don't really understand it. Dishiva just said I had to come and find you and tell you because if you don't come, he's going to be torn apart by Levanti before the Chiltaens even break down the gates."

"What? Why?"

Jass pressed his lips into a solemn line. "He's . . . done some really bad things. The sort of things no one can forgive him for, even if they believe he was under the control of that shit."

Control. "Leo's an Entrancer?"

"A what?"

But I had been asking myself, memory spinning back to moments when it had seemed like he could read my mind. Like he knew what was going to happen. He'd been the only decent Chiltaen I'd met, and I'd fought hard to defend him, lost many Swords defending him.

And now he'd used Gideon too.

My stomach churned.

"Fuck." I ran my hands over the short pelt of my hair. "Fuck!"

If I didn't go with Ezma she would get all the Levanti on her side, might turn them against Miko, but if I went, I was leaving Gideon defenceless, alone, fending for himself. And I couldn't. I couldn't.

"What did he do?" Amun's question was quietly spoken, but his fierce words reminded me how Gideon had let him stay behind in our first Chiltaen camp, knowing he would be killed. That Gideon had ordered us not to take the heads of enemies. That he had made a deal with the Chiltaens so more Levanti would be forced to fight. Had given up his saddleboys. Had slaughtered whole towns of innocent people. What more could he have added to his list?

"You know about the city? Mei'lian?"

Amun nodded. "And the attack on the deserter camp."

"Right, well, after that..." Jass flicked a look my way. Wary. "He sent a lot of the Swordherds away and...killed others. For conspiring against him, he said, but they were all people who spoke against Leo. I'm sorry," he added, looking fully at me now. "He killed Yitti. And some of the other Second Swords of Torin."

It was like someone had taken a club to my head. Either I staggered or the ground moved, and when Amun spoke it was from far away. Yitti. I had begged for his help. He had been taking them home and I had stopped him. And now—

I threw up, spraying my horror upon the grass at Jinso's feet. Self-blame swirled, along with anger at Leo and Ezma and anyone who had ever sought to control a Levanti. But beneath it all, the sick knowledge that Gideon hadn't needed controlling, hadn't needed pushing, to be capable of terrible things.

"Rah." Amun's hand was on my shoulder. I tried to breathe evenly, to suck in air and let it out with the same ease I'd possessed before Jass had spoken, with the same confidence in my goal. In Gideon.

Overhead, Jass whispered words of comfort to Jinso, and I

couldn't thank him for it. Couldn't focus. Amun said no more, neither man making any attempt to comfort me when nothing could be said. Under Leo's influence or not, the blood of my Swords was on Gideon's hands as Sett's blood was on mine.

For a time, I stayed crouched, unable to move, unwilling to look up and face either them or the decision I had to make. But time was not stopping. The night was getting no younger. And no matter how many times I told myself Gideon had become a monster, that everything he had done was wrong, that he deserved whatever was coming to him, my thoughts returned to imagining him alone and afraid.

And to the boy I had once been, sitting at the edge of the herd, ashamed.

I stood on legs that trembled more than I would like. I think Amun knew what I was going to say before I said it, something resigned and pained in his face though he said nothing.

"I'm going to him."

"If you can hear that and still go, nothing I say will change your mind," he said. "But what about the Levanti here? What about Ezma? We're leaving at first light, remember."

"You won't be back by then," Jass said. "The only safe way into the city is through caves that go under the walls, and it takes time."

My people or Gideon. I almost laughed at how little consideration I gave it. "I'm going. Amun, you'll have to take my place as Ezma's second. You know as well as I do what she's up to now."

"Yes, but I'm not you," he said. "People don't want to follow me just because I looked at them. I don't have your words."

I set my hand on his shoulder, forcing a smile I was far from feeling. "I think I taught you more than just how to be a stubborn ass, but either way, I won't ask you to go to Gideon for me, so this is the way it has to be."

He didn't tell me he thought Gideon deserved to be abandoned, that I was wrong to go, that I had to think of my people, and for that I was more grateful than for anything else.

"I know he's done—"

"Just go, Rah," he said. "I know. You don't have to explain to me. I don't fucking like it, but I get it. And you have to go or it will eat you up forever."

For the second time that night I pulled him close, crushing his shoulders. "I know you'll do me proud, Amun," I said.

"And I know you'll be a noble idiot. You always do such a fine job of it. Now get going, before you're too late."

I wished I could thank him for the selflessness it took to encourage me to do something he hated, but I couldn't. All I could do was take a breath and turn to Jass. "All right, show me the way."

22. MIKO

"*Tiateph*," I said.

"More emphasis on the *p* sound."

Tor had slowly relaxed as he taught me, moving from standing stiffly to attention to slouching, to sitting, and now lying across a bank of cushions in one corner, staring up at the rippling tent.

"*Tiateph*," I said again. And when he made no sign I'd said it any better, I kept trying. "*Tiateph. Tiateph. TeeeeahhhtePAH.*"

He rolled his head to look at me. "Are you taking this seriously?"

"Are you?" I snapped.

A frown lowered his brows, and somehow that silent censure was worse than even Minister Manshin's disapproving looks. "I'm here, aren't I?"

I sighed. "Yes, and I know I can never thank you enough for all you do to help me, but it's been a long day and I'm tired and Levanti is—"

"Not as difficult as Kisian."

"Do you always have a retort on hand to make me feel foolish and whingy?"

Tor laughed, a sound rare enough to take me by surprise. "Absolutely, Your Majesty," he said, raising himself on an elbow. "I consider it my most important duty. To stop you flying too high above us mere mortals."

"You," I said, "are a monster."

Almost I wished the words unsaid, playful as they were, but his lips twitched into a smile and the skin around his eyes crinkled. He saluted me in the Levanti way, one elbow still propping him off the floor. "It's my finest quality."

Before I could think of a retort, a Levanti voice sounded outside, and for the merest instant my heart constricted, sure Rah was back, but Shishi hadn't so much as lifted her head from her place curled up in the middle of the floor. With a grunt of effort, Tor was up and striding to the opening, as though it had been his job to welcome people in and out of my tent.

A few brief words outside and he was back. "It's Amun, Your Majesty. Amun e'Torin. He says he has a letter for you."

"A letter? From whom?" But of course, Tor just shrugged and I shook my head. "Doesn't matter. Tell him to come in. Are you able to—?"

Tor broke in upon my question with a bitter "It's what I'm here for, isn't it?"

Before I could answer, Amun e'Torin stepped through the tent flap and stood wary and unsure of his welcome. I knew their last names came from the herd they were a part of, yet it always surprised me to find Torin who were so very unlike Rah in appearance. Amun was about half a head shorter than his one-time captain, his face broader, with a jaw so square it didn't only appear chiselled from stone but could have been used as a chisel in its own right. He had deep-set eyes with something of a mournful shape, but that could merely have been the gravity of his mission.

I must have spoken a welcome for he saluted, uttering a respectful Levanti greeting, before holding out a scroll sealed with Kisian wax. My hand trembled as I took it, hunting a hint of who it was from and finding no sigil.

"It came from Kogahaera," Amun said through Tor's translation.

"It was given to Jass en'Occha, who brought it out through the narrow cave system with him when he came to fetch Rah."

Even as Tor spoke he flicked a glance at me, tension filling the tent. I had taken the letter, but did not drop my arm, my whole being seeming to freeze in place. "Fetch Rah?"

Amun grimaced, glanced at Tor with something like belligerence, and set his already square jaw hard before replying.

"He left," Tor translated. "A message came for him too. It is... hard to explain, but it seems like Gideon is in a bad way, and Rah is going to him before the Levanti tear him apart."

Rah, departing on the eve of a potential battle, leaving to save the very enemy I had come here to oust. It would be more complicated than that, and he wasn't *my* Rah, and yet the hollow sense of abandonment couldn't be quietened.

"I see," I said, because I had to say something, had to appear cool and unconcerned, like the vagaries of the Levanti marching with us meant nothing to me, though I had a hundred questions. Why had Gideon e'Torin's people turned on him? What did the Kisians in Kogahaera think? And most importantly, why Rah? What was Gideon e'Torin to him other than a herd brother?

In the end the only one I could ask was "He went alone?"

"Yes, Your Majesty. With Jass en'Occha to guide him. I am to be Whisperer Ezma's second in his place when we leave in the morning to sweep the area for other herds."

I nodded, nothing else I could do. "Thank you."

A salute and Amun was gone, leaving Tor standing tense, hovering like he wasn't sure whether he ought to stay or go. "They've been friends a long time," he hazarded after a silence. "I don't know if friendship can survive this, but... Rah is... always very honourable. He does what is right even if he hates it."

"I understand. I hope he has no cause to regret his decision. You may go and rest now, Tor. Thank you for your help with the speech."

He nodded and then, remembering his position, bowed and was gone.

I didn't immediately crack the seal on the letter, but stood holding it alone in the centre of my tent, unsure what I most wanted and feared it to say. Was it a reply from Emperor Gideon? The same Emperor Gideon Rah had gone to save? It seemed unlikely, but then who? Sichi? Edo? I had no idea who was in Kogahaera with the false emperor's court, and able to put it off no longer, I broke the seal. Red wax flaked onto the floor as I unrolled the letter.

Dearest Koko, it began, and heart constricting, I looked to the bottom to see Sichi's name signed in flowing black ink.

Dearest Koko, I read again. *You must forgive the presumption of our former friendship, for I write to you in desperation and wish you to remember what we once were to each other. I feel neither of us was entirely honest that last morning in the bathhouse, but I know you and I have always shared a will to survive and prosper, and I beg that you will not hold my choices against me.*

Emperor Gideon is lost to us. I believe he has been for some time, but the situation is precarious and no one dares challenge the power Dom Villius has acquired here. I fear to say more, and can only beg your help. Were you to march to our gates in peace, there is not one Kisian or Levanti present within these walls who would fight you, but the Chiltaens could well make an end of us first. We have lost so much as an empire, lost so much as individuals, as families, and the Levanti here doubly so. And thus I write to beg you to stand with us. To fight with us. To stand side by side, Kisian with Kisian, Levanti with Levanti (for I know you march with many) against the enemy that has most harmed us both.

I pray. Your ever-affectionate friend, Sichi.

I stared at the page, the words seeming to reverberate on and on in my head like the ringing of a dozen gongs, drawing forth memories. Of Tanaka. Of Edo. Of Sichi. Of a simple time when we had only dreamed of a future, not had to fight for it. Much easier to dream, to claim ideals, to believe I could do it better without ever being tested, but to be the one standing up and making decisions was not an enviable position. Sometimes there was no right decision, sometimes we made the wrong call, or could only see the wise path in the painful glare of hindsight and would have to carry our wrongs with us forever. Already I carried the souls of so many, and I had only to close my eyes to see the slaughtered people of Syan lying dead in the road beneath my horse's hooves because I hadn't had the right words, because I had been the wrong leader, because I had let my righteousness overtake my judgement.

And now Sichi begged for my help. Not only for herself, but for all the people who had, for one reason or another, ended up at the Levanti court in Kogahaera. My righteous self might say they deserved it for their poor choice, for allying themselves with a false leader, but how could I blame them? I had failed my people at Risian, but long before that Emperor Kin had failed the north of his empire by giving in to hate and anger and hurt. In truth, their defection, even Grace Bahain's plans, had nothing to do with me and everything to do with the legacy two people had left the empire with their pain.

I began to pace, the scroll clutched in my hand. Rah would do what was right, even if he hated it. He did not grumble or complain, did not even seem to weigh his options, just saw the right path and took it no matter how dangerous. I had not Rah's sight, but one path before me could protect innocent Kisians, could save Kogahaera and Sichi, while the other was the surer path to conquest. To success. To the reclaiming of the empire no matter how many of its people lay dead in payment.

I didn't need Rah's sight to know which was the right way.

I stuck my head out through the tent flap, shocking the guards. "Your Majesty! My apologies, we—"

"No time. I need the council recalled. Now."

None of them needed to be dragged from their mats, but fatigue was present in every face and we had to wait while General Mihri dressed. Though I had not specifically requested her, Whisperer Ezma was present once again and was, without Rah, the sole Levanti representative.

"What is this about?" Minister Manshin demanded in a low voice, bending down beside me instead of taking his place at the table.

The question had been on everyone's lips, but he was the only one to demand the answer before deigning to join us. A man expecting to have to talk me out of a poor plan. After Syan, I could hardly blame him, but so public a display of his failing trust was too much.

"I shall inform the council of my purpose as soon as everyone is ready," I said, more bite in the words than I'd intended.

He straightened. "Your Majesty."

His place was on my left, and while he knelt, Minister Oyamada shifted his weight to my right. He had done a good job getting the majority of my army here and setting up camp, in keeping an eye on the Chiltaens as well as the Levanti court, but with Manshin's arrival he had been relegated back to a position of little importance. At a traditional court in Mei'lian, he would have had hundreds of secretaries and administrators answering to him as he oversaw everything from supplies to trade to laws, but here he was just in Minister Manshin's way. The army had been his sole domain too long.

"We cannot wait until the Chiltaens have attacked Kogahaera," I said, taking courage in blurting my stance as General Moto was wont to do. "Information from within the city says Gideon e'Torin is no longer emperor and the Kisians who were once his allies will surrender to us. So long as they aren't all slaughtered by Chiltaens first. If we wait, far too many Kisians will die, and that I cannot allow."

In the moment of silent consideration that met this I knew they were all thinking of the disaster at Syan.

"Might we ask where this information has come from?" General Mihri said, not with disbelief but not totally without it either.

"It came in a letter. From Lady Sichi Manshin."

Eyes flicked my minister's way, but it was Mihri again who said, "Who has reason to be on the Levanti's side given her marriage to their emperor. With all due respect to His Excellency, I would not trust her word on so risky a change of plan. To attack the Chiltaens before they move on Kogahaera would be a dangerous move."

"Then let us attack them *while* they are attacking Kogahaera," I said.

"And risk facing the full Chiltaen force on our own if those in Kogahaera sit back and leave us to it," General Moto grumbled.

"Is it true that Captain e'Torin has left us?" General Mihri interrupted abruptly.

Of course the news had gotten around. He could hardly have departed without being seen by the soldiers on watch. I could tell them what I understood of his purpose, allay their fears, but to do so would be a betrayal of trust.

"He has," Minister Manshin replied, and I wondered who had told him and what he knew. He might well be glad of it, of the removal—temporary though it might be—of a man he saw as a danger to the empire's future. To me.

"Well, the desertion of Rah *e'Torin*, on the eve of battle against Gideon *e'Torin*, only strengthens my dismay that we are trusting the Levanti"—he looked at Ezma—"to leave in search of more of their own people. I do not trust their intentions any more than I trust Lady Sichi's account of the false emperor. My apologies to you, Minister, but if ever there was a time for honest speaking it is now."

"An apology to the minister, but not to the Levanti leader whose honour you just impugned?" General Yass said, his voice deceptively cool. "I see now how it took Kisia so long to accept us as anything more than barbarians to be rid of."

General Alon murmured agreement beside him, and a prickly discomfort spread through the tent that had nothing to do with the proposed change of plan. Our history with the various mountain tribes was bloody and unpleasant, I knew, but I was less familiar with that of their inclusion in the ranks of our army. All too well could I imagine these same men speaking such worries about allying themselves with warriors from the mountains. As an empire, we seemed to identify ourselves by who was most hated, who was least like us, even if the answer was sometimes other Kisians. Damn northerners. Petty southerners. I'd long wanted to heal our internal divisions, but it was Kisia's relationship with the people around us as much as with each other that needed to be restored.

"I hardly feel it is of value to discuss such things at present, General Yass," Mihri said. "Whatever our past, it is the Levanti we are speaking of now."

"The Levanti with whom I have much sympathy. It seems every great nation has a use for the blood of our warriors, but request respect and fairness in return and we are told we ought to have been grateful we were allowed to die for you in the first place." He looked at me, a deep, old anger hot in his eyes. "As General Mihri wished to make it known he is against our alliance with the Levanti, I wish it to be known that I am for maintaining this alliance, Your Majesty. And that I honour you for respecting them and their autonomy in the face of such opposition."

He settled his hands in front of him and looked in turn at each of the others around the table. He had finished speaking but had not finished fighting, his challenge asked of every one of us. Ezma showed no sign she had been listening, but General Yass had not spoken for her as much as for his own people.

Minister Manshin broke the tension. "No matter how we feel about a Levanti alliance," he said, the way he said the word *Levanti* making it clear how he felt, "it is folly to even consider going into battle against two armies when neither is focussed on us at present."

Folly. I turned and Manshin met my stare without a blink. "I made the wrong choice in Syan, and it led to too many innocent deaths," I said. "I will not make that mistake again. And yes, even Kisians who chose to ally themselves with a false Levanti emperor are still Kisians. We cannot let more of our people die at the hands of Chiltaens. We cannot let yet another city fall. They will not be expecting us to attack. They will be expecting us to sit back and wait. That is in our favour."

"Speaking of the happenings at Syan, you must also consider what it will look like to anyone wishing to discredit you, Your Majesty," he said. "The story of what happened is already getting around. Were people to see Empress Miko going from slaughtering innocent people to attacking one of her own cities, it would be difficult to ensure such a tale was not misconstrued."

Stung, I demanded, "How could anyone mistake my purpose when it is the Chiltaens we are attacking, not the city?"

"Anything someone wants to use against you can be used against you, Your Majesty."

I wished I could believe there was no threat in the words, but however calmly spoken, however much someone else might miss it, I had too often been the subject of his critical gaze of late to be hopeful.

Murmured agreement made its way around the table, and I could not shake the feeling they were closing ranks. I'd had the same sense of being trapped back in Mei'lian while Grace Bachita made his play for the throne, so easily did the men who held power on the council accept one of their own over someone who would actually fight for the empire, not only themselves. It was maddening to feel like the only one who could see how dark Kisia's future looked if we did not change.

They had moved on to discussing when would be a good time to join the battle and how best to keep watch on its progress as though there was nothing more to say about my intention now Manshin had dismissed it. In that moment I realised I had not taken power. I had been granted it. Minister Manshin and Minister Gadokoi had looked me over, had considered how well I fit *their* plans and *their* vision, and whatever they had done in service of it had not been done for me. Even Manshin's sacrifice at Mei'lian, however noble it had been, had not been without calculation.

The power they had granted me. The power these men had granted me at Achoi. Willing to let this little girl play her games while they got on with the real work. Except I hadn't been pliable enough. Not meek enough.

I stood up, surprising the generals into silence. From her place at the far end of the table, Ezma smiled. Perhaps she knew how I felt.

"I thank my council for their advice," I said. "But as empress of Kisia it is my decision that we march out to meet the Chiltaen force tomorrow rather than leave Kogahaera to fight alone. There will be no further discussion about this. Kisia's army exists to protect Kisians, whatever the difficulty and whatever the cost. No—" I held up my hand. "I meant no further discussion when I said it, General Mihri. A more detailed plan will be forthcoming in the morning. In the meantime, I suggest you inform your soldiers and get some rest. You are all dismissed."

Hesitation slowed their movements, eyes turning to Minister Manshin as though expecting him to contradict me, to speak over me, but whatever he might have wished to do, he was my minister, not my regent, and could only rise with the others and bow. General Mihri was the first to stalk out, while the two generals from the mountain tribes bowed with the greatest respect—such things must always be watched, Mama had said, for whatever words people might hold back behind their teeth, rare is the man who can lie with his whole body.

I had expected Minister Manshin to linger, to stay and argue the point until we were both equally tired of the other, but he departed along with the rest, leaving only General Ryoji and Whisperer Ezma in the tent. The whisperer had her hands caught behind her back in the way of one intent on remaining. "Whisperer? There is something you wish to say?"

"There is," Ezma said. "But I will say it in private." She glanced at General Ryoji and, when he didn't immediately move, added, "If you fear designs on the empress's life you're looking in the wrong place."

Her words made me as uneasy as Manshin's capitulation, but I nodded dismissal to him. With a grimace and a bow he departed, leaving Ezma and me facing each other across the empty table.

"Well?"

She lifted her chin. "I have cause to call in the debt you owe me."

I tensed, wishing I had still been kneeling so I could reach for my wine bowl. "Your request?"

"I want Gideon."

"In what way do you mean?"

A tiny frown flitted across her face. "I mean that when he is captured tomorrow, his fate is given into my hands. As a horse whisperer, I am the only one who can decide upon justice when it affects multiple herds."

I was glad I had not told the council where Rah had gone, but I wondered now, looking up into the stern lines of her face, if she already knew. If that was the reason for her request.

They've been friends a long time, Tor had said. *Rah is always very honourable. He does what is right even if he hates it.*

If only I knew what right here was. Her reasoning made sense, and if Gideon had harmed the Levanti then surely it would be good for all of them to have closure, to have the relief of seeing justice done. But Rah and Whisperer Ezma did not get along. Tor had explained as best he could, yet I wasn't sure what to make of it, whether she was truly the danger he seemed to think her, or whether some objected to her as an unapologetic woman in a position of power.

"I am not sure that's something I'm able to grant you," I said. "I do not have Gideon e'Torin in my hands and may never have."

"But if you did?" When I didn't immediately answer, her eyes narrowed. "I hope I need not remind you that you stand in my debt. In Levanti debt. And if you wish us on the field with your army tomorrow that debt will increase. I do not take my people into battle for my own amusement. I do not let them die for the glory of others. If you want to keep Levanti allies, you must accept our ways and pay the requested price."

"Is there not something else—?"

"Gideon e'Torin, or we will not fight for you again." She drew herself up, towering over me. "Think about it carefully before you consider betraying me, Your Majesty. Your position means nothing to my people, but mine means everything."

She awaited no reply, but turned and went out, leaving nothing but the flutter of the tent flap in her wake and a sick swirl in the pit of my stomach.

General Ryoji waited outside my tent, his lips a compressed line of concern. "Your Majesty," he said, a wary look at the guards on duty. "All is well?"

His way of asking what Whisperer Ezma had wanted, perhaps, but I wasn't sure I could discuss her request even with him. Could there have been a worse time to examine the complications that came with my feelings for Rah?

"Indeed, General," I said. "But there is something I wish to discuss with you, if you'll step inside a moment."

He bowed and followed me into the warm tent, its floor old matting, while its table and divan were well-crafted things from a fine residence. There were a number of comfortable cushions, but I could not sit. Could not rest. I paced back and forth, trying to gather my thoughts.

"General," I said at last. "I know you were as much advisor to my mother as you were the head of her guard, so please, advise me now. You cannot have failed to see I am losing support. Not of the soldiers or even the Kisian people, though I will have to work hard to undo the damage I did at Syan, but—"

"You're worried about General Moto?"

"Yes. And...and Minister Manshin, though I fear to say so. His dislike of the Levanti has set us at cross purposes."

General Ryoji gestured to the divan. "May I?"

"Of course."

He sat with a tired little groan of effort and said, "You may like to stalk up and down the floor while you think, but I have been on my feet all day and think better without a cramp in my calf."

"That's just because you're old."

Ryoji grinned. "Lucky for you that I am since I'd likely be significantly less wise if I wasn't. Now, your council. Emperor Kin had many councillors over the years who did not agree with him or did not even like him and often said that inviting dissenting opinions was the best way to ensure good advice."

"You think I'm overreacting?"

"No, because you aren't Emperor Kin. Your mother once

434 • *Devin Madson*

observed that what is true for men in our society is rarely true for women. People respect a man until he proves himself unworthy. Yet people won't respect a woman until she proves herself worthy. You have the respect of General Yass and General Alon because as outsiders they suffer from the same prejudgement. They are barbarians, big, stupid men who need not be considered until they prove themselves otherwise. Same with the Levanti."

I slowed my pacing and halted, heaving a sigh. "Then how do I make them respect me? How do I prove it if nothing I have done so far—not even the taking of Syan—has achieved it?"

He leaned forward, elbows on his knees, chin in his hands. "You want my advice, but I'm afraid all I can do is lay before you two contradictory paths. The one I would have you follow as the commander of your Imperial Guard, with thought only to your safety. And the one I would have you follow were I not considering that and speaking only as Hade Ryoji."

The gravity of his words, of his tone and his bearing and his expression, acted upon me like a weight and I sank to the ground, kneeling with my hands clenched upon my knees. "Tell me," I said, breathless.

"All right, first, as the commander of your Imperial Guard, I advise you to swallow your pride. Ask them for advice you don't need. Play the part they want you to play. And make peace with the fact that the men who control your army will always have more power over it than you do, but if you let them get on with it without interference, they will let you do what you wish with the rest of the empire."

"Be a puppet ruling in name and not in actuality?"

"Exactly. It is safest not to fight powerful men. Most are like sleeping snakes. Content to lie still while the world is the way they wish it, but fast to strike should you seek to oust them from their warm rock."

I nodded slowly, thinking of the generals who had granted me power and how fast they could take it away. "And the other piece of advice?"

Ryoji's lips twitched into a rueful smile. "Overturn the rock. Get rid of them all. Replace them with people who are loyal to you, or even better, people who share the same vision for Kisia as you do. Rebuild the whole system of administration if you have to." He shrugged. "It wouldn't be easy and it wouldn't be quick. Change everything too fast and you'll carry no one with you. Change too slow and you'll give them time to fight back. It would take careful planning, patience, and determination, and you will put your life in constant danger to see it done."

"Yet it is what you would ask of me. For yourself."

"For Kisia and all Kisians." He sat back. "You have allies in this already. General Yass and General Alon would be on your side. I do not pretend to know what the Levanti want or whether they will stay, but keeping them while you can is wise for your protection. And you may find a few surprising allies in places you don't expect. Enemies of your enemies."

"Such as?"

He shrugged again. "For the most part it's hard to tell while the empire is so fractured, but of those close to hand I think Minister Oyamada is more valuable than he appears. But there will be plenty of time to discuss such things and observe those around you if you choose to walk that path. Think about it," he said as he got to his feet. "Because once you start there's no going back. It's not a small task, but a lifetime commitment. I am not sure your mother could have done it, but you…"

The words hung there, as close to a declaration of faith as he would allow himself at so precarious a moment, a moment when he had shown exactly where his loyalties lay. With Kisia. With me.

"Get through tomorrow first," he said when I didn't answer.

"Then we can talk again. What happens at Kogahaera could change much."

"About tomorrow," I said, gnawing my lower lip.

"What about it?" There the wary Ryoji I knew so well.

I met his gaze, something rueful in my own. "I have been informed by newly arrived Levanti that there are some Kisian soldiers to the north. I don't know how many, but enough that the Levanti who found them called it an army."

His eyes narrowed and I knew what he was thinking. I ought to have informed the council about them, but I hadn't. Had never planned to. Not from the moment the words had left Rah's lips. What trust I'd had with Minister Manshin had been strained to breaking point over my refusal to get rid of the Levanti.

"More soldiers?"

"Yes, some of the northern battalions cut off from the main force, perhaps, I don't know."

"It seems most likely. What are you thinking?"

Gnawing my lip again, having gone over and over the idea that had sprung into my head, hating that the best way to be sure of them was to leave me vulnerable. "I am thinking," I said slowly, "that you have to go. Alone." He parted his lips to retort, but I hurried on. "If they are northerners you are the best person to rally them. And you are the only person I trust now. Others can ensure my safety, but no others can ensure these men will fight for *me*."

Ryoji frowned, thinking through my words for a long time. A thoughtfulness I ought to value, but which only made me fidget impatiently. "There is much in what you say, Majesty," he said at last. "But there will be many questions over where I am if, as I recommend, this is to be kept between us."

"That cannot be helped. We will think of some story or other to account for your sudden absence. A letter. From a dying...aunt.

Something better than that," I added when he laughed. "I am tired and have run out of good ideas."

"It'll have to be better than that, because you can be sure more than one of your generals is already suspicious that Rah e'Torin is away on a secret mission for you."

"How I wish that was true. He isn't even on a mission to aid the Levanti."

His brows lifted, perhaps at the bitterness in my tone, perhaps at the still more knowledge I had kept from my council.

"I understand he is saving... a friend in trouble."

"Interesting timing." When I made no answer, he added, "I'll think of a good lie. As long as you're sure about this. Your reasoning is sound, but it goes against every instinct to leave you at such a time, even with men I trust."

"My generals may disagree with me, but I think we are not yet so far beyond disagreement that they would consider killing me. Kisia is not secure enough and they are not united enough. And if we win tomorrow, perhaps they will not dislike me so much after all."

"I dislike the idea of you riding into battle without me."

"I did it at the battle of Risian. And at Mei'lian. Of course I would rather have you with me than not, but there will be plenty of soldiers to protect me, and I am quite capable of looking after myself."

It was false assurance, I knew, but how could I admit I was more afraid of my own generals than I was of the coming battle?

I may not have said it, but he seemed to understand all the same. And in a gesture so much more that of the surrogate father he had been, he set his hand on my shoulder and squeezed. "I know you are, Miko, you are everything I trained you to be and everything that would have made your mother proud. Take care of yourself while I am gone. Be careful who you trust and who you put your faith in. Watch everyone."

I nodded, having no voice with which to thank him. There was a sense of rightness about the moment, of comfort, but I was sure though we didn't speak it we were both thinking the same thing. Wondering if Mama was still alive. If we would ever see her again. If she would truly be proud of me. Of us. And in the wake of such a moment I couldn't but fear I would lose my way as she had done. That one day grief and anger would destroy me too.

23. CASSANDRA

As our body slipped toward sleep, my consciousness shifted away, flitting like a firefly through the night. It had been far smoother in Saki's hands, the sense of flying with purpose, in one direction, not this wandering and loss.

The voice drew me first. Unus, his whisper a frantic, breathless thing. "He must be dead. There is still pressure, like...like a weight against my skull, but it's only coming from one place now. I don't know. I...don't know what's going to happen."

"Whatever it is, I'm here."

No reply, just the touch of a forehead to my shoulder and he was gone, cold air opening up around me. Dawn brightened the sky out the window. Birds were waking with their morning songs, and servants were moving on quiet steps through the house. Minister Manshin's house.

I sat silent and stared as Kaysa stared, waiting, listening, needing to be sure we were alone. No other sounds, no shifting of fabric or weight, no footsteps or voices.

Kaysa?

Her fingers stopped tapping on the windowsill. "Cassandra," she said, a whisper spoken to the cool glass. "What do you want?"

To stop Leo harming Empress Miko.

A little sneer turned her lips. "Saw that, did you?"

I did. And I don't know what weird shit is going on with him, but—

"Weird shit? How can you say that when we've shared a body all these years listening to the call of the dead? He's like me, Cassandra. Trapped. Forced into being something—someone he's not because they are stronger than him. Unus is not the same person as the others. Here. It's even in the book you ought to have read."

She lifted us off the window seat and strode to where a short pile of books sat upon a table. I recognised the one we had taken from the Witchdoctor before she slid it from the bottom. Its spine cracked as she opened it and began rifling through the pages, all dry and smooth between her fingers, until she found the one she wanted. Running a fingertip along a line, she started to read.

While most souls split by this anomaly are one of a pair—each a half soul born into different bodies—there are very rare instances where one of those halves is further split. Split in half again is the most common of these, but higher degrees have existed. In one particular case, that of Memara 21, the already split soul was further divided into six, each therefore technically one-twelfth of a soul, as half already resided inside the Mystic. Adding to the rarity of this case, all seven (the Mystic and the six Memaras) were born of the same mother in the same birth, an anomaly I have only seen a handful of times.

She looked up. "Do you see what I mean? The six Memaras are the same person, but they are connected through Unus. Their Mystic. And the sheer... *force* of them has all but destroyed him. Only now that so many of them are dead is he beginning to have any control over himself."

How many of his other halves are left?

"Two. Septum and Duos. God only knows why I'm telling you this."

I could feel her fear like leaves trembling against my skin. In all the time we had lived side by side in the same body, I had never felt so present with her. My fault, I knew, for never letting her be anything but a beaten-down voice in the back of my head.

And if they were both dead?

"We don't know. Without one of them he might die. It has to be Septum though, he's the only one that has no weight. They're all connected, you see. Unus can block the others out for a short time now they're weaker, but he's not strong enough to stop them seeing his thoughts. Speaking through his lips. Filling his mind with their... nonsense. Which is why I want to help him. Why I understand him."

Guilt stabbed deep at how she had been forced to live, lacking all freedom. I tried to imagine it, imagine the fear I had felt whenever she forcefully took control of my body, except it had been for her whole life. I had always been stronger. She'd never really had a life at all.

For a time, neither of us said anything. I could not read her thoughts, had never been able to even when we shared a body, a mind. Perhaps because she had been forced to make herself small, or because my own troubles and thoughts had always been so loud.

"How are you?" she asked, eventually breaking a silence that had become almost companionable.

Frustrated. Useless. Trapped. Sorry.

"That is probably the most honest thing you've ever said to me." I wasn't sure what to say to that. "And the empress?"

Tired. And swamped with guilt and grief. But she's determined to help her daughter now, even though she was ready to die back at the Witchdoctor's house until he saved her.

"He didn't save her. You did."

It was a statement of fact, not spoken to make me feel better, only to correct a mistake, but it struck me with more force than she had intended or could even guess. I had tried to save her, had gone into Hana's head to shout at her, had shaken her and insisted she could not give in, but she had died anyway. Died with my hands upon her, leaving my soul to tumble into this new empty vessel. Only I'd brought her back. Somehow, I had brought her back.

Only to make no difference. We had achieved nothing. Had not even reached her daughter, let alone been able to help her. Able to change the world.

"You should go before he comes back," Kaysa said. "Just in case it's not Unus."

I was reluctant to leave, more comfortable there with her than I could remember ever being, a warm sense of having come home after a long time away. But it was too dangerous to stay longer, so I shouted until the empress woke and I was once more gasping for a full breath that wouldn't come, cold upon damp sheets.

"He really is a mess," I said, sharing all I had discovered with the empress as we lay sluggish and dozy on the mat.

She definitely said there was a chance killing Duos could kill Unus too? That they might not survive without the other?

"Assuming Septum doesn't have enough soul to maintain the link, I suppose so. Asking the Witchdoctor would be better than asking me though."

He isn't here.

"Neither is Duos."

No, but if killing Duos could kill Unus, then killing Unus—

"Could kill Duos."

We lay still, heart pounding. It could work. One more assassination and we could be rid of them all. Forever. No more rebirths. No more manipulations. Gone. The final completion of my contract with Secretary Aurus.

It won't be easy.

"No, but it—"

—would change everything.

Hard to imagine going back to a life that wasn't ruled by this man. This problem. That with one strike of a blade we could save Miko. Could save Kisians and Chiltaens from dying for one all-too-powerful man's delusions of grandeur.

To see it through would be difficult. We'd done difficult jobs before, jobs with a narrow window of time to kill, or where there was likely to be a dozen others around at the same time. A man who could read your mind and knew you were coming was far worse, yet it was Kaysa I thought of. Kaysa, who had found a purpose in Unus, in at last being able to help someone, in healing some of her own hurts by fixing another troubled soul. God, how she would hate me for this.

There isn't another way. We can't do nothing.

"I know."

Dawn light speared through the high window, turning everything it touched to pale gold. It was the hour of the dawn prayer, and panic jolted through me. Leo could be next door with Yakono. Could have heard all of our thoughts. All our plans.

Heart thudding, I strained to catch the sound of Leo's voice through the wall. Nothing. To be sure, I rolled over and said, "Do you know why the devotees of the One True God pray to the rising sun?"

There was a pause and a shifting of weight. A clink of chain. And it was Yakono who replied. Just Yakono. "No. Is it not to thank God for providing the day?"

"No, it's not actually part of the devotions to the One True God, but you see, when the missionaries first came to Chiltae it was part of our religion, to pray for the rising and the setting of the sun, so they just...let us keep doing it and said it was part of their religion too. To lessen resistance to adopting a new god."

Allovian had whispered the truth the day he'd found me locked in one of the storerooms at the hospice. The other children had wanted to stop me making my prayers so God would strike me down as I deserved.

"A Blessed Guard told me all about it when I was young. I think of him whenever I make the morning prayer, more than God. Blasphemous, isn't it?"

Yakono shuffled against the wall. "How... cynical."

"Of me or of the missionaries who brought their God to us?"

"Both?"

I laughed and rested my head against the wall. "What were you brought up to believe in?"

"The Ethical Precepts."

"The... what? Are they a... group of gods, or...?"

"Oh no, not gods, we don't believe in any great... unknowable being. Just in, well, a way to live that's right. You don't worship or pray to them, you just practise. There is a sort of confession, like what your priests do, where daily failures to live by the precepts are turned into moments of learning. We sit down together in the evening to share our failures from the day and what we did to make up for them, what we learned from them, and what we would do differently next time. It's a very... comforting thing, really, knowing every day you will fail and that's all right, because you can be better tomorrow."

"To fail again?"

It was his turn to laugh. "Yes, but it's never the same failure if you learn from your previous mistakes."

"Let me get this right, your religion is that you live to fail every day?"

"And to learn from that failure. Yes."

It sounded both terrifying and exciting, the idea of not bowing to a mystical entity, just trying to live a good life. But the amount of work, of self-awareness, of... openness and honesty and trust it would take was staggering.

"What are the precepts?"

"Be honest with yourself and others. Be generous with your time and heart. Show courage in the performance of the precepts. Lift others with kindness. Be trustworthy and repay all trust with loyalty. Help those in need. Selflessness is—"

"Wait, you live by all of those?"

"I try to."

I let out a breath I'd been holding, making my chest ache. "I think maybe you are the best person I've ever met."

"That's not the goal. I don't live by them to be admired, or to be better than others, rather so I am free in my own conscience. So I can live and die knowing I did the best I could."

So many questions were piling up, but someone was coming along the passage with quick light steps, so I held my tongue, not wanting to be overheard. In the back of my mind, Hana was wrestling with the problem at hand, trying to figure out how we could kill Unus without him knowing we were coming. Perhaps we could make use of his visits to Yakono? Perhaps even ask for Yakono's help? It didn't matter which of us killed him as long as he died.

Do you think he'll succeed in turning Yakono to the faith? I asked, thinking of Leo's intoxicating voice as he read.

You make it sound like a disease rather than a religion, and not in and of itself a terrible one. Captain Aeneas was a good man and a devout believer. Both are possible. Now go back to your flirting and let me think.

Flirt—

Shhhh.

The footsteps had faded away, leaving us alone again.

"Cassandra? Are you all right?"

My chest constricted at the words so few people had ever asked. "Yes, I'm fine. But tell me, why do you think assassination is important? Apart from the desire to ensure a respectful end for people who would be killed anyway."

"Ideologically?" Yakono asked, his voice muffled. "This is perhaps a cold way of thinking about people, but I see people as being a bit like plants. In a garden, not every plant is made equal in terms of what they give to the garden as a whole. There are plants that shade others, that provide homes for creatures, or food, while others are parasitic and give nothing back. If we can get rid of some of those plants, the garden flourishes. Societies are the same."

"You want to make a difference."

"Ideologically, yes. But in practice I do not consider myself, or anyone, infallible enough to make nuanced decisions about who serves society and who takes from it."

"What if you could be sure someone had done great wrong?"

He shifted against the wall, and his voice grew less muffled. "You're talking about Dom Villius, aren't you?"

"Yes. How important, would you say, given your research into the Chiltaen political situation, is his death to the future of Chiltae?"

"That depends on the future you want it to have. I'm not a prescient. Not even an expert on Chiltaen politics. But that he has an almost terrifying level of control through numerous avenues is undeniable. If you agree with his philosophy then that's a good thing. If you don't it's cause for concern."

"Are you always so sensible?"

"I try."

Cassandra. I've got an idea, the empress said. *You aren't going to like it.*

She was right. I didn't. But we were running out of strength, running out of time, and the faster we could move the more surprise we could maintain. It wasn't like we'd had any better ideas. Or any other ideas at all.

"Cassandra?" Yakono said, after we'd been silent for a long time. "Are you sure you're all right?"

"Yes. But I need you to do something for me. I'm afraid it might go against your precepts a little, but... I need your help."

"If it helps you it cannot be against my precepts. And even if it was, I would do it."

I closed my eyes, the constriction in my chest hard to dispel after such words. "Thank you," I managed, hating how pathetic my reply sounded, how weak and pitiful and full of...sentiment.

It's harder to care than not to, the empress said. *It takes more courage and strength to care, not more weakness. For what it's worth, I'm sorry you don't have more time to get to know him better.*

Against the wall, I heard Yakono shift about, and I wished I could see his face, could see his expression, could put more than imaginings to the sound of his voice. "What is it you need me to do?"

———◆———

Yakono's shouts brought footsteps running along the passage. The door slid and the room filled with guards and servants, and I flopped back and moaned as dramatically as I dared.

"She needs a physician," Yakono cried from the next room. "Take her upstairs and call for a physician."

I had asked him to say those words, hoping the general panic would keep them from realising it was advice from a prisoner, and it seemed to work.

"Yes, quick, you, pick her up," one of the men said. "Carry her to the receiving room. You, send someone for Master Ao. We can't—" Whoever had been speaking broke off to hustle others about their tasks. Someone else shouted for everyone to get out of the way. Another voice called for water and tea and food to be brought up and a clean robe found and many other things lost in the swirl of noise. A swirl of noise beneath which Yakono's voice was swallowed, and I hoped he would not later suffer for the part I had asked him to play.

Carried like a sick child, we were jolted along the passage toward the main rooms. There, I listened for Leo's voice, but there was no sign of him, only a hum of panic as people afraid of angering him hurried about their tasks.

I was set lightly down upon a divan and risked opening my eyes to slits. No Unus, but Septum still lay upon the opposite divan. Of course he had not moved. Could not. Yet.

Don't think too far ahead, just focus.

"What's going on?" Kaysa, an edge of panic in her voice.

"She was having a fit. We've sent for Master Ao."

"A fit?" Kaysa's voice reached a higher pitch, but anyone who didn't know her, didn't know me, probably wouldn't notice. Nice to know, after all this time, that she did actually care.

Opening my eyes, I let out a groan and tried to sit up, failing the first time, which didn't even need to be feigned I felt so weak. The second attempt sent shoots of agony branching down every muscle and tightened knots around my heart. If I wasn't careful, I wouldn't need to fake how bad I was.

"I'm fine," I cried out, trying to sound fine, to sound calm and collected though it came out like the weak complaint of a child. "There is no need to trouble Master Ao. I just need rest and I will be well."

Are you ready? I said.

Yes.

You will have to be totally quiet.

I know.

No screaming.

I know.

And you're sure you can?

I was so close to handling him last time. Trust me, Cassandra.

And I was surprised to find I did.

Goodbye, Your Majesty.

Hana, she corrected. *Goodbye, Cassandra.*

I got to my feet, preparing to walk back to my room, and didn't have to fake the weakening of my legs that dropped a knee from beneath me. I had been moving forward and the tumble threw me toward Septum's divan. To fall atop him would be too obvious, to fall too short more obvious still, but his hand sat right near the edge and as my knees smacked into the wood, I gripped the divan for support.

It was the merest brushing of skin against skin, but the empress leaked out through the contact and was gone, leaving me a shrivelled husk in her absence. I felt so empty without her, so wrong, so broken, and I slumped onto hands and knees on the floor, barely managing to make the pained moans we had planned to cover any small sounds Septum might make at her arrival.

"No," I said as again someone suggested running for Master Ao. "No, I just need rest. Kaysa?"

She was there at the sound of her name, crouching close but not close enough, the deception she feared most that I would try to return to our body. Without the empress I wasn't even sure I could. There was every chance I had long been trapped here.

"Kaysa." I lifted my head but did not move. "Tell them I'm fine and just need to return to my room to lie down."

Whatever her doubts, she nodded and stood. "There is no reason to be troubled," she said to whoever was still present. "She just needs rest. We cannot have her worn out with our worrying when His Holiness needs her well. Help her back to her room and have her meal served there."

Someone argued, but the words were all becoming distant. Unimportant. All I could focus on was the weave of the matting floor beneath my hands and the inhale and exhale of my rough breath through a mouth that hung open and would not close. I had hardly the energy to wonder how the empress was getting on inside Septum, whether the other Leos would know she was there, whether I could ever get her out. She could get trapped in there, as I had gotten trapped in her skin.

A hand gripped my arm, helping me up. The room spun, but before I could get my bearings, we were walking, my feet dragging with each step back along the passage. It seemed to be my whole world now, this corridor and my room, nothing else existing. Not the gardens outside, nor the empire, not even Genava, though I had such fond memories of the city in which I had suffered a lifetime of pain and doubt and confusion.

The whole house spun around me, but I held in bile with clenched teeth and allowed myself to be lowered onto my sleeping mat, murmuring assurances that I would soon be well if only I could be left to sleep.

They must have believed me for they left, soft footsteps exiting into the passage and closing the door behind them. I was glad they had gone and yet to be so alone when I felt so ill, when darkness was closing in, was frightening. It had been comforting to think that if I were to die in this body, at least I wouldn't be alone. In a twisted way it was amusing that letting the empress go was what might finally kill her. Kill me.

I rolled against the wall, shivering so violently my teeth clacked. "Yakono?"

"Cassandra."

Tears pricked my eyes at the sound of his voice. I was not alone. "Are you all right?"

"No," I said. "No, but it's all right." It wasn't, but I couldn't say so, didn't have the energy to reassure him. "Thank you for earlier. I'm... very glad I met you."

I'd never said anything like it to anyone, and it all felt wrong and yet so right, the knowledge the end was upon me freeing my tongue. "I'm sorry I can't stay."

"What do you mean?"

He sounded concerned—concerned! Tears rolled down my cheeks and I could not stop them. Didn't even want to.

"Yakono, will you talk to me? Tell me a story."

"Any story in particular?"

"A story that makes you happy."

Yakono shifted his weight against the wall, fabric catching as he got himself comfortable. "A story that makes me happy?" he said, and I closed my eyes at the deep, warm roll of his voice. "Well, one memory I always look back on fondly is the day Master Luko brought my sister Sara home. I'd been living and training there for three or four years, long enough to forget about life alone on the streets, but she arrived and stood hunched in the doorway like a wild animal, her arms folded, watching us prepare our evening meal like she thought we were going to cook her."

He chuckled at the memory but I could not, the breath needed for such an action locked in my chest. It came out in a slow rattle, and I focussed on his words to keep from panicking.

"Even when we set food on the table, hoping to tempt her to join us, she wouldn't move from the door. And when we started our evening discussion of our failings, she looked at us like we were mad."

The room darkened as he spoke, but at least it had slowed its spinning. Every breath was a hard thing to draw, seeming to come through the tiniest of holes.

"And I remembered what it was like, living on the streets, being cold and starving and sick, only to have a hand held down to me, to pull me up off the hard stones and into a new life, and to see the realisation dawn across Sara's face was like living it all over again, and she…"

He must have kept talking, must have gone on shifting his weight against the wall and laughing his low, rumbling laugh, but as life leaked out of me on the last of my breaths, I knew no more.

# 24. DISHIVA

Leo was out there. He was fucking out there standing at the head of the Chiltaen army, and for a full minute I couldn't move, could only stare at him and want to be sick. Beside me, Lady Sichi seemed similarly afflicted. We had rolled him into the pond. He hadn't been found. I'd checked. Four times. He was still there. Still dead. Yet there he stood outside the gates.

"That's bad," I said.

An ill-assorted collection of the remaining Levanti and Kisians had gathered on the narrow wall. It wasn't as thick and sturdy as the city walls of Mei'lian had been, but it would hold a while. Hopefully long enough for us to come up with a better plan.

Standing in the dawn sunlight like the god he thought he was, Leo spread his arms and called up to us. In Kisian first, but Sichi's gasp prepared me for when he switched to Levanti.

"My dear friends," he said, making my skin pimple with a chill shiver. "My soldiers were marching here to be of use to your cause, to *our* cause—"

"Horseshit," I muttered, looking at the array of siege weapons they had with them.

"—but it seems whatever friendship I believed we had, whatever partnership in looking toward the future, I was alone. I don't know what you were told, but I was murdered." He paused dramatically upon the word, and I glanced along at the gathered Levanti. Already the Kisians were scowling and muttering. "Murdered," he repeated. "By Empress Sichi and her supporters. You have a choice. You can give the empress up, and I will take my army and leave. Or we will have to see God's justice done by force."

Had he demanded Gideon he might have gotten what he wanted, but Sichi had become as beloved of the Levanti as of the Kisians, and the outcry against his demand rang along the parapet. She remained standing proud beside me, but I could hear the ragged edge to her every breath.

On her other side, Edo whispered to Nuru, who leaned toward me. "Any sign of the Kisian army?"

"Nothing."

"Do you think Lady Sichi's message got out?"

She had sent her letter with Jass the previous day, but there was no way to know if he had even reached their camp yet, let alone gotten a response. "I hope so," I said, trying not to consider what could have held him up. I had to believe Jass had gotten through all right, both for himself and because I had no idea what I would do with Gideon if he didn't.

Nuru passed the message back. Edo gave a little nod and, drawing himself up, stepped forward. "It is not murder when you commit treason against our emperor," Nuru translated. "You were discovered in the act of manipulating and assassinating Emperor Gideon e'Torin, a crime for which you would have been executed had you not turned on his empress and been killed in self-defence. Do not think you can peddle your lies here anymore, *Priest*."

"Whose word do you think carries the greater weight of truth, Lord Edo? Or should I say, Grace Bahain." He made a little bow in acknowledgement of the title Edo now carried. "An overwrought and emotional empress"—Sichi growled in the back of her throat— "or a true child of God given new life to fulfil his purpose?"

"Even were she overwrought, I would still take Empress Sichi's word over yours, you Chiltaen snake."

Hisses spread along the narrow parapet. Bows held below the edge of the stonework were passed from hand to hand, other hands shifted toward sword hilts, only a few Levanti glancing Sichi's way as though considering their options.

"It's a pity you have so hastily condemned all the people who stand with you, Lord Edo," Nuru whispered to me as Leo replied. "But you never had your father's courage and wisdom, did you?"

"The courage to shame my family by throwing my cousin, our empress, at you like meat to dogs? No, I haven't got that kind of courage and wouldn't want it when I can stand up and fight for my people. You are nothing but Chiltaen oppressors in different clothes. You will get nothing from us."

"Are you sure those are your final words, Lord Edo?"

"No, my final words are 'Go to the hells, you shit.'"

An angry cheer tore through the Kisians atop the wall, fists and bows and swords lifted into the air. It was all noise to me, but they chanted, and proud looks were thrown Edo's way. At least we could be sure they followed him, whatever else might happen, and for a moment I thought we might even get through this.

Until they launched the catapults. Enormous stones flew, swelling panic in place of cheers. Soldiers pushed to be out of their paths, and down in the courtyard Levanti started shouting. The first boulder crashed through the parapet, scattering stones and soldiers like they were nothing but sticks, sending them flying.

I heard no order, but all around me archers nocked and loosed, and Edo was shouting. I gripped Nuru's arm. "We have to get Sichi out of here!"

She was no warrior. Nuru and I carried our blades, but neither of us had bows or javelins and were just in the way. Yet Sichi hesitated, determined she ought to be a leader, be seen. Until a second boulder slammed into the base of the wall, shaking it so violently she gripped Nuru's arm and capitulated.

Our plan had been to retreat into the courtyard and help where we could, with the injured or with supplies, but barely had we reached the stones than Lord Nishi strode toward us in a towering fury.

The man snarled in Sichi's face, Leo's name all I understood. The rest of Leo's followers had been secured in the city, only the rich Kisian they called Lord Salt allowed to remain out of respect for his title. I had said it was a bad idea, but I wasn't pleased to be proved right.

"What the fuck is wrong with him?" I demanded of Nuru while Sichi replied more calmly than I could have.

"He thinks Leo is still alive and we're just hiding him."

"What? Has he looked at who is out there attacking us?"

"Sichi is attempting to explain that," Nuru whispered. "But he's insisting on searching the manor. He says he has concerned soldiers and servants who will help him."

I stared at the railing lord, waving his hands around in a rage and not letting Sichi speak more than a few words every time she opened her mouth. Another boulder roared through the air, smashing through a nearby section of wall. Lord Nishi merely glared at it.

"In the middle of a battle he's going to take soldiers to search for the priest who is actually outside the walls?"

"Yes. That's about the gist of it. He seems to think the Chiltaens will stop attacking as soon as Leo, or his body, is given over respectfully."

Before Nuru finished speaking, the Kisian lord spun on his heel and strode across the busy courtyard toward the manor, exactly as if there were no wounded soldiers or stones or bodies, as though no battle was happening at all.

"Shit," I said. "If he finds Gideon, we're in trouble."

Nuru grimaced. "Would he know about the caves?"

"He might. He's Kisian. I don't know what he knows."

"Then go. Find someone you trust to guard the passage if you can, else stay yourself."

"What of Si—"

"I can guard her." Nuru set her hand upon one of her sword hilts. "I'm as capable and well-trained as any Sword, even if I'm not Made."

I hadn't doubted it, but with Lord Nishi disappearing into the manor I didn't have time to reassure her, only to nod and run, hoping they would be all right until I returned.

Servants and soldiers alike were hurrying through the entrance hall carrying bundles of arrows and cloth and water, stones and old blades and food, the chaos here a quieter mirror to the chaos outside. I could only hope our walls and gates would stand long enough for supplies to matter.

After the bustle and noise of the hall, stepping into the empty cellar was like stepping into another world. There was no sign of Lord Nishi or any of his supporters, and hoping it would stay that way, I shifted the stone cover and dropped the short distance into the narrow underground passage. Light from the pair of lanterns we'd left glimmered on the damp walls, filling the cave ahead with a pale glow, their flicker the only movement or sign of life.

"Gideon?" I called as I ducked beneath the low arch.

Air ripped and a blade halted before me, all threat and no welcome. At the other end of the long, clean edge was Rah. Tired, thinner, dirty from the caves, and with the shadow of old bruises on his face, but still Rah with his intent gaze that looked right through me. Our eyes met, but he didn't lower the sword.

"Dishiva," he said.

"Rah."

Gideon lay against the cave wall where I had left him, twitching and trembling in his sleep. Rah's gaze shied sideways with mine. "What's wrong with him?"

"Tep gave him something to help him sleep. It just hasn't been restful. He'll probably wake soon, and you'll wish he hadn't."

"Why? And why send for me?"

I folded my arms, no longer afraid he would use the outstretched weapon. "Because you were right, but you shouldn't have been." I gestured around. "This should have worked. Would have worked. Gideon was making it work. But that fucking little monster ruined everything. Everything we could have had and could have been. He gets inside your head, like a voice. A feeling of peace. A raging attack of noise, whatever he needs to—" Unable to find words, I mimed tearing something apart with my hands.

"He's an Entrancer."

"A what the fuck?"

He finally lowered his sword, nicked the edge of one of his fingers, and sheathed it. A tired sigh led his next words. "Ezma told me. She said that's how our herd masters have been controlled. She's a believer in the One True God, but she thinks Leo is a fraud and the real Veld is a Levanti." He ran a hand over his face, leaving it dirtier and more lined with fatigue. "I think she wants to build a holy empire on the plains."

"But she's a horse whisperer!" The words were out of my mouth before my cynicism caught up. "You're serious, aren't you? Is that why she was exiled?"

"Yes. Tor's been working on the book, by the way, but I don't know how much help it will be now."

There was something disconnected about having a conversation about Veld and Leo and Ezma here beneath a Kisian manor, but even more so about having it with Rah. I ought not to have been surprised Tor had confided in him, but for weeks this problem had consumed me and weighed its horrors upon me, and I had felt alone. Even with Sichi and Nuru and Edo. Rah knowing, Rah talking about it without questioning its truth, lifted a fear I hadn't known I was carrying. Someone believed me. Someone who hadn't been there, who hadn't seen it firsthand, believed me.

Unable to voice such feelings, I gestured at Gideon. "He's a mess. I think he's afraid and...fragile." I touched the side of my head. "He's had Leo in here too long. He did it to protect us in the end, but...he couldn't fight when it mattered and is...tortured by the things he's done and can't undo."

"Yitti." Rah's voice was even, a determined state of calm hiding his pain. "Who else?"

"Oh, Jass told you, did he? I told him he shouldn't. But I guess he didn't want you to come all the way only to find out and still feel obligated to look after him. Trust Jass to think like that."

"Unlike you?"

"Unlike me. I have to be more pragmatic."

"But not pragmatic enough to kill him and make it easy."

I shook my head. "No, but it was close. I had to watch them die. I had to listen to the condemnations come from his lips in his voice, watch him smile while it happened. So even though I know, I *know*, it wasn't him, I can't separate the two. I figured you're the only one left who gives a shit about him who can."

Rah turned, watching Gideon twitch in his half doze, and I was glad I could not see his expression. "Thank you," he said, the dull tone tightening a fist around my heart. "But you didn't answer my question. Who else?"

"Is that a question you really want me to answer? Now of all moments?"

"No, but I need to know."

I couldn't meet his gaze. "Yitti," I said, thinking it would be easier to start with the name he already knew, but it stuck in my throat like blades. "Himi. Istet. And Lok. The rest were Bedjuti, not your Swords."

What was there to say? Rah's face was a dead mask behind which he held his pain close, and there was nothing I could do to lessen it that hadn't already been said. Perhaps it would have been kinder to kill Gideon after all.

At last he nodded, a slow, regretful motion as much thanks for my honesty as acknowledgement. "I should go." He glanced up at the cave roof through which the distant thud of steps could be heard. "Are you going to be all right?"

No would have been the honest answer, but there was nothing he could do to help. "I think we can hold them off. Sichi sent a message to your empress, so hopefully she's on her way. If not, do tell her when you get back that we'd rather like some help."

He nodded, looking again at Gideon. "I'll do that. Not that she has any reason to trust me now."

We stood a minute in silence. Rah kept his back to me and I let him keep his pain, knowing there was nothing I could do to lighten it. Eventually, he heaved a sigh and stepped toward Gideon, tentative like a hunter.

"Gideon?" Rah knelt, his hand on Gideon's shoulder. "It's Rah. I've come back for you."

His voice cracked on suppressed emotion, and I had to swallow a lump in my throat and fight the urge to leave. This was too raw a reunion to be present for, but until I was sure Rah could manage him, I could not go.

"Gideon, I'm—"

Gideon rolled, lashing out with his fist. Rah flinched but caught it, only for Gideon to lunge at him with a mangled cry. For a moment they were a mess of tangled limbs and sharp grunts before Rah pinned him to the ground. "Stop trying to hit me, you idiot," he growled. "I came to save you, but I could just as easily leave you."

"Rah?" A sob broke upon his name, and Gideon shoved Rah off him. "Get away from here. Go. Go! Don't let him find you."

"I am going, but I'm taking you with me."

The man who had once held all the Levanti hopes in his capable hands clung to Rah like he was drowning, gulping lungfuls of grief. His whole body shook and tears streaked down his dirt-smeared face, and I had to look away and remind myself he had not ordered those deaths. Remind myself that what Gideon had been through deserved kindness. But it was hard to think of Yitti and Himi and Istet and believe it.

Rah murmured words I tried not to hear, speaking over Gideon's every attempt to explain or beg him to leave, until at last he fell silent.

"We're getting out of here," Rah said. "You can lean on me most of the way, but you're going to have to walk. You can do that for me, can't you?"

He was treating Gideon like a troubled horse, and I wondered if it was easier to think that way, to solve the problem at hand rather than try to grapple with reconciling all his different thoughts of Gideon.

Rah started to his feet and I stepped forward, stopping as he shook his head. Whether it was because he feared I would spook Gideon or because he understood how difficult this was for me, I wasn't sure, only grateful.

"You can go," he said when he had Gideon on unsteady feet. "Jass is waiting. He'll help me if needed."

That Jass was so close but I would not see him hurt more than I expected. We had both chosen to put helping our people before each other, before the hope of a relationship that might not even last beyond these shores, yet his strong arms wrapped around me would have made the world feel all right for a few blissful moments. Instead he had his task and I had mine, and Sichi and Nuru might already be in need of me.

"We prepared some supplies for the journey," I said, pointing to the two satchels sitting against the cave wall. "Give one to Jass for me and say...say thank you. Again."

It was not enough, but it would have to do. Rah nodded, his lips twisting into a wry smile, one that contained all the things we had never said to each other and now never would. I had to make peace with that, as I had to make peace with being parted from Jass. All I could do was trust they would make it and turn away, my heart as full as it was broken.

———————◆———————

The floor shook as I reached the top of the stairs. I steadied myself against a wall, shouts sounding through the tumbling of dust and the cracking of timbers. Nearby, a pair of servants huddled in a doorway, watching me as I ran on, back into the bright daylight.

A boulder sat in the crumbled ruins of the steps, making a jagged jumble of the stones. They shifted under my feet, sliding as I tried to run down them. The courtyard was a mess. Stones broken from the wall scattered the ground, along with fallen arrows and a smattering of bodies. A boy was running along collecting the arrows, and two Levanti healers knelt beside a screaming soldier. It was all too much with the stink of dust and blood and the thunder of a ram beating against the gates.

"Have you seen the empress?" I shouted at a passing soldier, but he didn't look around, let alone answer. The gates were holding, but the wall was a mess. Some archers were still atop part of it, but most soldiers were gathered inside now, tense and waiting. I headed for the flash of a crimson surcoat.

Edo stood in the centre of a large gathering of soldiers, shouting orders. They watched him with the confidence I'd once had in my leaders.

"Edo!"

And now here was I, breaking in on his speech. He looked around at his name, relief flashing across his face. Before I could ask my question, he pointed in the direction of the stable. "Empress Sichi" were the only words I understood, but they were all I needed.

He picked up where he had left off as I pushed my way back out through the crowd of soldiers, stinking of sweat and fear.

The main stable yard sat in the shadow of the north tower, its decorative stonework watching Levanti gather with their horses. Made tense with fear and noise, the animals were twitchy as everyone rushed to saddle their mounts. Loklan dashed about, helping with anything he could get his hands to, a dozen people calling to him all at once.

"Loklan!"

He looked around, wiping sweat from his eyes. "Captain! Itaghai is here and ready."

Oh, to be a captain again, to be on my horse fighting the way I understood, the way I had trained. But that was not my path now.

"You ride him," I said. "I have to find the empress."

"Me?"

"Yes, your horse was left with Ezma. You need a mount more than I do."

He gaped at me. "Are...are you sure, Captain?"

I wasn't. "Yes," I said anyway, telling myself that if I couldn't trust my horse master with him, I couldn't trust anyone. "I know you'll take care of him. Fight hard."

"And you, Captain. I saw Nuru and the empress climbing onto the stable roof earlier."

I didn't stay to ask why or to thank him, too afraid I would rescind my own offer. I left him to it, ignoring all the calls and shouts as I edged back out through the press of horses and Levanti, mud and hay trampled beneath hooves and boots.

On one side of the main stable building, a rickety gate made for good footholds, and I pulled myself onto it. From there I could reach the edge of the roof. My hands and arms protested my weight, but I dragged myself up onto the roof's slippery slates.

Sichi and Nuru stood at the far end, each balancing on the roof as they peered through a gap in the stones. They had their heads together, talking fast, but turned at the clinking of tiles beneath my boots.

"Rah came," I said. "They've gone. You should get out of here too; I'm not sure how long we can hold out if the other empress isn't coming."

I didn't need to ask if there had been any sign of Empress Miko. Their expressions told me we were alone.

"I've been trying to persuade Sichi to leave," Nuru said with a glance at the empress—a different woman in her borrowed armour. "But she says a leader doesn't run."

"Sure, but what is she the leader of at this point?" My foot slipped and I only just managed to save myself from sliding down the roof by gripping the ridge. Sichi had half lunged to save me, but straightened when I shook my head to show I was all right. "She cannot lead the Levanti into battle, and Edo has the Kisians. If Leo wants her, we need to get her out of here."

"I am here as you speak," Sichi said in her imperfect Levanti. "Speak me. Not Nuru."

Stung by the reproof, I looked right at her. "You have to leave. It isn't safe here. You don't want to get caught by Leo. Go, through the caves. If you hurry you might be able to catch up with Rah and Jass and Gideon, they won't be moving fast."

Nuru translated, leaving Sichi biting her lip. She looked around at the courtyard, at the fast-crumbling wall and the gate beginning to splinter. We had soldiers and riders, we had archers and blades, but when the Chiltaens got through they would crush us into our own walls until there was no one left.

"Your presence will make no difference to the outcome," I said, and cruel though the words might be, they were true and she knew it.

Sichi nodded.

"Good. Now go, before—"

A rush of air overhead heralded the passing of a huge boulder. Its shadow swept over, and stone smashed stone in a burst so loud I pressed my hands over my ears.

The crashing ought to have faded away, but it grew, a thunderous cascade of tumbling rocks. Stones burst from the middle of the north tower, and the whole thing toppled sideways like a dropping tree. Chunks spewed out across the courtyard, but the bulk of it crashed outside the wall, hammering the track leading into the mountains. A track that buckled under the weight, the ground beneath it subsiding as though struck by a giant fist.

The caves.

Cold dread shot through me even as a fierce cloud of dust blew over us. It stung my eyes and tore my breath from my body, each tiny stab of grit against skin nothing to the overwhelming fear of what I might have just lost. Jass had been down there.

Hunched over and coughing, Nuru said, "Was that the caves?"

I dared not speak lest my words make it true, but Sichi nodded.

I hadn't noticed how much the ground had been shaking until it stopped, the remains of the tower settling, only small rocks left to trickle down its slopes. Inside the compound, cries rose from the injured, followed by calls for healers as people scrabbled at the rockfall, looking for survivors.

"Fuck," I said, and the word just didn't seem big enough to encompass the full size of either my fears or my shock. I couldn't bring myself to move.

"All right," Nuru said. "That's that plan gone. No way out. What now? The gate isn't going to hold much longer."

She was asking me like I had an answer, but my brain seemed to have filled with dust. Every thought skittered away and I stared at her, trying to focus, to think, able to do nothing but suck fast breaths and hold down panic. Leo was out there. He was coming for us, and there was nothing we could do to stop him.

Sichi spouted a stream of rapid Kisian, pointing to the other side of the compound, and even before she had finished, Nuru was nodding.

"Some of the south wall has broken away in places," she said. "If we go that way, we might be able to find a way through, or somewhere we can climb down without the Chiltaens seeing us."

It was a terrible plan, but it was the only one we had.

Thrusting aside all thought of Jass and Rah, I drew a deep breath and followed Nuru and Sichi to the edge of the roof.

All was chaos in the courtyard. The dust had turned everything hazy. Footsteps hurried past. Someone nearby was crying. I dared not look, just hurried in Nuru's wake, afraid of losing her in the confusion. All around us horses whinnied and snorted and people were shouting, punctuated by the ever-present rhythmic boom of the ram hitting the gates. It was speeding up, the inevitability of the end making my pulse roar in my ears.

Darting and dodging around rubble and people, Sichi led us across the yard, her surcoat flapping behind her. It was easier to follow than Nuru's dark leathers, and we made it to the opposite wall without losing each other in the rows of Kisians lining up amid Edo's orders.

"Let's see if there's a way up on this end," Nuru shouted. "The front stairs are too close to the fighting, and these ones are broken."

She had barely finished the words before she was off, heading in the direction of the south tower now looming its height alone. A single point in a broken crown.

Rubble littered the ground, and we had to watch where we put our feet or risk tripping. "Shit, there's nothing big enough," Nuru said as we reached the stairs at the base of the tower. "Shall we go up and see if there's a way down?"

Sichi started up the stairs, her hair beginning to pull loose from the topknot she'd tied. Nuru followed, glancing back to be sure I was with them. Two at a time up the stairs to the top of the wall again, everything that had happened between the army's arrival and now like a bad dream. They were still out there, still hammering their way in, still loading rocks into their catapults and raining them upon us, intent on our destruction.

"Look!"

Nuru pointed. A dark smudge sat on the horizon behind the Chiltaens.

Sichi darted to the parapet, stepping upon a fallen rock to get a better view. When she turned, a broad smile stretched her lips, a little laugh tripping from her tongue. "Miko!"

The dark smudge owned crimson banners.

"Yes!" Nuru cried. "They're coming!"

"We just have to hold out until they get here." I tried to measure the distance, but all I came up with was too far away. "We had better hope that gate holds."

A large rock sailed over the wall and smashed into the upper floor of the manor. Timbers splintered and a section of roof sagged, spilling tiles.

"Yes," Nuru agreed. "Because heading back to the house is out of the question now too."

The gate shattered, the end of the ram sticking through the hole like an iron fist. The courtyard filled with shouts as the Kisians and Levanti lined up, weapons drawn and ready.

"Shit," I said, as Sichi scowled at me and gestured angrily.

"She says you need to stop talking," Nuru said. "You said we should use the caves a moment before they caved in, now this."

"It's not my fault!"

"Tell that to the gods."

The ram tore the gates as it was withdrawn, and a shiver of

mingled anticipation and fear moved through the waiting soldiers. At Edo's command, arrows flew through the opening before the onrush of Chiltaen soldiers. Half a dozen fell, trampled beneath the feet of their own comrades, and my skin chilled.

Leo was coming.

"We have to get out of sight," I said, looking around. The manor was out, as were the stables and most of the outbuildings, even the caves. Everything else was close enough that he might see us or hear us or whatever the weird mystical shit he did was. I pointed up at the south tower. "Up there. Quick, go!"

I shoved Sichi toward the stairs as she exclaimed, and guessing her complaint, I said, "Yes, the very same sort of tower we just saw brought down by a single rock, now get going."

"Are you sure—?" Nuru began.

"It's a terrible idea, but we don't have another one," I said. "Leo isn't infallible. He can't be everywhere. All we need to do is get out of his range and hold out until the Kisians arrive."

Sichi led the way, the hammer of our footfalls echoing as we wound our way up each flight of stairs. Every floor was a small room, bare of all furniture or crammed with so much one couldn't enter. At the first that looked liveable—a room with a small table and cushions and a long couch under the narrow window—Sichi stopped to catch her breath. The space was dusty and unused but comfortable, and Sichi leaned against the wall. From the window, I could see the courtyard, but it was too hard to make out any individuals in the moving mass of fighters, horses, dust, and blood. But I could have seen Leo's banners from twice the distance. One was coming this way.

"How far up are we?" I asked, gesturing at the next flight of stairs.

Nuru and Sichi exchanged words. "Halfway."

"Only halfway?"

"It gets rickety the farther up you go," Nuru said. "This is safe."

"Safe from falling, but maybe not safe from Leo." I peered out the window again. The banner had disappeared, sending my heart leaping into my throat. "We should keep moving."

Sichi held up a hand, seeming to beg a moment to rest. I couldn't say my legs were looking forward to more stairs, but neither was I looking forward to more Leo. He might already have seen us. Have heard us. Have caught sight of Sichi's bright crimson surcoat and followed it through the dust as I had. "Just a few more floors and we can rest again."

Nuru translated, and with a reluctant nod, Sichi agreed.

Three more floors brought us to another furnished room, where I knelt on the sagging couch beneath the window. "The Kisians are almost here," I said, eyeing the broadening shadow approaching the back of the Chiltaen lines. They had surely seen them coming by now, and I could imagine the confusion as the rearguard became frontline fighters.

"Can you see Leo?" Nuru was at my shoulder, her hair tickling my cheek. She pushed closer to the window, but it wasn't wide enough to stick her head through so she settled for pressing her cheek to the stone. "I can't see anyone."

"A banner was coming this way before, but it disappeared." I itched to look again and had to sit on my hands to keep from pushing her aside. "Hopefully he didn't see us."

Sichi spoke, giving me a look.

"She says everything else you've said has come true so far."

"I am not trying to curse us, the worst possible things just keep happening on their own, all right?"

"That's not very comforting."

A door banged far below us, followed by distant footsteps. "Dishiva?" called a voice we all knew so hatefully well.

Nuru glared at me. "Maybe stop talking from now on."

"It's not me, I—"

"Dishiva," he called again. "I know you're up there. You can't stop me taking her."

Behind me, Sichi let out a harsh puff of breath. I turned to find her hands shaking. "Do you have a knife?"

"She has one of mine," Nuru said. "I have my other and my swords."

"Well, that's something."

"Do we hold our ground here, or...?"

The room was not large, but large enough for a messy scrap. Better still, being above him meant he'd have to stick his head above the edge of the stairs and risk attack before he could see us.

"Here seems as good as anywhere."

"Planning to kill me again, Dishiva, Defender of the One True God? It hasn't been working out very well for you so far."

My hands clenched to fists. We had killed him twice now, but the shit just kept coming back. I let out a hard exhale and gripped my sword hilt. Not usually a good choice for close confines, but I wanted to slice his head off the moment it appeared, while keeping as far away as I could.

"My dear Sichi," he called out when I made no answer, his voice seeming to come from a few floors below us. "I am desolated you would hurt me so. I thought we had something, you and I."

Sichi stepped closer, Nuru's knife in her hand. By her grip she'd never been trained to use it, but anger can make up for much. Gesturing for her to stay where she was, I stepped forward, a slow heel to toe on the creaking floor.

The battle outside sounded very far away.

"You and I could achieve so much together, Sichi," he said, Nuru translating for me in a low hiss as he went on, earnest rather than mocking now. "I know you want a powerful position from which others cannot control you. I can promise you that. No one tries to control a man chosen and beloved of God."

"Except for God," I muttered, quiet enough there was no way he could hear me.

"Yes, but everyone is part of God's purpose, Dishiva," he called back. "As you ought to have accepted by now. How much stronger you would be if you did."

I suppressed a shiver and crouched by the railing where his head would soon appear. "I got a copy of your holy book, you know," I said. "And had it translated. Fascinating read. Man dies in a throne room. Dies in a cave. Keeps coming back. But honestly, I don't see how all the dying is helping you. No one is even seeing you do it."

"Your expert opinion is greatly appreciated, Dishiva."

More a snap than the boastful answer I had hoped for, but he was close now, maybe only two flights down. I leaned forward, peering through the railing. I glimpsed him, head turned up, eyes on me, an instant before the screaming hit me like a club. The floor slammed into my back and I pressed my hands over my ears, sound ripping through me on a tide of voices.

And was gone. I lay sucking breaths, Nuru and Sichi staring in mingled horror and fright as Leo's footsteps kept approaching up the stairs.

"Did I hurt you, Dishiva? It's only fair after everything you've done to me, don't you think?" Such anger in his words, such bitterness, but I could do nothing beyond feel a flicker of pride that we had pushed him so far.

Sichi held down her hand to help me up. "I think..." I began as I took it. "I think you have to look him in the eyes for him to do that."

I'd looked at him in the garden house. He'd goaded me into looking up before the ceremony too, it just hadn't felt as strong. Not as much anger behind it, perhaps.

"You're right," he said, not having to shout now he was so close.

"I was not as skilled in my younger bodies. A pity really; so much more I could have achieved."

Once more, I edged toward the stairs. He appeared before I could get close enough, and I flinched back, bracing for the pain and the noise, for the voice that never came. Recovering, I lunged, but he had hurried up the last few steps and blocked my blade with his own, grinning hatefully over the sound of the metallic clang.

"You think you've angered me, Dishiva?" he said, advancing a step. "You've caused me considerable pain and annoyance, but how can I hate you when you keep doing everything I need you to do? The cave was the greatest gift you could have given me. And letting Sichi stab me in the back—I couldn't have planned it better myself."

He stepped forward, pressing me back. "Get on the stairs," I said to Nuru, looking over Leo's shoulder rather than risk his gaze. "Stay behind me."

"Is that your plan?" He advanced another step. "To keep standing between me and what I want?"

"Whatever it takes."

The stairs creaked behind me. Slowly backing up however many flights of stairs were left was not the best plan, but once again, it was the only one I had. That and hoping he would give me an opening. Or that the Kisians would somehow guess we were up here and save us.

Leo chuckled, and it was such an effort not to look at him. "They are never going to know. And won't get the chance anyway."

He slashed at my face, and had my reflexes been slower he would have sliced my cheek. I backed onto the bottom step, heart hammering my panic.

Nuru and Sichi hissed desperate words behind me, but I couldn't focus on them, only on the man I watched out the corner of my eye.

"What a waste of time this is, Dishiva," he said, advancing slowly. "You are going to run out of stairs."

"Before you run out of mocking things to say?"

"Oh, I have an unlimited supply of those." He jabbed at me and I leapt back, catching my foot awkwardly on the step and almost falling. Hands caught me from behind, steadying my retreat as he lunged again, the flash of a grin all I saw above his blade.

Sichi cried out, and I had to fight the urge to turn and see what was wrong as Leo advanced another step. An open floor yawned above us.

"She said you're running out of floors," Leo said, matching each of my steps back with one forward. "There are only three above this. Oops. What was that about hoping the Kisians would save you?" His gaze flicked to the window, and mine followed as he looked back.

The strike to my mind was fast and vicious, a fist clenched over all thought. I stumbled back, crying out.

Just let go. It is pointless to fight. It only puts Sichi in danger.

Hands gripped me. Pulled. I jolted and wriggled and fought to be free of them, sure they were the claws of monsters dragging me into an abyss.

Just lie still. Don't fight. It will soon be over.

At a sharp cry, the dense fog faded and I was lying on the top step, battered from thrashing. Something flew over my head. Leo cried out again and snarled as a broken table leg hit his raised arm. Someone helped me up. Nuru, from the smell and the tight grip of her long fingers. Sichi's hurried footsteps behind heralded another flying table leg.

"You're going to run out of furniture even sooner than you run out of stairs," he said, speeding the last few steps and sending us scurrying across the dusty floor toward the next flight.

"Stay behind me!" I called to Sichi and Nuru, unable to turn. "Don't look at him."

"You'll look at me eventually. It's what we do, look into each other's eyes; that's why people find the mask so uncomfortable to be around, because you can't see the eyes behind it."

He kept approaching, not bothering to swing his blade now, his smile and his continued approach all the threat he needed.

Until he leapt two steps and slashed at my face. Pain ripped across my eye and the bridge of my nose, and heat leaked down my cheeks. I couldn't see and blundered back, everything a blot. Nuru swore. Her shaking hands touched my shoulder. My arm. My cheek. "Fuck! Dishiva? Look at me."

I could turn toward her voice but couldn't see her. There was red and darkness and a blur of shapes, but no Nuru. No Leo.

"Oops." He laughed. "What happened to your eyes?"

One moved when I shifted my gaze, the haze of darkness shifting with it as though something was trapped in my sight, but the other...I touched my face with my free hand, fingers finding an empty gash where an eye should be, hot, wet blood and fluid dripping down my face.

"Stay back, you piece of horseshit," Nuru snarled in front of me, her footsteps loud on the stairs. Was she standing in front of Leo? I couldn't tell. Couldn't think. I kept trying to open my eyes like they were stuck closed.

Nuru screamed, the ragged sound I had heard torn from my own throat. "Changed your mind yet, Sichi?" Leo said. "I might spare her life if you do."

For a glorious moment, angry heat seared away all my pain and fear, and I lunged toward his voice. The blur of a figure flashed before me and I hit him, sweet-scented woollen fabric and the smell of wax sneaking between breaths of my own blood. We tumbled, limbs slamming against steps, everything a whirl of different pains and the gasp and blow of his breath so close it warmed my skin.

We hit the floor below in a tangle, him beneath me. Feeling

for his collar I hauled him up and smashed his head down on the wooden boards. "Fuck you," I snarled. "Just die. Die and leave us alone."

He laughed—a weak, breathless, mad sound. "That's not going to happen. You can't escape me, Dishiva."

I made to slam his head again, but his knee rammed into my chest, knocking breath from my body. Feet scuffed as he got up, his outline flitting across my good eye. I tracked him through the haze, a joyous possibility occurring to me as I got shakily to my feet. "You can't get inside my head now," I said, lunging after him. "You've fucked up your own biggest weapon."

Floorboards creaked beneath him. I followed the sound, adrenaline all that kept me moving like a stalking lion.

"I am going to be the end of you. I am—"

Noise slammed into me. The floor trembled. Stone scraped and tumbled and someone screamed. It might have been me as a board snapped under my feet in a rip of timber. Leo cried out and the floor fell away, casting me into emptiness and pain.

25. MIKO

My horse stood as steady as a rock. Its stillness helped me be calm, or at least appear so. There was no being calm anymore.

Before us the city of Kogahaera stood proud upon its plateau, the governor's manor beset by a Chiltaen army. One of the great towers had fallen, leaving only one reaching for the sky. I wondered if it would ever be rebuilt. If Mei'lian would ever be rebuilt, or if we would leave the ruins of this war scattered like scabs across the land.

"Might I take this opportunity to dissuade you from ordering us into this fight?" Manshin said. We had stopped a little distance back, waiting for everyone to gather, he my only companion at the head of my army.

"No," I said, not turning to look at him. "You may not."

For a moment there was no sound beyond the growing restlessness of the soldiers behind me, all shifting feet and murmuring while their comrades gathered along the ridge.

"It's dangerous."

"Hardly. We outnumber them." I turned to look at him. "I told you, I will not sit by and watch another of my cities get destroyed. Or more of my people be slaughtered."

He met my gaze, no smile in his eyes. "They aren't interested in the city. If they were, they wouldn't have attacked at the most defended part. The part filled with Levanti warriors. They want the same thing we do, the end of this false emperor, though why is something I would very much like to know. It bodes ill to have so many Chiltaens seemingly rogue this far into our lands."

"Shall we wait and ask them? After they've defeated the Levanti and turned around to man the walls themselves? If they get in, they will be harder to root out, and I would rather not exchange a Levanti court allying itself with the local Kisian lords for a Chiltaen one intent on our further destruction."

Whether because one of my points had finally found weight with him or because further argument was pointless, Minister Manshin made no answer. I had gotten so used to heeding his advice these last weeks that to sit there and spit on it felt churlish. So far had we fallen from our mutual respect, had it ever been mutual at all.

"*It is safest not to fight powerful men,*" Ryoji had said, and gods how I wished he was here now, no matter how much more I needed him to fulfil his mission.

I risked a sidelong look at Minister Manshin, catching a frown that made deep ridges of his brow.

"Are we ready?" I said.

Manshin heaved a sigh. "Yes, Your Majesty."

"If you cannot agree with this plan on its military merits, at least be grateful for the opportunity to save your daughter." I touched the pouch in my sash where I had stowed Sichi's letter. "If we sit here and let the Chiltaens win, she will either die or be taken prisoner. You cannot want that."

"It matters little as she's no longer a daughter of mine."

I turned at the bite in his words, so angry and dismissive. "Because she was forced or manipulated into this position? It is hardly fair to disown her for that."

"If I am not to tell you how to lead this army, I would ask you not to tell me how to feel about my daughter marrying a barbarian."

Rather than face censure for his lack of respect, he turned to address the army at our backs, calling to the generals, who called to their commanders and their captains until the preparations were a storm with us its eye. There was no turning back now.

"For Kogahaera!" I cried as the shifting mass of my army reached a restless peak. "For Kisia! Let's make them regret the day they stepped across our border!"

I kicked my heels to my horse's sides, and on a tide of thundering hooves and shouts, we surged toward the Chiltaen army hastily regrouping to meet us. The wild exhilaration of riding at the head of an army toward an unknown fate filled me with the sense I was flying. Or falling. The destination a painful inevitability I could not draw back from, could only face with all I had.

It was the battle of Risian over again, the distance everything and nothing in a blink as we crashed into their front lines. A handful of Ryoji's guards charged in beside me, one tumbling at the piercing tip of a Chiltaen spear. Hooves and metal and mud and short cut-off screams and we were through their first line of soldiers, our horses knocking them down and trampling them into the ground.

There was no time to think, only to react, to lay about me with my sword and be grateful for the guards ever at my side. A blade sliced at my leg and an arrow ripped by, the guard on my right plunging the tip of a spear into a Chiltaen's neck. Their armour was the green and blue of an army half merchant owned, half commanded by the Nine, both splattered with mud and blood.

We had not planned to punch all the way through their lines on the first charge, yet Chiltaens fled my horse's hooves and I was soon well into their army, ranks closing behind me. My handful of guards clustered close, pressed on all sides by Chiltaen soldiers drawn to my banner. I could retreat to the safety of my army or press on to the Kisian banners ahead.

It was the decision of a moment, no time to fear, only to ride, forging a path onward through enemies as I would have to do off the battlefield every day if I wanted to succeed. With gritted teeth, I appreciated the living metaphor as I urged my horse on. Through slashing blades and screaming men. Through crowding bodies and blood. Panic and hate.

One of my guards fell, but I could not stop. Kisian banners were close. Hot blood the same crimson colour sprayed as I slashed at the enemies closing in, nothing skilled in my desperation. The tip of a spear grazed my horse's neck and plunged on into one of my guard's legs. He cried out, jabbing at the soldier even as someone else tore through him in a spray of blood. The Chiltaen dropped, and there in a cluster of Kisian soldiers was Edo. Edo I had never thought to see again, standing in full armour like the soldier he'd never wanted to be.

"We've cleared a path for you, Your Majesty," he said, and it was a stranger who spoke, a stranger with the face of a friend I'd known all my life.

There was no time to speak to him, not even to thank him, only to push on with my guards and feel foolish that I'd needed rescuing.

With Edo's soldiers all around, it was easy to ride the rest of the way, though I rode through ranks of unknown Kisians loyal to the Bahains, unsure of their hate. The broken walls of the governor's manor drew close, and with my remaining guards, I rode in through the shattered remains of its gates.

Within the walls, Levanti and Kisians fought side by side amid the wreckage, scattered stones and splinters of wood, bodies and limbs and blood strewn across the ground. I turned a circle with my horse, looking at the ruins of the manor and the fallen tower, and at the knots of injured people gathered in the safest corners of the yard.

"Your Majesty." Edo had followed me and I turned, fearing to look at him and yet wanting to with the same fervour. I had wanted so much to see him again, to know he was safe, but under better circumstances.

"Lord Edo. I—"

"We are grateful for your arrival, but these are my soldiers. Do you agree to leave this battle to me, or will we have to put you under guard?"

The authority with which he spoke sent a delighted shiver through me even as I bristled. Where had this Edo been all my life?

"I have no intention of overthrowing your command, Lord Edo," I said. "But I feel that you and I need to talk."

"We do, but Empress Sichi needs to speak to you first. Will you go to her?"

"Of course. Where is she?"

Edo gestured toward the southern tower, a great gaping hole in its side. Dismounting, I left my horse and my injured guards behind, and walked with him over the rubble. He said nothing as we hurried along, Edo at a pace that had me jogging to keep up. Had Sichi taken refuge in the tower? Was she all right? I had so many questions I could not ask for lack of time and breath and courage.

The entryway to the tower was dim and dusty, and I paused on the threshold while my eyes adjusted to the low light. Footsteps were tramping heavily on the stairs, and two Levanti appeared, a body held between them. Another Levanti, her face covered in blood, her body limp.

The two Levanti nodded to Edo as they passed in a respectful way, and he nodded back, his gaze catching to the woman they carried until they disappeared through the door. More questions were added to my mental list, questions I couldn't ask as Edo hurried for the stairs.

After the first few flights, the tower seemed to be nothing but steps, even the raging sounds of battle fading away beneath the ragged drawing of my breath. I wanted to rest, but Edo did not stop, and I hurried after him, my legs on fire.

At last he slowed, glancing back, a grimace all the gratitude I got for having followed as we emerged into the dusty remains of a sitting room. Sichi knelt at the table like one inviting me to join her for tea, but the strangeness of it was nothing to the unexpected surge of emotion at seeing her again. We had been different people the last time we met.

"I often think of that morning in the bathhouse," I said, my first words breathless and unplanned. "Did you know then? About the Levanti and the Chiltaens? Is that why you asked what I knew?"

Sichi didn't flinch at the attack, merely gestured to the opposite side of the table and said, "I knew some. Nothing of the Chiltaen plans, but I was aware of my uncle's alliance with Gideon and his intention to overthrow Emperor Kin."

"You could have told me."

"And risked my own execution and the destruction of my family for treason? Or to endure many more years pretending I would be allowed to marry Tanaka? You should know better, Koko. When a woman is given the opportunity for power and freedom, she would be unwise to let it go by, no matter the cost."

"I was fighting for Kisia."

"So was I. It was just a different Kisia."

Edo shifted by the stairs. "I must get back," he said. A bow, a murmuring of "Majesty," and his footsteps were fading away on the stairs, leaving Sichi and me facing one another under the watchful eye of a young Levanti woman. She hadn't moved since I'd arrived, her statuesque presence in the corner of the room intimidating. Like Tor, she had the long hair of one who hadn't been initiated into their warrior herd, and I wondered if, like Tor, she could understand every word I said.

"You don't have to worry about Nuru unless you plan to hurt me," Sichi said.

"I would only do so if you plan to hurt me."

Sichi smiled. "Then I think you can safely join us. There is something I want to ask you."

Her plea for help had brought me here, yet I moved warily toward the table. It was more difficult to kneel gracefully in armour stiffened with dried mud and blood, and across from her I felt like an animal rather than an empress. She had all her old grace and poise, but she was not the same Sichi. She had hardened.

"What is it you wish to ask?" I said, settling my hands in my lap.

"Whether I ought to take my own life."

I'd not known what to expect, but the question, so blunt as it was, shocked a small gasp from me. Unfazed, Sichi said, "My father is your minister of the left, I understand. What you may not understand is that he's not a forgiving man. My grandfather was one of the traitor generals who chose to fight for your father—"

I flinched at the open admission of my true father's existence, despite our privacy.

"—He made what my father always called *reckless decisions*, designed to embarrass our family name. He often said the only reason I was kept at court, why he was always under such scrutiny, was because my grandfather had left people unable to trust the name of Manshin. You may imagine how amused I was to learn he had done the very same thing in choosing to support you against Grace Bachita. I wonder if he realised, in that moment, he had become the very thing he had been fighting against."

I could have answered, could have told her I feared her father's disintegrating loyalty, but it was a weakness I wouldn't give anyone to use against me. So I merely lifted my brows and waited for her to go on.

"Personally, I doubt it," she said with a shrug. "But whatever he can reason through accepting in himself, he will not extend me the same courtesy."

It matters little as she's no longer a daughter of mine.

"Your silence is all the confirmation I need. He will shame me. He will force me into another marriage. He will not allow me any autonomy."

The first emotion pierced the ice of her demeanour—sharp, raw panic. It was there and gone in a fleeting twist of her mouth. Outside, the distant sound of the world changing on a tide of blood went on.

I reached across the table, only to pull my hand back and return it to my lap. "He may be my minister, but I am the empress and I promise you amnesty. There will be no repercussions from your choices, and you may remain with me or make your home wherever you choose."

"By myself? Or with Nuru perhaps? With my own position and money and no need of a husband to wipe clean my sins with marriage." Her look was pitying. "Men do not let women attain such dreams of freedom. Especially not my father."

"But I am the empress, not your father," I said, knowing too well how close I stood upon the brink of an untruth. Taking his daughter's side would only push him further away, but more than any other choice I'd made, the one before me was the difference between the easy path and the right path. I could give Minister Manshin his daughter, could win back some of his loyalty, or I could fight for her as I had always wanted someone to fight for me.

It was the easiest decision I had ever made.

"I give you my word," I said. "Your father may fight me over it, but I will take you under my protection, not his. Please, don't let him, or any other man, win. We could achieve so much together."

I hated to pressure her, to tell her how to feel and what to do, but

I could not bear the thought she would give up her life for nothing. I told myself Kisia needed her. But in truth, I needed her. I needed not to be alone anymore.

Although the Levanti behind her made no move, she seemed wholly connected to Sichi in the silence that followed, each aware of nothing but the other's existence. Without looking at one another, they nevertheless seemed to come to an unspoken agreement. Sichi nodded. Not a happy movement, not even a determined one, more the offhand sort of nod one would carelessly give a servant bringing tea. She was with me. For now. It was the best I could ask for.

While we had been sitting in the still, quiet tower room, the battle had continued outside, changing in tone as it ebbed and flowed around us. Now the sounds of panicked shouting caught my attention and I jumped up, hurrying to the small window. The courtyard was a mess of Levanti, Kisians, and Chiltaens, inside as well as outside the walls, but where my army had been the aggressor crushing the Chiltaens into the compound, there was now another bulk of Chiltaens behind us.

I stared, my heart seeming not even to beat for the time it took me to realise what had happened. They must have known we were coming, have split their force and left half to lie in wait.

The rear of my army was turning to face them as the first half of the Chiltaens had turned to face us, the lines all chaos, and my heart sped, kicking up thunder like the charging Chiltaens. My head swam, and the floor seemed to shift and toss.

"Shit," Sichi said, appearing beside me, and it was a moment before I realised I was laughing. Whether at the sound of so coarse a word on her lips or at the vast understatement it was, I wasn't sure.

I had no words of my own, but before I even thought to run, I was on the stairs, clattering down wood and stone and out into the weak daylight. Sounds crashed over me. Everywhere the press and movement of soldiers. Wounded propped the crumbling walls and the dead lay staring, trampled into the mud, the glory of battle nowhere to be seen.

Edo was there, shouting to his soldiers.

"Back on the walls!" he called as I joined him. "Quickly! Take out the front lines!"

His archers ran for the stairs, needing no second order. Some Levanti followed, one of them relaying orders. I stood, unsure what to do or say while everything moved around me. I had left my generals behind, and now I was trapped far from where I needed to be. Would they worry I was dead? Or think me hiding?

"Run and tell Oshar their horses would do better up front," Edo went on, a glance all he'd thrown me as he went on shouting, every bit the commander. "The rest of you, push forward. Let's get rid of the Chiltaens in here so Empress Miko's men can focus on the Chiltaens out there. Form up your lines. Stay together."

Shouts of "Yes, Your Grace" jumped around, and his soldiers hurried off.

He grimaced, nothing left of the pretty Edo I had admired as one admires a portrait. Here stood a man forced to become something he had never wanted to be, only to find he was good at it. A twist of envy choked all thought of compliment. My soldiers were loyal to their generals, not to me, and Minister Manshin or General Moto had commanded every battle we had fought. My presence had always been as nothing but a figurehead. Edo had become so much more in so short a time.

"I need to get back to my men," I said, able to think of nothing else to say.

"The remaining Chiltaens on this side have clumped up around the gate," he returned. "Getting through is not going to be easy. You're safe here."

"I don't want to be safe, I want to be leading my soldiers. Emperor Kin would not have hidden."

"Emperor Kin would probably have left us to our fate." They were bitter words, built on his father's anger at being left to defend Syan alone. "You don't have to be the same ruler to be a good one."

Not only did he have more respect from his soldiers, he was being wiser too. Stupid to be angry at him, but knowing Minister Manshin didn't need me out there was not helping. If we made it through this, it would be off the back of his skill as a commander, not mine.

Edo watched me warily. He looked like a man who had other places he needed to be, and I had never felt more like a burden while needing nothing.

I could run into the battle with his soldiers, but I would just be a target, and if I died, who would take over? Manshin? Leaving Sichi doubly alone and in danger and the empire in the hands of someone who would kill every Levanti if he could. I'd ignored all my advisors' continued insistence to be safe since escaping Mei'lian, but standing there on the brink of drawing my sword, I considered what would be lost if I died. Tanaka and I had dreamed of a different empire. A fairer empire. An empire no longer built on the hate of our ancestors. If I let it fall into the hands of my army, there was no saying what would emerge the other side.

I needed to survive.

Edo made to turn away about his tasks as shouts began cascading from atop the wall. An archer pointed toward the approaching army, and unable to tell whether the news was good or bad, I sprinted for the stairs. Edo followed, bounding behind me. Atop the nearest section of wall, I pushed to the front and, hands on the parapet, stared out at the battlefield.

Where the Chiltaens had charged in to pin my army as we had pinned theirs, a Levanti army now stood. Three long lines of riders charged toward the recently arrived Chiltaens, and my heart soared. I knew not whether it was Ezma or Rah who led them, but it didn't matter. They had remained our allies and they had come.

"Yes!" I cried, lifting my fists into the air.

"Friends of yours?" Edo said, a little breathless beside me. Wary whispers spread through his archers. Farther along the wall, even Edo's Levanti weren't cheering.

"My Levanti allies," I said. "Is that so surprising when you have your own?"

His smile was strained. "At least we might get out of this alive."

Shouting an order to his men on the walls, Edo strode back down the stairs, surcoat billowing. I followed, hating the feeling I was a dog at his heels. "Push through!" he shouted to the soldiers near the gate. "Let's get out there!"

He didn't look back as he ran, throwing orders left and right while I remained, just me and my small knot of guards with nothing to do but watch on as other people fought my battle. I let him go and held my ground, reminding myself of all I needed to stand for, all I needed to survive for.

I helped where I could, aiding the wounded and hunting supplies, and for the first time I didn't escape from my guards but kept them with me, watching for danger. Edo's soldiers were respectful but wary, and though it broke my heart, I hadn't time to trouble myself with its implications, only to help.

By the time the Chiltaen army had been defeated, I had no energy left for joy or satisfaction, only a numb sense of gratitude that it was over. I had done nothing, but it was over. Yet my work was only beginning. All too soon Whisperer Ezma stood before me, tall and blood spattered and menacing in her crown. She was enormous atop her grand horse, but rather than dismount, she spoke down to me. "Your Majesty. Where is Gideon e'Torin?"

"I understand he was dead before the Chiltaens attacked," I said,

shaken from my stupor. "Killed by Leo Villius, but the story is...
confusing. You have my thanks for arriving when you did."

"Your thanks is not required. I have much to see to."

Other Levanti swarmed around, some familiar, others not, all on
their great steeds, stopping only to greet one another and check their
mounts for injuries. One or two had started on the heads of their
fallen, and there were enough dead Levanti scattered through the
courtyard that they would be at it for a while.

"You will have to tread carefully," Edo said, drawing close and
speaking low as he watched Ezma depart. "Don't demand the loyalty of those who fought for my father yet."

"Why not? Without Emperor Gideon there is no other ruler to
rally behind."

"Not unless you force them to elevate one. They are wary of
your Levanti."

"Say the people who sided with a Levanti emperor."

"And had great cause to regret it, and no reason to think the
Levanti Gideon called enemies are their friends. It's complicated."

I bristled, disliking his paternal air. "I am a Kisian, fighting for a
Kisian Kisia, what does it matter who my allies are?"

"Would you say the same if someone allied themselves with the
Chiltaens?"

"No, but they are our enemies."

"And the Levanti have not been?"

"The Levanti have no power here anymore. There is no reason
to fear them."

His look was full of disbelief. "Just...leave it a few days. Prove
what sort of leader you are. Give them some time."

Time during which Minister Manshin could turn them all
against me. Panic flooded ice through my veins, and clenching my
hands to keep them from shaking, I said, "I could have every one of
them executed if they refuse."

"To what end?" he said calmly. "So you can rule through fear? That isn't the sort of leaders we wanted to be, Koko."

The very softest of his words were a punch that left me winded and speechless, ashamed to the depth of my soul. He could have kept speaking, could have moralised and crushed me, but instead he smiled, a weak, disappointed thing, which was almost worse.

"I will leave you to consider, Your Majesty," he said, bowing. "There is a lot to do here before the sun goes down."

He walked away, and only then did I see Minister Manshin standing close by. How much had he heard? Enough, I thought, by his scowl.

"That was a disaster," he said without preamble as he approached. "But I am glad to find you safe, Your Majesty."

"And you, Minister. Our alliance with the Levanti bears further fruit."

Around us, everyone was busy. Wounded soldiers were being carried or tended in place, broken piles of stone were being picked through for signs of life, horses were everywhere in an ever-spinning dance of velvet skin, and through it all Kisian and Levanti congregated in their separate groups, some exultant, some sombre, but always separate.

Despite the noise and the people and the activity, no one came near us. He looked at me as I looked at him, left to imagine all the things he wanted to say. That he had warned me not to attack. That we ought not rely on the Levanti. That their arrival had been lucky, not the outcome of good planning.

He said none of it, just "My daughter?"

"Here. Safe," I said. "She chose to surrender herself, and I have accepted her into my custody. I intend to pardon her and dissolve her marriage if she wishes, but have not made any plans yet for her future."

"*You* haven't."

"No, *I* haven't."

Somehow, I managed to keep my voice steady. Somehow, I looked him in the eye and did not flinch. Did not bend. Did not break.

"Very well, Your Majesty," he said, and with a stiff, cold bow, he turned away. With the regal stride of a man robbed of his vengeance, of an object upon which to vent his fury, the man who had once been my most trusted minister walked away.

26. RAH

We left the sounds of conflict behind, but replacing it with the echo of our steps and ragged breaths was hardly an improvement. The journey in through the caves with Jass had been a special sort of nightmare, all dark shadows and low, jagged roofs and the feeling of weight pressing down on me, enormous and inevitable. It was almost a blessing to be able to focus on Gideon, no matter how heavy and awkward he was.

Jass ambled ahead, disappearing at intervals to double-check the path before returning. I envied his ease.

"You've been through here a lot," I said as he strolled back to us, his lantern hanging unheeded from his hand. I held mine high, my arm tense.

"Quite a few times," he said. "Mostly I carry messages and supplies. And help people escape."

"For yourself or for Dishiva?"

He lifted a brow as I caught up with him. "Both?"

"Are you one of her Swords?"

"Technically she doesn't have any anymore, but before that yes, and before that no."

At my side, Gideon staggered on, dragging his feet. He leaned heavily against me like the effort of being upright was too much.

"But you help her anyway?"

"It's complicated. And honestly, due respect and all that, but I don't owe you an explanation."

He went ahead again, not looking back as he slid through a narrow crack into the next cave, turning dark to light with a swing of his lantern. His humming echoed in the next chamber. I could ask him to help me get Gideon through the narrow opening, but I already felt like a burden he didn't want to deal with.

"I'm sorry," Gideon said, the words an airy warmth against my cheek. "You don't have to do this."

I hadn't planned to talk to Gideon until we were out of the damned caves and maybe not even then, maybe never, but his words triggered a burst of anger that made me hot from head to foot. "Oh yes?" I snapped. "And what should I do instead? Leave you here? Good. Excellent. I hadn't thought of that, what a grand idea."

The ground shook. A distant roar stampeded toward us like a galloping herd. Lightning cracks echoed, and the shaking became more violent, sending us stumbling back from the opening. Ahead, Jass shouted, but it was just useless noise beneath the rumble and crack of tumbling stone.

"Get down!" I shouted, pushing Gideon before me. He stumbled a few steps and fell as a fist-sized rock smacked into the ground near his feet. More came down around us. Fear spiked like cold knives, and I dragged Gideon into the arch between caves, stopping as a waterfall of dirt poured from the ceiling in the hollow behind us.

"Shit!"

Still clutching the lantern, I threw myself on top of Gideon and curled over him as best I could, tensing. Small stones hit my back, nothing to the crack and roar of shifting rock that lasted both a heartbeat and an eternity. Until slowly, it began to fade. The last stones to hit me bounced off, and I heard them fall. Heard Gideon's breath. Felt him alive beneath me though every breath tasted of dirt and dust.

I coughed, but it didn't help. Dirt seemed to clog my throat all the way down.

Somehow the silence was worse than the roar, every small, close sound serving only to intensify it. I lifted my head. My lantern lay half buried in the dirt slide, illuminating a thick curtain of golden dust filling the space. A small space, enclosed by a slope of dirt at one end and at the other by fallen stones. A large rock had wedged across the narrow arch between caves, protecting us from skulls full of rock. Although if we couldn't get out, dying slowly from thirst or hunger or both was unlikely to be an improvement.

I swallowed a shard of panic and took a deep breath, trying to stay calm. Gideon hadn't moved. I rolled him over. "Are you all right?"

"Great," he croaked, punctuating it with a cough. "Is that daylight?"

I looked up and gasped as a sharp and increasingly familiar pain stabbed into my ear.

"Rah?"

With a hand to my head, I examined our new ceiling. There did seem to be a glimmer of daylight above. Too far to reach, even with the right tools.

"Rah?"

"I'm fine." I dropped my hand. The pain in my ear subsided to a mere constant ache.

Carefully I got to my feet, dirt sliding off my back. Three strides took me to the lantern and I pulled it out, blowing dirt off the glass and cleaning it with my sleeve. Anything rather than look at Gideon.

Despite his silence, I was sure he was watching me.

I looked back up at the glimmer of daylight overhead, that tiny hole the only ingress of air into our small, dirt-filled hollow. "Well, we're fucked," I said, kicking away some dirt at the base of the slope. More slid to take its place. "There's no saying how much rock is between us and a way out."

I thought of Jass and then very deliberately stopped thinking about Jass. Most of the cave-in seemed to be behind us, but perhaps that was just wishful thinking.

Gideon sat up, one arm curled around a bent knee, the other stretching and bunching fingers in the soft dirt beside him.

"At least we have some food and water." I patted the small satchel I'd been carrying and silently thanked Dishiva for her foresight. "So we can live longer and not miss a second of this thrilling stuck-under-a-mountain-of-rock experience—"

"Rah."

"—although it will mostly be just sitting in the dark once the lantern burns out. But maybe we'll be lucky—"

"Rah."

"—and the roof will collapse on us and end our suffering."

"Rah, I'm sorry."

I rounded on him. "Sorry for what? For killing Yitti? Or for killing Himi? Or is it Istet you're sorry about?"

He sucked a sharp breath and let it go, followed by another and another, beginning to tremble. *It wasn't really him*, I told myself. *It wasn't really him.* I ought to sit with him or apologise or do anything at all except stand and watch him suffer, but even when he gripped his hands together so tightly his fingers turned white, I didn't move. All I wanted to do was shout. He had been willing to do anything to achieve his ends. This had only happened because the cost had always been too high.

It wasn't really him.

I backed against the opposite wall and slid slowly to the floor, our feet barely a pace apart. Being present was the best I could do.

While tears leaked silently from his eyes, I concentrated on my own breathing, seeking to keep down my panic. Perhaps we would be able to dig our way out. Perhaps Jass would get help.

I risked another look at Gideon, scrunched into a ball and shaking. It was like looking at a different man. My Gideon was bold and sure, expressive and capable, my First Sword, my idol. This Gideon was a mess.

But he's still your Gideon, a traitorous part of me said, and trying not to think about Yitti and all the Swords I had failed time and again, I shuffled over to him. I had no comforting words, but I had an arm I could lay over his shoulders as he had once done to me.

Gideon leaned away with a wet sob, but I held him in place, wrapping my other arm around his chest and locking my hands together. Habit took me the next step, sitting my chin on his shoulder, my nose finding its old place pressed to the side of his head. We'd spent long evenings sitting so around campfires back home, the jut of my throat against the curve of his shoulder—two shapes that did not fit and yet felt so right.

I ought to have pulled away but didn't. He smelled of dirt and blood and sweat like he might have done after a hunt, and for a moment we were home on the plains waiting for the cooling winds of the Eastbore to roll in. When they came, we would strip off our tunics and let it chill the sweat from our skin, before tying up our sacks of meat and riding back to the herd. But we weren't home. We were stuck beneath the ground outside a Kisian city, far from where I'd planned to die.

"Do you remember the day you taught me how to skin?" I said, speaking to the side of his head, prickly with short regrowth. "We rode so far from camp that I worried you'd gotten lost." I breathed a laugh. "But you had thought far enough ahead and found a nearby waterhole for when it got messy. Enthusiastic, I think you called my knife skills at the time. It had been such a hot summer, I don't think you even tried to persuade me not to jump in, did you?"

We had stayed all afternoon, splashing each other and sitting in the water, able to talk and laugh and just be in a way that wasn't always possible when constrained by responsibilities. At the time I hadn't considered I could have learned to skin in camp, that it had not been his responsibility to teach me, that it was yet another occasion Gideon had gone out of his way for me. And even now as I considered it for the first time, Gideon trembling in my arms, I told myself it was just how we had always been, nothing more. He'd made an impulsive young man's promise to my dying mother to look after me. It hadn't been his job, and no one would have held him to it, but he had.

Because he loves you! Sett had spat the words at me back in Mei'lian, and I had been avoiding thinking about them since. Love meant a lot of things in a herd.

"You weren't a very good swimming teacher though," I went on, because continued avoidance of difficult topics seemed safest. "You wouldn't even get in the water that summer we spent with the Sheth. I know you said you didn't like their games, but it was because you liked to be the best at everything, wasn't it?"

Gideon didn't answer. He was still shaking, but his breathing had eased to a more natural pace. I reached for the water skin Dishiva had packed. "Here, you might feel better."

Yes, because a drink of water could absolutely help wash away feelings of guilt, I thought, and immediately chided myself. It hadn't been him. But I had been me when I had given Sett his death sentence. Did Gideon know? He must; there had been so many witnesses.

He took the water skin but didn't pull the stopper. "Not because I wanted to be the best," he said, making no effort to free himself from my hold. "Because you were having plenty of fun without me."

A more pathetic admission had probably never passed his lips, and for a stunned moment I couldn't accept that confident, glorious Gideon had ever thought it, let alone believed it.

"That Sheth girl was very pretty," he went on, still not moving. "What was her name again?"

"I don't remember."

He pulled the stopper. It took three goes to get it loose, but at last he managed and tipped the skin to his lips before handing it back to me. I'd thought to save my first sip until later, to stretch the water supply, but suddenly my mouth had never felt more dry.

I let him go and took a sip.

"Lahta," Gideon said abruptly. "Her name was Lahta."

I got up and strode the length of our tiny prison before spinning back to face him. "Why? Why does it matter? That was… ten cycles back. More!" I turned on the rocks piled between us and freedom. "What the fuck are we just sitting here for anyway?"

I dropped to my knees and, fuelled by a furious energy, began picking up rocks and throwing them aside. The rockslide was full of sharp edges, but I kept digging, dirt clogging my fingernails and stones scraping my palms. My fingers soon ached from being jammed into the pile, like the sheer force of my desperation would get us out of there.

After a time, Gideon took off his crimson surcoat and joined me. He knelt an arm's length away and pulled stones off the pile, his movements so slow and disinterested it was all I could do not to shout at him again. He was exhausted. He needed rest and care. He would get neither if we died here.

"Don't you want to get out of here?" I snapped when he took a particularly long time between lifting one stone and throwing it onto the pile we were building.

"Not really."

The unexpected answer drew my attention. "What?"

His gaze didn't shy away, his dark-ringed eyes full of fatigue and hurt and a frightening determination. "It would be easier not to, don't you think?" He picked up another rock and threw it aside. "You think you're hurting. You have no idea what it even means."

My heart felt too constricted to beat anymore. "I'm...I'm sorry about Sett," I said, the words the most useless things I'd ever spoken.

"Me too."

Gideon didn't look up, just set another rock aside, his fingers trembling. I had expected him to let his anger out on me as I had with him, but he just slowly moved rock after rock like he hadn't heard.

You think you're hurting. You have no idea what it even means.

With every rock I moved, more dirt and stones cascaded to take its place, a never-ending barrier between us and freedom. If any freedom existed on the other side at all.

When my fingers began to cramp, I sat back, stretching them with a frustrated growl. The ache in my ear had remained throughout, and I wondered if it was possible for a body to fall apart from misuse.

Gideon stopped too, but I worked my fingers and forearms like he wasn't there, bending and stretching and rubbing my tense limbs.

"Here."

He held out a hand. He'd never asked before, always just started working my muscles, but nothing was ever going to be the same again.

"I'm fine," I said, and he lowered his hand with a twitch-like shrug.

I kept pressing my thumbs hard into my forearms, annoyed by how skilled I knew Gideon was. Somehow I managed to hate myself as much for wanting him to offer again as for being angry he had offered at all. None of my thoughts were fair or kind, but I couldn't help what spewed from my heart. Even my own guilt over Sett could not detract from what he had done.

While I eased my tight muscles, I listened to the increasing pace of his breathing, to the rasp as it quickened, leaving him no air in his lungs. It sounded like it hurt, like he couldn't long keep it up, and fighting against the angry belief he deserved it, I went to him.

"Here," I said, gripping his shoulders. "Breathe with—hey!"

He pulled away, gasping as he scrambled across the rock floor.

"I'm trying to help you," I snapped, shuffling forward. "Just come—"

Both hands to my chest, he thrust me back with more strength than I had thought he possessed. "Don't. Want," he said, each word a ragged gasp as he pressed his hands against his chest. "Don't."

"I don't give a single horseshit what you want, you need to breathe."

I moved forward only to be thrust back again with a strangled, desperate wail. He scrambled toward the rockfall like a frightened animal, chest jerking with every rapid emptying of his lungs. "Don't. Want. You."

"Well, I'm sorry, but none of your new friends are available so you're stuck with me."

Poor choice of words, but he rolled onto his knees and elbows and rasped, and hoping he had worn himself out, I shuffled closer. If I could hold him against me, encourage him to breathe, he might calm down, but at the first sound of movement he sat up. "Let. Me." He crossed his arms over his stomach. "Let. Me. Go."

"Gideon, please." Moving fast, I gripped his face before he could pull away. "Gideon. It's me. I'm here. I came for you. Now please, just breathe with me. You're going to be all right."

He yanked out of my hold and swung his fist at my head. A Gideon at full strength could have knocked me flat on my back, but he was weak and clumsy and I dodged. Only for his left to crunch into my cheek. I fell back, pain splitting through my ear again, and for a moment I was back in Mei'lian with Sett pounding my face. But Gideon didn't hit me again. He drew back and lay on the rough stone floor, wheezing.

His panic seemed to be easing, his breaths taking longer to draw and release, so I lay where I was and hoped my own slow breaths might carry away the pain stabbing deep in my ear. It didn't help.

Slowly, peace returned, the pair of us lying in the dirt, focussing on the rise and fall of our chests. I dared not move, as much out of fear it would set him off again as it would make my ear worse. This was not a good time. It was never a good time for debilitating pain, but if there could be a time that was even less a good time than usual, it was this fucking time. If I didn't get up and dig, we were dead.

Gideon shifted, fabric catching on the rough stone. Something moved at my hip and I opened my eyes as he drew my knife from its scabbard. Panic launched me from the ground, but it wasn't my throat he sought. He pressed it to his own, a strangled cry all I could achieve as I gripped his arm and his hand. Blood rose beneath the knife edge, running down the blade to the hilt and onto our fingers. He roared, trying to wrench away, and with nothing but fear filling my body to bursting, I slammed my boot into his shin.

The shock loosened his grip, and caring nothing for the sharp edge of the blade I yanked it from his hand. He lunged after it with a hoarse, heartbreaking wail only to lose his footing and fall. Upon hands and knees he gasped, blood dripping from his neck.

"Shit, Gideon!" I dropped beside him as he tried to rise, but his knees gave way and he stumbled into me, still grabbing for the blade in my hand. I slid it clattering away across the ground. "Stop, please!" I begged, trying to see how much damage he'd done, but he wouldn't be still. He sprang after the knife, and with my ear screeching its pain, I leapt after him. We crashed onto the rock-strewn floor in a tangle of thrashing limbs and blood and I might have been his worst enemy by how hard he fought.

Instinct and desperation were all I had as I gritted my teeth and pinned him down, grateful for his weakened state. Knee in his back, I held his arms and waited for him to stop thrashing. Eventually he stopped, the movement of his back rising and falling with his breath the only sign he was still alive. I dared not let go yet, afraid he would go for the knife again, but if I didn't look at the wound in his neck soon, it wouldn't matter.

"Just let me die, Rah," he said, cheek pressed to the stone floor, his eyes closed. "Just let me go."

"No. I did not come all the way back here for you to give up."

"I deserve it."

I'd condemned Sett for less, but I had already mourned Gideon once. I refused to do it again. "No."

"Please. You could do it. It's the fate a horse whisperer would give me."

I dropped my forehead between his shoulder blades. "No. If they knew everything they wouldn't. And I won't. I'm too selfish."

A sob shook his body, but it was a weak thing, quiet and broken. "This isn't going to get any better," he whispered.

I had thought the same after leaving Whisperer Jinnit. The shame had been so heavy that I'd almost walked alone out into the wild plains to let the gods punish me. But every day the weight had grown more bearable. Never gone, never forgotten, but I had grown the strength to carry it with me and still move.

"That's not true," I said, still resting my head upon his back. "It will. It will, and I'm not going anywhere. Sorry, Idi, you're stuck with me."

His tears ran onto the stones. "It's been a long time since you called me that."

"I guess we haven't been close for a long time, you know, even before all this shit. But you're not getting rid of me so easily. Can I look at that wound now without being punched in the face?"

"It's fine."

"Let me see it."

"Can't while you're sitting on me."

"All right, I'm going to let you go, but if you fucking fight me again, I'm going to…make rope out of fucking dirt or something, I don't know, just don't do it. I'm tired."

I let his arms go and eased myself off his back. With a groan of effort, Gideon rolled over, having the audacity to look anxiously at me. "Are you all right?"

"I'm fine, absolutely fucking grand," I said, lowering the hand I'd pressed to my ear. "Stuck under the ground and probably going to starve to death, but never been better."

"You're shit at this."

"Having to stop you trying to kill yourself was not part of my training."

He looked away. "Then your teacher had poor foresight."

"Most of the time you were my teacher."

"Yes. I know. That was the joke."

"Ha ha. Now lift your chin and stay still."

Thankfully he seemed to have given up and tilted his head back, exposing the cut in his neck. Blood smeared his skin down to his collarbone and the cut had a ragged edge, but it wasn't deep enough to have done real damage. I let out a long breath. "Thank the gods," I said. "It's not too deep. I'll bind it up as best I can, but I'm no—" I almost said Yitti's name. "Tep," I finished instead, hoping he wouldn't notice the slight pause or the sudden speeding of my heartbeat. "It won't be anywhere near as good."

I stretched over to grab the crimson sash Gideon had dropped with his surcoat. Silk probably wasn't the best material for this, but it wasn't like we had a lot of options. I held it out, waiting for him to lift his head. He did so with a pained hiss and let me slide the sash beneath his neck. It was a long piece of material, but all it needed to do was put pressure on the cut, so I tied a simple knot. "You're tying a red bow around my neck?"

"Damn right I am," I said, not slowing my task. "If you didn't want a red bow you shouldn't have cut yourself."

He rolled his head and shot me a weary look. "Right. I'll remember for next time."

"Good." I tugged the knot tight enough to maintain pressure, checking he had enough breathing room with two fingers slid beneath the fabric. "And in the meantime, you look very pretty."

With the makeshift bandage tied, I rolled onto my back beside him and waited while the initial throb of pain in my ear died to what had become its interminable sharp presence. Thankfully, he didn't take the opportunity to jump up in search of my discarded blade. We might have been stuck under the ground with no way of getting out, but at least for the next few minutes I didn't have to move.

Gideon rolled his head to look at me. "I'm sorry."

"Don't be." Keeping my head turned to look at him made my pain worse, but I couldn't bring myself to look away when I could grit my teeth and be there for him. "I get it. I mean, I don't get it, but I get it."

"Did I already tell you you're shit at this?" A tired smile twitched his lips. I couldn't help but smile back.

"You did, but by all means tell me again."

I looked back up at the shadows dancing on the stone above us, and as I breathed through the stab of pain that came with moving my head now, wondered distantly how much longer the lantern would stay lit.

"You're hurt. Did I—?"

"I'm fine," I said.

I could feel him looking at me.

"I'm fine," I repeated. "You didn't hurt me."

"You're also a shit liar."

"Fine, I'm in pain but it's not your fault and there's nothing you can do, so can we just not talk about it?"

His hair scraped the stone as he turned away. "Sure. Let's talk about the weather. It's quite cold in here for this time of year. I wonder if it will rain."

"My ear hurts, all right? Yes, it sounds stupid, but that's what it is."

He turned back. "It doesn't sound stupid. Which ear?"

I pointed at my right. "It's like someone is sticking a knife in there. This isn't the first time, but I've got no idea what starts it or what I can do to get rid of it. Nothing seems to help except putting up with it or sleeping it off."

It was so easy to fall back into the old habit of talking to him like we were friends, like nothing had changed. But we weren't, and it had.

"Can I help?"

"No," I said. "It's fine. I'll just lie here until it fades off a bit, then we should keep digging."

"Do you really think there's any point?"

I looked around at our stone prison, a spike of panic thrust aside the moment it appeared. "I don't know, but I'm going to try anyway."

We lay for a while without speaking, the silence of our stone tomb seeming to press in upon us. Overhead the tiny hole leading to the outside world still owned the bright light of day.

"When did the pain start?" After the long silence it was almost strange to hear his voice again, disembodied in the small space.

"This time or the first time?"

"Either. Both."

"After the rocks came down. And I don't know." That was a lie, but "after your brother pummelled my face into the road" wasn't the wisest response right now. Everything was fine while our conversation held to a thin crust of friendly topics, everything beneath it too raw to risk.

He made a little sound I knew well, like a small click of his tongue and a *hmpf* of air. He knew I was lying, but he didn't ask again.

Breathing deeply in and out, the pain slowly became a more manageable ache, and I gingerly sat up. "I wish I knew what the fuck it was," I muttered, every part of me exhausted just looking at the mountain of rock we still needed to move.

Gideon shifted beside me and the water skin appeared before my face. "Some water might help."

He hadn't gone for the blade, but he was pale and looked exhausted, and the hand holding the water skin shook. I took it and, pulling the stopper, wet my lips while he looked in the satchel.

"Perhaps something to eat too." He pulled out a thick patty of browned rice. "Here."

I took it, watching him. At a quick glance I would have said he was unchanged from the man I had last seen sitting on the throne in Mei'lian, but although he stood as tall and as broad, there was something fragile in his stance, something unsure and curled in. He watched me in return, eyes bright though they sat in deep pits.

"I'll eat this if you eat one too," I said, nodding at the rice patty. "Otherwise I can wait."

He knew me well enough not to doubt my stubbornness, or that I would use his care of me against him if I had to. "All right," he said, taking another rice patty out of the bag and holding it up in salute. "May the gods watch over us."

It seemed unlikely so far from home, but I watched him take a bite rather than say so. The rice had a sweet tang, but every mouthful was an effort for my jaw, leaving me eating as slowly as he did. But it filled my stomach, and when we had finished, we each took a sip of water and lay down on the slope of dirt. I wanted to keep digging, but Gideon looked like he would collapse if he didn't rest.

"Do you remember that time you dropped a whole handful of pepper nuts into the stew pot?" I said, trying to keep his mind on good memories. We'd been tracking a herd of deer one winter, a group of assorted Swords under the command of Ekka, the old tracker of the First Swords. It had been as much hunt as training exercise for the new saddleboys and girls. Gideon had been there to help, and had been put in charge of cooking the first night.

Beside me, Gideon chuckled softly. "Good, cleansing food."

"Cleansing! Yes, my nose was dripping for hours. And Lamh cried."

"Very cleansing."

A laugh bubbled up through all the fear and grief and shook my body intensely. Once I'd started it was hard to stop. "You laugh," Gideon said. "But Ekka said it was a very remarkable dish, remember?"

"And with such a straight face."

"He was crying too."

Tears had leaked silently from his eyes as he chewed a mouthful. Tears sprang from mine now as I laughed, knowing there was a deep sadness beneath the joy for all we had lost. Gideon's laughter was a quiet, exhausted thing, all breath.

"He wouldn't let me near the spice pouch again," he said. "He gave it to one of the saddleboys to look after."

Still I laughed, unable to stop now I had started, but I thought of Juta and Iya and Fessel, cooking for us because Swords did not cook for themselves. There was so much I wanted to say, so much I wanted to talk about. There had been a time when we had shared deep conversations about tenets and gods and herd plans, but nothing was safe now. Memories were all we had.

"I remember thinking how horrified the cooks would have been," I said. "But Ekka told them the food had been delightful. Tihum snorted, do you remember? I don't know how you managed to look so innocent."

Gideon didn't answer, and I turned my head in the dirt to look at him. His eyes were closed, but he opened heavy lids and quirked a sleepy half smile. If I ignored the blood-soaked sash around his neck, his pale, drawn face, and the deep rings around his eyes, he could have been my old Gideon, the pair of us having stayed up late to lie beneath the stars and talk about everything and nothing. Perhaps if I kept talking, he would fall asleep.

"I laugh, but I tried it again once when I had a blocked nose," I said. "I don't think I ever told you. We'd...grown apart a bit by then, or whatever happened. Either way, I snuck a full pinch into a bowl of soup and can confidently say it cleaned me out for a few hours. I only did it once though. I don't know if you've ever had pepper nut on your hands and rubbed your eyes, but it's...not good."

He gave no sign of hearing me, but I kept talking. "I had to use half my day's water ration to clean it out, and it still burned for hours. Captain Tallus said it looked like I'd been stung by wasps."

Gideon's eyes remained closed, and his chest rose and fell gently. I heaved a sigh. Exhaustion lived in my bones these days, but though I could have slept, what purpose was there in being well rested, only to soon be dead? At least with Gideon asleep I could dig without worrying about him. Much.

I waited a few long minutes, watching the rise and fall of his chest and the flicker and twitch of his eyelids until I was sure moving would not wake him. No fresh blood had escaped beneath his makeshift bandage, and thrusting aside fears he had already lost too much, I rolled away and got to my feet.

My knees protested against more kneeling on stone, but I settled in front of the rockfall and dug. Stones, handfuls of dirt, large rocks I needed both hands to shift—I moved them all, only for more to replace them in a never-ending face of earth. But like I had often found at times when many heads needed to be cut, there was peace in mindless activity. I dug, barely thinking at all, just seeing the next stones and moving them like I was a physical force more than a flesh-and-blood man.

When my forearms and fingers began to ache, I stopped to stretch them and check on Gideon. He had rolled onto his side but was still asleep, his brows contracted into a troubled frown. I wondered what he was dreaming about and how he would be when he woke. I wasn't sure I had the physical strength left to fight him again.

I kept digging. Time meant nothing. There were just rocks and dirt and aching hands and stinging knees and the smell of damp earth stuck so far up my nose it might never come out.

The lantern began to splutter. It had possessed enough oil for hours, but it seemed those hours were almost up. I ought to have been more afraid. Overhead, the hole in the ceiling had grown dark.

I dug until the lantern's sputters became frequent. Stretching, I got up to check on Gideon once more, to remind myself he was there, that he was all right, that I had come back for him like I'd said I would. Whatever dream he'd been having seemed to have passed, his breathing so shallow now I had to bend close to be sure he breathed at all. But whatever the ravages apparent on his face, he was still warm and vital, his breath a soft dance of life across my fingers.

I had just returned to the rockfall when the lantern died. Darkness swallowed me, its silence seeming deeper as though the light had roared. I reached out, comforted by the feel of the rocks, by the knowledge that nothing had ceased to exist because I couldn't see it.

I wished I could hear Gideon breathing.

The rocks and dirt clattered upon the floor as I started digging again. My fingers were almost numb from the work, their tips cut and bruised. One might have been bleeding, but apart from a sense of damp warmth it was impossible to be sure. It didn't matter. I needed to dig. Every time I considered stopping to rest, I thought of the tiny stone space, of the half-empty water skin, of the prospect of dying here in the dark. Of Gideon. I could give up on my life, but never on his. We had eaten rice patties together because he had wanted to take care of me and I had wanted to take care of him, not because we cared for ourselves. The realisation left me breathless and I shied away from considering it further, the space beyond that thought intense and frightening. Better to dig and not think than risk thoughts I could not draw back from.

A distant clatter echoed near my hand. Followed by a whisper. I shook my head and kept plunging my fingers into the rockfall and dragging free stones and dirt. Gideon moved in his sleep as, far away, someone shouted. I blinked, wondering if I had fallen asleep. Perhaps I was just dreaming about digging because digging was all I had now.

I kept working, accompanied by the clatter and scrape of distant sounds. I understood none of it until someone said, "It can't be much farther; this is the way to the next cave."

Jass. That was Jass's voice. Jass and replies in Kisian. Jass and the sound of digging and shifting rocks. The realisation crept upon me, tingling my skin from my toes to my scalp. Jass was close by. He was coming.

"Hey!" I shouted to the stones. "Hey! Jass! Jass!"

"Rah?" Movement and excited gabble followed. "Rah, are you all right?"

"Fine, just trapped," I called back, tearing rocks away now. They had to be close. We were going to get out of this. We were going to live.

"We're coming, just hold on a little longer."

Afraid I was hallucinating, I kept digging, listening to the scrape of shovels and willing them not to vanish like the echoes of a cruel ghost. They got closer and closer, clawing at the walls.

Light pierced the stones, pouring through the first small hole. Voices followed. More light as rocks and dirt were pulled away, and I flinched back, the brightness an assault on my eyes.

"Rah." A hand touched my arm. Voices milled. Footsteps. They had come. It was real. We were going to get out of here. Tears rolled down my cheeks in relief I couldn't voice.

Then Gideon cried out.

The footsteps stormed around me. Lanterns flashed, but I forced my aching eyes open. A pair of Kisian soldiers had hauled Gideon to his feet, his eyes bleary and disoriented from sleep. "Emperor Gideon e'Torin," one said. I didn't know the rest of the words, but they were harsh and clipped in anger. I hunted Jass in the milling bodies as the men dragged Gideon toward the hole I'd dug in the rockfall. Toward what moments ago I'd thought of as freedom.

"Rah." Panic and confusion filled his voice as he was carried past. "Rah!"

The scuffle of footsteps faded as they moved into the next cave, leaving me blinking rapidly in the light. Alone.

27. DISHIVA

I opened my eyes. Opened them again. Tried to blink the darkness away and remembered what had happened, slowly, like rising from warm water into cold air that nipped at my skin and made
my bones ache.

Every part of me hurt.

I parted my lips and managed a breathy groan. There was weight
on my face. A tightness around my head. My hand found fabric.

"You've lost an eye," said a familiar voice, calm and motherly
yet far from the one I wanted to hear. Whisperer Ezma cleared her
throat. "And the cut across your nose is deep, but has been stitched.
The other eye is scarred but should heal."

"Great." The word rasped and I cleared my throat. "Sichi?
Nuru?"

"Fine."

"Leo?"

"Gone."

I could still feel the floor cracking beneath me. Falling away. His
shocked cry dropping into dust. "Dead?"

"We found no body, and a number of Levanti are missing. No
doubt these things are connected."

"Missing?"

"We don't know what happened. Everything was rather chaotic."

I groaned, trying to make sense of her words. "Where am I?"

Fabric rustled as she moved. Closer. I wished I could shift back, but even a twitch of muscle ached. "You're in a house in Kogahaera, along with the other injured Levanti who are still with us. As I understand it, a rock hit the tower beneath you, taking out a corner of stonework and ripping a hole in the floor. You fell through it."

I remembered falling, but not landing, not hitting anything hard on the way down. My body remembered though, every inch of me bruised.

"The wreckage was searched, but no Leo Villius. His followers are saying he has been renewed by God."

I patted the bandages, relieved to see a shift in the darkness above my left eye. I didn't want to touch the other.

"Dishiva." Ezma's tone was urgent. Low. Ill-ease broke through my lassitude. "This has happened for a reason."

"For a reason—?" I bit off the sudden flare of anger so hard my teeth clacked.

"Yes," the horse whisperer said, her caressing voice too close. "Because you are special, Dishiva. Because you are here for a purpose. We are all a part of God's purpose, but you...I have been waiting ten years for you."

I could see nothing, yet the room spun around me, such an odd sense of displacement that I doubted I could reach out and touch anything solid. If not for the pain, I would have been sure I was dreaming.

"I don't understand," I said, the thud of my heart uncomfortably loud within my darkness. There were little sounds of movement and murmuring around me to prove we weren't alone, but the way she shuffled closer made me feel all the more isolated.

"You are the one they call Veld, Dishiva, not Dom Leo Villius, whatever he might claim to the contrary. You."

They were ridiculous words. "That," I said, trying to maintain an even voice, "makes no sense. I am not even a believer. I was only given this position because he wanted to punish me. And besides, Veld dies and lives again, and I've seen him do it. I've seen him die twice and come back." My words became a desperate hiss. "I have no such pact with a god."

"You don't need one. The original translation doesn't specify death in its true, bodily sense, but in the way a heart breaks and one dies inside. Suffers. Hurts."

Almost I tore the bandage from my face, sure I could rip away the darkness and everything would be back to normal. But there was just nothingness and her voice, pressing in on me like a suffocating weight.

"You don't believe me."

"Of course I don't believe you, it's ridiculous. If he's not Veld, why does he keep coming back?"

"I don't know. I've been trying to figure that out, but the information is vague and unhelpful. Yet I know he is not the one I've been waiting for. You are."

"I am not even Chiltaen."

"Nor is the faith. There are many passages proving Veld is Levanti. 'Wide-open plains.' 'On thunder of hooves.' 'Painted dedication to God upon their skin.' None of those could possibly refer to a Chiltaen cleric now, could they? And yet they are in the original book. Not the Chiltaen one of course. They changed and adapted what they didn't like. They were even so set on Veld being a man they mistranslated the leader with two voices. *Nyan* means male leader, but the faith does not allow for men to couple, which meant Veld was a woman, all well and good where the faith originated but unthinkable here where women are not highly valued."

They were all words I knew, but none of them fit into my mind, half sticking only for the rest to tumble out.

"A Levanti," was all I managed to say.

"A Levanti," she repeated. "A woman. One 'chosen to protect, whose *single vision* will build an empire.' You are already Defender of the One True God. Chosen to protect. Your body and soul sacred in the eyes of God. So, you see why I say this happened for a reason."

"No."

She shifted on the mat beside me, pressing ever closer with her voice and her scent. "Yes, Dishiva. Your fate is hundreds of years written and cannot be denied now. You are the one who will build a holy empire from ashes."

"No."

A gulf of silence sucked at my thoughts, and I had the urge to scream until she went away, scream at the world for having brought me to this place. I pulled at the bandage, linen unravelling. It stuck to some skin and drying poultice, but I ripped it free, blinking at the sudden ingress of light through the crusted lids of my left eye. She appeared, a blur owning vague disapproval. It sharpened as I blinked and forced myself to focus, unable to shift the thin film of rain behind which she sat.

"That was not wise," she said.

"What do you want?"

"What is meant to be."

"And what do you get out of that?"

Even blurry, the look she gave me was condescending, and I felt like dirt beneath her feet. "You will understand one day, Dishiva. Your time is coming."

"Horseshit."

"It has been written."

"So what? I could write your death now and it wouldn't change anything, it's just words on a page."

"The words of a prophet."

All the thoughts crowding my head had grown sharp edges,

jostling about and cutting each other and me with the anger that had shaped them. *Prophet.* The term sounded so wrong on her tongue. We used it for forecasting spring rains and the routes different herds used to cross the plains, not for the futures of individuals. Or gods. Or empires.

Ezma reached for my hand. Her grip was strong, and I was too stunned to pull away. "It is for the best you know the truth now. You can accept your fate. Make peace with it. Be grateful."

"Grateful."

"It is an honour to be a chosen. To be the one with single vision is the greatest honour of all."

Grateful, for pain and loss. For having my once steady sense of self stripped away piece by piece. For being the chosen instrument of a God I didn't want to serve.

Bile washed around the sharp-edged thoughts in my mouth, consuming them into angry words. I wanted to spit them all at her, but they owned vulnerable parts of my soul. What right did she have to my pain?

"Dishiva—"

"No," I said again. "I don't care what you think is going to happen, or what some long-dead man who drank too much wrote down. I am the only one who makes decisions about my life, and while there are many things I can imagine myself doing, building an empire is not one of them. Take your holy writings and scrunch them up for tinder. Your god will get nothing from me and neither will you."

"You are being narrow-minded and stubborn to your own detriment, Dishiva," she snapped. "To all our detriment. You sided with Gideon because he promised to build something you wanted, but now that you have the chance to build it you refuse to even listen?"

"Get out." My whole body felt hot with a rage and disappointment and hurt as I thought of everything Rah had told me about her, about what had been happening back home. "Get away from me or I will scream until someone throws you out."

Ezma let my arm go. "We will talk again soon," she said, stiffly calm. "For now, you should rest. Remember, whatever our pain, whatever our suffering, everything happens for a reason. Trust in that."

When she was gone, I wanted her to return so I could vent more of the fury dammed inside me. Propped upon hard cushions, I stared straight ahead, trying to make sense of the sounds and the shapes and the blur of shifting light while I worked my stiff fingers until I could close them to an aching fist.

"Everything happens for a reason." The insidious words ate at my mind, rubbing ragged against the Levanti belief that prophecy was only a guess, a likely outcome, that no matter how much one knew about rainfall patterns and the contour of the hills, the plains had an element that was ever-unknowable. As did life.

"Everything happens for a reason."

I was still opening and closing my fists when hurried footsteps approached and a familiar outline appeared. One far more welcome than Ezma's. Relief spilled through me, burbling through my lips on a sob.

"Dishiva! Shit, what happened? Are you—? Do you need—?" Jass looked around at the second person who'd followed.

"You've made a mess of my bandage, I see," they said. "Let me—"

"I want to be able to see."

The unknown newcomer shuffled. "Your eye—"

"I know it's gone. I mean I want to be able to see without this one being covered. Go away. No, come back. Tor. Tor e'Torin. Is he around anywhere?"

I didn't need clear vision to know the two men looked at one another. "He should be," Jass said at last. "He arrived with the empress's army. Why?"

"The book. I need...I need to ask him something important. Can you fetch him? He'll come if you tell him I'm here. I know he will."

A little snort of annoyance followed a murmured discussion, and the second man departed, leaving Jass standing beside me. With a pained grunt of effort, he lowered himself onto my mat, my first breath of him a mix of dirt and sweat.

"I saw the tower come down," I said. "I thought I'd lost you."

Easier to speak about that pain than the one curdling in my chest.

"I thought so too." He grimaced, but I couldn't make out the way his brow usually crinkled, and the hurt I harboured soured all the more. "And I did lose Rah and Gideon for a while. We had to dig them out. They were...very lucky, really. The way the rocks fell left them with a hollow, and they had food and water, but... well, I was worried. Whatever I might think about Gideon, no Levanti deserves that end."

He told me how the cave had collapsed, how he had dug himself a way out and run to the Kisian camp for help. I listened and sipped metallic water from the edge of a thin bowl, mind full of the questions I had for Tor.

The young Torin soon arrived, his all too vague outline approaching to join us.

"Captain Dishiva," he said as he saluted. "I'm sorry I could not get more information to you sooner. About the book, I mean. Everything got quite...complicated there for a while."

"I don't think it's likely to get any less complicated for some time," I returned. "But I didn't ask you to come to berate you. I have...some questions. But first, did you find out more? About Veld and how he...died?"

"I did." He knelt beside my mat, leaving Jass to hover. "You already knew about the cave—that was the last one I had when you…" He trailed off rather than specify the circumstances under which I had visited the deserter camp. "Well, the one after that took me some time to figure out, but it best translates as 'stabbed in the back by an empress.'"

I closed my good eye and, tipping my head back against the wall, laughed. It was all I could do, all it made sense to do, when it was already far too late. When we had, once again, helped him, having set out to hinder.

"You've already done that," Tor said, and it wasn't a question, but I nodded anyway, my stomach hurting from the laughter. My eyes stung as tears tried to fall.

No wonder that Leo had been so happy. He was playing with me. I had to think of it like that, not let myself fall into Ezma's belief that everything happened for a reason, that I was merely living out the words of a prophet, had to hold to the Levanti understanding there was no such thing as prophecy, only a likely outcome of events. An outcome I could change.

"Tell me about Veld," I said. "About the holy empire. What is it? How does he build it?"

Tor shifted his weight, fabric rustling at my side. "It's complicated, and honestly none of it makes a lot of sense. I may just be translating it poorly, but the book seems to…disagree with itself quite often. Often enough that I think it can't just be my translation at fault."

"What does it say?"

"That Veld is disbelieved and maligned, even by his own people. Yet is also revered. That he is both a warrior and a peacemaker. That his empire is both the salvation of his people and their destruction. There is a whole section I only skimmed through about where he was born and how he earned his name, but most of it isn't that detailed."

He shifted his weight. It sounded like it had nothing to do with me, but Ezma had spoken of a different translation, of a version of the book that wasn't Chiltaen. She had spoken with such belief, but if there was one thing I had learned, it was that belief was all too easily fashioned out of desperation.

"*I have been waiting ten years for you,*" she had said.

Desperation for purpose. For a belief that fit her view of the world. For a Levanti holy leader. A woman. It was only a wonder she hadn't twisted the details to fit herself.

"Why do you ask about it, Captain?" Tor said.

"Just…something someone said to me. Thank you, Tor, you've set my mind at ease. I'm sorry to have taken up your time."

"Whisperer Ezma, I assume, but no need to thank me, Captain, I'm glad to have been of use. Sorry I didn't get the information about Veld's next death to you in time to…stop it."

I turned my head, centring his blurred outline. "What comes next? After being stabbed in the back by an empress?"

"He gets betrayed, and then sacrificed by himself," he said. "Though I'm not sure how getting betrayed kills him. It also says that the foundation of Veld's holy empire is built on the death of a false high priest. I'm not really sure what that means either. Whisperer Ezma has a different copy of the book though, so if you have other questions it may be best to ask her."

"It is not a conversation I wish to have with her, so thank you, Tor. You've done a huge service to your people by translating that thing, and you ought to be proud, whatever anyone else might say."

He was silent a moment, before nodding. "Thank you, Captain."

With a scrape of his boot across the floor, he rose from my side, and lingering only to salute Jass and be saluted in return, the young man left.

I found I was clenching and unclenching my hands, taking a perverse sort of pleasure in the pain it wrought through my swollen, bruised fingers. Jass took Tor's place at my side, kneeling still and steady like a rock, and made no effort to stop me working my hands. He said nothing, just waited, and soon I found myself spilling all that had happened since we'd last parted in a tide of words. The defence, the Kisians arriving, Leo—all the way up to Ezma and her iron belief that I was Veld.

Jass listened, still and quiet, until I finished and he let out a puff of air. "Well, that's...a lot. Rah told me what she'd said about Leo and our herd masters, but I wasn't sure what to think of it all. But now, I—"

"It's true. It must be. It's the only thing that explains all this. She wants me to build a holy empire. She said this"—I pointed at my missing eye—"has happened for a reason."

"She would if she's trying to manipulate you into doing what she wants."

"Yes, but as much as it fills me with such fury to realise it, she's also right."

I could almost make out his sweet frown through the haze of my scarred eye. "What do you mean, she's right? Bad things don't happen for a reason, Dishiva. That isn't how the world works. You didn't do anything to deserve this, and anyone who says you did can—"

I squeezed his arm. "I know. But..." Missing Levanti, she had said. I had a hundred questions, but their answers were unlikely to change what I needed to do. "When we have a unique ability to help people, to change something for the better no matter how small, isn't it our responsibility to do it?"

"I don't understand."

"I'm going to ask you to do something you'll hate."

He snorted. "Wow, what a new idea. You've never done that before."

"No, this time you're *really* going to hate it."

28. CASSANDRA

The sense of owning a shell, of existing, grew upon me. A slow awakening.

Cassandra? Cass, is that you?

Hana. Her presence unsettled me, something so wrong in the sound of her words and the feel of her mind pressed against mine. We were looking up at a thick beam crossing the ceiling, dust dancing in the faint light. Nearby, voices mumbled in low conversation.

Did we... did I... die?

Everything slowly started to click into place. The sights and smells and sounds of the receiving room, the presence of the empress, and the comfort of a body not ill and in pain as Hana's had been.

Septum.

I'm sorry, I said. *Letting you go must have been a final stress we couldn't handle. There was nothing I could do.*

I had been too worn out to try, too connected to the failing body to feel anything but gratitude it would soon be over. Now my mind was bright and alive. I had been listening to Yakono. The empress's body must still be there, lying upon the mat against the wall. Had he noticed we'd stopped replying? Did he understand? Or care?

I knew it was coming, the empress said. *I knew, but... I thought I would... be there. At the end.*

Her grief was an odd, twisted thing, mourning the loss of her life though she still lived. It was like not having been present for the death of a loved one, except that loved one was her own body, a body she had thought of as so intrinsically herself.

Well, that's it, she said. *I knew I probably wasn't getting out of here, but now I can't. I'm... truly dead, aren't I?*

I wanted to comfort her, to tell her we'd find a way, but what way was there? My true body was still alive; I could hear its voice now, a voice I'd spoken with almost all my life, but even if Kaysa could pull me back inside, would there be room for Hana? Was that even possible? Surviving this had not been part of the plan, but that had felt acceptable while tired and trapped in her dying body. Now it was all wrong.

She must have caught that thought, for with the matter-of-factness of one trying not to dwell on something unpleasant, she said, *I suppose we had enough of a connection that you came to me when the... when my body died. I don't know how it works but lucky it did. Or you might have been...*

She didn't need to finish. I *had* died. I had felt the light and warmth leave my body, had felt myself drift away, fading to nothing to the sound of Yakono's voice.

I'm sorry I wasn't there.

No, I said, *don't be. I'm sorry it happened.*

This was more important.

Yes.

This. It was easy to forget we were inside another body, another mind, so completely did it feel like just the two of us.

I thought you said it was loud last time.

It was. Perhaps due to the proximity to another Leo, or the stress of the situation. This time has been quiet, like standing in an empty hall but... not alone, if that makes sense.

It did. She was here, but the feeling of... space was impossible to ignore. Not empty space, rather darkness full of people I couldn't see standing just out of reach.

Have you tried . . . communicating?

As subtly as I could to avoid detection, yes, but he feels very . . . cut off at the moment. We can move though, look.

One of my fingers lifted off the divan.

The plan had been to get into his head and learn to control him enough to kill Unus with these far stronger hands. We had expected the first part to be more difficult.

Perhaps it will get harder once Unus returns, I said. *Perhaps they're only really connected when at least one of them is nearby.*

You mean maybe Septum doesn't have the strength to link with the others over long distance on his own? That makes sense. He feels so weak. I've only seen a flicker or two to prove he's here at all.

Hurried footsteps hammered their way up the stairs. "Your Holiness? Your Holiness!"

"Dom Villius is out," Kaysa said, her voice drawing near. "What's the matter?"

"It's . . . it's Miss Marius, my lady. She . . . she's . . . I was just taking her food and tea, and she was just lying there, propped up against the wall, not moving and—"

"What?" Kaysa's voice cracked. "Dead? Are you sure?"

"Yes, my lady. I'm sorry, I—"

Rhythmic steps crossed the floor as Kaysa paced. "She can't be dead. I was just . . ." She breathed out shakily, and I'd never thought to hear such emotion in her voice at my passing. It felt wrong to be listening to it, for her to not know I was here, to let her bare her honest feelings in a way she would never have done had I been present.

Would I have been as moved by her loss? The question filled me with shame.

The maid sniffed.

"Calm," Kaysa said, hushing her like a mother calming an anxious child, and it was strange to hear such kind sounds coming from my mouth. "You did nothing wrong."

"No, my lady, but...well, His Holiness did say—"

"I'll tell him. You may go."

The woman sniffed again. "Thank you, my lady. But...what should we...do with her? She's just lying there and..."

"Lay the body out neatly for now. I'll...I'll be there soon."

"Yes, my lady, of course. His Holiness will want to perform the proper rites. Thank you, my lady."

Hana growled. That was her body. Her whole existence. She was an empress, a true daughter of the Otako line, and her body deserved to be honoured as such. Or at least given a proper Kisian burial.

Footsteps hurried away almost as quickly as they had come, leaving nothing but a humming silence and the pacing of Kaysa's steps.

She genuinely seems to care that you're gone, Hana said.

It's probably just shock.

Septum's eyes rolled. *You would say so. You know, you could...try to get her to take you back. Dying is very permanent. I have no choice now, already made my decision, but you...*

I made my decision too.

Yes, while constrained by pain and exhaustion. You're allowed to change your mind now you're not.

I didn't answer and she didn't go on, each of us trying to keep our thoughts to ourselves. She because she had her life to grieve, I because she was right. I did not want to die.

The slowing clop of hooves floated up through the open balcony doors. Kaysa stopped pacing, the room seeming to hum with the tension in her muscles. The time to change my mind had passed. Unus was coming. This was the only chance we would have to kill him and Duos together.

Footsteps approached. A voice. Definitely Leo, and yet the sense of empty space within Septum continued. No connection. No noise, just me and the empress and the empty sense of presence.

The door opened and a quick tread strode in. Halted.

"Unus?"

"Unfortunately for you, no," Leo said. A boot squeaked on the floor, and a gentle click heralded the door sliding closed. It took all our self-control not to look. "Doubly unfortunate. Dead, are they? A pity. They would have made it much easier to organise marriage with Empress Sichi, but no matter. I will make use of the other assassin and now have no reason to keep you alive."

"What?" she cried. "No!"

"I'm afraid without them you are quite useless, my dear. And in fact, given your expressed desire to help save Unus from me, you're dangerous. Safest dead."

"Unus! Unus, please!"

Scuffed steps backed across the floor, and we clenched Septum's hands into fists. Still no connection. Hana pushed gently at the edge of the nothingness. Unus was just there; we ought to have been able to connect. The distance had been greater at the Witchdoctor's house, yet there was nothing. We were still alone in our great empty cave.

I don't like this, she said. *It feels wrong. Like a cage. Do you think... do you think he knows we're here? Or suspected we would try this?*

I don't think so. He is behaving as though we're really dead.

She pushed again, harder, testing the edges. His footsteps stuttered to a halt.

Noise hit us like a speeding cart and we flinched, a cry pulled from our lips. Leo appeared overhead. "Well, look at that. Foolish to have so underestimated them."

"What? She's alive?"

Her demand was shrill, but I could not focus on it. On her. On the fleeting warmth that was proof she really did care. The connection flared hot and bright and loud, and I could see why the empress had struggled the first time she'd experienced it. This time she lunged us up off the divan.

Septum's muscles were stiff, but he moved with more strength than Hana's old body, and our hands closed around Unus's throat, tightening. Kaysa screamed and clawed at our arm as we squeezed, but I could not heed her. This was our only chance to stop him. To save Kisia. To save Miko.

His eyes rolled back. He was going to die. We were going to end him and be free of—

Unus gripped our forearms and kneed us in the balls.

I had used just such a move against countless men over the years, leaving them writhing, but I wasn't prepared. Not for the looming dread. Or the pain—an explosive sensation simultaneously the tingling of smacking one's elbow and the most excruciating thing I had ever felt. My stomach dropped. My knees buckled. And as I hit the floor, I knew exactly why all those men had been unable to fight back. Waves of nausea flooded in and I could not move, existing only as an empty husk of pain and misery.

I feel sorry for everyone I've ever done that to, Empress Hana said. *Almost everyone. Some of them really deserved it.*

Somewhere nearby, Unus let out a breathy laugh owning a manic edge.

"Hoping to kill us all, Cassandra?" he said. "The ultimate assassination. But now I know, and you…you are stuck in that empty, soul-sucking hole of a body I detest being connected to, and you are the one who is going to die. You thought I wanted Septum so you couldn't use him against me as some sort of weapon? Nothing so elegant. I just need him to die at the right time. Now you'll get to die with him."

I struggled up onto wobbly knees. Die at the right time.

At the right time, Hana repeated, a final realisation dawning over us both.

The balcony.

There was no time to think of something clever. No time to wonder if there was another way out of this. No time to think at all, only to act.

I ran.

The distance to the open balcony doors was at once impossibly far and no distance at all, our soft shoes thudding across the floor. No time for finesse. No time for grace or second thoughts. Time only to leap.

Breeze rustled our hair. Sunlight struck our face. The railing dug into our stomach and we threw ourself forward, sick fear dropping through us as we overbalanced. A rockery stretched below, all jagged edges and hard, skull-cracking rocks, and for a terrified moment I wished I could pull myself back. It might not be my body, but I would still die in it.

Dearest Katashi, I'm coming. I'm—

A hand gripped my ankle. My knee slammed into the railing, someone grunting with effort above me. "Don't you dare!" Leo snarled.

"Fuck you! Let go!" Our voice came out as Leo's, and not looking down at the rockery, we desperately wriggled and kicked and bucked, trying to pull free. Trying not to think about how much I didn't want to die.

I slipped, but a hand snatched at my other leg. "Cass!" Kaysa cried. "Don't!"

"Let go, Kaysa! This will stop him!"

"Help me pull him back," Leo said, pain shearing like a spiked collar through my ankle.

They hauled, strength born from desperation. Blood was rushing to my head, and the rockery swirled below us, promising death.

"Don't do this, Cass," she said, the words pushed through gritted teeth. "You don't want to die, I know you don't."

"But you want me to. Let go, Kaysa! This is your chance to have the body to yourself."

Figures appeared in the rockery, one carrying a white bundle under their arm. It was only two floors down, enough to kill us if

I landed head first onto rocks, but maybe not if they managed to cushion our fall.

"Fuck!"

We wriggled like a caught fish, and one of our soft boots began to slip.

"Damn it, Cass, I don't hate you. I mean, I do, but...I don't want you to die. I don't think...I don't think I can live without you."

Kaysa's words stole all breath from my lungs, and I stopped wriggling, twisting to see her. A glimpse of my own face set in determination, teeth gritted, and Hana took over, bucking our stolen body, desperate to finish the job.

I'm sorry, she said. *But there's no other way.*

There wasn't, but Kaysa had said she couldn't live without me. My heart ached like dozens of needles pressing into my chest.

My boot slipped. I was going to slide right out of her grip. Leo was shouting at the people gathering in the rockery, but they weren't ready, the bundle of fabric just a pile of linen, pale on dark stones.

I'm coming, Katashi. I'm coming.

"Please, Cass," Kaysa said, the words strained.

"No," I said. "But I'm sorry. For a lot."

It was all I could say. All I would. My shoe slipped farther, and she scrabbled to keep hold of me. Leo was still shouting, but I wasn't listening anymore. The rockery was just there. God, I wished we weren't going to go head first, but maybe it would be a quicker end, smashing our brains—

Don't think about it. It'll be over before it even hurts. And I'm with you this time. You don't have to die alone.

Yakono had been with me last time, in his way, and again I had the feeling of needles pressing into my chest and—

The shoe slipped.

Our weight tore through Leo's grip and we fell. Until something as light as a feather brushed my foot, and I was wrenched back until I was leaning against the railing. It dug into my gut and yet there was Septum, falling, falling, with nothing to stop him. To stop her. A strangled cry left my throat and I reached out, but the body hit the ground. A sickening crack drowned out every other sound.

Relief and guilt and grief vied for my attention, but I could only stare, numb, hardly even aware of the change in my body. Of the change in the mind now sitting alongside mine. Not Hana anymore. Never Hana again. Kaysa felt familiar and yet different, my body both comforting and all out of proportion.

Beside me, Unus had stopped shouting. And it was Unus now. I could see that with Kaysa's understanding, see the difference in the way he stood and in his expression. This man wasn't Leo in the same way Kaysa wasn't me.

Below, the people who had been trying to stretch a sheet between them slowly edged toward the body. It wasn't far down, but head first onto rocks had a finality about it. I could only hope she had been right and it had been quick.

"I see you liked *her*," came Kaysa's bitter words from my mouth. My mouth. My voice. The sense of slowly dawning euphoria was impossible to ignore. I was back in my body. I was home.

Unus looked up. "You've broken it. The reborn prophecy. He… wasn't supposed to die here. Not like that."

"Good or bad?" Kaysa asked, and Unus shook his head, folding his arms over his chest like the world was suddenly too cold.

"I don't know." He didn't look at us. "I don't know. That depends what Duos chooses to do."

"Surely there's nothing he can do now. Right?"

But fear lived in the depths of Unus's eyes, eyes I had seen full of the cruellest malice. The Leo who had killed Captain Aeneas was still out there, and we had just royally pissed him off.

29. RAH

I had no idea whose house it was and didn't care. The empress had taken over a fine manor, and my dirt-dusted boots slammed into the floor with every step as I hurried along the passage. I had not seen her since I'd arrived. No doubt she was busy with more important things.

There were guards outside Gideon's room—both men I had seen around since Syan. They eyed me warily as I approached.

"Rah." I turned to find Amun leaning in the opposite door frame, waiting for me.

"Amun," I said, something in his expression making every part of me tense. "How did it go?"

"Exactly how I said it would go." He pushed off the frame and faced me in the passage, ignoring the guards who were our only audience. "She put on a good show for Captain Menesor e'Qara and Atum e'Jaroven. Although perhaps that's a good thing since the Kisians would be dead if we hadn't been there. Your empress owes Ezma. You're going to have to speak soon if you don't want her to take every Levanti's loyalty."

"There's nothing I could say that would convince everyone."

"Then maybe it's time to stop worrying about dividing us. It's either speak or let her Chiltaen god have them."

Entrancers. How she had laughed.

"He gets inside your head, like a voice. A feeling of peace. A raging attack of noise."

Leo had broken Gideon. He had used us. Again and again he had used us, and if Entrancers were responsible for what was happening on the plains, he was probably connected to that too. As Ezma was.

My hands clenched into tight fists. Amun looked down at them. "What are you going to do?"

There was an unsure edge in his voice, but revenge hungered in his eyes. "I'm going to stop her," I said, causing Amun to smile a hard, humourless smile. "I'm going to stop Leo. I'm going to make them all wish they'd never looked at Levanti and seen people they could use."

He nodded, with me all the way. "If you put your case to the captains we found, they might still fight for you."

"We'll find out soon who stands with me, but I'm going to check on Gideon first and—"

"You're still putting him before us? You know what he—"

"Yes, I do know," I snapped. "I do. Imagine how you would feel if someone got inside your head and made you give those orders, if you had to sit and watch, a prisoner in your own mind, as people you cared about were killed because of your voice. Your position." Amun leaned away from my spitting vehemence, scowling. Unsure. "You can say it's his fault, but in the same situation would you have been strong enough to fight magic even our herd masters could not? If you can't be sure, compassion is the only option."

"You forgive him?"

I stared, owning no answer. I hadn't yet. Couldn't. Wasn't sure I ever truly would, but that was different to holding him solely to blame. "That question is unfair."

Amun looked away. "I'm sorry, Captain."

"No need. This is...not ground any of us have walked before. I'm not asking you to forgive, merely to focus your anger on the most appropriate person. Raging at Gideon will achieve nothing, however righteous it might feel."

He bowed his head. Saluted. "I still feel this situation needs you now. While Ezma is out on the battlefield seeing to the bodies."

"There is time. Making a move behind her back won't have the outcome we want, but come and let me know if anything changes."

"As you wish, Captain."

"And, Amun?"

He spun back, glancing at the two guards still watching us with curious looks. "Yes, Captain?"

"Talk to people. Listen. Feel the situation out. The newly arrived Swords are far more likely to be open around you than me. If I know who to talk to, who isn't sure about Ezma, it will help."

"I can do that."

This time when he saluted, I let him go.

I had expected to have to argue my way into Gideon's room, but one of the guards pulled open the door for me, sending a murmur of low voices spilling out. Worry sped my steps inside, into a dimly lit room possessing a knot of people. Lanterns lit the faces of Tor and Tep and a man I knew to be a Kisian healer. All three looked up as the door slid closed behind me.

"Rah," Tep said, his voice cool and unfriendly.

As cool and unfriendly as the room felt. My skin prickled in the chill air.

Gideon lay upon a mat, his appearance unchanged from how he had looked beneath the ground, right down to the dirt in his hair and on his clothes and the dried blood on his hands and neck. Only the crimson sash had been removed, Tep's handiwork replacing mine. The Kisian healer was murmuring to Tor, who nodded, glancing at me only to grimace.

Fear solidified like a stone in my stomach. "What's wrong with him?"

Tep shrugged. "The gods didn't want him saved, perhaps. Or he wants to die."

He had pressed a blade to his own skin, possessing a desperate strength I would never forget.

"Master Izaka thinks it's just fatigue," Tor said when the Kisian finished speaking. "He needs food and water and rest, but he might have lost too much blood. There's little we can do if he won't wake."

"He hasn't woken at all?"

"Not since he was put on the cart."

They had bundled us roughly into carts, guards sitting with us all the way. Gideon had slept. I had promised I wouldn't leave him and had crouched at his side, only to lose him upon arrival when a healer insisted on checking me over. At least he hadn't woken to find me no longer there.

The Kisian healer shrugged as he stood up, adjusting the satchel he carried with him. "He says we will have to wait and see," Tor translated. "He'll return to check on him later."

"Like it matters," Tep said. "Empress Miko will have him executed if he wakes, so it's better he dies now. Better still not to have made it out of Kogahaera at all."

"Go," I said. "Get out. I'll look after him."

Tep's lip curled, but he saluted and made for the door without complaint. The Kisian followed. Only Tor hovered, unsure.

"Have someone send food," I said. "Please. If he wakes, he'll need it. Something easy to eat."

The young man nodded and followed the others out, leaving me alone in a dim, cold space all too reminiscent of our chilly stone prison. I stared down at Gideon. At his dirty clothes and the dried blood on his skin and the way he lay curled upon himself in the cold.

Tor had gone, but I strode to the door and tried to speak to the guards outside. "Hot," I said, one of the few words I recalled in

Kisian. I mimed shivering. "Hot." I needed a cloth and warm water too, maybe some fresh clothing, so I added, "Bath," and tried to mime a jug of water, plucking at my clothing. The men looked at each other. Spoke. Nodded. And one started off along the passage. Hoping he had understood, I went back inside.

It was dark beyond the narrow window, somewhere between midnight and dawn. The house was quiet, not the quiet of peace, rather the quiet of whispers. Of alliances shifting and changing like windblown sands.

I sat at Gideon's feet and started untying his boots. Dirt crumbled beneath my fingers, the smell of it all too present. My hands ached from digging. They felt swollen and bruised and clumsy, and it took longer than I cared to admit to untie his boots and pull them off, scattering dirt and stones. I'd only just started on the first buckle of his leather tunic when servants arrived. Two men, one carrying a pair of braziers, the other two metal buckets held in animal-skin gloves. Neither spoke as they set the braziers in the corners, working fast to fill them with hot coals.

A tub arrived next, rolled in, a pair of maids following with steaming water jugs. I wanted to tell them not to bother as they lowered the wooden bath and began to fill it. I just needed one of the jugs and a cloth, but they hurried in and out without looking at us, and I was too tired to try to explain. Slowly the bath filled. Food came. Clothes too, a pair of soft robes with plain sashes. Towels. Soap. I knelt beside Gideon and waited until it was all done, the last of the maids hurrying away with her empty jugs and sliding the door closed behind her. Through the paper panes, the vague silhouettes of the guards on duty shifted their weight.

Gideon hadn't stirred.

"I think they are very keen to please the empress," I said as I went back to the buckles of his tunic. "The lord who lives here was probably loyal to you and needs to atone." I wondered what had

happened to them all. To Gideon's allies and the Levanti who had
been with him. To Dishiva. But the questions could wait. Waiting
would not change the answers.

Piece by piece I removed his armour. The plain tunic and breeches
beneath were Kisian by the feel and cut, but not so different to
what we wore against our skin. Dried blood stiffened the neck of
the tunic, cracking as I pulled it over his head. He stirred, enough
to draw his arms back to his body but no more.

I dunked a cloth into the bathwater and wrung it out before running it over his collarbone, smearing dried blood. Gideon flinched.
Rolled over.

"This would be easier if you could just get in the bath," I said.

"You get in the bath," he murmured, the words little more than
a breath.

"Trust you to be able to mouth off in your sleep." I took his
shoulder and rolled him back. "Here, let's get you in the damn
thing. It might wake you up."

He didn't answer, just curled his arms over his chest. His dark
skin had long owned a wealth of scars, but there was a new one on
his shoulder. It looked recent. I wanted to ask what had happened,
but even had he been awake the question was too dangerous.

I sighed and traced the crescent scar on his other shoulder, one
he'd gotten protecting me from an enraged boar the year we'd wintered in the hills. Always he had been there. The memory made
the same uneasy feelings from the cave swirl in my stomach, and I
pushed the thoughts away, edging back like I owned a dangerous
beast I feared to wake.

He killed Yitti, I reminded myself, setting off a spiral of
self-blame.

With a snort of annoyance, I untied the knot holding up his
breeches and yanked them down. The extra exposure to the
cold did nothing to wake him, and he lay in all his dishevelled,

long-legged glory as though he was a carving rather than a man. Each of his abdominal muscles a ridge, his thighs strong from life in the saddle—but for the blood he could have been a sculpture of Nassus. Not that I would ever tell him so. Too well could I imagine his self-satisfied smile.

"Come on," I said, gripping his shoulder and rolling him. "Time to wake. There's a bath. It looks warm and you stink."

He made a little grumble, but didn't move.

"Yes, you smell awful. Like a dead deer that fell into a bog."

Another grumble deep in his throat.

"And then got pissed on by a whole pack of sand cats."

One of his eyes cracked open a moment that was all glare.

"So insulting you is the way to wake you up. It's a wonder Tep didn't try it." I gripped his arm. "Up. Now. Bath. If you don't, your legs will rot and fall off. Sand cat piss can really burn."

It took a few false starts, and I had to bear most of his weight, but with much grumbling I managed to get him to the bath. He stepped in, one leg after the other, only to topple sideways, face first.

"Shit! No no no," I said, belatedly realising how bad an idea it was. "You can't sleep in the bath." I pulled his face out of the water. He coughed and his eyes flickered open like they were trying to focus on me, but he didn't fully wake. I tried letting him go again, only to catch his head as it slumped toward the water.

"All right, fine." I tugged at my own clothing as best I could with one hand, the other holding his chin up. The buckles were difficult, the ties frustrating, and by the time I was in my underlayer I was fed up and uncomfortable. Deciding it was good enough, I stepped in, struggling to shift his weight as I slid into the water behind him.

The tub wasn't big, but it was just large enough to fit us both with our knees bent. Not a comfortable position, but a functional one. With Gideon's head resting beneath my chin, his face turned to my shoulder, I didn't have to worry about him drowning. Taking up the cloth I'd had the foresight to hang on the side of the tub, I cleaned the blood off his neck and chest.

Even with a layer of clothing between me and the water, the heat eased tensions I hadn't known I was carrying. Alone it would have been pleasant, but with his weight against me and the prickle of his scalp beneath my chin, I could not relax. The discomfort of the intimacy was too present, and I hoped he would not remember. Hoped only I carried the confusion it provoked.

Dipping the cloth into the warm water, I scrubbed his skin, taking care to be gentle around his face. I wished I could clean away the ravages of the last few years and find the old Gideon underneath, ready with a smile and a laugh, but if he was still under there, I could not reach him, could only wipe away the dirt and remember who he used to be.

Although the braziers were slowly warming the room, the water soon chilled. It wasn't cold, but once the heat began to dissipate, Gideon shivered. He'd been asleep against me without any sign of life beyond the even rhythm of his breath, but now he twitched and rolled his head, a frown cut between his brows like he was having a bad dream.

"Cold," he murmured. His teeth chattered.

"All right, time to get out," I said. "But if you don't help me, I'm going to be dragging you by your arms. Can you sit on your own?"

He didn't answer, but he seemed awake enough that I risked edging out from behind him. My arse felt numb from the bottom of the tub, and when I stood, my wet clothing stuck to my skin.

Somehow, I managed to strip my dripping underclothes off without Gideon sinking into the water. Having wrapped one of the towels around my waist, I readied the other for him, but although the cold seemed to have woken him, it wasn't an improvement. He stepped out, his breathing uneven. He wrapped his arms around himself and looked into the dark corners, wide-eyed and gasping.

"It's all right," I said, towel around his shoulders, rubbing his arms. "You're safe." Probably a lie. "There's nothing to worry about." Definitely a lie. "I'm here." At least that was true, but he didn't seem to hear me.

Working fast, I dried him as best I could and got him into one of the robes. He was still shivering, still sucking deep, wild breaths, but he was clean and dry and dressed and sitting, and that was a start. I held out a slice of pear and he took it, looking my way but not seeing me.

"You need to eat something," I said, pulling on the other robe. It was soft and warm enough, but without layers or armour I felt exposed and wrong. "I'll eat if you do," I added, not sure it would work a second time. His breath quickened, true panic setting in. He gasped something that could have been an apology or just the rasping of his raw throat, crushing the pear in his hand.

"No no no, you're all right, I'm here," I said, caught between the urge to hold him tight and the fear he would fight me. I settled for having one leg bent in front of him and one behind, like I was a safe harbour if he needed it. "Can you try to breathe with me?"

"Go—away—"

"And leave you to choke to death or something? No."

"Don't—see—this—"

"You're embarrassed about this? Don't you remember the time I got so worked up thinking I'd been bitten by a snake that I puked on your feet?" *Or when you took my knife and tried to cut your own throat?* "Just shut up and breathe with me, all right?"

I drew in a deep breath, held it, and let it go against his shoulder. He didn't join me, but he made no attempt to pull away or tell me to leave, so I did it again and again until he drew a shuddering short gasp and then a longer one. When he took his first full breath, he released his clenched fists, and the wad of crushed pear fell into his lap. I kept breathing slowly and deeply until Gideon turned his head. "You can stop now, you know."

"No, I didn't know, because I'm not exactly an expert at this yet."

"Yet," he repeated with a bitter laugh. "You don't have to become one. You don't have to stay."

"I know."

He risked a fleeting glance at me, turning away as he met my gaze. He stared at my knee still bent before him, tensing like a man who wanted to move both closer and farther away and was caught in the middle.

"You really don't have to stay."

"I know. I'll have to go find out what's happening out there soon, but you're stuck with me for now, and I'll be back. Even if you don't want me."

"How charming."

"Aren't I just?"

I caught the flicker of his smile, like a glimpse of his former self.

"You should eat and rest," I said, finally shifting back and getting to my feet.

"So should you. I'll eat if you do."

"Using my methods against me now?"

"Whatever it takes."

I took a walnut and nibbled it, eyeing him. He did the same, no expression, no emotion, just a slow blink and the sluggish movement of his jaw. Whatever energy he'd mustered to talk seemed to have vanished.

Soon, Gideon lay down. No one had come to take the tray or the bath water, and with the world seeming to be asleep, I gave in to the fatigue pulling at my eyelids and stretched out on the mat beside him. He lay with his back to me, and though he must have known I was there, he didn't turn. When weak, tired sobs shook his body, I touched my forehead to his back, but still he did not turn. He cried himself to sleep, and only once he calmed did I let myself rest, forehead still pressed to his shoulder.

———————◆———————

I woke to bright light, my sleep having been so deep I couldn't recall dreaming. I'd rolled over in the night, and now Amun crouched in front of me. He lifted his hand from my arm. "Ezma is back."

The words chipped at my lingering drowsiness and I sat up, a glance at Gideon enough to tell he was still deeply asleep, curled upon himself. Amun stared at me like a man intent on pretending his one-time First Sword didn't exist.

"What is she doing?"

"Meeting with the empress."

"Shit." I leapt up, hunting around for my armour before remembering I had nothing clean or dry. "I need clean armour."

"I'm not sure what we'll be able to find, but I'll look."

There wasn't time to wait. I looked down at Gideon, still asleep. It was a small mercy. I didn't want to leave him, didn't want him to wake without me, but everything hung too precariously in the balance to wait any longer.

Empress Miko was holding court in a large, central room of the manor. A silk divan sat at one end, but although her guards were present she was not. Dozens of eyes watched me enter, not all of them friendly. I had grown used to Minister Manshin's scowling presence, but many of these were new faces. Lords, soldiers, and to my surprise, Levanti.

Lashak e'Namalaka stood to one side of the room with a young, unmade Levanti woman and a Kisian lady, her soft, elegant features carefully moulded into an expressionless mask.

"Captain Rah," Lashak said as I approached, saluting though

she owed me no such respect. The unmade woman saluted as well, while the Kisian just stared, something in the slight widening of her eyes seeming to look deep into me. "I think perhaps you have not met Nuru e'Torin and Empress Sichi e'Torin."

My heart thudded hard in my chest. Gideon's wife. I wanted to stare at her as she was staring at me, but I couldn't ask any of the questions that sprang to my tongue. Instead I uttered an inane greeting. At least I hoped I did.

"I need to see the empress," I said after saluting them both. "The...other empress."

Lashak grimaced. "She's meeting with Whisperer Ezma." She nodded toward a door behind the makeshift throne. "You'll have to wait. There are a lot of people here to see her, I understand."

I wanted to say Miko would see me now if I asked, but in the short time I had been gone, everything seemed to have changed. Perhaps I'd already worn out everything we'd had.

Empress Sichi spoke, her voice quiet but sure, like something finely wrought from steel. "Sichi wishes to know how her husband is," Nuru said.

I thought of the way his breath raced in panic, the way he had stared at unseen monsters around me, and the strength in his hands as he fought to end his own life. Unexpected anger bubbled. Stiffly, I said, "He's as well as can be expected."

The lady maintained her mask, but Nuru's brows rose. Shocked at my words or my tone, I couldn't tell and found I didn't care. They had been there. They could have helped, have stopped this, had they tried.

"I am very pleased to hear it," Nuru translated the lady's reply, and my anger festered all the stronger. Had she really cared, it would have been her, not me, who had forced her way into his room to look after him. I was probably being unfair, but I didn't care about that either.

We stood in silence a time, surrounded by the whispered susurrus of the court. I wanted to talk to Lashak about Ezma, about what had happened at Kogahaera, about the feeling everything was poised to tumble down at a single wrong word, but Nuru would have translated it all for Empress Sichi, so I said nothing.

The door opened. The chatter quietened as Ezma walked out, tall in her jawbone headpiece but made all the taller by her proud, upright stance and triumphant smile. She turned it my way, four long strides all it took to bring her before me.

"Rah," she said, savouring my name, the suppressed joy in her voice sending fear trickling through my skin. "I do hope you will be joining us for the ceremony tonight. It is important for us to show unity."

"Ceremony?"

"The Voiding."

My stomach dropped. A Voiding. There was no greater punishment for any Levanti, reserved for the very worst of crimes against a herd. The disrespectful death.

Bile burned up my throat, sick and hot and angry. I didn't need to ask who it was for.

"Empress Miko has been wise enough to give Gideon's justice into our hands," Ezma went on, the *our* a cruel barbed edge. "His fate is a Levanti matter, and if she wants Levanti support..."

The suggestion we were united on this, that no one could question Gideon deserved such a fate, sickened me still more. I wanted to spit in her face, and but for the watching audience and the hiss of Nuru translating behind me, I would have.

Ezma stared down at me, her very stance a challenge. She wanted me to argue, but a horse whisperer was the final arbiter of justice, and whatever the empress might have thought she was doing, giving Gideon's life to the Levanti was giving it only to Ezma.

A fierce whispering had broken out behind me. Perhaps Nuru

was explaining to Sichi exactly what Ezma would do to her husband. His branding scratched and sliced off. His death ensured in the darkest of places so he went unseen by the gods. His head left attached to his body so he was never to be free. I wondered if she would understand how terrible a fate it was.

"Two hours after sunset," Ezma said. "Here. Tonight. We have permission to shutter the windows against the moonlight."

Having gotten no previous reply, she seemed not to expect one now and, with a pleased little smile, walked away.

"Rah," Lashak began, but I was already halfway to the door Ezma had emerged from and didn't stop. It had closed behind her, and two imperial guards watched my approach with wary looks.

"I want to see the empress," I said, and gestured at the door. "Tell her it's Rah e'Torin and I need to speak to her."

They looked at one another, and seeming to understand my meaning if not my words, one opened the door a crack and spoke through while the other watched me, a hand near his sword. I might have tried to barge through had Miko refused, but despite the number of others waiting to see her, I was ushered in.

I had expected to find her sitting with her head minister, or at least a pair of guards or General Ryoji, but Empress Miko was alone. She had donned ceremonial armour, all flowing silk surcoat and gold fastenings, but despite her grand appearance her lips split into a broad smile at sight of me.

"Rah!" she exclaimed, and threw her arms around my neck, pressing close. Having barely expected a polite welcome, let alone a warm one, I was thrown off balance, no time to decide how to respond before she kissed me. The ferocity of it made my knees weak. So much had changed and yet nothing had. The smell of her hair, the feel of her against me, the strength and determination of her like a drug I could consume again and again and never be sated. I had not thought desire could make its way through the fear and anger and disgust Ezma had left me with, but it did. We had come so close to being together too many times, and I wished this could be that kind of moment, that I could give in to the yearning of my body in celebration of all we had won, but I couldn't.

Though I had taken her face in my hands, though I wanted her with every inch of my skin, I gripped her shoulders and set her from me. She broke from the kiss with a breathless gasp and stood looking up, still and unsure, her hands hovering between us.

"Rah?"

"It's Gideon."

"Gideon?"

"You can't give him to Ezma."

She frowned, and for the millionth time since we'd met, I wished we better understood each other's language. How could I explain? How could I appeal to her mercy? How could I even express how I felt without words that mattered to her?

I signalled for her to wait and hurried back to the door. Nuru was still standing with Lashak and Empress Sichi, and I beckoned. "Please come and translate. This is important."

The long-haired saddlegirl glanced to her companion for a nod of permission, which only deepened my dislike of the soft Kisian woman Gideon had married.

Wary, Nuru followed me back inside. Empress Miko hadn't moved.

"Tell her she can't allow Ezma to decide Gideon's fate."

Nuru bowed to the empress and began to translate, but where I had been vehement, she was respectful and moderate, Kisian in her tone as well as her words.

"I don't understand," was the empress's reply. She stood where I had left her, hands frozen. Hands that had pressed against my back and held me close only moments before. "Is it not right the Levanti decide his fate?"

"It would be if a true horse whisperer led us. If her judgement could be relied upon. If—" I huffed a breath, frustration overtaking me. How could I make her understand, whatever words I poured forth?

Nuru translated, but there being no end to my sentence, Miko looked to her in question. Nuru answered in her own words, and I wished I trusted her enough not to have to ask what she had said.

"I merely explained about Ezma having been exiled, which she knew, and a horse whisperer being the arbiter of law, which she understands," was Nuru's pettish reply. No doubt like Tor, she was sick of finding herself caught in the middle of such conversations, valued only for her ability to translate. "Now she asks whether you disagree with the decision Ezma has made regarding Gideon's fate."

"Yes."

Miko finally lowered her hands, the movement an acceptance of sorts that this stood between us now, though I could still taste her on my lips.

"I know he is your herd brother," Nuru translated. "But he took over my empire. My people—"

"And rid you of the entire Chiltaen army. Has he attacked you since? Or has he tried to make peace with your people?"

Empress Miko looked away, a scowl cutting between her brows that I wished I hadn't caused. Wished I could smooth away. But she had to listen to me.

"Nuru, please explain a Voiding to Her Majesty."

Hesitantly at first, Nuru began to explain. I watched Miko's face, wondering if she had spent enough time with us to grasp the depth of its dishonour. Her gaze flitted to me as she listened, a wariness in her expression now as Nuru seemingly spared no detail.

"Can you not speak to her about it?" Miko said when it was done.

I laughed, the sound full of bitterness, and said, "She sees me as a threat and will do anything to hurt me, even if it means using others."

For a full minute, Miko said nothing. She stood there in her glorious armour, her hair held up in delicate pins, and she looked at me as I looked at her, wondering if this was the end.

"I'm sorry," she said, the Levanti words ones I had taught her, ones I had taken such joy in hearing on her lips.

"Sorry?"

Anger was all that lived inside me now, anger at everything and nothing. At Ezma and Leo and the Entrancers, but also at Sichi and Miko and Dishiva, at Nuru, at a world that kept tearing at my sense of who and what we were.

"She says the decision has been made," Nuru translated. "There is nothing she can do."

"Nothing she can do?" The words were wrenched from me upon a seething tide. "Nothing she can do? You're an empress! This is your empire. These are your people. You gave his fate to Ezma and you can take it back. You can do anything!"

Nuru had been translating along, and at that Miko launched her own fury back at me, her teeth bared. "I wish that were true, that any of it was true. I have no position but the one I am allowed. The one I hold because I am difficult to get rid of, not because I am held in respect." She had pressed her hand to her chest, emotion ringing in her words. "We are not like you." She looked at Nuru, her meaning clear. Here, she was lesser for not being born a man.

Turning away, Miko drew a deep breath and let it out, the face she turned back as expressionless and mask-like as Sichi's had been. "The decision has been made," she said through Nuru's lips. "There is nothing to be gained from discussing it any further. You may take it up with Whisperer Ezma. If you explain your concerns, she may listen."

I stared, sure these couldn't be the words I was hearing.

"If there is nothing else you wish to discuss, I have many other matters requiring my attention. I'm sorry, Rah."

Her words stole the fire from my fury. I understood the politics of her position as little as she understood the issues between Ezma and me, or the severity of the punishment that had been chosen. Shouting would change nothing. Nor would pleading. Her apology was sincere, as clear in her eyes as her words. She didn't want to hurt me. She wanted to reach across the distance between us and touch me as I wanted to touch her, to be with her, but our moment had been lost, leaving us alone in our different worlds—worlds that had brushed against one another for a time but could never truly be one.

It was pointless to stay. Painful. So, I bowed. Saluted. And spoke the only words left for me to say. "There is nothing else, Your Majesty. Goodbye."

That word she knew, and her hand twitched as though to reach for me, and I had to look away. "Thank you for your help, Nuru. We can go now."

Together we walked toward the door. Miko did not call us back.

———————✦———————

I strode back toward Gideon's room, seeing and hearing nothing but the raging of my thoughts. Some terrible part of me wondered if Ezma was right, if he deserved Voiding for what he had done and I was just too close to him to see it. Or too angry with Ezma to accept it. I asked myself if I would have abided by the decision had someone else made it, but the answer was no. I would not let anyone do it.

I found Amun once again waiting for me outside Gideon's room. I grabbed his arm. "I can't stay here. No, let me finish. I don't expect you or anyone to come with me, but Ezma has condemned Gideon to Voiding, and I can't let her do it. I won't." Amun gasped and I hurried on. "I know you don't like him, but I'm begging you to help me. Me, not him. He would probably be happy to die right now, but this isn't his fault and I won't let Ezma kill him just to hurt me. We have to get him out of here."

"And then what?"

"I'll meet you somewhere as soon as I can. I'm taking him home."

"Home?"

"Home," I said. "You're welcome to come, or you can finally be free of me."

"No." Amun shook his head, his arms folded over his chest. "That's not how this is meant to go. You're meant to stand up to her. Protect your people from her. You're meant to help us, not run."

"What can I do? I can't stay here and fight her if it puts Gideon in danger. I can't. I just…I can't do it, Amun. I can't lose him again."

"Then don't stay. But take us with you." He gripped my shoulders. "You know about the Entrancers now. About the shit that Leo has been doing. We could find out more. Could go home and fight them. Fix this before the city states destroy us. But first you have to stand up and tell them." He flung an arm in the direction of the gathered Levanti. "Remind them we have our own home to fight for. You won't convince them all to walk away from a whisperer, but you can try!"

I met his furious stare, and it could have been any one of my lost Swords glaring at me through time. Instead it was all my guilt over their deaths concentrated into one remaining pair of eyes. Perhaps I could do it. Perhaps I could do both. Not all of them would come, would even listen, but enough might. Enough to undermine her plans. I thought of Empress Miko. I would be stealing away Swords that might have fought for her if this had played out differently, but it hadn't, and there was no way to change that now.

"All right," I said. "As many as I can. But you have to get Gideon out of here well before the ceremony tonight. Take him somewhere safe and wait for me. If I don't come…"

I couldn't finish that sentence, wasn't ready to consider what might happen if Ezma turned against me. "It's a deal," Amun said. "I'm going to need help, but I've got something of a plan."

While my plan, I thought as he saluted, could well be called more of a death wish.

30. MIKO

I paced the length of the room. Up and back. Up and back. A dozen times I had been on the verge of sending for Rah, and a dozen times I had stopped myself. Twice I had even considered pardoning Gideon e'Torin, but if I did it would be the last thing I did as empress. The only reason I still held any power was because the Levanti whisperer was my ally, not Manshin's.

I went on pacing, wearing myself out. Could I talk to Ezma myself? Was there another way to give her what she wanted? And if not, would Rah ever forgive me?

"I just...please help me understand."

Tor leaned an elbow on the table. I'd asked him to drink tea with me, to talk, but I hadn't been able to sit down. Every time I tried, anxiety set me pacing.

"They don't like each other," he said, shifting his tea bowl rather than look at me.

"But why? It does not seem to be this one incident."

He sighed and, in a bored voice, said, "*She* is worried he commands enough respect with the Levanti to threaten her position. *He* is angry because she shouldn't have a position. Horse whisperers aren't leaders, and she was exiled. And she left him to die."

My steps stuttered to a halt. "Left him to die?"

"He was injured. It's...a thing we sometimes have to do on the plains, but she didn't have to, she just—look, it's hard to explain."

"But they still follow her? I mean, you still follow her?"

His look was sardonic. "If your emperors are bad at their job do people still do what they say?"

"Sadly, yes. An emperor is a god."

"It's about the same. It's hard to convince people who have had respect for a position drummed into them that now that position means nothing." He shrugged. "She shows them all a respectable face. What reason have they to doubt her?"

I groaned, causing Shishi to look up from where she lay stretched upon the floor. "What can I do?" I said. "I need her support, but Rah is upset about Gideon's fate."

"A Voiding is...more extreme than I expected. I have more reason to be angry at Gideon than most, but I would not have chosen that fate. Even though he is the reason I don't feel—"

He shut his mouth upon the words, teeth snapping. Never had he come so close to admitting how much it hurt him not to be a member of his herd the way he ought to have been, but rather than finish the thought or meet my gaze, he sipped his tea. Well did I know that method of avoidance.

"Is there anything else you require?" Tor said, finally pushing the tea away. "I have things to do."

"Things other than educate me about your people?"

"Things other than talk about Rah."

I reddened, hating what he must think of me. Did he look at me like my generals and see only a foolish girl torn by love? I fell back on stiff pride. "If you wish to leave, do. But tell Rah—"

"Tell him yourself!" Tor stood so abruptly the table shook. Concerned, Shishi padded toward him, but the young Levanti ignored her sniffing at his feet.

He had that bullish look he got when his anger burned hot, and I swallowed mine, drawing a calming breath. "You know I can't."

"Well, you'll have to find a way, because I'm done. I want to fight, not talk. I want to do something meaningful, something that might help me feel Levanti again."

"But, Tor, I need you here. *We* need you here."

He spun a scowl on me, pressing his fist to his chest. "And I am sick of being needed, being wanted, for nothing but these words that were forced upon me, wanted only as a bridge between two peoples—between two *people*—and never for myself."

He seemed to regret the words and crossed his arms, rolling his shoulders forward. Such defensive fury. Such proud grief. Almost I reached out to say with a touch upon his arm what I couldn't put into words. That although we came from different places and had lived different lives, although we only spoke the same language because he had been forced to learn our words, I knew his pain because it lived in my heart every day, in my bones, in my soul. I had lost so much I could never regain.

"That's not true, Tor," I said. "The two—"

"Isn't it?"

His glare dared me to reassure him with a lie, but it wouldn't be a lie. I had gotten so used to his presence, to his prickliness and his watchful gaze, to the way he hunched his shoulders as though in apology for being a little taller. I didn't want him to leave.

But those words wouldn't come. Meant too much. Were sure to be sneered at. So I said nothing. And Tor, seeing my silence for the surrender it wasn't, snorted and turned away. I gripped his arm before he could go, and with my head empty of all thought, slid my hands over his cheeks and into his hair, and kissed him.

For a brief moment, I tried to pass through my lips all the words and feelings I had been unable to speak in the hope he would understand what I had meant, understand he was wanted and needed for himself, but it was all too brief a kiss. He did not pull away, but neither did he respond, and the tensing of every part of him sent panic ripping through me.

I tore myself away, all but darting back like a frightened cat, apologetic words spilling from damp lips. "I'm so sorry," I said. "I shouldn't have—I just, you…I…I'm sorry. Please forgive me. I don't know what I was thinking."

He had looked stunned, but at that his brows dove. "Then I will leave you now, Your Majesty," he said, bowing, all stiff, wounded pride. "Goodbye."

And with my lips still tingling in memory of a kiss that shouldn't have been, I watched him go. Unable to call him back as I had been unable to call back Rah.

Feeling every bit the pathetic, foolish woman they both surely thought me, I gritted my teeth on a frustrated scream and smashed the teapot off the table. Shards scattered. I didn't have enough time for this. Enough power for this. I had to let them both go if that was what it took. I had to be the Dragon Empress my mother had been and show the world nothing but ice.

When my first flare of rage passed, tears welled, and I crouched to bury my face in Shishi's fur, she the only one allowed to see my tears now.

———————◆———————

Thankfully, I had much to keep me occupied. Oaths to accept, lords to meet, soldiers to praise, and plans to make. Oyamada came and went in a flurry of secretaries, while Manshin received reports from scouts and generals. I could have left it all to them and rested, and the gods knew I needed rest, but I needed to be seen more. My position stood precariously upon the backs of the Levanti, and if I did not rebuild my position before they fractured, I would be left standing on nothing.

For weeks I had considered Gideon e'Torin my greatest enemy, yet as the sun began to set and his execution drew near, it was sick uneasiness I felt, not satisfaction. If I closed my eyes, I could still see Rah's face contorted into a pain I had never seen him admit, as he pleaded for the man's life.

You're an empress. You can do anything.

Having to admit it wasn't true had left a bitter taste in my mouth.

Nuru had told me to wear a soft, dark robe free of shimmering threads to the ceremony, so it was without my finery I made my way back to the main hall that night. For Rah's sake I had almost thrown her advice to the wind and donned my shiniest robe in the hope of drawing the gods' attention, but it would have been disrespectful and small consolation when he had asked for so much more.

The room was packed with Levanti when I arrived, every face solemn and strained. Few Kisians were present, only General Moto and Minister Manshin, a couple of soberly clad lords who had been part of the false emperor's court, and Lady Sichi. I joined her and Nuru on one side of the room, sliding into the shadows.

I whispered a greeting and received a strained smile. Sichi had not spoken about her relationship with the Levanti emperor she had married, but there was no grim joy in the hard way she clenched her jaw. She was not looking forward to this. I wondered what sort of man Gideon was that, despite all he had done, two such people as Sichi and Rah cared about his life.

It took time to find Rah in the crowd. The windows had all been shuttered and the lanterns were few and dim, but once I'd seen him, I couldn't look away. He still wore the dark robe he'd come to see me in. The fabric had been soft under my fingers, his body beneath it so warm and vital and everything I needed. I'd wanted to go on kissing him, to feel his strong arms around me, to utter the Levanti words I'd practised again and again that would allow us to lie together, but they had remained trapped on my tongue. Now if I forgot them there was no Tor to ask.

No. Don't think about Tor.

You're exactly the whore your mother was, said a dark part of my mind. *Trying to control people the way she did.*

But of course no one had ever said the same of Emperor Kin. Not even when he'd fathered an illegitimate heir.

Ezma entered, the bones of her crown darkened with soot. The Levanti saluted her in a silent wave of respect. Or most of them did. Rah didn't move. Neither did Lashak and a few others around her, or Nuru beside me. Tor had explained the tensions, but still I found myself gripping my hands tight. The air prickled.

Lifting her hands, Ezma addressed the gathered press in Levanti, her solemn tone vibrant with the passion of one supplicating gods.

"The herd is everything," Nuru whispered for Sichi. I shifted closer so I could hear. "The herd is life. Our herds are our family and our soul, and every Levanti makes a pact to serve the herd as the herd serves and protects every Levanti. That's how it's meant to be. Transgressions against the herd can result in exile, but there are crimes so great they are not merely a transgression against one herd but all. Gideon e'Torin has hurt all of us, not only those of us here, but every Levanti upon the plains. He has taken our names and our tenets, our purpose and our soul, and crushed them until they were devoid of all meaning. And he demanded we be grateful."

Even from the other side of the room, I caught the flicker of disgust on Rah's face and had to tell myself again there had been no other choice.

"It is with a heavy heart that my responsibility to you all requires me to condemn him to Voiding."

Nuru's already low whisper broke upon the last word. Almost every Levanti was looking at the floor, divorcing themselves from what was happening. I thought about Emperor Kin sitting on his throne, commanding the death of my brother. How many people watching would have opposed it had they been able?

"No one else's soul ought to be weighed down with the

consequences of this," Nuru went on when Ezma spoke again, turning slowly to address everyone gathered in the large room. "So I will perform it with my own hands. Bring him in."

People shuffled near the door. Heads turned. Necks craned. Rah didn't move. He stared at Ezma with an intensity that made my stomach flip. She showed no sign of discomfort, just stood waiting. Patient. Calm. Sure.

Whispering started. A lone head moved through the crowd. A Levanti woman squeezed into the open space around Ezma and spoke in her ear. Ezma bent to catch the words, only to snap her head back up, gaze like daggers as she hunted Rah.

What have you done? I thought, clasping my arms over my stomach. *What have you done?*

"It would appear Gideon e'Torin is no longer here," Nuru translated while Ezma swept the room. Her gaze locked onto me with such a flare of fury I was sure I really would be sick.

"Empress Miko," she snapped, in Kisian this time. "You assured me he would be well guarded. That he couldn't escape. What do you have to say?"

The few Kisians in the room visibly bristled, their defence of the respect owed my position shaking loose my terror. "He was. And he couldn't," I said. "I have had no word from my guards that anything was amiss."

Ezma bared her teeth, but before she could retort, Rah stepped forward. I drew in a breath I never wanted to let go, wishing I could pause time and step away, do something, change something, so I would never have to witness what was coming.

"I did it," he said, the tremble in Nuru's voice as she translated proving the seriousness of the admission. "I removed him from your justice, because while it is a justice you desire to give, it is not one you are permitted."

She broke in with an angry exclamation, but Rah shouted over her. "You are an exiled horse whisperer, removed from your position by a full conclave of horse whisperers. That alone makes you unqualified to mete out justice. Add to it your adherence to the faith of the One True God, and it goes against every tenet I have ever lived by to allow you to lead or condemn anyone."

Murmuring tore through the room, but Rah only raised his voice louder still.

"I am no one," he said, turning to speak to the crowd now. "I am no captain or herd master or horse whisperer, but the one thing I will always be is a Levanti. The one thing I will always fight for is the Levanti. I will not remain here to be led by anyone who harms us, seeking power for the sake of power."

His passionate vehemence sent tingles through my skin. But Tanaka had stood just so, denouncing the emperor, and died for it. The thud of my heartbeat was the echo of his head hitting the floor over and over again.

"I expect nothing of any of you," he went on, holding the room in a way I'd only seen Emperor Kin hold it. He spoke and they all listened. Even the Kisians who could not understand his words were entranced. "I will no longer stay to fight the wrong battles. The plains need us. Our people need us. We have a point of vengeance to settle with the Chiltaens and their false priest, but after that the plains call me home. Any who wish to come are welcome regardless of which herd they came from. We are all one now, and I will fight for anyone who fights with me."

He turned on Ezma, and in barely a whisper, Nuru translated, "May the gods damn you when they weigh your leaden soul."

No one stopped him crossing the floor. No one stopped him pushing his way through the crowd or stepping through the door. No one stopped others from joining him, peeling off and striding in his wake. Lashak and Shenyah and many others whose names I did not know. They flooded past Ezma, following him into the night as she spat a proud reply. My hands itched to reach out, to pull Rah back and fix everything that couldn't be fixed. I ought to have seen this coming, but I had been foolish and naive and oh so hopeful, blinded by his respect and his love.

Love. What a ridiculous choice of word in the circumstances.

"What is she saying?" Sichi hissed at Nuru, who stood with her hands clenched to tight fists.

"She is reminding us of everything Rah e'Torin has done wrong. She says he abandoned training to be a horse whisperer because he was selfish. She says he wouldn't have stood up for anyone else in Gideon's position. 'I have only ever given to the herd, to my people, even when I was thrown out for caring more for Levanti souls than my own position. I have done all I could to accommodate Rah e'Torin's views, seeking anything but division in a time when we need to be united, but this I will not stand for. He is an exiled exile, a former captain removed from his position by his own Swords, who has failed you again and again.' "

Some who had begun to follow Rah stopped to listen. Others were long gone. Some looked from Ezma to the door, the decision heavy on their shoulders.

Their divisions ought to have meant nothing to me, but I held my breath and hoped as fervently that many would leave as that many would not. I believed in Rah, but it was Ezma I needed, Ezma I had made my alliance with. I needed her and her Swords.

No one spoke as the crowd shifted and split. There was no shouting or raging or even looking at one another as each Levanti made their choice to walk or stay, the respect they showed for each other's autonomy a strange and beautiful thing to behold.

"You do not have to stay," Sichi said, quiet and close amid the solemn footsteps. She was looking at Nuru, who didn't turn. "Do not let me decide your choice."

"I am not," she said as Levanti continued to brush past us on their way to the doors, dodging around anyone who chose to remain. "It is for me I have made my choice."

On the other side of the room, General Moto and Minister Manshin whispered together, and the knot of tension in my chest tightened.

Slowly, movement ceased, leaving a diminished presence in the room. Half, perhaps, had remained of those who had attended. It was impossible to tell from Ezma's expression if the outcome was more or less than she had hoped. More or less than she needed. Than I needed. My gaze kept sliding to Manshin, his head still bent toward my most powerful general.

When all movement settled, it was not her people Ezma looked at, but me. "Our alliance was founded upon a mutual desire to bring Gideon e'Torin to justice," she said in Kisian, standing tall and proud despite her loss. "As you have betrayed us upon a final point, giving in to the importuning of your lover"—she spat the word, such disgust in her face I could summon no part of the pride born into me—"there is nothing to be salvaged from this night's work. Congratulations, Your Majesty, on ridding your lands of Levanti."

No bow, no salute, no nod, nothing but a disdainful look, and she turned away. Words to the remaining Levanti. A gesture to her apprentice. And she too strode out. Her people followed, each there and gone as they filed through the double doors, leaving behind a handful of Kisians, Nuru, and a desperate need to call them back lodged in my throat.

"Run after Rah e'Torin," I said to one of the guards by the door, the words bursting from my lips without thought. "Tell him I request speech with him before he leaves."

It was a foolish, desperate plea, and yet it ought to have been obeyed. A nod, a bow, a murmur of "Yes, Your Majesty," and the guard ought to have hurried away. Instead, he looked at Minister Manshin, who shook his head. The man did not move.

"Did you hear me?" I said, my voice shrill. "I commanded you to—"

"He heard you, Your Majesty," Manshin said in his calm way. "But no one is running after the Levanti to beg us into more debts we cannot repay."

He nodded to General Moto, who headed for the door without looking my way. "General Moto," I said. "General Moto, I have not given you permission to leave."

The man shrugged a shoulder as though to dislodge an annoying fly, but did not turn. He took the guards with him, the doors closing with an echo of finality behind them all. Mere minutes ago, the room had been full; now there was just me and Sichi and Nuru. No guards, no generals, no lords, no Levanti. I felt exposed, like I had forgotten to dress.

"You may leave us, daughter," Manshin said, not having the kindness to even look at her.

"No."

"No? I am your father, and that is a direct command." Anger edged his voice, but he kept his expression neutral. The mask we all wore to cover our hurts.

"As you have told me twice since my return that I am no longer a daughter of yours, I will stay." She wore the same mask, so much hurt she wouldn't let him see. What right did he have to it anymore? "Unless you intend to have me carried forcefully from the room, I suggest you make peace with that."

"Very well, but I will not have *her* here." He jabbed a finger at Nuru. "There is no reason for a Levanti to be present, and I will have her forcefully removed, don't think I won't."

No one could have doubted it from his tone. Stunned into a sick silence, I could only watch Nuru and Sichi share a look, a nod. And Nuru, scowling at the man who had once been my most trusted supporter, walked out.

Once the door had closed behind her, Minister Manshin clasped his hands behind his back and stood before us, Sichi and I recalcitrant children.

"Explain yourself," I said, because I had to say something, had to maintain the pretence I was in control.

"Explain what? You have failed in your leadership, Your Majesty. I and many others risked our lives in the hope you would be the leader we needed to unite the empire. Your ability and your sense and your passion for Kisia appeared, at the outset, to be unparalleled. It mattered not that you were a woman. Then."

"But now it does? Have my breasts gotten in the empire's way?"

He gave me a disdainful look, disliking the frank speech he had previously encouraged. "Hardly, Your Majesty. But whatever your reason, you have continuously put the furthering of the Levanti cause above the needs of your own people and kept their company in preference to the Kisian allies you ought to have been cultivating."

"They are the strongest warriors we have," I said, clenching my hands to keep in my rage. "Capable of being either our greatest allies or our greatest enemies, and I know which one was better for Kisia."

"Even in that you have failed us." He looked around the empty room. "They appear to no longer be here."

I did not answer, and he began to pace a slow length across the floor. "You once had cause to admire my dedication to the empire, Your Majesty. That dedication is unchanged; I am only sorry you now have reason to damn it." He spun, looking me in the eye. "I am taking command of the empire in your place. Do not contest it. The generals all support me in this move."

How Jie would have laughed. He had said one of his generals would take his throne, that our names meant nothing anymore. Power rested in the hands of whoever commanded the army, leaving both Otakos and Ts'ai as irrelevant as each other.

"All hail Emperor Manshin?" I said, lifting my chin in challenge.

"Hardly. The reason we thought you would be so strong an empress is because you carry both the Ts'ai and the Otako name, making you an important symbol for those who still care about such things. You will sit on the throne, but your generals, your councillors, your guards, and your governors will take their orders from me."

"So I am to be a puppet?"

"A figurehead."

"You are so sure of your support?" I wanted it to be a challenge, but even to me it sounded like weak hope.

"Your council and your generals care for the empire as befits their positions. Kisia must come first." His smile had a pitying quality. "You may be able to go on convincing commoners that you are a god, but Emperor Kin set a long precedent. They knew he was no god, that Kisia was not his by right. It is not yours by right either. It belongs to its people and you must serve those people, whatever it takes. To which end, I have accepted a renewed request from the Chiltaens to sign a treaty reinstating the border. Your marriage to Dom Leo Villius will finally be able to seal peace after all."

I staggered back a step, drawing a breath into lungs too tight for air.

"What?" Sichi gasped, finding her voice first. "Leo Villius? Father, he is a monster. He can get inside people's heads. He can—"

"I understand the Levanti did not like him," Manshin interrupted. "That his religion went against theirs. He would not allow them to cut off heads as they are wont to do, or burn their bodies. Upholding one's beliefs in the face of barbarism is hardly monstrous. Regardless, you are not a Levanti, and neither is Miko."

Miko. It was like I was a child again.

"The Levanti didn't dislike him for his faith, Father. He is... unnatural. A cruel, manipulative—"

"Enough! You are overwrought by your so-called husband's poor treatment of you. May the experience teach you wisdom. Unlike your barbarians, Dom Leo Villius will treat Miko with the utmost respect."

I tried to remember the man who had sat across from me in Mei'lian and plotted treason. A man who had stayed at his position though his family estate and his daughter were in danger. His determination and drive still stood before me, but he was a cold shell of his former self. Just as Mei'lian was now burned out and empty.

"A treaty with Chiltae," I said as calmly as I could manage, choosing a different angle of attack. "That restores the border *they* marched across. Restores the peace *they* broke. We give it back to them when all they have given us is thousands of dead to bury and dozens of burned cities and towns. Why? Why would we do that?"

"Because further war would last years and risk so much more. We have no idea what the Chiltaens have on their side. They are rich. They may have more mercenaries, or get more if pushed, and—"

"And if you sign a treaty with them, how many years will it be before they break it? One? Two? This cycle just keeps turning, getting faster and faster as we pour more hate into it. A piece of paper and a loveless marriage are not going to change that!"

"Perhaps not, but they are too strong to conquer. So it is peace now or risk being destroyed."

"The people will not stand for it. Not after what they have done to us. Neither will they accept a Chiltaen emperor."

Manshin lifted his hands, his calming gesture only increasing my anger. "He will not be an emperor. He will be your consort only. And Kisia is well used to the rotation of war and peace with Chiltae. We fight them, then we trade with them, and for the common folk, the world goes on. This time it was the barbarians who incited the violence. Blame ought to be cast where it is due."

I knew the Levanti had been forced into service, knew that if the

Chiltaens were offering peace it was only because they were afraid or had some devious plan, but what did it matter what I knew anymore?

Manshin spread his hands again, placating a rage I had not loosed. "I serve the empire. The oaths I swore, I swore to the people of Kisia, not its rulers, and by your very own wisdom this is the best course of action. 'A small chance of a big success, or a big chance of a small success,' you said, and peace is not worth risking on our pride."

I hated how logical it was. Hated he was using my words against me. Hated there was nothing I could say to change it. He would not have made such a move without being sure of his position.

"How long have you been planning to turn on me, Your Excellency?" I said. "How long have you feigned loyalty?"

"I have always been loyal to what you wished to accomplish, and I still am," he said stiffly.

"Bullshit. You are loyal only to your own whims like every other two-faced councillor and opportunistic general in history. Tell yourself lies if it makes you feel better, but it doesn't change the truth."

"Whims? Caring what happens to Kisia is a whim? Like sleeping with a Levanti is a whim?"

Rage propelled me a step forward. "I didn't sleep with him," I hissed. "I have done nothing wrong. Nothing you wouldn't have just looked the other way for had I been a man."

"But you are not a man."

"And that's the real problem, isn't it? It was fun to let me play the leader when you thought you could control me, but the moment I started questioning your advice and making my own decisions you were too afraid to trust me. It's pathetic."

He stepped in, meeting me in the crackling space between us. "You were supposed to be a symbol of strength. You were supposed to be a symbol of wisdom, the pure goddess who would fight fearlessly for her empire, inspiration for the soldiers."

Pure. Symbolic. Not a woman with a mind and a body and a

heart. I bared my teeth, the fury of a hundred forgotten empresses spitting between them. "From such a pedestal how could I do anything but fall?"

We glared at one another. "You should have listened to me," he said.

"And you should have trusted me instead of undermining me at every opportunity."

Manshin snorted. "I did no such thing. You were capable of that without my help."

"Capable of retaking Syan. Of reclaiming Kogahaera. Of marching an army on a false emperor and winning."

"And losing half your army to an ambush."

"And destroying all of Grace Bahain's in an ambush. You are too ready to give full weight to my errors and none to my victories. Did Emperor Kin lose battles? Yes. Did he lose soldiers? Yes. Did he give ground at the border? Yes. Did he lose half the empire to my father? Yes."

For the tiniest moment I thought I had him, but with a snort, Manshin looked away.

"What a pathetic thing," I said. "To hold a woman to higher account than a man."

"Trust you to see things that aren't there."

"How dare you."

"Merely an observation, Your Majesty."

The return of the respectful address hurt as much as his switch to my name had, and I spat at him, loosing all my pent-up rage. He flinched back, but shock soon twisted into disgust. "Very ladylike. We are clearly finished here. While you maintain a respectable face to the world, you will be respected by the court. There are many worse fates, Your Majesty."

"Like being forced to marry Leo Villius and watch him take over my empire."

"He is a priest, not a warrior."

"You are making a big mistake with him, Father," Sichi said.

Manshin looked at her with the same disdain. "Threats are beneath the name you were born to."

"How strange. I was sure I heard you threaten to forcefully remove Nuru from the room if she did not leave on her own."

"This interview is over," he said. "You both ought to rest. Tomorrow I will inform you of the council's plan for the treaty and your marriage, and where we intend to base the court now Mei'lian has been destroyed. By the very people you insisted on allying yourself with."

It was one last parting jab. I couldn't pass up my own. "The very people you wouldn't be alive without. The very people who saved us again and again and again."

He deigned no reply, just bowed, mockingly deep, and turned to the door without so much as a glance at his daughter. And that was it. I would not call him back. Would not plead.

No Manshin. No army. No allies. Not even Edo or Rah or General Ryoji. I was alone.

Sichi's hand slid into mine, her skin soft. I blinked back tears. She didn't speak and neither did I, the pair of us standing there in the smothering silence of the empty hall.

When I thought I could speak without my voice breaking, I looked at her. She looked back, and my heart broke anew. Whatever hope I had wanted to see, whatever strength and determination would have steeled my resolve was absent in her face. We had each other, but no allies. No resources. No power. No plan. Nothing.

I returned her wan smile, tears running down my cheeks. I let them fall. There was no point pretending. The same hopelessness I saw in her eyes, she would see reflected in mine.

We were alone.

31. DISHIVA

Warm and strong beneath me, Itaghai was my anchor, the rocking motion of his slow gait more lulling than the sweetest cradle song. If not for Jass, I would have dozed off long since.

"I know you've had some bad ideas in the past," he said, looking up from where he walked alongside. "But this one...Are you sure about this?"

"That's the...seventh? time you've asked that question."

"I'm not getting a good answer."

"What would be a good answer?"

He stared ahead at the moonlit road, empty but for us. The wind was cold and damp, but at least it wasn't raining. I was starting to cling to such small mercies. "No. I think *no* would be a good answer."

I sighed, tired to depths I hadn't known I possessed. "But I am sure. Sure I want to do it. That it's important, not that it's a good idea or will work out well."

Jass said nothing for a while, the whip of the wind and the clop of Itaghai's hooves all that marked the night. I closed my aching eye. A healer had replaced the bandage over my empty socket. I needed it, but the pressure around my head was only making my headache worse. I ought to wait. To rest. To go when I was better. Jass had uttered so many sensible suggestions, dancing around the desire to outright tell me not to go at all, but the longer I waited the greater the chance I would be too late.

"You said they took more than a dozen Levanti captive," I said after a time.

"I did."

"Oshar amongst them."

The young translator was barely old enough to be Made, ought to have lived a life that looked nothing like the one he had. But our herd masters had been manipulated. Gideon had chosen to stay, to conquer, to build. Leo had ruined it all, and now I would be damned if I would let him down too. Let them all down. Matsimelar had died for my mistakes. Oshar would not die too.

"No one else can do it, Jass."

He walked on, his hand looped in Itaghai's reins, his shoulder close enough that I could touch him if I reached out, that his arm would bump my leg if he drew any nearer, and yet he had never felt farther away.

"He can't get into my head with my eyes damaged," I went on, unsure if I was trying to convince him or myself for the dozenth time, the same doubts running through my head again and again. "And with the name of defender, I'm protected under church law. Tor checked."

We had found him packing saddlebags when we went for Itaghai, and I'd asked him that one last question. "It does say the defender is protected by God as the defender protects God," he had said. "And it looks like it's always been a position. There is always a defender, though who holds the position changes."

We had thanked him and wished him well and gone our separate ways.

"That no one else can do it doesn't mean you have to," Jass said, not looking at me. "Or even that you can."

"No, but it means I'm going to try."

He puffed a heavy breath to the night and looked up at the sky. Only a single moon there, a sight I was getting used to. "I hope one day you will consider your own safety before you do these things."

"Do you? You should probably leave then, because I'm going to disappoint you."

Jass's laugh was a weary thing. "I know, and you know I won't. I'm just being selfish because I don't want to lose you." He glanced up at me then, a fleeting, wary look. "I fret. And worry. And I hate it."

"I know." I reached out and touched his shoulder. "We both walk tough paths; they're just different paths. Nothing happens for a reason, but we can choose to do something with the fate we're dealt or just complain about it. If I don't...do something with this..."

He gripped my hand, squeezing it to his shoulder. "Who'd have thought losing an eye would help you see more clearly than me."

"I'm also older than you."

"Not by that much!"

I met his gaze with steady disbelief. "Which term of service are you in?"

"My first."

"Exactly."

"That is hardly conclusive evidence!"

"Then I'm not sure what is."

He tried to glare and managed only a few seconds before it became a laugh, and for a moment we weren't on our way to yet another parting. Except that we were. The heart-pounding urge to turn around welled up, only to be shoved aside. I had the ability to help. I was the only one who did. Could I live with myself if I didn't?

The Chiltaen army had retreated, battered and beaten, but had not gone far. Only far enough for safety while they rested and regrouped and decided what to do next.

"We must be close," Jass said. "I can see men watching us from the trees."

I could see only haze myself. "Many?"

"Enough."

"Then it's time."

He took three more steps and halted. Itaghai's hooves scraped the stones. "Are you sure about this?"

"Eight times."

"All right, I'll stop asking." He lifted his hands to help me down, and while I hated being injured enough to need assistance, there was joy in the strength of his arms and the closeness of his body, and the warmth of his breath as it ghosted across my cheek. Then he let me go, and I was standing alone upon the road beside him, unable to say goodbye.

I touched his arm, wishing I could see him more clearly but grateful for his solidity. "I can't tell you I'll ever think of my own safety first. Or ask you to do so, but..." I drew a breath and let it out, shaky and uneven. "But I promise I will come back to you if I can. That I hope... one day no one else will need me, and if on that day you want me..." My voice suspended upon a mixture of fear and emotion I could not swallow. I ought not to have said anything, but I was sick of doubting. Sick of not speaking. Of protecting myself with a silence that cut deeper than any admission.

Jass breathed out. "This is where we're doing this?" he said, a laugh in his voice. "I love you and goodbye?"

"It could be our last chance, so... yes. Gods know it would have been easier not to care for you, but you were you, and now it's too late. Really, it's your fault for being who you are."

"Thank you?"

"You're welcome."

His laugh owned no humour. "I didn't want to say anything that might pressure you to change your mind, but if this is what we're doing then gods be damned, Dishiva, you are the most stubborn, tough, selfless person I have ever met, and often you make me want to tear out the hair I don't even have, but I started out staying to help others and ended up being here only for you. Oops."

"Oops indeed," I said, returning the gentle kiss he offered with more passion than was safe in that moment, but I might never see him again, no matter how determined I was to get through this, to have a future.

Itaghai gave a restless snort. We had lingered too long, and I pulled away from a kiss that left me breathless. "Ride fast," I said, taking a wobbly sidestep so he could reach Itaghai. "Don't look back. Please. For both of us."

He tried to smile, but it twisted into a grimace. "I'll wait for you, Dishiva. However long it takes."

"And I'll come back to you, however long it takes."

Jass crushed me in one last fierce embrace, holding me so tightly to him that for a moment I couldn't breathe. He let me go as hurriedly and was in the saddle before I regained my balance. Hooves scraped. The bridle clinked. Itaghai turned, and unable to bear more words, unable to bear another touch lest we never let go, Jass dug in his heels and sped away, the flick of Itaghai's tail the last thing I saw before they disappeared from my scarred vision.

Hoofbeats clattered into the distance, leaving me with the whip of the chill wind and the emptiness of night all around. Now, even if I wanted to change my mind, I couldn't, and that was more comforting than I had expected.

Drawing a deep breath, I pulled up the mask Leo had forced on me at the ceremony, settling it as comfortably as I could over my bandages. Then I walked.

The white clothing I'd been given was thin and far from clean, but it felt like armour as I walked alone along the road. The watching Chiltaens had only to see me to know me for what I was, to know I was untouchable. Bit by bit, the sense I was being watched deepened. Soon, steps crunched at the edge of the road. I walked on like I hadn't heard them.

"Defender," a voice said, wary. I couldn't understand any of his other words, but at least they didn't sound combative.

"I want to see Leo Villius," I returned, and surely they would know the name. Understand my purpose.

"Dom Villius?"

"Dom Villius."

More footsteps joined us, their figures vague outlines. Voices whispered. I flinched at a touch to my arm, but the firm grip made it easier to walk. I didn't want to be grateful for anything, but I hadn't realised how much I'd been struggling. Pain had just become...normal.

I staggered as we left the road, the ground uneven beneath my feet. Thanks to the white robe and mask, they steadied me with more kindness than I'd ever seen a Chiltaen show, and anger bubbled inside me. If nothing else, my voice gave me away as Levanti, but while I wore the trappings of their culture I was allowed to be human.

Other voices rose around us, followed by little sounds of activity. Of horses and cooking and the flap of tents in the wind. The Chiltaens guiding me called out to others and were answered, still no words I understood. But no one jammed a knife into my back or slit my throat, and I was led on through the haze of unfocussed shadows.

Eventually we halted amid whispers. More talk. Men came and went. Then I was led forward toward the hazy light of a tent, its fabric brushing the top of my head. The men helping me inside let go, and I took my first deep breath of incense-laden air.

"Ah, Dishiva," Leo said, his voice a sudden shock though I had known where we were going. He sounded no worse for his fall through the floor, assuming he was still in the same body. "So clever of you to think of using my cruel joke against me. Now if only it had been a cruel joke, how foolish I would look."

His footsteps crossed a carpeted floor, the shape of him drawing closer but not close enough to be in focus.

"Positions in the church are not hereditary," he went on. The soldiers who had brought me were heavily breathing statues around me, their shadows falling across my vision. "My father was the hieromonk, but that does not make me the hieromonk. It is the hieromonk's job to name an appropriate successor, a task my father abstained from doing, sure naming me would lead to his death, while naming someone else would fracture the fragile alliance we pretended to have."

His robe swished as he moved slowly around the tent, trailing fabric.

"How fortunate that I had the foresight to name a defender in his place, ensuring that when he died, Chiltae's great faith would continue to have strong leadership. Because he is dead, you know, killed by the very assassin he once sent to kill me. Which makes you, Dishiva, the hieromonk of the One True God."

I tried to focus on his face, hoping it was another of his cruel, manipulative lies, but it was all too believable. Too believable that he'd had a long game, that he'd played me, that he'd used me against myself. Again. I wanted to be sick.

"No."

"Oh yes, Your Holiness. You now carry the title even though you are no believer, making you a—"

"False high priest," I finished in a breathless voice. "You named me defender so I could die for you at the right time."

In the silence I heard the wet click of his lips spreading to a toothy smile. "Your cleverness is what makes you so much fun. Luckily there's still some time left for us to play. A pity, however, that although you have so much power, I'm the only one who can translate your commands. Oh, great and wise leader of the church."

The room spun. I ought to have found something clever to say, have sought a plan, but in the hazy shadows of my new world I could think of nothing but a man with strong arms who had held me to him and accepted me for everything I was and everything I wanted, though it had been the hardest thing he could do.

I'm sorry, Jass. I'm afraid I might not be coming back after all.

# 32. RAH

We walked. We walked from the open gates out into the night. We walked though some of us had horses, though I itched to run, to see Gideon safe with my own eyes. And though we walked in silence, we were not alone.

I led Jinso, Lashak e'Namalaka on one side, Shenyah e'Jaroven on the other—two Levanti I would never have met in another life. Kuroshima Shrine, Amun had said, and Shenyah had known it. Had ridden there as one of Gideon's guards upon his marriage and was able to lead the way.

It was late when we came to the bridge. The dark shadow of a river roared beneath it, and lights glimmered on the opposite bank. I stopped, causing a cascade of halting steps behind me.

"I think I should go ahead on my own," I said, turning to Lashak. "It might scare them to have so many Levanti appear without warning."

And there were many. There hadn't been time to count, but the sight of them following me had constricted my throat with emotion I wasn't ready to deal with.

"Both for the townspeople and Amun," Lashak said. "I'll stay here with the others until we get your signal."

She didn't need to tell me everyone was tired, that I shouldn't keep them waiting long—I knew it.

Leaving her to explain, I patted Jinso's neck and walked on alone.

The bridge was a steep arch, and at its peak I could hear nothing but the rush of water beneath me. I was on my own now, but I didn't speed my pace toward the flicker of lights on the other side, worry beginning to gnaw at me. Whatever I would find when I arrived, I would not be able to change. Any number of things could have gone wrong in their escape. I might find no one here at all.

Jinso's hooves echoed upon the stones as we descended toward inevitability.

A collection of houses sat nestled in the dark trees, the only light the welcoming twinkle of lanterns set either side of the mountain stairs. Shenyah had said the shrine was up there, that our horses wouldn't be able to make the climb, and as I looked around for signs of life, a shadowy figure waved from the lee of a house. I recognised Amun as he stood, but he was alone. My stomach turned over as he approached.

"You found us, I see," he said, his gaze unfocussed like he had been dozing.

"Gideon?"

His lips twitched in wry amusement. "He's fine. Or...alive at least, I'm not sure he's ever going to be fine. He's sleeping." He jerked his head toward the house behind him. "A lot of the houses are empty. We found a mat. Loklan and Esi are sitting with him."

"I don't—"

"They're Jarovens. Dishiva's. They were in as soon as I said you planned to deal with Leo. Their story is...wild, honestly. You need to talk to them."

I nodded. "We need to do a lot of things. I didn't come alone."

Amun's eyes widened, and he looked fully awake for the first time. "How many?"

"I don't know. More than I thought would listen to me." The

look in his eyes grew hungry. "I didn't want to scare anyone without warning, so I left them with Lashak on the other side of the bridge. Ezma was...not happy."

He hadn't wanted to save Gideon, had only done it for me, but a spiteful grin stretched his lips. "I wish I could have seen it."

"I'm sure you'll get another chance. I don't think we're rid of her."

Amun's smile became a grimace, and he gestured toward the bridge. "Shall I fetch them?"

"Yes. I want to see Gideon. Where did you put your horses?"

"I'll take Jinso, you go on. I can see you won't relax until you've seen him."

I hadn't noticed I was shifting foot to foot, making Jinso twitch with my nerves. I gave Amun the reins with a wry grin.

Dim light welcomed me into the house, emanating from a second room deeper inside where voices hissed like sand. They stopped at the sound of my footfalls, and two faces looked up. They sat side by side against the wall, two young Levanti who had surely expected a far different life to the one they were living.

Neither spoke, but both looked to the man lying on the mat. Gideon was dozing, fitfully shifting in a way that had crumpled the blanket laid over him. His dark robe was the same colour as the short growth of hair on his head and chin, everything about him soft and tousled, only the bandage on his neck a stark reminder of his desperation to die.

"He's been asleep most of the time," one of the Levanti said—both familiar from our time marching with the Jarovens. "We're worried he doesn't want to wake up."

"Did you try insulting him?"

They looked at one another. "No?"

"It works surprisingly well." I knelt beside Gideon and ran my hand over his hair, his warmth releasing a tension inside me. His brows twitched into a sleeping frown. There was much I wanted to say, but with Dishiva's two Swords watching on, I kept it all to myself.

"We were going to let him sleep until morning then try to get him to eat."

"It's not your job," I said. "Thank you for sitting with him, but he's my responsibility, not yours. No one should have to take care of him after what he did."

Neither answered, but their silence was acknowledgement enough. Outside, low voices were rising. "If you could extend your kindness and sit with him a few more minutes I would be grateful. I'll be right back."

Both saluted, and glancing a last look at Gideon, I walked out.

Amun and Lashak were outside, a slow tide of Levanti crossing the bridge behind them. I had expected a few to follow me, had known I wasn't entirely alone in not trusting Ezma or in wanting to go home, but to see so many... My heart swelled with a pride I hadn't felt for a long time, and for a moment I couldn't speak, could only watch them spread out around the clearing and begin setting up camp. Quiet. Wary. This the unsure beginnings of something bigger than all of us.

I was exhausted. The doze with Gideon in the early hours of the previous morning all the sleep I'd had since leaving the Kisian camp with Jass. Yet these Swords had followed me. Had trusted me. I could not rest until I was sure they had all they needed. That was the responsibility of a captain after all.

"Well, Captain," Lashak said, coming to stand beside me. "What now?"

"Truthfully, I don't know." I grimaced, glad she couldn't see my thoughts at that moment, couldn't feel the bite of fear at how poorly I had led my last Swordherd. "We have plans, but there is a lot of work to do. A lot to discuss and decide. How to deal with

Leo. When to go home. Whether we stay here or move on. And we'll have to elect a Hand before we can do any of that."

"And give everyone time to rest and grieve. We've lost a lot."

Agreement was unnecessary, and for a time we stood in silence and watched the beginnings of a camp rise around us. It wouldn't be a full camp until tomorrow, or until we decided where to go. For now all we needed was somewhere to sleep and to know our horses were safe. Everything else could wait until morning.

Amun soon joined us. "Esi says Gideon is getting more restless. She wants to know what she ought to do."

"I'll go to him," I said. "I shouldn't have left them to the task so long." I gripped his shoulder. "Amun, if you would take the position, I would gladly have you as my second. You are all I have left of my old Swordherd, and I value your expertise and honesty."

He saluted. "I will take the position and fulfil it with honour." I hoped he would not think, as I did, about what had happened to my last second.

"That takes a weight off my mind. Now I must relieve the Jarovens watching over Gideon."

"Before you go, Captain," Amun said. "A piece of the honesty you value." Before he spoke I could feel every part of my body tensing as though preparing for a hit I did not want to take. "Not everyone is happy that Gideon is here. You'll have to tread carefully if you intend to keep him with you. I may be able to swallow my anger and accept him for your sake, but not everyone will. What I'm saying is—"

"It's a risk," Lashak interrupted. "Especially if you intend to lead this herd more...democratically than has thus far been our way. If enough people object..."

They shared a look.

"You want me to abandon him?" I said. "An honourable way to begin."

"We didn't say that." Amun folded his arms. "I just wanted to warn you that there is already talk. You may have to accept that a time is coming when you have to give up on him. Some people cannot be saved. Some people cannot be redeemed. There are dark places too deep to ever see light again, and as a captain you must put your herd before all else."

Mere moments ago, I had stood there with hope, confident that we could all build something new and strong together, could make our way home together, but already that dream had burst. Exile had not only taken lives from us. Not only taken our freedom. Our pride. Our blood. It had taken our unity. Our forgiveness. Our trust. We were not truly Levanti anymore. We were survivors.

The story continues in…

WE DREAM OF GODS

Book FOUR of the Reborn Empire series

Coming in 2022!

ACKNOWLEDGEMENTS

So many people work on these books of mine, and they are all amazing, from my agent (yay, Julie!) and my editor (Nivia Evans, the true genius here) to the cover artist, art director, and publicity team. I've thanked them all before many times now. The team at Orbit are wonderful, and I feel daily grateful for the effort they put into these fantastical tomes of mine.

Normally, as with my previous books, I would list all these people and the tasks they do and thank them individually (and if you want to see such a list, check the back of my previous books; all the people I work with are amazing), but this book was wholly written and edited in the Times of Covid 2020 (it's October as I write this), and instead of my usual acknowledgements, I want to thank all the little things in life that have kept me more or less sane this year.

- Black rice crackers. True champions.
- My weighted blanket, even if it does like to slide off the bed.
- Sniffing ground cardamom (it smells nice, okay?).
- Plants.
- Renovating. It's so cathartic building and decorating things with your hands.
- The new wheelbarrow with a wheel that CAN'T GO FLAT.

- Numerous rewatches of *Pride and Prejudice*. Again. Also *Emma*.
- Watching livestreams from Melbourne Zoo. Giraffieeees!
- Plants.
- My discord fam (Flaaaaaaps).
- The Bunker.
- Plants.
- Zoom chats with my daughters on the other side of the world.
- Anxiety meds, oh how I love thee.
- Bed.
- Hibiscus and rosehip tea.
- Plants.
- The YouTube channels where they just play with Thomas the Tank Engine toys, thereby entertaining my child for endless repetitive hours so I can sometimes work.
- Lists. Of anything. Everything. Lists are amazing.
- History books. For some reason, nonfiction has been much easier than fiction this year.
- And last but definitely not least—PLANTS. Our house is getting full of plants.

extras

meet the author

DEVIN MADSON is an Aurealis Award–winning fantasy author from Australia. After some sucky teenage years, she gave up reality and is now a dual-wielding rogue who works through every tiny side-quest and always ends up too over-powered for the final boss. Anything but Zen, Devin subsists on tea and chocolate and so much fried zucchini she ought to have turned into one by now. Her fantasy novels come in all shades of grey and are populated with characters of questionable morals and a liking for witty banter.

Find out more about Devin Madson and other Orbit authors by registering for the free monthly newsletter at orbitbooks.net.

if you enjoyed
WE CRY FOR BLOOD

look out for

LEGACY OF ASH
The Legacy Trilogy: Book One

by

Matthew Ward

A shadow has fallen over the Tressian Republic.

Ruling families—once protectors of justice and democracy—now plot against one another with sharp words and sharper knives. Blinded by ambition, they remain heedless of the threat posed by the invading armies of the Hadari Empire.

Yet as Tressia falls, heroes rise.

Viktor Akadra is the Republic's champion. A warrior without equal, he also hides a secret that would see him burned as a heretic.

Josiri Trelan is Viktor's sworn enemy. A political prisoner, he dreams of reigniting his mother's failed rebellion.

Calenne Trelan, Josiri's sister, seeks only to break free of their tarnished legacy, to escape the expectation and prejudice that haunts the family name.

As war spreads across the Republic, these three must set aside their differences in order to save their home. Yet decades of bad blood are not easily set aside. And victory—if it comes at all—will demand a darker price than any of them could have imagined.

ONE

Preparations had taken weeks. Statues had been re-gilded. Familial portraits unveiled from dusty canvas and set in places of honour. The stained glass of the western window glittered in the afternoon sunlight. Come the hour of Ascension it would blaze like fire and cast an image of divine Lumestra into the hall so that the sun goddess too would stand among the guests.

It would not be so elsewhere. In the houses beneath Branghall's walls the part of Lumestra would be played by a doll, her limbs carved from firewood and her golden hair woven from last year's straw. There, her brief reign would not end with the fading of the sun. Instead, hearth-fires would usher her home on tongues of flame.

The chasm between rich and poor, ruler and ruled, was never more evident than at Ascension. Josiri strove to be mindful of that. For all that had befallen his family, he retained comfort and privilege denied to many.

But a prison remained a prison, even if the bars were gilded and the guards polite.

Most of the guards.

"That will have to come down." Arzro Makrov extended a finger to the portrait above High Table. "She has no place here, or anywhere else in the Tressian Republic."

Josiri exchanged a glance with Anastacia. The seneschal's black eyes glimmered a warning, reinforced by a slight shake of her head. Josiri ignored both and stepped closer, footsteps hollow on the hall's flagstones. "No place?"

Makrov flinched but held his ground. "Katya Trelan was a traitor."

Impotent anger kindled. Fifteen years on, and the wound remained raw as ever.

"This was my mother's home," said Josiri carefully. "She would have celebrated her fifty-fifth year this Ascension. Her body is ash, but she *will* be present in spirit."

"No."

Makrov drew his corpulent body up to its full, unimpressive height. The setting sun lent his robes the rich warmth of fresh blood. Ironic for a man so pallid. The intricate silver ward-brooch was a poor match for his stolid garb. But without it, he could not have crossed the enchanted manor wall.

Josiri's throat tightened. He locked gazes with Makrov for a long moment, and then let his eyes fall upon the remaining "guests". Would any offer support?

Shaisan Yanda didn't meet his gaze, but that was to be expected. As governor of the Southshires, she was only present to ensure Josiri did nothing rash. Nonetheless, the slight curl to her lip suggested she found Makrov's behaviour tiresome.

She'd fought for the Council at Zanya, and on other battlefields besides, earning both her scars and the extra weight that came with advancing years.

As for Valmir Sark, he paid little attention. His interest lay more with ancestral finery ... and likely in broaching Branghall's wine cellars come Ascension. Josiri had heard enough of Sark to know he was present only to spare his family another scandal. The high-collared uniform might as well have been for show. Sark was too young to have fought against Katya's rebellion. And as for him standing a turn on the Hadari border? The thought was laughable.

That left Anastacia, and her opinion carried no sway.

If only Calenne were there. She'd always had more success in dealing with the Council's emissaries, and more patience. Where in Lumestra's name was she? She'd promised.

Josiri swallowed his irritation. He'd enough enemies without adding his sister to the roster.

"The portrait remains," he said. "This is my house. I'll thank you to remember that."

Makrov's wispy grey eyebrows knotted. "Were it up to me, I'd allow it. Truly I would. But the Council insists. Katya Trelan brought nothing but division and strife. Her shadow should not mar Ascension."

Only the slightest pause between the words imbued challenge. Josiri's self-control, so painstakingly fortified before the meeting, slipped a notch. He shook off Anastacia's restraining hand and took another step.

Yanda's lips tightened to a thin, bloodless streak. Her hand closed meaningfully about the pommel of her sword. Sark gazed on with parted mouth and the first spark of true interest.

"It is my hope," said Josiri, "that my mother's presence will serve as a message of unity."

Makrov stared up at the portrait. "I applaud your intent. But the lawless are not quelled by gestures, but by strong words, and stronger action."

"I've given what leadership I can."

"I know," said Makrov. "I've read reports of your speeches. I'd like to hear one for myself. Tomorrow at noon?"

It was an artful twist of the knife. "If you wish."

"Excellent." He raised his voice. "Governor Yanda. You'll ensure his grace isn't speaking to an empty square? I'm sure Captain Sark will be delighted to assist."

"Of course, my lord," said Yanda. "And the portrait?"

Makrov locked gazes with Katya Trelan's dead stare. "I want it taken down and burned. Her body is ash. Let her spirit join it. I can think of no stronger message of unity."

"I won't do it," Josiri said through gritted teeth.

"Yes, you will." Makrov sighed. "Your grace. *Josiri.* I entertained hopes that you'd lead your people out of the past. But the Council's patience is not infinite. They may decide upon another exodus if there's anything less than full cooperation."

Exodus. The word sounded harmless. The reality was punishment meted out for a rebellion fifteen years in the past; families divided, stolen children shipped north to toil as little more than slaves. Makrov sought to douse a fire with tinder.

"Your mother's memory poisons you. As it poisons your people." Makrov set his hands on Josiri's shoulders. "Let her go. I have."

But he hadn't. That was why Makrov remained the Council's chief emissary to the Southshires, despite his advancing years and expanding waistline. His broken heart had never healed, but Katya Trelan lay fifteen years beyond his vengeance. And so he set his bitterness against her people, and against a son who he believed should have been his.

Makrov offered an avuncular smile. "You'll thank me one day."

Josiri held his tongue, not trusting himself to reply. Makrov strode away, Sark falling into step behind. Yanda hesitated a moment before following.

"Tomorrow at noon, your grace. I look forward to it." Makrov spoke without turning, the words echoing along the rafters. Then he was gone.

Josiri glanced up at his mother's portrait. Completed a year before her death, it captured to perfection the gleam of her eyes and the inscrutable perhaps-mocking, maybe-sympathetic smile. At least, Josiri thought it did. Fifteen years was a long time. He saw little of himself in his mother's likeness, but then he'd always been more akin to his father. The same unruly blond hair and lantern jaw. The same lingering resentment at forces beyond his control.

He perched on the edge of High Table and swallowed his irritation. He couldn't afford anger. Dignity was the cornerstone of leadership, or so his mother had preached.

"When I was a boy," he said, "my father told me that people are scared and stupid more than they are cruel. I thought he'd handed me the key to some great mystery. Now? The longer I spend in Makrov's company, the more I suspect my father told me what he *wished* were true."

Anastacia drew closer. Her outline blurred like vapour, as it always did when her attention wandered. Like her loose tangle of snow-white curls and impish features, the robes of a Trelan seneschal were for show. A concession. Josiri wasn't sure what Anastacia's true form actually *was*. Only black, glossy eyes – long considered the eyes of a witch, or a demon, bereft of iris and sclera – offered any hint.

The Council's proctors had captured her a year or so after the Battle of Zanya. Branghall, already a prison in all but name, had become her new home shortly after. Anastacia spoke often of what she'd done to deserve Tressian ire. The problem was, no two tales matched.

In one, she'd seduced and murdered a prominent councillor. In another, she'd instead seduced and murdered that same councillor's husband. A third story involved ransacking a church. And then there was the tale about a choir of serenes, and indecency that left the holy women's vows of chastity in tatters. After a dozen such stories, ranging from ribald to horrific, Josiri had stopped asking.

But somewhere along the line, they'd become friends. More than friends. If Makrov ever learned how close they were, it wouldn't be the gallows that awaited Josiri, but the pyre.

Pallid wisps of light curled from Anastacia's arched eyebrow. "The archimandrite is foolish in the way only clever men are. As for afraid? If he wasn't, you'd not be his prisoner."

Josiri snorted. "My mother casts a long shadow. But I'm not her."

"No. Your mother lost her war. You'll win yours."

"Flatterer."

The eyebrow twitched a fraction higher. "Isn't that a courtier's function?"

Genuine confusion, or another of Anastacia's little jokes? It was always hard to be sure. "In the rest of the Republic, perhaps. In the Southshires, truth is all we can afford."

"If you're going to start moping, I'd like to be excused."

A smile tugged at the corner of Josiri's mouth. "If you don't show your duke a little more respect, he might have you thrown from the manor."

Anastacia sniffed. "He's welcome to try. But these stones are old, and the Council's proctors made a thorough job of binding me to them. You'll fail before they do."

"You forget, I'm a Trelan. I'm stubborn."

"And where did stubbornness get your mother? Or your uncle, for that matter?"

Josiri's gaze drifted back to his mother's portrait. "What would she do?"

"I doubt she'd put a mere *thing*, no matter how beautiful, before the lives of her people." She shrugged. "But she was a Trelan, and someone once told me – though I can't remember who – that Trelans are stubborn."

"And none more than she," said Josiri. "I don't want to give up the last of her."

Anastacia scratched at the back of her scalp – a mannerism she'd picked up off one of the servants in her frequent forays to the kitchens. Her appetites were voracious – especially where the manor's wine cellar was concerned.

"Might I offer some advice, as one prisoner to another?"

"Of course."

"Burn the painting. Your mother's legacy is not in canvas and oils, but in blood."

The words provoked a fresh spark of irritation. "Calenne doesn't seem to think so."

Anastacia offered no reply. Josiri couldn't blame her for that. This particular field was well-furrowed. And besides, good advice was good advice. Katya Trelan had died to save her family. That was her true legacy.

"I should tell her how things went," he said. "Do you know where she is?"

"Where do you think?" Anastacia's tone grew whimsical to match her expression. "For myself, I might rearrange the window shutters on the upper floor. Just in case some helpful soul's watching? One who might be agreeable to expressing your annoyance at the archimandrite where you cannot?"

Josiri swallowed a snort of laughter. Regardless of what his mother would have done about the painting, this she *would* approve of. Humiliation repaid in kind.

"That's a grand idea."

Anastacia sniffed again. "Of course it is. Shall we say nightfall?"

That ran things close, but the timing should work. Makrov was due to hold celebration in Eskavord's tiny church at dusk. Afterwards, he'd make the long ride back to the fortress at Cragwatch. It all depended on whether Crovan's people were keeping watch on the shutters.

Still, inaction gained nothing.

Josiri nodded. "Nightfall it is."

Each creak of the stairs elicited a fearful wince, and a palm pressed harder against rough stone. Josiri told himself that the tower hadn't endured generations of enthusiastic winds just to crumble beneath his own meagre weight. He might even have believed it, if not for that almost imperceptible rocking motion. In his great-grandfather's time, the tower had been an observatory. Now the roof was a nest of fallen beams, and the walls stone teeth in a shattered jaw.

At least the skies were clear. The vistas almost held the terror at bay, fear paling before beauty. The town of Eskavord sprawled across the eastern valley, smoke dancing as the Ash Wind – so named for the cinders it gusted from the distant Thrakkian border to the south – brushed the slopes of Drannan Tor. Beyond the outermost farms sprawled the eaves of Davenwood. Beyond that, further east, the high town walls of Kreska nestled in the foothills of the Greyridge Mountains. All of it within a day's idle ride. Close at hand, and yet out of reach.

But it paid not to look too close. You might see the tabarded soldiers patrolling Eskavord's streets, or the boarded-up houses.

The foreboding gibbets on Gallows Hill. Where Josiri's Uncle Taymor had danced a final jig – where his mother had burned, her ashes scattered so Lumestra could not easily resurrect her come the light of Third Dawn. It was worse in the month of Reaptithe. Endless supply wagons crept along the sunken roadways like columns of ants, bearing the Southshires' bounty north.

Duke Kevor Trelan had never been more popular with his people than when he called for secession. The Council had been quick to respond. Josiri still recalled the bleak Tzadas-morning the summons had arrived at Branghall, backed by swords enough to make refusal impossible. It was the last memory he had of his father. But the Council had erred. Duke Kevor's execution made rebellion inevitable.

Another gust assailed the tower. His panicked step clipped a fragment of stone. It ricocheted off the sun-bleached remnant of a wooden beam and clattered out over the edge.

"I suppose your demon told you where I was?"

Calenne, as usual, perched on the remnants of the old balcony – little more than a spur of timber jutting at right angles to a battered wall. Her back to a pile of rubble, she had one foot hooked across her knee. The other dangled out over the courtyard, three storeys and forty feet below. A leather-bound book lay open across her lap, pages fluttering.

"Her name is Anastacia."

"That's not her name." The wind plucked a spill of black hair from behind Calenne's ear. She tucked it back into place. "That's what *you* call her."

Calenne had disliked Anastacia from the first, though Josiri had never been clear why, and the passage of time had done little to heal the one-sided divide. Anastacia seldom reciprocated the antipathy, though whether that was because she considered herself above such things, or did so simply to irritate Calenne, Josiri wasn't sure.

"Because that's her wish. I don't call you Enna any longer, do I?"

Blue eyes met his then returned to the book. "What do you want?"

Josiri shook his head. So very much like their mother. No admission of wrong, just a new topic.

"I thought you'd be with me to greet Makrov."

She licked a fingertip and turned the page. "I changed my mind."

"We were discussing the arrangements for *your* wedding. Or do you no longer intend to marry at Ascension?"

"That's *why* I changed my mind."

"What's that supposed to mean?"

A rare moment of hesitation. "It doesn't matter."

"I see." Steeling himself, Josiri edged closer. "What are you reading?"

"This?" Calenne stared down at the book. "A gift from Kasamor. *The Turn of Winter*, by Iugo Maliev. I'm told it's all the rage in Tressia."

"Any good?"

"If you admire a heroine who lets herself be blown from place to place like a leaf on the wind. It's horrendously fascinating. Or fascinatingly horrendous. I haven't decided yet." She closed the book and set it on her knee. "How did the meeting go?"

"I'm to make a speech tomorrow, on the topic of unity."

She scowled. "It went that badly?"

"I didn't have my sister there to charm him," Josiri replied. "And . . . he reacted poorly to mother's portrait." No sense saying the rest. Calenne wouldn't understand.

She sighed. "And now you know why I stayed away. If Makrov reacts like that to Katya's image . . . I didn't want complications. I can't afford them. And I *do* want this marriage."

Josiri didn't have to ask what she meant. Katya in oils was bad enough. Her likeness in flesh and blood? Even with Calenne at her most demure and charming – a rarity – there was risk. With every passing year, his sister more resembled the mother she refused to acknowledge. Perhaps she'd been right to stay away.

"You think Makrov has the power to have it annulled?"

She shrugged. "Not alone. But Kasamor's mother isn't at all pleased at the match. I'm sure she's allies enough to make trouble."

"Kasamor would truly let her interfere?"

On his brief visits to Branghall, Kasamor had seemed smitten. As indeed had Calenne herself. On the other hand, Josiri had heard enough of Ebigail Kiradin, Kasamor's mother, to suspect she possessed both the reach and influence to thwart even the course of true love, if she so chose.

"On his last visit, he told me that I was the other half of his soul. So no, I don't believe he would. He'd sooner die, I think. And I . . ." Calenne shook her head and stared down at the book. "It doesn't matter."

Josiri frowned. "What? What doesn't matter?"

Calenne offered a small, resigned smile. "I've had bad dreams of late. The Black Knight. Waking up screaming doesn't do wonders for my mood."

The Black Knight. Viktor Akadra. The Phoenix-Slayer. The man who'd murdered their mother. He'd taken root in the dreams of a terrified six-year-old girl, and never let go. Josiri had lost track of how often in that first year he'd cradled Calenne as she'd slipped off to broken sleep.

"Is that why you're back to hiding up here? He'll not harm you, I promise."

"I know he won't." Her shoulders drooped, and her tone softened. "But thanks, all the same."

She set the book aside and joined him inside the tower proper. Josiri drew her into an embrace, reflecting, as he so often did, what a curious mix of close and distant they were. The decade between them drove them apart. He doubted he'd ever understand her. Fierce in aspect, but brittle beneath.

"The world's against us, little sister. We Trelans have to stick together."

if you enjoyed
WE CRY FOR BLOOD

look out for

SON OF THE STORM
The Nameless Republic: Book One

by

Suyi Davies Okungbowa

On the continent of Oon, there is no destiny but the one you make.

A clever scholar seeks forbidden knowledge.

A mysterious warrior wields forgotten magic.

A fixer's daughter schemes for political power.

From city streets where secrets are bartered for gold to unpredictable forests teeming with fabled beasts, three lives collide ... and their tangled destinies will bring down a storied empire.

Prologue

Oke

The Weary Sojourner Caravansary stood at the corner of three worlds.

For a multitude of seasons before Oke was born, the travel-house had offered food, wine, board, and music—and for those who had been on the road too long, companionship—to many a traveller across the Savanna Belt. Its patronage consisted solely of those who lugged loads of gold, bronze, nuts, produce, textile, and craftwork from Bassa into the Savanna Belt or, for the even more daring, to the Idjama desert across Lake Vezha. On their way back, they would stop at the caravansary again, the banana and yam and rice loads on their camels gone and now replaced with tablets of salt, wool, and beaded ornaments.

But there was another set of people for whom the caravansary stood, those whose sights were set on discovering the storied isthmus that connected the Savanna Belt to the yet-to-be-sighted seven islands of the archipelago. For people like these, the Weary Sojourner stood as something else: a vantage point. And for people like Oke who had a leg in all three worlds, walking into the Weary Sojourner called for an intensified level of alertness.

Especially when the fate of the three worlds could be determined by the very meeting she was going to have.

She swung open the curtain. She did not push back her cloak.

Like many public houses in the Savanna Belt, the Weary Sojourner operated in darkness, despite it being late morning. During her time in the desertlands, Oke had learned that this was a practice carried over from the time of the Leopard Emperor when liquor was banned in its desert protectorates, and secret houses were operated under the cover of darkness. Even though that period of despotism was thankfully over, habitual practices were difficult to shake off. People still preferred to drink and smoke and fuck in the dark.

Which made this the perfect place for Oke's meeting.

She took a seat at the back and surveyed the room. It was at once obvious that her contact wasn't around. There were exactly three people here, all men who had clearly just arrived from the same caravan. Their clothes gave them away: definitely Bassai, in brightly coloured cotton wrappers, bronze jewellery—no sensible person travelled with gold jewellery—over some velvet, wool, and leatherskin boots for the desert's cold. Senior members of the merchantry guild, looking at that velvet. Definitely members of the Idu, the mainland's noble caste. Guild aside, their complexions also gave that away—high-black skin, as dark as the darkest of humuses, just the way Bassa liked it. It was the kind of complexion she hadn't seen in a long time.

Oke swept aside a nearby curtain and looked outside. Sure enough, there was their caravan, parked behind the establishment, guarded by a few private Bassai hunthands. Beside them, travelhands—hired desert immigrants to the mainland judging by their complexions, what the Bassai would refer to as *low-brown* for how light and lowly it was—unpacking busily for an overnight stay and unsaddling the camels so they could drink. There were no layers of dust on anyone yet, so clearly they were northbound.

"A drink, maa?"

Oke looked up at the housekeep, who had come over, wringing his hands in a rag. She could see little of his face, but she had been here twice before, and knew enough of what he looked like.

"Palm wine and jackalberry with ginger," she said, hiding her hands.

The housekeep stopped short. "Interesting choice of drink." He peered closer. "Have you been here before?" He enunciated the words in Savanna Common in a way that betrayed his border origins.

Oke's eyes scanned him and decided he was asking this innocently. "Why do you ask?"

"You remember things, as a housekeep," he said, leaning back on a nearby counter. "Especially drink combinations that join lands that have no place joining."

"Consider it an acquired taste," Oke said, and looked away, signalling the end of the discussion. But to her surprise, the man nodded at the group far away and asked, in clear Mainland Common:

"You with them?"

Oke froze. He had seen her complexion, then, and knew enough to know she had mainland origins. What had always been a curse for Oke back when she was a mainlander—*Too light, is she punished by Menai?* people would ask her daa—had become a gift in self-exile over the border. But there were a few people with keen eyes and ears who would, every now and then, recognise a lilt in her Savanna Common or note how her hair curled a bit too tightly for a desertlander or how she carried herself with a smidgen of mainlander confidence. There was only one way to react to that, as she always did whenever this came up.

"What?" She frowned. "Sorry, I don't understand that language."

The housekeep eyed her for another moment, then went away.

Oke breathed a sigh of relief. It was of the utmost importance that no one knew who she was and what she was doing here, living in the Savanna Belt. Because the history of the Savanna Belt was what it was, a tiny enough number of people who originated from this side of the Soke border looked just a bit like she did. Passing as one was easier once she perfected the languages. Thank moons she had studied them as a scholar in Bassa.

She drank slowly once the housekeep brought her order, and she put forward some cowries, making sure to add a few pieces to clearly signal she wanted to be left alone.

Halfway through her drink, she realised her contact was running late. She looked outside again. The sky had gone cloudy, and the sun was missing for a while. She went back to her drink and nursed it some more.

The men in the room rose and went up to be shown to their rooms. Oke peeked out of the curtain again. The travelhands were gone. One hunthand stood and guarded the caravan. One stood at the back door to the caravansary. The camels still stood there, lapping water.

Oke ordered another drink and waited. The sun came back out. It was past an hour now. She looked out again. The camels had stopped drinking and now lay in the dust, snoozing.

Something was wrong.

Oke got up without touching her new drink, put down some more cowries on the counter in front of the housekeep, and walked to the front door of the caravansary. On second thought, she turned and went back to the housekeep.

"Your alternate exit. Show me."

The man pointed without looking at her. Oke took it and went around the building, evading both the men and the animals. She eventually showed up to where she had left her own animal—a kwaga, a striped beauty with tiny horns. She untied and patted it. It snorted in return. Then she slapped its hind-quarters and set it off on a run, barking as it went.

She waited for a moment or two, then dashed away herself.

Going through a secluded route on foot, while trying to stay as nondescript as possible, took a long time. Oke had to take double the usual precautions, as banditry had increased so much on the trade routes that one was more likely to get robbed and murdered than not. Back when Bassa was Bassa—not now with its heavily diluted population and generally weakening influence—no one would dare attack a Bassai caravan anywhere on the continent for fear of retaliation. These days, every caravan had to travel with private security. The Bassai Upper Council was well known for being toothless and only concerned with enriching themselves.

The clouds from earlier had disappeared, and the sun beat mercilessly on her, causing her to sweat rivers beneath her cloak, but Oke knew she had done the right thing. It was as they had agreed: If either of them got even a whiff of something off, they were to make a getaway as swiftly as possible. She was then to head straight for the place nicknamed the Forest of the Mist, the thick, uncharted woodland with often heavy fog that was storied to house secret passages to an isthmus that connected the Savanna Belt to the seven islands of the eastern archipelago.

It didn't matter any longer if that bit of desertland myth was true or not. Whether the archipelago even still existed was moot at this point. The yet undiscovered knowledge she had gleaned from her clandestine exploits in the library at the University of Bassa, coupled with the artifacts her contact was bringing her—if either made it into the wrong hands, the whole continent of Oon would pay for it. Oke wasn't ready to drop the fate of the continent in the dust just yet.

Two hours later, Oke looked back and saw in the sky the grey tip of what she knew came from thick, black smoke. Not the kind of smoke that came from a nearby kitchen, but the kind that said something far away had been destroyed. Something big.

She took a detour in her journey and headed for the closest high point she knew. She chose one that overlooked a decent portion of the savanna but also kept her on the way to the Forest of the Mist. It took a while to ascend to the top, but she soon got to a good enough vantage point to look across and see the caravansary.

The Weary Sojourner stuck out like an anthill, the one establishment for a distance where the road from the border branched into the Savanna Belt. The caravansary was up in flames. It was too far for her to see the people and animals, but she knew what those things scattering from the raging inferno were. The body language of disaster was the same everywhere.

Oke began to descend fast, her chest weightless. The Forest of the Mist was the only place on this continent where she would be safe now, and she needed to get there *immediately*. Whoever set that fire to the Weary Sojourner knew who she and her contact were. Her contact may or may not have made it out alive. It was up to her now to ensure that the continent's biggest secret was kept that way.

The alternative was simply too grave to consider.

orbit

Follow us:

f **/orbitbooksUS**

/orbitbooks

/orbitbooks

Join our mailing list
to receive alerts on our
latest releases and deals.

orbitbooks.net

Enter our monthly
giveaway for the chance
to win some epic prizes.

orbitloot.com